THE MOMENTS LOST

THE MOMENTS LOST

A MIDWEST PILGRIM'S PROGRESS

* * *

BRUCE OLDS

FARRAR, STRAUS AND GIROUX

New York

FARRAR, STRAUS AND GIROUX

19 Union Square West, New York 10003

Copyright © 2007 by Bruce Olds
All rights reserved
Distributed in Canada by Douglas & McIntyre, Ltd.
Printed in the United States of America
First edition, 2007

Grateful acknowledgment is made for permission to reprint the following material:
April Galleons by John Ashbery, copyright © 1984, 1987 by John Ashbery. Reprinted by
permission of Georges Borchardt, Inc., for the author. Excerpt from "The Dry
Salvages" from *Four Quartets*, copyright © 1941 by T. S. Eliot and renewed 1969 by
Esme Valerie Eliot, reprinted by permission of Harcourt, Inc.

Library of Congress Cataloging-in-Publication Data
Olds, Bruce.
    The moments lost : a midwest pilgrim's progress / Bruce Olds.—1st ed.
        p.   cm.
    ISBN-13: 978-0-374-11821-1 (hardcover : alk. paper)
    ISBN-10: 0-374-11821-3 (hardcover : alk. paper)
    I. Title.

PS3565.L336M66 2007
813'.54—dc22

                                                                                2006029464

Designed by Gretchen Achilles

www.fsgbooks.com

1   3   5   7   9   10   8   6   4   2

FOR NANCE, NOVA—
AND IN MEMORY OF MY FATHER
AND GRANDFATHER

✦ ✦ ✦

The true history of life
is but a history
of moments.

SHERWOOD ANDERSON

All history is nothing but myth . . .
each moment fades each moment
into the realm of the imaginary.

PAUL VALÉRY

CONTENTS

✦ ✦ ✦

BOOK ONE

PILGRIM

Tamarack   *3*

Chi-Town   *28*

Mart   *104*

BOOK TWO

PROGRESS

Keweenaw   *175*

Red Jacket   *259*

Ana   *346*

Family Plot   *451*

Appendix, Notes, Citations   *463*

Acknowledgments   *467*

PILGRIM

♦ ♦ ♦

As I walked through the wilderness of this world,
I lighted upon a certain place where was a den,
and laid me down in that place to sleep;
and as I slept, I dreamed a dream.

JOHN BUNYAN, *The Pilgrim's Progress*

TAMARACK

◆ ◆ ◆

On the tenth day of the eleventh month, 1880, at precisely nine past noon, Franklyn Tyree Lattimore Shivs was born to Augustus I. and Narcissa Shivs-née-Wills in the second-floor bedroom of their whitewashed clapboard, shiplapped, cedar-shaken mainhouse in the affluent farming community of New Menomonee, Wisconsin, some dozen miles northwest of Milwaukee.

No doctor stood in attendance, no certificate of birth was applied for or secured, no announcement was placed in the local newspaper, and, because none then was extant, no relative was notified. History failed to acknowledge its most recent arrival, as it did the disconcertingly curious fact that he had been born with one eye, his left, the one gray as gun grease, cocked obliquely open, and, so his parents shortly would conclude, sentiently seeing.

Odd. Decidedly so. Odd-got and odd-born. Odd child. If not so odd that his mother, middling conversant in such and the selfsame, was upon first infant sight of her son not rendered too disencumbered or fractured of wit to quote, as she never failed to call him, the Old Top Bard Himself: "'Tis the error of our eye—that *armed* vision—directs our mind.'"

SWAMP CREATURE

He endured his childhood, he would insist everafter, altogether alone—save for his dogs, of course—if, incidentally, in the company of his mother

and father, on a dairy farm abutting a swamp, the Tamarack, where, on select summer nights, the swamp gases phosphoresced steady as beacons, or,
rather, flicketted in stroboscopic fits, their shimmy, flare, flameout and flit
playing tag and tagalong, self-immolating before rekindling in firedrakes
and fantails, in licks called *ignes fatui* ("foolish fire"), will-o'-the-wisp, fox-
fire, friar's lantern, corpse's candle, *noctilucae terrestia.*

Ensorcelled by them from the first, the swamplights—those about
which his mother once had read from their encyclopedia, "Occurring most
often on windless nights well after sunset, when approached, they appear
to recede, often reappearing in another direction, behavior leading to the
folk notion that they are the work of a mischievous spirit intentionally
leading seekers and pilgrims astray"—he had throughout his childhood
been repeatedly admonished by his father to "stay clear of the Tam," those
unfarmable acres the paterfamilias was in the habit of referring to as "the
cess," the "drossy wet neck" of which he likewise was in the habit of loudly
vowing to someday "wring bone-dry."

But that night, in the schorl-dark of his bedroom, ears forfeit to the
swamp's jatter and chirr as he stood at the window absently clasping and
unclasping the twin blades of his parents' birthday gift, the Buck jackknife
inlaid with oolite and staghorn, he decided—in his own mind, quite mo-
mentously—that being all of eleven now, he was old enough deliberately
to end-run, if not cavalierly to disregard, his father's wishes.

Stealing down-grece, striding over the snoring Tick, his terrier,
clumped at the base of the stair, he slipped out the front door undetected
and tiptoed across the porch, making straight for the barn. Feeling for the
lantern along the wall, he found it, struck a long Lucifer match, unlooped
the handle from its nail, then settled it on the ground as he fetched to a
knee, flipping open its glass panel before wristing the vent-cock and in-
serting the flame. The lantern caught easy, its fourteen-candlepower light
oiling up the barn walls to magnify the stall rows where the cows lay mute
and uncaring, chackling cud, swishing tail.

Lowering the flame to a steadier, less light-blinding burn, he headed
out of the barn and across a gap of ground that was rock strewn but reasonably flat, then a stretch of tallish grass that gradually dipped toward
a pitchy brake of stiffer rushes and stalkier reeds. The sky, he noticed—
impossible not to—was pressed immodestly near, nearly naked, its moon
nigh full, the stars as cloves of ice.

Toting the lantern shoulder high and steady, its light-loft torchlit the tress of the trees dead ahead and beckoning, not far. Reining up, he looked back, his sight line cutting the house in half. The roof and some of the second floor were all that he could see—his bedroom window, the moon on its pane a chrome eye.

"Moon paint," he thought. "Puck."

The piped peeps of the peepers surged and receded, singing crescendo/diminuendo waves in oscillating accord with his plotching farther in, quieting as he approached, upswelling as he passed, a diapason. And then he was fully into it, among treespread onto floor sponge burlapped and nappy through the soles of his shoes, the fluxion, flex, sway and giveway, springy as a cushion of mattress. The deeper in he went, the less tentative he felt, less apt to step through bottom. He felt his feet getting wet, squishy in their socks, a pair of "soakers." He was going to catch hell when got back, a bawling-out, but found he cared less. Like walking in chews across heels of bread.

The moon had melted the mud.

He hadn't expected it to smell like rotted eggs. Phew!

Fancied, then, that he could feel the wind of the planets as they wheeled in their rounds, sounds of passage, musical spheres. The moon has a way, perhaps, of massaging a pulse from the ground.

Extinguishing the lantern, he stood there a moment, self-blackened, before lowering himself to a knee, Indian scout, immediately feeling better, less exposed for the crouch. Something unthinkable rustled his hair, migrated its surface, crisscrossed his scalp, inched down his neck. Procession of spider? Scrutiny of grub? Leech? He felt it hook in, sink a footing, probe, then drill, root 'neath his skin. He swatted. Deadfall inside his shirt. Yeesh!

Which is when, roughly, he saw them. They weren't there, and then, roughly, what had not been, was.

Twenty, twenty-five yards ahead, a glade of lucent mist, and on the mist and of it, and of the mist and through it, glosses of pink sheen, wafers of red, lobes of bluish green, pleats of membranous yellow merging with flounces of purple that wobbled, roopled, minnowed and weeviled. And, then . . . fled.

The lights skated plasmas and muscosas of air as if skimming a sentient surface, one he slogged over and through as if reeled onward, into the dark, amidst the marl of everything he could not see, not thinking, bereft of thought and right cogency, until, expecting each to be his next, squelching further on far from sure-footed, keeping his eyes fixed fast on the lights, the closer he came, it suddenly dawned upon him, the farther they moved off, backpedaled, waltzed in reverse, tattered apart, trailed off and away, draining *in situ* until they had petered to nothingness. His three feet forward, their six feet back. His eight, their twenty.

Pulse step by pulse—of panther's paw?—he pounced, raced headlong, unheeding on the hurtle, only to have the dunes of ectoplasmic light distill to dissolve before his eyes, an in-essence more porous than powder; tachistoscopic.

He fell.

So—though he would arrive at its meaning only later—that was the first lesson: what is bequeathed you, however beautiful, when pulled even with at last, falls apart, goes to pieces, evanesces, in the dark, over and over again. The moment, present, always, past.

Impermanent as the vapor of angels.

FATHER

Before it was half over, his mother had fallen into the habit of calling it "the Summer of the *Fledermaus*." Bats were a seasonal fact around the farm, but that summer—he must have been twelve, thirteen maybe—the local population seemed inexplicably to have soared by magnitudes of infestation. Indeed, so conspicuous had become their amassed flocking that his father, the very night before what happened happened, had remarked over evening stew that they were so plentiful now, they had become "nuisance enough to spook the cows."

Twenty-four hours later, Franklyn, having been called down to wash up for supper, was standing at the kitchen sink hard at the hand pump when his gaze was drawn through the windowglass to the image of an object at no little remove from the house, out across a stretch of yonder pasture. Size, shape, angle, contour, color—he could delineate nothing with any salience. Even when the figure appeared to move, a fluttering of black flaps in relief against a white field—crows feeding on a carcass of summertime snow, he would remember thinking later—even then, he hadn't a clue.

Until he heard the sound. Or rather, his father did. His father heard it first.

"Damn!" He was on his feet at the kitchen table. "Stay here."

Franklyn stood, mindlessly pumping, feet stapled to the floor, as his father charged out the kitchen door, past the privy, through the barnyard, blew past the barn, the dovecots, his shed, sped along the pond, past the silo, the millrace, through the pasture gate, into the pasture and across it, full tilt, not stumbling.

Willing himself, belly full of bees, Franklyn released his hold on the pump handle and crossed over to the door, staring through its screen. It would occur to him later that he never had seen his father, who customarily typified what his mother always called a "plodder," move so swiftly or sure. Beeline. Something about his father's purposefulness, quality of voice. Franklyn suspected he might have use of his help.

He was out the door and halfway there when his father turned and yelled, "Kerosene!"

Altering his course without breaking stride, Franklyn sheared for the barn, located the tankard, not frantic, raced back through the pasture, hands full and encumbered. He could see his father bent over the spot, back to him, kicking at something in what appeared to him as all of an infernal fit. By the time he reined up even with him, he was clean out of breath, the stitch in his side a tug like a suture that was playing his ribs for a cinch.

It was a cow, one of theirs, and she no was longer standing but supporting herself propped by her rear legs alone, down on her knees, V'd, bipod, having been *brought* down, felled and foundering, her rump hoisted in the air as if slung there. Franklyn was drawn at once to her eyes, eyes open wider and redder than he ever had seen any cow's before and which bulged with what could only be fear and panic even as they rolled wild'd in bewilderment. From her mouth, open as the *baa* of a shearling lamb's, resonated a baritone of mucosal bleating around and past a lax slab of pink tongue that lolled out and over her massive lower jaw like an unspooled band of wet rubber, even as her nostrils dilated and contracted in rapid bursts, blown strings, pomellated knots. The pools of piss and piles of shit lay everywhere; she floundered among them, the strew of them there.

Snatching up the cannister of kerosene from his son, the father unscrewed its lid, turned it bottoms up, and began shaking it, dumping its contents, flinging it in long flumes over her head, back, shanks, flanks, the liquid landing in splashes that splotched the black-and-white Holstein hide enough to dislodge some of the bats, the ones that loosed their holds here and there, rose up, flapped off, but not all of them, not most, not nearly enough.

They appeared to be hundreds—or at least enough to bring down a heifer—and they clung to her like a last meal, bunched at her neck, corsaging her nose, clumped to her backside, under and along the basket of her belly and groin, bouqueted at her udder and teats, a school of winged sharks lost to the frenzy of its feeding.

He could see—she was chum.

Her back legs gave way then, and, as she collapsed, overcome and unsocketed, her mass met the ground with a *humpff*, full brunt, before rolling onto its side, her lungs heaving hugely against the slats of its ribs.

They were about to lose her. Perhaps she had been lost all along.

His father retreated, took three steps back—Franklyn counted—stood staring as his son stared along.

"Go home," he said, not looking at him. "Go home, boy."

"Yes, sir," said Franklyn, making no move to obey. His eyes were fixed on his father's, whose own appeared to have lost track of their presence, the tense of this present, so monocularly trained were they on what they beheld. "Can't I stay?" he said at last. "I'd rather stay."

Summoning one last mighty effort, expending what she could afford to ill spend, the cow endeavored to jolt her way to her feet, craning crazily at the neck, cords taut, muscled herself partway up, bucked herself to her haunches, performed a sort of demivolt, then sank back, slack, before beginning to thrash, legs and hooves feebly bicycling.

She wasn't bellowing anymore. Her bellowing had ceased, if not the gurgling that was not immediately apparent to Franklyn as that of a cow's. Though it was only when they went for her eyes that his father reached into the breast pocket of his bib overalls and fished out the safe of matches, sliding it open like a desk drawer. Extracting a match from the box, he struck it, then flicked it at the heap. When it failed to catch, he struck a second, then a third, another, then another still, struck every match in the tray, tossing each in rapid succession . . . *fluuuf!*

The flames engaged, vectored, spread, rolled horizontally across the carcass until, describing the veer of a vertical leap, they hurled upward, a collusion of boas. The smell of charred cow coursed up Franklyn's nose, chafed at the roof of his mouth, scalded the back of his throat. He sensed the lining of his lungs sear, stung acrid as outcry, raw as regret.

And then it was night and they gunned thistling up out of the flames, black burrs finning, shrapnel aflame.

Combing the crown of his balding head with a calico kerchief, his father clumsied his arm about the startled shoulder of his unwitting son and insinuated an assuasive, rough tender-meant tug. A hug?

"Let's home," he said. "She'll keep 'til morning."

Through the dark, its moment at their backs, they humped their horror home.

How speak the substance of a shadow or endow a vapor with its valency? How give his bedeviled dust its due?

Like that Fourth of July when Augustus Shivs, flare-blind and smoldering, staggered through the backdoor blistered, blasted, tattered to effigy, having blown himself nigh sky-high. Though for all his grinning through the raccoon mask of black powder you might have thought, as did his son, that he just had returned from a leisurely day at the races. Had to hand him that, his moment of special grace.

"Can't see jack," he had joshed, barking a shin on the stove while ripping the still-smoking shirt from his back. "Somebody, woncha pleeze, hand me the crook of a cane."

Then the hours at the kitchen table, refectory, trestle, swabbing his eyes, rinsing them with saline back to some semblance of sight, Mother extracting each of the black grains of unburned powder embedded beneath his flesh like kernels of pepper, squeezing them out, tweezing them out with tweezers or, the deeper ones, a sewing needle, placing them, seeds in a saucer, hundreds, like lice, daubing at his wounds with rubbing alcohol. And Father the while, good soldier, nary a word in complaint save the occasional sharp in/uptake of breath and good-natured, "Oooo. Now that's a beaut, that one was."

"Watch this," he had instructed wife and son later that evening, forfeit to high spirits, almost antic, playful as Franklyn ever would see him as he arranged what shreds remained of the shirt in a heap in the front yard before flicking several matches in its direction. The flag of cloth sizzed, sneezed, effervesced froth-white with spark, and when wife and son had started some, he had japed, "Lucifer's blouse!"

The Fourth was his father's holiday, the only one he took more personally than his own birthday, and when Franklyn—vague recollection—

once had dared ask him why this was so, he had consented, that once, to explain: "Noise, heat, smoke, motion, light, brilliance, color, form, flight—it's all there, Latty, a feast for more than the eyes."

An amateur pyrotechnician just amateur enough to pose a danger, at least to himself, the one pocket of his life not laundered of risk was that in which reposed his fireworks. Which was what his workshop was about, his "powder lab," the "fire lathe," the off-limits, twelve-by-twenty-foot tarpaper-roof shed located out back, hard by the barn where he made and kept his "pyros." Atelier, refuge, it was where he repaired to perform, as his son conceived of it, his miracles of fire, the wonderwork of pyromancy, and, as that son would apprehend only much later, seek right respite from the ways of his wife.

Franklyn remembered that quite clearly, his father not saying much, if the little he did with a rude, blunt-nosed eloquence. No lessons imparted, philosophies shared, no attitude encouraged or endorsed about how properly to repose in the world, no bootstrap or cracker-barrel advice, a reticence so organic he typically exercised the option only under duress, the while counting upon the need not arising, as if he were hoarding them—words for a rainy day that he knew never was coming?—saving them back in case he should have need of them later, in heaven, perhaps, or elsewhere.

Did his father know the world, what was going on in and across it? Or if he knew, care? Certainly he never communicated the sense to his son, but then, he wasn't the sort to share his counsel or strut it, commend consolation, ignite debate or stoke it, proffer congratulation, talk sex, politics, business, or religion, cajole or gladhand, trade barbs or bon mots, josh around, or call his one and only affectionate nicknames—horsefly, pissant, buzz cut, bullethead, bucko, bucky, buckaroo, spike, spud, sluggo or stretch, slim or stubby, satchmo or socks or sprat or sprout—and so remained for him, the son, much the insular cipher, a man defined by the uneasy space of his silence, a silence so transparent that when he entered a room he did so without being seen, yet whose greatest pleasure in life was to punch open the sky in parasols of flame in order to scrawl there his signature in every fiery color of the palette.

The Shivses kept cows, milch cows as his mother called them, black and whites, Holsteins, half a hundred head. Still, it would not have mattered to Augie Shivs had the Holsteins been Herefords, the cows bantam roosters, and their acreage sown with barley and beets. What mattered more, as his mother was prone grandly to repeat in her moments of more regal self-regard—the farm had been bequeathed to them upon their betrothal by *her* parents—was that they were "landed."

Augustus Shivs may have embodied the stoicism one associates with the stereotypical Midwestern farmer, but he was singularly unsuited to managing a farm, save precisely where he succeeded in doing so, incrementally into the ground. It wasn't neglect. Augie Shivs was no piker. It was sheer ineptitude, temperamental incompetence.

At last, he was a dairy farmer who almost tragicomically despised dairy cows. They were docile, and he disliked docility. They were stupid, and he disliked stupidity. They were ugly, and he disliked ugliness. They were dependent, and he disliked dependency. They were slow, ungainly, bereft of personality, and he disliked all of those—because the qualities were so pronounced in himself? And they were bovine, and bovinity he could not abide. Nor was he overly fond of rolling out at 4:00 a.m. to milk them, as he was the less so of turning in at eight in order to roll out again at four to milk them again. And again. And again. Seven days a week, 365 days a year, year after year for the rest of his natural-born life.

"I am so dang tired of teats, boy," Franklyn recalled him remarking near the end. "Tired of puttering around the arse-end of cows. Flat-out, udderly beat. Cows is cows. Awesome dumb. And bad smelling. Dumb as the dung they dump where they do."

Most dairy farmers pet-name their cows—Maysie, Daisy, Elsie, Sal. Not Augie Shivs. He called each one the same thing—Fucking Dumb. It was the sort of existence that cornered a man, set him to chewing off his leg before blowing out his spirit, until in time, as his own father had done before him, he went out for a fag and disappeared—*poof!*—a man literally up in smoke, this abiding archetype, the father who abandons, then vanishes.

That final morning, the one over which Franklyn later would reproach himself for failing to intuit what it portended, Augie Shivs addressed his son at more length than he had, it seemed to Franklyn, the previous thirteen years sum. The date—helpful, perhaps, to nail these things down—was the year of "the Crisis of '93," the one history shortly would immortalize as that of the "Wisconsin Death Trip," the year the banks failed, loans were recalled and farm foreclosures soared, black diphtheria ran rampant, killing children by the score—whole families wiped out, and the "Wisconsin Window Smasher," the berserker Mary Sweeney, went on her rampage in the northern part of the state, near Ashland, breaking more than one hundred panes of glass before being arrested. The year, too, that a spate of inexplicable arsons swept downtown Milwaukee, as did a rash of barnburnings near Madison, and more inmates escaped from the madhouse at Mendota State than in any similar period before or since.

That morning, then, milking the cows as they always did, teat stripping in silence perched side by side upon their stools amid the feculent amalgam of hay, sawdust, mud, and cow pie strewn about the floor, the splish of warm milk *chi-tinging* its plangent tin-rain rhythm against the curved sides of the pails—had they kept cats, as cats, by farmers, typically were kept, they would have been on the prowl about then, plaintively mewling for their share—without missing a beat or even looking his way, he of a sudden began.

"Frankie"—he never called him that, always Franklyn or Frank or, occasionally, Latty; should have known right there—"every man worth a jackleg has a dream, but hardly a one has a passion, and those who do, well, recognizing it ain't so easy. And in time? Before it's too late? Passed too far on by? Shoot, that's just damned difficult."

Franklyn looked up and over, not a little startled. His father appeared to be speaking to the cow, addressing the bulge of its udder.

"So, now, you do yourself a favor and don't let that happen to you, hear? Quit your listening to what any man may tell you and find the one row that's for you and hoe it on down and for all that it's worth. And then no excuses, none. You keep to your way of it, come what may. No quit. None of this running out on yourself way a hermit crab sheds its own shell. You keep 'til what's done is well done."

Augie Shivs paused then, quit milking, looked at his son.

"'Cause life'll be a damned misery if you don't, 'til you reckon your own way of it and no kind word from another living soul. No, you make your purpose your passion, and you make 'em both yours, alone."

Augie Shivs appeared to be deciding something then—which words to use, perhaps, or whether to use any at all.

"The mind's one crafty bastard, Frank, and it'll try to talk you into thinking you can go it alone. Don't listen; it lies. 'Cause it's not enough, nor meant to be. Gotta listen to your heart, see? Gut, too. And eye. See it all, all through, all around. And when you trip into trouble—and you will, someday, happens to us all—no place left to go, nowhere to turn, nothing to hold to, then you listen to your soul. Could be carnal, too, you know, in part. Often thought it so, the soul."

And then he did the unthinkable: hitched up off his stool, strode over, stood behind his son, bent over, and kissed him on the top of his head, through his hair, whispering in his ear, "Swear it, Frank, your oath honor bright, that you'll not let it cut you down to size, your life."

And so he had sworn, however confounded. Carnal souls? It would be years before it roosted home with him—it was the only counsel with which his father ever had favored him, as the only real advice. This man, anonym, whatever, whoever he was, or once had been.

BOOK SCENTS

The farm was going slowly to seed, the house less slowly to pot.

Mother briefly considered selling out altogether, then selling off in lots, going so far as to advertise "two-acre parcels for sale, prime farmland," before hiring on a man, Jonah Fineshriber, a non-Orthodox Jew. A god-send, he took things in hand from day one. Wasn't long before he took her in as well, moved into her bed. They were never to marry but lived out their days as if they had, scandal of the neighborhood, a fact each seemed too much by a tad to relish. Whether Jonah knew something Augie had not, or whether the fire had simply scared them off, the bats never returned. Not one.

Franklyn stood quits awhile with school, intending to pitch in around the farm, lend Jonah, whom he genuinely liked, a hand. Didn't last, of course, a season or two. If his heart wasn't in it, his mind was so much the less. It was as his mother had predicted: "You'll not make half the farmer your father did, and your father was no farmer at all."

Some children bloom, others blossom, but she saw the way of it, his growing into himself, too deep, far, too fast, furling inward as the folds of a flag, knew him well, too well, perhaps—mothers can be like that, if fathers not—well enough to know that rather than reprove him back to school, with which he plainly had grown bored, she had better say what in fact begged its saying.

"You'll read," she said. "Just that. You won't school, can't farm, you'll read. What harm? You've the mind for it, even Jonah says so. Why not?

Grab a seat, pull up a chair, can't hurt. Books for fireworks. Now there's a half-fair trade, and you the best of it." She paused. "And do you know why?"

He had to allow as how he did not.

"'Cuz language is power is why. Only sort that matters. 'Tis what I wish for you, Latty, to see not only the more you would see, as you do, but their right words."

He had been reading, so his mother always would swear, since the age of three—Henty, Fenn, Ballantyne, Kingston, writers for boys, the so-called Big Four, though young as three, in his opinion, rather strained credulity. And yet, it was true that he could not recall a time when *Famous Frontiersmen, Pioneers, and Scouts*, or Ned Buntline's dime seafaring novels had not occupied the selfsame place upon the selfsame shelf above his bed. Later, of course, as is the wont of boys, those who will be boys at least, he had been drawn to Scott, Dumas, R. L. Stevenson, Irving, and Fenimore Cooper's Leatherstocking tales, to Verne and Wells and Hugo, *Quo Vadis* and *Ben-Hur* and *Taras Bulba*, to *The Adventures of Robin Locksley*, *Captains Courageous*, to *Gulliver's Travels*.

New Menomonee recently had built a commendably forward-looking "free" public library of which it was justifiably proud, a new addition occupying the second floor above the firehouse—odd site, surely, if better than none at all, though peculiarly prone to the *lectio interrupta* of fire bells and Klaxons, as, too, the updrafted aroma of wet horsehide and horse-appled straw—and it was there that he spent such time as Jonah might spare him, in fact a generous lot, trawling the stacks, omnivorous mole. He could not have known it then, of course, but he was about to embark upon the best times of his life, and this, in its way, was sad. "I would be as free as air," wrote Melville, shortly to become a favored author with him, "and I'm down in the whole world's books."

Anything serves to transform a person's life.

Her name was Palmer, graduate of the inaugural class of the new Chicago University—soon to become the University of Chicago—where she had been tutored by Veblen and Dewey and introduced to, before becoming a devotee of, the newly published sex theories of Havelock Ellis. ("The absence of flaw in beauty is itself a flaw.") She had noticed Franklyn's habitual stalking of the stacks, this reserved, almost diffident, well-mannered, if uncommonly self-conscious, seriously quiet young man, serious enough that, coupled with the inordinate amount of time he spent lurking about the place, he inevitably piqued her interest. Something about him, or to him. She approached him.

He immediately—well, not immediately, perhaps, but soon enough—thought her uncommonly, if unconventionally, attractive. Took note of certain attributes. Lithe and extraordinarily small-breasted, her pole-vaulter legs—what little he could see of them, never enough—appeared to thrust upward past her—what?—hips? armpits? eyes? Her waist was small, her tonneau tiny, her skin the texture of mole. "Ballerina," was his first thought. "This ballerina of books."

Introducing herself, she proffered the requisite inquiries and, after he had answered, sheepishly, made what struck him as a curious offer. She would, she said, if it was not presuming too much, and only if he had no reservations, be pleased, insofar as time might allow away from her other, more "official" duties, to assist him in formulating a more "systematic and rigorous" method of achieving what she understood to be his aim.

There was about her something unfathomably sad; he sensed it straight off—though his notion of what was and was not fathomable was then still as shallow as show tunes—a woundedness about her glaucous-green eyes, some radiating aura of fragility, and perhaps that explains why he answered as he did, "Thank you. I'm game if you are. In harness then."

Hours, days, weeks. Months. Became years, as, at Blake Palmer's behest, his life became little but one opened book after another. Millennia later, nothing better to do, he undertook to compile a bibliography of that time and, some one hundred titles in, abandoned such bibliotheca as duller than dentifrice, mindless citation. Though it doubtless bears mention that, because she had minored in French literature—her fluency in the language was faultless—she understandably banged *that* drum louder than some others. Punished it at no little length for Voltaire, Rousseau, Montesquieu and Montaigne, Balzac and Zola as well (though his admiration for the latter, however leavened by the unreadability of the work, soared inestimably when he stumbled upon that author's scrupulously accurate self-description: "I am only a scientist"). Beat it for *Bovary*. Bashed it for the *Education*. Bludgeoned him with her demand that "With Flaubert, you must go farther, indeed no less than as far as is possible, then still farther than that."

He would, he knew it even then, have found himself utterly at sea without her. Knowledge might be out there for the taking, but how know which to take and which to leave, in what quantities and order? Or, once taken, where to put it, how to shape it, hook it up, plug it in with all the more to be had? It took the sort of knowing he did not have and which she, decidedly, did. What he owed her was beyond owing; some debts never can be repaid.

> **If you are involved in life, you see it badly; your sight is affected either by suffering or enjoyment . . . I am leading a stern existence stripped of all external pleasure, sustained only by a kind of permanent rage. [One] should have neither religion, country, nor even any social conviction [but] cultivate an ego and *live in one's den*.**
>
> **Every beautiful thought has a beautiful form, and vice versa . . . You cannot remove the form from the Idea, because the Idea exists only by the virtue of its form. An idea without form is impossible, as is a form that does not express an idea . . . What I love above all else is form, provided it be beautiful, and nothing else . . . What seems to be outward form is actually essence.**

He could not have said, then, whether he agreed with every Flaubertian word, only that he was exhilarated by his desperately wanting to; unaccountable, the felt connection. And when she determined that his ground had been well enough laid with Baudelaire, Verlaine, Rimbaud, Mallarmé, Bertrand and Villiers de l'Isle-Adam, Nerval and Laforgue— the lot begat, as she never failed to insist, by Poe, viz., "There neither exists nor can exist any work more supremely noble than this very poem—this poem *per se*—this poem which is a poem only and *nothing* more—this poem written *solely* for the poem's *own* sake"—AND it bears mention (so will be), that little known then, utterly forgotten now, was that the work of most of these writers was available in translation in an obscure publication, *The Chap-Book*, published by the Chicago firm of Stone and Kimball, scarce ninety miles south—she presented him with the orris-work-covered notebook she had purchased for the purpose, instructing him to copy the words conscientiously twice a day, once upon waking, again at bedtime, this midnight lucubration:

> *There is nothing truly beautiful but that which can never be any use whatever; **everything useful is ugly,** for it is the expression of some*

*need, and man's needs are ignoble and disgusting like his own poor and
infirm nature. The most useful place in a house is the water-closet.*

Gautier's words in his preface to *Mademoiselle de Maupin.*
And why, she quizzed him. Why was this? How so?

"Because," he intuited, "man is a creature of abject want ahead of dire
need, base desire before necessity? Because life is a matter of aoristic ex-
crescence? Because fantasia and phantasmagoria, reverie and dream, are
more beautiful than brute experience? Because the lyric of a poem sustains
life no less than a loaf of bread, and there is no place without eyes to see
us? Am I close?"

"No." She smiled indulgently. "Not close. Correct. You are learning."

"In other words," he said, "music over meaning?"

"In other words," she said, "quite so."

Not that it was solely this sort of Symbolist thing. She grilled him, for
instance—gruelingly, relentlessly, without accommodation or apology—in
Machiavelli, and Hobbes, and Burke, had him read the pre-Raphaelite
William Morris's *News from Nowhere* and *A Dream of John Ball*, and even,
for awhile, until he dug in his heels so deeply that she eventually was
obliged to relent, had him studying, and with no little rigor, Jacob Riis,
adamantly insisting that *The Children of the Poor, Out of Mulberry Street*,
and, especially, *How the Other Half Lives*, were "essential reading for anyone who would call himself a thinking, educated, decently informed
American." Into the same category fell Frank Norris's *McTeague*, a book—
a noisome travesty, as he considered it—he both loathed and despised as
much as any she ever thought to assign.

In the end, though, it was as it ever had been: *It is the woman in us /
That makes us [read and] write— / Let us acknowledge it— / Men would be
silent.*

PALMS

Their relationship sustained Platonic. The age discrepancy. Seven was a
long lot of years, doubly so at their ages. And then she recommended a
book, *Reveries of a Bachelor*, Donald Grant Mitchell (writing as Ik Marvel), a book unlike anything she previously had suggested.

In sum, an old bachelor sits fireside at midnight smoking his cigar and
reminiscing—here the faintest whiff of Huysmans (whom he had, at the

time, yet to read: *Why stir when one can travel so magnificently in a chair?*)—
about bygone loves and love affairs, only to conclude that men and women
might most purely experience the "entireness and total unity" of sexual
union without benefit of marriage.

Charming enough was his judgment, but strange and—strangely—
strangely powerful, just powerful enough to suggest that love existed *not*
for marriage but for its *own* sake, a beauty to be embraced in the moment,
as it did that women were not angels, far from it—not the ones he always
had presumed them to be at any rate—but blood and flesh and, as such,
quite delectable enough.

And there were its lessons: that beauty does not mean but simply is, as
weather is, a state of volitionless being; that passion is not fuss, so ought
not fret, like fire; that while love is the possession that consents not to possess, it never is selfless but insists, mandates, consumes, immolates—the
love that loves to love too well, wholly, too much, always: the Meaningless
Intensive.

All this was news to him, of course, which only goes to how young,
inexperienced, hopelessly idealistic and romantic, how nescient and naif
he really was.

She took the initiative. It was all hers to take. "Welcome to Eros," she
whispered in his ear, then nipped at its lobe, drawing blood. *"Meum et
tuum."*

Bewildered, he momentarily was caught at cross-purposes with himself or, rather, his notion of himself, and if it was different with Palmer,
that was because *she* was—indeed, unlike anyone he ever had known.

He felt flattered, decided to like it, did, muchly. He hadn't known you
could do all those things, the different ones, the ones he liked, came to like
more, if certain ones more than others. And all the pet names she taught
him: the harness, chandelier, cinch-and-saddle, bandolier, the ball-and-
socket, trapeze, slingshot-and-swing, shoot-the-moon, high-and-uncut,
the cut-your-suspenders-and-go-straight-on-up.

Of course, there exist secrets in the skin, within and deep beneath it.
Everyone knows this, but he didn't, not then, or the way they might be
made to yield, all those moments bred of their moments *in* those moments. If he had much to learn, and what he had to learn was everything,
his inexperience was part of his attraction for her. Initiation.

"Sex is for knowing someone," she told him, pillow-talking, "and, too, oneself. The worst sin in the world is to fornicate apologetically. Never be ashamed to lust. Be impatient. Insatiable. Ravish. Just / don't / rush. I need to sense your avarice, Frank."

What response was he to make? "This is how people get power over one another," he thought, remembering Blake: *"He who desires, but acts not, breeds pestilence."* As, too, his Nietzsche: *"Thou goest to woman? Do not forget thy whip."* Which, naturally, would not do. Stammered monosyllables instead.

They made love everywhere no one would think to look, everywhere secret, hidden, dark, inside her Barclay Street flat, number 10, and once, that winter, outside, bundled up in the snow, on the roof, beneath the moon, drunk on Madeira and stars.

"I know," she said that time, "let's pretend it's a belvedere, one in Paris, France."

Stripped naked afterward and made snow angels while she mouthed in French the names of constellations, she so singularly ignorant of axial spin, galactic drift, celestial churn, the speed of light, and how time was too slow, beats behind and fracts, so that looking at the stars was looking at the past. History overhead. Distance × velocity. Not meant to last. Every moment, every moment together their bodies wound tight, set to spring, each to the other.

"To be alive and free for a few hours is all there is," she said, once back inside, after they had finished a second time, her words afloat on the fragrance of her cubebs, the postcoital cigarettes she favored late at night in bed, blowing polygons at the coffered ceiling like vowels of candied smoke. "There is no more."

"Sure there is," he said, tapping his temple. "Nothing but more."

"Ah," she said, "your buddy Flaubert." And quoted him. "'Some fatal attraction draws me into the abyss of thought, down into those innermost recesses.' Fine, but what for?"

He shrugged, looked long miles through the cut jade sage of her eyes. "No what for. Just is."

Her husband, a teacher of high school English, had died two years earlier of tuberculosis. "Twenty-two months," she said. "Twenty-two most precious months." Brushed at a housefly of tear. "He always said the bugs would get him before the worms." And fetched, somehow, a smile.

Sometimes the two of them read, in unison, the *Rubaiyat.* It was all the rage then, and she owned the five successively revised editions of FitzGerald's translations. *Drink and be merry for tomorrow we die. A Book of Verses underneath the Bough, / A Jug of Wine, a Loaf of Bread—and Thou.*

Called him private names: Thesaurus Man, My Poetic Phallacy, because his vocabulary had begun posing a problem. Already rangy, it was daily enlarging, cellularly multiplying, and, unlike with people's names and faces—or their life stories, which he seldom retained—it seemed to her that once he had suffered exposure to a new word, he was incapable of forgetting it, as he was compelled less to induct than to crowbar it into every conversation, for he found it impossible, apparently, simply to whisper words to himself, then place them in his pockets.

"Do you know how you feel when you're inside of me," she asked, "when you make me come?" Took his hand in hers, placed it to the hammer of her heart. "Like this," she said, "exactly." Sweet as muscovado.

The world was a beautiful place now, one that, later, he would recall in the context of Bacon's maxim: "No beauty without strangeness," and which read more precisely, "No excellent beauty that hath not some strangeness in the proportion." And this, it began at last to dawn on him—slow learner, interminably so—was some exigent part of what Blake Palmer had been and continued tutoring him toward: to see in such a way that one sees nothing save that one sees beauty, nor less so in that which but a moment ago had appeared disproportionate, disfigured, and deformed. Because that was its power, beauty's, as, too, its ultimate value. She knew, as he had yet to learn, that it commanded regard, beauty, and regard for it was what she wished for him to show.

"Beauty, Frank," she lectured him, "is not erasable, but that which erases, and its power is precisely that foaled of its promise to please and be pleasing, pleasure and be pleasuring. Dark magic, that, for it is no less than to gain control over another by satisfying the other's most ardent desire through the usurpation of all will and all reason. Pure effect and no cause, it entices, lures, seduces, propels and impels, enthralls and enthrills, and, ultimately, my love, it entraps.

"We wish to delight in it, have commerce and couple, become one with it, in this way better to complete the whole of ourselves, and yet, in wishing to possess it, we inevitably are possessed by it. We desire what we cannot abide."

Women, head swimming, was all he could think, that must be what all this talk of beauty was about. What else, after all, had Bacon meant by strangeness if not the uncanny, the other, the divine, and what could be more divine to a man than a woman? "Women consider that they supply the beauty," he recalled Schopenhauer having remarked. Well, didn't they? For if not women, Woman, who?

Well, it could be argued, perfectly pointless, pretentious too, to talk about beauty this way, abstractly, and yet, there was, to him, nothing pretentious or abstract about it. More than some aesthetic principle, concept *aéré*, idea or ideal, more than some theory *fixe*—or so he was becoming convinced—beauty was the way a scent feels, color tastes, sound smells— a surd hircine?—the way emotion bleeds. It was esters and ethers, elixirs and electuaries, alembics, and it was dreams. Because man is a dreamer of woman, always was and will be.

Perhaps, who knew, it was this that his father had meant by "the carnality of the soul." The mind was a man's only weapon? Okay. His primary responsibility might be to meticulously assemble his intellectual armamentarium, but, by God, to quote his father, there was more to a man than his mind, and he must learn to grasp the moment as the cunt grasps the cock. How was he to know—child!—how quickly joy expires once the mysteries of any flesh are solved, as if one could live within and through words alone, yet get off scot-free, without being required to open a vein and unwell oneself, black as every ink—

> *who believes*
> *in the power of beauty*
> *to right all wrongs.*
> *I believe it also.*

—until the sky unspooled like a scroll upon which to inscribe among its moments— person, place, object, event—the few that mattered most: *N'est-ce pas beau comme la littérature?*

So it was, at any rate, that in those days he dared to compose on the fly his first extended poem, one, ostensibly, about poetry, for about what other subject might he pretend, bereft of pretext, to poeticize?

Brief excerpt:

> *. . . what more, then, dare we ask our poetry* do
> *save soar, climb, pivot blued altitudes,*
> *hoverhigh, noon-high awhile fumed on flames (azured, oranged),*

then plunge back burnt black-through, charred of tongue, or
failing that, pull up a chair, strop itself in, and
hazard its unsung flight once more, all-new.

To terror it is that beauty must bend,
as by terror it was that beauty was bred.

This shaping of a sensorium.

TIME'S UP, AND AWAY

In time, and, so it proved, *just* in time, he began mulling the advisability of
leaving. When he inadvertently caught the two of them *in flagrante* in the
barn in the middle of the day—his own mother, Christ!—he reckoned it
was time to stop thinking and just go. Hightail it. Save he had no money,
none that would last him a month, not in Chicago.

"Chicago! But why Chicago?"

"They're hiring, Mother. Some kind of spree. *Inter Ocean. Evening
Post. Trib.* Saw it in our *Journal* just the other day."

"You're sure about this? Thought it through? It's what you want
to do?"

"Think so. Don't need me around the place, not anymore. I'm no
farmer, we both know that. Not that I don't like it here well enough, just
don't belong."

"But how will you live? Until you get hired, I mean. If you get hired."

"I was thinking—"

"A month. Float your boat for a month, enough to get you on your
feet, find a place, find work, some cash in your pocket. How's that?"

"You can afford it? A month, I mean, if you can't, I'll—"

"A month, one month, no more."

"All right then, that should do 'er."

"That better. So one favor first."

"Sure."

"Write."

"Every day."

"No, when you can, now and then. So then it makes you happy?
Going?"

"I dunno, guess so, feels right, yeah."

"Good. Trust to your head and the eyes the Lord gave you, you'll be fine. They're level enough."

"You'll be okay? You and Jonah?"

"Don't worry about us. Write when you can, visit when you want. Go seek your fortune."

Palmer would understand, of that he had no doubt. There would be no scenes, recriminations, words that once spoken could not be retrieved. It hurt like hell to go smash, it stung, but she would agree, for the best. He took it for granted she would. What did he know? Of another's soul? And if she didn't? Gosh.

"No regrets, my love," she said, trooper, time come—she was so far ahead of him—"not one. Rainbows and blue chiffon, Frank, bouquets and bonbons, that's how I'll remember us, still young."

The gratitude he ought have expressed was precisely that which he was incapable of expressing. Too shallow, callow, too stuck on himself to see straight, and no time, if less inclination, to attend to the required unsticking.

"You're going to fall in love with that place, kiddo. The first expression of American Thought as Unity, that's what Henry Adams calls Chicago. One must, he said, start there. You're doing the right thing, Frank, you are, the only thing. Everyone's got to start somewhere. Do you realize how lucky you are to do it there, to start at the very beginning?"

He could not have known how much he was going to miss her.

"I'll write," he said, and when she shook her head, insisted, "but really, I will."

She only smiled, her sadness. "No, but you won't."

"But—"

"You won't, and it's perfectly all right. Better this way, love. I could not bear it otherwise. It falls to neither of us to reinvent the other. We're each doing what each should be doing. So now promise me. You won't. Write."

So he did. Promised. And kept it. His word. Time come. It was hard. But kept it. Gesture of faith in the silence. Wrote, not a one.

The Silver Cyclone out of Milwaukee's Everett Street station on the Milwaukee Road along the Hiawatha Corridor, the one hugging the shore of Lake Michigan falling south, departed thrice daily on the roughly ninety-mile trip that when accomplished without delay or sidetrack took exactly two hours and more. A third-class, one-way ducat, fifty cents. One of thirty passenger trains fanning into and out of that city each day crammed with one hundred thousand passengers.

Franklyn never had ridden a train before, what his mother, for some reason, always had called "the Kelockity." He would recall little of riding one now. The porter awakened him upon arrival by a jostled shoulder, the narrowing rails, as if by sorcery or sortilege, having slid together behind him, squealing ladders of steel.

Shock City, Hustle City, Packingtown, Porkopolis, Hog Butcher, Wheat Stacker, Freight Handler, this robust metropolis—originally Checaugou, "wild onion" in the indigenous Potowatomi dialect—so unafraid to be openly demonstrative. 1,698,575 souls (by count of the last census), three out of four of them immigrants or the offspring thereof (98 percent white)—prying their living amid the liquor purveyed by some 6,400 to 12,000 saloons (the figure fluctuated daily), the dozen major gambling syndicates, and the rampant lording of vice presided over by hoodlums, gangsters, and three-penny thugs.

Wickedest City in the World. One, as Mr. Dreiser soon would inveigh, "packed to the doors with all the riffraff of a thousand towns." "An overgrown village ruled by barbarians," one wag had called it. "A gigantic peepshow of utter horror, but extraordinarily to the point," yet another. "A frontier town grown fat on bread and circuses. A great, gorgeous, gaseous hussy dressed in red satin with a heart as big and gaudy as her clothes and her language."

Franklyn carried a pair of tattered rattan grips—grips he shortly would pawn for a creel-size tote of incarnadine Brussels carpet embroidered with acanthus and orange blossoms—with his father's initials, A.I.S. (the I for Icilius), embossed in gilt. Strapped 'round his waist, zippered inside his father's soft leather belt, was the money his mother had advanced him. His pocket bulged with coin; the heft of its weight jounced when he walked, its silver sound chunky and chingling against the watch fob and jackknife.

He felt flush, if likewise naught but at sea. Only to be expected, he thought, to picture oneself the yokel, Yahoo, the figure of fun just off the boat, in from the provinces, the unreconstructed hayseed and rube, country lout and rusticon. A literary trope, sure, but wasn't it the truth, regardless?

The air pulsed, *pro*pulsed, he sensed it right off, the buzzsaw and throb, rumpus and thrust, the almighty *throstle* of its thrum. He had heard someone liken it once to living inside the belly of a hydroelectric plant.

Not that he found it unpleasant, could not honestly have said that, the strangeness and size of it, magnitude of its push, the velocity he sensed as a squall—or turbulence, perhaps, better word. Noisy, though. The *clitter-clat-brang* of the surface cars, throaty brattle of the nearby El—the three-year-old, double-track Union Elevated trains, 1,600 a day rumbling, *Looping* thund'rous on their rails above the pedestrians below like, or so he conjured it, so many electric eels shrieking in their throes. It got inside your teeth is what it did, the din, bedlam of sound, the pandemonium.

He spat.

"Let's see," he thought to himself, swiping his lips with a coat sleeve and lowering one of the suitcases to the banquette. Patting his breast pocket, he fished out the map, then the address of the *Trib*. Madison and Dearborn. Southeast corner. Ten blocks. Shank's mare. He'd walk.

Headed east down Van Buren toward State, heart of the commercial district, past the aptly named Monadnock Building on Dearborn, the one where the businessmen called "cliff dwellers" quartered. Head back, back arched, neck craned, eyes sliding up up on up the vertices of the tallest buildings he ever had seen, could never have dreamed, the peekaboo sun slanting through in sparks off the soar of them, glare off their glass in his eyes, and then the river up his nose like a spignail. He smelled scuffs of fresh-brewed black coffee, cooking candy-caramel, cottoned candy, burnt nuts and licorice, cinnamon buns, spiced plums, and underneath those— up from the South? West?—what he took for the insinuating assault of the notorious Yards, all their 450 acres of abattoirial stench.

Swift, Armour, Libby. Furnace of factory, stockyard, incinerator, steel-work, slaughterhouse, cannery. The Yards—more formally the Union Stockyards and Transit Company running north to south from Thirty-ninth to Forty-seventh Streets, east to west between Halstead and Ash-land—employed fully a fifth of the city's workforce, the fluctuating 25,000 to 40,000 souls indentured for 15 to 20 cents per hour to any one of the 100 meatpacking firms that slaughtered half a million hogs, sheep, cattle, and nags each year within the vast, eviscerated urban prairie of blood spill, pig squeal, knife rip and meathook, orts, offal, and flyblown flesh that con-tained enough holding pens to quarter, concurrently, 50,000 sheep, 75,000 cows, and 300,000 hogs.

Up State Street then beneath a pizzicato rain raw as whips as, over-head, brisk winds steered bruised clouds the color of beets and swart schooners of sea sky swooned through gaps ragged as riprap. The Palmer

House, Sherman House, Marshall Field's, Siegel-Cooper, Schleisinger and Mayer, Mandel Brothers, Sears, McClurg's Bookstore on Wabash, said to be the largest in the world. On through the new, thumping heart of this city not one hundred years old, burned black to the ground but thirty years before, rebuilt bigger now, resurrected better, rearisen of its own char as the "I Will, Can Do-opolis," "The City on the Make of No Past," the very one where no story ever was so long that it could not be made shorter, if no less complete.

So that it was that very afternoon, fresh off the street, when he was hired and assigned his own corner, Armitage and Clark, newsboy, colporteur, *Trib* hawk, a foot, as he chose to consider it, if by the tip of a toe, in the door. And if he was slightly older than the typical newsie and the spot slightly out of the way, out of the Loop, more than a mile north of the river and not a prime location, off the old beaten path, well, then, he would reckon a way to steer all that to his advantage.

As a succession of nameless others had failed there in the past, he resolved to make it the hottest corner in the city, penny a pop, nickel on Sundays, and, so, in the ensuing weeks proceeded to so outperform expectations—he soon settled upon a shtick, song and dance, an act, part of which was to trick himself out like Santa or Napoleon, Uncle Sam or Lady Liberty, Buffalo Bill or Blackface Blackie (he eventually succeeded in prevailing upon the *Trib* to help defray the cost of the props) or, sometimes, draped in a sandwich board emblazoned with the day's banner headlines—that three months later he was invited inside, drafted onto the second floor of the five-story *Trib* building—only later would the paper make its move to its landmark seventeen-floor "skyscraper"—into the newsroom, the pressroom, where he was put to work as a "copyboy," eight dollars a week.

Ten, twelve, fourteen hours a day, six days a week, up and at 'em at one—he didn't mind the late hour; nonmatutinal cerebration—to the summoning mantra of "Boy!" beneath the profane-laced lash of head office boy Jimmie Durkin, James Aloysius Durkin, his thirty-year-old boss, fetching rough drafts and pencil-edited and reedited versions of stories and heads and cutlines, ferrying cut-and-glued paper—the cheap, grainy, mustard-colored stuff, rough as sandpaper—about the cement-floored, cigarette/cigarillo/cigar-and-cheroot carpeted room, to and fro through the maze of desks and aisles, dodging the ubiquitous gaboons to the arrhythmic clatter and riot of Underwoods and the LePaged gluey whiff of the paste pots. So that as the year stalled out, impatient to be shed of its past, or perhaps fete what might lie ahead, he had run away into text. This new vocabulary of type. One cold and hard. One fast.

"Thirty!" Durkin would sing in the finest Irish tenor he ever had heard, dismissing him at day's end once the paper had been put to bed, while everywhere in America the batteried, neon century was turning, somewhere around the carousel of its corner who knew what headlines buoyed upon the billows of this brash, beckoning, barrel-chested city, in its new winds the old dreams of the young.

And Franklyn Shivs, his mind speeding silver, wishing to stay abreast, sprinting to keep up, pull even at last with an age about to be over, the one of absolutes, answers, clarity, and meaning, of mapped directions ordered and true. Striving now—all were striving—each more wayless than the next, desperate to outdistance the news.

CHI-TOWN

* * *

Newshawk, copyboy, morgue filer, picture chaser, cutline writer, obit writer, legman, Saturday-night rewrite, Sunday-night slot, Franklyn rose steadily if unspectacularly through the ranks, catching his first real break when Durkin, left shorthanded by an outbreak of Spanish flu, tapped him to cover Saturdays, a job requiring that he answer the bank of phones on the copy desk; deliver all finalized copy to the city editor, E. S. "Teddy" Beck, for his sign-off before chuting it by pneumatic tube down to the composing room; track the fire-alarm buzzer (nicknamed the joker)—note the number and pattern of alarm bells to determine the location and size of the blaze (a "4-1-1" was all hell broken loose); and hang out with the night rewrite crew until the city edition had been put to bed around three in the a.m.

"And if something big breaks after one," Durkin instructed him, "you get on the Graham and ring up Calumet 4-1-2."

"Calumet 4-1-2?" Franklyn asked, innocently enough. "What's that? Stillson's?" The latter being, as he knew, the saloon across the street favored by the scribes after hours.

Durkin shook his head. "Nah. The Everleigh, son. That's the fuckin' Everleigh."

Franklyn shrugged the universal "search me" gesture.

"Whorehouse, son. It's a whorehouse. Shit, it's *the* whorehouse."

Paid most of a living wage, he lived mostly within his means, on the cheap, alone, in a bare, draughty, acceptably dank garret-keep no larger than a cuddy that featured as cotenant a recalcitrant coal-burning potbelly he promptly named Nerval. Requiring stiff verbal coaxing, sometimes a swift kick in the slats, it eventually would snuffle, snort, sigh, wheeze, rattle back from the dead with enough *Sturm und Drang* to jar the windowpanes. Its glowing cast-iron paunch, he soon enough drunkenly discovered, was an object you did well to steer clear of.

The attic, one of the few he could find that did not require he deposit an arm and a leg up front, was in the old Frederick Dent Grant mansion on the Near Northside, on Dearborn, easy walking distance to the Newberry. The northern limit of the burned-over district, where the Great Fire of '71 had breathed itself out, was but some ten blocks north, at Fullerton.

He hauled his coal up from the coalbin in the cellar by the shuttleful in fetch-and-tote, rope-handled zinc scuttle-hods furnished by the super. The pull-chain water closet was out in the hall, on the landing, as was a sink for cold-water sponge baths. But the cousy featured decent light and a good lot of exposed, periodically too-hot-to-touch brick at either end where a pair of massive chimneys thrust through. He called it "my gloomy endroit, my claustral coop."

Writing his mother to have Jonah ship down the books he had crated before leaving, when they arrived he lined them across the floor, spines aligned, plumb along the baseboard in back of the mattress-upon-pallet that served for his bed, jelly and jam jars filled with Indian Head pennies for bookends. Other details included: the impossibly acute angle at which the ceiling downsloped, obliging him to duckwalk his way around all but the very center of the place; the way the warped floorboards croaked like flatulent frogs; the spirit lamp he had purchased secondhand upon which to singe his Turkish coffee thicker than bisque and as black; the haul of tanbark he took it upon himself to store in a heap in the corner to intermittently spread in the cobblestone street to muffle the incessant night-and-day clip-clop of horsehoof and creak of carriage wheel—Studebaker Brougham, Oldsmobile Landau, the endless procession of stanhopes, victorias, phaetons, and cabriolets, fiacres, and barouches; the way that in winter he could hear the water clack to ice in the sink in the hall and in summer the tugs bugling on the Chicago River through the open windows—blasts of pain blotting out bleats of agony, as he conceived of them—to the fresh-roasted whiff up from the nearby coffee warehouse.

But above all, more than the rest, there was the mental upholstery that was his thoughts. He had been scarcely a month or two on the job when he found himself compelled, typically late at night, to compose a piece he always would think of as *The Unfurnished Room*. Over the years, he would return to it again and again, much as many do a diary, but at its birth, intent upon imbuing it with what he conceived of as his own distinctly Midwestern Modern(ist) sensibility, its very beginning began:

At night and abed, amidst the dark and alone, I paint my vacant walls, scrawling there the outlines of my nightmares as with the ash of my eyes. These grays against blacks. Their dry tears entangled.

Then laugh at the stupid art of it.

I room. Am a roomer. Bed-and-boarder. I rent. New American me. New home. Hopeless. Rootless. Alone. On my own. But free?

The unfurnished room welcomes us, the hopeless homeless, hapless, unacknowledged unknown. Not forgotten because never remembered. Tramp. Transient. A traveler. All those like myself. Who trawl.

Here I dump the disarray and discard, crude filth of brain and of body. Lay in my larder. Lay down my soul.

The room, I feel, has eyes of its own that press down to the bone, pierce in, punch through, hook onto like hands. The room, I suspect, thinks me a fool, means me harm without name. Is it haunted? It begins to haunt me.

No houses for homes. Rooms, only. Hotel rooms, laundry rooms, lunch rooms, wine rooms, each ashen as smoke, more joyless than snow. This New World America. This New Home is cold.

My room always takes me back. So I go. Back. Return to the place I can go. The one I know best. Others have it far worse, perhaps. Who knows? At least its fears are familiar. I must parley a truce with its ghosts.

I throw off my covers, slip from my bed, walk to the window, naked with stars. I sign each one, compose for the occasion: "Save the roomers." I sign: "Save all those whose moments are spent in unfurnished rooms painting the walls with their fears."

The stars have gone now. But where? Out? Sucked into my mirror, all blent with its silver? Empty as eyes?

Night coffee. Cigarette smoke. On my bed I lie naked, buried alive up past my eyes in the light of my nakedness, scrutineer of my fears.

In the morning the jaws of the sun will come into my room to chew me awake or eat me alive. Fill the space of my room with the buzz of bright bees. Inside my head. Inside my sheets. I am afraid of nothing but fear. And my bed.

What can it mean to wake in sunlight, yet see only darkness? To awake to one's teeth hallucinating outside one's head? One's tongue, detached from one's mouth? Tapping out messages, receiving the same? In code.

The mind churns to spittle, whispers me Milton: Which way I fly, is hell.

He wasn't poor—his salary had been bumped to fifteen dollars a week—but, rather, decidedly poorish. When he ate out, which he seldom did, typically surviving on macaroni and cheese, tamales and chowchow, redskin-potato salad, the occasional radish, green tea, he did so at rathskellers and *beerstubes*, bon tons, chop-suey joints, chuckwagons and hash houses, "one arms" and greasy spoons, or one of the Clark Street penny-lunch counters on Toothpick Row, favoring whatever was being offered as the twenty-cent table d'hôte, then bagging home for next morning's breakfast whatever foodstuff and potable, vittle, victual, or viand he had failed to polish off.

He rode the El, omnibuses, or streetcars instead of paying for hansoms and hacks. Had his shoes stitched and resoled rather than buy new. Let his hair grow too long between visits to the barber. Labored diligently, if with but sporadic success, to avoid cultivating dear habits—tobacco, gambling, alcohol, whores. In time, discovered Ben Abramson's Argus Bookstore south of the Loop, source of the best commercial scopophilia in the city.

He endeavored to persuade himself that strolls around Washington Square Park or bicycle "scorches" along the lake—the bike, generically called a "wheel," was his first significant purchase, an inexpensive, silver-and-black Pope "Safety"—or, in winter, skating on the Midway Plaisance,

or spending Saturday afternoons ensconced in an armchair in the poetry
room of the Newberry reading Emily Dickinson constituted a rewarding
social life. And when he had had enough of the latter or required more,
when he grew overtaxed or restless or bored, he exited through the library's south door, crossed into its front yard—colloquially called Bug-
house Square, Chicago's version of London's Hyde Park or New York's
Union Square—plunked himself down on a park bench beneath a flower-
less crabapple, and fished from his ruck an eminently affordable McIntosh
apple and a plug of black licorice, or simply gazed at the sky long enough
and with sufficient intensity to convince himself that he could, applying
his powers of concentration alone, sculpt clouds into shapes.

And, if he had a spare nickel, which was seldom enough, he hoofed it
the three blocks over to the Noose Coffeehouse in Towertown, wondering
as he blew and sipped from his saucer, what Tick was up to and Palms,
typically in that order. Because, much as he might have preferred otherwise, he was in no position to cab it with some swell gal over to the Blue
Fountain Room of the LaSalle, or the Egyptian Room of the Blackstone,
or any room whatever of the luxurious Sherman House, or even to the
glitz and ritz of the Frogs for an evening of highballs, woodcock on rye-
toast points, olive-stuffed squab, Pont l'Eveque cheese, *canard à l'orange*,
haricots verts, and broiled lobster, or a bottle of Château d'Yquem and
shrimp soufflé, or Oysters Rockefeller, clam consommé, planked steak
chasseur, or Filet à la Rossini, and a nice Liebfraumilch or Montrachet at
the Tip Top Inn on Michigan Avenue, overlooking the lake. Capped off
by—what?—Baked Alaska? Bananas Foster? Cherries Jubilee? Floating
Island? Blancmange? *Crème fraîche*? *Mille-feuille*? *Flambeuax à la Poire*?
Peach Melba? Jellied madrilène served in silver *écuelles*? *Sorbet au Kirsch*?
Sacher-torte and *schlag*? Platters piled high, wide, and handsome with sack
posset, frangipane, profiteroles, bonbons, and petits fours? After which,
perhaps a round or two of skipping the light fandango—the Bunny Hug,
Turkey Trot, the Two-step and Grizzly Bear, the Boston Dip and Hesita-
tion, the Texas Tommy—into the wee, sparkling, purry, champagne-pink
hours getting comfortably numb on Pommery Sec or Ruinart Brut. Hell,
he couldn't even afford a night out at Kolze's, Colehour's, Excelsior Park,
Ogden Grove, Fischer's Garden, or the Edelweiss or the Bismarck, the
city's better beer gardens.

There always were the pleasures to be had from haunting the book-
shops, of course: McClurg's on Wabash, Browne's in the Fine Arts Build-

ing, Powner's secondhand for stowaway first editions, or from eating pompano beside the onyx-black pillars and shimmering glass fountains of the peach-blossom promenade of Peacock Alley, its rhythmic splash and syncopated splash the chuckle of all lakeside Chicago. But Congress Street was a hike, even by bike, and the Auditorium Bar, while the bar snacks were free, criminally overcharged for a bumper of beer. You needed to be in the mood and the money, and he seldom was either. His single indulgence in those days was shagging it out to West Side Park at Lincoln and Wood of a Sunday afternoon to sit for a dime in the cheap seats with a frank—called a "red hot"—a beer and to cheer on Mordecai "Three-fingered" Brown or watch "Big Ed" Reulbach mow 'em down, or Tinker throw to Evers on to Chance.

For the most part, then, he was content to vagabond about, scuffing, but not . . . quite, and not . . . always, for aside from the insomnia by which he found himself increasingly plagued—sleep had become for him, as he thought of it, a matter of barbed wire, a thing to climb over or through—there also were those dark moments when the loneliness grew so acute that decisions, choices, judgments, distinctions, selections, priorities, resolutions all were impossible to summon, and the broad shoulders of the big city seemed then to droop and slacken, rendering what otherwise was so gay grittier than he could bear, the day a swart-faced affair, gray and hodden-gray, rain-smudged, slush-bound, soot-hung, square, dismally drabbish, oppressively opaque—soiled laundry, cindered air, dead pigeons and gulls, ossifrages, rats, raccoons, everywhere—and sometimes, however bright and balmy the noonday, it went all black, black as atrament, though he bore it best he must.

Later, of course, he would feel sheepish about it, confess regrets, apprehend that he had not earned the right to such emotions, the way characters in novels do (or are said to), but, rather, had assigned them to himself by imposition. Still, lonely as he was, he found himself faced with the same truth everyone must face sooner or later—namely, that people are impossible, life is less than what it is cracked up to be, the world is a singularly unattractive place in which to be obliged to pass one's time, Creation is the greatest botch and put-up job ever invented, the truth is unfailingly unpleasant where not insufferably bitter, love is powerless to make anything right, and scarce a book is worth its rereading, if foremostly those that had made that year's brand-new adman's brainchild, something called "the bestseller list."

To wit:

1. *To Have and to Hold*, Mary Johnston

2. *Red Pottage*, Mary Cholmondeley

3. *Unleavened Bread*, Robert Grant

4. *The Reign of Law*, James Lane Allen

5. *Eben Holden*, Irving Bacheller

How live one's life properly in such a world, he wondered, amid such dreck? How do that? Well, one didn't, he supposed. One held one's nose and tiptoed as one tread. One read the rereadable few, the while wondering what it would feel like to *be* a skyscraper, or perhaps the El itself, the way it crept, insectlike, caracole to life, some saurian millipede, its spine alive with the skitter of a roach going nowhere save diverticular, looping its Loop. Save that—downtown, underground, skybound—what possible difference? He still was left gnawing his insides out by guess and by golly, morning, noon, night, forfeit to his—what?—folly?

Part of the letter he intended to post off to his mother: *I feel myself ebbing away sometimes. All sailed out. Past seas unseen, even by myself. Atrabilious eyes. All the salt gone out of things, the mustard besides. Debility everywhere. Pitch and tars. Stuck. I feel like a ropedancer watching his own shadow do the skipping. Everything worse, or worse still. And there I dwell, a ruin in advance of his wreck. Not even the Sirens sing to me.* And so, of course, never sent. But instead: *Hope this finds you tip-top. I am doing aces. Like my job. They treat me well. The pay's okay. The city's swell. My love to Jonah. Say hey to Tick. Miss you guys. Love, Latty.*

In the end, he bought himself a secondhand medicine ball, a pair of Indian pins, a new jump rope, and a pair of boxing gloves and began to work it off, as he presumed, by trying to work it out. Wind sprints, shadowboxing, sit-ups, push-ups, pull-ups, none of which took, until he began with the shadow play, practicing hour on end using his arms and hands and fingers, legs and feet and toes to make imprints on the walls and ceiling. Not animals, living things, neither so much as a *fantoccio*, but oddly configured, intricate shapes, indelible designs, caliginous geometry. Mudras. This ganty show.

"No man can escape this city," his future friend Swatty Anderson soon would write about Chicago. "When you have been sick of it to the very marrow and accepted it, then at last, walking hopeless, endless streets—hopeless yourself—you begin to feel its beauty, its half-wild beauty . . . Something half-wild and alive in yourself is there, too. The city you have dreaded and feared is like your own soul."

"I must," thought Franklyn. "I should. Shall. Why not? Compile a list. Random order. All that renders this . . . waking, worth it."

1. "Un Coup de Des"

2. Women's backsides

3. Mescal (all brands)

4. "The Large Bathers"

5. Terriers (all breeds)

6. "The Maple Leaf Rag"

7. Baseball

8. Women's breasts, and eyes

9. Autumn (November in particular)

10. Emily

Reasons enough, more or less?
The price of solitude seldom is cheap, but at least one owes no debt.

CUB TO CRACKERJACK

He liked his work enough to be perceived as uncommonly devoted to it, a "grind," and because he was well mannered—if none disagreed more passionately, few did so more agreeably—and gave the impression of being naturally unguarded and guileless, if disarmingly frank, he personally was well liked by some of his colleagues, though far from all. Too solitary, after all, too unapologetically eccentric as well, what with his preference for working unshod at his desk draped in a black-and-white checkerboard shawl fringed with hand-twisted tassels and wearing his mop of ungovernable sandy hair wildly askew—uncropped, jackstrawed, unscrewed—as well as his irrational partiality for fancy weskits and vests, his one visible concession to citification—although, in time, they came to be pocked with burn holes; he was a notoriously sloppy smoker—along with his favoring sponge-bag, triple-pleated trousers and the butter-toffee snap-brim he wore correctly downturned in front, upturned in back, and canter-cocked at a severe forty-five-degree angle over the right, always the right, always at forty-five degrees, eye. Well liked, then, but *not* popular, a fact of which he decidedly was aware but could not be bothered to bother about save on those occasions when he was assigned to "team cover" a story and found himself more cold-shouldered than not by his so-called brothers-in-arms.

Notwithstanding, he was marked a "comer," and certainly he slogged the hours, performing his duties at a higher pitch and with more raw enthusiasm and manifest flair than most, if not as brilliantly as some. His superiors, appreciative of his attitude of assiduity as much as his ability, were patient with his shortcomings, chalking them up to inexperience rather than to what he knew they were in fact—some manner of disconnect between who he was and what he was being paid to do; square peg/oblong hole.

A reporter, he quickly learned, must listen and observe in close, what they liked to call "telling" detail; must intuit ways to place his sources at ease long enough to extract from them that which the story demands; must develop a nose for the feint of the feigned and the false; must not shy from insinuating his way into situations where he otherwise has no business being, protocol be damned; must never be reluctant to ask the dumb and/or obvious question; and must nurture in himself three qualities above all: an arched-brow skepticism, a bulldog doggedness, and a pair of antennae cocked curiously to the world, its doings, and those who inhabit it.

Learning the city, acquiring an intimately savvy knowledge of its physical and psychic geography—the location of the closets where all the skeletons have been and are buried—was important, too, of course, and whenever he found himself at a loss, assigned to a "story"—which he came to understand was the misnomer the profession insisted upon applying to its reports, accounts, data inputs, and dispatches—in an unfamiliar place among unfamiliar circumstances, he simply walked up to a cop and begged directions and, so, got to know them some. Tough lads, most of them, Irish, and grabby.

The other requisites of the job, he might, as in time he did, learn to cultivate. It was the natural curiosity, as he came to consider it, the unflagging inquisitiveness that he apprehended was going to pose a chore, be-cause to be curious about something necessarily is to care enough about the something one is being curious about to be curious about it in the first instance, and, as a rule, he was not, though he did his level best to mime his way through. What he *did* care about was his copy, and this soon proved, to his astonishment, as much a liability as an asset.

He had been, perhaps, less than a year on the job when it was confi-dentially conveyed to him by his boss that the powers that be felt he was prey to certain "excesses," an "overzealousness" is the way he put it, that betrayed itself in an appetite for "a perfectibility of product that on daily deadline is a luxury we cannot afford." Nor were they entirely wrong. "History on the fly," "better first than good," "go with what you've got," "let the facts speak for themselves," "less is more," "make a little do for a lot," "what you don't have today you'll get tomorrow," "catch as catch can," "brevity is the soul of wit"—such canards and chestnuts drove him to the verge of distraction, for it wasn't enough that he be thorough, conscien-tious, solid, reliable; he was compelled to completeness, definitiveness, to the all of a thing or its nothing. Sketchiness made him squirm, as did sprawl.

Worse still, his boss was pleased to inform him, was his "obsessive, pointless, striving for sentence-by-sentence perfection." And, once again, he was not wrong, for Franklyn wrote his ledes the way others chewed gum or bit fingernails or picked noses or gnawed pencil erasers or chain-smoked or masturbated: compulsively. By night's end, the floor beneath his desk typically was ankle-high in the litter of discards and rejects, this rising tide of crumpled paper, a risen sea of simile. He did not really write, he sometimes thought, so much as rewrite, revise, emend, incessantly.

"We're not word slingers here, Shivs," his boss admonished him. "We're not versifiers. We're type scribes, not inscribers in stone. Who do you think you are, the Satyr of Fucking Metaphor?"

Well, how argue? They wished above all to inform; he wished nothing but to create form. No gulf ever yawned so wide. Not that that stopped him from registering his reply.

"And words aren't hash," he shot back. "They're for sculpting poetry—or lies."

The Satyr of Metaphor indeed! Such a thing to say. Why? Because when he wrote he wished to experience the erection of his soul? Writing was fucking, was it not? Fitting the phallus of the word to the vagina of one's thought (in a manner of speaking)? His boss smirked, scowled, dismissed him for both a metaphrast and a topologist—though he was left to suggest the words himself. Well, better those than some damn clerk of mere fact, the way they typed them out in short sentences and shorter graphs, active verbs, vivid nouns, adjectives as mortal enemy, concision, concretion, coherence, continuity, clarity, the vaunted single focus, that of the stenographer, its linearity.

Well, they insisted that language existed to communicate. He was convinced it ought to express. They sought at all cost to privilege the story. He cared only for its sensibility. They believed in cause and effect—indeed, took them altogether for granted. He cherished anacolutha and non sequitur. They strove for certainty. He thought the concept a myth masking the aporia beneath. They genuflected before the gathered facts. He was indifferent to all save his own intuition, and to its manner.

How keep from feeling what he began to feel, then, that he was a dunce among dolts, a dotard among dumbos and dopes? True, they were dedicated to their so-called prole craft, had to hand them that, their earnestness. It was almost quaint, the devotion they displayed to their ink-stained clichés, the "tricks of the trade," the mindless allegiance professed to what it pleased them to call a "fraternity." Problem was, how impudent, impertinent, how audacious, really, when one considered it, that they dare pretend to know what *interested* most people, what those people *needed to know*, what they alone were permitted to define as *the news*, which information merited *package and play* and which did not. Not news, he thought. Be honest. Call it what it in fact was: the despotism of topicality. Could anything be more presumptuous than to arrogate to oneself the sort of daily discrimination to decide, edition by edition, what *the citizenry* should be told and how and where and when and—sometimes, if more seldom—why?

"Your purpose here," he was instructed, first day on the job, "is to report the reportable facts, to observe, collect, compile, chronicle, not to understand, apprehend, evaluate, analyze. Don't give me motive, Shivs, give me incident, give me the five *w*s, not psychology. Embellish to your heart's content—inflate, conflate, sensationalize, we can work with that, we do it all the time, just don't—do not!—narrate. Savvy? You're a reporter, so—report."

In the end, he sensed that, while they liked his work well enough, the (over)polished product, tropes and all—particularly when placed alongside the monotonous mediocrity that characterized 90 percent of the copy that routinely made it into the paper—they scarce could stomach the something about him they recognized as shadowing him like a pall, the one that left him feeling increasingly outside his element—fish out of water, beached whale, white elephant, unicorn, fifth wheel, all such figure—never quite one of the boys, the gang, the club, the network, the one not often enough defined, as he considered it, as "those who, given time enough, write *worse*."

What was it that Flaubert once had written to George Sand? Something to the effect, wasn't it, that, "the Press is a school that serves to turn men into brutes, because it relieves them from thinking"? How, he wondered, how in good conscience summon the temerity to disagree?

THE IROQUOIS

One late, late December midweek afternoon, specifically the Wednesday after Christmas following a late-ish, if too liquid holiday lunch break across the street at Stillson's, he found himself walking off the head-fogs, alone as always, east along West Randolph.

He walked carefully, eyes glued to the sidewalk, not only because his every step was an effort to avoid misstepping in errant swerve or sottish sway, but because the walkway stretched out before him was patchy with ice. It was cold—8 degrees F., according to the clock atop the Farmer and Merchant's Bank. His breath blew white as rime.

He was a couple of blocks north of the *Trib*.

Reaching absently inside his overfrock, he inadvertently brushed the pair of brass knucks he latterly had begun carrying in a scrimshaw, clip-on case in his inside breast pocket, fished the fobbed watch from his vest. Later, he would wonder why he had thought to do that just then, was left to conjecture that, in the face of a vision as otherworldly as the one with which he found himself confronted, he could only have wished to assure himself that he remained fixed in space as he did anchored in time, Earthbound Central Standard, spatially tethered, temporally aligned.

It was shortly before 3:30 p.m.

Halting abruptly in his tracks, he closed his eyes, opened them again. He still was in the Loop, West Randolph, and they had not gone away, the fairies, these diaphanous, miniature fairies clad in luminous pinks and tufts of blue fur, green fuzz, white fluff, red down, silvers and golds, and they wore fairy dust fizzed in their hair, frizzed on their heads in traceries of sequin, the glitter and glitz of them, drizzle of argentine stars.

Their wings fanned out, up behind their backs, fins confected of gossamer webs of feather and plume, and their faces were masked beneath smears of smudged makeup, masks contorted in shrieking and screams, but not the screams of fairies, as fairies do not scream, but those of young girls, mere kids. And as they clambered up, out from beneath the concrete before him, weeping and wailing, faces sooty and tear streaked, filing through the coalhole in the paving from the chute below, they were hoisted up before being hustled along by a clutch of gaily dressed women and black-bundled men.

A fire truck clanged by, whistles, bells, Klaxons, gongs, then a pair of red-and-gilt circus wagons—spoke-wheeled, five-ton LeFrance Metropolitan steam-engine pumpers propelled by a galloping team of seventeen-hand-high, fifteen-hundred-pound, dapple-gray Percheron geldings, their coats a-lather, manes a-fly, the reporterly details he hastened to jot in his notebook.

The Iroquois Theater, 24–28 West Randolph, was only the latest among the city's three dozen playhouse/music halls, as it was its solitary "million dollar" one, or so it advertised itself, the actual cost being roughly half that. Coincidentally, he had covered its sold-out opening not five weeks before, the night a box seat, normally a one-dollar ticket, had fetched a princely $225. Helluva impressive venue. "The Temple of Beauty," they called it, or, alternatively, "The Best Theater on Earth." Benjamin H. Marshall, architect. Modeled after Paris's Opéra-Comique. Indeed, so taken had Franklyn been with the place that he had found himself shamelessly pumping it: "'Tis sure a palace of seldseen splendid dignity, as near ideal as can be imagined. Chicago's playgoers have their temple of resplendence at last, one unrivaled in all the West."

What he had failed to write, because he had failed to notice—an oversight for which he would flog himself in due time—was that there was an utter absence of telephones, marked fire exits, ceiling sprinklers, fire hoses, sand and/or water buckets, fire axes and/or hooks. No fire-alarm system, either—button, bell, tocsin, siren, no horn, as, too, no exhaust ducts, ceiling flues, or working ventilators to the roof.

Pretty, though. Six stories and sixty-three hundred square feet of pavanazzo marble, obsidian-stained mahogany, curly ash wainscoting, beveled mirror, crystal chandelier, elliptically groined vaulted ceiling arch, terra-cotta and hand-painted tile, tessellated floor, oriental rug, velvet drape, empire-green damask drapery and portiere, Waldorf wall tapestry, double-wide sweeping staircase, plinth, obelisk, balustrade and colonnade, esplanade and espalier, antique-gold green-and-rose paint, ogee, ormolu, white-marble wall dado, filigreed candelabra, Etruscan-crystal bowl lamp and faux-gold flambeaux, Corinthian-leather settee, the lot spacious enough to seat 1,600, hold 1,724, 35-cent standees included, and accommodate 38 backstage dressing rooms, the main floor alone being 70 feet across, 110 feet deep, 100 feet high.

Its owners certainly had crowed loudly enough in all the papers: "America's most modern fireproof playhouse!" "A completely fireproof structure, guaranteed!" "Our more than two dozen exits can empty our building in under five minutes!" "Absolutely fireproof!"

From where he was standing, he clearly could see the 52- or 60- or 66-foot-tall polished-granite or Bedford-stone facade of the front entrance, its twin 32- or 35-ton Corinthian columns sentineling the 10 or 12 glass-and-mahogany or oaken front doors, illuminated, as he knew, by 2,000 or 2,600 Edison Mazda lightbulbs, a berg of glittering pillar, pilaster, pedestal, pediment, cornice, and cartouche.

A dozen hose wagons, hook-and-ladder trucks, steam-engine pumpers were aligned along the curb even as a conspicuously linked, lacquered, buffed-and-burnished crowd gathered near and beneath the red-and-white-and-royal-or-cobalt-blue awning jutting out over the broad, snow-covered sidewalk: derby hats, tuxes, minks and muffs, beplumed bonnets, winking diamonds and emeralds, glistening pearls, sterling silver, solid gold.

He scanned the roofline for the telltale outline dark smoke makes against light sky. Nothing. But he could smell it, and it, the smoke stench, strengthened.

He ought by rights have crossed the street, collared a cop or fireman, perhaps the barrel-chested, six-foot-five assistant superintendent of police, Herman "Wonder Shoes" Schuettler, or the enormously unpopular, walrus-mustachioed, sixty-five-year-old, white-helmeted fire marshal, Henry "Two Fists" Musham, inquired what was up, going on, how widespread, intense, and "alive" the fire. Instead, playing a hunch, he raced east on West Randolph—by some ambulatory miracle failing to fall, though his feet, playing the pavement with scant purchase, splayed as they fished for a footing—turned north on State, then ducked west into the cobblestone alley called Couch Place that he knew ran behind the north wall of the theater out toward Dearborn, directly across from the building—the old Tremont House Hotel—housing the law, dental, and pharmacy schools of Northwestern University. By the time he made the alley—an isthmus of ice no more than twenty feet wide—he was winded.

Edging tractionless onto the aisle of glaze ice—slippery as greased glass rendered the slipperier still by the shellac of wind at his back—he inched flatfootedly forward, moving farther into the alley, *seeing* it at last, choking on its sound, the gorge of sound that gored the space between his ears until he no longer could hear. Whoosh of his blood? Whump of his heart? Nothing. Heard nothing. The sudden silence. Watched himself watching a silent film.

Creatures, objects, falling, second floor, third, jumpers, figures gowned in plunging flame. He could see but not hear the flames fanned cluster-fat by icy winds, feel but not hear the roaring winds, splat of human flesh, crunch of human bone. Many were on their knees in what appeared an attitude of prayer, flames caressing them alive, whirling gyres, swirling hives, monks bunched within habits of fire. They shivered, writhed, rolled frantically side to side or lay upon their backs, surf tossed, furiously bicycling as if pedaling for their lives. Others, muscles involuntarily contracted and flexed, assumed the physician's "pugilistic posture," one or both arms outflung and fixed before them as if to ward off a blow before pitching forward onto the pavement flaking apart in clumps. Melting shapes, shadow-burnt, melded with and into alley walls, oozed across and onto alley floor, mouths open wider than hippos'.

"They *must* be shrieking," he thought. "I can *see* them shrieking, so why can't I hear?"

Flames spewed in orange somersets out every rear exit and window. The alley was a funnel that tunneled its air toward and on top of them, fueling the flames in cyclonic tents and fluttering sails, lancinating billows that sucked, licked, tongued and kissed, nipped and chewed the skin. Flesh churned loose of its bone base lifting away in nifty charred flags. Nifty? So it struck him then. Blisters, bubbles, flurry of beard froth.

He was close enough to see faces unfurl, the very *idea* of a face. It felt wrong to look, keep looking, describe looking, to watch them slowly unshape, crimp, crumple, curl free in tatters, behold how likenesses can stop resembling themselves, likethat, features slide from skulls. A violation, this desire to *see*, see around, all through, seek the face, face into and up to it, stare into the pit of hell, out the other side, and, mesmerized, not blink. He wished to avert his eyes. Except, had he wished to, he would have, and did not.

"Death is dumb," he thought, "dumber than sad. Must hurt. So hot. So cold. Too bad."

He had smelled this smell before.

He fought the impulse to pitch in, lend a hand, make himself useful, and this, he discovered now—to his horror or merely chagrin?—was far easier for him, as he considered it later, than, by all rights, it ought have been. To remain the voyeur, use this pen, jot in this notebook, write these words, catalog these details of death, ignore the rest.

"Steady now!"

Someone was yelling, actually shouting, a real person, in real life, and he could hear him!

Up there, one hundred feet up, men—how many?—were clutching to a window on the opposite side of the alley, the Northwestern University building. They had hold of long ladders and scaffolding planks and were feeding them fishlinelike through the window, aiming, it appeared, for one of the landings of the wrought-iron fire escape bolted to the theater's rear wall, a maze of black grille descending in a tiered series of ladderless

Z
Z
Zs,

each of which writhed with bodies burning or burned or soon to be.

Several lay still, smoking upon their sides, but most still were alive, hundreds were, or appeared to be, if unable to jungle-gym down because the gangways were blocked at intervals by fire-launched shrouds that flapped out blown-open doors and blasted-out windows. Nor could they retreat, turn back, retrace their path against the crush of the crowds surging on behind them.

A second round of planking levered from a second window ledge, found its way uncertainly to a second, lower landing. Yet a third of makeshift ladder spanned across to an opposite window. Those marooned on the receiving side who by dumb luck found themselves in the right spot—sixteen-year-old Hortense Lang and her eleven-year-old sister Irene, as he would report later, or Carrie Anderson and Mary Marzein of

Elgin, or grotesquely burned grammar-school teacher Alice Kilroy of 67 Oregon Avenue, perhaps three dozen all told—undertook to hoist themselves aboard and scramble on hands and knees, scuttling on all fours to safety.

A few lost their balance, misstepped, slipped, tried to right themselves, hang on, improvise a handhold, foothold, dangled a moment, fell, alley floor speeding to meet them. He hadn't known—why would he?—that from one hundred feet up a human body, a child's best, can bounce, or bound: *Ker-cruk. Ker-crunch.*

And then a traveling tendril of orange-angry flame shot straight across, midair, far enough to tongue-lap the wall of the university building opposite, and those caught midcrossing were blackened midgesture, frozen by fire. Following which they fell. Save that, being dead when they did so, perhaps "toppled off" or "dropped" are better words, the way one might through the trapdoor of a gallows. *Whooof!*

"Pay attention!" he heard himself shouting—at himself. "Get it down! Miss nothing! See! Around! Through! The moment!"

It increasingly was apparent that the metal fretwork could not much longer bear the burden of such amassed deadweight. A loud jolt, then, as the entire framework began to unbuckle before jerking brute-loose of its fastenings, abruptly dropping several feet—uncabling of an overcrammed elevator—the wrenching sound of its rusty anchors weighing, iron torquing in capitulation. The sudden sag kicked dozens off their feet flinging them from the landings to the ground, ragdolled, eighty feet down, some of whom survived owing to their landing square upon the accumulating cushion of corpses on the cobblestones below.

In one long, not ungraceful, swan-sweeping motion, the top of the framework at the third story relinquished its grip and tore free of the wall—crumble of mortar, chunks of brick—pitching out and away where, for the briefest of moments, it swayed suspended in place, stairway to nowhere, its shrieking occupants, mendicants now, clutching at rungs, clinging to rails, clawing at one another's backs, necks, heads, hair, limbs, eyes, and then . . . they tumbled. Roman candle, human torch, they tumbled in vertebrae plunges headfirst to the ground.

He noticed that, as they hurtled—reporter's detail—the hair of some of the women streamed upward, long strands on end, manes tailing straight above their heads in smoking streaks and contrails.

Where, he wondered, were the damn firemen? Scanned about. No standpipes here or hydrants. There were, he knew, 92 or 123 engine companies in the city, roughly 1,300 firefighters, 27 hook-and-aerial ladders. Musham was renowned for his repeated boasting that 35 of the former could converge on any site in the Loop in less than 20 minutes. He glanced at his watch—surely it had been 20 minutes—shook it, held it to his ear, still ticking.

It hadn't been half that.

"The Deadliest Blaze in Chicago History." (The Great Fire of '71, the one apocryphally ignited by the lantern-kicking cow, the one that had burned the city to the ground, had killed 250, not half the tally of what it was to be here.)

"The Second Worst Fire in the United States."

"The Fourth Most Lethal Fire in the World."

Newspaper headlines, as if words could darn a shape for suffering, the needless deaths of 602 human beings from 13 states and 85 cities and towns, 420 of them women, more than 200—212—children.

Each of the papers, all eight or nine of them, floundered less for the right words than for those they reckoned would best sell: *consuming holocaust, superheated frenzy, oven of death, blistering hell, raging inferno, searing caress, seething volcano, fiend of the fire feast, beast of the fire fiend, blazing vortex, hurricane of flame, whirling maelstrom, devouring fireball, den of terror, smoldering sepulchre, chamber of horrors, withering blast, vision of Dante, dance of death, wild hegira, fiery furnace, sea of fire, burning dervish of ecstasy, angry demon.* Words and more words, as if tagging horror with a label, branding terror with a name might make it more palatable, plausible, less pointless.

His own story, the *Trib's*, would appear the next day on the front page beneath the headline:

MORE THAN HALF A THOUSAND PERISH IN MAD PANIC AT IROQUOIS THEATRE— WOMEN AND CHILDREN PURSUED BY WAVE OF FLAME

The play had been a matinee, a three-act, eleven-scene, sixteen-hundred-costume, three-hundred-actor performance of *Mr. Bluebeard* starring Eddie Foy (in the role of Sister Anne), a "Musical Extravaganza direct from London's famed Drury Lane Theatre," which, prior to hitting town by way of Pittsburgh, Indianapolis, and Cleveland, had enjoyed a successful sixteen-week run at the Knickerbocker in New York City.

It was roughly 3:15 p.m., the second act. The song-and-dance renditions of "Daylight Is Dawning," "Songbirds of Melody Lane," and "The Beer That Made Milwaukee Famous" just completed. On the stage—34 or 38 feet deep, 40 wide—before the 25 or 30 footlights against an illuminated, painted floral backdrop depicting Bluebeard's castle garden, eight chorines/choristers/coryphées—Lola Brand, Daisy Beaute, Maxine Richards, Aodaoin Romaine, Gertrude Lawrence, Daisy Williams, Madeline Dupont, and Ethyl Wynne, each clad in their Florodora outfits—and their Hussar-uniformed, nameless cadet partners, eight pairs, a double octet so-called, were going through their assigned paces hand in hand, crooning, hoofing it *allegro moderato* slathered in dreamy silvers and blue-green-golds to Herbert Joseph Dillea's twenty-six-piece orchestra version of "Let Us Swear It by the Pale Moonlight."

A standing-room-only crowd—two hundred of it sardined four deep along the back wall and side aisles—1,924 all told, easily the largest audience of the show's thirty-seven-day run, which had been drawing underwhelmingly. Christmas holiday, the day before New Year's Eve, nineteen aught three, holiday break, school vacation time, the audience was fraught with kids clad in their new—eminently flammable—Christmas duds.

The cadets sang: "We love you madly, so make no noise, but come join the boys, on condition that the moon is shining bright."

To which the chorines replied: "The reason we allow this liberty, is because you wear a smile that says it's right."

And then in unison, "Let us swear it by the pale moonlight!"

In the front row of the parquet, orchestra level, sitting her velvet-covered, hemp-stuffed seat, Hazel Coulter, 18, of 4760 Champlain Avenue, whose eyesight was better than 20/20—she worked for a microscope lens-grinding concern in the Loop—thought she saw something. "A few, tiny wreaths of curling blackish smoke" near the top of the red velvet curtain, the proscenium arch, stage right. Then, a second or two later, "an orange-red glare," followed by a six-inch flicking tongue of whiter fire licking upward along its side fringe, catching its top border, traveling across, running there awhile before a clutch of glowing embers, cinders, and what appeared to be pieces of burning lint or shreds of canvas cloth or bedsheet began floating, fluttering their way to the stage floor. Hazel noticed that the costumes of some few of the chorus girls, all of whom were by now gazing uncomprehendingly upward, were on fire, and that their wigs were mops of smoke.

At the same time—perhaps a few seconds in advance of Hazel—the assistant electrician, Patrick McNulty, his eyes drawn to what his ears had heard—"a sort of sputter crackle"—looked up from his backstage perch fifteen feet above the ground, stage right, upon the metal-grid light bridge. First a spray of spark, then a flare of flame, its "flash glare," then a billow of smoke as the hot reflector of the 110-volt carbon-not-calcium arc-amp spotlight—4,000 degrees F.—ignited the top fringe of the "tormenter," the curtain concealing the wings from the audience. Fire spread along its edge, leaped to the heavier, oil-painted arch-drapery drop curtain, the one slotted third back in the series of four. McNulty yelled something to the flyman on the catwalk above him, John Farrell, who leaned over and out and, slapping, tried to snuff the flames with his hands, falling two inches shy and receiving seared palms for his pains.

The dancing slowed, untracked, lost sync, stopped. The music stopped. One by one, the bassoonist in the lead, the musicians abandoned their instruments and began exiting through the orchestra-pit door beneath the stage until only Dillea and six others remained. The dancers, those who had yet to collapse—as had Daisy Williams, for instance, into the arms of her partner, Jack Strause—disappeared precipitously into the wings. Backstage a bell rang, the signal to lower the fire curtain, which was not, yet, lowering.

Hazel Coulter rose in her seat and headed for the center aisle.

Onstage, out of the blue of the increasingly acrid air, forty-seven-year-old Eddie Foy, Jr., aka Edwin Fitzgerald, wearing silk stockings, garters, high heels, chemise, and shoulder-length blond wig—"Not half-bad," thought Hazel—tottered on his spikes and, in his nationally famous squeaky-door-hinge voice, called as he might for attention, order, calm, reason, endeavoring to talk people, Hazel included, back to their seats.

Turning to Dillea and what remained of the bassoonless pit orchestra, Foy said, "An overture, please, Herbert. Something rousing, I should think. 'The Sleeping Beauty,' then. 'The Beast.' Let's hear it out and loud. Play and keep playing, please. Tchaikovsky." But, by then, only a single violinist remained, and, however *furioso* he fiddled while the Iroquois burned, it was only the rising sound of wood crackling like kindling that the audience heard. When a banner-size chunk of burning scenery plunged to the stage at his feet, furry with flame, Foy, squeaking, fled.

Which is when someone backstage started shooting—or tossing grenades. One, two, three, four, five reports in a row. Rivets. Gunshots. Bomb blasts. *Ka-boom* and *ka-blam*. Another. Another still. Pause.

McNulty knew, as Hazel did not, that the reports signaled the snapping of either the eleven miles or 75,000 feet of two-inch, heavily greased Manila rope, the bursting of the guy lines used to support the 3,000 square yards of canvas-and-gauze main drop curtains, as well as to harness the 40,000 cubic feet of painted-canvas scenery flats and 280 separate squalling pieces suspended in the two fly-galley docks of the rigging loft, stage left. As the makeweight wooden batons bashed into the floorboards across the deserted, smoke-palled stage, and the burning rope lengths, squawking pipe fragments, and every pulley, light, light rig, and sandbag rained clobbering down, the backstage electrical switchboard shorted out, plunging the theater into fiery darkness, one punctuated by a peculiarly high-pitched caterwauling.

"Drop the curtain! Drop the curtain! Lower the fire curtain!"

Someone was yelling. Foy? Hazel thought so. Which curtain was, or was supposed to be, had been advertised as being, made of asbestos. Up onstage, what she construed as Bluebeard's garden, Hazel noticed, was ablaze.

Each of the aisles, right, middle, left, was logjammed with patrons thrashing their ways toward the twenty-four or thirty unmarked exit doors obscured behind heavy drapery so that not a one—each designed to open in, not out, insofar as they opened at all—was visible; most were locked and cross-barred, a policy aimed at discouraging gate-crashers and seat-cheats.

In the first row of the Dress Circle balcony, Charles Thompson, 32, of 294 Orchard Street, was on his feet, mesmerized by the bedlam below as an arpeggio of emotion surged up from the ground-floor parquet to the upper gallery, the balcony above Thompson's, where in excess of five hundred people sat bug-eyed and finger-pointing, glued to their thirty-five-cent seats as bewilderment became apprehension, apprehension turned to anxiety, anxiety slid toward fear, fear finned to dread, dread horror, horror terror, terror panic, and panic red-amok frenzy.

"And then people were fighting to gain the center aisle," Thompson was to remember, "clambering over seats, climbing over each other, children being crushed beneath the feet of strong men, women falling and being trampled, the elderly being elbowed and flung aside. Nobody helped anybody else. Nobody helped anybody but themselves."

Several women and young girls who leaped hand in hand from the higher balcony were broken in half on seat backs or impaled on the iron railings of the Dress Circle.

Backstage, William Sallers, retired city firefighter and the lone fire-man on duty, grabbed a couple of cannisters of Kilfyre, a commercially produced bicarbonate of soda fire-retardant mixture—three dollars a tube, retail—tore them open and began slinging handfuls of the white powder upward at the flames. Effective as birdseed.

The red, allegedly absestos curtain began slowly to lower, but in its inching descent hung up, snagged, jammed, seized on the side where a galvanized iron light reflector attached to the proscenium arch had failed to retract, only to stop dead twenty feet short of the floor, even as the other side continued merrily upon its way, finally drawing up a-kiltered and cockeyed no more than a dozen feet above the stage, black smoke churn-ing thickly through the gap.

Hazel Coulter began running—difficult maneuver in a mob. Charles Thompson fled. The 280 or 348 performers and stagehands trapped back-stage flocked to the stage-door exits while sceneshifter John Massoney and theater engineer Robert Murray tried and repeatedly failed to jump high enough to grab hold of the stuck curtain, to dislodge and yank it down.

Someone bulled open the iron, double scenery doors backstage just as a wire-meshed skylight on the roof was broken through. Subarctic fresh air ripsawed through both openings, sucked in, pinwheeled, whirligigged, married, as the stage became a wind tunnel—draw of chimney flue. The partly lowered, anchorless curtain blew outward, gusting, billow of para-chute, flapped voluminously once, and, being nothing but asbestos-free treated cotton and mineral wool, disintegrated back to front: *flooosh*.

Fists of fire punched into the theater, hoop-rolled onrushing out and over, then fanned fat and outspread, a voluptuous canopy of super-radiant air across the backs and faces of the fleeing audience—moment of acetylene.

Onstage, benzine-painted sets, gauzy scenery, eight thousand linear feet of white-pine frames, braces, and profiles, along with their 1,500 sheaves and rollers, went up like tinsel and lace. Flame wed to chemical fume globed forward, licked every nook, lashed every cubby in vaporizing waves that consumed the heavily draped and tapestried lavishly curtained loge boxes, gulped the green-gold-red veneers of the balcony facings, leaped the sidewalls, vaulted to the ceiling, and, searing over the seat tops of the parquet, swept their velvet-and-hemp stuffing bare, gobbling their plush, cabernet-red rail cushions.

The structure, that part of it built of steel, brick, and cement, remained standing; scarce fifty thousand dollars in damage.

Its chromatic, polycolored parasol glass dome—the oculus, so-called—did not.

Charles Thompson heard it first. Sound burst. "Like lightning," he thought. "Jagged."

Turning toward the sound, he gazed up into a monsoon of glass as it plunged on the freefall from the shattered eye in the roof ninety feet above. Ingots, icicles, some large as organ pipes, acquired speed—plummet of javelin. Those caught in the jaws of the lancinating shower were chewed to pieces—shred. Bodies came apart in seams, avulsion of sinew, snipped thread.

Later it was discovered that what had not annealed had vitrified: dead.

Fleeing Couch Place, Franklyn headed back toward the front entrance, where, turning the corner onto Randolph, he saw more or less what he expected to see: a street cordoned off to all but emergency vehicles. As he hastened forward, he began counting, quitting when he reached seventy: hose wagons, ladder trucks, paddy and patrol wagons, public works vehicles, ambulances, rockaways, hearses, omnibuses, appropriated hansoms and requisitioned hacks, tallyho coaches, grip cars, two-horse Dixon transfer vans, halted trolleys, stalled streetcars.

The sidewalk in front of the theater was partitioned by a perimeter of city-issue sawhorses patrolled by a phalanx of what appeared to be in excess of one hundred blue-uniformed beat cops armed with batons and swagger sticks, nightclubs and billies and megaphones. Inside the perimeter, dozens of police and fire brass, city officials and working press convened, convoked, conferred, actors playing their parts in a cast cast far in advance, one besieged by the thousands of rubbernecking onlookers who milled the sideways beyond the sawhorses, wanting answers, needing them more, demanding news, dreading its receipt, only to hear: "Get back away from there now. Move along. Let the gentlemen do their work. You'll know what we know as soon as we know it. Right now, we know what you know—nothin'."

Franklyn's immediate challenge was to seek the system at the center of what was little more than bedlam. As he had come to learn, one of his first lessons on the job, there *always* is a system, the one arranged on the fly to sift chaos like seed. The human response to devastation is as predictable as it is unfailing: intervene, cope, manage, organize anarchy, disarm pandemonium, blunt pain, restore order, perspective, proportionality, some semblance of normalcy, what passes for sanity, up out of havoc hatch control and command, tactic, strategy, at least long enough to stanch the wounds and bury the dead. Salvage remains. Mission accomplished. Duty discharged. Denial to follow. And then the damn dread. The nightmares that haunt, the ones awaiting in bed.

Is chaos still chaos when it is fractionally contained and controlled? When it has been taken authoritatively somewhat in hand by the paid professionals? When a shadow of structure, however hastily improvised, has been implemented, a nascent order inchoately imposed? Perhaps, then, it is merely crisis.

The one in place here, he quickly ascertained, the *system*, was as simple as it was unpleasant: Get quick to the still living inside. Bring the still living outside. Carry the still living next door. Try to save the still living. Bring the dead outside. Cart the dead away to funeral homes and morgues. 182 to Rolston's in Adams Street, where they lay five-deep in the parlor, four-deep in the annex. Roughly 235 to C. H. Jordan's on East Madison, where by midnight some two thirds had been identified and tagged, while a crowd of one thousand–plus managed by two dozen cops waited silently in the street until 2:00 a.m., when they were permitted to file past the bodies lying three-dozen-deep in ranks, rows, and echelons. Forty-five to Carroll Brothers on Wells, fifty to Buffon's on Wabash, some of the most severely burned—thirty-six women and children—to Sheldon's on West Madison, as well as anonymous miscellaneous others to Perrigio's on State, Gavin's on North Clark, the county morgue on Polk Street.

The smoking interior of the theater had been illuminated by fifty arc lamps courtesy of the Edison Company. Police and firemen entered, hunching close to the floor holding kerchiefs to their faces, reemerged cradling a corpse or slinging one upon a shoulder, placed it upon the sidewalk, out of the snow, beneath the front canopy—eventually the bodies lay exposed, Franklyn estimated, eighty-five to one hundred feet to either side down the sidewalk—where it was lifted onto a blanket or stretcher or gurney before being trundled by whomever wherever elsewhere.

Immediately east of the theater, (John R.) Thompson's "A Ladies and Gentlemen's Lunch Place" quickly became the provisional infirmary and jury-rigged morgue. There the police ambulance corps, the Red Cross corps, a hastily assembled team of some two dozen doctors and nurses, most of them mustered from Northwestern University and headed by Dr. G. Frank Lydston, improvisationally bent to the battlefield business of doing what they might to preserve such life as lent itself still to preservation. Triage.

Franklyn noticed that many of the would-be rescuers and retrievers made but a single trip inside, that that was all they could bear. Having seen what they had seen, they found themselves on the sidewalk outside the theater, fallen to their knees or flat on their rumps among the sea of lifeless bodies, staring fixedly at nothing, or heads buried in their hands, silently crying.

So chockablock with death was the sidewalk in front of the luncheonette that Franklyn was obliged to step over and around the tarmac of bodies to get to the door, though once inside, what struck him was less the appalling number of dead—the final figure, once again, would tally 602—or the unearthly wailing and shrieking of the few left alive or yet to die, than the starkly surreal contrast—for they often lay side by side—of those burned "beyond recognition" and those pristinely unmarked. The juxtaposition jarred.

Across marble tabletops, atop granite counters, amassed upon the floor, bodies writhed or lay blackly inert, some crisp as Krispies, some beyond charred, others mere parts, detached and disarticulated. More than half of them appeared to be women and children, three quarters perhaps, difficult to say. Some had no discernible head or skull or dura mater. Others had no discernible face. Some faces bore the deep imprint of shoe and boot. Some bodies were bent double. Others were jackknifed in two, chest flipped front to severed back, back of head come to repose upon hump of butt, or just dangling free. Some had no arms, legs, hands, feet; others no fingers or toes. Some had had their nose reduced to raw red stub or blackened plug. The fluids and oils of bodies suppurated everywhere, ooze of scorched skin everywhere, less skin than—what?—skin *melt*. Franklyn noticed how many appeared possessed of strafed and mutilated hands, as if they had clawed at something ragged.

He succeeded in eliciting a comment from Dr. H. K. Montgomery, or, rather, he eavesdropped as the doctor remarked to a nurse, "I was with the Army of the Potomac in the war. Rescued 150 people in the Great Fire. I have seen the wreckage of explosions, but never have I seen anything as frankly horrible as this."

At one table, Franklyn watched as Dr. Lydston labored over the untouched, open-eyed, fully clothed, perfectly pristine body of what appeared to be a girl of sixteen. Massaged her chest, auscultated, rubbed her hands, poured brandy down her throat, hypodermically injected a quantity of nitroglycerin. All to no avail.

"Dead," he said finally, before moving down the line. At which she sat bolt upright, which is to say bolted upright, quickened into a sitting position, asked with more curiosity than incredulity or alarm, "Where am I?" slid altogether gracefully from the table, and fled out the front door, disappearing into the crowd outside before anyone could lift from their presence of mind the language to stop her. Anabiotic.

Other physicians, stethoscopes slung about their necks like horse collars, shirtsleeves rolled past the elbows, side-wound from body to body, what was left of them, shadowed by nurses carrying oxygen tanks for which there proved infrequent call. Scissored off clothing, dabbed on unguents, olive oils, lotions, lanolins, applied cotton bandages, administered brandy, debrided and debulked as they were able. Nurses slid mirrors beneath nostrils or were dispatched by doctors to Dyche's Drugstore on the corner to fetch black coffee, "ardent spirits," cardiac stimulants such as strychnine.

"He's dead," became the mantra. "She's dead." "This one's dead." Dead and dead and dead. Which dead were then removed from their places upon the four-by-fifteen-foot tabletops and either fetched below or ferried away.

Bishop Peter Muldoon of St. Borreomeo's and Father McCarthy of Holy Name Cathedral strode up and down the aisles, intermittently pressing their lips to the T of a crucifix, mumbling Latinate prayers the while fishing from beneath their vestments as the need might arise, as it seemed never to cease to arise, their portable holy viaticums. Too much and too many, they couldn't keep pace. It was Muldoon, finally, who announced in English, "I am granting general absolution to all here."

Franklyn's attention was drawn to the far-most corner and to what he ever would recall as "The Corpse." A woman, beautiful, roughly his own age, had been emplaced or come to perch propped upright, braced against the rear wall, eyes closed, and, though naked to the waist, bereft of mark, blister, or burn, immaculate still, if apparently quite whole. Silent as plaster, of course, and alabaster white. And then, as he watched, rapt and transfixed, she began, almost imperceptibly, to stir. Shoulders to shift, spine to slide, head corona-ed in shining, flaxen hair to tilt. To the left, as he recalled.

What triggered the gesture he never would reckon—some vibration of the El through the wall?—but it was only when she gradually, as if in slow motion, reached her point of no return and toppled abruptly over, that he fled in a daze for the door. She had—it was in his notes, though he had no recollection later of having made them—been torn clean in twain beneath the navel, little but a fair-breasted torso.

Leaving Thompson's—still others, he learned later, were being vetted at the Sherman House, Kohlstaat's restaurant, Bullard and Gormully's, some few up on the eighth floor of Marshall Field's—he interviewed some cops and firemen, endeavored to secure a reliable fix on the lay of the land inside the theater, gathered little enough save the secondhand stuff about the glass dome, a detail, so it would prove, that none of the other papers had. The consensus seemed to be that fewer of the victims had died from their burns, than from smoke inhalation and/or suffocation and/or having been trampled and/or crushed during the mass melee and stampede for the bottlenecked exits.

"They're stacked up in there like cordwood on the landing of the promenade," one firefighter, a grim, grime-faced Crawley Dake, told him, referring to the elliptical, marble-beamed, 18-foot-high lobby of the 60-foot-high, 80-foot-wide Great Court. "Hundreds, wedged. Mass tangle fifteen-foot square, eight high. Choke point. More up on the second and third floors, angles at the head of the stairways. Can't see three feet in front for the smoke. Steam's rising all off of 'em. Pulled 'em down with pike poles, peeled 'em off."

Franklyn espied Police Chief Francis O'Neill. Chief had a way with his words. Good copy. "Hey, Chief. Inside. Tell."

"Ah, young Shivs, is it? Well, Shivs, ever see a field of timothy grass blown flat by a summer storm? That's the look of things then, at the balcony exits. Jammed up in the doorways they are, ten-deep. Lying like shingles, lad. Field of toppled corn. Some still alive when we reached them, but at the bottom, you see, pinned down, jumbled in, too deep to pull free. The deadweight. Poor souls. Heard the moans and whimpers, I did. Saw the fingers twitch, the hands. By the time we could get to them, untangle the ones above to lift away those below, it came too late. Poor souls."

A film of glister entered the chief's eyes as he damped and cleared his throat. "Ah, the children, Shivs. So many wee ones. And to think then of the vultures and jackals who thought to maraud among 'em. Why, the damn bone-picking ghouls. A dozen looters we nabbed. Appears they gained entrance posing as rescuing angels, they did. And may the lot roast in their own special hell." The chief was a chewer; he spat, skid of chaw across snow.

Franklyn had, he reckoned, enough; more than. Needed to check in now, confirm whether they wanted him at the office or to keep working the story, dictate what he had over the phone. But—wait! Wasn't that Bishop Fallows? St. Paul's Episcopal? Source he'd once tapped for another story.

"Bishop!" Flipped open his notebook.

"Ah, Franklyn. The tragedy." The cleric cocked his head toward the theater. "Just come out. Ghastly thing, Frank, altogether beastly. I happened to be passing by, been over to Field's, you see, when the commotion began, so found myself enlisted for the rescue. Had no idea."

Black smudges raccooned eyes that appeared more vacant than not. "I was just out for a shop, you see, a little browse over to Field's," he reiterated, "when I saw them. I was out in the street, and there they were, beating against the locked doors. Saw them through the glass. Should say I heard them as well. The human animal wailing, howling his doom. The way we live our last mortal moments." He peered absently about, vectorless. "Sorry, lad. Sorry."

"No, please, Bishop, go on. Please continue."

"Well, what more is there to say, son? The bodies lay in piles, Frank, actual enormous mounds. Tons of flesh, human flesh, and all of it dead, burned, blackened. And the children, utterly crushed, as if hurled from a great height. And the women, all bent, their fingers clenching the iron sides of the seats so strongly they were all torn and bleeding. Oh, Franklyn, how they must have suffered! We removed one couple, husband and wife so it appeared, burned to form a death hug, fused fast for all eternity. We tried, but they refused to unembrace.

"I have seen the great battlefields of the Civil War—I was, as you know, attached to the Wisconsin Infantry—and I tell you, lad, 'tis no scintilla of exaggeration when I say they were as nothing to this."

Franklyn thanked the Bishop, wished him godspeed, elbowed his way through the swollen crowd—1,000? 2,000? 5,000 now?—tracked down a phone box a block farther on. "Come on in," he was told. "You're to be point on the lead piece. Rewrite."

Replacing the receiver in its rack in advance of picking his half-shell-shocked way along Dearborn, whom should he descry then, himself in much the same state, but Eddie Foy.

"Mr. Foy!" Piaffering down-street, Franklyn could see that Foy still was clad in his costume and greasepaint and that he tottered precariously on the high heels that for some reason he had failed to remove. "Mr. Foy. Shivs here. *Tribune*."

"Yes? What can I do for you? Shivs, you say?" Franklyn nodded as Foy extended a hand. "Very well then, Shivs, how can I be of service?" He was coatless, having left, as he explained half ruefully, his Astrakhan frock in the theater in the rush.

"Mr. Foy, how was it exactly? Inside, I mean. How did it go?"

"Ah." Foy shook a solemn head, grave with gathered gravitas, a gesture of contrapuntal absurdity in light of that voice, scarce the pip of a squeak. "Had I played my part better, perhaps some few more would have escaped intact. As it was, I don't know what I should have done to prevent what occurred from occurring. In all honesty and candor, I can think of nothing, nothing more I could have done, should have done, and yet . . ." The tinhorn voice faded, trailed all but off. "I cannot help but feel that I did pathetically fail the dead.

"They had, you see, sir, come out to see no other than yours well and truly. I was the reason they were there, the reason they died. 'Tis not easy, sometimes, being Foy, not nearly so easy as some might presume."

Franklyn thanked him, wished him well, was wished well in return, then hoofed it back to the paper, composing the lede in his head as he did so: "More than 500 people were burned, suffocated or trampled to death late this afternoon when the stage of the city's newest theater, the Iroquois on West Randolph Street, was enveloped in an enormous globe of fire the insatiable flames of which rolled across the audience consuming everything in their rapacious path."

He scratched it as best he could in his notebook as he walked. Hmm. "Rolled" across? He could do better than that. Verbs. Would he never learn? Take to heart what Baudelaire had taught? *The verb, angel of movement.* Chronic weakness, that. "Suffocated" or "smothered"? "Enormous" or "immense"? "Insatiable" or "devouring"? He would need discard "rapacious" altogether.

Well, he would work it hard when he got back. This was one occasion, at least, when they dare not object to his cranking up the heat. And in the meantime? Endeavor to brush aside the impulse to collapse, for he felt, by rights, that he ought to be permitted to wail away the night against the wind, gnash his teeth, beat his breast, shear his hair, rend his clothes, talcum his body with cinder and ash, hack gashes in his arms and legs and stain himself most bloody. To absterge that alley and launder the land, dress the wounds of the wounded and gather the bones of the dead, flense and bury them in a single grave, faceup, perhaps—those still with faces— a hollow reed placed between what might remain of their lips extruding aboveground to provide the proper pathway for the transmigration of their forsaken souls.

Instead, much later, having polished off his story, he skipped the saloon, went straight home, smoked most of a pack, flopped into bed, and dreamed of home, of Tick and Blake Palmer and his uneyed descent through the sump of the Tam where no light prevails nor fire might abide.

Restless night.

BILL

If his work on the Iroquois did not immediately win Franklyn the coveted accolade "crackerjack," it certainly raised his stock, position, and profile in the newsroom, nor only with his colleagues and bosses at the *Trib*. In the ensuing weeks and months, he was assigned a series of follow-ups that entailed interviewing as many of the survivors and family members of the victims as he could track down, a semiregular feature that proved enormously popular both with the public and with the paper's advertisers, as well as with those of his coworkers who were not so consumed by professional jealousy that they could not appreciate a good story when they read one.

Naturally, certain perquisites thereto accrued, not the least of which were a significant bump in pay and being granted the latitude of a modest expense account. Novelty of novelties, he soon found that he actually had a little loose change to spare at week's end. Not enough to move into new digs, of course—he coveted no design on doing so in any event; the flaws of his own were its foibles, and they suited him—but at least he could afford a more regular haircut and the occasional shoeshine, a new weskit now and then, an extra half-pint or six-pack or two. More important, he was assigned to the labor beat, if only after a bout of rather vigorous arm twisting on the part of his bosses, to replace Tom McKey (pronounced "Mackie"), who had taken a comparable position for more than comparable pay on the *Morning Telegraph* in New York City.

If Franklyn was hesitant about taking the job, it was only because he knew that, at the *Trib*, the position carried with it a most peculiar status owing to the paper being so inordinately, even boorishly proud of its long-standing reputation as the city's leading antilabor mouthpiece. That said, because the job was considered a plum, his being tapped to fill it only fed the competitive envy that, in Franklyn's opinion, certain of the more seasoned hands seemed to feel increasingly at liberty to express in his presence.

Until he officially vacated the post, the lame-duck McKey—queer one, too; not only did he eat Spanish onions as if they were Winesap apples, but it was his habit to buck-and-wing it light-footedly across the newsroom, desktop to desktop, upon completion of a "corker," the while chanting, "Stuck it to the Reds, stuck it to the Reds, stuck it to the Reds again"—would take him in harness, clue him in, introduce him to the personalities and players, ins and outs, acquaint him with the ropes.

"I shall do the job in accordance with the level best of my abilities," Franklyn dutifully told Teddy Beck, "but I want it understood, and understood clearly—I do not dance. Ever. Or cut anyone's idea of a rug."

William Dudley Haywood seldom set foot on a public street without first donning his trademark black Stetson, size XXL, and hand-tooled Corinthian black-leather cowboy boots, size thirteen extrawide, and yet, when he paid his first visit to Chicago, he deliberately chose in the blunt face of the inhospitable winter weather to go about bareheaded and shod in all-business brown brogues.

Fresh from a flag-desecration affair in Colorado stemming from his role in the bloody Cripple Creek metal miners' strike there—a charge on which the courts hastily had acquitted him—the secretary-treasurer of the nation's most radical labor union, the Western Federation of Miners (WFM), slipped hatless into town, went quietly about his business inside Anarchists' Hall on Lake Street, and slipped back out without a whisper from any of the newspapers, not surprising in light of the fact that, in those days, in those parts, scarce a soul knew his name.

Ostensibly in town to pay a visit on his editors at Charles H. Kerr, publisher of the *International Socialist Review* (*ISR*)—its masthead listed him as a "contributing writer"—the real object of his visit was to meet clandestinely with his colleagues, among them the Socialist Party president, Eugene V. Debs, seventy-five-year-old Mary Harris "Mother" Jones—the so-called Miners' Angel, and WFM president Charles B. Moyer, and to arrange for the printing, publication, and distribution of a quarter-million copies of what would soon become known as "The January Manifesto," reading in part:

> Universal economic evils afflicting the working class can be eradicated only by a universal working class movement. Such a movement . . . is impossible while separate craft and wage agreements are made favoring the employer against other crafts in the same industry . . .
>
> One great industrial union embracing all industries—providing for craft autonomy locally, industrial autonomy internationally, and working-class unity generally . . . must be founded on the class struggle . . . with the recognition of the irrepressible conflict between the capitalist class and the working class.
>
> The growth and development of this organization will build up within itself the structure of Industrial Democracy—a Workers' Co-Operative Republic—which must finally burst the shell of capitalist government, and be the agency by which the working people will operate the industries and appropriate the products to themselves.
>
> One obligation for all.

A union man once and in one industry, a union man always
and in all industries.
Universal transfers.
Universal label.
An open union and a closed shop.

Addended to the manifesto was an invitation that read: "All workers
who agree with the principles herein set forth, will meet in convention at
Chicago the 27th day of June, 1905, for the purpose of forming an economic organization of the working class along the lines marked out in this
Manifesto."

That the claque should have chosen Chicago for its revolutionary
purpose, Franklyn was to reason later, only made sound and fitting sense.
Between the Haymarket Affair of 1886 and the Pullman Strike eight years
later, the city had played host to roughly five hundred labor disputes,
though how many more had transpired in the decade since, no one seemed
to know, save for "lots" or "plenty" or "a passel," or, if one were a Tribbie,
"too many."

From ten in the morning to six at night, beginning on Tuesday, and
every day for the twelve consecutive days of the convention, Sabbath included, Franklyn sat in the roped-off press gallery on the second floor of
Brand's Hall on the corner of Erie and North Clark Streets, quaffing
cheap beer bucketed up in bumpers and growlers from Schmidt's Saloon
located on the floor below. Sweating copiously out his shirtfront in the
sweltering, smoke-wet, ninety-degree heat, he suffered to take meticulous
notes as he suffered the tedious parade of speakers: Debs; Mother Jones
(clad even in that oppressive heat in her signature black bombazine
mourning and black pancake bonnet); Moyer; Socialist Labor Party president and propagandist par excellence Daniel De León, "the trade union
wrecker"; A. M. Simons, editor of the *ISR*; a dozen nameless others—
as they trooped in apparent lockstep to the platform to regale either the
186 or 203 assembled delegates representing either the 40,000 or 60,000
or 90,000 workers—socialists, anarchists, Marxists, rainbow unionists—
most of them card-carrying members of the fearsomely militant WFM.
The hall so stank of perspiration, cigar, flatulence, mildew, and sloshed
beer, that Franklyn could actually see it. Like being gloved, he thought, in
an infragrant pall of brown exhaust toasted to the texture of mundungus.

As long as he could rely upon a prepared text, Haywood, while no rabble-rousing fire-eater or silver-tongued stormy petrel of the William Jennings Bryan school, could, in his way, perform the first-rate orator. Earnest, animated, blunt spoken, a bearish man possessed of a magnetic presence, Bill Haywood was perfectly capable of putting across a speech. Bringing the hall to order by banging a two-by-four upon the podium once, twice, thrice, pause, once, twice, thrice, pause, he began:

"Fellow workers, we are here, at this our Continental Congress of the Working Class, to confederate the workers of this country into a working class movement that shall have for its purpose the emancipation of the working class from the slave bondage of capitalism. There is no other labor organization that has for its purpose this exalted object.

"The American Federation of Labor, which presumes to be the labor movement of this country, is NOT"—clobber of two-by-four—"a working class movement. It does NOT"—clout of two-by-four—"represent the working class. It is a CRAFT movement, a TRADE movement, and as such represents the worker by skill alone. It does NOT"—belt of two-by-four—"represent by class. It represents only the labor aristocrat.

"When the corporations and the capitalists understand that you are organized for the express purpose of placing the supervision of industry in the hands of those who do the work, you are going to be subjected to every indignity and cruelty that their minds can invent. You are also going to be confronted with the so-called labor leader, the AFL man, the Gompers man, who will tell you that the interests of the capitalist and the working-man are identical.

"The truth is that there is a continuous struggle between the two classes, and this organization will be formed, based, and founded upon that struggle, having in view no compromise and no surrender, and but one object and one purpose, and that is to bring the workers of this country into the possession of the FULL value"—swack, split, splinter of two-by-four to kindling and toothpick—"of the product of their toil!!"

Applause, tentative at first, spotty, then groundswelling, cartwheeling, tumbling in wave upon wave. Kettledrum stomping. Stamping. Pounded staves. Cheers cresting. Crescendo roar. Tympani. Cymbals. Cowbells. Horns.

Franklyn jotted in his notebook, "Haywood, interview!" Then, in a moment he would find it impossible to explain later, not least of all to himself, rose to his feet, removed his vest, and whirled it lasso-and-lariat high above his head before sheepishly glancing about. "Whoa, boy," he thought. "What was *that* about?"

Over the next two weeks, Franklyn interviewed for his series "The Radicals" not only Haywood ("King of the Underground Cowboys"), but Moyer ("The Conservative's Radical"), Debs ("America's First Socialist"), De Leon ("Militant Professor of the Working Class"), Mother Jones ("The Miners' Angel")—he didn't like her, trust her, found her nothing but a demagogue, a cold and colorless one at that, though he did a decent enough job, he felt, too decent perhaps, of camouflaging his antipathy in his story—Emma Goldman ("An Anarchist Without Answers"), and the faux-folksy, cracker-barrel-philosophizing, poker-addicted local attorney Clarence Darrow ("Attorney to the Underdog").

Following Tuesday's largely ceremonial opening, Franklyn had requested, and eventually was granted, an interview with Haywood, to take place at John Barleycorn's, out of the way, on Belden. Rumor had it that Haywood had little use for teetotaling. Franklyn increasingly had little use for it himself.

Beating his subject there, Franklyn bellied to the bar, ordered a shot and a draft—*Edelweiss*—a combination just then beginning to be called a boilermaker, lit an unfiltered cigarette—*Sweet Caparol*—spraddled a stool and began mentally flipping through the litany of questions he had prepared. When Haywood did not show, he ordered another beer, forgoing the shot. Then another shot, forgoing the beer. Then another beer, which he decided to nurse.

Forty minutes later, which is to say forty minutes late, the thirty-six-year-old, rosacea-and-roseola-ridden Haywood appeared, his right eye every bit as bald white and ball dead in its bare-open socket as a shark's. No wonder, Franklyn thought, that his detractors called him Cyclops. "Lost it as a kid," he explained later, "whittling. Slingshot. Won't wear a patch. Pirate's act of vanity."

His Stetson and its brim giving the impression of arriving fully five minutes in advance of the rest of him, Bill Haywood strode through the doorway shoulders down and wide-walking. Well over 230 pounds and half an inch shy of six feet—though he appeared formidably taller owing both to his three-inch bootheels and the high crown of his cowcatcher hat—he bore the determined brawn of a burly man, one whose bulk demanded it be reckoned with: ox-yoke shoulders, ice-block chest, tree-trunk legs, the all of him: oaken.

"Battering ram," thought Franklyn at once, a man likely at his finest when fully aroused, one accustomed to moving within his own rawly wild, elementally violent weather.

As he neared, Franklyn discerned that Haywood's other eye, the good one, his left, smacked of load-heavy luggage, as if having been saddled too long with having seen too much or, perhaps, with having to do double duty in compensation, make up for lost sight—or time.

"Mr. Haywood!" Franklyn lifted his butt from the bar stool and waved him on. "Here!"

Rack of shoulder. Keg of chest. Jut jawed. Lumbering. *"Tribune?"*

"Frank Shivs, sir," extending a hand.

Haywood tugged at his hat brim, became momentarily embrangled in its band, extended a meatsome hand in response. Franklyn found his own vise-gripped and engulfed, lost in the rough hollow of the larger man's own as Haywood grabbed a stool, straddling it like a saddle. Left his hat on.

"Barkeep!" Knuckle rap against bar top. "Bourbon and branch water. And for my friend here . . . ," turned expectantly to Franklyn.

"Boilermaker," mumbled Franklyn, sensing himself shrink inside his shirt in the presence of the larger man's own.

"Boilermaker," repeated Haywood to the bartender. "So then, friend, ask away. Reckon I might see fit to answer some."

The romantic thing to say would be that he smelled of prairie and wide-open spaces, save that he smelled of printer's ink and pipe tobacco and of the pomade he wore larded-on too thick through his hair. The romantic thing to say would be that his voice resonated with the wildness of the still Wild West, save that it was soft as a girl's, on tiptoe, at dawn.

When his drink arrived, he tossed it back—"Bottoms up!"—ordered another, pulled from a pocket a calabash pipe, filled its bowl with burley unpacked fresh from its pouch, lit it to a fine-glowing brew. Franklyn would learn later that the pipe chiefly was show. Bill much favored cigarettes, rolled his own, called them "quirlies," or, less often, "swagger roots."

Franklyn lauded his Tuesday speech, expressed a warm and genuine interest in such ideas as he assayed—few enough, frankly—even ponied up for his drinks, but whether it was owing to his wariness regarding the antilabor *Trib*, or that he was peculiarly reticent around strangers, or merely some phlegmatic quality hewing to the nature of the man, Bill Haywood, Franklyn shortly discovered, was perfectly incapable of extemporizing in anything approaching a manner that might make for good copy.

What was it, Franklyn wondered, that the man's thoughts should so wretchedly fail to shape themselves into sentences, as that such sentences as he succeeded in shaping should so stubbornly refuse to unstick themselves from the roof of his mouth where, iciclelike, they hung gnarled in glues of syntax. It was as if he expressed himself through a set of ill-fitting dentures, the words, which is to say the act of saying them, appearing literally to pinch like . . . cheap spats?

Well, sometimes these cowboy types, thought Franklyn, were not exactly the most garrulous studs in three states, though in light of his performance at the lectern—the man had been genuinely eloquent, even moving—how explain . . . this? Bill Haywood incontestably was the most maddeningly inarticulate man Franklyn ever had known, his own father excepted. Until, after yet another halting, sputtering, unintelligibly awkward, nonresponsive response to yet another perfectly kerosene-clear question, he suddenly fished from his inside coat pocket a wallet-size buff-colored booklet, placed it upon the bar top, and slid it toward Franklyn.

"Here, friend. Go ahead. Take it. I got others. What you're after's all in there. Personal stuff, too. Biography facts. Suchlike." He, no other word, twiddled, his thumbs. "Wish I spoke. Off the cuff. Locute. Never have. No good at it. Stumblebum.

"A speech, now that I can give. Though, even then, rostrum's a damn scaffold. Missed my schooling. Never even read Marx. Now? Can't make heads or tails. Folks say I oughtta read this here Georges Sorel." He pronounced it "Surl." "Some Frenchie. Hear of him?" Franklyn allowed as he had not. "Well, may be as I'll give 'er a shot, one of these days.

"Lucky for me hardest-working man don't make the best talker. I'm no damn theoretician anyways. Never was. Sure as hell ain't no *pol*itician." He took a drink. "Dumb ol' shirtsleeve *tac*tician, that's me. Two-gun Western man. Real action's in the fields and factories anyways, mills and down the mines. Point of production. Trade-union action. Control of the shops. That's first. Workers' state later. What we're after here, this new union I mean, what we're calling the International Workers of the World, ain't nothin' but socialism with its working clothes on, that's all. And"—he winked—"guns ready.

"Tell you this, friend. I don't care a snap of my fingers"—he snapped his fingers—"whether the *skilled* worker joins up or not. Not right now. We're going down into the gutter to get the *mass* of workers. Get 'em and lift 'em"—raised both of his arms above his head—"up."

Drained his drink, ordered another. "Could talk a dream, though, if yer interested." Franklyn nodded. "Well, then, here goes. It's that someday the battle'll be over and won. No owners, no workers. New society, new man, new factories, ones with dining rooms, best food, music played by the best players, gymnasiums, swimming pools, private bathrooms, all marble."

He said these things in all sincerity, yet with the utmost dispassion, as if, Franklyn thought, his "dream" was so self-evidently right, so practically attainable, so nonvisionary and counterutopian, it required no elaboration or embellishment—"without tremolo"—as Franklyn soon would learn was one of his favorite phrases. Bill Haywood was about the farthest thing from a natural wit, wag, or raconteur Franklyn ever had encountered, but he packed the irrefutable punch of a presence—one happening, or about to happen, or on the verge of happening, always. A living event of a man. Human occasion.

He was, apparently, far from finished. "On one floor of this new plant, best masterpieces of art. First-class library, another. Roof converted to gardens. Workrooms the best conceived. Work chairs all Morris. So when you tire, you can relax. In comfort. Way a man has a right."

He paused again, stared into and through his glass as if reading runes. Franklyn was about to say, "Mighty fine dream" or words to that effect, when Haywood remarked, "So whaddaya say, friend? How 'bout we high-tail on outta here, pronto. Go scout us up some *fire*works."

"Reckon I'll pass," thought Franklyn. Said instead, "Aw hell. Why not?" A night on the town with Bill Haywood. Could be interesting. Might even be something in it for his piece. "Something in mind?"

"Ever been over to Everleigh's?"

"The Everleigh Club?" The "Ever" came out way yelpy, an octave too high. "Uh, no. Too rich for my blood. You don't cat around that place on a reporter's salary, not on this reporter's salary anyway."

"Aw, come on, friend. My dime. I'm feeling flush these days. Deep pockets." He shoved his arms into his coat pockets past their elbows, grinned. "See?" Then, nodding toward the door, headed out in a headlong rush while Franklyn saw to the tab, more than a little startled at how much more they had drunk than merely their share. By the time Franklyn followed him outside, Haywood already was aboard and waving him on toward the streetcar.

Sprinting to catch up, he stumbled, almost went down, swanned his way toward equilibrium, found himself about to lose the better part of a foot to the roll of the rail-bound wheel. Which is when Haywood reached down, grabbing him by a forearm and shoulder, and swung him up hard—and in. Light as leaves.

They plunked down side by side.

"Still got that little book I give you?"

"What?" Franklyn worked hard to catch his breath.

"You know. Back at the bar."

"Oh." Franklyn patted himself down, still dazed, rifled his pockets, came up empty. "Mr. Haywood, I . . ."

Haywood was laughing, sides heaving like slabs, laughter fit to fit the man, beat the band, be hogtied. "First off, son, do me a favor and cut the crap. It's Bill, savvy? Second"—he reached into his pocket—"here. You left it. Reckoned you'd be needing it soon enough." He finger-drummed its cover as he passed it back. "You need to read this here, son. Right quick.

"Now"—he broadly smiled—"you find a place it'll stay put, then hang on to yer hat with both hands. We're in for a time of it, boy. Tonight we are. Boy-howdy if we ain't. Only question is, we gonna blow the roof off the joint? Or we gonna git ours blowed first?"

That silent laugh, those heaving sides. Couldn't be but a dozen years between them, yet Bill Haywood made him feel like his pup. As if reading his mind, Haywood reached over and mussed his hair. Kid sitting in the bleachers.

"That's some mop you got going there, son. Gonna go over top-dog at Everleigh's, just see if it don't, see if they just don't put a curl in your wave and a rod in your cod, stiff as that old cob of a stalk."

"God love it," Franklyn thought. "Western talk." Scanned the booklet's cover: "Sabotage," he read, "by Emile Pouget. Translated from the French and with a new introduction by Arturo Giovannitti, anarchist." Slipped it into his pants pocket and buttoned it down. Cushion as he rode.

THE EVERLEIGH

The monocled, strabismic Minna Everleigh threw open the front door on Chicago's worst-kept secret. "Well, I'll be. Look who's back. Hey there, Mr. Haywood! Or should I say, howdy?"

The woman's empty cigarette holder, ivory and gold, was gaudily studded with what appeared to be real diamonds, and she clenched its ebony mouthpiece between her gap teeth, removing it at intervals to hold it dramatically aloft as she exhaled imaginary smoke.

"Howdy, Min," said Haywood, removing his Stetson and clutching it belt-high, rotating it by its brim with both hands as he averted his eyes and scuffed at the ground with a boot toe. "Bully to see you. Again." Soft as a girl.

"Well, you gonna stand there impersonating my coatrack, or you gonna come on in and make yourself to home?" She half-turned her head back inside, called, "Lookee here, girls. It's Big Bill."

Stepping inside, Franklyn heard giggles, whispers, strains of soft piano, a gold-leafed baby grand, as he shortly was to discover, played in the most delicate legato manner by the tuxedoed "Van-Van the Piano Man," aka Vanderpool the Professor. Discerned tunes: Chopin, then Tin Pan Alley, then Gilbert and Sullivan. A blue parrot on a perch squawked, "Welcome to Everleigh's," then loudly whistled, wolf.

Minna looked Franklyn up and down. "And he's got himself a moppy-haired pup in tow." Addressed him directly: "That's some chevelure you got going there, kid. *Très* cute."

"Pup?" thought Franklyn. "Jeez." Said, "Not a chevelure, ma'am. This here's a coiffure. Bouffant. Pompadour. This here's whatfor."

She looked dark, then dour, then burst out laughing. "Ha! So, pup, gotta name?"

"Oh, sorry, Min," said Haywood. "This here's Frankie Tribune."

"Tribune? You mean like the paper?"

"No, Min. I mean he *is* the paper."

"Reporter, eh? Well, then, I'll be hogtied. Isn't that what you say, Bill? The way you like 'em? Hogtied?"

"Aw, Min. Hush."

She turned to Franklyn. "We get our fair share, sure do. Newspaper folk. Owners, publishers, editor or two, not reporters much." Wink. "Oh,

I could tell you some stories, young man, that I surely could, except"—she shook her head as she raised her hand like a pledge—"I can't, shan't, won't. Discretion, discretion, discretion, that's the art. Without it, might as well douse the lights and ring down the curtain."

Bill Haywood stood nearly six feet in his argyles, and Minna Everleigh—who let it be known she preferred the appellation "resort keeper"—easily looked him even in his solitary eye. "You know why they call him *Big* Bill, don't you, hon?" she asked Franklyn.

"Aw, Min," said Haywood, actually blushing. "Cut it out now."

She smiled as if indulging a child. "Whatever you say, *Big* Bill." Winked again, at Franklyn, cahoots. "So here. Give 'em up and hand 'em over."

She passed Haywood's coat and hat to a disarmingly, because frankly virginal-looking, if equally pretty, even more scantily clad young woman who dutifully disappeared with them all seesaw and swish around a corner.

Franklyn had had occasion to pass by the three-story, fifty-room, double-manse brownstone known as the "Crown Jewel of the Levee" more times than he could recount and, being a reporter, had heard second-, third-, and fourth-hand several of the more lurid stories associated with it. Of a piece with New Orleans's Storyville District and San Francisco's Tenderloin, Chicago's Levee was the city's designated vice enclave, part of the crime-ridden, politically corrupt First Ward stretching south of the Loop around South Dearborn and Archer and Armour Avenues where they were bisected by Twenty-second Street. The Levee—the Everleigh itself was 2131–2133 South Dearborn—also known as "The Segregated District," marked its official boundaries as Eighteenth Street on the north, South Wabash on the east, Twenty-second Street on the south, and South Clark on the west.

There, the blocks ran shank-to-flank with "vice resorts," "disorderly flats," or "establishments of chance reputation," as they sometimes were called—barrelhouses, burlesque joints, bagnios, bawdy houses, bordellos, assignation hotels, call flats, panel houses, goosing slums, deadfalls, opium dens (also called "hop" or "yeast joints"), casinos, dance halls, free-and-easies, honky-tonks, nickelodeons, peep shows, massage parlors, porno dives, Turkish baths, and precisely 121 brothels secretly owned by some of the city's wealthiest businessmen, each of them permitted to flourish with the tacit approval of the local ward bosses and aldermen Bombastic "Bathhouse" John Coughlin—"the Bath" for short—and Brainy "Hinky Dink" five-foot-one Mike Kenna.

Known as "Da Boys," the pair, in conjunction with Police Captain Ed McCann and his cops on the take, received their under-the-table cuts from "made" characters Ike Bloom—who ran both Bloom and Freiberg's Dance Hall and Bloom's Midnight Frolics Café, "the flashiest drops in town," according to the *Trib*—and Big Jim Colisimo, an ex-city street sweeper partial to year-round white seersucker suits and four-alarm "red ink" spaghetti. The towering, lantern-jawed Colisimo, who was rumored to be raking in fifty thousand dollars a month, ran two dozen brothels, including the Victoria and the Saratoga, the latter farmed out to his on-the-muscle boy, Gentleman Johnny "The Fox" Torrio, whose protégé was a gun-happy mug out of New York's Five Points, one Alphonse Capone— known around town as Scarface Al Brown.

About the Everleigh Club itself Franklyn knew just enough to know that he didn't know the half of it, as the half that he did was mainly statistics:

—Having opened on February 1, 1900, some five years before, it operated in a milieu of roughly 5,000 prostitutes and 1,000 places of prostitution citywide that generated a cumulative $15,000,000 to $25,000,000 annually, the Everleigh alone accounting for a weekly $2,500.

—While the typical "streetwalker" was fortunate to clear $150 a month, the "fillies" at the Everleigh pocketed that much in a single week, not infrequently three times that amount.

—Ada, older by two years, and Minna, the more outgoing, were the sisters, originally from Evansville, Indiana, who owned and ran the place. Daughters of a wealthy Louisville, Kentucky, attorney from whom they had inherited their stake, they had named their house in honor of their grandmother, who customarily signed her letters to them, "Everly Yours."

—The "Peccable Ladies," as the newspapers routinely referred to them, once had been described, courtesy of the *Trib*'s own Jack Lait, by way of the homology "What Christ is to Christianity, the Everleigh sisters are to pleasure," though they remained themselves scrupulously chaste.

—Doling out $75,000 a year in operating expenses, 40 percent of it to servants—cooks, maids, musicians, dancers, upkeep crew—another 20 percent in protection to the cops, they still managed to clear twice that figure in pure profit.

—Rumored to employ twenty-five cooks on a rotating basis and another twenty-five full-time servitors, the club was known to serve the best fried-chicken dinner, lay on the best buffet, and stock the most expensive wine and champagne cellar in the city—"no beer, no booze, no Raleigh Rye"—charging $12 for a bottle of champagne in the parlor, $15 in the boudoir, either Cliquot King or Mumm's extra dry.

—Admission was "men only," solely by letter of introduction or engraved invitation. Clients, in order to secure the prized return invite, were expected to drop a minimum $50 per visit—dinner alone, wine included, was that much and up—and to favor the girls with a 20 percent tip on top of their fees.

—To become a member of the "Elect Stable of 30"—called "butterfly stock" by Minna—a girl in addition to certain physical attributes and proofs of experience—"no virgins, no amateurs, no young widows or local girls need apply"—was required to meet rigorous standards of robust health—"no rales, no gleet, no clap, no pox"—good grooming, well-spokenness, and breeding. Fully half were said to be under eighteen; as Franklyn shortly was to discover, they looked it.

Taken in harness by Minna—Bill, meanwhile, seemed to have vanished without so much as a godspeed—the pair disappeared arm in arm down a milelong Aubusson-carpeted hall appointed with potted ferns and bamboo palms, Greek god-and-goddess statuary, suits of knightly armor, bottom-lit vitrines of iridescent abalone, and crystal chandeliering beneath which bright peacocks sipped from flame pots on the floor. Franklyn felt his feet through the soles of his shoes melting into the pile underfoot—toes through swamp mud.

"When we bought in for $55,000," remarked Minna—Ada, apparently, was overseas "recruiting"—"the property was worth $150,000. Since then, cellar to garret, we've sunk in another $100,000, with plans to spend that much more again. See here?" She gestured toward a fancily filigree-engraved spittoon standing against the wall. "Pure gold. $700. Twenty of them throughout the house."

"Fourteen thousand in gaboons?" asked Franklyn, doing the math.

"Only the best," she replied, plucking a piece of fruit from one of the many horns of plenty arrayed with salted cashews and pecans, bonbons, candied cordials, marzipan, nonpareils, balancing it like a mint by her upturned fingertips for his inspection. "Nectarine? They're white."

When he declined, she continued. "Champagne buckets, too. Gold.

Six pianos here, all grand. Upstairs, fifty brass beds, marble headboards, custom mattresses, double thick. Mirrored rooms. Five thousand dollars each in mirror glass. Excellence, Tribune, excellence in excess. Without it, why bother?"

Rounding a corner, they headed down yet another hallway, where the lighting was more moodily muted. Gold silk flowed in five directions. Yellow canaries in yellower cages warbled their yellowest tunes. Along the corridor lay a dozen continuous reception rooms or miniparlors, the bowers so-called, each tastefully draped in damask and tapestry, each bearing an inscribed brass door plaque: "Gold Room" (containing a fifteen-thousand-dollar piano gilded down to the gold plating atop its ivory keys); "Silver," "Copper" (with its hammered brass walls), "Green," "Rose," "Red," "Blue" (featuring blue divans, blue Ziegfeld and Gibson Girl embroidered pillows, blue afghan throw spreads), "Ebony," "Moorish," "Egyptian," "Chinese," "Japanese" (boasting carved teakwood thrones and yellow pongee-silk ceiling canopies). Each room was outfitted with a fountain that spouted scented water at timed intervals—lavender, jasmine, oleander, lotus, lilac, columbine—mixed with potable aphrodisiacs. "My secret formula," whispered Minna.

Girls, many of them approaching womanhood, adorned each of the sumptuous, resplendently appointed rooms—appointed, in part, as Franklyn was to discover, with a concealed cosh in the efficient use of which each of the butterflies had been scrupulously drilled. Most lolloped semi-lasciviously in various stages of undress: unlaced corsets, undone garters, rolled sheer hose boasting the never-ending seam running beyond the knees straight on to paradise, dangling stiletto heels, boots high to the thigh; glimpse of buttock, peek of cheek, glance of breast, bit of nip, peep of pantalet. Others played backgammon or cards—a few, chess.

None of them sipped absinthe or smiled whitely as the pair strolled by, nor did they lick their lips, moue their mouths, pout their eyes, flutter their lashes, part their fluey thighs, nor submissively bend their creamy necks in the universal come-hither gesture of contra-aversion, although some brazen few, he could not help noticing, assayed, as it were, the Grecian Bend with provoking croups.

"Our philosophy, Tribune, is simple," remarked Minna. "It is that what goes on here entails—pardon the pun—more than commerce. Indeed, that it is an art, an ancient art, and that those who practice it are the keepers of a long and honored tradition. The girls are reminded each day that they have the entire night before them, that one fifty-dollar client is better than five ten-dollar ones because it requires less wear and tear, that youth and beauty are all they have in this world, and to preserve and prolong their gifts, which are precious but also fleeting, as best they can manage. And to take precautions. 'We shall have no trick babies here,' I tell them. 'You must stay respectable by any and all means.' I insist that they remain about their persons more scrupulously clean, and about their presentation of the self more conscientious, than any class of woman.

"Listen, Tribune, when you have visited brothels all over the world, from the House of Seven Stories in Tokyo, to Mahogany Hall in Washington, to the Rising Sun in New Orleans, to the House of All Nations in Seattle, to Marseilles, Singapore, and Honolulu, you know some of whereof you speak, so when I say that there are mattress whores, and then there are Everleigh girls, the distinction is everything. A whore performs a service, delivers for pay a product—she is a commodity, little more. An Everleigh girl follows a calling by perfecting her craft, pride in courtesanship. We do not run a sex mill here, Tribune. This is no bust-out or kick-up joint, no goosing show. We offer a once-in-a-lifetime experience. You shall find no air walkers here."

When he looked at her quizzically, she pointed to the sign on the wall.

> IT IS NOT UNLAWFUL TO SELL COCAINE.
> IT IS NOT SOLD HERE ALL THE SAME.

"Dope fiends, Tribune. Coke heads. Abusers of encaine. 'Tis by the bounce in their stride that they give their game away."

Beyond the lavishly accoutred parlors lay the art gallery, a library (stocked with "the classics only, no erotica"), the music room, and the billiards room. (There were, apparently, both a bowling alley and a Turkish bath in the basement.) Farther on, the walnut-paneled dining room with its fifty-person-capacity mahogany table clothed in Irish linen and Spanish drawnwork was set with Sheffield sterling-silver cutlery and Baccarat crystal, and beyond that lay the Grand Turkish Ballroom: mosaic-patterned parquet floors, marble fountains, crystal chandeliers, orchestra loge. The famous blocklong buffet was laid out inside an exact replica of the Pullman railroad buffet car, save that it was attached to a greenhouse hung like Babylon to the rafters in rafts of orchid and orange blossom.

"We could continue on upstairs," said Minna, "but you'll be seeing it for yourself soon enough." And then, altering her tone, "As I've some matters to attend to, I need take my leave here. Enjoy, Tribune, enjoy, and come back and see us—anytime."

Thanking her profusely, he retraced his steps to the buffet—hot-buttered snails, fried oysters, Welsh rarebit, deviled crabs, Lobster Newberg, quail on toast points, broiled squab, capon, pheasant, guinea fowl, as well as au gratin cauliflower, creamed-spinach cups, Parmesan potato cubes, both pear and cucumber salads, stuffed artichokes, white-asparagus bernaise, candied carrots and yams, and every species of lettuce known to mortal man. The tour had whetted his appetite; he was most curious about the caviar. Heaped a plate—Limoges—headed for the art gallery trying with partial success not to spill.

His mouth was swishy with fish egg when she approached. He gulped, tongued at his lips, swiped his mouth with a napkin, noticing at once that hers was a body containing each tuck and curve of the royal goods. "A real peacherino," he thought. "Bee's knees, cat's pajamas, a Trilby if ever there was one." His stomach growled.

"Come," she said, slipping her hand into his. "This way. Follow me."

Her hand was soft, warm, dry, sorbefacient. Up the runner-carpeted stair, winding as a windlass, greens, blacks, reds, golds, an oriental of entwined designs, arabesque and quincunx. Weight rods of wrought brass. High-gloss mahogany bannister, handrails, capitals, finials. He noticed it all. The too humid lilt of her fragrance, the shade and texture of her too shiny hair, her too creamy skin, too rouged and too blushed. Face, nose, chin, contour of breast, lift of tush, heart curve of ass. He imagined each inch of her mesial groove. Thought, thinking of Palmer, "Don't rush."

She was wearing the strappiest, highest high heels he ever had seen in his life. "Must be like putting your ass on a pedestal," he thought. "To balance, gotta throw back the shoulders and arch the back, thus making the breasts appear bigger, the stomach flatter, the legs longer, tighter, more toned, tensed, as if by—yes—arousal. The degree of added protrusion of a woman's buttocks when she is wearing heels this high has got to be—what?—25 percent? More?"

There existed, he knew, he had read it somewhere, a mathematical formula pertaining to the phenomenon, something, he recalled as he ascended in the wake of her wiggle, along the lines of $(S+C) \times (B+F) / (T-V)$ viz., (Shape + Circularity) $\times$ (Bounciness + Firmness) / (Texture − Vertical Ratio Symmetry, i.e., ratio of waist to hips). A perfectly good and useful logarithm, so it struck him, and one he had found frequent enough occasion gainfully to apply in the past. Utilizing a scale of one to twenty, the lower number being least desirable, a perfect score, he knew, was eighty. She wasn't an eighty—he had yet to encounter an eighty, had begun to suspect that eighties were roughly as numerous as unicorns—but for the moment, in the moment, she was damn well and away close enough.

Her boudoir bore a ceiling. "How brazen," he thought. One deeply mirrored, catoptric, crystal chandeliered. Rice-paper propeller fan, blades like fins. Gold bathtub. Sprays of fresh flower stemmed up from hand-painted, enameled, bone-china vases. Oils in gilt frames, Impressionist stuff. Monet, Manet, one or the other—no nudes. Travertine marble-manteled Italianate fireplace. Velvet drapes sans tassels or togs. The walls were not flocked in red flocking. Brass bed. Headboard and foot, testers, canopy. Étagère. Armoire. Chiffonier. Verdu and silverized stuff. A pair of armchairs, damasked. Tête-à-têtes to match. An ornamental censer burned incense—not patchouli. Pomander and sachet.

The room was warm as flesh.

She lay him down upon his back upon the bed, knelt to, removed his shoes, slipped off his socks, tugged off his pants in yanks and shrugs, teased down her chemise—or camisole?—plucked her nipples some, gumdrops and pom-poms. Tongued the tip of her tongue to the bud tip of them. Made a fuss of rolling down a single stocking, slow as silk, a show of showing off her bum. Got up and crossed to the washstand where she filled the basin from a pitcher, then used an eyedropper to add several dribs of purple liquid.

"Wait," he said. "What's that?"

"What? This?" She held up the dropper, shrugged. "Dunno, potash or something, pomegranate. Supposed to be a disinfectant."

"Permanganate of potash?"

"Yeah, guess so."

Having dunked and wrung the washrag, she knelt to him once more, took him in hand, prodded, palped, the way they do when checking for what's untoward. Kneaded his crotch all 'round with the rag. Fetched another to dry him down, dry as June.

"There," she declared. "Clean as Cavendish. Let's spoon."

Took him in and around, rimming glans, upon her tongue, then head-first down, the stalk of him within her O, its moist surround. Slowly deep and slidden slow, inching all, clenched chute of sleeve, until he was finished before he'd begun, cleaned and emptied, cum and gone.

"You . . . you swallow?" he said. Rhetorical question. Palmer hadn't, not once, and they had done this a lot.

"Mmm," she said. "Always. Way we're taught. French way, they call it. You learn with oysters. Just protein. No harm."

"Maybe," he said, endeavoring, if not entirely succeeding in regathering his far-flung wits, "maybe we could do it again? Later? I mean, if you want to. Didn't really see it coming that time. Caught me, pants down."

She laughed. "We'll see. I'm not the only one, you know. Plenty of oysters in the ocean. It'll cost, though, unless you paid for time. Then you can do whatever, however, for as long as you want. Did you pay for time?"

He shrugged. "Dunno. Maybe. Friend of mine did. Whatever he paid, I'd say I already got my money's worth."

Fetching to her feet, she rearranged herself in the mirror, reappointed, redid her hair, hooked up, clasped in, buttoned down. Neither washed nor rinsed. Or gargled. Remarked, "Adieu. You're cute." And left the room.

Sometimes the element of mystery, anonymity, impersonality, keeping it between strangers, rendering it all business, illicit sport, play for pay, divertissement, little more than a roll in the hay, sometimes to grab it, slam it, blam it, bam it, wham it, thank you madam it, to fuck and go, fuck and leave, fuck it, fuck you, fuck godspeed, to fuck and then run for awhile by the lake, to clear one's head, cool one's loins, sometimes that can . . . enhance things some, add to the thrill, frisson, sense of transgression.

He never had gotten her name, didn't recognize her soul, had failed to ask, didn't want to know.

He saw her later that evening, smiling like a forceps, and then, never, ever, again.

It was going on four a.m when they strode more unsteadily than not into the smoke fog of the candlelit grotto that was Big Jim Colisimo's Dollar House Café and Resort on the southwest corner of South Twenty-first and Armour Avenue, 2126 South Wabash.

Cornering a white-linened table near the back, they ordered beers from a monkey-suited waiter, lit up cigars long as umbrellas, and sat listening to the Big Jim Orchestra—a piano, cello, two violins—play *Madame Sherry*, *The Chocolate Solider*, *The Red Mill*. The place was rife to the rafters with swanks and swells, bigwigs, bigger wheels, whales and cheeses, dapper dudes and lacquered dames, too many of whom pretended to speak French. Diamonds, or their facsimiles, were splurged everywhere around. The kind of dive where men were weighty with scent as well. Franklyn had heard of the place, of course, and, of course, had never been, though Bill, apparently, had.

"I know Jim some, sure," he said, between numbers. "But listen, son, we'll have to leave it at that, *capisce*?" A strange look did not come into his eye, nor, come to think of it, did he shift uncomfortably in his chair. At no little length, a too shiny tuxedo—blocky black hair, fat head, jagged white scar sawtoothing neck to jaw—came over and tapped Haywood meatily upon the shoulder. "Boss wants you, Billy," said the tux, not gruffly. Franklyn noticed the bulge beneath his coat near the breast shaped like the grip of what was called around there a rod or betsey or gat.

"Sure, Al," said Haywood, rising to his feet, turning to go before turning back again. "You best stay here, Tribune. Hold down the fort. Be right back."

Bill and the Scarface Tux peeled off, the former in the lead by an arm, disappearing through a side door, leaving Franklyn Shivs to ponder how much the latter, save the womanish eyes, reminded him of the hammerhead shark he once had seen at the Shedd Aquarium. He suddenly realized he was remarkably thirsty. Stubbing out his cigar, he ordered another beer, yawned.

"Shit," he thought. "If I was any kind of reporter . . ." Stopped himself, derailing the thought. "Christ! Who am I kidding? What am I supposed to do, burst through the door, notebook blazing? What I need here is one of those Nock Volley guns. Least it would give me a soldier's chance. Either that, or balls bigger and brassier than the nonchalcenterous pair I'm wearing. Ach! Leave it alone, Latty. Leave it the hell alone."

The beer came. He drained it without coming up for air, then ordered a shot, double. Cutty Sark. "Keep 'em coming," he told the waiter. Why not? The drinks, so he had been given to understand, were on the house—and he was off the clock.

During the ensuing ten days of the convention, brought to a close with a rousing rendition of the hall singing in unison "The Internationale"—*'Tis the final conflict / Let each stand in his place / The Industrial Union / Shall be the human race*—which, all said, was, he had to confess, rather thrilling in a faux-millennial, ersatz-chiliastic sort of way—Franklyn managed to speak with Bill Haywood on a number of on-the-fly occasions, though not one at such length—the man was a human whirlwind—as he might have preferred, not length enough, in fact, for a simple doch-an-dorris. No matter, he had most of what he needed from the booklet, the *Sabotage* one, though he had yet to get around to reading the slimmish volume save for a hasty perusal of its introduction in which the translator, the Italian anarchist, had taken its author to no little task for his advocacy of the public destruction of all private property.

The "biography facts" to which Haywood had referred were contained on a single blue-lined typewritten notecard slipped between its pages. They read:

Born, 1869, Salt Lake City, Utah, son of Pony Express rider and
    miner.
Age three, father dies, pneumonia.
Age nine, loses eye to knife whittling slingshot; drops out of
    school; enters mines for first time, Ophir, Utah.
Age 15-18, hard-metal miner, Humboldt County, Nevada.
1889, marries Nevada Jane Minor, Humboldt County; works as cowboy,
    nearby Hoppin Ranch.
1896, working Idaho silver mine; hears speech by Ed Boyce, WFM
    president; joins union; contributor to WFM Miner's Magazine.
1900, member WFM executive board.
1902, WFM secretary-treasurer; moves to Denver; contributor,
    International Socialist Review, Chicago.
1903-1905, coordinates Cripple Creek, Colorado, miners' strike;
    arrested, jailed, acquitted.

Over the past week and a half, Franklyn had become privy to certain other facts as well, most of them, although Haywood never said as much, not for public consumption. That his marriage, for instance, was nothing short of a calamity, Nevada Jane having early on become an arthritic, bedridden invalid who could not abide being touched, and who had fanatically embraced faith healing and Christian Science—"Scientism," as Bill called it—both of which her husband thought "a slew of superstitious horseshit and mystical raving."

For her part, Nevada Jane understood little about, as she professed less interest in, unionism. What she did know, and permitted to flourish, was the deepening resentment she harbored against "the movement," which she blamed, rightly, for Bill's long absences. He loved her, or claimed to, though in fact he effectively had abandoned her to her "invalid's half-life," as he called it, and was widely known back in Denver as a regular patron of both Lillian Powers's Cupola and Jennie Rogers's phallic-faceted House of Face and Mirrors, as, too, the none-too-discreet lover of the wives of any number of his cronies, chief among them his own sister-in-law, Winnie Minor. To his credit, he continued to dote upon his children, Vernie and Hen, both of whom he had midwifed himself, at home, and whose locks of red hair he habitually wore braided into a watch chain.

There was about Bill Haywood, Franklyn had begun to understand, more than a little of the maieutic. If it wasn't his own babies, then it was his union, a baby of a different sort, one he had taken it upon himself not only to birth, but to close-vet through its infancy while tending to its long-term well-being. Odd image: Bill Haywood, Accoucheur to Organized Labor.

At last, what emerged from the convention, if only after two weeks of interminable posturing, mind-numbing rhetoric, internecine bickering, and increasingly petty wrangling, was the creation and ratification of the IWW Constitution. The *Trib* ran its preamble on an inside back page in ten-point type:

The working class and the employing class have nothing in common. There can be no peace so long as hunger and want are found among millions of working people and the few, who make up the employing class, have all the good things in life.

Between these two classes a struggle must go on until all toilers come together to take and hold that which they produce by their labor through an economic organization of the working class without affiliation with any political party.

The rapid gathering of wealth and the centering of management of industries into fewer and fewer hands make the trade union unable to cope with the power of the employing class because they foster a state which allows one set of workers to be pitted against another in the same industry, thereby helping to defeat one another in wage wars. The trade unions partner with the employing class in misleading the workers into the belief that the working class has interests in common with its employers.

These conditions can change and the interests of the working class be upheld only by an organization in which all its members in any one industry, or in ALL industries, if necessary, cease work whenever a strike or lockout occurs in ANY department thereof, thus making AN INJURY TO ONE, AN INJURY TO ALL.

The *Trib* ran Franklyn's seven-parter, "The Radicals," in order: Debs, De Leon, Darrow, Jones, Goldman, Moyer, Haywood. But it was only with the appearance of the final piece that readers by the thousand called or wrote in, hundreds canceled their subscriptions, and advertisers—none of them major, thank god—pulled their accounts.

What had touched them off, apparently, boiled down to a few paragraphs near the end of the story:

Said Haywood: "I am no angel and do not wish to be portrayed as such. Violence is not part of our policy or credo, and we try conscientiously to avoid it where we can. We are not Spanish *anarquistas*. But people need to understand, as our forefathers understood, that there are times when violence not only is justified, but necessary. A responsibility. A duty. A patriotic act. I will not back down from doing what is necessary in order to see justice done.

"We are fighting a war. It is a class war. And it is a war that will be fought and won by the rules of war. If that makes me a militant or radical or subversive or undesirable or incendiary or Red or whatever word people prefer to use to describe people like me, so be it. I think it makes me a patriot.

"Nor am I alone. There are hundreds of thousands just like me, and we are not going away anytime soon. Steps must be taken. Steps will be taken. But that does not mean that violence is a sacrament. It seldom is that. I can admire and praise old John Brown without wishing to emulate his example unto the gallows and into the grave.

"I despise the law. I am not a law-abiding citizen. No true socialist could be."

It has been said that it is not the sentiments or words of men that make history, but their actions and deeds. How doubt, then, that in W. D. Haywood, the New Union Movement in this country has found its history maker.

Publicly, of course, the *Trib* stood by the story, the syntax and diction of which Franklyn had taken the liberty of cleaning up considerably so as not to humiliate the man toward whom he had come to feel no small modicum of affection. Privately, not only was his boss officially reprimanded for permitting the story to run as written, it was made clear to Franklyn that this "sort of thing will not be tolerated in the future," that it was not sufficiently "*Tribune*-esque," that it lacked "right balance," and that if he could not see his way clear to "handling your beat in a more thoroughly professional and professionally restrained manner," perhaps another position could be found for him where "such restraint is less at a premium." The society page was mentioned, as was the mail room.

It was perhaps a week later when Managing Editor James "J. K." Keeley, who seldom condescended to speak with anyone in the newsroom save his city editors, stopped by Franklyn's desk. "So," he said, in his affected, up-from-the-slums, plummy Brit accent, "would you say that you are happy in your work here, Shivs? Do you like your job at the *Tribune*?"

Keeley, whose mincing stride was that of an abject sufferer of chronically fallen arches, spoke in a voice distinctly redolent of the clown honk of a seal, a voice that emerged from the chlorotic pallor of the terminally deskbound. An asymmetrical smear of uncommonly sparse, ginger mustache glistened primly askant the nonextant rim of his nonextant upper lip. Insufferably pompous, commensurately patronizing, Keeley was, as everyone knew, if one helluva newsman, a draconian and tyrannical snob.

"Perfectly right," said Keeley, when Franklyn, mortified into silence, failed to respond. "No answer is an answer, too. I merely was wondering, you see. One never can be too lax about taking the temperature of one's gainfully employed chattel. But permit me to suggest, young fellow, that it might behoove you to think about it and"—he paused the pause of cheap punctuation—"to *continue* thinking about it."

When, in the weeks and months that followed, his copy, as he could not help but notice, was targeted for the sort of heavy-handed editing that was less diligently scrupulous than pettily scrutinizing, Franklyn surmised—they never came right out and leveled with you about such things, of course—that he had been placed on the notorious *Trib* short leash, the same leash—noose, really—from which none was permitted to slip free, or ever had.

Something about the Haywood piece had squarely struck the proverbial nerve, provoking a range of quite violent emotion in a range of otherwise quite rational people and, apparently, placing his own job, as he considered it, in no little jeopardy.

Later, long after that job was little but an unfondly forgotten memory, Franklyn would, most often while sunken irrevocably in his cups, wonder why the hell he ever had consented to take it, or, once having done so, failed in that moment to muster the nerve to tell Keeley precisely what he knew in his bones about Bill Haywood: that during the two weeks he had spent in his presence, he had come to sense about him a gift for romantic readiness and hopeful idealism, for commitment to pursuing both his personal grail and the fulfillment of some Platonic conception of himself, that was as chivalrously large as that of any man he ever had known.

Instead, stung and intimidated, rendered in the moment every bit as unlanguaged as Bill Haywood himself, Franklyn Shivs, much as his father before him, had sought the serenity of silence. And, perhaps, he could not help thinking, just perhaps, he had done so precisely because that posture, its sanctuary, however conceivably craven, was the very one that so singularly, lamentably, but altogether uncannily, suited him.

THE BLOOMING OF THE NEW

Insofar as the Chicago Renaissance was a renaissance, it was only as Henry Louis Mencken, a Chicagoan neither city born, bred, nor transplanted, anointed it such while writing from New York City looking fondly, if rather too rosily, back a decade after its advent, said advent occurring either March 5, 1909, or November 25, 1910, both dates possessed of their partisans. Mencken's exact words, in the magazine *The Smart Set*, being: "Chicago is the only genuinely civilized city in the New World. It takes its fine arts seriously and gets into such frets and excitements about them as are raised nowhere else save by baseball, murder, political treachery, foreign wars, and romantic loves." Which, thought Franklyn later, was no more than half true, for Chicago never was as civilized as from afar the Sage would have had his readers believe.

What the "renaissance" was, in fact, was the coincidental conflux of just enough avant-gardist "arty" types at the same time in the same place—

painters, sculptors, musicians, playwrights, actors, novelists, poets, journalists, editors, publishers—that the sum of their work in conjunction with their public postures and pronouncements, as well as their private behaviors, registered with the public as a communal voice raised on behalf of a new way of seeing, feeling, thinking, and living. As for what that "new way" was or was striving toward, what it might portend, no one seemed to know, save that it must dispense with the "old" and embrace the "future."

The second date, the 1910 one, marked the opening performance— Franklyn was not in attendance—of Oscar Wilde's *Salome* at the Auditorium downtown, featuring the internationally celebrated Aberdonian soprano and dancer Mary Garden's rendition of "The Dance of the Seven Veils," about which Chief of Police Leroy T. Steward, who *was* in attendance, found it fitting to remark, "She wallowed around like a cat in a bed of catnip. If the same show were produced in the Levee, it would be called cheap and disgusting."

The first date, the 1909 one, had marked the publication of the inaugural issue of the *Chicago Evening Post*'s *Friday Literary Review*, the soon-to-be-fabled *FLR*, the first truly modern, stand-alone newspaper literary review in the world, the one that all those to follow would enthusiastically embrace as their blueprint, an event at which Franklyn not only was very much in attendance, but perched ringside. Ostensibly, of course, it had nothing to do with him—he was one of its avid readers, nothing more— but any dolt could discern that, as its stated mission was to "strike the first blow in revolutionizing the way in which the new, *Modern* literature of our nation's future is perceived," and in light of the fact that it was being published by the most culturally elitist, politically conservative, socially mandarin of the city's nine major dailies, something not insignificant had occurred. It scarce hurt, of course, that it also sold books by the gross or that it circulated by mail order to London, Paris, and Berlin.

The *Trib* being the *Trib*, it deftly countered the competition not by initiating its own book section or replacing its genteel, rebarbatively anti-Modernist lead critic, Elia W. Peattie, with someone less retrograde, but by hiring its first sob-sister columnist, the thirty-three-year-old Margery Currey, an erstwhile Evanston High School English teacher and wife of Floyd Dell, the twenty-three-year-old wunderkind assistant editor of the *FLR*. Margery knew Franklyn's work back to the Iroquois, a fact she revealed to him over lunch at Stillson's—Mrs. Dell, thought Franklyn, while none too comely, was cordial as cognac, an old soul, smart one as well, Vassar grad—and before meal's end she had invited him up to the couple's "crib" in Rogers Park, northmost enclave of the city.

The apartment, on Morse Avenue, was in a nondescript building on a nondescript residential street two nondescript blocks from the lake, four from the nearest El stop. Called in those days a "four-in-one flat," it proved a peculiarly cramped space, as one virtually bereft of furniture. Magazines, journals, newspapers, books lay strewn about like confetti. There were no chairs. You sat as you could ad-lib a spot upon the whichaway bookstacks or made do tailorwise upon one of the throw cushions, lounging among the oversize, overstuffed, crudely embroidered pillows nesting among the reading material littered about the bare, hardwood floors.

Floyd, kimino clad, rep tie Windsor-knotted for a belt, saw to the meal: Lobster Thermidor, a couple of bottles of cheap California white wine, a Caesar salad before which to genuflect. "The cheese," Floyd explained. "Proper ratio of romano to Parmesan, not too finely crumbled, just that hint of anchovy, capers, and the romaine toss, more gentle than vigorous."

Well, and well: laughter, lobster, wine, provocative talk about literature, art, books, painting, unembarrassed badinage about sex and politics and the politics of sex. Franklyn began to feel slightly at home here in a way that he did not at his own place, where he slept, or sometimes did not, or, too often of late, slept it off.

After dinner, while Marge somehow negotiated the folds of her flowing oriental robe long enough to clear, stack, rinse, and wash, the two men, at her insistence, retired to the drawing room with yet another bottle, a pair of jam jars, and cigarettes. When Floyd kicked off his shoes, Franklyn did the same. Leaning across to light his guest's cigarette before sitting back to light up himself, *Richmond Straights*, he blew rings while Franklyn French-inhaled. Exchange of smoke signals.

Gaunt, pale, neurasthenically delicate, the not undashing Floyd had yet to affect, as he would in the years ahead, his lobelong sideburns, sketchy mustaches, pince-nez, malacca walking stick, and yellow kid gloves, black stock and high collar, the gunbarrel-long cigarette holder, green eyeshade visor, and spats, as he would begin openly cheating—though neither of them, apparently, considered it that—on his wife.

The Dells, so it turned out, were "Varietists," the sort who kept indiscreetly displayed upon their living-room wall the full-frontal nude self-portrait they had had painted by a locally prominent miniaturist (Martha

Baker) shortly after Floyd's arrival in the city (from Davenport, Iowa). As such, they constituted a species Franklyn knew about in theory only, namely, that couples ought engage in what typically are considered illicit—or, at least, nonbinding—multiple sexual relationships as a way, or so Floyd explained it, of "transcending mutual envy by honing one's mental hygiene and sharpening one's spiritual affinity or 'comrade relations.'" Franklyn never had encountered a couple practically devoted to "free love" or "free unions," as they were sometimes called, or, as the Dells preferred, "soul mating."

Vaguely aware of Floyd's reputation as a gifted conversationalist and raconteur, Franklyn was about to learn what Floyd's many friends already knew: how in the midst of some Dellian disquisition about the aesthetics of Richard von Krafft-Ebing's *Psychopathia Sexualis* or Debussy's "Prelude to The Afternoon of a Faun" or the cultural symbolism of the current rage for two twins over a shared double bed, you would find yourself pulled up short just long enough to wonder over the fact that this young man was but twenty-three years old—though he looked and acted ten years older—and would be astonished all over again by the breadth of knowledge at his intellectual fingertips. Impossible to find fault with Swatty Anderson's later assessment that "he was exceptionally brilliant, and regardless of the subject at hand and whether he knew anything about it, had the ability instantly to grasp the whole meaning and then elaborate upon it at length—by wit and by fancy—carrying it farther and deeper than anyone else, and, usually, correctly."

"I deplore it," Floyd suddenly remarked without preamble.

As it seemed the right thing to do just then, doubtless the only thing, Franklyn went ahead, asked, "What's that?"

"Why, the contemptuous degradation of girls in men's minds, their implicit attitude, as of some hungry tramp toward an apple tree laden with fruit, that women are something to be picked, plucked, and consumed, an object to be eaten, enjoyed, tossed aside. Such behavior is that of the lords of the earth toward a slave class.

"As society presently is constituted, the tyranny of class distinctions must remain inescapably at the center of romance and relations between the sexes. There is a political and polemical element to all of this inequity—or should I rather say, iniquity—and one way of attacking it, besides that of birth control, of course, one route to true purity, is to grant woman their birth-rightful suffrage."

Suffragettism and the enfranchisement of women were "going" topics just then. Franklyn thought the subject plainly silly, or, rather, the fuss and the furor, the arguments against. That a woman should be barred from casting a ballot in a political election owing to her anatomy struck him as self-evidently dumb. Besides, he failed to see where men had done such a splendid job of exercising the privilege. Why not share the power, or shift the blame?

"As the principle applies to every other area of this godforsaken life," said Franklyn, "why not at least be consistent? Make the vote a woman's prerogative."

"Ha! Prerogative indeed. And it is precisely that prerogative that will make it possible, and for the first time, for men to be truly free."

"Preaching to the choir, Floyd."

"Wine?"

"Please." Franklyn extended and steadied his glass while Floyd poured, brimful.

"To cease treating women as frivolous, that's the thing," he continued, "helpmates at best, accessories at worst, feudal dolls over which to drool, servant girls, broodmares, a thing to knead and delve like so much dough, instead of independent creatures with minds of their own, deliciously free, apart and original, feminine. Heaven!"

"On earth."

"Ha! Yes, on earth. To restore to women what is rightly theirs"—he paused, as if waiting on a drumroll—"their *wildness*.

"Varietism does not work, you see, when conscience is absent and ego present. It leads, then, only to sex anarchy and conjugal bankruptcy. But otherwise, in every way, it is the ideal state, the natural condition of marriage, for then it openly recognizes the *total* liberty of the other. Being free to have all the love affairs one might wish is a supremely right thing to do—to take a lover, or as many lovers as one may choose."

He did not pause to take a breath—astonishing, thought Franklyn.

"I once had a lover of mine tell me, 'You can go or you can stay, you are welcome to do either, but what you cannot do is stray.'

" 'But it is necessary,' I told her.

" 'What,' she answered. 'To fuck about?'

" 'But of course,' I said. 'Because of the beauty of women, you see. Complicated and painful, of course, but necessary.'

" 'But why?' she wished to know.

"'But why not?' I said. '*How* not? Better that life should lose its savor? My dear, it is just such relations, call it philandering as you will, that renders getting out of bed in the morning something more than mere existence.'"

"Oh my," thought Franklyn. "Brilliant as he is, the man is one of those born idealists to whom it simply does not occur to endorse a position or espouse a theory that he does not himself endeavor literally to practice in his own less practical life."

Not that Floyd Dell ever was simple. Indeed, he could be, as he so often would prove, a bundle of cross-purposes—his favorite writer was Whitman, his favorite Whitman quote, "Do I contradict myself? Very well, I contradict myself"—one who wore, as it were, flannel shirts but silken underwear.

"You know, Frank, for what it's worth, if you didn't work for the *Trib*, I'd have you writing for us in a jacklight. I've read your stuff. Marge brought it up. Damn swell." Another pause, briefer. "Say, why don't you do it anyway? Come ahead and write for us."

"What? Nom de plume?"

"Or de guerre. Why not? Been done before."

"I appreciate the offer, Floyd, I do, but I couldn't write unsigned for the *FLR*. Anonymity'd eat me alive." Placed his empty wine jar on the floor, crackled his knuckles, stretched longitudinally, unstringing his hams. "Sound like some damn prima donna."

"Not at all. Nothing wrong with a little ego. Wouldn't give a tuppence for a man without one. Like to see you over there, though." Loosed the Windsor knot. "Art! Christ! What the hell is it anyway?"

"Dunno, Floyd. All I know is, the bitch oughtta be let alone by guys like us. Got enough rubes sleeping with her already."

Franklyn felt his eyes flung from their focus, room-spun and swimmy, suddenly found himself wondering about Marge. Where was she? Where'd she go? Bed, musta. He really did need to take his leave before he said or did something for which he would be unkindly remembered in the morning. He liked this Floyd, he did.

Getting to his feet was going to pose a chore. Ordered his brain to order his body to behave, then chanced his move: whoa there, pard! Bad angle. Halfway home, sank hopelessly back to the floor, five hundred pounds of imbecile. Floyd was up and over, helping him to his feet. Where the hell was the door?

"Flattered," managed Franklyn. "Am. Bad timing. 'Nother day."

Floyd had him by a shoulder, guide-dogging him toward the door. "*Any* day," he said. "I mean it, Frank. Open invitation."

And with those words, their italicized stress—it is difficult to truly understand virtues one does not oneself possess—Franklyn Shivs felt all his bruising begin to fade, to lift away, to heal, and to mend. Floyd Dell, bless him, felt like a possible friend.

Seven years before, the Iroquois had burned, taking 602 souls with it and clinching Franklyn's professional reputation, one risen, as he never failed to think of it—and he tried never to think of it—of their ashes. Seven years. It seemed to him an eternity—not nearly long enough.

On December 22, 1910, at precisely 4:00 a.m., the Yards caught fire.

In the northeast corner of a basement room saturated with animal fats and saltpeter preservatives, the hide room of the Nelson-Morris warehouse, Plant 7, a six-story cold-storage building on Loomis between Forty-third and Forty-fourth, one boxed in by an adjacent seven-story lard house to the north, a solid brick retaining wall to the south, a warehouse to the west, and a railroad track parked unpassably with boxcars to the east, one packed with thousands of head of cured hogs, a fire broke free.

For the next 26 hours—hours during which $500,000 in property was destroyed and 21 firefighters, including 51-year-old Chief Fire Marshal "Big Jim" Horan, 29 years on the job, as well as three nameless civilians, lost their lives—the fire havocked. The civilians remained nameless to Franklyn, at any rate, for he made it a point to remain ignorant of them.

He was not at home when the call came through to his empty apartment but, rather, waking, wherever, whoever she was this time, before shagging it into work. And when he caught wind of what was then in the midst of its happening, *all over again*, he Elled it home, where, even as he climbed the stairs, he could hear the phone ruckusing off its hook.

Opening his door, he walked inside as the sound spanked off the walls, vivid as a sun through his head, as did, in the clamor of the moment, the formal definition of the word "phone": "A ringing in the ears through holes in the air." Just so. Sonic perforation.

Yanked his blanket from its bed, snatched up a pillow, strode over to the black Bakelite tabletop number and, swaddling it 'round and muffling it down, throttled the son of a motherless bitch until every last breath of its radial rising had been wrung from the howl of its malignant black throat. Then fished the lighter from his pocket, a Zippo or Galoot, flipped back its lid—*chikt*, thumbed it to a leap of high flame—*thrrrrp*, stood over the lot heaped upon the table, and, lowering the heat of its lick to a dog-ear of cloth, tongued the fuck-all ablaze.

Crawled into bed, back ironed to the wall, and . . . watched. Watched that Bell-fast black cowboy burn out its ride.

In a drunken moment, or at least one fallen considerably shy of perfect sobriety, he decided to quit. Truth was, conditions for too long had been intolerable. He hadn't had a pay hike in years. The last time he had put in for one, it had been summarily dismissed. His bosses had made it plain that they considered the quality of his coverage several shades too Red. And what once had been little but a behind-the-hand whisper campaign, about their grooming a successor to horn in on his beat, lately had become an open secret. Besides, he did hanker to see his name in the *FLR*, an ambition he no longer was keeping a secret, least of all to himself.

There was an opening at the *Inter-Ocean*. Jack-of-all-arts—painting, music, dance, theater, books included. City's raggiest rag, low man on the food chain, lowest paying, and, so, most fun. Arranged to interview with an editor there named Walter Noble Burns. Nailed the interrogatory, was led to believe he had the gig, upon which they promptly hired the son of a friend of the owner's family. There were other openings on other papers—copy editors, rewrite, sports, general assignment. None interested him.

He noticed the advert, of all places, in the *Trib*:

Wanted. Chief Correspondent and Columnist for metropolitan weekly newspaper with growing circulation. Successful candidate will have at least three years full-time newspaper experience reporting, writing, editing, layout, photography helpful. Knowledge of Slovenian helpful but not required. Contact George Ivan Molek, editor-in-chief, Proleterac, The Proletarian. P.O. Box 3204, Chicago, Ill.

He was familiar, if only by reputation, with *Proleterac*, the city's socialist weekly. Curious, then, that he should give the position more than glancing consideration, if only because it always had been his conviction that it was to a reporter's decided advantage—where not his professional duty—to abstain from political dabbling. Which was why, or so he rationalized, he never had affiliated with a party or registered to vote, as he seldom had found it profitable to argue the point with anyone save other newsmen, who at least had some visceral feel for the logic behind the castrato's posture, one for which he had on more than one occasion been damned by those outside the fraternity for a decadent dilettante and elitist, and, once, more memorably, a "chicken-hearted Tory."

For much the same reason, save when he was too drunk to give a damn, he typically made a conscientious point of steering well clear of those conversations, discussions, and bar-side flaps that took for their subject the relative merits of this or that candidate or party, policy, ideology, or philosophy. Not that he was entirely disinterested. He tended to track political goings-on much as one might the baseball scores, as a form of sport, something to keep abreast of in order to remain minimally conversant. But beyond that, in all candor, such matters bored him. Dull as doughnuts, twice as hollow.

Had he been asked his political druthers, he was far from certain he could have supplied anything approximating a coherent answer, save that he was neither Republican nor Democrat, and the third-party Progressives, insofar as he understood anything about them, while capable by fits and starts of a certain energy, he found mainly middling, muddling, and unpersuasive. He agreed with Mencken: Theodore Roosevelt had about as much public spirit as a cat.

Politics, it seemed to him, was about one thing only: power and its wielding. Pursuing it, acquiring it, using it, keeping it. So then, went his thinking, disperse the stuff. Diffuse and defuse it. Divvy it up, spread it around, water it down. Restrict, constrict, proscribe, circumscribe. Decentralize—or defer. He imagined he was partial to parties and candidates who would see conscientiously to that. Unfortunately, he had yet to run across many, or, come to think of it, any. TR broke monopolies and busted trusts, precisely forty-three of them over seven years. Thereby? Gathering more power unto himself and that of his cronies. Bad business all around.

As for socialism, or, as he was wont to think of it, "the collective, coequal ownership of the ways and means of economic production and distribution of goods and services," he simply didn't believe it—which is to say, in it. He reckoned he could applaud it in theory, but socialism, in practice, had man precisely backward. Human nature might be many things, but one thing it was not and never would be, was nonacquisitive, leveling, or other than supremely self-interested. Nor in this regard the least chance of reform. Sooner jar a rainbow or nail water to a wall.

The problem, as he surmised it, had been put first, and best, by Rousseau, some 150 years before: "To find a form of association which will defend and protect with the whole common force the person and goods of each associate, and in which each, while uniting himself with all, may still obey himself alone."

Himself alone. As well as all together. As one. One as we. A polity. How, that is, make $1 + 1 = 1$? Could that be done? Perhaps, perhaps it could, though not without first overturning every mathematical law invented by mankind or subscribing to the sort of voodoo calculus espoused by the most literal-minded Trinitarian.

More disturbing still—for he detected it suffused so palpably through the air he might have said he was aware of *seeing* it there—was the growing inclination, not yet a groundswell, to anoint and sanctify "the worker" as some sort of new saint. What was it that Gene Debs had been quoted as saying in the newspaper just the other day? That "there is no good capitalist and no bad workingman. Every capitalist is your enemy and every workingman is your friend." Such remarks spoke for themselves—they were demagogic, and equally stupid.

Perhaps it was the lingering residue of covering labor for the elitist *Trib* all those years, but his own sense of "The Workers" was that they were as vain, self-aggrandizing, sentimental, and grasping a bunch as the very "bourgeoisie" to which they—or rather, their more articulate partisans—claimed moral superiority, as if being poor and/or put-upon, underpaid, hard laboring, *exploited* in a word, endowed them with some aura of nobility. Sorry, but he did not believe for a second that, afforded the right opportunity and for the right price, all but the paltry few would sell their so-called brothers in solidarity down the proverbial river and do so in less than an eyebat.

No class has a monopoly on virtue, any more than any race is predisposed to vice. So the powerless deposed the powerful, only to become the powerful in turn, who in turn yet again were deposed by those more powerless still, and so it went, and so it goes, 'round and 'round, on and on, ad nauseam ad infinitum. Pascal, he thought, Pascal was far from wrong: "Anyone who tries to act like an angel is acting like a beast."

No, socialism was no different than any hundred other faiths one might wish to name. So long as the salvation it vouchsafed was perceived by the faithful as serving its material self-interest, the faithful would rest content to believe. As soon as it was not, not. It was the same scam Christianity had been running from time immemorial: to sell, all evidence to the contrary, the proverbial pig's ear for the silk purse or, in Franklyn's less genteel imagery, to trick the dumb and the desperate into believing that what in fact is shit smells like clover and tastes like crème brûlée. In the end, Franklyn had roughly as much use for socialism as does a dog a fireplug. Not a word of which he intended to breathe to George Ivan Molek, as the moment, in time, might arise.

From time to time Franklyn wondered where Bill was, what he was up to, how his cherished dream was progressing, and whether, having become "Big" Bill at last, he had become any more eloquent in his foibles or articulate in his habits. The last he had heard was much the same as the rest of the nation, that after languishing some eighteen months in prison, he had been acquitted in Idaho of the bombing assassination of the antilabor former governor and wealthy newspaper publisher Frank Steunenberg, though not before TR had seen fit to publicly declare Haywood an "undesirable citizen," thereby turning the trial into a national cause célèbre, Haywood's attorney, Clarence Darrow, into a household name, and Big Bill Haywood himself into Still Bigger Bill, if not so big that he did not still publish the occasional article in the *ISR*, his latest entitled "With the Copper Miners in Michigan."

Today not far from the site of the first claims located in the copper country are the deepest shafts in the world. Number "three" shaft of the Calumet and Hecla mine is an incline 8,290 feet deep. The Tamarack mine shaft Number "four" is a vertical hole in the earth's crust, 5,100 feet as the plumb line falls.

Here are vast deposits and veins of copper which occur in conglomerate and amygdaloids. These valuable resources of the earth have come into the possession of a few individuals who have grown marvelously rich at the expense of the underground toilers. Here is located the Calumet and Hecla property which has been the greatest dividend payer in all the mining world. Organized in

1871, since that time it has paid $107,000,000 in dividends. In 1907, every man of the several thousand employed returned to the company more than $2,000 over and above the wages received, all running expenses, improvements and development work. Of the latter it is said that six years ore supply has been blocked out, ready for extraction.

The Calumet and Hecla Company has adopted a system of paternalism towards its employees, which holds the workers in a state of feudalism very peculiar under a capitalist regime. This company own 117 square miles or 74,841 acres of mineral lands. Upon this company land, temporarily leased, the workers have built hundreds of homes which they *must* vacate at short notice when they leave the company's employ. The company owns 1,200 dwelling houses and in these the workers *must* live and for this privilege the company *must* receive 6% interest on their investment in addition to the cost of maintaining the houses.

There are eight company schoolhouses where the children are taught by company teachers—a company manual training school—a company high school—there are 30 churches of different denominations all of which the company has aided to erect and helps to maintain—there are newspapers owned by the company—there is a company hotel—a company club house—company library of approximately 30,000 volumes, books chosen by the company, newspapers in 20 different languages, and these are not sufficient for the requirements of the men as there are 30 different nationalities represented on the payroll.

There are company stores where the men are expected to trade—a company hospital where mangled men get well or die under the attendance of company doctors—on company grounds is built an armory of the state where sons of company men are drilled in the art of murder and taught to shoot that they may protect the company's property rights.

The dominating influence of the company in all walks of life has bred servility on the part of the miners and creates an atmosphere entirely unlike any western mining camp. The spirit of the slave is not confined to any particular nationality, but here seems to be more pronounced in the Cornish and Italian—the Finnish miner being decidedly more progressive. Miserable are the conditions in the copper mines, but the wage slaves are awakening and organizing.

Soon, very soon, they will strike.

So now he knew. Haywood was in Upper Michigan, the U.P., its Keweenaw Peninsula, organizing the copper miners, and, knowing Bill, endeavoring in the meanwhile to convert them to "industrial socialism" over boilermakers and bourbon in the bars or during the course of an affable stroll to the nearest cathouse.

DELL'S CIRCLE

That summer, shortly before or after Franklyn was hired by *Proleterac*, the same summer during which Floyd Dell was named editor in chief of the *FLR*, the Dells moved a forty-five-minute streetcar ride south of the Loop to a neighborhood known originally as "The Corner." There, by mutual agreement—or acquiescence, for it was Floyd who had suggested the arrangement, the "disaggregation," as he called it, one which Marjy had seen fit amicably enough, if not unreluctantly, to accommodate—they took separate, though abutting, quarters.

Since become The Colony—or Jackson Park Artists' Colony or Fifty-seventh Street Group or Stony Island Bohemia or Young America or The Beloved Community—it was an L-shaped rabbit warren of single-story, single-room, storefront-windowed rental units—twelve dollars a month, fifteen dollars for those with indoor toilets—clustered about Fifty-seventh and Stony Island Avenue just west of Jackson Park, near the University of Chicago, where it occupied the whitewashed, gingerbread-trimmed concessionaires' buildings of the old fairgrounds of the Columbian World Exposition Midway. Now it was about to acquire another name, one that would prove more enduring: Dell's Circle.

The structures, thought Franklyn, when he helped Floyd move in, resembled nothing so much as sugar cubes. While most were possessed of postage-stamp-size, tree-shaded backyards with outhouse, and all boasted a potbellied coal-burning stove and iron sink with cold running water, most were unequipped with indoor toilet, bathtub, or hot water. All in all, an odd place accustomed to attracting even odder residents.

The Colonists, as they were called, were a free-spirited, free-loving, fun-loving bunch pledged to their religious reading of the *Lantern*, the city's underground weekly, and quoting often, and liberally, from Murger's *Scènes de la Vie de Bohème*. To the extent that Chicago's renaissance would come to mean anything meaningful, that meaning would germinate among them. But it was not until the Dells arrived with the example of their Varietist marriage and unaccountable knack for attracting a critical mass of friends, colleagues, acquaintances, acolytes, and hangers-on, that that meaning spread beyond its more parochial boundaries and caught on with the city at large.

Its high-beating heart, all soon recognized, was Marjy Currey Dell's Stony Island Avenue studio-salon with its secondhand-oriental-rug-draped window front, triptych screens, Szukalski statuettes, and baby-grand piano, the only place to go, as everyone acknowledged, if one wished to talk one's head off deep into the night while eating heartily and for free. Marjy—soon to be known as "the pollen carrier" after her wont for hostessing what she called her "creative copulations"—was partial to serving chop suey, chow mein, foo yong, or what have you, out of large, communal buckets, the lot washed down with several bottles of the department-store wine she kept generously stocked and ever on hand.

It was her place, not Floyd's, that was the cynosure of the vanguard of the city's avant-garde, and during the cenacle's days of res gestae, Franklyn routinely found himself at its vortex, if typically feeling more ill at ease than not, largely owing to Floyd's puckish insistence upon portraying his decision to leave the "capitalist" *Trib* in order to write for *Proleterac*—as well as the occasional review for the *FLR*—as some emblematic gesture of self-martyrdom.

"Cut it out, Floyd," he finally was compelled to admonish him.

"What?" All innocence, feigned.

"You know what well enough. You've got half the kids who come around here convinced I'm some sort of sacrificial lamb to god knows what. I can't abide it. Really, I cannot. All this . . . these, starry eyes."

"But aren't you?"

"You know damn well I'm not."

"What then?"

"I don't care about any of *it*, Floyd. I care only about writing about it. They're good kids, most of them, smart, if a little lost, but Christ! They come over asking questions, which is fine, but then they expect answers, which I don't have. That's your department. I listen. I watch. I've my thoughts. That's all."

"I know you do. So share them. You do it on paper. You do it with me. Do it with them."

"No good at it. Besides, why? Toward what end?"

"Oh, I don't know. The future. How about that?"

"Ah, the future. Yes. Well, perhaps in the future then, not now."

"But now *is* the future. You can see it written all over their faces. Tell me you can't."

"No, no, I see it all right. I do. It's just that . . ."

"What?"

"I'm trying to duck through moment to moment, you know? Me, myself, I, out on my own limb. I start dragging people out there with me, bough's gonna break."

He laughed. "Frank, you are an ace, but the way you hold back, the way you *look* at people—or don't. You *avert*, Frank. Everything sidelong and slant. What I don't get is—why."

"You think I look, what—sneaky?"

"No, not sneaky. More like—ach, I dunno. Abashed maybe. Ashamed."

Franklyn shrugged. "Feel like an intruder sometimes. Interloper."

"So?"

"What?"

"So what are you ashamed of?"

"Christ, Floyd, what not? Other people, I suppose. The world. *Their* world. The one they've made of it. The being in and of it. Complicit. I reject it. And its salvation."

"Your fellow man?"

"Not *my* fellow, Floyd. Yours maybe, not mine."

Floyd's own place, unlike Marjy's, had no indoor toilet, had nothing much, save what Franklyn had helped him move in: a battered writing desk spattered with kalsomine/calcimine, a dozen orange crates brimming with books, his typewriter and its stand, a fireless cooker, patent coat and trouser hanger, a ratty old couch, no bed, candles in wine bottles. And it was there, on occasion, that a select group of them, having done up Marjy's, would adjourn, typically in the wee-est of wee hours. Floyd operated best post-midnight; more than four hours of sleep a night and, as he told Franklyn, "I can scarce dig myself through the day."

"The Floyd Sessions," as they soon acquired the reputation, were something to behold, and Franklyn felt favored to be included first among the beholders. The content of the sessions, while wide-ranging, leaned toward certain common themes collected under the name—Franklyn could not have said who first coined it, young Hecht probably—"The New Gospel," as in "The Gospel of the New": the liberation of the individual; the redistribution of wealth; the relativization of morality; the realization and fulfillment of the self; life lived as a self-consciously visceral experiment; the power of the romantically inclined will. This nexus of art, mysticism, and power politics.

Weighty enough, save that Floyd proved singularly adept at packaging them as so much lighthearted playtime where toys were ideas and their free association, association that by night's end often enough inclined toward the carnal. Floyd wasn't hosting orgies, not exactly—the key to understanding leftist sex is to realize that it is less about orgasm than oracle and oration—but to describe the sessions as chaste would be less than scrupulously accurate. They decidedly were not, say, Mallarmé's "Mardis," 87, rue de Rome.

"Let us look at what the New, or what some prefer to call the Modern, means," he would say, the while pacing furiously about the room chain-smoking his *Richmond Straights* as, ashes flying, he addressed his shoeless pilgrims, gunnysacking acolytes, fresh-faced newcomers, the street-hardened vets slouched casually about his cramped "shed," as he called it. "It means flouting the accepted rules, flaunting the going conventions, dashing the current icons and idols, and opposing the genteelists, chauvinists, xenophobes, philistines, provincialists, and moralizing moralists—in short, *épater le bourgeois.*

"It means giving the boot to the Victorians and Puritans, monitors, censors, cops, and prudes, the prigs, the pretentious, petty, prissy, pompous, the too easily patriotic. It means getting shed of sanctimony, stodginess, stuffiness, stinginess, and sentimentality, mediocrity and monotony and melodrama. It means ridding oneself once and forever of all that is prosaic, mundane, pedestrian, boring. It means, boys and girls, leaping feet-first into the *mix.*"

Dramatic pause. "And what is the mix? Why, it is love, and life, and love of life in the Now of the Moment, the New Moment, its Next and its Next." Though precisely what constituted that moment in all of its concrete particulars was, naturally, left open to contest and disputation, which it was, nor infrequently, deeply into the dawn.

As if on cue, Floyd would bang into some stray stick of furniture, stumble, stub a toe, bark a shin, scrape an elbow, curse loudly, resume talking as if nothing in the world had happened. Talking took Floyd Dell deep, so deep that the rest of the cosmos ceased materially to exist. He became, then, all mind, self-absent, as also, ironically, absentminded, and it was this quality—Franklyn thought of it by now as "the Dellian sensibility"—that was the source of so much of the charm for which he fast was becoming so well known. Coupled with what Floyd himself called "enlightened ironism," it was an aesthetic that found its purest expression in self-effacing wit, latitudinarian empathy, and mutual tolerance. It was why Franklyn liked him, had liked him from the first, as, too, why they liked each other.

Floyd being Floyd, he might, on occasion, tumble toward declamation, but he did not blowhard or bloviate, make speeches, lucubrate, or deliver lectures—Franklyn never heard him do so, at any rate—but spoke as he always spoke, off-the-cuff, ad libitum, with an easy nonchalance, collegial openness, and casual self-possession, if—true—with enough needless-to-says, notwithstandings, never-and-nonetheless, in-any-events, moreovers, insofar-ases, futhermores, and be-that-as-it-mays, to punctuate a codicil.

Whether the subject at hand was a Shakespeare soliloquy or the lesser subtleties of sex, the shortcomings of the prose-poem or what he described as Nietzsche's "gospel of laughter," the man was wholly incapable of billingsgate, rodomontade, or flapdoodle, just as he was seldom less than the picture of jittery poise. Jittery, because on such occasions he invariably became a mass of vellication: head bobs like a pigeon hunting seed, foot taps, finger drums, knuckle cracks, handwrings, thigh whacks, neck cranes, shoulder shrugs—he convolved them off the cuff in the fiercest of herksome jerks one rotation after the other as he, oblivious to the lot, proceeded to pace, left hand shoved, palm outward, deep in his hip pocket, with each step clenching and unclenching its fist so that the left cuff of his pants hiked an extra three inches above his shoe top.

"A cakewalking chicken wearing a bustle," an image someone—Hecht, probably—once had suggested. Well, the remark required no one-upping. At last, it lent him the aspect less of impatience than of being on the clock, perpetually late for an appointment with . . . lost time?

———

A parade of mainly motley, mostly youthful, never less than unorthodox characters passed through the Dells' charmed circle that summer and fall. To recite but a fraction of their names, as Franklyn later was fondly to do—for he met them all, became acquainted with several, familiar with a few, friendly with a couple, and with one in particular much more—would be to fetch to mind a yellowing photograph of a moment ambered in time.

And, indeed, there once had been such a photograph—Franklyn had seen it countless times at Marjy's, propped atop the closed lid of her piano in, as he recalled, a cocobolo frame—a convivial, Gordon's Gin–soaked summer group shot taken by—whom? someone famous? probably, by now—down at the lakefront, Jackson Park.

And yet, because so many of the faces in the snapshot later became both so widely recognized and recognizable—before, most of them, returning perforce to obscurity—to endeavor, now, to lift from the image a meaning would serve only to confound. Unpublished, unproduced, unpatronized, unshown, unsponsored, long before fortune or fame—the street, then, only knew their names.

There was, for one, the distinctly charmless, nervous breakdown–prone, perpetually glowering, perpetually perspiring, perpetually muttering "Mad! Mad world! Quite mad!" Dreiser himself, neck carbuncles, potato face, marauding libido, the whole unpleasant hulking nine yards of him just then in town working on *The Titan*. He *was* famous, as was Upton Sinclair, whose own libido was little but a source of self-torture, and whom Franklyn found frankly creepy as he minced about bitterly complaining of how horrified he had been to discover that "I have been made a celebrity, not because the public cares a tuppence about the workers, but because it fears eating tubercular beef." But they, in terms of contemporaneous notoriety, decidedly were the anomalies.

There was the unnaturally silent, eighth-grade-educated Carl Sandburg, drawing his salary in those days from a business efficiency newspaper (*System*) and the *National Hardware Journal*, who preferred strumming his banjo to running his mouth, willing only to recite what he called "the shortest poem ever written": "Born. Troubled. Died"; his wife, Social-Democratic Party activist Lilian Steichen, sister of photographer Edward, who spoke often and passionately about how their father had forfeited his health to the copper mines of Michigan's Upper Peninsula and who habitually addressed her husband as "My Comrade"; the impossibly young-looking, improbably brilliant Ben Hecht; the exotically Jewish Edna Ferber; poor, ever poorer, mad, ever-madder Vachel Lindsay, nicknamed Nick after his proper first name; Edgar Lee Masters, Clarence Darrow's well-connected, wealthy former law partner; Maurice Browne; B. J. O. "Bror" Nordfelt; the "Harvard Boys" Arthur Davison Ficke and Witter Bynner, whom everyone called Hal; the *Trib*'s art critic, Harriet Monroe; George Cram "Gig" Cook, author of the "radical" novel *Chasm* and, later, founder of the Provincetown Players; Lucian and Augusta Cary, Floyd's new assistants at the book review; Cook's lover, the poet Eunice Tietjens, later to become Harriet Monroe's assistant at *Poetry*; the journalist Fanny Butcher; Floyd's lover, the photographer Marjorie Jones; Hecht's friend, the long-haired, bowlegged, increasingly toothless, Tabasco-sipping, tobacco-stained, stammering star drinker *beau renegade* boho par excellence Max "Bogie" Bodenheim, the soon-to-be notorious "Isaiah of the Butterflies" and "Cubistic Nightingale of the Lost Land of Poets," bearing "the look of a pensive Christ" fresh from his dishonorable discharge from the U.S. Army; his lover, the ballerina Fedya Ramsay; Critchfield adman Sherwood "Swatty" Anderson and his painter brother, Karl. One and all, anonymities then.

Because the then-unpublished Swatty was, despite being a good decade older, as much an admirer of Floyd's as was Franklyn, Franklyn came to know him better than most, and one of the first things he came to know, perhaps the very first thing, was that Swatty was convinced—a conviction he shared with his poetic counterpart Dr. William Carlos Williams, if absolutely no one else—that there not only should, but must exist a distinctly non-European, indigenously American style of artistic self-expression. And that that style, which he dared call "the way of the future"—or, more often, simply "the future"—was colloquial, vernacular, ordinary, simple, earthy, rough and unmanicured, unwashed, even crude, and more intuitive than intellectual. "Our all-American idiom," as he called it, "autochthonous and atavistic, ad hoc and raw."

"Shivs." Franklyn remembered being dropsically cornered by him at one party or another that summer of nothing but parties—Swatty, who by nature was effervescent in any case, could not, for the life of him, hold his liquor; a single highball set him to staggering or, rather, swaying in place. "Shivs, what a man has to do is feel into a thing. Understand? *Feel into.* What people think and say? Doesn't mean cowlick.

"Reason? Erudition? Eloquence? Elegance? Finish and refinement? Polish and perfection? That lot's the bollocks. Stick 'em in the sunless place 'neath ruined hats. If we are an unsubtle, childlike people, which we are, in thought and in fact alike, how should we expect our arts to escape that reality?

"No. You show me what a man knows here"—tapping his heart—"and here"—rubbing his belly—"and here"—cupping his genitals—"that's all I want to know. All I need to know. Tits and cunt and fundament. Pussy and ass." He muttered it, mantra, over and over. "Live deep or not at all."

The carnality of the soul? Mind in hock to the body? Franklyn wondered. Consciousness stripped bare that it might better be caressed, ravished, raptured? The cock fitted to the penetrated form of its thought? Idea mouthed, tongued, fellated in silent speech? Cognition through coition? Hmm.

It was Plato, he knew, who had contended that the soul could see, perceive quality. Was one to trust what one saw, then, or what one sensed or heard? Or need the senses be so divided, so opposed?

Swatty knew full well as he knew it well before the rest that he was the one, sui generis, hapax legomenon. And this included Dreiser, about whom Swatty, same party, or perhaps another, had confided to Franklyn, cocking his head in the great man's direction, "The poor fellow cannot write for sour apples." And this was an opinion Franklyn never could bring himself to contest, for he found Dreiser's prose—his own decidedly mixed notice of *Jennie Gerhardt* had latterly appeared in the *FLR*, not that the novel's author ever condescended to discuss it with its reviewer—so pathologically off-key, pathogenically out-of-gee, that he could not help but suspect that the man wrote with a pen the ink of which plopped fartlike from its nib in turds of brown mud, mud thick, mud turgid, mud gum, mud dispensed in mud-bound brown tubs. Not that turgidity, or pleonasm for that matter, is the worst sin in the world. Still . . .

Swatty, who prior to his arrival in the city had spent his life going slowly so insane that it eventually had landed him in a padded cell inside a Cleveland mental ward, argued his prejudices—which respecting Dreiser amounted to the criticism that "he is all experience, all subject matter, and no skill—of imagination, technique, or style"—more valiantly than any man he ever had known, Floyd included. And those prejudices, as over the summer and following fall Franklyn became familiar with them, were legion, as they all, in essence, were one. To wit—and quoting him, as Franklyn either would overhear Sherwood telling another or be told by him directly, typically when in his cups—

"Women are at their best as receptacles, their worst as thinkers."

"Boys fondle, men fornicate."

"Make no promises, proffer no compliments, pay no court."

"One dislikes going to bed with freeloaders, however pretty."

"The only gift a woman ought expect from a man is the privilege of being permitted a glimpse of his soul and his genius and to bask in their harmonies—in bed."

"No kissing, no hugging, no words of love—and not a dime."

"No matter how naked a woman is, she never is naked enough."

"No man can rise to the top with a loving woman clinging to his genitalia."

"Female virtue, where not a fiction, is a cabal for the undoing of the free will of free men."

"Around a woman, a bed is not a bed, it's a workbench."

"No one betrays a man more quickly than the woman who claims to love him."

"Women aren't for men to understand or lovers to enjoy. They're for anthropologists to study and cryptologists to decode."

"Looking for loyalty, honor, and fidelity in a woman is like hunting for the unicorn. It's rumored to exist, but no one has ever seen it."

"The woman who fails to fall willingly into a man's arms is only to be pitied for the opportunity she is missing."

"There is something very wrong about a woman's soul sleeping alone."

"The most fastidious lady is at last only a reproductive machine painted up in order not to appear too unappetizing."

All this sort of thing, this rather—what?—epigrammatic vulgarity and smutty posturing, however amusing in its way, was owing, as both Floyd and Franklyn knew even then and so forgave—forgiveness, accommodation, allowance, slack being first among the unspoken requirements if one was to remain his friend—to Swatty's being as yet unpublished, and so unrecognized, and so unappreciated, and so, so terribly, gruesomely insecure. "The most insecure man alive," as Floyd often called him. As, too, the one most self-convinced of his own genius.

Naturally, once their relationship had evolved to the point where Franklyn reasonably could get away with doing so, it had been necessary to ask him why, the why of his way.

"I began writing to keep from going crazy," he said simply, "or crazi*er*." Swatty never was reticent about referring to his "crack-up" or "breakdown," his "time off." Indeed, he often used it, quite shamelessly, to attract the sort of women he called the Nurse Nightingales. "And I keep on writing, because if I stopped, I fear what might happen."

"That being?"

"That I would lose myself and never find me again, my way back. I have been there once already, Frank, and once, trust me, is enough. All that nothingness, the knowing who you are, in there, inside, but no way to get to it, at it, touch it, close the distance, to make contact."

Swatty at his Swattiest was a man who sensed about himself the capacity for cool magic and dark genius, and so people were drawn to him, as Floyd and Franklyn were drawn to him and to his wild aura, one he could not be bothered to harness precisely because he was too self-immersed to live other than utterly outside the lives and opinions of others. For all his pathological insecurity, Sherwood Anderson was never at war with the world. How could he have been? He never cared enough about it to join combat. Or, as he did, chose to say the hell with it, as it had nothing whatever to do with him.

Regrettably, what neither Franklyn nor Floyd foresaw, or could have foreseen, was that what Floyd called Swatty's "fissure of insecurity," ran so darkly deep, it would prove, in time, his undoing.

That fall, by order of Mayor Harrison, who finally had had enough of its "infamy, audacity, and indecency," the Everleigh was shuttered, though not before the sisters threw a last, late-hours farewell during which Madame Minna declared for the benefit of the press gathered in the Moorish Room, "I am not sore about it. I never was a knocker, and nothing the mayor can do will change my disposition. I will close up shop and walk away with a smile on my face.

"Still, it is difficult to conclude that the crusaders have this day not made fools of themselves by their failure to separate the wheat from the chaff, the flowers from the weeds, by throwing out the baby with the bathwater.

"We were expert in the finer shames. We were respectable and clean. We were professional in the best sense of the word. What's more, we were solvent. Instead, we were touted as the force of evil itself come to spoil God's own Eden. We never, ever, were Babylon.

"Had we been consulted in the matter, we would have been open to constructive adjustment. We were not consulted. We never were con-sulted. We were judged and, I fear, sadly misjudged. By fools, as I say. And yet, fools are the very ones to win such battles as these.

"That said, gentlemen, as nothing in this life lasts forever, why not go down with a cheer and a good belt under our belts? What's done for is good and done. We are washed up here. All that is left is to clean out. Per-haps there is something to be said for getting out while the getting is good. Perhaps, let us pray, there is some grace to be had in that."

It took the sisters less than a week to put their affairs in order and exit the city on the Twentieth Century Limited en route to a six-month vaca-tion in Europe, beginning in Rome, after which they retired to New York City, taking with them the gold piano, a quarter million in diamonds, $150,000 in paintings, rugs, furnishings, and books (one thousand vol-umes of fiction alone), and a million in cash, enough, at least, to bankroll their living high on the hog ever after.

A year later to the very month, the police, armed with warrants for 135 named "resorts," conducted a weeklong, top-to-bottom raid of the Levee, which effectively put it out of business, "dooming its dives and darkening its red lights," as the *Trib* put it, "for all time."

The district had been pinched at last, and with it, thought Franklyn, some precious piece of his more checkered past.

MART

◆　◆　◆

The story Van Molek told Franklyn—he called it "the Lynching Story"—was about the time he was working in the U.P., Michigan's Upper Peninsula, editing the Slovene socialist newspaper, the weekly *Glasnik*, circulation three thousand, founded 1901.

He was twenty-three, twenty-four years old, resident in the States no more than a handful of years, only recently having become a citizen. Hired the year before by the Boston-owned Calumet and Hecla (C&H) copper mines of Red Jacket/Calumet, he had landed the job with the aid of his U.P. relatives whose expatriation had preceded his own, this the same job that, each time he told the story, he condemned as "fit neither for monkeys nor mules. Living people alive in a grave. Who lives this way? I tell you, corpses live better. At least a corpse does not worry, sick with fear."

It was the same job that, as it had with so many beside whom he had worked underground, had come within literal inches of costing him his life, as, in fact, it had cost him an arm at the elbow, a loss for which C&H—"the Outfit," as he called it—had compensated him by providing medical care at its company hospital before cashiering him outright. He lay flat on his one-armed back for weeks as, behind it, the company Xed his name from its payroll.

While such amputations scarcely were anomalies in those parts in those days, the paucity of prospects for a one-armed Slovenian ex-miner who spoke rudimentary English eventually led him to accept the editorship of *Glasnik*, a position that, while paying far less than the worst scut work in the mines, as far as Ivan Molek was concerned, "could have paid nothing at all, and there would have been more profit in it than going back down in that hell's place."

He was on the newspaper job some sixteen months when, having for some time been laboriously working a pair of sources, a visiting divinity student and a church sexton, he succeeded in confirming that the local Slovene parish priest, Klopchich, was buggering on a metronomically regular basis certain of the lambs of the flock he was being better paid to shepherd than mount.

"The truth being the truth regardless," Molek felt the story ought be published "to its depth and to the end," a position that placed him at odds with the paper's ownership, which insisted that Bishop Eis of Marquette be privately informed of the "allegation," after which His Holiness might determine in his divine wisdom whether he wished publicly to disclose the matter.

Molek, properly mortified, properly resigned. "The bitter bread of journalism," he called it in his front-page farewell, though not before referencing, however obliquely, "the scandalous affair of the sodomite priest," the mention being just enough—the whispers at that point had exceeded the whispering stage—to prompt Klopchich immediately to call for a "public gathering to clear the air" to be held in his church, St. Joseph's, where he would "explain all."

Some three hundred faithful amassed to listen to the priest parrot his speech. He was a martyr, must endure the foul and unfounded slander of his good name, suffer calumny against his spotless reputation, was being dragged unjustly through the "mire and murrain," placed most cruelly upon the rack, the charges were baseless, he had nothing to confess, let those without sin, et cetera.

This was the story Molek told, how he advanced down the center aisle toward the priest, striding to the front to address the audience by addressing the truth, a thing that, so he had noticed, the priest conspicuously had failed to do. The crowd, most of which did not know him on sight but were aware that he had but one arm, rose in stages to its feet. "It's him," it collectively shouted in Slovenian. "It's Molek. Kill him. Kill the one-arm. Hang him! Lynch him!"

At which point the crowd became a mob, spilling into the aisle, blocking his way, falling upon him omnium-gatherum and en masse with a flurry of punches and kicks. Molek was about to black out when Joe

Shtrucel, skinning his police revolver, elbowed his way in, reached down, hooked his arm under and about Molek's shoulders, yanked him to his feet, and shouted—"Police! Peace!"—before firing a single shot into the rafters. At which the crowd, recoiling, dispersed, the incident summarily ended, and the priest was discovered to have performed the divine miracle of rendering himself invisible.

"I had been, what you say, naïve, yes?" Molek would remark each time he told the story. "So I was young, yes? So young I thought a priest must live to what he taught others. What did I know? I thought he must live not as you and I—young, healthy, alive. That he must be some angel. So, I was a child. Now I know better. Now I know a priest, even a priest, is of the flesh and the blood. That even a priest has a right to love. That a priest is a priest but also a man. Think on this. Why? Why would a man be a priest? Why? Many reasons, maybe.

"Or maybe just one."

Molek always maintained that the reason he hired "Frenk" was owing less to his skills as reporter and writer, which he was happy to acknowledge were considerable, not at all because of his politics, and even less on account of his Slovenian ancestry, about which he appeared to know less than nothing, than because the thought of an erstwhile employee of the "greet Cheecago *Treebune*," a semicelebrated one at that, fetching a one-armed, immigrant, Slovene fourth-grade-dropout a cup of coffee or firing up his cigarette was one that tickled him so.

For his part, Franklyn had taken the job because, in truth, he needed the money—it paid a living wage, seventeen dollars a week, a slash of some 50 percent from his *Trib* wages, true, but the typical factory worker was then supporting a family on little over twelve dollars a week—and because, no small concern, Molek had assured him that he could write at length about any subject that might strike his fancy as long as he conscientiously covered his beat in the meanwhile: "the comings and goings" of Chicago's burgeoning Slovene community. It scarce hurt, of course, that George Ivan Molek, as Franklyn had sensed from the moment they shook hands, was a fundamentally decent man, a far better one, he suspected, than he was himself.

In fact, Ivan's reputation among his West Side folk was that of a soft touch and easy mark, for he temperamentally was disposed to trust people implicitly, was drawn instinctively to championing underdogs and their causes—those of the poor "bohunks" or "hunkies," as they pejoratively were called—was by nature an infracaninophile whose generosity of spirits was nigh pelagic, and was possessed of a mind both as alert and wide-open as his heart was capacious. Dark-haired, deep-eyed, every bit as diminuitive as Floyd Dell, Van Molek played fair, shot square, and, certainly his most admirable quality, refused to be bullied or intimidated. He also was fanatically driven, undeviatingly focused, and obsessively single-minded, loathed all manner of small talk and parties (especially those thrown in his behalf), despised frivolity of all stripe, and was constitutionally incapable of laughter. One of the few men Franklyn ever had known wholly lacking a sense of humor, both about himself and others. Remarkable, all the more so in light of his genuine fondness for Mark Twain.

Despite their being the same age, having coincidentally lost their fathers at the same moment in their lives, and, in time, developing a healthy, even profound mutual respect, the two immediately developed an adversarial, at times even fractious relationship. Ivan thought Franklyn "dégagé," chided him for the Slovene equivalents of a feuilletonist and dandy, pasticheur and fainéant. Franklyn thought Ivan oversolemn, mocked his accent to his face, and insisted upon calling him "Wee Van," a nickname he detested.

They quarreled from the first like an old married couple, nattered, needled, bickered constantly, and, finally, quite harmlessly, but where they found common ground, it trumped their differences twice over, for each valued excellence of process above all else, just as each held holy *total* freedom of self-expression. Upon these two principles the two were in lockstep and would brook no compromise.

Ivan was married, as he described Mimi to Franklyn, to "a nonsocialist, Slovenian Catholic beauteecian from Calumet, Meecheegan," by whom he had one child, a three-year-old boy, George Ivan Jr., though Mimi was just then, as she would seem ever to be as long as Franklyn knew her, pregnant again. Ivan, on the other hand, easily was the equal of Bill Haywood in his distaste for religion, and Franklyn could not help but recall the way Haywood's marriage had scuttled upon the shoals of religious schism, though he had to confess that Ivan and Mimi, at least in his presence, seemed to have reached some manner of truce, if not accord, upon the subject.

He also, was Van Molek, possessed of an abiding antipathy for Karl Marx, as he was a fawning admiration for Eugene Debs. As Franklyn was to learn, socialism Molek-style had little to do with "revolution"—sabotage, insurrection, bomb throwing, armed uprisings, guerrilla warfare—and everything to do with what he called "my four P's": progress, pragmatism, practicality, pacifism.

Their very first exchange upon the topic, second or third or fourth week on the job:

Ivan: "One third, Frenk."

Franklyn: "What's that?"

Ivan: "One third of all wealth in America, owned by two trusts."

Franklyn: "You don't say."

Ivan: "Morgan. Rockefeller."

Franklyn: "Ah, must be comforting."

Ivan: "What's that?"

Franklyn: "Believing in a thing—doctrine, creed, system, philosophy—the way you do, as much as you do, to be that, I don't know, *sure.*"

Ivan: "Comfort? No. Human nature, I think, Frenk, to need a purpose, direction to living. But not just belief, anyone can believe, a papist believes. It is in what the belief, that is what matters, no? Believing in the right, with all the heart. Believing to act. Acting, action, not belief, that is more important. To live it, Frenk."

Franklyn: "Sounds awfully, I don't know, crusade-y or something."

Ivan: "Yes? Well? So?"

Franklyn: "The evil men do."

Ivan: "Yes, well, yes, they do, sure, sometimes. Most men, though, they are not evildoers. They are, how you say, they walk through their sleep."

Franklyn: "Sleepwalkers."

Ivan: "Sleepwalkers, yes. I think, maybe, you cannot arise before you awake."

Franklyn: "Poetic, Ivan, watch out." Molek purported not to read poetry. Thought it "not productive."

Ivan: "Socialism is not a poem, Frenk."

Franklyn: "This I know, which is part of its problem, though that it is on the side of the angels I have no doubt, which is another part of its problem."

Ivan: "Why you say this, Frenk?"

Franklyn: "Because it makes a poor fit."

Ivan: "I do not understand, what fit?"

Franklyn: "Those angels, we humans."

Ivan: "Ah, I see. But not so poor, I think, sometimes. Moments."

Franklyn: "No, you are right, not so poor. Even poorer, poorer still."

Ivan: "I wish you understand, Frenk. You don't understand so good sometimes."

Franklyn: "Can't argue with that. Most of the time, not a clue."

Ivan: "I give you. Clue. Here. The cannibals, they come."

Franklyn: "Cannibals?"

Ivan: "Vampires, yes? Parasites. All the world, she be bought up and sold now."

Franklyn: "Bought up and sold?"

Ivan: "Nothing left, no more. The whole world, she is owned. Nothing left to claim for. Only each country to claim from another."

Franklyn: "Didn't know. Interesting. Well, there's always the moon. Look, what I will give you, Ivan, is that capitalism tends to flatten out the nuances in a culture, grinds everything down to the sausage of commerce."

Ivan: "Tolstoy, Frenk. You know Tolstoy, eh? You like Tolstoy, yes? Everyone like Tolstoy. Tolstoy, he says, 'Socialism, she be the name of my one desire.' Pretty good, no? But she is not yours, eh, Frenk? Not your passion. She is just an idea, one more idea, a thought, up here, inside your head, on the air, in the sky, yes? A cloud, yes? Like other clouds. But socialism, she is no cloud, Frenk. She is the sun, the only sun, the only one. What does a cloud do, Frenk? Nothing. Floats, drifts, disappears, poof. But the sun—ah! She shines, Frenk, no? She glows, warms, lights the day, makes us grow. Without the sun, we die, all of us, everything, no? This is not so? I die. You too, Frenk."

Franklyn: "More partial to moonbeams myself, boss."

Ivan: "So socialism, she is a desire, yes. A belief, yes. A faith, yes. But more, Frenk. A practice, action, a practice in practice, action in action. A way of living, being, not just thinking. Living in the light, in the sunlight. Beautiful!"

Franklyn: "Uh-oh. Beauty, Ivan? Like art? Music? Like, heaven forfend, poetry?"

Ivan: "No, Frenk. Better. A vision. *Useful* vision. A meaning. *This*, the beauty. Equal justice, common humanity, people to people. Your beauty,

Frenk, it is of a single pleasure, no? One person. Now, tell me, please, what is the meaning of such a beauty? What is its use? What does it *do*?"

Franklyn: "It has no use, Ivan, none at all. It *does* nothing. If it did, it no longer would be beautiful. No revolution, however just, ever is beautiful, just as no utopia, however beautiful, ever survives."

Ivan: "Ach, leave to a side this talk, utopia, revolution. I do not talk revolution. I talk choice. There is form, yes? And *re*form, yes? And these two, they do not *con*form, yes? They do not, how do you say, when two things do not fit?"

Franklyn: "Jibe? Gel? Comport?"

Ivan: "Comport! Yes. They keep bad company, these two. The vision divides, it breaks in half."

Franklyn: "But Ivan, I don't need such a vision. I already have enough vision to last me several lifetimes. I've had more of the stuff than I can bear. What I need is less vision, not more."

Prompting then the shaken head, exasperated sigh and shrugged shoulders, the upflung arms, and, of course, as Ivan stomped away, the mutter in Slovenian that, judging by its tone, Franklyn construed as neither sympathy nor agreement.

Proleterac was owned by a publicly traded joint-stock company, the Jugoslav Workman's Company, the majority stockholder of which was the well-heeled, culturally influential Slovene Socialist Club. Modeled after the *Appeal to Reason*, the enormously popular, half-million-circulation, national socialist weekly that had been the first to publish in its entirety Upton Sinclair's *The Jungle*, *Proleterac* more recently had duplicated the feat with Zola's *The Three Cities*.

Proleterac had nothing approaching the reach or coverage of an *Appeal to Reason*, of course, or, for that matter, a Chicago *Tribune*, or even an *Evening Post*, but the city's Slovene/Slav/Croat/Czech community clustered on the Southwest Side, the Czech Pilsen District, so-called, now numbered well above a quarter million. Although the community increasingly was spoking out west toward the Cicero suburbs, Franklyn did not want for readers, many if not most of whom subscribed both to the socialist *Proleterac* and to its counterpart, the Catholic *Amerikanski Slovenec*, the first Slovene newspaper in America, founded 1891.

Ivan had established his offices adjacent to Frank Mladich's tavern in the National Hall, Mladich's being the city's "Slovene Hub," a cavernous, real workingman's saloon where a nickel bought you a Poor Man's

Bloody—a mug of beer well mixed with a double shot of tomato juice (also called a "Red-eye"), a dime got you a Yorsh—the same, but with vodka, and another dime a Ditch—whiskey, water, rocks.

The tavern's basement was a recently abandoned bowling alley where the former proprietor once had styed a pair of pet pigs which he had fattened on a strict diet of bar scraps. Mladich, at Ivan's urging, latterly had outfitted the cellar with a dozen cots for the benefit of homeless Slovenes or, as the occasion arose, for drunks to sleep it off: flophouse space. Franklyn had himself spent his share of nights there, less because he was particularly besotted than because he often worked late into the night and, rather than inconveniencing Ivan and Mimi, who lived nearby, found it convenient to billet there. His place on the North Side was an hour away.

He would bed down in the dark again tonight, and again, tonight, in the dark, he would find himself talking alone, aloud, to no one, himself included, before, feeling bushed, rubbing the tangles from his eyes, clasping his hands behind his head, and staring straight up in the dark, or what he took for straight up, thinking, "Be afraid, pal. Be very afraid of shapes that spin, their slant of sunlight's speed, of every middle come unfixed . . . Oh, for pity sakes, what I am yabbering about now? Let it go already, Latty. Go to sleep. Let it alone. Leave it be."

Thirty seconds later, certainly no more, dreamland.

(L***) AT FIRST SIGHT

Funny how anything happens.

A party at the Dells'. Nothing but parties that summer. Brats, burgers, Marjy's chop suey, Hungarian goulash, and hunter's stew, beer, lemonade, gin served in sherbet glasses. The room that night was overcrowded, overheated, musky, giddy, all schmooze. Leaning out of the way against a wall, not for support, just against it, slightly, his left hand fisting a longneck blistered with sweat, Franklyn Shivs took stock of the fact that he was not yet drunk. Steamy night, open door, lamb's wind off the lake, Japanese lanterns, colored candles in apple-juice jars.

He felt a rile of temperature, rankle of light enough that his eyes were drawn that way, toward the front door, its frame, the way one's gaze might be said to climb the string up the tail to its kite the same. He looked, that's the point, like leaning into the field of a photo, then recoiling at the sight, felt what he could only describe as a rush of awe, and of fright. Spooked him, frankly, the sheer force of it, the—what?—delight? if by delight is meant being whisked on beryllium wings to lands sweet strange 'cross sweeter seas. *The point of vision and desire are the same. / . . . It is desire, set deep in the eye, / Behind all actual seeing, in the actual scene, / . . . in a room . . .*

She wore a yellow rose. Above her breast, she dared. Upon her chest a yellow blossom. The way her bosom . . . bloomed.

Blue eyes blue enough to fall into, down, down through, then bathe there, turning . . . blue. "Secrets there," was his surmise. Her brows were broad, high upon high, arched, and oddly inactive.

Her vanilla hair appeared veneered, and ornamentally curled—marcelled? Onduléed?—and she wore it tucked beneath a casque of an uncanny match with the blue of her blue blue eyes.

Recalled Rilke, as he once had written of his Lou: "I have never seen you without thinking I should pray to you."

"So what to think," he thought, "and say, and do? Fall prostrate upon the floor, perhaps?" Because "where does something like that come from? What does something like that do? Breathes, all right. And walks, too, I bet. But what else? With what? And whom?"

"Lust is the ultimate goal of almost all human endeavor," he remembered Schopenhauer having written, and, remembering, agreed.

Uh-oh. Marjy was walking his way, smiling, arm in impossible arm. No place to flee, fewer to hide. "Shit!" Deep breath. "Relax. Remain cool, Ace. Think. With your eyes."

Over there. What was that? The bucket. Ice? Yes. Ice would do.

Too late.

"Margaret Anderson?" Marjy said. "Frank Shivs. Frank? Mart Anderson."

"Delighted," said Margaret Anderson, placing her left hand, its five fingers outspread, over the space of her heart, as if she feared it was about to leap from her breast, taking the rest of her with it.

This startled him, not the gesture, but the word. That she should speak, actually speak, in words. Mere words.

Canting her head, she batted her eyelashes, opening and closing of a boudoir door. Her neck, he noticed, was impossibly overexposed. He might have soaped in her suds, or swooned: ayapana, opoponax, chypre, champaka, stephanotis, sarcanthus, seringa. The world, of a sudden, was good, quite, and this was its bouquet.

"How address a deity?" he thought. "On bended knee? Head bowed?

Eyes averted?" For words were bound to fail. (Goddesses fly faster than the speed of their sound.)

"Miss Anderson, charmed." Charmed? Had he actually said that? Charmed? What the hell! "A rose for the occasion, I see. So yellow. My favorite color. Almost as beautiful as its wearer." Oh, for Christ sake!

She did not blush. He noticed that. Not the sort who easily would. "Please," she said, "it's Mart"—smiled indulgently—"I insist." She was used to this.

"Mart's written a few things for Floyd," said Marjy. "Calls her the most enthusiastic reviewer he's ever published."

"Actually," said Margaret Anderson, "he said that I wrote more effusively—I believe it was 'effusively,' he may have said 'ecstatically'—than anyone in the history of book reviewing." She laughed. So she could laugh. Wind chimes, water bells, Aeolian harp. "But I think he was purposely exaggerating."

"Oh, I doubt that very much," said Franklyn. "I'm quite certain he meant every word."

In fact, Floyd had mentioned this one to him, his newest recruit, though he pointedly had not mentioned . . . the rest. He already knew, then, that she was so wildly intemperate, willfully extreme, unblushingly rapturous, and breathlessly gushing in her opinions that Floyd had been obliged on more than one occasion to run a companion review for right balance. Blue sparks, singing stars, spinning suns, so Floyd had said.

She smiled, politely, withdrew a cigarette and holder from her purse.

"Right now," said Marjy, "she is editing *The Continent*. Do you know it?"

"It's a religious magazine, Lutheran," Margaret Anderson volunteered, running her tongue left to right along the line of her upper lip, the fullest, most everted, bee-stung lip, thought Franklyn, this side of a department-store mannequin. Her mouth, he noticed, appeared cemented into an ongoing moue, as if having just finished pronouncing the word 'yum' or 'you.' She fitted the filter of the fag to the mouth of its ivory-gold holder. "Not that I'm Lutheran, or religious. Well"—she sighed, louver of dove wing—"it's a job, if not quite a living."

She was, she told him, "lodging it" at the Y downtown, though she had it in mind to purchase a pair of tents and pitch them by the lake, "just for the summer."

"Frank is—" said Marjy, addressing Mart.

"Oh, I know quite well *what* Mr. Shivs is," she interjected, failing to add, "if not yet who."

"What could she be?" thought Franklyn. "Twenty-four, if that?"

"Frank, please," he said, fumbling for his lighter. "You leave me feeling absolutely ancient. Mr. Shivs was my father." Awkward pause. "So, you claim to know who I am, do you? Perhaps, then, you wouldn't mind too awfully refreshing my memory. I sometimes forget myself." Did not add, "Especially around a woman like you. Not that there are any women like you."

"Not who, what," she said, warming, "but nothing would please me more." And shot him a look a hairsbreadth this side of brazen. "You write for *The Proletarian* about wild characters like Big Bill Haywood and his Wobblies, and how anarchism is to socialism as bomb throwing is to attending a bomb-making class, and how both are to politics as Modernism is to art, and from time to time, as at present, you cover the comings and goings of Mr. Roosevelt and his new Bull Moose Progressives, whom you personally much admire, but find politically weak broth indeed. Am I close?"

"How?" he began. "Why?" he continued. "Where?" He drew to a close. Out of interrogatives. For once.

She ignored him, continued to worry her cigarette in the mouth of its holder.

"What's wrong?" he said. "Can't you smoke it crooked?"

"Certainly," she shot back, "but with less pleasure."

"So now you know, Frank," said Marjy, with a wink, "our Mart is no mere decoration, however decorative she may appear. I would leave her all to you, but she really does need to make the rounds. Come along, dear."

As they turned to go, Mart leaned in, said something to Marjy, turned back. "Nice meeting you—Franklyn." Her smile was less polite this time.

He met hers with one equally his own, a half-slooching, long-strooling grin that sloothered his face like a groomsman. "The pleasure is mine, and the privilege, Mart."

And then, gazelle, she was off, waltzing adagio, three-quarter time, the sort of woman who does not come and go but makes her appearance and takes her own leave propelled by little more than the invisible power of her provocative soul.

"Now there," thought Franklyn, "is a woman who does not need anyone telling her how gorgeous she is, having heard the word every day of her life. Nobody's girl, that one."

There is being smitten, which, of course, he was, and there is being smote, which, of course, he also was. Still, every beautiful woman one encounters is not encountered expressly to be fucked. Once, perhaps, yes, that might have been true. Such indiscriminate fornicating could have been pardonable. "Annexing with abandon uncharted female isthmuses," as he recalled the wonderful phrase. But not now. He wasn't some candy-eyed kid, not anymore.

Where beauty is perfection of form and that form is female, he was, he knew, too often that form's prey. More than merely susceptible, he found himself routinely powerless before the promise of its secret grace, as, too, intent upon the possession of its providence. This longing for what he never had had, but sensed he had lost, or squandered. And the fact that Margaret Carolyn Anderson was more than just beautiful, that she so clearly superseded the word, that she required of the mind that it invent a new language, definitions, criteria, nomenclature, other rubrics and rules? What, he wondered, might *that* portend? Because he could not begin to think. The most he knew, *all* he knew, was that he was possessed of just enough imagination to believe in a miracle when he saw one.

The next time he saw her was later that evening, the party—rather than adjourning to Floyd's, as was customary; too hot—having migrated of its own momentum onto the Jackson Park dunes. Naked, she wore nothing but the moon. He wore much the same. They all did. Nothing out of the ordinary. Among the Colonists, nude bathing—not yet called skinny-dipping—was all the rage (as were belly dancing and doing the hula, the still-popular tango and Cherokee Indian stomp, *bout-rime*, haiku, working the Ouija board, tossing the *I Ching* and yarrow sticks, dream interpretation, word association, charades and scavenger hunts, blackout sessions and hyperventilation, blindman's buff). This, at a time when for a woman to swim in public typically was considered "racy," and proper upper-class girls bathed privately in their nightshirts.

In the park, high upon the sand, he was much more than slightly drunk and, though naked, felt warm. Knees to chin, butt to sand. The lake was black as coke, *el mar*, no boats or ships at sea, an expanse of glistered tar.

Someone had brought along a flageolet, someone else a flute. He heard a pennywhistle whisper, arpeggio octaves, sounds of pipers down the strand, expanded guitar, gypsy violin. Up the shoreline some yellow pit fires flared, here, there, cat's-eye orange, a necklace strung with torch. Some danced about and by their light, Druid silhouettes. It was, his sense of it, long after midnight.

High on his dune, some little remove, he watched her sperm about below, dolphin some, water prance, galoosh and glissade, splash and sploosh, wade, splish and fin, swim effortless the waves. Broad of shoulder, slim of hip, long of neck, pure-sure of herself as a swan. No suggestion of self-consciousness, inhibition, misstep or false move, singly at home in the pelt of her skin; he had his fill of her form for free.

"Speed," he thought, "and harmony. She's tidal, a hegemony of one."

Her meaning for him at that moment was the meaning of music, the way music means without meaning to. Nothing could have been clearer to him than his own lack of clarity, so thought unclearly, "Sea spawn and sea wrack, a nearing tide, she swims in beauty, in and of it, swims inside herself," *a naked woman shining in her courts, she draws a toil of waters . . . bobbing landward, a pace a pace a porpoise.*

Eeling out, she rose, phosphor-cum-pearl, walked aways nearer, toward where he was watching, not seeing him, her thatch a vast fluff, red-gold. Snatching up a towel, she robed it about herself, tucked it up under her arms, grabbed another, stood with her back to him turbaning her hair. The wings of her back were bare, the backs of her well-muscled thighs, her calves were toned.

When he felt himself sating, felt her with his eyes, inside, himself inside her, swelling and, gathered, gathering, refusing to flag, he rose to his feet, clambered down the dune, stumbled, fell, sand in his eyes, tumbled to his feet, half blind, crisscrossed the beach, hit the water running, *blash,* moment of shatter and foam, the one where language no longer matters, nor a moment, not one, too soon.

FIRST BLUSH

If he entertained notions of embarking upon *l'amour fou,* he hadn't a clue what he was letting himself in for or what he intended to do. She having, according to Floyd, gone forward and pitched camp on the lakeshore north of the city on the Cook/Lake County line above Glencoe off Braeside, he decided to go up there.

"You might want to think twice about that, Frank," said Floyd, upon learning of his plan.

"Why? Why twice? Because she's so pretty?"

Shook his head. "Of course she's pretty, prettiest girl in Chicago, and, of course, pretty girls come with their own special set of problems. But no, I mean, because she's so . . . Mart."

"Meaning?"

"Meaning—well, meaning you should talk to Marjy. Talk to Marjy, Frank, before you go hotfooting it after this one."

"Marjy? But why, Floyd? What's the mystery?"

"Just talk to Marjy, okay? Do me the favor. Do yourself the favor. I'm not the one to rain on your parade."

"Rain? Why rain?"

"Marjy, Frank." Asseverative, dead earnest. "Talk to her."

But of course he didn't, couldn't, permit anything to stand in his way. He had a hunch he was not going to like what Marjy had to say, and whatever she said, he knew he was bound to disregard it. No, he was going up. In his mind's eye, he already was there.

The spot—he had coerced Floyd into supplying a map—proved a broad, sparsely wooded, isolated and unpoliced sash of sand covishly well sheltered beneath a 150-foot-high, steeply pitched bluff, down which someone had managed to haul enough lumber to patch together a series of five wooden platform floors upon which perched a contiguous clutch of substantial duck-canvas khaki tents, three facing the lake, the remaining two—one, the kitchen—facing one another across a stretch of further platform flooring, the open-air picnic dining space. Each tent and its wood porch extension contained military-style cots, deck chairs, secondhand Persian rugs, and was strung with laundry cord from which hung its denizen's wire-hangered wardrobe. Cooking was by campfire. She called it "My North Shore Gypsy Camp," which is exactly what it appeared to be. Smelled of fish fry and frying bacon.

She didn't live there Crusoe'd to herself, of course. Her divorced sister, Lois, and her two children, as well as a hometown chum named Harriet Dean—the dark-haired, rather butch-looking "Deansie" had lived next door to Booth Tarkington back in Indianapolis—plus her Negro maid and young son, constituted the "family."

"Franklyn Shivs, my god! To what do I owe this unexpected pleasure?"

She sounded winded. Glistered with sweat, she had, she said, only just returned from her Sunday-morning swim-and-sprint. Her tangled hair was wet; wore nothing but her bathing suit.

He was about to reply, when, having ordered him to sit—"Grab some wood there, bub"—she abruptly excused herself, ducking into her tent in advance of reemerging flimsily half robed and brandishing lighter, holder, and half a pack of cigarettes—*Laurents*, what else, a hard-to-find, expensive French brand, blue box, gold band. Plunking down across from him at the picnic table, she fussed some with the spray of narcissus, daffodils, and jonquils vased upon the table in what he recognized as a Provencal bowl, fished out a fag, poured herself a cup of java, plucked a single green grape from the bunch plattered atop the table, and popped it like a peanut into her mouth.

"Now I'm jealous," he said.

"What?"

"Of that grape." He pictured her in peplum and hemp sandals, Roman empress palankeened aboard her barge. "I've come to ask you to dinner, Mart." Beat her to the matchlight. "And to see your digs. Floyd was being fatherly," he lied. "Asked me to drop by." Wristed out the match after lighting his *Sweet Caparol*.

"Floyd's a sweetheart. Marjy, too. Think they'll stay together?" She inhaled deeply before exhaling with a peculiar sort of languor, letting the holder dangle, rather too dangerously in his opinion.

"Often wondered the same myself," he said. "Floyd has his notions, needless to say. I love him like a brother, but sometimes his brilliance is, well, too brilliant for his own good. To answer your question, who knows. Make an interesting couple, though."

"Oh, agreed, fascinating," she said. "Ordinarily I don't like groups, can't abide them, coteries, salons, so forth. Such people devitalize me. The Dells' is the only one I frequent, only one in the city worth frequenting." She paused, flipped her hand toward the tents. "Welcome to Arcadia, by the way. This must seem all rather, well, curious to you. Or quaint. Both perhaps."

"Not at all. I'd say more intrepid than quaint. Just call me a camp follower."

"And I'm a poor gypsy."

He smiled. "Yes, a gypsy at her ease among Persian rugs."

She smiled back. "Poverty may be more than a state of mind. I'm certain it must be. But that is how I prefer to think of it. Something wondrous always will happen if only one permits it."

"Micawber."

"Perhaps, but how much more marvelous the imagination. Life is quite beneficent enough if one insists upon its being so. So, I do—insist."

"And I insist," he said, availing himself of the opening, "that you come to dinner with me."

Now she did frown. "Well, I simply wouldn't think of it."

His face must have fallen a million miles—certainly he felt his heart sink into his shoes—because she immediately remarked, "Oh, my. Please do not misunderstand."

"I understand perfectly," he said. "But might I inquire, why not?"

"Oh," she exclaimed, "no. You don't understand. You're offended, and it's all my fault. I said it perfectly wrong. But the truth, I'm afraid"—here it comes, he thought, shoulda listened to Floyd, she's got a damn *boy*friend or something, betrothed to some bloke back in Indy—"is that I do not dine. Not anymore."

"You—do not dine?"

"Correct. I do not dine."

"You do not eat dinner."

"Well"—she smiled, imp—"of course I eat dinner, silly. I am a regular eater, healthy appetite, eat like a horse, I'll have you know. Breakfast and lunch as well."

"Then you are right, I don't understand. You eat dinner, but you do not dine."

"Correct. I do not dine. Formally. In public. Anymore."

He was perfectly perplexed. "Would it be overstepping to ask why?"

"Not at all. It's because eating, I've decided, is a perfectly private affair, or ought be. Food is about intimacy, among other things, wouldn't you agree?"

"Well, I wouldn't *dis*agree. Never thought of it that way, is all."

"What I mean is," she continued, "one shares an altogether personal relationship to food. At least, one does if one properly understands anything about it. Indeed, in my opinion, it is one of the most intimate of art forms."

He smiled. "In your opinion, however humble."

"All right, all right. I've my share. Guilty. But the truth is, I have eaten 'out' before, in restaurants, clubs, so forth, and each time I do, I find it one of the most excruciating experiences of my life. To dine, in public, in a new place, unfamiliar place, unhomey, on edge, on show and display, people watching, perfect strangers gawking, ogling your every bite, sip, mouthful, swallow." She shook her hair. "No, really, it is all just too much. Nerve-racking in the extreme, and, I've no doubt, unhealthy. Such degustation cannot be salutary for the digestion."

"In your opinion."

She laughed; wonderful.

"But certainly," he said, "you are aware of why they, as you put it, gawk."

"Yes," she said, no longer laughing, "I do. I do know why, and do you know what?"

Shook his head, no. A lie. He knew. As he likewise knew that, in her most private person, she must of necessity be inclined to barbicans, bartizans, bulwarks, and berms; the self-vigilance of beautiful women.

"It displeases me." She was firm. "Is it my fault I look this way, some magazine-cover cutie? Matinee girl? I know that much about myself. I attract, and because I do, I worry, sicken myself with it, that should I appear less than—"

"Thrilling?" he volunteered. "Stunning? Flawless?" He paused. "Well, I reckon any defect *is* ten times worse in a woman."

"Well, exactly," she replied, not hesitating. "So, you see, I could accept your invitation—I am, believe me, flattered that you thought to ask— but I fear the evening would be a disaster, and, while I have experienced my share of those—enough, at least, that they ought no longer faze me— I would not think of visiting such a calamity on you. It would be perfectly pointless." She glanced about. "I would ask you to dinner here, but, as you see, I cannot imagine that this is what you had in mind. What did you have in mind?"

"Dinner," he said. "Drinks, dancing, the Drake. Something fancy. Champagne and silver slippers. For a start. The moon and stars. For dessert."

"Ah, I see. Thought that might be it. Squired about on the gentleman's arm. A date." She glanced toward the lake. "And then what, Shivs? What then? Would you be my gaoler? Would I be your muse?"

The inspiration descended from god knows what planet. "I know!" he said. "A picnic. Do you picnic, at least?"

"Picnic? Why, certainly I picnic. I adore picnics. Who doesn't?"

"Then that's it. We'll picnic. I know just the spot. Will you picnic with me, Anderson? A sort of day trip, train trip. I'll see to everything, you see to the rest. Are you game?"

"Game is something I've never been accused of not being. When? Where?"

"Let's leave it a surprise. Is that too corny? You pick when. Just make certain it's a day without rain."

She laughed. "Let me get back to you. I need check my calendar first, but we'll do it. You're on. You've your date."

They spent the rest of the morning and most of the afternoon talking, or, rather, in deep, deeper, ever-deepening conversation, the art of which, he discovered, she lifted with a consummate ease to a level—altitude, really—the likes of which he never had experienced. At first, it was all about her. He asked, she answered, he listened, content to do so, and always in the back of his mind whatever seed Floyd had planted there.

She was from Indianapolis, six years his junior, the oldest of three sisters reared in Youngstown, Ohio, "that disgusting milltown," where her "gentle, henpecked" Scotch-Dutch father, to whom she ever would remain "Martie," managed both the city's utilities and transportation system and was "most unhappily married" to her mother, "The Tyrant," who had turned their home into "the Great Divide." As a child, she had "fallen madly in love" with the piano, in which she majored for three years, not degreeing, at the Western College for Women in Oxford, Ohio, before arriving in Chicago to clerk at Browne's bookstore and edit *The Continent*.

More interesting to Franklyn was that she swam, sunrise and -set, often at midnight, particularly in the rain, during lightning storms, after which she ran; exercised with Indian pins twice a day; rode and jumped horses on weekends; devoured caramels and chocolates when she could afford them; purchased a yellow rose fresh each day for a nickel, pinning it to the breast of the only blouse she owned, a powder-blue georgette number with ruffles about the wrists, which she wore smartly pressed beneath a darker blue, tailored suit, also her one and only; owned one hat, the one he had seen that night at the Dells; wore but a single glove, the right one, it being the hand she "hated," while overfavoring its mate; smoked like the proverbial chimney; gathered her own firewood but could not boil a proper egg, though she was "an artiste of omelettes"; was an accomplished pianist—practiced "at least two hours" each day in the Fine Arts

Building downtown on a Mason & Hamlin grand, the only brand of ivories she would consent to tickle—possessed of a "positive weakness" for Chopin and the performances of Paderewski; wrote in front of triptych mirrors in order to "observe my reflection from a variety of angles"; and insisted that she had been "ecstasied from the age of six," always appearing as if she had that moment "emerged from a scented boudoir."

And then, because she opened the door and pointed the way, they talked of other things. Of sea orchards, sand colors, wind harps in cedar trees, flame flowers, the way rain slides, blackbirds on green grass, rose-cuticled moons, the restless silver routes of stars, the pace of winds and patterns of clouds, burning high noons, lotus pools, night poppies, dream-colored wings, the way that rushes whispered, of pipers at the gates of dawn. Talked of slant light upon poplars, shaken dew, the shiver of winter wheat, warm white gulls above cold blue waves, yellow butterflies in yellow corn, the sweetness of salt, currents on the upper air, sunlight through cab and chablis, the lisp of autumn's reeds, sea grass and shore grass, red-pine and resiny trunks, bird cry in hollow trees, hammocks of shadow slung in the sun, street lamps washed by summertime rain, cream of moon in chardonnay sky. Of pagan temples and Chinese gardens, old pagodas, their ivory silence, almond trees the frost has burned black, bitter fruit, the pulse of city streets at night, scows misty-wet with mizzling rain, Assyrian incense, Arcadian quince, torn lanterns that flutter a-fly with their rips, Phoenician silks and satins outspread, garlanded gods undone by their hubris. And of the white graves of goddesses, wounds of new ruins, sorrows that suffer and snuff out the sun, the thunder of horses' hooves stamping steep over cliffs, all the hollows where pain is golden and rich, all the roots of the earth and foams of perpetual sea.

And then they talked of still other things, and talked, and talked, and nothing they talked about, insofar as Franklyn was able to surmise, sounded an alarum. So maybe he would talk to Marjy after all, listen to whatever it was she might have to say. It had only been the better part of a day, true, but it was a beginning. It was something.

Knowing her, getting to know her, having known her, would prove, among countless other things—trial, tribulation, travesty—difficult. Already he could sense it was not going to be easy, mainly because there was not a blessed thing, so far as he could determine, that was easy about her, or might prove easy. Save her looks, which were nothing but easy, on the eyes. She left a guy gasping, so it struck him, ate oxygen like bonbons, a presence as present as any he ever had experienced, the precise obverse, it occurred to him, of his father's. Not that he minded. Shifted the burden, is how he considered it. Besides, nothing comes quite so naturally to a reporter as to ask questions, then sit back and listen avidly to the answers, and, in this respect, he found her nothing if not accommodating.

"I am no partisan of the simple life," she confided to him one day, "whatever that may be. The so-called salt of the earth holds no charms for me. Living the life of *people*, in the midst of their everyday vibrations, their *abrutissement*? No, I intend to live life unhampered by such sanity. Live the life of people? Perish the thought! Who knows how many essential emotions one never would experience? I see no future in being an ordinary person. It fails to interest me."

How to reply? Decided to quote Nietzsche: "'When I am among the many I live as the many do, and I do not think as I really think; after a time it always seems as though they want to banish me from myself and rob me of my soul.'"

"Yes," she replied. "*Daybreak*. Quite so. My favorite work of his. How did you know?"

She had her detractors, of course. The exotic and too beautiful always do, and, as she was both in like measure, she attracted and repelled more than her share. "Impossible" was the word they bandied about, or, just as often, "insufferable." Impossibly discriminating, insufferably temperamental, impossibly superior, insufferably smug. A mutual friend, Eunice Tietjens, the poet, once described her as possessed of a "savage scorn of everything she does not understand." And might well have added, thought Franklyn, "does not care to understand." This the same Eunice who once remarked to him that "she is so like some antique goddess of dawn, Aphrodite herself could hardly be move lovely." It was a comment that put him in mind of Hecht's own: "She is a Dido in Carthage, the laconic high priestess high on her hill of High Art looking down with Olympian hoots on the grumbling, grubby streets."

She did not pretend that such remarks did not bother her. "I know what they say about me," she told him. "It is because they see what they see to the exclusion of me, my interuterine nature."

"Pardon?" he said.

"I prefer to nurture myself than to be nurtured by others, that's all. To live in a *self*-affirming fashion rather than to fight and confront. I am not out for combat, however much I may find the dialectic of intellectual dispute invigorating."

"Ha!" he exclaimed. "I imagine you do. Because you never lose, even when you are dead wrong."

"But why should I? Lose." She shook her head. "I do not lose, because I refuse to."

Which was altogether true. He never had, nor would he ever know her to lose an argument, with himself or anyone else. "It is not that my critical faculty is infallible," she said, "or my standards of taste superior, or my rules of behavior impeccable. They aren't, save in everything that matters. Anyone can be discerning; it is being discriminating that distinguishes knowledgeability from mere knowing. It is simply that my nervous system is constitutionally incapable of abiding having things taken out of my hands.

"I know, Shivs, that my life is one based on manias, and I know how this frightens people, most people, puts them off, but it cannot be helped, nor, in all candor, do I wish to help it. Take me, leave me, but I will be loved or left unloved for who I am. And I *will* be loved, on my own terms, as I will love on mine.

"Life is rapture, or meant to be. Hardship, discord, poverty, none of those, not for me, too jarring, jejune, too out-of-gee. Life is for rejoicing. Tell me you disagree."

He thought about this a moment before replying, "My mother once told me that life is something to get over, escape as best one can manage it with one's self still somewhat honorably intact. I do not believe she was wrong, nor do I believe, are you."

He had another question, and, as she was bursting so with answers, he found it difficult—reporter's reflex—not to ask away. She was, it occurred to him, the best individual human copy he ever had stumbled upon.

"What is it," he began, "that frightens you so? Why are you, and you know that you are, always so high-strung, high-flown?"

She immediately became defensive. "I will have you know that I am frightened by nothing and afraid of no one."

He held up both hands, stop signs. "Mart the fearless, no sal volatile or *sal soda* for her. Still, every *profound spirit needs a mask*, no?"

"Fond of your Nietzsche, aren't you? Well, mask. Sure. Or ventail."

"Ventail," he repeated. "Very good. Now, an honest answer, please."

She glowered or glared, one of the two. Loathed, freely admitted it, the way she looked when she was cross. "Fine," she said. "You desire an *honest* answer, then you shall have one." Sighed. "Nonlife. There! Will that do? That is what I fear, what frightens me, *terrifies* me. Does that answer?"

Apparently it did not, for a rant—the very word—one for which he was ill prepared, ensued.

"All that does not stir, rise, mount, ring, resound, resonate, accrete. The presence opposite you that remains inert and flaccid when you are breathless . . ."

"At last," he thought, "we may be getting somewhere important."

". . . the presence in which nothing arrives, that leads you to nothing and considers it something, that solicits your interest only after both the subject and object have been long decided, when all that is rich in substance has been drained away, when the talk has been bypassed and the idea reduced, the presence that puts you in prison and keeps you there since you cease to exist the moment it speaks.

"It is the theme that never is allowed to develop, the orchestration that never is listened to, the enthusiasm that is labeled naïve, the originality that goes unrecognized. It is the lyrical turned into the practical, the political preferred to the psychological, the empty space that insists it is full. It is the noncontributor who just *must* contribute, the uncharming who *will* thrive and flourish, the limited who limit, define, impose, insist, who establish their superior pose, its chains and shackles, the ones that bind, even as the poseurs look down their nose.

"It is all those who avoid going to extremes save when they go to extremes to avoid them. Those who value above all things circumscription, circumspection, discretion, proscription, propriety, officiousness, and who wish at all cost to live lukewarm, tepid, in between, and to take as I was taught from a child to take—all things in moderation and measure, never feeling anything too deeply, for look at last where it lands them: smack in the middle of nowhere!

"You wish to know what frightens me, Shivs? *That* is what frightens me, all of it, because I know it too well, know them, all of them, and I know they would starve me to death with their lack of excess, their absence of soul, with their fucking—yes, *fucking*—petty small-mindedness, their small hearts blacker than coal."

She appeared, to his bewilderment, to be silently weeping, or on the verge. He wished to kiss away her tears—and did not dare.

"I see myself swimming in famished circles," she managed, voice cracking, "desperate for meat, drink, mead, ambrosia, elixir of the gods, some *nectar*, and all I am offered"—she brushed at her tears, snuffled some, spat the words— "is *vinegar*."

"Christ!" he thought, aghast. "I had no idea. How *much*, how *very* much, she must hate her mother."

A Saturday, and with it, rains. So they swam. Her place. Gesture of lustration. Instead of talking, ran. Thunder, lightning, wind, her element. She smoked more than he did, yet he could barely keep pace. And then, while the skies lifted, cleared, as the thunder moved off, they roasted corn on their cobs, double-baked potatoes in their skins, drank the wine he had brought, some of her gin, washed dishes in the sand, rinsed them in the lake, played chess (badly), backgammon (less so), during which she spun some Chopin, Schumann, Paderewski on her Victrola, made plans for two Saturdays hence.

Out of the literal blue, she began. "Men may run the world, and they are welcome to it, but they do not run me, *nor* are they welcome to it. Let them rule the universe, I shall create my own. The problem with men is simple."

"Oh," he interjected, "that I do not doubt, and thank God."

"The problem with men," blithely on she went, "is that they cannot tell the difference between love and death. They war, that is *their* idea of being most fully alive: conflict, combat, triumph, defeat, the glorious pursuit of self-annihilation in the name of bashing and bludgeoning the perceived enemy, the competition, in the name of winning for winning's sake. And this is utter madness. Which is why they so often betray us, because they are too stupid to know the difference between heaven and earth."

He thought he noticed something then, in her eyes, or back of them, something trying to wrest its way to the surface.

"I talk too much," she finally said, and when he began to object, "You're sweet, but no, I do. I always have."

"I don't know," he replied. "Perhaps. Perhaps if you think you do, you do." All this talk of talk. He had something more he wished to . . . talk about. "We all are beaten before we begin," he continued, and when she knit her brow, raised his hand, traffic cop. "No. Bear with.

"We all are beaten before we begin, beaten by the game, the game of language. Which is what it is, a game. The most complex game in the world, granted, but still, a game. Abstract ideas do not exist apart from it. The unconscious cannot be explained by it. Words—talk, if you will; writing, if you must—create thought, not vice versa."

What the hell, he suddenly wondered, was he driving at? And whatever it was, did it matter, amount to more than squat? And then, no less suddenly knew—nothing possibly could matter more, or be more fraught.

"Language is a game, just not one to be won or lost. To be played, only. The mug's game, then. A game the only object of which is to reach the understanding that the game *is* a game and that its field of freest play is consciousness.

"We are imprisoned in language, and its sentinels are sentences." He paused. "I adore the way you talk."

"Paraphrase a poem," she said, matter-of-factly, "destroy its poetry."

"True," he said. "And yet, more words? What for? This is a serious question, Mart, one I never have answered or had answered to my satisfaction."

"Oh," she said lightly, "but isn't it obvious?"

"Don't doubt that it is—to you."

"For beauty, Shivs, just that, because beauty alone is what saves us from death. And this is what we share, you and I, those like us, the great secret: not that life is beautiful—any dolt can see that it is not—but that the beautiful is life."

"*That* is beautiful, Mart, the thought, almost as beautiful as its speaker." And then the words were out of his mouth before he could retrieve them. "You are beautiful, you know, really the most beautiful woman in the world." She adjusted her posture, appearing distinctly unembarrassed—or flattered. "I'm sorry. I find it beyond my means to regard the beautiful in silence."

"But *not* beautiful," she sighed. "Lovely, perhaps, a lovely freak of nature." She took her next-to-last drag. "Everyone's darling, the gods, apparently, included."

"But surely you are aware of the effect you have on men, present company no exception."

"Oh, I am more aware than you know, just as I am aware that is it not me who has that effect, but the way I appear. I find it"—searching—"tedious."

"Beauty?"

"Men," she laughed. "Present company excepted, of course."

He smiled. "So did you ever wonder, then, what it is really?"

"What?"

"Beauty."

By the light of the moon there was the resumption of thunder on the lake and lightning across it. They had talked themselves out. He had, at any rate. Besides, he needed to be going. She drew on her cigarette, the thousandth of the day, glow of orange dot in darkness. Stubbed it out in the sand. Upon his skin, hers as well, the air felt damp.

"I don't trust it," she said suddenly.

"What? Words? That's wise."

"No. Beauty."

"Wise, too. Dangerous business. 'Her pure and eloquent blood,'" he quoted Donne, "'spoke in her cheeks, so distinctly wrought / That one could almost say, her body thought.'"

"Now that," she said, "*is* beautiful."

"Yes, it is."

"At least mine has integrity."

"What's that?"

"My body."

"Ever hear the expression, too much of a good thing?"

"Last swim?" she said. "I know it's late."

"I'm game. Suits me."

"No. Let's not. Suits."

"Well"—he was less taken aback than immediately anxious—"if you're all right with it."

"Don't be silly. I know you've seen me naked, Shivs. I know you were watching. And I know what else."

"You know?"

"I know."

"And?"

"And what can I say? What is the correct response here? What would you have me say?"

"How about that you don't find me disgusting and loathsome and a beast?"

"Well, of course I don't find you any of those things. If I did, would I—would *we*—be sitting here right now? You *are* silly."

She laughed, got up, disappeared into her tent. A light lifted up inside, buoying her silhouette. The sky fattened and flicked, a rear of sky, its rim. She returned with a pair of towels, one for him. Tossed it his way, playful.

"Race?"

He sighed, shook his head no, let his shoulders sag, then, without warning, took off, sprinter out of the blocks. She had sensed it coming. They beat it neck and neck through the dark, slapping barefeet across bare sand, arrived at water's edge winded and sweating, began stripping off their clothes.

"Come on, slowpoke," she said, already in to her ankles.

He followed, chromed in moonlight, the naked form of her a stork wading whitecaps curled as commas, beards of torch. A breeze arose. Down from the stars, satin on air, he smelled the scent of her scent, perfume of planets.

They both were bare.

He was a hard-on hard on her heels. They plunged side by side, heads first, bruising their bodies, shedding their skin. It felt to them both like hours. Worlds. They finned toward the one world's rim. Dove inside strokes of lightning, kabuki. Swimming down the moon.

DEATH IS A MOTHER

That summer, his mother died. Jonah had written him in advance, "Your mother is dying. She asks for you. Come home."

He got what often is called roaring drunk instead. Because how could he? Go? Really? Really how could he?

Drunk as he was, he managed actually to pack a bag, call a cab, actually succeeded in boarding the train (stumbling), actually got on (swaying), actually sat down (reeling). Which is when he knew, actually knew: "This is wrong, *very* wrong, actually, all quite actually wrong." Stepped back off (stumbling), backpedaled (swaying), almost tumbled off the platform onto the tracks (reeling), found the train-station bar (lurching). Poured himself into a booth.

"That's all dead now," he thought sloshily, lipping a brew. "All dead. Gone. Tick. And me less myself. Not myself, nope, no more. And Palms."

Raised his glass: *"Timor mortis conturbat meum."*

And literally wept in his beer.

There was an exchange of legal-type letters. The farm would go to Jonah until he moved off or died; then it would be Franklyn's. Fine. He wanted nothing to do with it. There was a settled sum of money, extra spondulix. He would need to keep working, would have in any event, but he was about to start eating better, drinking better, too, as, in kind, more often.

She had bequeathed him what she had bequeathed him. "A good lot of temperament," he thought. "That's what."

Not a bad son, it would have pleased him to argue, a weak one, because he could not see her dead face, face facing it, or talk about facing it, or keep himself from thinking about or conjuring it every day all day long. She was dead, now he wished her gone, to stay away, keep her damn distance, every day, the distance of the dead. He was familiar with what the poet had said, about how when you get close to death, too close, you no longer see it. How when you become its intimate, you can look it straight in the eye and still miss it, look right past it. Ask a cop sometime, medic, ER doc, combat soldier in wartime. It was true enough, until—nice theory, nice try—someone you loved actually died.

He did not believe in romanticizing death, making more of it than the nothing it was, soft-pedaling or mystagoguing it, the several consolatory fictions and well-heeled lies the left alive tell themselves to cushion their pain, anesthetize, help them survive numbled day after day. How nothing could be more natural, for instance, than this positive turn of the wheel of life, its cyclic step in another, more beneficent direction, some launching, as Melville had it, *into the region of the strange Untried*. How life and death were little but opposite sides of the same coin, the same reality only differently perceived, imbricated dimensions of the same existence, covalent planes of a common array of cosmic facets, the shitless reward for having endured all the shit, the unavailing need.

Nor did he believe in being haunted by it, its ritualizing, in commemorating the dead and their dead lives. He carried no brief for eulogies and encomiums, epitaphiums either, for coronaches, dirges, requiems or requiescats, memento mori and apopemptics, death masks, funerals, wakes and burials, mausoleums and gardens of marmoreal repose, the sideshow panegyrics, paeans, encores and second acts, in shriving or stringing it out.

Her death was no wound in time, not in his. He felt on its account no loss of self, looming mortality, need to mourn. Or howl. He felt as he preferred to feel: nothing. Less. He was not disposed to caterwaul.

It was just a hole, in life, time, someone's soul, figurative, real, let it go. Death was no distinguished thing, but the trampiest of tramps, and one tramp is much like another—here today, gone tomorrow, now you see her, now you don't, out of time, out of sight, out of mind, gone as a ghost, forever. The only closure he required was that of nothingness, meaninglessness, *inanima*, void, to think of her as reposing facedown in the pile of her own unyielding yardage. And wasn't it what he required that mattered, and not anyone else, least of all herself? Because she was beside the point, beside herself, quite dead, and death is nothing, save to the living, which is what he was, and she wasn't—alive, anymore. Christ, she hadn't believed in it herself!

The egg in his throat was as the pit of a peach, large and hard and fruitless.

"When you're dead, you're dead," she had told him, if once a hundred times. "Nothing sweet about the sweet hereafter, that's why they call it death and also why they don't call it life. Last things are last things, not the beginning of something else. People die, in order, out, easy, hard, day, night, afraid or not, happy, sad. When I die, when I'm dead, let me be dead, please, let me rest in—well, just let me rest, because I'm bound to anyway, whether in peace or peat moss or pain. Mortality's a bitch only for the living."

"This is what time does," he thought. "Twirls you rear to front until you find yourself facing backassward, looking at your past as if it were the present, even as you are lowered to the grave, wondering the while where and how it all went so wrong. We squander time as if it were the sky discharging the whiteness of its rain and life little more than death's dress rehearsal. We oughtta be ashamed."

So he put it all on Jonah. Apologized at unseemly length, trusted him to understand, forgive, "you know how it is." Wished him well with the farm. Prayed that she had suffered as little as possible, but *please* spare him the details.

What might it mean to be motherless? he wondered. Books, treatises, screeds, manifestos, epistles, the most eloquent sermons had, he knew, been written upon the subject. Poems composed, paintings painted, operas operatically sung. But the best he could do was: "Something vaguely different from being fatherless, as nothing especially special, where not spectacularly less special than that." Because, if not a quotidian occurrence, then certainly a prosaic one.

One's mother, dead. Happened, time come, to everyone. No? Every mother. Every kid. So what all the fuss and furioso? Gone as gulp, whiskey past ribs. He felt no more or less orphaned in the world than he ever had been. One always is alone; born that way, lives, dies. Persuading oneself otherwise, scamming oneself long enough to pretend that one might connect or care—how in good conscience dare? You can't outpace dread.

"We will," he thought, "remember about the dead the little we will, and regarding the rest forget, as surely as the dead have forgotten us. It always is later than we think. We are handed the time of our life, and what do we do but immediately set about its killing?"

It wasn't death that was the squandering brute, but life. And now, it, life, had gone and killed his only mother, as in time, he reckoned, it would kill her only son. What alternative, then, but to bury her deep in his belly and be done? THE END.

"'I have my dead, and I have let them go, and was amazed to see them so contented, so soon at home in being dead.'" Rilke knew. Though it ought be said that he did, in fact, spare a thought for her that day, fancied he could see the maggots invest the folds of her flesh in the fallen form of her through the flannel of her cerecloth and cerement.

"Life is a martingale," he thought. And ordered another beer. "And death, the imbecile, is naught but death. No one mourns the dead. They mourn the loss of their investment in them."

No agenbite of inwit for him. No. None of that for Franklyn Shivs.

IN TRAINING

Mart Anderson found herself ushered onto the train early of an extraordinarily sunny mid-September morning, poised to head north along the lake. She wore her yellow rose.

"Trust me," he said. "This once. No questions. Not one."

"All in your hands," she replied, settling into her seat as the train jerked once, lurched forward, chugged out. "Curiosity checked at the door. Will we have fun? Must be exceptional, wherever we are headed."

He smiled, placed the wicker basket on the floor between his feet using a heel to sled it sclaffing partway beneath his seat. "It is. Was when I was a kid, anyway. We'll see. Haven't been back since."

She lit a cigarette. "Astonish me."

"Coffee?" he asked.

"Oh," she said. "You're a marvel."

"Have to be black, I'm afraid."

"Better be." And warmly smiled.

Fishing the thermos from the basket, he unscrewed the cap that doubled as a cup, poured it half full, handed it off, taking care not to slosh against the sway of the train. "Hot. Careful."

She sipped. "Ah, brilliant." Lounged back. He noticed that she had brought along reading matter, as had he. *By Sappho* was hers. His, the collected Dickinson, nonvariorum edition. She blew at her coffee, dragged on her *Laurent*. "Go ahead," she said, nodding at the book, "I dare you."

"What?" Glanced around the car, roughly one third full. Why not? Once, he had known them by the score. Now, he could remember but the one, number 1129. Recited its eight lines, softly.

"Oh, bravo!" she said. "More. You read flawlessly." Reached for the book, took it from him, riffled to a page, read the whole of number 640, repeating the final lines, *And that White Sustenance— / Despair—*.

"I often have wondered," she said, "why."

"What's that?"

"Well, why white? Why not black, or blue? Are those not more typically the colors of despair?" He nodded. "Then why white? Of all the colors she might have chosen to couple with despair, she chooses white, the color of purity, virginity, angelic light. And why sustenance? Despair as sustenance? What am I missing?"

He closed his eyes, sinking back behind them. "I *see* it this way," he said. "White is the color of no color, noncolor, uncolor, the color of absence, not-thereness, the never-been and is-no-more, once-come-and-now-gone, the color of numbness. Think, um . . . think of the whiteness of the albino-blank page, the space between the words and lines, or their erasure, *néant blanc*."

Paused, to see the more he might. "Or try this. The whiteness of the eye spooled back in its socket, the bloodless, passionless, pale, and denatured, the bleached, blanched, leached, and blenched, the belly of the beached blue whale."

Clenched his eyes more tightly closed still. "What color is a skeleton?

Skull? Winding sheet? Shroud? Or, perhaps, she felt that purity itself was a kind of despair, its sterility, isolation, suffocating air."

He opened his eyes—to her stare. "It is said," he said, "that she wore white herself—or wore herself white, perhaps. That she dressed in nothing but white day after day after day down all the days of her life. Remained in her room, den, hibernacle—recluse, withdrawn, out of sight. White like a wraith, the wraith of her room, ghost, cloud, docked wing of dove, dead planet, moon, someone but spectrally there. The color of apparition and afterthought, the *nuit blanche*, the collapsible non. And never published in her lifetime, not a word.

"So, perhaps, who's to say, she bore her life like that, whitely, in despair." Suddenly came to him. "As she herself put it in number 709, 'We—would rather from Our Garret go / White—Unto the White Creator— / Than invest Our Snow.'" Suddenly sheepish. "Does a single word of that make any sense whatever?"

"Brilliant sense, Frank."

He may have blushed. "As for why sustenance," he said, "well, you are familiar with the expression 'the wholly pleasurable consolation of melancholy,' perhaps? Burton, I believe. When despair is *all* you have, it becomes what your life feeds upon, becomes your only source of nourishment, connection, solace, the only thing that prevents you from starving. One can only suspect that in her room, wombed, it always was winter, year-round, wind broomed, rocky in its wintry ruin. 'Tis a paradox, despair, or can be, the very thing that keeps you from despairing."

She leaned slowly toward him, placed her hand—feather on wind—over his. They did not touch much, still. It almost was shocking. His trembled beneath hers, alive. "You understand," she said. "You see her. How? Is that possible?"

Felt his hand crumpling into a fist beneath hers. "You might say I know a little something about white, that's all." Paused. "Sorry, I feel like I'm flinching all over. Would you mind terribly if we talked about something else?" Weak smile. "Anything would do."

"What do you suggest?"

Did not hesitate. "Us. How about us?"

"Us? I was not aware that there was an us." Withdrew her hand. "Is there? An us?"

"No," he said. "Yes. I suppose there is, and there isn't. Yet."

"Friends," she said. "Fast friends."

"Yes, that. But—"

"Difficult, Frank, is it not," she interjected, "picturing oneself a unit with anyone. A matter of breathing, its perfect rhythm. How does one create such synchronicity with another? Four lungs at once." She sat back, silent a moment, long gaze out the train's window. When she finished her coffee, he lifted the cup from her hand.

"More?" She shook her head no. He poured himself another, spilling some. She lit another cigarette. He watched her sit. Picture. Perfect. Radiant. He was not yet near worldly wise enough to understand that there were women like this, untouchable women who could not abide a man getting too close, crowding them, presuming to share their space, and that *this* one was the paragon of the type.

They changed trains in Madison; almost there.

Later, having deboarded, she visored her eyes with a hand against the vault of the sun, surveyed the tree-atolled lush green of the countryside. Wisconsin farmland, heart of the heart of.

"Beautiful here," she said, panning the panorama. "Fragrant, the grass. Reminds me of home. Not *always* a good thing. More contour here, I should say. Where are we, exactly?"

"You promised, remember?"

"I did, didn't I? Well, lead on then." She nodded toward the depot building. "I shall be needing to make a brief stopover first. Powder my nose, run a comb, reappoint, freshen up. Woman's prerogative."

"Oh, by all means, though I would be remiss if I did not remark that I cannot imagine how the vision of radiance standing before me might be rendered more radiant still—not without blinding the whole world in the process."

She laughed, but did not blush. He noticed that. "You *are* sweet, Shivs, on occasion, really you are, but now you must cease and desist or I shall feel obliged to tell you that I find flattery tiresome in direct proportion to its earnestness, and we shall spend the afternoon squabbling over those of your compliments that I choose to find insufficiently complimentary.

"I know this leaves you at a natural disadvantage, but, once more, the woman's prerogative, and I always have found same peculiarly pointless save as it is exercised exquisitely and to its hilt. Now, be a dear—here— take my book while I duck inside. Won't be but a jiff. Promise.

"And Frank?"

"Mart?"

"Try not to despair dead away, or whitely, while I am gone. Or wither, you know, wilt from the lack of radiance."

CAVING IN

"I *am* sorry, Frank, but I cannot. Just"—shook her head NO!—"can't."

"But . . ."

"No. But you go ahead, I insist."

"But . . ."

"I shall wait here. Leave the basket. I'll read. Over there." She pointed to a picnic table beneath a grove of alder.

"But . . ."

"I cannot go in there, Frank. Impossible. Forgive me, but no, simply impossible. I really am *so* sorry. If only I had known."

They stood side by side queued up at the entrance. Leaves fell like greenbacks interleaved with gold coin. She brushed one from her brow. He plucked another, from her hair, a flaming maple, then pocketed it, intending to press it like a lilac when he got home. Bracket of fire.

Once, there had been no queues like this. Cave of the Mounds, Blue Mounds, had been little but a locally popular freak of geological nature, an enormous subterranean hollow lurking tucked beneath the southern slope of the 1,700-foot-high East Mound of southern Wisconsin in what formerly was the lead-mining district of Dane County, some twenty miles west of the state's capital, Madison.

The cave was on old Brigham property, their farm. From where they were standing now, you could just make out the redbrick remains of Brigham's smelting furnace through the tall trees to the north. After the last of the family died off, or so the story—the old man allegedly was the county's first white settler, 1828—the new owners set about blasting limestone from the nearby quarry, one of the explosions, owing to an overload of dynamite, gouging an entire rock facing clean off, revealing a gigantic gash, a cavern of Galena dolomite thrusting on the sloping horizontal some 700 feet underground.

This proved an anfractuous mineral trove, room after room, chamber upon chamber, gallery stacked atop gallery, a netherplace pocked with perilous pits and drop-offs, fraught with crawlways, narrows, galleys, me-anders, rock waves and wind passages, plinths, pillars, chimneys, smoke-stacks, columns and domes of wet rock and subterranean, otherworldly waters: a river, a waterfall, spillways, reflecting pools. These sancta.

Once word got out, folks flocked by the thousands until the spot be-came so overrun with rock hounds, spelunkers, curiosity seekers, and pic-nickers, that at the behest of the geology, geography, and archaeology departments of the University of Wisconsin, the local authorities moved in, closed it off, rigged up wooden walkways, catwalks, handrails, and lighting, commissioned tour guides, then reopened it as what is called in the parlance a "show cave," charging a nominal admission fee, to see.

One of the few family outings of his childhood worth, as he recalled, the trouble.

"If it's the bats," he said, "not to worry. I checked. They've been mainly cleaned out."

She shook her head. "No, it's not that. I just can't, is all. I am sure it is every bit as beautiful as you say, but, Frank, under the earth? All the way? Inside of it? Down below? So . . . enclosed?" She made the universal sound for shuddering before, actually, shuddering.

"So, you're claustrophobic. Didn't know."

"No, I'm not, it's just that, well, does the phrase 'buried alive' mean anything to you?"

"You've a premonition the cave's going to collapse?"

"No premonition, just the thought of it." Shivered again.

"Ah, I see. Well, then nothing for it, as you say. Too bad. Doesn't mean we can't have our picnic."

"No, and we shall, but you go on ahead. You must, I want you to, and you must promise to tell me all about it when you get back. Take notes, mental notes, I'll want to hear everything."

He was chapfallen. This was not the way it was supposed to have gone. "It's wrong," he said. "Leaving you alone out here while I go intrep-idly spelunking? Not right."

"Oh, don't be silly, silly. I'll be fine. I've my book, yours as well." She brandished them. "I'll read. Plenty to do. You'll put me off my feed the rest of the day unless you go ahead. I mean it now, go."

"You're sure."

"Just"—she flaggled her book hand toward the entrance—"please, go."

Less than an hour later, he was back, finding her, as she had said, sitting at the picnic table, having raided the basket for a radish. Reading Sappho and gnawing on a radish. "Helluva combo," he thought.

When she saw him coming, she closed the book. Plopping down across from her, he lit a *Chesterfield*, lit her *Laurent*. "So," she said, smokily, "tell. All."

"As beautiful as I remember," he said, "though not as beautiful as it might have been." Puffed. "*Should* have been."

"Really? Why?"

"Because you weren't there." He glanced about. "Let's move. Too much traffic. I know a spot. Bound to be there still."

He grabbed the basket, she her Sappho. They tracked to the stream without difficulty, walking the length of its low bank. The woods around had grown up, tallish now, girthy boles, overhung boughs. No thickets, sparse underbrush. Fallen leaves emblazoned the earth: rich red brownie, half-burnt orange, green. Wisconsin late September. They scuffed them up in crunches. The brook chuckled, smoothing over slabs of stone, tumbled terraced rock. A chute of water softly chuting, sifting, soft and easy churn. They arrived at a flat place, creekside clearance; a clearing in a woods.

"Here," he said. "Okay?"

"Heaven."

He fished the tablecloth from the basket—red-and-white checks, swear—flappled it open, billowed it up, then down, pillowing it lightly upon and over the ground. They sat, he tailorwise, she lengthwise, head propped by an elbow, lounger. He had at the basket. His belly squawked; pigeon sounds.

"Hungry?" she teased.

"Famished. And thirsty. Wine?"

"Of course."

He passed her a stemmed glass; cheapware, odd number of a second-hand set.

"Well," he began, cranking the corkscrew, "you go down a flight of wooden stairs, three dozen steps, I counted, like descending a throat of rock, stone windpipe, dimly lit, damp, chilly, guide said fifty degrees at fifty feet down—and I'm boring you already, aren't I?" The cork popped, making the universal cork-popping sound: *puck*.

"Cut it out," she said. "Keep talking and pour." Held out her glass, into which he tipped a finger's worth of white. He waited. "Mmm," she said, holding out her glass again. "More."

"Cold enough?" he asked, filling her glass. "We could stick it in the stream."

"Perfect," she said. "So, then?"

"So then you wind on down between rock walls thirty feet high, another flight of stairs, another, seventy, seventy-five feet at its deepest, some spots narrow enough you have to shuffle sidewise to squinch through, so low you have to duckwalk, the while feeling you're inside of something far bigger than yourself, whale belly of rock, hard womb. All these formations and forms, colors and textures of rock, fluid rock, *flowstone* they call it, like the Painted Waterfall, this twenty-foot-high pouring of pitched rock, glossy spillage of polychromatic stone." He sighed. "Not doing a good job of this, am I? Making you see it."

Her eyes were closed. "I see it perfectly," she said softly. "Don't stop."

"But not just rock, because there's water, too. Surprising, the amount. You smell it, sense it, hear it, too, plopping, plinking, ploofing, sweating down the walls, slishing along the ground. Had me thinking, despite all the stoniness, rockiness, maybe a cave's more feminine than masculine, all the moistness, perviousness, penetrability." Paused. "Yielding."

She opened her eyes, extended her empty glass. "Yield me another, would you?" He poured. "Thanks," she said. "This is good. Keep going."

"Water's what accounts for all the dramatic stuff, speleothems and so forth, stalactites, stalagmites, trilobites, helicites, soda straws, cave bacon, pearl oolites, calcite grapes, aragonite orchids. Water as artist, sculptor. Look, I know this stuff only because you told me to pay attention, so I did." Drained his glass, poured himself another. "What is it, do you think?"

"What's that?" she said dreamily, eyes still closed. The flare of her nostrils, vibrissae, even those, excited him. Why?

"The quality alive inside stone? What is it, ya think, that moves when the earth moves?"

She had switched to lying flat on her back, hands laced behind her head, listening—or so he presumed. For all he knew, she was falling or had fallen fast asleep; she did not stir beyond the regular slow rise and fall of her breasts inside her blouse. He wanted nothing more than to lean over and kiss her neck, its Bosphorous. Instead, said, "When you're down there, you lose track of time. My watch stopped. Off history's clock. Odd. Felt like years."

"Should have gone along," she murmured suddenly, eyes still closed. "Should have talked me into it. Why didn't you, Shivs, talk me into it?"

"Well, let's go back then, do it, after we eat. We'll go down, do it together. Why not? I'm game if you are."

"No, I can't."

"But I thought you just said . . ."

"I know. I did, but I can't. I don't. Do them. Can't. Caves."

She right-angled up, upright at the waist, jackknife, then bent farther over still, hunching to touch her fingers to her toes before grabbing them, sustaining the position a moment before unfolding to sit on her soles.

"Of course, the classic interpretation," she said, "is that caves—dens, lairs, nests, hives, cocoons, so forth, your whale's belly, so to say—that all such inner sancta symbolize rebirth, which is what is happening when you enter, then reemerge, having experienced again the womb of your mind, this dark, placental, private, concealed interior space. Free for the first time, again. Born, again.

"But"—she gestured toward the picnic basket—"I don't agree."

"I agree," he said, undertaking to unpack, "with your disagreeing. A cave's a cave. This one's uncommonly pretty, granted, but beyond that? Being born again? No, being born again is how I feel when I'm with you."

"Flattery, Shivs. You've been warned once already." She laughed. "Few years back, serious now, I was in Egypt. Wanted to see the pyramids and so forth, lost library at Alexandria. So I find myself near this spot called Uweinat, above the shallow well there named Ain Dua, the Cave of Swimmers. I had been admonished not to miss the cave paintings there.

"Inside, all over the walls, were these petroglyphs, pictographs of giraffes and cattle and so forth, men in grotesque, feathered headdresses, imprints of human palms, made, it appeared, by outstretched hands against the walls upon which had been blown pigments to create the image, as if in negative, the image as residue of their makers, trace of their presence left behind. Mythogram, story, *shul*, sign. A silent language, it impressed me, universal sign language of the glyphs of caves: Chauvet, Altamira, Lascaux, name one. And there were hundreds and hundreds of what appeared to be swimming figures, barely human figures at swim in the middle of the desert."

He passed her a plate, knife, fork, spoon.

"And," she continued, "there was the story about the woman, nameless woman, faceless. She had died inside that cave, though how or why no one seemed to know. This was years before. They had found her lying off in the deepest corner upon her back along a rock shelf. Ribs shattered, wrists broken, but she was fully clothed and had been bundled with the greatest of care and concern in a sort of slant-cut silken bedspread, perfectly mummified, pristinely preserved, rendered parchment by the desert upon her ledge of arid sleep.

"And her face, it was said, and her body, had been colored in the hues and very designs of those upon the cave walls, duplicates upon her flesh as if she had been trying to emulate, blend in, merge, become one with. A form of cave camouflage, perhaps, this broken human object of stolen dyes and sacred pollens and images. Ocher face, blue eyes, vermillion hair, saffron knees and pubis, rings of pink thighs to her ankles, these bangles, bracelets, hoops of bright pigment, a corpus of coded signature.

"So, I found it a fearful place, I did, as all holy places are, right? As they must be, perhaps, the *tout autre*. And so I could not remain there. It was cold, getting dark, the swimmers were drowning, each upon their walls, and I, I felt, was drowning with them. Each moment I stayed there I was becoming more a part of something I had no business being part of. Difficult to describe, a terrible, horrible kind of holiness, trespass upon hallowed ground, until I began to suffocate. I was being smothered alive in there, by the cave, no air. Too late, I thought, all, too late. I ran out of there in tears."

Having turned several shades of white, she was breathing heavily as she threw back the rest of her wine. "I never have told that story to anyone before," she managed weakly, "not a living soul."

"You need food in your belly," he said. "Here." And passed her a drumstick.

"I believe," she said evenly, recomposing, recoloring, "that caves are containers of fear, or of its consciousness, our subconscious fears, here on earth, our communal fear, terrestrial fear, and that such fear lingers in those lairs, subterranean and wholly alive."

IN CHARACTER

Looking back later—well, it *would* be later, wouldn't it?—looking back on what transpired later that afternoon—the nuances and subtleties of the way it unfolded, turns of mood, oscillations of tone, alterations of pitch, travels of cadence, so on—trying to recompose in his mind the wherefores of what occurred and the whys of it having occurred in just the way it oc-curred was, he found, ultimately pointless.

They had polished off the bread (black), the cheese (Black Diamond), the fruit (black plum, white peach), the fried chicken and bakery-made strudels. He had rebasketed the remnants and they were well into their third bottle of wine, a red. A Mason jar of high-octane applejack still awaited in the wings. The talk had turned personal. He had steered it that way.

"A source of strength," she was saying, "to go it alone. There is a void, my freedom fills it. None of this clinging to, clingy as clematis."

"Egoist," he said.

"Yes," she said, "that would not be wrong. At least I do not behave selfishly and call it selflessness. Why is it wrong to be more interested in one's own thoughts and feelings than in the objects and events outside oneself? What vanity worse than gainsaying one's vanity?"

The wine had found his head, and, it occurred to him, if it had found his, then surely it had found hers.

"I believe I love you, Mart."

How had he pictured she might respond? Had he pictured anything at all?

"You may," she said, "but you do not, or, perhaps you do, in your way, which is to say, as long as we are saying, that you wish to make love to me, as many men have wished, but you do not wish to love me to live with me. No man possibly could. Or, if you believe that that is what you want, then permit me to disabuse you of your belief, because you could not, nor I with you, not without eating each other alive. And, as I disapprove of cannibal-ism in all its forms . . . Look here, Shivs, real love is not about wanting the other, it is about wanting the other's happiness, and sometimes it is about loving them enough to respect their solitude.

"I realize we have known each other only—what?—four months? but you must understand by now how *hard* we would live on one another. I do not function in intimate association, and were I to succumb to your charms, which are considerable, and I say succumb, not surrender, I would, be assured, not be responsive, not as you would have me be, fantasize my being." She turned her wineglass upside down. "Better to remain friends than risk ruin upon such shoals."

"But risking ruin is precisely the point," he said, startled by his own directness. "'Love,'" he quoted Yeats, "'is all / Unsatisfied / That cannot take the whole / Body and soul.' Surely you know what you mean to me."

"I know," she said, "that you are my great, good friend, and that I like you immensely, enjoy your company, the meeting of our minds and souls. And that you make me laugh and think. No small things, those."

"No," he said. "What you *mean* to me—to *me*."

"But how could I know that, Frank? How could I possibly?"

"Everything."

"But you mustn't say such things! No person means everything to another. If they did, the world would come screeching to a halt and the two of them with it. It is not healthy to say such things, as it doubtless is less healthy to think them."

"Fine. As you will. I won't."

"Good, that's settled then."

"Doesn't change for a moment the fact that I cannot live without you."

"Is it the wine, Frank? I do not doubt that you *want* me, and I respect your desire, I do—far be it from me to slight it—but this is purely lust talking, and that is something I know nothing about. I regret, I suppose, not being possessed of the Turkish delight temperament, for I am certain that I have missed and will continue to miss some of the bread and wine of life, but I shall not apologize for my absence of desire. There, is that clear enough for you?"

He was drunk. Not all the way, not yet, but well enough along, knew the feeling, friends with it, longstanding. Where *was* that Mason jar?

"I *am* sorry," she said, "but it is a form of madness, this pairing off, the world well lost, the base, mindless, *formless* exchange of animal appetites. I prefer to reserve my insanity for art—and ideas."

"You mean ideals, don't you?"

"Perhaps. Yes, perhaps I do."

"Then you are wrong, Mart. The notion that there exists some mystical soul communion that lies beyond carnal ecstasy, some magical carpet ride to a higher spiritual plane, is a pernicious myth. Gratification in physical consummation is simply that, not that there is anything simple about it, nor ought there be."

"Fine, then I am wrong. The fact remains, you need accept what I have to say. Why, Frank? Why won't you?"

"Because," he quoted, "'love, resistless love, my soul invades; I see the right, and I approve it, too, condemn the wrong and yet the wrong pursue.'"

"Ovid, yes, fine, but this is not interesting to me any longer, this . . . repartee. Nothing could be less interesting. You are on the verge of complicating things irrevocably. Perhaps you already have."

He did not intend to say what he said then. "My mother died. Earlier this summer."

"Oh, Frank!" she said. "I *am* sorry."

He shook his head. "Perfectly tactless of me. I am quite over it, not that there was anything to get over, particularly."

"Oh, well, of course there was. There always is. This explains it then. Oh, my."

"Didn't go to the funeral, haven't visited her grave, if she has a grave. For all I know, she's ashes in an urn, cremains in a shoe box . . . or amphora . . . or columbarium." Lumpen throat. Coughed clear of it. "Look at us, sitting by a stream in the sweet setting sun lying out upon the green green grass getting drunk and arguing about life and death and love. You might think we were . . . poets—or lovers."

"I think we are both too infantile to be either." She laughed. "I know I am. I have yet to enter that cycle of life in which one puts away one's childish things." She sighed. "The truth is, I do not care for the vision of myself I see in your eyes. It is that of the wolf, and it"—she pursed her lips—"whistles."

"Do you really loathe me so much?"

"I do not loathe you at all, save when you act like some goatish schoolboy. Try to understand, I am not your text made flesh. I do not need you to compose or complete me. Thank you for the offer, I *am* flattered, but I choose to narrate myself."

He was feeling beyond incautious now, feeling very little, frankly, the most familiar feeling in the world. Holding the Mason jar in both hands, he lifted it head-high. "Here's to you, Mart, and to your *amitié amoureuse*. Deathless, mademoiselle, absolutely deathless."

She was ashen-lipped. "This does not become you."

"What? Being crazy about you?"

"No. Well, yes, that too. I meant"—she nodded toward the jar—"that, the volte-face it grants, the *in vino veritas* of it, turning picnic into debauch. Your being drunk."

"I am that, quite so. Your point?"

"What do you want, Frank? What are you after?"

"Easy. To stop feeling I need to scream all the time. And you, I want you."

"You need to scream? Right now?"

"Now, all the time, always, since I met you."

"But—why?"

He shrugged. "How not?"

"Where?"

"What?"

"This need to scream. Can you place it?"

"Begins above the neck, between the eyes, behind the eyes, inside, then moves down to my crotch, and, sometimes, if more seldom, comes screaming across the sky."

"How big?"

"Big? Don't know. Big, bigger than I am, and deeper."

"What does it look like?"

"Hard to see, save at night. Late at night, sometimes, I can see it. Like a cube, cube like a throat."

"Color?"

"No color. Colorless, clear, clear through."

"Texture?"

"Facets, angles, lots of angles, slant."

"Does it move? Ebb, flow, place to place? Roll? Does it come and go?"

"No. Expands, contracts, like breathing, lungs." He paused. "Is this really necessary? Where *are* you going?"

"For the moment, yes, it is. Hollow?"

"No, full. Scream's in there, solid."

"And it makes you feel—how?"

"Like screaming."

"More?"

"Like crawling into a tunnel. Well, sometimes."

"Other times?"

"Drinking, getting potted, blotto, blind."

"Scared of it?"

"Maybe. I dunno, a little."

"Why?"

"That maybe it really *is* hollow, empty inside, nothing there, lot of dead air."

"Why?"

"'Cuz the nothing there's gone off, something foul."

"Yes, your conversation. Why say such unpleasant things?"

"Because what is foul is faith, belief, conviction, commitment. Rancid, those. Because, I know."

"Know what?"

"That were I to start, I'd never stop."

"Believing?"

"Screaming."

"But still you feel the need."

"Yes, save when I drink, drink it away, get drunk, and . . ."

"Yes?"

"When I'm with you."

"Not fair, not fair at all."

"Just true."

"I won't save you, Frank. I cannot complete you, fill what is empty, provide what's not there. That's not my job at all."

He wasn't seeing straight anymore; she was in triplicate; couldn't bring his eyes together to single focus, synchronize his sight. She blurred.

"I think," he began—well, what *did* he think?—"I think you should respect a person who is run over by love, the way I have been run over, and"—he would wonder, later, about his choice of words, but in the moment, at the moment he spoke them, they were the only ones he could count upon himself to accommodate—"I think that you should swallow me, all of me, because I want you to, and because the body contains the art of its own language. What reposes there demands expression, desires it, wants, needs, lusts after the expression that must be shared, appreciated, enjoyed."

Nothing like an articulate drunk, she thought. Or, perhaps, he did.

"I want you to swallow me, Mart, all of me, to the hilt, eat me alive, as I would eat you."

For just a moment, she appeared poised to storm off, rose to her feet instead, walked over, only a step or two, leaned down, and slapped him hard, flush across the face. "Fuck you, Shivs," she said, softly. "Fuck you."

His response to this—while he was aware that he been struck and that she had been the one doing the striking, he felt scarcely a thing—was not rational, which is to say, far from stone sober. Flinging the Mason jar, empty by now in any event, into the stream, its thin-sharp shatter against rock, explosion of glass, shards through smoothness, struck him as not *exactly* that which dirt clods make upon coffin lids. The slap, then, hadn't hurt half as much as it had startled him, though it must have accomplished *some*thing, roused, *a*roused him in some way, because the next he knew, he was at his pants, zipper of his fly, unzipping. Or trying to.

She was half crying, but through her half tears she did not fail to notice his fumbling. "Stop it, Frank! Don't be ridiculous. Listen. Are you listening? Listen to me!"

He had heard her, of course, but he didn't want to listen anymore. What he wanted to do, although he wished to do it with her—or, if it came to it, *to* her—did not entail listening.

"Put yourself away," she said. "Back in the box, inside the cube, with all of you."

He tried, but found himself too drunk to comply, couldn't find a grip, no traction. Gave it up, relinquished the rarebit, let it be, what it was, a dangle, a-dangle, four sails to the wind, swaying as he swung—aspargus stalk, pollywog, collop of crimpled pasta—before slewing toward her, alongside, orbiting his face across the gap between them in a single glide, angling in-toward as he laced his fingers into her hair at the back of her head and brought her nearer, pressing.

She did not resist. They did not kiss. He kissed her, half missed, caught a lick of lower lip, oddly angled, a little wild. Well, not tame. Drew blood.

"No," she said simply, and disengaged, pulling back and away.

His left hand inadvertently brushed her right breast, circled back uncertainly, came to rest, curled and cupping. She said nothing, just removed it, said, "No touching."

Placed his left hand on her right shoulder, right upon her left and, pawing, pushed, not hard, firm, pressured her remorselessly back, until she was down and he was reading air, Donne's "Elegy 19," the words, just there: *License my roving hands, and let them go / Before, behind, between, above, below.*

There is a right way, proper way, perfect way for a man to embrace a woman. The gentle, slow sliding of her body downward, the kiss delivered leaning in from above, her head bent back tenderly exposing the throat, so forth, so on. Or, alternately, while standing—which they weren't, at this point—the wrapping around of the arm, one hand squarely to the base of her spine, the firm but gentle pressing in-toward, stomach to stomach, torso to torso, chest to breasts, cheek brought to rest against cheek, deep breathing through hair, the sinking into, cleaving unto, clinging one to the other, et cetera.

So this wasn't going to be any of that. Romantic crap.

What he wanted, wished for, desired with all of his appetite in the moment, was not her, not alone, but to stand outside of time, with her, but upon his own. Demolish it, time. Or bring it forth broken and scuffed to its gorgeous knees, fuck it full-all from behind hard and *per annum*, make it die. To make the present stop, stall, arrest, to still and to seize. He wished, that is, to do what he wished to do, give himself, of himself, all, up her.

Or *to* her. But take, share, have, this . . . pair.

Found himself spraddled over her, planted atop, legs astride, knees at her hips, shanks akimbo clenching inward with the inner half of his thighs pressing the straddled full weight of the V of himself against her midsection, pinning her plumb in place. She did not struggle, squirm, yell, scream. Nor did she spit in his face.

But neither did she yield.

"I can smell it all over you," he slurred. "Your monthly mudge, your shallow hole, your rose on wet and rosier rose. Your red. I can smell the form of your form—your soul. Catamenial."

His lips fell radially, smile upon her neck, its bend and curve, its round; his nose was up inside her hair. He breathed, took his tongue, its tip, wet it some, placed its lick to the eave of her chin, ran it there around, the way a moment looms, then drowns.

Reached back behind him then, felt for her skirt, found it, fumbling, slipped his hand clumsily beneath its hem, sledding it smooth up her leg, sweep of upraised ride up rise of undraped thigh, warm, soft, moist, firm. Unfastened, somehow, the clasps on her camiknickers, slid them down, hiked his hand farther, 'round, higher too, past curves, berms, hairy-pin turns, shell-pink mist, fished the fen of her villous squim, sifted her quiff, entangled its trim, this velutinous this.

His hand scythed, splaying it open delta-wide, drenched itself, musk, but it did not yield, much, enough.

He lowered his face to hers. "You're a virgin, aren't you?" he whispered.

She turned her face sharply to one side, came up swiftly with her arms to push him off at the shoulders. Surprisingly strong; the swimmer. Muttered, "Hell!"

"You are!" he said.

When he refused to budge, she—but before she could, he had her, shackle, at each of her wrists, wresting them back down to either side above her head, clamping them firmly in place, trying not to wrench or yank or manhandle but manacle, handcuff, stake to the ground.

"You're . . . hurting . . . me," she said, sounding far angrier than hurt.

He felt her helplessness, and it honestly excited him, fueled. *He* was hurting *her?* What could she possibly mean? *She* had hurt *him* worse than he ever could hurt her. He could never hurt her enough, never.

She whipped her head back to face him face-onto-face until the tips of their noses were touching. Forcing his fingers into her mouth, he made a fist, inside, womb of hand in womb of mouth.

"How's this?" he hissed. "Let's tear each other in two."

She bit down hard, enamel. He was drunk, but not that drunk. It hurt. When he saw blood at the corners of her mouth he wrenched his hand away and out, unjawed, indentured with her indents; souvenir.

"Get off of me, you son of a bitch!" He saw into her eyes where red daggers flew, vaginas dentata-ed, brass bullets, too. "Get off of me," she cried. "Get off of me now, or I swear I'll scream so loud, they'll hear me back in the Loop!"

Chicago.

Rolled off, lay on his back beside her, chest heaving.

"Goddamn it, Mart. Goddamn it. Goddamn it all to hell." Spent.

She was on her feet. Her back was to him. He could not tell if she was crying. Finned in and out of focus. "Mart," he said. "I, I—I think I'm going to be sick."

Rolled onto all fours, staggered partway to his feet—sky, earth, horizon, reeling—lurched sidewise trying to hook into a footing, grab some deck, could not—cannot find your feet when your legs are gone missing—found himself sprawled, prick out, flagging, facedown in the grass being sick. Thought he heard her say, "I'm leaving."

"Wait," he managed weakly, even as he thought, "This is what happens when you forget your Flaubert, when you dare venture outside your den, when you turn your back on the throne of your chair." The lesson so hard in its learning.

The price of beauty is self-denial. Knew the truth of it better than he knew the nose on his face, but for a while she had had him forgetting.

"Witch," he thought then. "Lamia. She can only be a witch, or whatever word rhymes with the 'b' of her broom."

AFTERGLOOM

It seldom had given Franklyn Shivs pause to conceive of himself as a functioning drunk. So long as he continued minimally to do so, enough to earn a living, say, and content in that, so what? To realize, however, and, further, to acknowledge to himself—once he had sobered up, days afterward—that he also was—well, what was he exactly? Whatever he was, it jerked him up short, that this should be in him, inside of him, festering.

Not that it stopped him from drinking. Precisely the obverse. It was the way he went about trying to kill it off, make it relent, go away and leave him alone, by trying to drown it in seas of booze, inland lakes and Amazons.

So it was the ensuing Saturday, the day when ordinarily he would have been up to see her, the day he ought have been up there, first thing, hat in hand, bouquets of yellow roses and cases of caramels, humbly apologizing until he was cyanotic in the face, doing his best to make amends, mend fences, put things back right, say and do whatever she may have required of him, it was that Saturday that it arrived in the post.

Wanting a drink, desperately in need of one, he poured himself a large tumbler of tomato juice instead, a little ice, lots of pepper, lemon, lime, Tabasco, found a chair, lit a cigarette, fiddled awhile with a pair of dice. It was well after noon, but he was still in his urine-stained robe, clad in a week's worth of bristle. Pressing a cold compress to his forehead, he pinned the envelope to the tabletop with the tusk of an elbow, one-handedly knifing open the flap and fishing out its contents before letting the envelope flop to the floor.

Three pages, typewritten (not a good sign), sans salutation (ditto). He read:

Having composed the following, I debated all week about posting it off. That I do so now is for my sake, not yours. I need to say these things, and, also, apparently, share them.

I know who I am, as you do not, neither who I am, nor who you are. I know who you are. Perhaps I always have. Certainly I know better now. I shan't tell you who you are, for I no longer am interested in telling you, and you need discover your self for yourself. I wish you luck in doing so, as you will need it, but you shall need to do it without my help.

I bear you no ill will. I should, but I do not. I will miss our
friendship. I will remember it always, but what we see too clearly
loses its charm, what we understand too perfectly forfeits its
mystery, so its allure. This but one among the many lessons I
tried to teach to you, and failed.

There is more, little enough of it about you, save in the most
indirect way. Men, by which I mean all men, men in general, are my
issue. I am able to say now with the utmost certainty that they
always have been, as they doubtless shall remain. This is no one's
fault. Not yours, neither mine.

I do not like them, you see. I am perfectly capable of liking
the few I may choose to like, as I chose, however briefly, to like
you, but I do not like them as a lot. I do not like the way they
look at me. I do not like the look of them. I do not like the
differences between us, the way they are furry where I am smooth,
stiff where I am soft, the way they go out where I go in, are cold
when I am hot. The way they are so flat where I am not, and take
so much license, presume too much liberty, believe the world is
up to them first, last, exclusively.

Why ought I feel differently, even if I could, which I cannot?
Why ought I desire to pleasure such creatures, conceive of my bed
as theirs, my body as their bait, feel obliged to reduce myself on
their account to the sum of my body, its parts, my face, its
entrances, gates? Why ought I feel compelled to let to the like of
them the room at the inn of my womb? Why? Because I have some
stuff--all right, lots of stuff--that they might grab and poke
and harpoon?

I am not cut out for any of that, to be somebody's or anybody's
wife, fiancée, betrothed, girlfriend, passing fancy, or enchanting
lakeside summertime lay. Idol, token, icon, trophy, ideal, trinket--
no! And no again. I ca<u>nnot</u> be some man's mate. I never was, never
have been, never wish to or will be, because--<u>it is not me.</u> My
essence, nature, fate.

Men, when I think of them, which I seldom do--until there was
you, you who seemed better, true-blue, new--men mean to me what
they always have meant. Permit me to list a few: syphilis,
gonorrhea, chlamydia, cystitis, perineal warts, papillomavirus,
genital herpes, anal fissures, hepatitis B, trichomoniasis,

chancroid, pubic lice, scabies, Candida, oral thrush (I had
mistyped it thrust; applies as well), unwanted pregnancy (and so
the butchery of abortion), ectopic pregnancy, cervical cancer.
Death. Where not so much the worse.

There is something very awry with them, men, their erections,
explosions, so very like a bomb, or gun. Sperm bullets, is how
I think of them. So why would I wish to be shot, suffer such
wounding? I abhor it, as I abhor all violence. No, I will not be
shot, or shot at, or shot up, or shot at all, thank you very much.
A woman never would do such a thing to a man or another woman,
or, for that matter, a dog.

I am for dwelling in jouissance, a state of gentleness and
gentility, of tenderness, the mutual, mutually respectful bestowal
and exchange of sensual pleasure. It would be of little comfort to
you to know, to any man to know, how utterly unnecessary such a
state makes men. All men.

Puny, syllable-poor, underendowed subject, men, so manly, macho,
so tediously male. And useless, just as useless as a clock without
hands in that very climactic moment when time peters out with a
whimper--or premature bang, oops--forever. The cuckoo, as cuckold,
uncocked.

If one looks hard enough, searches long enough, anyone can
find what they seek. What it behooves one rather to remember is
that whatever one may find, however much it may satisfy one's
desire in the moment, it seldom approximates the truth, much less
passes for its meaning in time.

Our natures, so opposed. You in desperate need of self-
completion, myself so exquisitely complete and completed, replete
in and unto myself, alone. In this, both blameless. Call it a matter
of timing, if you wish. But think, what could you have offered me?
What taught? Sexual abandon? How to spelunk? I had and have no
desire to learn the latter, and the former is terrain we had so
often trod that its ground had become as plowed under as last
year's refrain.

I do not forgive you, because there is nothing to forgive. Forget
your perfect offering. There is a crack in everything, the most
perfect vase. It is how the light gets in.

Cruel to be kind, Shivs. Sometimes. Sometimes cruel to be kind.

From time to time he would see her at the Dells', laughing, breathless, beautiful as ever, always alone, and unavoidable. Their mutual friends knew nothing about what had transpired that day, suspected nothing beyond what was entailed in the phrase "falling out," and, as the people in their set were falling in and out all the time—one needed a playbook, a scorecard to keep track, so convoluted were the pairings and unpairings, couplings and uncouplings—the nature of their relationship, or absence thereof, merited no comment whatever. Only Floyd and Marjy were to become, in time, possessed of more than their suspicions.

It was painful for him, and not only because it so often was so damn awkward. She, on the other hand, appeared pained not at all, appeared nothing but her transcendentally radiant self at all times, in every situation, under every circumstance. But it continued painful for him—it was months before he could muster an expression that was not a grimace or scowl, each more hangdog than the next—and her apparent talent for flying so high above it all rendered his pain only the more painful still.

Well, he had desired her, hadn't he? Desired her desire. That was his great sin. Cardinal, mortal, whatever is more. Whether it was love or lust or something else entirely—well, what *was* love anyway? And she had desired him not, nor his desire for her. Of course, he understood the reason now, and so must only learn to accept it, live with it as best he might, arrive at some accommodation and accord. And yet, if the gesture of purest aggression is to withhold, hers had been an act, as he felt and experienced it, of the most savage and retributive denial, one made all the crueler by her greater native generosity of spirit and soul, a generosity which, when placed alongside his own, was vast as yeasty seas.

Desire absent obstacle is the death of desire, that much he knew, how one only knows what one really wants once one has arrived at that which prevents one's having of it. Contentment equals the death of possibility precisely because desire exists only in excess of the desired object's ability to satisfy it, and because that object is desirable only commensurate with its capacity, potentially, to disappoint. But what did it profit him now, to understand that people fall in love only at the very moment, those moments, when they are most terrorized by . . . hope?

She had made him feel so alive, damn her. She had fueled like a flame the guttering light of his life, only to douse it doubly dark once again.

The Chinese, he knew, had a proverb: *Wherever you look, there's something in the way.* And wasn't *that* the truth. The lot, naught but humiliation.

To fall heels over head for a daughter of Lesbos, one of Baudelaire's *femmes damnées*, a tribadist, no less. Perforce it left him talking to himself: "Lousy choice, Ace. How could you possibly be so stupid? Christ, what a dope!"

How exorcise an engram?

That August, the nation's preeminent opponent of nuance and ambiguity, as, no less, its foremost champion of all that is earnestly clear-cut, happily unsubtle, pure-black-and-purer-white, having earlier bolted the Republican Party in gleeful dudgeon, had marched through the Loop, teeth bared, at the head of a phalanx of suffragettes to the Progressive Bull Moose Party convention at Orchestra Hall. There, Hull House's Jane Addams had seconded the nomination of the notoriously thin-skinned Theodore Roosevelt for president, an event Franklyn begrudgingly had covered for *Proleterac*, the while plying himself with Turkish coffee in a half-failed effort to stay awake long enough to do so.

Now, in October, on the evening of the fourteenth, having been shot point-blank in the chest with a Colt Police Positive .38-caliber revolver, serial number 58714, by one John Schrank, a saloonkeeper, in front of Milwaukee's Hotel Gilpatrick, the profusely bleeding candidate had been conveyed by train to Chicago's Mercy Hospital where he met with the press in his room, an event Franklyn covered as well.

"Theodore Roosevelt being Theodore Roosevelt," Franklyn's story began, "the Bull Moose candidate for president perched on the edge of a Mercy Hospital bed paste-faced and bleeding at the breast from an assassin's .38-caliber slug lodged three inches deep in the fascia of his chest cavity behind the right nipple and, struggling for breath—and thirteen days shy of his 54th birthday—proclaimed himself 'prepared to carry on the fight so long as breath remains in my body.'"

What Franklyn admired about "the Colonel" (TR's address of preference) was his energy and raw physical courage, his life force and will. What he did not admire about him was much of the rest, none of it worth mentioning.

ALONE AGAIN

It was at one or another strategically drunken moment at one more interminable party or another when Franklyn Shivs found himself alone with

Floyd Dell, an increasingly rare and precious thing. Or, perhaps—always possible—they were staggering in mutual solitude along the lakefront. No matter, either serves equally well, save that it had to have been winter by then—bleak. Franklyn wore his coat flyaway-open, where the wind had wedged it. In the mood for taking some stock.

Floyd, of late, was in the midst of becoming increasingly political or, at least, seriously committed to contriving some sort of shotgun marriage between social consciousness and art, his "unholy alliance," as Franklyn called it. Indeed, Floyd's first book, a collection of essays—biographical sketches, actually—entitled *Women as World Builders*, was just then in galleys at a local publisher, Forbes and Co. Its subject, feminism, so-called even then, was treated by him—Franklyn knew these things owing to Floyd having asked him to proofread the work in manuscript, a trusting gesture—as an explicit form of radical politics as expressed through the psychologies of each of the ten women it profiled: Isadora Duncan, Jane Addams, Emma Goldman, et cetera.

It was an approach that furnished the book's author just leash enough to write at no little length about what he chose to call "the ethics of the new eroticism" and to enumerate all the ways in which those ethics were changing women and society, and women *in* society, for the better, "demanding everything, including a larger political life, a larger motherhood, and destroying institutions to that end as it becomes necessary."

For himself, while taking genuine pleasure in his friend's publishing success, Franklyn found the entire premise harebrained. Erotic ethics? The very phrase was an oxymoron. Not that he had the heart to tell Floyd that what he had written—written quite well, in fact—was wholly wrongheaded.

More latterly, Floyd had begun perfecting his Poe. Others conjectured Baudelaire or Rimbaud, but no, it was Poe. Not only had he raised the mustache and affected the spit curl, he had succumbed to supplementing his sartorial repertoire with orange ties, white pants, Byronic collars. Franklyn considered that he would not have been *too* surprised to see him sporting a raven upon his shoulder, as it is said do certain pirates, parrots.

"Question, Floyd."

"I like your questions, Frank. Fire away."

"Can great beauty and concupiscence on the one hand, like Mart's, say, and great intelligence and perspicacity on the other, rightly coexist? In a woman, I mean. Is that possible, do you think? Are they compatible? Or must one be more absent to permit the other to flourish and flower? Does brilliance in a woman inhibit eroticism? After all, if anyone might be said to be an expert on the subject—"

"Ah, back to Mart then, are we?"

"Never left." He sighed. "Hard to let go. Revelation, how hard." Paused. "Didn't even last that long, our . . . whatever it was, yet felt like all of a lifetime, the way it played out at such a pitch. Besides, and feel free to keep this to yourself, it really was a privilege, pleasure too, sweet pleasure, at moments anyway, to be part of something so . . . beautiful."

"Time, my friend. Time turns the trick, and tricks there are, aplenty, everywhere you turn."

"I know, I know," he said, then mustered somehow, from somewhere, a wink. "Believe me, I am working on it. Now, if I could just persuade my dreams to jump on board with the rest of me."

Post-Mart—which is how he thought of it—Franklyn's life became almost unbearably simple. No ambitions, not the need. Obligations, none. Loyalties the same, or roughly. Attachments, equally. Complaints as regrets, the same, precisely. Passions, the one only. Isolations and solitudes, abounding. Renunciation, self-abnegation, everywhere. Descent into neutrality, mental hopper empty, files of the heart, shred clean.

The *only* way to be free: *Indifference before all.*

The technical term for what he was becoming in her wake was "adiaphorist." Life passing him by? Oh sure, in a sense, but then, perhaps life was as overrated as its living so clearly was overvalued.

The drink helped, the pornography, the occasional whore or one-night. Had he been a gambler he would have gambled, a user he would have used. "Better a hundred anonymous fucks than one between lovers," he thought, because that is the way he was thinking then, as if nothing could have made more sense than to live in accord with the old folk maxim that "if you do not deflower one thousand virgins, you will receive one thousand lashes for lack of the proper initiative." Learning not to mind.

Learning to keep Goethe in mind: *Individuum est ineffabile.* Learning to ponder the moral ramifications of what he had done that day and discovering that he could not, for the life of him, think of a single one. Which, finally, was the wonderful thing about doing something inconceivably dreadful—you hardly ever remembered it later.

Besides, morality, what was that? What was it anyway? He wondered. A lie of childhood? Perhaps the biggest one of all? Little but lip service, a thing to be chatted up as sport and divertissement, a winked-at vice about which to talk a good game, cherries on one's sundae, sprinkles on one's cone, syrup over ice cream, bananas in one's float. Morality was the malt in the malted milk, that's all.

"The world plays as it always has played," he thought. "With fulhams, off the square, on the rig, nothing trig about it. No, nor fair. But what sort of man am I, to persist in loving someone incapable of returning my love?"

The answer did not please him.

Love. Is that what it had been? But how was he supposed to know? How does anyone? What was it, after all? Love. A psychosomatic condition? Cognitive one? Psychotic episode or break? The Dubious Volition? Altered state? Emotional attrition? The fucking flu? Sharing of a mutual illusion, the one mutually consented to? Was it a semantic nicety? A conventional code word for conduct unbecoming? A temptation of nature in one's youth that as one aged culminated in an impulse to puke? Divine Inexplicability? Execrable timing? Inner fire? Celestial light? Gift of grace? Existential choice? All that is deaf and dumb? Infinite space? Ever-presence of an ongoing moment? The Ultimate Dissolve? Or perhaps it was just a tic or tingle, a twitch or an itch. Love, the Nervous Habit, one among the hundreds of crazed and crazy feelings that lay siege to the seizure of a terrorized, susceptible soul. Some half-assed knowledge in the blood? Scrotal distraction? Perhaps it was terminal illness or, as she had insisted, a form of death. Or perhaps, as had he, still did, the vision of a vision conceived upon conception. Did we choose it, or it us? Did it matter? Probably not. All that mattered was that it existed, or did not.

And if the latter? Well, pretend then, how about that? That it meant something, anything, anything at all, something to do in the meantime, fall in love, with love, the idea and ideal, the notion that one has the gall to survive what amounts to its null. Surrendering that which you do not possess to another who does not exist save as a notional lie.

Love was impossible, yet impossible not to, precisely because no one wants to be loved, everyone wants to love. Being loved, the beloved, the noun, the object, is intolerable. The only value of love lies in loving, being the lover, the verb, the genesis and initiative, the actor. *God so* loved *the world* . . .

To be the object *of* not only is to be passive but menaced, threatened, placed in positive danger, at the beck and call of, to risk being exposed, stripped naked, humiliated. And how not hate that, and fear it? It is the actor, rather, the lover who holds the cards and pulls the strings, demands and insists, who is possessed of power, because even in the face of denial and rejection, it is the lover who can continue to crave, desire, possess, choose to endure, persist despite the pain. It scarce requires an alienist to understand that when the giver is the sole arbiter of the receiver's worth, then the latter has power over the former, absolute power, and because he does, she fears and hates him, fears the fetter with which he would fasten her freedom. Love's yoke.

Margaret Anderson did not loathe Franklyn Shivs owing to his having behaved like a monster and beast, but because he had deprived her, through the passion of his pursuit, of the one thing she valued above all else: the power of her own passion. He had overpowered it. It was that which she could not abide, as it was that for which she would—despite her disavowals to the contrary—never forgive him.

And this is why we say, some of us do, that LOVE KILLS.

"Our proper bliss," wrote Pope, "depends on what we blame."

So how get over her? But perhaps he did not want to. Perhaps no one ever does, or did, their first love, first true love, only great love, if that was what it had been. By which he meant what? "Great" love? Something about lasting, he supposed, enduring, abiding, staying even unto suffering all corruption of the flesh, the withered limbs, bloated belly, wimpled buttocks, wilted skin, wrinkled lips, sagging breasts, absent hair, so that what once merely had appeared beautiful, the figure of its surface, over time in fact *became* beautiful, the beauty of one's being, its very air.

Well, never again, he vowed to himself, would he permit beauty, however dazzling, to so cloud his vision that he could not see through to what mattered more: the carnality that crucibles each soul. Because he could do that. Knew how. Long practice. To harden up his heart. All it took was a little keratinizing of one's pericardium, cuticle, callus, nothing magical, little more. Bitter kernel. Turning flesh to bone.

PLAYING HER PART

A postscript of sorts.

Years later, roughly ten, long after she had begun publishing her *Little Review*—subtitled "A Magazine of the Arts, Making No Compromise with the Public Taste"—in room 917 of the Fine Arts Building downtown, its door stenciled with the single word *WHIM*, the same magazine in which both Swatty and Ernest Hemingway would enjoy their first taste of respectable publication, Franklyn dropped her a note.

At the time, he had nothing but—time; it was all over his hands. He had had to secure special permission for the pen and paper in advance, solicit for someone to write down his words—as he couldn't, then—but playing the angles, in the end, he had managed to manage them both.

He had—as everyone had, everyone *he* knew at any rate—been following the case in the papers; he had the rags read to him by the trustees. She was living in New York City by then, having left Chicago years before, and it was there, in her little magazine, commencing with the March 1918 issue and continuing into the winter of 1920, that she had been publishing installments of the novel seriatim, the first time it saw print anywhere in America (Ezra Pound, her foreign editor, had secured the rights), some thirteen or twenty-three excerpts in all, thus proving to the world what Franklyn had known all along, that she was, as she called herself, "a serious editrix of impeccable taste, if one unable to make or create," but both talented and nervy enough to wrench into print the unprintable words of the world's first Modernist masterpiece.

On October 14, government officials—specifically John Sumner's New York Society for the Suppression of Vice, known more popularly as "Sumner's Vigilanti," the same already having confiscated and incinerated the entire print run of three previous issues, viz., Lestrygonians (1/19), Scylla and Charybdis (5/19), Cyclops (1/20)—placed her under arrest, charging her with "purveying obscenity"—the Nausicaa section containing the Gerty McDowell episode—tried her on December 13, convicted, fined, and fingerprinted her.

She faced jail time, something that, under the circumstances, at *that* time, given *his* circumstances, Franklyn found so deliciously ironic, he could not bring himself to reference it in his letter. The postmark, if she noticed it, would give away the game in any event. As he dictated it, the note was a brief one, the entire contents of which read:

Dearest Mart,

Fuck 'em. Refuse the fine and do the time. There are worse ways to pass the days, believe me. Fling it back in their faces, do the time, and you shall win the day. As, too, shall the book. And such a book. The tongue the inventor wagging the tail of its dog, or the other way 'round? And what matter, for it is the masterpiece of our time, probably all time. You are just the one to make so dramatic and defiant a gesture. You, who so value your total freedom, should know that it is only when one has nothing left to lose that one is utterly unconstrained. I hope that you do not find this communiqué presumptuous. I do not care if you do.

Bless you, Mart, for publishing Ulysses. Because of you it lives and always shall. Remember, the writer's word can be no more obscene than is the painter's hue immoral. So dream, then, as Valéry admonishes us, dream as I do that time is no more for thee to hate me.

Between hard hammers, Mart, as ever, beats my heart.

Whether she received or if she received actually read the note, he never knew. Of course, she did not serve a day in jail. He had not expected that she would, not if she could find a way, any way around doing so. For all of her florid rhetoric about personal freedom and individual liberty, he knew that the only sort that genuinely concerned her was the license to run radiantly roughshod in the moment as the spirit might move her or as it suited her to indulge some divinely inspired whim, the while complaining that such license was not enough, would never be enough, because the world, as ever, conspired against her toward its proscription.

Well, she was Mart, the delightfully deliberate dilettante, she who insisted that as life was a lyric, it must be lived as a poem, and no poem, she would be glad to tell any soul disposed to listen, ever was lived vegetating in a cell, ripening behind bars, parading its rotting narcissism in a void, much less a cell too cramped comfortably to contain an ego the size of an oil derrick, one immersed in its own private destiny, enmeshed in itself alone, yet no more connected to the living of its life than a novelist to the draughting of his novel.

Where there is a corpse, there is a mystery, and Mart was incorporeal. Moerdrices always bring something to the scene of their crimes, as they always leave something behind, but she had left nothing, not even by mistake, nothing that he might so much as embalm, enshrine, or burn outright in effigy, nothing he might so much as stash in an urn. It was, he knew, what made her so special and, too, what made her so not.

Certain extraordinary creatures have a meaning. That such a meaning eludes us, that it is one that in the moment we cannot discern, makes this no less true. Who was she? Who had she been? Who become? A secret? Mystery? Great love?

"A spirit," he thought. "*Res nullius*. Or a future. If always the future of one."

What is the great truth about great beauty? He could, as he would, quote her own words: "Nothing satisfies but what confounds. Nothing but what astonishes is true."

Square the sun, box the moon, drape each Station of the Cross, what difference between them? This terror? That love? At what cost?

Hearts can be fragile, but also quite fierce. What matter if one's own is broken along the way? It mends, scars over, heals itself, hides its hurt, keeps feeling, endures. So long as it beats and the blood moves in its passage, it knows it is inevitably cursed.

Into and out of one another's lives we travel through and on through, little more one to the other than our most answered and unanswerable prayers, and what remains of the heart is only enough to shear itself sundered with the sight of its thoughts, enough vision to undo its own due. And so, thought Franklyn, might God bless her and keep her and grant her her peace, and might he absolve her of each of her sins, for he would not, nor could he. Wasn't his place. Hadn't the vision. He no longer could properly see—blind and imprisoned, hard cell.

The love unseizable you came to bring
Passes, in a shiver, breaks Narcissus, flees.

It was true, he thought, this much was true: the broken bones of the still beating heart.

HISTORICAL MARKERS

Looking back, Sherwood Anderson would recall the period as containing the moment when "a cult of the new sprang up . . . clutched out of the seething mass of new forms," just as William Carlos Williams similarly would observe that "there had been a break somewhere, we were streaming through . . . Nothing was good save the new. Infinite fracture and disunity," and Gertrude Stein would memorialize it as "a time when everything cracks, where everything is destroyed, everything isolates itself."

Thirteen years before, in 1900, the very year Franklyn Shivs had arrived in Chicago, an obscure forty-three-year-old Austrian physician, Sigmund Freud, had published his first book, *The Interpretation of Dreams*. The Prussian philosopher Friedrich Nietzsche, eleven years insane with neurosyphilis, died, age fifty-five, at Siberblick, Humboldtstrasse 36, Weimar. And Gertrude Stein, an Allegheny, Pennsylvania–born, twenty-six-year-old medical student at the Johns Hopkins University and erstwhile psychology student of William James at the Harvard Annex (later, Radcliffe), began her first lesbian affair before leaving on her inaugural visit to Paris; she was followed a year later by a Spanish teenager named Pablo Ruiz, an aspiring artist.

That same year, Theodor Herzl redoubled his recruitment efforts on behalf of a small movement that was coming to be called Zionism, and Paul Cézanne, having turned sixty-one and with little more than six years to live, still was a reclusive, diabetic, paranoid, misogynistic, anti-Semitic, politically reactionary, critically shunned painter working in a small studio attached to his family home at Les Lauves on a hill above Aix-en-Provence in the south of France.

That autumn, the German physicist Max Planck postulated the existence of the quantum, and on the last day of November, some several months before the posthumous publication of *The Will to Power*, Oscar Wilde—masquerading as Sebastian Melmoth, wallpaper critic—was found dead in his Paris hotel room.

Less than two years later, the president of the United States, Theodore Roosevelt, took the unprecedented step of employing the offices of the federal government to intervene in a labor stoppage, the five-month-old anthracite coal miners' strike in western Pennsylvania, justifying his action on the grounds that to have done otherwise would have been to encourage what he called "socialistic action."

During the last month of 1903, near Kitty Hawk, North Carolina, the Wright brothers performed the first successful, power-driven, heavier-than-air machine flight, and that spring Pablo Ruiz moved to Paris for good, even as Adolf Hitler was flunking out of the Linz high school where he had been a classmate of Ludwig Wittgenstein's. In New Orleans, meanwhile, the cornetist Charles "Buddy" Bolden was pioneering a peculiarly American form of music called jazz, allegedly a Mandingo word meaning "acting crazy-like," and a New York City insurance executive named Charles Ives was placing the final touches upon a musical composition he called *Ragtime Pieces (Dances)*. And in that year's presidential election, the nominee of the Socialist Democratic Party, Eugene V. Debs, polled almost half a million votes, a figure that the winner, Theodore Roosevelt, found "a cause for concern."

In September 1905, in Zurich, Switzerland, a twenty-six-year-old Albert Einstein submitted to the journal *Annalen der Physik* a little-noticed paper that contained the curious equation $E = mc^2$. Seven months later, San Francisco was rocked by the most devastating earthquake to occur in more than a century, and six months after that, shortly after the Austrian opthamologist Eduard Zirm performed the world's first successful corneal transplant, Paul Cézanne died on October 22, 1906, at the age of sixty-seven.

Between March and July 1907, Pablo Ruiz, now Picasso, began and mainly completed work on a squarish, eight-foot-high painting—243.9 × 233.7 cm; 96 × 92 ins.—called *Les Demoiselles d'Avignon*, a depiction of five, naked, anatomically impossible, voluptuized, Africanized whores, an iconic image so aggressively *outré* that he refused to show it publicly for almost a decade. At much the same time, having previously departed his native Dublin for the Continent, an unpublished author with failing eyes crafted a short story he called "The Dead," even as he embarked upon a longer piece he tentatively entitled *Stephen Hero*; it would require another seven years for James Joyce to hone "Hero" into *A Portrait of the Artist as a Young Man*.

That summer, on June 5, Buddy Bolden, not yet thirty, but having riffed his last, was committed to the East Louisiana State Hospital for the Insane, where he would live the next twenty-four years until his death. And on All Saints' Day in Paris, France, the tubercular, dwarfish, pistol-packing—it was a *boudledogue*, actually—Alfred Jarry, Yeats's so-called Savage God, drank, drugged, absinthe-ed, and ethered himself to death at the age of thirty-four, leaving behind his unpublished absurdist master-work, *Gestes et opinions du docteur Faustroll, pataphysicien*. That same year and on into the next, roughly two thousand anarchist bombs exploded in the streets of Barcelona.

A year later, in 1908, the self-named political exile Vladimir Ilyich Lenin moved intact to Paris the entire apparatus of the Russian Social Democratic Party; an Idaho-born former classroom teacher named Ezra Pound left what he termed the "half-savage" country of his birth for Europe; the IWW, better known as the Wobblies, declared its rejection of political action, calling instead for the overthrow of capitalism using the Sorelian syndicalist tactic of a general strike of all workers and the establishment of a classless socialist society governed by industrial unions; Arnold Schoenberg began writing "atonal" music, music that would lead him to develop the twelve-tone system he employed for the first time that year in part of his String Quartet No. 2; and the company owned by and named for Henry Ford manufactured in Dearborn, Michigan, the first Model T automobile.

In 1909, at a meeting of the American Chemical Society, Leo "Doc" Baekeland unveiled the patented material he had created two years earlier and which, in deference to its chemical name—polyoxybenzylmethyleng-lycolanhydride—he called Bakelite, the world's first all-synthetic plastic, an occasion that dovetailed almost too neatly with the publication in Paris of the First Futurist Manifesto in the February 20 edition of *Le Figaro*, authored by the movement's founder and financier, Filippo Tommaso Marinetti, the self-described "caffeine of Europe." Later that year, a twenty-six-year-old Rutherford, New Jersey, GP, Dr. William Carlos Williams, a college chum of Ezra Pound's at Penn, self-published the straightforwardly titled *Poems*, his first book of poetry, and Gertrude Stein self-published her first mature book-length work, *Three Lives*, the first English edition of which would not become available for another twenty-four years.

In 1910, in Milwaukee, Wisconsin—the same year T. S. Eliot began composing "Prufrock," Rainer Maria Rilke published what would prove to be his only novel, *The Notebooks of Malte Laurids Brigge*, Igor Stravinsky produced the first of his major ballets, *The Firebird*, and both William James and Mark Twain relinquished their respective great ghosts—Emil Seidel was elected the first socialist mayor of a major American city. And on a chicken farm in suburban Westport, Connecticut, a soft-spoken, hermetic, freelance commercial illustrator and Cornell University grad named Arthur Dove, nicknamed "the Whispering Kid"—beating Wassily Kandinsky to the punch by mere months—was painting a series of pictures, the *Six Abstractions*, the first purely nonrepresentational art, which he called "extractionism," created in the West.

The following year, in England, the physicist Edward Rutherford discovered the atomic nucleus, and Kandinsky, in Germany, published *Concerning the Spiritual in Art*, his seminal attack on naturalism, materialism, objectivism, and picturism, and his defense of and advocacy for abstraction in painting. Before the year was out, Gertrude Stein completed work on the thousand-page masterpiece she was to dedicate to Sherwood Anderson, *The Making of Americans*, a text begun nine years earlier and destined to go unpublished for another fourteen.

The year after that, shortly after the sinking of the *Titanic*, a Memphis, Tennessee, bandleader, William Christopher Handy, composed "Memphis Blues," the first blues piece ever published, and Paul Valéry, Stéphane Mallarmé's most brilliant disciple and protégé, began work on the extended poem that was to clinch his reputation as the aerialist of the chaste celestial and azure upper air, *Le Jeune Parque*. That same year, in the course of a single sleepless September night, a tubercular, Prague-born, German-speaking Jew named Franz Kafka wrote his first mature story, a hallucinatory, relentlessly interior text he called "The Judgment"; Gertrude Stein published her first words in America, a pair of "word portraits" about Picasso and Matisse; and thirty-nine-year-old Dorothy Richardson repaired to her cottage in Cornwall to begin writing *Pointed Roofs*, the first volume of her thirteen-volume autobiographical novel, *Pilgrimage*, a forty-year endeavor during which she would invent a new literary technique called, as first coined by May Sinclair by way of William James, "stream of consciousness."

In January 1913, a few short months before he met Lev Davidovich Bronstein for the first time, in Vienna, Iosif Vissarionovich "Koba" Dzhugashvili, a Bolshevik organizer and Lenin loyalist, changed his name to Stalin, as Bronstein earlier had changed his to Leon Trotsky. Four months later, Adolf Hitler, then twenty-four, after failing the admissions exam to its Academy of Arts, left that same city, where he had been living in a men's homeless shelter, and went to Munich, Germany, where he found employment painting postcards.

And on March 24 of that year, a Monday, precisely twenty days after the creation of the U.S. Department of Labor—the stated purpose of which was "to foster, promote, and develop the welfare of the wage earners of the United States, to improve their working conditions, and to advance their opportunities for profitable employment"—and five months after the publication in the city of the inaugural issue of Harriet Monroe's *Poetry* magazine—the Armory Show exhibition of modern art, or, rather, the more generous half of it, some 634 pieces—opened in Chicago, having arrived from New York City for its mounting the week before.

Franklyn's Armory Show piece, headlined "The Moment of Cubism," filled the entire news hole of that week's edition of *Proleterac* save for the news briefs, obits, birth and wedding announcements, and crime blotter; the paper didn't run cartoons or sob-sister columns. It was the heftiest, as it was certainly the longest story he ever had written as a journalist, and the fact that Ivan had consented to run it in toto was a gesture of magnanimity, not only in terms of play, but because insofar as Van Molek concerned himself with pursuits such as painting, it was to appreciate the way legibility and literal representation might best serve to portray poverty, class struggle, the socialist Utopia, or to create uplifting pictures of dumb and radiant nature, not underlying essences or sublime and significant form, much less little cubes juxtaposed just so on a canvas. Ivan Molek was with Frank Shivs nothing but the soul of human decency, ever, but his notion of terrific art extended scant farther than the Ashcan Eight.

In any event, the piece had run (and run and run, to Franklyn's way of thinking, ad nauseam), and so, when it was warmly received by professional colleagues and readers alike, and even, later, acknowledged to have played rather a critical role in rendering the Armory Show such an extravagant success, no one was more surprised than thirty-three-year-old Franklyn Shivs.

Cubism wonders aloud, upon the canvas, what might be the form that furnishes the most felicitous fit for what it endeavors so fully to formulate—namely, the spirit of a future, the very one whose arrival is now. It is not, then, about technical virtuosity or facile fabrication in the service of achieving lifelike representation or resemblance or painterly verisimilitude, but, rather, a search to recognize and depict, in and as image, the ambient essence of a moment.

It is not just that these pictures look strange or shocking—were that the case, they might be dismissed as mere novelty—but that if what they convey is true, then seeing no longer is believing, perception's relationship to reality is problematic at best, there not only is more to life than meets the eye, but that which does is not the half of it, hindsight is anything but 20/20, a picture is worth far less—and more—than a thousand words, that which causes need not effect, time may be of the essence but that essence is distinctly entropic, and all is flux, fluxion, drift, fiction. Shift holds sway, whirl is king, chaos rules, unity is rumor, harmony a unicorn, salvation a myth, God a fraud, and we all are missing not only the boat, but the one and only time of our lives.

The bad news the Cubists betide is that the human condition is broken, fragmented, in disrepair. The good, that we can, should we choose, gather up its pieces and patch ourselves together again in new, more honest and enriching ways. The Cubists are not out, as their countless critics are so fond of vociferously repeating, to destroy art. They propose, rather, to *italicize* and **boldface** it, to fly it like a banner. Yes, Cubism produces anxiety in the viewer—the stirring of that anxiety is altogether deliberate—but in so doing it invites wonder, affords the viewer the seldseen opportunity to experience the delight of reckoning a private path toward the moment, not the one of "I see *it*" but, quite simply, freshly, seeing.

Such, at least, the merest sampling.

UP NORTH

The call came from Ivan in what typically is called the middle of the night or, less frequently, the hour of the heather of bones. Jerked awake, he picked up only reluctantly. He despised the telephone.

"Pack your bag, Frenk."

"Ivan?"

"Wake, Frenk. Pack."

"I'm going someplace?"

"Oh, yes."

"Where, Ivan? Why? Where to?"

"Come in the office. Then the train."

"Where, Ivan? What train? The train where?"

"North, Frenk. The news."

"What news, Ivan? What's the story?"

"One I never expect to see in my lifetime. Come in, Frenk, we talk there. Important, this story. Not poems. Not pictures. *Real.*"

What Franklyn was thinking and feeling, he could not have said. Coffee. Perhaps he was thinking coffee.

It was brewed when he arrived, hot and black, aroma of morning, black steam at his eyes every day of his life. Ivan didn't touch the stuff himself, literally could not stomach it. Things like this, you see, kindly gestures, good man. Ivan shoveled Franklyn a mugful as he slid into his chair.

"Here, take, drink."

Franklyn took it, two hands, cupped, peace offering, sweltering high summer day, five a.m., stifling already. Scalding coffee in mid-July; nothing better. Sweating through his shirt in canoes, he blew at the cup, sipped, while Ivan straddled the corner of a desk.

"So?" Franklyn asked. "What's up, Wee Van? Sounded all *enthused* on the phone. Something got you enthused, Ivan? Why the mystery?"

"See you packed," said Ivan, nodding to the valise on the floor at his feet.

"To the gunnels," he said. "You weren't real specific."

"Copper country," he said. "Going out, all up and down the range, whole Keweenaw."

Franklyn knew Ivan had relatives up there, friends from his Calumet/Red Jacket days. "When?"

Ivan shrugged. "Tomorrow, next day, next week—soon. They're wanting to shut it all down. Tight. Every mine."

"Who's behind it? Know?"

He smiled. "WFM. Wobblies."

"Haywood?"

Nodded. "Gives us—what they call it?—insider's track."

"With Haywood?" Franklyn shook his head. "Haven't seen or talked to Bill"—counted mental fingers—"must be seven years. Doubt he remembers me at all."

"No. Remembers. Reads, too."

Franklyn frankly was surprised. "How'd you come by that?"

Hoisting a zippered, leather portfolio from the desktop, Ivan tossed it bulging into his lap. "All in there, names, addresses, cash, so on. You stay at the Arlington, by the train station." Bar-stooling from the desk, he walked over to a wooden filing cabinet, jerked it open, returned with a book. "For the ride up."

Franklyn scanned its cover. "Already read it."

"When?"

Shrugged. "Years and years."

"Read. Again."

"Agitprop written by a propagandist masquerading as a novelist," he replied. Ivan understood English better than he spoke it.

"No," he said, "truth written by a novelist, one knowing fiction from fact."

"Some distinction there I'm missing?" asked Franklyn, going for his goat.

"I tell you, Frenk, sometimes I—"

Raised both hands, stickup. "Some things are better left unsaid, eh, boss? Most things, maybe." Unzipped the satchel, slipped *Germinal* inside. "I'll get the story, if there's one to be got. You know I'll do that, get it all, then some."

"And first," said Ivan. "First and fast. Nothing magic to a story."

Franklyn ought not, he reckoned, have chortled as he did, then burst into fits of marginally maniacal laughter, but at the time it seemed the only pardonable response. "Good one, boss," he managed, wiping his eyes with the heels of his hands. "Nothing magic, very good."

"Crazy, Frenk," he said. "Crazy as crazy pup, you are. Go on now. Ticket's in there." Gestured to the pouch. "Call down when you get there."

Franklyn clutched the satchel, fetcheled to his feet, saluted his best mock'd-salute, grabbed his valise—it contained his new copy of Bernard Hart's *The Psychology of Insanity*—and headed for the door.

"And, Frenk?" Slewed back around. Ivan was tentative, chewing something over, nothing small. "The drink."

It was the first he ever had mentioned it, and while ordinarily Franklyn would have shrugged it off with a jape or taken exception, he felt compelled, for Ivan's sake, to pretend to a measure of . . . sobriety. "I shan't say, 'Not a drop.' Can't. Wouldn't be true, you wouldn't believe it. So, no promises, okay? Save the one. I'll file my stories, file on time, they'll be the best I can manage in the moment, best *we* can do. Don't ask for more, boss. Please."

Molek nodded, an understanding. "You could be a good man, Frenk, I know. So much talent, good heart. But up here"—he tapped at his temple—"trouble."

Franklyn smiled. "Ain't *that* the truth? Nothing but."

"Be well, Frenk. *Do* well."

Franklyn had heard him, but was he listening? Sometimes the future has eyes in the back of its head, and the present marches lockstep in place.

The train sped, stinging on its spur, rails astrum with steely song. Closed his eyes to the throck of its throstle, watching the images play against his innermost eyelids.

"Thornveld," he thought, drifting. "North to its impenetrable white. Star point. Some flicker of available light."

And drifting deeper. "Upland. Upland and inland. Landscape of inscape. Something lies somewhere. Must. A through path where *no white-ness (lost) is so whole as the meaning of whiteness.*"

Up North. The U.P. Quest and a journey. The ache of some incipient loss.

> To seduce
> A fact into becoming an object, a pleasing one, with some
> Kind of esthetic quality, which would also add to the store
> Of knowledge and even extend through several strata
> Of history . . .
> Connecting these in such a dynamic way that one would be forced
> To acknowledge a new kind of superiority . . .
>   . . . but in any case the thing's got to
> Come into being, something has to happen, or all
> We'll have left is disagreements

JOHN ASHBERY, *"One Coat of Paint"*

BOOK TWO

PROGRESS

◆ ◆ ◆

*This miry slough is such a place as cannot be mended:
it is the descent whither the scum and filth that
attends conviction for sin doth continuously run;
and therefore it is called the Slough of Despond. For
still, as the sinner is awakened about his lost
condition, there arises in his soul many fears and
doubts, and discouraging apprehensions, which all
of them get together, and settle in this place: and this
is the reason of the badness of this ground.*

JOHN BUNYAN, *The Pilgrim's Progress*

KEWEENAW

*   *   *

T he last time she had been this sky-high was when she had been a
little girl and *Oee*, her da, had swung her to the sun and back on
the vulcanized tire suspended from the low-boy bough of the
butternut in their backyard while she squealed in delight and shrieked,
"Higher!"

Now she was ascending, buoyed in the belly of a cloud car, up through
sixteen hundred tethered feet of midair.

But then, altitude always had been her issue. Endowed with it from
the outset, even as a child, especially as a child, it had been, as she considered it, much the defining fact of her life. The torturous wait to grow into
herself, to persuade her body—the one that had seemed in its girlish un-
gainliness so often to be literally possessed of a contrary mind of its own—
to behave. The self-conscious effort to bat aside the impulse to stoop,
slump, sag, backhunch, bow, shrink, neckbend, and duck while gradually
developing the womanly grace to complement her stature.

Not that she was circus-freak tall, but she was tall enough that she
could not recall a time when the remarks, rude stares, wisecracks, and
nicknames—*korenjak*, they called her, giantess—as well as the occasional
catfight, had not been a self-conscious fact of her life. When you are a
thirteen-year-old girl and you already stand half an inch over fully six feet
in your stockings, then you are virago-tall, Amazon-tall, you tower and
traject in a way that fitting in, hiding out, stealing away, or being left alone
is impossible. Inconspicuousness had never been on her dance card.

Not that stature didn't have its advantages, ones that could be manipulated to your benefit. You were compelled, for instance—unless you
chose deliberately to withdraw and retreat, hover averse and gun-shy on
the peripheries—to cultivate your talent for intimidation and accommodation the same, as how equally to put people off or place them at their
ease, depending. You learned, of necessity, how to read human nature in a
hurry, as you did how to callus your skin. Because most people were going
to be more than benignly curious, they were going viscerally to react, to
use your seventy-four inches as pretext either purposefully to ignore, inap-
propriately approach, or—the more extreme cases—confront and affront.
They were going to attribute, in other words—project onto you a panoply
of assumptions and expectations, each more unfounded than the next.
Prejudgment.

All of which inevitably saddled you with a certain . . . *slant* on the
world, a different, more altitudinous angle, one that, while hardly unique,
was far from ordinary. So that while Ana Clemenc—pronounced "Klem-
anch," accent on the second syllable—née Klobuchar, never would have
apologized for her . . . prodigiousness, she had decided early on deliberately to propagate an electric presence so blazingly outsize, a personality
so positively surcharged, an ego so impregnably impervious that it would
throw her literal shadow deep in the figurative shade. It would not, she
vowed, be her "high-ness" that people would remember, but her Ana-ness.
Ana, *mochan kot hrast Amerkanka*, the one strong as an American oak.
And, indeed, so successfully had she managed it, that now, in the prime of
her twenty-fifth year, she was perceived by others not only as imposingly
tall—no getting around *that* fact—but altogether irrepressible, impossibly
impetuous, and famously disposed to outbursts of the most blunt-spoken
truculence. High, but high-strung.

Down there, one thousand feet below, it was gala time, midsummer's
fest, this annual affair. Just as it was, unbeknownst to all but a privileged
handful—Ana decidedly *not* among them—the last weekend before the
great strike. Electric Park and its illuminated **E*L*E*C*T*R*I*C P*A*R*K**
sign, as well as the 880 swaying Japanese lanterns strung everywhere around
its dozen acres, fell slowly away as they climbed. It was, she thought, like
going for a vertical ride in a lightbulb, perhaps the bladder of a bubble as
it was blown to a ball, or a diving bell, say, ass up—pontoon. This enormous laundry basket of wickerwork harnessed and slung to its overhead
balloon. She was boating on air in a charioteer's chair, is how it felt to her,

the while dragging the horizon with her as the pilot bailed ballast bags of sand, a process, according to the pilot, called relection.

They floated straight up, tethered by guy lines to the ground, a captive flight, so-called. No sense of jolt or soar, scarce one of sway and ascent. You didn't take off in a balloon, she discovered, but levitated in place as the world reeled silently away underfoot. High currents prowled the flesh of her face, surfed the strands of her hair, sifting in ruckles and riffs. Leaning out over the side of the nacelle, she breathed them in mint-cool, then half-braced/half-cocked the knuckles of her lower spine against and over the rattan-and-wicker rail of the sky galleon's gondola as she glanced upward smack into its interior hooped halo, the balloon's nonhydrogenated, flap-valved, rip-paneled, multigored envelope, its heated bulge comprising some seven thousand yards of lacquered and shellacked Japanese Suchan pongee yellow-silk gold-beater's skin.

The balloon rose slowly as a beach ball globing toward a prolapsed sky. Reminded her of an image she once had seen in a book—odd that she should remember it now—Redon's so-called eye-balloon (*The Eye Like a Strange Balloon Mounts Toward Infinity*, 1878, charcoal and chalk, 42.2 × 33.3 cm), the one the artist had drawn in tribute to Poe.

"Into the Mystic," she said.

"What is that?" asked her husband.

"Oh, I was just thinking how sad it is." She watched the pilot fiddle with this valve, fuss with that dial, worry the lines and levers like joysticks, their lives reposed in the intricate calculation of his hands. He was no barnstorming Lincoln Beachey, but little Dumont knew his stuff—aerostat master of airborne dexterity. He had posted his motto upon a plaque above the controls:

FEAR IS FOR THOSE WHO BELIEVE THEY HAVE A CHANCE.

She drew her husband near.

"Sad?" he said. "I thought you would be thrilled."

"Oh, Josef, I am. It is wonderful, really. The best birthday gift in the world." She smiled and placed her hand upon his shoulder.

"Then why so tristful, wife?"

She sighed. "This good and decent man," she thought. "Simple, straightforward, earth's salt." Sighed again, said, "It is just that . . ." Shook her head.

"What? What is it, wife?"

"How the time for the mystics is past, the seers, savants. Time now for the voyeurs, instead of *voyants*." She huddled closer, nestling some, press of tall breasts to his sternum. "An end to it all. From up here you can see it, clear as windows. No more voyagers, no more frontier. We no longer are so small. Why, we have breached the very heavens—in the eye of a ball!"

They were just south of Osceola here, the "location" where not twenty years before, when she was five, she had lost her grandfather to the great mine fire, twenty-seventh level. The flames had incinerated thirty that day; her father had been lucky to escape with bad burns.

Uncoupling from her husband, she let her eyes rove, watching the world's rim run away, bent as a boomerang beneath the horn of its moon, Orion and the Hunter so low they seemed even to eavesdrop. From up here the lake looked unwild, she thought, laid out flat as a fantail, sheet-metal blue. Isle Royale, its many holms, loomed fifty miles offshore, its cheroot of land—spooled out long as old Cuba—comprising, as she knew, four hundred square miles and half a million untrammeled acres that, as the season might determine, was transformed into either a lump of black mud or a floating blue jewel. And just beyond—there!—Thunder Bay.

The Keweenaw jutted on out to the tip of its shoot, peninsular claw of headland, a cape curved as a hook from its hand. South to north the villages were as gems on a bracelet: Eagle River, Eagle Harbor, Copper Harbor, old Fort Wilkins at its northernmost lip, an end-of-land place strewn starry across a vault of dark ground. And just eight miles off, just there— that was home. The steeples, spires, campaniles, and carillons—thirty-three churches all told—the chimneys and smokestacks of Red Jacket and surrounding Calumet Township. She could just lift it clear: smoke climbed from their cloacae, clematis.

The Jacket's lights were just blinking on along Fifth Street and Sixth, the stores, hotels and hostelries, grand opera house, one hundred taverns and bars, their signs and marquees nervy with neon. The tall, multitiered, cantilevered shaft-houses of the mines—she lost count; too many—looked squat and squashed down. And out the other way, to the south, Houghton and Hancock, the twin sister towns connected by the Portage, the cummerbund of water that, along with the trains—Copper Range, Mineral Range, Keweenaw Central, DSS&A, Northwestern, CM&SP—was their lifeline, solitary connection to the world wide beneath and beyond.

"So this is what they mean," she thought. "This feeling of almighty grandeur atop the top of the world, sixteen hundred feet." And that but a fraction of the distance the men traveled in the opposite direction, that her own Josef traveled six days a week in the tar-paper dark.

Leaning over, she looked straight down into incandescence: the carousel, maypole, Flying Dutchmen, Dying Wings, more than one hundred rope, basket, rocker, and boat-lover swings, the twelve thousand square feet of dancing pavilion, roller- and ice-skating rinks, bandshell, velodrome, merry-go-round, the steam-driven Ferris wheel on the crescented boardwalk, the ongoing hammer-and-drill contests, Cornish-style wrestling matches, greased-pig chases, horseshoe pitching and discus throwing, an Oz-scape of lights and calliope sounds among the thousands at their evening picnics: pasties, saffron buns, currant cookies, cardamom cakes, rhubarb and thimble-berry jams.

"Being up here," she said, "so high, you feel that there might actually be some."

"What is that, wife?"

"Spirits. Gods, maybe. That this height of air might be their lair. A lot of nonsense, I suppose. Still, it is a feeling." She hesitated. "You, too?"

He shrugged. "There is but one God, and his home is heaven, not here." He paused. "Listen, Ann, I have been meaning to . . ."

She placed two fingers to his lips. "Hush. Listen."

"What now?"

"Hear it?"

"Hear what?"

"The music."

"All I hear is—"

"Music of the spheres. Seven spheres."

"What spheres?" he thought, shaking his head. "What music? My wife will not bear me children, will not go to church, yet she hears what is not there."

Sighing, he reached for the uncorked bottle of cheap champagne that was included in the price of the flight as his wife, forfeit to the lift of their sky loft even as it pillowed against the grain of its gravity, sensed their rising higher, octaves up the index of night, attics of air. The sun, sunken, sinking in a half-darkened sky; the earth, abstract, less painting than grid, blocs of design, flattened with distance, untextured by color, its elements of space running irregularly toward the next and the next. The horizon bowed, subtly.

Had she a peach, she thought, she would have ventured a bite before flinging it whole into the apricot light rouged rust by the risen air of the mines. "No escape," she thought, "not even here." Copper sought out, ground in, layered deep through the dermis, reddened the very skin of the sky.

Josef peeled open the bottle, working its cork with his thumbs until it *puck*ed free of its glass mouth to an outfizz of foaming pink spillage overflown from its neck fraught with double the bubbles owing to the altitude. Dumont lit his lantern—nightlight.

"Here is to the world at your feet, wife," said Josef, nodding the bottle at Ana before snitching a swig and handing it over. Wringing it by its neck, she drank, again, then again, handed it back. Bubbles up her nose like the spread of a starfish.

When the first volleys whizzed by, mortar rounds—*phitt, phatt, phutt*—she squealed trills and clapped her hands, stifling the impulse to jump up and down. An apex of skyrockets and Bengal lights overspread overhead, vast umbrellas opening in smaller parasols and canopies of smoke, corymbose spectacles of tumbled, trellised silver, churned golds, spattered blues, pitched reds, patriot cream in a black-and-white world. They kept coming in launched waves, a technicolorate cyclorama of sunburst, moon blossom, flower bloom as she watched agog at the explosions of shower-down sparkle, pinnacle, and plunge—squiggle, squib, wriggle, daub, spun rowel, blotch, girandole, pinwheel, blob—in whirlygigs, teetotums, and banderoles. Pageantry of sky-high processional.

Her husband's eyes were wide with the reflection—spume of yellow spray, flume silts of flame-out, teardrops of flare—caught circumnutate in their orbit, star-spangled glare.

More whistled by. Catapults of color, trebuchets of light, ovations of blurt, high bursts of bumbershoot. Clapped again, schoolgirl, while her mind did a dance: Virginia reel, Irish jig, buck-and-wing, Highland Fling. And then the lampblack fell open, time-lapse of willow tree—*zraaaad*—and she:

"Oh Josef! My god! I feel . . . kissed by neon, frocked—in bliss."

She began, as from a balcony, to sing the words to an old song: "Oh, to travel in the clouds." Found she had forgotten the rest, then tendered him a kindly half-kiss. "Can we stay here forever and ever? Oh please, Josef, can we?"

"Happy twenty-fifth, wife. Happy you are happy."

"Time to go down," said Dumont in his Brazilian-Portuguese accent. "We go back."

The yellow-kid-gloved "Little Icarus," as he advertised himself, wore a straw boater above a pair of snug-fitting goggles, a full four-point chin-chafing collar and slick four-in-hand tie, plaid knickerbockers, and upon his spatted feet argyle stockings. A pair of pink boutonnieres blossomed from his lapels, and a gold bracelet graced his left wrist, from which dangled a St. Benedict's medal and, farther up his arm, near the elbow, a tiny strapped-and-buckled-on clock that he called a "wristwatch," a device designed for him, so he never failed to boast, by his "close friend" back in Paris, Louis Cartier, to enable him more conveniently to keep time while aloft.

"Oh, no!" said Ana. "I want to fly all night—for the music."

"We valve down," said Dumont to Josef, reaching for the release line.

"Oh, why does everything beautiful always have to end?" she said.

"Beauty is what you pay for," said Josef. "Costs more up here than down there."

"The sky is a face," she said suddenly, apropos of nothing. "The stars are its eyes. Fireworks the smiles and laughter."

Josef, having heard her, pretended to have not, even as the kettledrum finale, petard upon petard, chewed concussive hole after hole in the night sky. Flashbulbs of sound.

"Why," he thought, "must she always insist on being so . . . she."

His Ana.

BOOTS ON THE GROUND

Franklyn Shivs lost count of the number of switchovers the train had made somewhere south of Green Bay, Wisconsin. Not that it mattered, so long as he arrived on the Mineral Range line out of Hancock, which—rumpled, unshaven, rail-weary, and so caffeinated with coffee that his eyes beat like bongos—is precisely what he did, debarking at the Calumet Station, Red Jacket Depot, late on Sunday, last train of the weekend. Moment of ubiation.

If his fellow travelers followed suit as he stepped from the train, he failed to notice, but then he considered them less passengers with whom he just had shared a trying and protracted journey, than wearied and wearisome specimens of humanity with whom he shared nothing but the common air they had had no recourse but communally to breathe. This the same air he had during the trip done his level best to render disagreeably smeared and smokishly befouled, as he likewise had to bartizan his berth with the extracted contents of Ivan's portfolio strewn haphazardly amid ashes, butts, and sloshed coffee on the seat beside him. He had spoken to nary a soul throughout, exchanged glances with, smiled at, nodded toward, said hello to, bestirred himself to offer a helping hand to fewer still—save the porters, whom he generously had tipped while instructing them to "keep the black coffee flowing and be kind with the alkalithia nor go light on the linctus."

There remained certain elements of his job that he could not abide, those to which, despite a dozen years doing it, he had properly to reconcile himself. And none was more distasteful or dispiriting than the way that, in order to "get" and "break" a "story," one too often was compelled to venture into the world outside of one's den and have commerce, actual personal contact, with so many of its inhabitants—any of them, or one.

And the only solace—and it was not even that, really, but compensation—besides one's paltry paycheck, or the negligible, wholly transient rush one received from seeing one's words in print, or being afforded the opportunity to know someone like Floyd Dell, or the occasioning of the seldseen occasion when a source like Bill Haywood, say, became something slightly more, was the simple fact that the job demanded that one's mind remain open, active, alert, and alive. As for the rest of it, having traffic with the rich, famous, and powerful, or an appreciative relationship with one's readership, or a hand, however minor, in ensuring that the citizenry was kept well informed and its press unfettered and free, or a voice that might be listened to when weighing in on issues construed to be of public concern, or of fooling oneself into believing that anything one wrote materially mattered much less resembled anything like the truth, he was having none of it.

Not that he was wallowing in jaded cynicism or jaundiced self-pity, but to find himself, in his so-called prime, a respected part of a so-called fraternity that its more respectable members sanctimoniously insisted played a "vital role as democracy's last line of defense," or were the tellers

of truths that would set men free, or the voices of the voiceless or com-
forter of the afflicted, or some other such laughable rodomontade was, as
he considered it, the ultimate in bitter irony. It made him want to drink
and keep drinking, where it did not induce in him the impulse to do bodily self-harm.

As someone who over time conscientiously had studied the lay of its
peculiar topography and so might perforce speak with some authority
upon the subject, one did not, unless one was a half-wit, go to a newspaper for reality or truth. One went to it, if one chose to go to it at all,
for "the news." And too often, the one had nothing whatever to do with
the other.

What, after all, had his coverage of the Armory Show to do with the
truth of the art on display? What had his coverage—or absence thereof—
of the phenomenon that was the IWW to do with the reality of the hopes,
desires, passions, and dreams that had fueled it? What had his reporting
on the Iroquois fire to do with the real horror experienced by those who
had died or the damage done to those who had managed to survive or the
wreckage strewn like blasted craters across the stricken lives of those who
had lost their most precious loved ones? The entire enterprise was the cru-
elest of cruel hoaxes, one made all the crueler by the self-aggrandizement
so ritually engaged in by those who were its most ardent partisans and
practitioners.

Was he ranting? He didn't *feel* like he was, but then, how know? The
train ride had succeeded in setting on howling edge each of his more sensitive, coffee and tobacco–stained teeth, and the sooner he could find a
place to floss them, the better.

The two-story, twin-chimneyed clapboard station house, he noticed—or, rather, his nose did; odor of turpentine—recently had been
painted some midnight-frolic shade of green—fir green, evergreen, forest
green, fever green, forever green—or so it appeared in the dark. An Illinois
or Wisconsin barn green perhaps? Barn-wood green? "Does it matter?" he
thought. "Yeah, probably does, as much as the next thing.

"It smells different here," he thought. "Better, somehow. Cleaner.
More . . . northerly. Pitch-piney or something. Resiny. Earthier. Sandier.
And quieter. Can something smell quieter? More still anyway, Sunday
still."

Late July in the U.P. Warm. Not sweltering, but sticky. And buggy.
Which made it feel warmer somehow. Why was that? And why was he

fixating on "nature" stuff? Colors, smells, sounds, fir trees, temperature, humidity, bugs. Hmm.

There was a station light, and it was flocked with moths, making the white light in its out-throw appear to flicker with the falderol flap of their thousand wings. He watched, transfixed. It was, he thought, as if light were music and to more clearly hear it they must move in, head toward, chance the closeness, account for the vibrational center of its source, helix in and twirl, endeavoring to englobe the light-globe for the pure, beguiled joy-ousness of encircling. Or perhaps they construed the light for the naviga-tional fix of the moon, a moon that millions of years of evolution had tutored them could never be reached, so that now, having reached it, they became confused. The luna moth, he recalled reading once, secretes a chemical signal that can be scented by an inamorata up to a mile away; he might have sworn he smelled it now.

"Or perhaps they're not drawn to the light at all," he thought. "Per-haps they're attracted to the illusion of darkness beyond it. Perhaps they're only trying in their dumb, mothy, entirely praiseworthy way"—an effort with which he certainly could empathize—"to return to the enchantment of the dark, the rapture of its trench, the bunker of the Mach band, the re-gion surrounding a bright light that appears darker than its neighbors." So, "Go moths," he thought. "Go with godspeed. Solve the mystery. Fetch down the very music of the moon."

Pricked out of his reverie by the hollow-needled plunge of a prong, the hypodermic sharp stylet stab at his neck, the one meant for his jugular or carotid, he swatted and squashed it, bloodily dispatching to its deserv-ing, slapdash death the first of the thousands of saliva-armed female mos-quitoes that he would with extreme prejudice slaphappily terminate in the weeks and months to come. Ivan conveniently had failed to mention that the state bird of Michigan's Upper Peninsula was the skeeter, and no won-der—they were big as beagles.

His nose nosed a whiff of something extremely wrong, and it was only then that he noticed the heaped shape darkly clumped upon the ground a ways up, fifty yards perhaps, off to one side along the apron of the road running back beside the station. As he walked toward it, the smell strengthened and intensified, grew so offensive that as he drew up, unable to brave another step, he sensed himself about to retch.

The horse lay upon its side so blackly alive with blo flies, so hived with them, that it was impossible rightly to reckon the color of its coat. The basket of its flyblown belly was visibly bloating, and he prayed that it would choose some other moment to explode in a maliferous splurge of sarcomatous entrail and ort. One of its eyes, the only one he could discern in that infernal darkness, appeared to have been plucketed clean away, taloned or beaked by crows or some other carrion fowl, perhaps a flock thereof, or some nocturnal, fangy vermin of one genus or another. The empty socket was the correct size and shape of the hollow of a pewter ice-cream scoop. He wondered what color the eye once had been; settled upon fulvous, or sard.

But noticed no blood, not a lick, until, backpedaling for the assault of the smell, he already had stepped in it. Startled, he was well into the banana-peel slip of an ignominious pratfall when, flinging his bags clear in the nick of, he torqued his body, wrenching it into a posture that might permit him as he fell to brace himself with spread hands, locked wrists, stiffened elbows and arms, absorbing the brunt of the impact at the cuffs of his shoulders before immediately pushing bloody-handed back to his feet. He could see now that the ground was puddled with horse blood, which in that moonlight, though he presumed it would have been true of any moonlight, looked oil-slick black; grease ice.

"What Conradian heart of darkness is this then?" he asked himself, and, receiving no response, for he had spoken the query aloud, retrieved his grips, crossed the street, and entered his hotel—the frankly seedy lobby of which contained no samovar, settee, potted palm, or propeller fan. This was the aforementioned Arlington, which stood around the corner from the carcass on the diagonal down a block from the train station.

Taking possession of his key from the pock-faced desk clerk who evil-eyed him pastily from beneath his green eyeshade, he immediately noticed that the surface of its well-worn brass—the once deeply etched "7" of which was all but invisible—showed the effects that the acidulous secretions of hand flesh often eat into metal when rubbed and dandled over time.

Toting his own bags up the stair—creak, croak, groan, give—he unlocked and swung open his door, lugged them inside, tossed them at the foot-end of the bed, heel-kicked the door shut behind him, eyeballed the facilities, and slipped off his shoes before launching himself from a standstill, butt-bouncing in place midbed, the mattress of which immediately struck him as little but a swaybacked, lumpetty raft of springs in dire need of lubrication.

As he lit a cigarette, his eye was drawn to the carpet, a hand-tufted Axminster (were he not mistaken) with cream ground and trellis border, which, while visibly frayed, was, were one to go with the flow of its figure—an arabesque or quincunx, vermiculate and fraught with intricate lemniscates—marginally hypnotic. He was, in any event, moderately buoyed by its being there.

Further detail of the concrete variety: the depressing, gun-gray paint gummily impasto'd over the off-plumb walls; the saggy, flaking, water-waffled ceiling bereft of Tiepolo-esque cherubs and clouds; the chairless, lead-glass-paned secretaire topped with the pro forma ceramic ewer; the ruffled, tasseled, rose-colored satin-shaded floor lamp; the wall mirror about which less said the better; the single, pitiably forlorn rose drooping petallessly dead in its cut-glass vase; the tessellated, undormered, ungabled window looking out onto the depot, and, down the way a considerable stretch and cattywampus, the imposing twin-spired, red Jacobsville sand-stone church, St. Joseph's Slovenian Catholic, dedicated 1902, the very site of Ivan's lynching story.

He tried a piss; no blood—yet. Badly needed a shower, the very one he could not indulge as the hotel was equipped with tubs only, an appliance to which he was decidedly averse. Disrobed and cold-sponged instead, using the Albion milk-and-sulfur soap provided, Kildare brand, then flossed, the while quoting Emily aloud: "I should have liked to see you, before you became improbable." As, too, Miss Gertrude Stein: "Once upon a time I met myself and ran." He was hungry, he suddenly realized, quite famished, actually, and, so it seemed, in unseemly need of a steadying drink.

Having unpacked and tricked himself out in a fresh set of duds—eschewing anything black or flowery, as both, he knew, attracted bugs—he scuffled downstairs, inquiring of Mr. Green Eyeshade—the Green Cipher, as he took mentally to calling him, the Original Mr. Whiteout, Merz or Muir; he intermittently would get it wrong throughout his stay—the quickest way to the nearest saloon, one he at some length succeeded in locating, for the *putz*, he suspected, deliberately had misdirected him.

The place, he was surprised to see, was, for that hour, doing a land-office business. He noticed a sign in the front window:

FRESH LUTFISK
Available Daily
Limitless Quantities
from unpolluted sky-blue waters

Rummaging up an empty stall in the rear against the wall—the much-carved-in, shoulder-high wood partitions front and back were trimmed with frosted, engraved glass panels—he side-reeled his way into it, waved over one of the backroom barmaids, ordered three boilermakers "on the double," a term—boilermakers—he found himself having to explain.

"Ah," she said, quizzically—her eyes, he noticed, were green as gherkins—"you mean three whiskeys, beers back? Three beers, three bumps." Eyed him no less quizzically a second time. "Never heard that one before, boilermakers. Not from around here, are ya?"

"No," he said, not wishing to get into it with her. "Three whiskeys, beers back then."

"What's yer choice?"

"Any whiskey'll do, top-shelf. But make it rye. What beers?"

She sighed, putting a sound to her boredom, letting him know she had been asked the same question too many times in the past hour, before monotonally rote-reciting, *"Bosch, Sauna, Calumet's Pride, Park Elite, Haas Special Brew, Castle Brew, Soo, Iron Mountain, Philadelphia Porter, Grand Rapids Silver Foam, Detroit Bohemian, Mundus, Goebel, Koppitz Pale Select, Voigt's Rheingold, Tivoli Altes, Regal Special, Columbia Select Export, Stroh's Brown, Pfeiffer's Wurzburger, Zynda's Culnebacker."* Tapped an expectant, not quite impatient foot.

Some of these he recognized as Detroit brews, others he never had heard of. "One each of *Bosch, Calumet's Pride*, and *Soo*. Or no, make it *Sauna*."

She shrugged, left, returned trayed, placed upon the table three shots, three opened twelve-ounce bottles, three seven-ounce beer glasses, called *schnitzs*, or "snits." Handing her a fifty-cent silver piece, he instructed her to "keep it," received no thanks. Lined them up side by side, filled each of the glasses with a fine *schaum*, threw back the first of the shots, drained the first of the beers, tossed back the second whiskey, glanced around, mulling it a moment before deciding that—nope, he never had seen so many white men in one place before, not white like this, not white in this way, white as whey, the white of men who spend their lives deep beneath the ground whitewashed by the dark; nonapricate. Because the flesh on display—he could see that much even by the amber-dim light of the bar—the bare arms, thews, sinews, the biceps like shotputs, were so uniformly white they were nearly translucent. Nor merely Nordic white or blond Scandinavian pale, but vole white, albino white, mole white. Save, of course, for the ground-in red dirt creasing the deep lines in their faces and those in their hands midst calluses no less callused than scutes. And short, most of them. Noticed that, too. Well-muscled, but undersized. If there were three dozen men in the bar, he rough-reckoned fully half of them had to be under five foot five.

A couple more *Bosches* and not a few scrumpy ciders later, leavened by little but a basket of bar nuts and farings, hard-boiled eggs, some potted soused herrings, the hour was later still and he was well oiled enough that he found himself, jackknife in hand, whittling idly if no less compulsively into the soft wood of the stall walls, a practice to which they seemed content to turn a blind eye here, even as he half listened to the serenade issuing in full and finer fettle from the far end of the bar:

For singin' and for minin'
They've somehow got the knack,
It's second nature to that class
Of lads called Cousin Jacks.

They come from distant Houghton
And Hancock on the Hill,
And here in Calumet you bet
We're hammerin' on the drill.

Amongst you slackin' bohunks
Do justice if you can,
There's none that can come near compete
With good ol' Cornishmen.

Staggering clear of the place as night passed into day elbows first—"cannon drunk" they called it up here—he undertook to compass his way back to the hotel, pausing just long enough to piss bloodily upon a hydrant, stile, tree trunk, or lawn troll, saluting the night, as he considered it, with a cavalier's dash—"Back in the pissoir again!"

Navigating by way of the horse-carcass site, he discovered that it had been removed and disposed of—carcass, not site—save for a single hoof, an *ungula*, which after trying and consecutively failing to flip it over with the side of his shoe, he booted savagely down the road, not waiting for it to kick-cannishly knockett to a standstill where, in the morning, he would find it stood upright on end, a dead-silent *clop*. Symbolic of something, he reckoned—*must* be—if without knowing quite what.

JOSEF

Josef Clemenc was a good man and better miner, good enough to be one of the few Croatians to have broken through the notorious "Cousin Jack ceiling" and, after rising through the ranks, to have joined those select few—predominantly Cornishmen—who were paid to apply their intimate working knowledge of the art of explosives and demolition to the blasting of rock and mineral in order to extract therefrom precious metals and ore, the "red gold," copper lode core.

> *A skilled miner, one who takes full advantage of cleavage, jointing, and bedding planes, and of the varying strengths of different rock forms, and of the fundamental principles of physics, will accomplish better results with half the drilling and half the powder, than can be secured by a beginner or an ignoramus.*
>
> *—The Copper Handbook,* 1900

A miner, one like Josef, was just that, not some mere laborer who happened to work underground—drill attendant, tool nipper, mucker, trammer, swamper, gobber, trackman, lander, timberer, mill runner, plat man, pipe man, chute man, shaft man. Not that he was a living legend on the magnitude of Nikolai Temelcoff, the daredevil Macedonian up from Toronto. Nik, who somehow had succeeded in overcoming what the rest of them could never quite manage, the quotidian dread of having to "go back down"; who was possessed of "a nose and a knack," for the paths a vein traveled through its rock; who, at times, seemed able literally to see in the dark, and whose favorite saying was "The dark is time, time is money,

money buys my children the light." And Nik, who not only had suffered enough broken bones that he walked with a limp, but who had saved more than a few, including Josef, from being buried, broken, alive.

The Macedonian was one of the few who worked "on contract," as did only the best—two in twelve, according to company figures—instead of, as did Josef, "on the clock," so that he was paid by the running cubic foot or fathom mined, the amount of rock "moved"—as in "the more you break, the more you make"—rather than straight by the shift.

But Josef, at thirty-two, was good, a veteran, seasoned, knowledgeable, solid, dependable, and skilled enough that there wasn't a miner manning a "two-man" who, Croatian or otherwise, would need think twice about taking him on as his drill partner. He knew the dangers and how to identify them, the various looks of deep rock, how to read a surface for potential hazard, and was diligent in doing what he might to minimize risks as he encountered them. Nor was he less fierce in the pride he took in doing his job "on the square and the snuff" than any Cousin Jack you might wish to name.

Josef Clemenc was a miner, a copper miner, and all that that meant, what it cost and exacted, took and extracted. Not an obsessive or a prodigy, perhaps, matador and virtuoso, not the Macedonian, but one in the only way that mattered, in his blood, to the bone, in each ache, scar, callus, and bruise, each breath breathed down below and metallic taste—"Macabre taste," as Rupert Brooke so knowingly once had described it, "the taste of copper"—of his tongue.

Josef had been an infant when his family had arrived from the old country—apparently, he had taken his first steps while at sea, an occasion that had earned him the cognomen "Sealegs"—and had listened to the story of the passage a thousand times. It had been hard, hard enough that his mother, who never had fully recovered from his birth, had fallen almost immediately ill. The ship's doctor had been unable to break the spike of her fever. Seventeen years old, she never made it to Castle Garden.

His father had had relatives in the U.P., *sorodnike*—aunts, uncles, cousins—so, after arranging for her body to accompany them, father, son, and casket had traveled by train from New York to Chicago, switching there onto the CM&SP, the Chicago, Milwaukee & St. Paul line, and from Chicago, averaging twenty-one miles an hour, straight on to Houghton, while Josef walked the aisles learning how to fall and regain his feet, accommodate the bump and sway of the train, reckon the balance and counterbalance of upset. In time, Josef had matured into a man extraordinarily steady on his feet, one with a gondolier's grace, whose feats of agility in the underground "drifts" others would undertake only with backup.

His childhood, spent in the bosom of extended family, had not been unhappy. They were poor, but everyone was poor. Still, gradually he had become confused. By the time his father, who worked the mines as a trammer, remarried—to his fifteen-year-old cousin once-removed, a devout Catholic girl who claimed to see what was not there, angels, everywhere—Josef was just old enough that the disparity in their ages was not disparate enough. Nor did it help that his new stepmother was, in her way, quite attractive, or that, while devout, was when going about the close quarters of their two-room shanty, singularly uninhibited about her body, as she seemed wholly unaware of its effect upon him. He had endured the torment of his adolescence fraught with more than his share of lurid sexual imagery.

At twenty-three, still a virgin—he refused to frequent whores, having in the meanwhile embraced, and with a certain overzealousness, the dogma of his stepmother's church, the *cerkev*, the C&H-built St. Joseph's—he had married. The courtship had been brief, perhaps too brief, but having wooed as best he could, when he had asked and she had assented, he had leaped. She had been sought-after, had had a raft of suitors, was considered a catch, this six-foot-two-inch Slovenian beauty, Ana Klobuchar.

Save that now, nine years later, still no children. Not that they hadn't tried, at first. Because she had been willing, at first. Wished to please and gladden him, at first. She came from solid mining stock, keenly appreciated the rigors of the work, the risks her husband braved each day that they might make a home, rear a family. If he wanted kids, then she would do her part to provide them. She believed this her duty, at first. And, at first, she was nothing if not dutiful.

She even consented to accompany Josef to church each Saturday evening and Sunday morning, where he prayed that the two of them might be fruitful and multiply. A "good Catholic," her husband, observant, obedient, the orthodox and steadfast believer, one whose emotional connection to the Latinate rituals and rites was, she knew, palpably real and profound. And while she did not, nor ever could persuade herself to share the unshakable reality of his faith, at first she had respected and even admired it, for that faith, the miracle of it, was that which he buckled on like a broadsword and brandished like a breastplate each time he went back down.

"Without it," he once had told her, "I do not know that I could do it. There are no atheists in a mine. Well, except the Macedonian, whose only god is himself."

But as time passed and they remained childless, the counsel of the priest—"Be patient, my son; all in God's time"—wore thin. She could sense that he felt wronged, victimized, put upon, a feeling he couched in religious terms.

"What sin have I committed," he had implored the priest, "that I remain by family unblessed? Am I not his servant? Is he not my lord? Why do my prayers remain unanswered? Is it a test?"

"We are all sinners, my son," the priest had answered. "The Lord's ways are a mystery. It is not for us to question them, only to forbear. Patience, my son. You still are young. Your wife still is young. There is time. With God, there always is time."

But time for Josef, Ana sensed, was running increasingly short. She could feel his searching, trawling for a reason that his mind might accommodate, his having begun to question not his god, but his wife, her faith and religious commitment, which, as they both knew, did not run nearly so deep as his own. What distressed him more so, however, was the unpardonable license she so regularly took with her criticisms of his holiness, the seventy-eight-year-old Venetian Pius X, and of his being "so almighty drunk," as she put it, both on his own "infallibility" and his *"ignis ardens,* his professed ardent love for what he calls his Immaculate Mother, the Blessed Virgin Mary."

She might approve, as she had, of his beatification of Joan of Arc, but with his encyclicals privileging private charity over social justice, condemning the separation of church and state, and indicting "the synthesis and poison of all heresies that is Modernism and Americanism, and whose only intention is to annihilate Christianity and use the human intellect as an insidious plot and unholy design to attack the fountain of Divine Revelation," she passionately disagreed. "This bad pope," she called him, pointing to his institution of "the Anti-Modernist Oath" as a requirement for all those standing for the priesthood as evidence of his "ungodly arrogance and megalomania."

It was a Sabbath, after church—when else?—that they had had it out. Her twenty-fifth birthday was in the offing, he already had made arrangements for the surprise of the balloon ride, and when he had dropped a harmless reference, as he considered it, to the sky ride "up there, nearer my God to thee," she had replied, "Better God than the pope."

"But he is the pope," Josef had replied. "He is God's first own in human form, our earthly lord."

"Then he is a bad god," she had retorted. "He is everything that is wrong about the church."

"But you must not say such things, Ann. He cannot be wrong. He is the pope. *Papez*."

"So *you* say, husband. I say otherwise. I say as I see."

"No, not I. I do not say. God says."

"Then God says wrong."

"Ann!"

"What would you have me say, husband? That I agree with every word that is uttered by such a *stupid* man? As God gave me this body, so, too, he gave me a mind, my own, one to use as I might see fit to use it, and what my mind tells me is that this pope is not worthy, not fit, that he—"

"Enough! You shall not vilify our holy father. It is sinful talk, a sin to say such things. I will not abide it, not in my house. Why, Ann? Why must you? The pope is bad, God is wrong. These are serious matters. Have you no fear of the Lord, wife? Can you not see that your words have"—he hesitated—"consequences?"

"What do you mean, Josef? What are you saying?"

He regretted it later, of course, but in the moment his mind had been blank, white with every color of anger; his tongue alone had worked.

"Why do we remain childless, Ann? Hmm? Why? Why do you fail to give me children? Give *us*? Why are we punished? Why is there a curse on this house?"

"You feel cursed, Josef? Punished? Then, husband, it is you alone who feels this way. Some things are not meant to be as we would have them be. Perhaps children are not meant for us. Perhaps we must find our meaning in other things. There is no shame in it. Is that it, Josef, that you feel I shame you?"

"You ask why," she had continued, "why we are childless. I shall answer. We are childless because you have not gotten me with child. Do you hear me complain of this? Do you hear me say I consider you less a man? That I feel less a woman? You do not. What is it, husband? That you feel you are disappointing your precious pope? That you offend him by not doing your part to strew the earth with more pope-fearing Catholics, *good* Catholics? If that is what a good Catholic is, then I am among the worst. Until this *wicked* pope dies, or comes to his senses, or is forced from his high and mighty throne, I shall have no more of him. Or it."

"But what are you saying, Ann? What can you mean?"

"I mean that in the future you can find your way to St. Joseph's alone. I wish nothing more to do with it."

"But surely you cannot—"

"But I can, husband. I do. No more, Josef. An end."

"Ann, be reasonable. You cannot, in a moment, decide to stop going to church, our church."

"*Our* church? No. *Their* church, built and paid for by the Outfit."

"What I mean," he had said, "is that you cannot choose to stop being Catholic. You were born, baptized, confirmed, reared Catholic. You *are* Catholic. Saying you are not does not make it so. Absenting yourself this way does not make it so. I think, perhaps, that you are not entirely in your right mind just now. We will discuss this later, when you are."

"No, Josef, we will not. Never again will we speak of it. Never again shall you question my decision. You need not agree with or respect it, but you shall not hold it against me, not if you love me. You do love me, do you not, husband?"

"Annie, of course I do."

"I know you do, and I you." She had taken his hand in hers then, kissed him on the lips. "Not another word, then."

He did not resist or recoil, no suggestion of rebuke or reproach, but neither, she had noticed, did he return the gesture with discernible ardor. "It is going to be fine," she had said. "Everything is going to be just fine."

He continued to love her, *did* love her, he told himself, and believed it, every word, even as he knew she loved him and believed that even more. Certainly their matrimonial commerce continued regular, what he considered regular, if no longer so . . . calisthenically. There was nothing to complain of in that regard, lest it be her indefatigability. He did not begrudge her her appetite. Besides, as far as he was concerned, the oftener, the better the odds of getting her with purchase.

Still, there were those times when he was not nearly as . . . up to his duties as she was to hers, a shortcoming for which she had yet to utter so much as a word of blame or to make him feel inadequate. That said, her stamina, at times, *was* daunting. Twelve hours a day, six days a week wrestling brute rock a mile underground, such *obertaim*, such work, drained the sand from a man, any man, save perhaps the Macedonian, and there were nights when Josef Clemenc simply was too *zmatran*, tuckered, done in, played out, to do anything but collapse into bed unmuscled, aching-limp with fatigue. As he had explained to her on countless occasions: every night, love, sometimes more than once a night, my love, simply was too much for a man to muster or manage. It was beyond his capacities, my darling, such wherewithal. He might be a working stiff, but good lord, woman, not on nightly demand.

Well, she fixed a fine meal and ran a well-scrubbed nine-hundred-square-foot tar-paper-roof company house respectably on budget and kept her person more than reasonably fetching and hadn't a shrewish bone in her overripe body, the body he conceived of as belonging to that of a princess, his, the way it spoke to him of unfathomable riches, fabulous secrets, hidden wishing wells, unattainable dreams.

And more than all that, she understood and appreciated the thanklessness of the life, its difficulties, dangers, rigors, asperities. Having been bred to it, she was at home with its climate of hardness, the routine of risk, momentous uncertainty, how appallingly cheap the work could render a life, the way those pits could swallow a man whole and spit him back out again, broken bloody to pieces. As well as the necessity not only of scraping by and doing without, but of doing so midst terrain that when it was not being unremittingly remorseless, could be mercilessly brutal, and without flinch or complaint in the rugged, stony face of it. A miner's wife. One, in fact, who so appreciated her role, she was bestirred to work twenty-hour weeks at the hospital vetting the maimed and the mutilated, washing their whites and scrubbing their bedpans for fifty cents a day. Her choice, not his.

So when he caught himself, as he did more often of late, wondering why he couldn't have a wife "like everyone else's," it made him feel small and petty and mean. He looked around him, at other marriages, and not a one was flawless, and most were fragile, where not troubled or damaged or worse. Worse than his. Far worse.

Ana was special, if one wished to use that word, possessed of real substance, integrity of heart and of soul. Everyone said so, even those who did not particularly care for her and her irreligiosity. And smart, quick-minded, nimble of wit, certainly of a more intellectual bent than himself, naturally more inquisitive about the world, temperamentally more open to the promise of all it might offer.

He, on the other hand, his faith aside, saw only what he saw—the here, the now, the what is and was there at hand and in front of his nose. And, in truth, about these he might miss little enough. But she saw something more. The ought be? Could be? Must? He could not have said. It was something he never could right reckon, this quality her Slovenian kin, his in-laws, called "reading every side of the state."

She actually had completed two years of high school, an accomplishment he could only begin to imagine. Hell, she read books, actual books, and in *English*, often two and three at a go, nor a single one the Bible. So, perhaps, in her way, she even was extraordinary. Must be. She read *poetry*. But did he really need extraordinary? Did he even want it? Well, it was what he had, what he was saddled with, with Ann, and no sense trying too hard to kick against his stall. He never had known anyone so invested in infusing life with the question of its presence. Fierce, his Ann, and when armed with single-minded conviction—and she seemed always armed with single-minded conviction—ferocious.

Not that he was overmuch experienced in the art of it, but he sensed, as do even the most insensitive of men, that a woman, most women, a wife, is not so easily knowable. Parts might be—available, so to say— oddments, episodes, *segmenta*, snapshots, but seldom the whole. And Ana—this he *did* know—comprised more parts than a puzzle, or, rather, any number of puzzles patchworked and pooled, those of sea plain and ocean floor, bathysphere, tidal soar. It was less, he thought, that a woman like Ann was endlessly mysterious, than that some essence or essential piece of her, some dimension or depth, remained private. Deliberately withheld? Purposively secret? Strategically hidden? Consciously absented? How know? Her. At core, her immaculate core, this intimacy at arm's length.

Perhaps a woman could be truly close, enjoy that unbuttoned interior commerce only with another woman. Still, left a man feeling . . . gypped, slighted, cut out, deprived of his full share, and duped, and had, and illused. This positively felt feeling that you were missing out on something without knowing exactly what it was you were missing, save that it must be worth knowing, worth having, and if only you could get to it, get at it, be granted a brief caress, your life would feel less . . . eclipsed. But of course you couldn't, because you were a man.

Well, he doubtless was being perfectly ridiculous. What did any of us ever know, really know, of another? How much did we really *want* to know? Not much, most likely. Certainly less than we might claim. And doubtless better off, to remain estranged. For were man to know woman and woman to know man each in their respective infirmities, how not turn tail and run? Where else could such *mutual* knowledge possibly lead, save to the end of ourselves, our days and our lot, the Don't, I Could Never, I Can't and Shall Not.

No, he would trust to the infinite wisdom of the Lord, however inscrutable: kneel to his prayers, attend to the mass, confess, take communion, say after me, plainsing, Gregorian chant. And observe, do penance, his Hail Marys, Our Fathers, his Stations of the Cross, all fourteen, do as *Papez* bade him do, his sacred Catholic duty by his sainted—he insisted—still Catholic, impossibly barren wife.

"Lucky man," he reminded himself. "Lucky I am to have her."

So this was the question Josef Clemenc was left to answer on his own, at night, in his bed, nor feeling ever more alone, his dilemma as one with his desire: how does a man live happily with a woman who has become to him a stranger, one incapable of sharing his vision of himself, and of his dream, and of what their life together should be? How does one properly love the apostate, or lie down with the rocky of womb?

BY THE SHORES OF

Across the whole of the Keweenaw there could not have been a dozen Indians who had yet to surrender to town living, drift north into Canada, or retreat to the wilds of Isle Royale. Every so often the stray, diehard, pedicular holdout, appearing wild-haired and weather-rent, might be spotted stocking up on bulk staples at Chynoweth's, or ducking into Martini's for tobacco or liquor, or stalking the aisles of the Glass Block Shop for sundries, but for the most part they seemed content to keep to themselves in their shanties and outcamps in the proximate deep woods. Called "tawnies" in the local parlance, they in fact were Ojibwas, or as some preferred, Chippewas or Anishnabeg, the original inhabitants of the peninsula.

They hunted, trapped and fished, dug roots, harvested morels, gathered nuts and picked thimble berries, foraged grubs, tapped maple trees for their sap to make syrup and sugar, winnowed wild rice, carved fetishes, tokens, totems, and charms, built travois, crafted birch-bark canoes, sang, dance, gambled, took sweat baths in bark sweat lodges, trafficked in their *manitous* taking special care to dodge the Williwaws and Windigos, buried their dead in aboveground bark cribs, and, so the popular consensus, necro-manced nature while smoking a narcotizing red sumac/birch-bark blend they called *kinickinick* and drinking too damn much for their own good or anyone else's. Rumor had them interbreeding their half-wild mongrel dogs with the diminishing stock of native timber wolves. God knows what all and whatnot.

"Goddamn heathen pantheists!" was the going townie oath, which, strictly speaking, was wrong. They were animists, lived the ambient senso-rium, Spinozists untamed. They praised every and all.

In any event, what is helpful to understand is that when Ana had her "encounter"—revelation, epiphany, what have you—it occurred in that context.

It had been some months earlier, the November previous, a Saturday minty-white, misty-wet with menthol rain, its early-morning sky wide as wax. She was alone, out hounding agates along the lake. Lacustrine agates, then, a variety of quartz, subspecies of chalcedony. November was the month to agate-hunt owing to the season's fierce westerly storms, that be-ing the time when the gravels carried closest to shore and the waters, once the weather had moved out, were at their least choppy and churned.

Beneath spat sleet, the sky was an amalgam of noncolors: Chablis, ecru, stilbite, *au lait*, smaltine and salt, sperrylite, saltine, putty and chalk, oyster, clam, calibreccia, cuttlebone, bonemeal, gesso and grout, tartar, co-conut meat, abalone. All of which rendered the day flat and faceless, bereft of dimension and contour, yet brittle as coral.

Her "spot" was a half-acre horseshoe cove, fir-lined, high-bluffed, a raw-sandy place of endless stile and stria, exposed root, not a structure in sight, not a roof. Head canted and down-bent, scrutinizing eyes fixed on the bed of wet pebble and chert arrayed at her feet like doubloons and ducats, pieces of eight, she methodically scruffed off and skreeted each foot—crunch-*ett*/pause/crunch-*ett*/pause—her breath blowing white in fur fists. Like hunting land mines. At her belt she wore a crandell.

Stooping at intervals to scoop one up, then another, she wiped them on her slacks, rubbed and dandled, palming them over and over, weighing the heft of their worth, then tossed them aside or deposited them in the zinc pail she carried by the long loop of its handle. Agates, after all, were not just lying about in plain sight, fallen fruit to be plucked. You had to chip away, break apart the husk of outer rock to get at the prize pithed at its pit.

She had been doing this since childhood—her private collection numbered well above one thousand—so she knew each of the types: tube, moss (or mocha), (tiger's) eye, leopard skin, shadow, ruin, fault, fire, plume, onyx, orange swirl, jasper, geode, sagenite, variegated, fortified, blue and crazy lace, water-level. Knew the "agate within the agate," each unique, pretty as snowflake, but better, because stone abided and endured.

Beauty, however much it sorrowed her to consider it, was hard to come by in the Keweenaw, but where it existed, its source most often was Lake Superior. And an agate, as she thought of it, was like owning your own private piece—the lake compressed and made . . . indurate, its durable rhythm and sway, waves arrested in rock. If you looked long and close enough, she thought, you could discern in a pebble miniature topographies, whole countries, continents, worlds, planets, agate universes and multiverses, ones you might clasp snug within the fold of your fist.

"Better than seashells any day," she thought, though she never had been to a sea.

Her eyes were glued to the ground, visually sifting the types, when she heard it, the kind of sound about which you immediately wonder, "Did I just hear that, or did my ears imagine it?" Because she sensed the sound as a presence, the way one feels a cloud when it scrolls past the sun on lidded eyes, ghost through wall.

Turning her head in reply, she lifted her eyes toward the bluff line of the thickly pined sand slope. Difficult to see through the chowdery mizz. The air struck her as texture, substance: powder, talc, batter, bisque. Shrugging it off, the sound, she attended to the business at foot, underfoot, only to hear it again, *musical* this time, an exhalation *sordamente*, some alto of octave.

Why did she think the sound was a panther and she its chosen prey? And still it drew her hither, tugged her toward, on, along, up the steep sand of the slope. Still gripping the pail, doing her best not to spill, she yanked herself up the incline, toehold, handhold, foot and knee, one-handing her way by the haphazard network of black, nakedly exposed roots poking here and there at gnarled angles, knags up through damp sand.

Achieving its crest, she found herself atop its hem, winded with exertion. Brushing herself off, she stood listening, regaining her breath, ears cocked to the high wall of trees before her—conifer, spruce, hemlock, red, white, and tamarack pine, jack and pitch, cedar, beech, balsam, birch—knowing she must go in there, *would* go in, but, in the margin of the moment, threshold and hesitant.

When the sound arose again, no louder but sleeving higher, that which a magic carpet might make were the carpet a sleigh, ethereally eerie, this *altitude* of music, she walked forward, slipping through and into the pages of the album of trees where the mist was less, sleet thinned, darker the greens and grays. The lake was on her right and she could hear its lisp as it lipped the shoreline in liquid slurps and chuckle-head chews, but nothing glittered through, no spools of silver, spangles of matelot blue. She could not see its scrim-shine for the density of tree.

Kept walking, in.

Tripping over deadfall, she all but fell, righted herself, resumed, before, startled, halting in place as, at some remove directly ahead and amid the trees, she watched the sound rear up, its figure unfold. Nemoral spirit? Manifest soul? *Materia prima*? Corpus of God? Goddess of tree? Male, female, some of both, a little of neither? As the words, then, had yet to be coined, certain ones did not, in the moment, suggest themselves: mutagenic, biomorphic.

Fossilized piecements of what appeared to be mirror—chips, chippets, chads—dangled from the figure's bark-and-moss body, appearing to drip-drool by the thousand, tiny tiles, a pouring of geometry, system of chrome. She sensed sadness here, a terrible beauty, one stillborn, and it radiated from the figure like magnets, infinite in its ancientness.

And then it spoke, invisible voice but clear. "Come nearer."

Approaching warily, she drew near enough to see herself reflected, fractured in the hanging gallery of mirrors, her face, its features abscissed and scissured to a thousand jagged shards. The figure—she could see it clearly now—was canopied in leaf, fern, compost, and mulch draping past its shoulders in a fantastic aigrette thickly sprigged with owl plume, hair-pipe, quahog shell, plug.

It spoke again. "Are your eyes open?"

The voice sounded to her older than winter, twice as wise, gathered from a far-flung place, faraway time.

"Yes," she managed. "Open. Yes."

"Good," it said. "Now open them wider."

"Yes," she said.

"See me," it said. "When you look at me, see me. When you see me, see yourself. Is it not true? You see your many selves."

"Yes," she said, running her fingers over the many remnants of her face as she watched them fade the way ice melts, emulsion across glass plate. "I see myself in pieces. Broken. Vanishing."

"And is this not true?" it said. "A truth of heart?"

And now, and of a sudden, there was a dark hole in Ana's breast the size of a silver dollar, the orb of an eye that opened slowly if more widely still, enough to permit her heart to fist through the gap where it lay fully exposed upon the outside of her chest, whumping wildly, strong as any healthy pink baby. Vapors rose off its ventricles. She inhaled them, attar and sachet.

"Yes," she said. "I see it now. My original face. How do you empty a heart of its secrets? My heart. Its rue."

"There is a great circle," it said, raising its limbs, wingspan, before hooping them forward in an enormous bear hug as the mirrors swayed and stroked, nicking one another with a musical chinkling sound, wind chimes and water clocks. (Celesta? Cembalo? Glass armonica? Valiha? Ravanastron or Theremin?) *Etheria musica.*

"At the center of the circle live my people, and whilst whither the circle moves"—the figure swept its great hoop of musical wing here, swooped it over there, then back again—"so there are my people, always within the circle, always at its center.

"So this is how I know. Because it is given to me to know. My people are gone now, every one. I alone remain. I *am* the circle. I contain its center. The center is myself, the Uroboros. Do you believe me?"

"I believe my eyes and my ears."

"Good. The circle is the form. The form is sacred, form of forms, its design. Pure thought thinks it into being. That which designs and constructs, that which is constructed, are indivisible. The actor is his act. Nothing is beautiful apart from life, and life is that which dies.

"So it is that I alone was sent to study in solitude the habits hidden of this bush, to know its unknowable meanings, inhabit its messages and align the great drum of my heart to the hum of its rhythms. They would have me wear its ways like skins.

"Before the gods existed, the *manitous*, these woods were holy. Later, the gods settled here and so followed my people. In those distant days, a tree could move a soul. Do you understand?"

"Nothing. Yet."

"Then that is enough for now. The tribes were created in language. Yours call this the talking-upon-paper. Picture sounds. The world can be written in its reading."

"I still do not understand," she said.

"Good. Then you have discovered something."

Odd, then, for Ana felt a sudden need to confess, deep need. But what? She did not know. And more, to be absolved.

"You," said the figure, "you have been chosen. So you must go away now. Go to your home. Feel the sadness. It is permitted. Transfigure yourself. I can tell you no more. There may be other days. So long as there are songs, there must be singers to sing them. For now, beware, or you shall find yourself fallen asleep in another's dreams."

And then the mist was back again, rapidly rolling in, doubly thickened, enclosing the figure in the wings of its cape. She watched as it was carried off and eased away, its shape become shadow, its ascent an eeling of chrome-colored smoke. She imagined a climbway of dream, its flight path white as white tundra.

Weakly waved, then turned, and, weak-kneed, walked away.

So that was the day Ana Clemenc began to see and hear what was or was not there.

But what tell Josef? What say, and how? How manage its sense, give him to understand what she herself did not understand? "Snap out of it, wife," he would say, or something similarly colloquial, as if it all had been a trance or intoxication. And how blame him? For perhaps it had. It was not unheard-of, after all, for those who suffered from long-term heavy-metal copper dousing to hear and see things that others did not. Retinal hallucination, auditory transport.

Walking home, she decided to leave it alone, say nothing at all, and better left. Better, at least, than something that would make her sound madder than the March Hare she knew her husband reckoned she already was. There was, after all, nothing sayable to say, was there? Great Circles. Sacred Forms. Transfigurations. Falling asleep in another's dreams. It was simply too . . . misty. Perhaps, she thought, one of those poets, one of those she had been reading in the library of late, perhaps a Longfellow, say, might know how to go about making something of it. She hadn't the words for a vision: *By the shores of the Great Blue Gitch.*

The way the mist breathes blueing in ages.

So, once having decided, she began to run—a rain had begun, cold quill plunge, rain *en brosse* and pennate—even as she sensed the tall trees closing like a trapdoor behind her, and did not stop until she was home, two miles, more. And there, in the front yard, her mind outracing the pace of her lungs, she vomited, astonishing the autumn grass with a substance black and hard and soft, cold and smooth and hot—hurl of bolus. The putamen chucked up from the peach.

Her *pes*, her dog, Liberty—Libby for short, or Lib, a vizsla—suddenly appeared, braving the rain she customarily could not abide, sniffed about, ventured a lick, then pinned back her ears before raising her hackles, baring a fang, and snarling. Backing off in a fit of barking and growling before emitting a gut-shot whimper, she bolted across the yard and, tail tucked, low-bellied it down the street.

Fetching the shovel leaning against the side of the house, Ana scooped the expectorant up, carried it through the sleety rain into the backyard and, once out behind the crib of chink-wattled planks that housed her *kopisce*, her ganister-lined kiln and the pile of native sand heaped beside it, buried it deep among the brown-dead gladiolas, rhododendrons, nasturtiums, hyacinths, and hydrangeas. Buried it much as a rock hurled upon water buries its reflection in the splash and ripple of its aftershock.

"There," she said at last, spanking the ruptured, rust-veined, wet-reddened earth with the flat-back of the shovel. "Out with all the old, in with all the new." She felt as relieved as if she had rid herself of the shackle of her shadow. Felt . . . freed.

The rain lessened a moment, lull, then, abrupt as a clap-stick, picked up, redoubled, its noise a steady scatter in the trees, dumb music inside its certain speed. Rain the size of seed, then bulb, then bumblebee. The storm broke with a blast, vengeful and vast. Espaliers were toppled, pergolas and trellises tossed, craticles, too, dead flowers shredded, shrubs shorn. Entire gardens were turned upside in and wrong-side down. At least it wasn't snow.

Orchards were stripped bare of the sum of their fruit. Vineyards bled copiously. Fields lay pillaged and cratered, their crops bent at unnatural angles, whole harvests gone a-sack. Windows were smashed, doors blown in, roofs lifted, silos and stables battered and bashed. A few houses were leveled. The ardor of nature's order rolled across the artifice of human arrangement thoughtless as dice.

Ana weathered another seven months, laboring into midsummer until, at last, she cracked. Unable to sustain the facade, she renounced her membership, relinquished the ghost, quit the church, abstained of the host, and, damning the priest for a poofter, banished the name of the pope in her presence.

A not unsmall copper crucifix adorned the wall above their bed, which, during the nine years it had hung there turning successive shades of verdigris-green, never had been removed from its spot, not even to be polished or properly cleaned. One morning, not long after the balloon ride, while Josef was at work, she removed it from its mounting and, sliding open the deep bottommost drawer of her dresser, slipped it horizontally into one of the bread-box tins inside of which she kept her agates, burying it layered down beneath them—enshrouded in stone.

When Josef crawled into bed that night, he eyed the vacant spot, a cross of clean paint, its patibulary outline starkly white against a wall dark with dross, and, knowing better, wagered not a word.

HOMEWORK

"Where am I going?"

This being the question Franklyn repeatedly had posed to himself on the train ride up.

"Where am I?"

This being the one he asked upon awaking next morning to what he construed for the cock-crow of more than one rooster.

Both were decent enough questions, and he had been diligent about girding himself for their answers—doing his homework, reading through, poring over, jotting and digesting his notes, studying and committing to semiphotographic memory the contents of Ivan's portfolio, the three-inch-thick stack he had taken to thinking of as "The Thornveld Dossier," the object of which not only was to establish the frame of a context but a palpable *feel* for that context's history, its interior perspective. For the reporter on far-flung assignment, writing becomes a place in which to live and, too, better breathe.

Whether history might be said to possess a meaning, while not an unmomentous matter, was one that would keep for another day. In the meantime, Franklyn understood that absent the historical "back story," the subtext of the who, what, and where of this place and its people, such meaning as might be had must remain wholly elusive. Thus had the train ride constituted a not undesperate delve among the information Ivan had compiled for his edification, a single-minded dredge after those dots and their connections that might result in a picture containing some clue of larger sense. The rest he would need to fill in on the fly, the data dance, catch-as-catch-can, off-the-cuff, seat-of-the-pants, the way every reporter works.

One word had kept recurring to him as he had read: gothic. Couldn't get away from or past it. But "gothic" less in the sense of uncanny, supernatural, ghosty, or bodey, than of bleakly exotic and desolately atavistic, half savage and grotesque. And dark. Deep winter, deep forest, deep muscle dark.

Insofar as he had read Ivan's materials rightly, the U.P. always had been, still was, less the America of Emerson, Whitman, and Thoreau, than of Hawthorne and Melville and Poe. Something, not to sound portentous, about man being coerced by the elements and constrained by his circumstances into having revealed to himself the nethermost fringe and peripheral extremes of his nature.

A testing place, then, crucible, or so his impression. The kind of unsung surround no one thought much about unless they were unfortunate enough to find themselves living there and, as they did, preferred, as they might manage, to forget. Not that there weren't those who must be possessed of an abiding affection for it, the land of their birth, but sentiment is sentiment, however true or false.

So far as he could surmise, what seemed to inform the place above all, as what defined it the more so, was simple: geography and climate. The former being a matter of remoteness and isolation, the latter of inclemency and harshness, both being a matter of northernness, northerliness, northwardness, of latitude. The peninsula lay just below the 47.5 parallel north, the same which to the east intersected the very northmost dome-jut of Maine. In the summer, night did not fully fall until after ten p.m. Nature, then, determined human behavior in ways that were inconceivable to anyone living anywhere else.

There are places in this world where the northland ends, where northern lands end, end in farmost edges, fore-thrust tips, trackless and undifferentiated expanse. The Keweenaw was such a place, an ongoing frontier, one as fully distant north of Detroit in the same state as Detroit was west of Washington, D.C. And those who lived in such places knew, or upon promise of mortal pain came quickly to learn, that theirs constituted a reality less forgiving than others, more ubiquitously impinging, one of no negotiation, from which there was no escape but accommodation only, or resignation. The meaning of north, the first among many, was that one treated it with imprudence and lack of humility, took it for granted, only at one's peril.

Franklyn had done his share of musing upon the subject—the assignment required he do no less—and so he knew how Poe once had written that north *is a wild weird clime that lieth sublime / out of space . . . out of time!* That the poet Herbert Read had defined *The Way North* as the *Way into the Unknown*. That the Russian writer Mariusz Wilk once had remarked that *North has no form. It is a state of endlessness, bottomlessness, shapelessness, indefinition, suspension. The other world shines through it, the point where the world meets the beyond*, as had the Canadian poet Henry Beissel that *North is where all the parallels . . . converge to open out . . . into the mystery surrounding.*

The national epic of Finland, the *Kalevala*—translated passages of which Ivan had included in the dossier—contained, as he did not fail to notice, the lines: *dark Northland, / the man-eating, the / fellow-drowning place.*

No coincidence, he thought, that the lowest circle in Dante's hell should be reserved for the frozen lake where the unendurable cold was generated by the flap of Lucifer's wings: the hell of ice. Or that the Bible, in the book of Isaiah, located Satan's dwelling place as *in the sides of the North.*

North, as he considered it, kills. Kills the light, soul, dissolves wit, freezes thought in the midst of its flow.

And gray. North is gray. Evanesces, northward. Dark rumor, rumors of dark and of dungeon.

North locks down time as it opens up space, enforces departures and partings, ensures no return, no open way. North is no turning back.

North is where pleasure goes to waste, to perish dead away. Last exile, no quarter, where no cold heart melts nor high spirit plays. North is far, and farther away.

North is not for but against, its grain on the counter, wills its own way. Is the enemy, home to the hostiles, barbarians, berserkers, pagans, the savage and alien invader. North vanquishes, untamed and unconquerable. Sires struggle, midwifes madness. North is Generalissimo January, where death goes once it has died.

The Song of the North is a posthumous dirge, mourns for itself without elegy. North eats raw nerve.

North is wolf.

North is the last to be searched for and mapped, and, once found, as Rabelais's Pantagruel discovered, that which it communicates, it is capable of expressing only in frozen words as they thaw: *Hin, ticque, torche, lorgne, brededin, brededac, frr, frr, frrr, bou, bou, bou, bou, bou, bou, bou, bou, tracc, tracc, trr, trr, trr, trrr, trrrrrr, on, on, on, on, on, ououououon, goth, magoth.*

North the unspeakable, subzero, zero-sum.

North the all-encompassing, overwhelming presence of an absence; an elsewhere that is here, everywhere; a far-awayness finally arrived; an other world that is this one and no other, where nothing awaits but more waiting.

North the nothing that is wild, lonely, whirls like snow wheels, winded, night after night.

North the deep, steep, the vast and the void. North the not nothing, not quite.

North is no relief.

North the question: where did my days go, and where, too, my life?

North the caducity of self, its avalanched soul.

North the assertion: remote things matter, isolation endures, the silence of solitude can shatter like glass, everything that succors and sustains, proffers solace and promise, is perishable; nothing lasts.

North is about surviving—North.

North is the end at the end of the world, space and time both, all edge and no margin, the stark made sublime.

North is the end, of North, North away.

So then, an outpost of world, ship's prow of land, a jutland, the Keweenaw, one hyperborean enough to be characterized, as its native "Yoopers" were wont to joke, by "fifty weeks of winter, and two of bad sledding," one that for six months in twelve was snowbound and ice locked; come winter, waterways were unnavigable and all trace of overland routes simply disappeared. One wherein, as one of the early Yoopers had written, "the Ice King rules with terrible swift severity," and summer, however hot, lasted not long enough to dispel the lingersome taste of winter.

A Keweenaw winter typically dumped two hundred inches of snow across the befallen peninsula in a succession of gales, squalls, blizzards, and storms, during which winds could top fifty miles per hour and temperatures tip toward thirty degrees below zero, even as the frigid sun shone in sunbeams toothed as icicles. May snows were not uncommon, and while a frozen Lake Superior *was*—"roofed over," they called it up here—there were those who recalled those anomalous Mays when their horse-drawn bobsleds and carioles had sleighed the ice bridge between the peninsula and Isle Royale, some fifty miles out in the lake; limestone sea.

Here was a flayed, closed-down place, then, one where when out hiking its winter woods, even clad in the appropriate footwear—the two pairs of woolen stockings, the nepe wraps encased in felt-lined rawhide shoe-packs, finally the snowshoes—one still might expect, upon doffing one's gear, to take three or four toenails with it. A place where people were more apt to ask, "Where is here?" than "Who am I?"

In fact, the U.P., according to Ivan's materials, had begun receiving weekly mail by stagecoach (summer) and dogsled (winter) up from Green Bay, Wisconsin, two hundred uninhabited miles due south, fewer than fifty years before. Had been unreachable by telegraph until well after the Civil War; news of Fort Sumter had not filtered through for more than three weeks after its fall. The first macadam road still was not yet thirty-five years old, the first railroad line younger still, and phrases such as "cooped up," "socked in," "frost jacked" and "froze stiff," "cabin fever" and "stir-crazy," "snow-blind" and "shack-wacky" were more than mere figments of speech—as were nausea and hallucination, providence and prayer.

The Yoopers' designation for the rest of the world was "down-below," a hyphenated noun spoken with a combination of condescension and awe. Down-below was everyplace else, and *here* was "up north," a phrase that elsewhere might signify a direction or destination but in the U.P. was synonymous with "above" and with "home," the one singly unto itself, isolate, alone.

He hadn't run across the fact in Ivan's files, but Franklyn knew that it had been only twenty years since Frederick Jackson Turner had read his paper "The Significance of the Frontier in American History" before the Congress of Historians of the American Historical Association at Chicago's Columbian World Expo, the frontier being, as Turner defined it, "the meeting ground between savagery and civilization," the border place—or moment—in which "the bonds of custom are broken and unrestraint is triumphant."

What Turner was describing, thought Franklyn, the more "civilized" cynosures of Red Jacket/Laurium and Houghton/Hancock notwithstanding, fit the Keweenaw's profile perfectly, save that the peninsula was a patch of frontier left *behind*, *a* frontier to the rear of *the* frontier. So that inasmuch as it remained frontier*like*, it did so as an expression of backwash and wake, a consequence of having been passed by and over as not worth the labor of its settling: too inhospitable, hostile, too hard. An enduring extreme, then, this increasingly seldseen entity in 1913 Midwestern America.

And it was that very quality about the place, its extremeness in a word, its drasticity in another, that also kept it so impregnably armored, therefore so forbiddingly aloof and unapproachable, therefore so partitioned, protected, preserved, pristine, so embryonically insulated from the impact of the rest of the world. A natural boondock; *Nova Zembla*. This was thought by some to be a good thing and by others to be beyond merely bad, the very bane of their drab and narrow existence.

Whether living above and on what the miners called its "surface" or working far beneath it, deep inside it, slagging, slogging, shagging, boring through, and blasting, wresting its interior *out*, the Keweenaw was for even the hardiest of stoics a difficult place to sleep through the night and awaken each morning to the rest of one's life, a life over which one was granted scant dominion save by blind chance or cruel hazard. One lived on edge because one lived on *an* edge, this razor ridge of land, in control of little but one's own meager efforts to manage, make a stand, cope, bear up, endure, get by, weather through, stay afloat, hang on, eke out, persevere. One either callused up and outlasted, or one quit and fled, caved and came apart, lost track of one's wits, gave up, left oneself for dead, free of the weary dread of each moment at last.

Life was no cheaper here than anyplace else—as it decidedly was no nobler; no triumph in overcoming, outlasting adversity, no honor and dignity in perduring, only survival, survival only, not dying—but it was, for all of its hardscrabble, tumbledown, rough-and-tumble ruggedness, more perilous, precarious, problematic. And always, always humbling. What was weak wore fast, wore down, wore through, wore out. Weak was what weathered badly and was ill tolerated, and strong was what might be rewarded with some shot at subsistence and solvency. And what was broken, once broken, remained ever after, broke.

Hard times in a harder place, existence spread thin and stretched, stressed to a certain limit, that moment where something or someone or both has to give, to bend—or break. And what is given, another inevitably takes. So that holding on and holding out, hanging in, making a go and making do, beating the odds and the elements, besting the worst and giving better than one got, yet still keeping on, by faith or by hope, was much the art of it. Save that neither of those—faith, hope—would feed you or your family. Life, such as it was, as frustum.

This, at least, was Franklyn's aborning sense of the "picture" he had lifted from the reading he had done on the train, the picture the frame of which he was about to enter as . . . what? A Knight Without Armor in a Savage Land? Some card-carrying Paladin? He hadn't reckoned that part yet.

Sometimes wisdom says ruckus. These Yoopers, the ones in his picture, with only errands in their eyes, hastening, snowshod, from one loneliness to another.

FACTAMENTA, STATISTICA, HISTORIANA

Prior to Étienne Brûlé—pronounced "Ateeyen Broolay"—the Keweenaw—pronounced "Key-wuh-nuh"—as the whole of Michigan's U.P., had been terra incognita. Tabula rasa as well. There was no history, not a recorded one, one written and/or published. So is unrecorded history really history? Franklyn wondered.

What there had been was the space and its silence, that broken only by oral tradition, collective memory, tribal legend, and personal exploit, now each as lost as musical notes to the air save to its few players and performers, keepers and tellers, the tongue-to-ear storyers who conveyed to their listeners what they might hear and hope to hold on to, memorize and preserve. For the Ojibwa, to possess the spoken word, display verbal facility and oral fluency, was to wield the first scepter of identity, so notice and recognition, so cachet, so power. Not by coincidence did so many preliterate cultures impress their counterparts as being possessed of subtler, suppler, more nuanced memories, as if their minds were tablets of stone and the spoken word a chisel.

What safely say, then, about such a history? Franklyn mused. That it would of necessity be agile, rhythmical, perhaps even rhyming? Playful? A game of crambo? That the spoken words employed in its telling would in their sequence and structure lend themselves most felicitously to retention, repetition, easy recognition? One could say little more, he thought. This matter of mnemonics.

Save that such history, however imperfectly or fragmentarily preserved, had gone wholly unshared save among the natives themselves. No Scheherazade. No *Thousand and One Nights*. No one else was listening, not even God. Not the Ice King. Not the North Wind himself. None wished to hear—deaf ears. The discipline of history is mystery. So perhaps the land knew, the bones scattered, strewn, forfeit to its darkness, a history in the bones. Did they gleam? Did they glow like radium in their beds beneath the earth? The land wasn't saying. Sentinel of secrets, centuries of seasons, seasons of silence.

Until Brûlé. Étienne (Stephen) Brûlé. It was Brûlé who gave first voice to the place, this Frenchman who, so Franklyn had gathered from Ivan's papers, was to the native Lake Superior Ojibwa—whom the French called Salteaux—much as Natty Bumppo had been to the Hudson River Valley Mohicans: First Listener, explorer, pathfinder, bush scout, interpreter, and *truchement*, paragon of the continent's fabled *voyageurs* and *coureurs de bois*.

It was Brûlé the dragoman who before Champlain and Nicolet, Sagard and Perrot, had been the first white to lay eyes upon Lake Superior, this inland hinterland sea comprising the largest body of fresh water in the world: 32,000 square miles of liquid, 2,700 linear miles of shoreline, 350 miles across, more than 1,300 feet deep, its 2,900 cubic miles of water more than the rest of the Great Lakes combined. As it was Brûlé who had been the first to set foot upon the Upper Peninsula and, in time, the Keweenaw—or *Kakiweonon*, as the Ojibwa pronounced it, "the place where they traverse a point of land."

That was 1620, give or take, by which time the Paris-born, illiterate, thirty-year-old Brûlé had been living among the Indians *as* an Indian for more than a decade. He spent the next three years on the futile scent of the *miskwabik*, the "red metal" or "magic stone" of the copper deposits rumored by them to be located somewhere along the lake's southern shores under the round-the-clock surveillance of *Gougou*, the cave-dwelling firebreather twice as high as a ship's mast. His verdict in the end: "'Tis the fag end of all creation, or I should rather say, its wreck." Not a nugget up-turned.

Eleven years later, the Indians killed him during a quarrel over the copper's still secret location before ceremoniously consuming his heart—an act, however savage, that was considered by them a tribute, as they were wont to cannibalize only the hearts of those they believed worthy of the compliment, a man's manliness, his courage and doughtiness being quali-ties they believed might literally be assimilated upon its consumption.

So the narrative had begun there, its Once upon a Time. Small won-der, thought Franklyn, that its opening paragraph was given over to the quest for copper and the spirit of violence that that quest, so time would tell, inevitably was to entail.

It was another forty years, according to Ivan's meticulously ordered chronology, before Fr. Dablon, a French Jesuit Indian missionary, pub-lished his uncannily accurate map of the region depicting the Keweenaw as a fifty-mile-wide peninsula vaulting talonlike from the mainland on the northeasterly diagonal a full seventy-five miles into Lake Superior, includ-ing, as he noted, "all places on this Lake where true red copper is said to be found." It was a cartographic feat that would go substantially unbettered over the next 150 years, years during which the copper lodes lay singly undisturbed, their quality a mystery, their extent unsuspected, while first the French, then the British, finally the American trade in fur and liquor among the Indians flourished unabated.

By the time Michigan became America's twenty-sixth state, in 1837, the Keweenaw, despite more than two hundred years of intermittent ru-mor and counterrumor regarding its "red gold," remained wholly trackless and equally uninhabited save for the Ojibwa and the "gallinippers," which vastly outnumbered them. The common wisdom? That the godforsaken place was uninhabitable by any but its indigenous timber wolves and black bears, deer, moose, lynx, beaver, and snowshoe hares, the red-tailed hawks and bald eagles.

And insects. The billions of blood-slurping, flesh-chewing insects, the Keweenaw being the only place on earth, so the jape, where you could be exsanguinated and/or cannibalized by skeeters while standing brow-deep in snow, and where they swarmed so thick in their schooling that it was said they could, as it had been documented on more than one occasion actually occurred, suffocate a horse.

Known in those days as Ultima Thule, "The Region of Perpetual Snows," the peninsula then boasted nary a single settlement, nor had a foot of its mosquito-infested wilderness interior been officially explored. In fact, the first such effort occurred only in 1840, the year state geologist Douglas Houghton undertook a series of scientific expeditions that eventually cost the delicate, five foot three, thirty-six-year-old father of two his life when his boat capsized in Superior's high-running seas during a post-sunset snow squall three miles off Eagle River.

Prior to his drowning, however, he had submitted to the state legislature his "Copper Report," a document that upon its public release the next year was so widely disseminated in newspapers, brochures, pamphlets, and various international journals that it occasioned the first broadscale mining rush in American history. The Lake Superior Copper Contagion, as it popularly was called—fever, boom, mania, grand dash, bonanza—gained significant momentum only two years later, when the Ojibwa ceded to the United States their remaining Michigan lands, some twenty-five thousand square miles, under the Treaty of La Pointe, clearing the way for the establishment both of a small federal military garrison, Fort Wilkins, at the peninsula's northernmost tip, and a U.S. mineral and land agency office at nearby Copper Harbor. The latter quickly became the staging arena for hundreds of prospecting forays into the interior, as it did, in 1850, the launching point of the first federal geological survey of the area that, upon its completion, set the price of land at $1.25 an acre.

As the rush peaked, then appeared to peter out in the summer of 1845 without a significant find, tent settlements and camp shanties began sprouting up a dozen miles south of Copper Harbor near both Eagle Harbor and Eagle River. And it was there, in March 1846, due east of the latter place, that a team of German miners, having driven an adit roughly seventy feet into the cliff face of the two-hundred-foot-high Greenstone Ridge near its trap-rock base, struck what it later described as "a great native mass," a mass so great that its separate slabs were found to weigh as much as fifty tons each. A year later, the site was being worked by more than one hundred miners employed by the Pittsburgh and Boston Mining Company. Two years after that, "the Cliff," as it was called, was yielding more than a million pounds of pure, native, mass copper a year.

At much the same time, a similar underground "mass" was discovered just off-peninsula, some sixty miles southwest near the Ontonagan River. Named "the Minesota Lode"—one "n," after the hastily assembled, New York–based company that owned it—it became by the early 1850s the richest copper mine in the world, one that shortly would disgorge a single, detached, 527-ton nugget forty-six feet long by twelve to nineteen feet thick, the size of a school bus, estimated to be worth some $150,000. Mineral rock is rated on a scale of one to ten according to its ductility, the low number being softest, the high number, diamond, for instance, hardest. Copper ranks a two. It required, using hammer and chisel, well over a year to break down the Minesota nugget and haul it to market.

Yet a third site, "the Central," was discovered five miles north of the Cliff and immediately proved so fruitful that it turned a profit during the maiden year of its operation, an unprecedented accomplishment.

If, as Franklyn recalled Tocqueville having remarked about America, "there is a sort of heroism in the greed for gain," then heroism was about to proliferate throughout the Keweenaw as it was swarmed at its eriferous north and south ends by the predictable steady stream of speculators, opportunists, fortune hunters, and profiteers, who in their wake spurred the equally predictable rudimentary gestures toward development. By 1862— shortly after a copper-mining section had been designated on the Boston Stock Exchange—Eagle River, seat of the newly formed Keweenaw County (formerly Houghton County's northmost half), boasted a population of three hundred. Copper Harbor, perched at its tip, was the site of four hotels, a general store that sold beef "by the carcass" for ten cents a pound, a church, and a lighthouse.

Still, while some one hundred joint-stock companies tried mining copper on the Keweenaw prior to the end of the Civil War, as did another two hundred freelance ventures, and though some few succeeded in producing an aggregate fifteen million pounds of copper a year—Keweenaw mines supplied some 70 percent of the copper used in the war, just as it accounted for fully three quarters of the nation's overall production—nine in ten failed, losing a cumulative $20 million in the process, four times more than they returned. In the sixty years between 1850 and 1910, investors poured roughly $60 million into roughly fifty companies, not one of which turned a penny of profit.

There were exceptions. The Minesota paid dividends of $1.75 million on an initial investment of $350,000. The Cliff, the stock of which peaked in 1858 at $300 a share, returned $2.5 million on $110,000, roughly 2,000 percent. But by 1870, both sites had played out—the Cliff never made it past a depth of 1,700 feet—and the entire enterprise was being written off as "the subterranean lottery," a phrase coined by Horace Greeley, who, after visiting the region, had chosen to invest heavily even in the face of the fledgling industry's first strike. A wildcat at the Cliff over wages, it lasted a week, accomplished nothing, and was blamed on what its managers called "the foreign portion of the mining populace." A skilled miner working six-day weeks and ten-to-eleven-hour shifts was then making roughly forty-five dollars a month.

Despite the spectacular, even sensational early success of a handful of "mass-fissure" mines, the future of copper mining on the Keweenaw circa, say, 1870, remained problematic. The reason was simple enough. Everyone insisted upon looking not only in the wrong place, either to the north or south, the vicinities where the initial discoveries had been made, but to the wrong form: the easily detectable, recognizable "mass." The single anomaly was the Pewabic Lode at the Quincy Hill site—"Pewabic" an Ojibwa word meaning "Iron Man"—near the twenty-two-mile-long Portage, along either steep bank of which the twin hamlets of Houghton and Hancock shortly were to rise and, in time, boomishly prosper. There, a new form, the amygdaloid—from the Greek for "almond-esque"—had been uncovered and, throughout the 1860s, begun slowly, if steadily, to produce.

At Quincy, copper was entombed in calcified lava-flow beds, basaltic lava sheets pocked with thousands of almond-shaped gas cavities—according to Ivan's notes, called "vesicles"—containing copper-particle deposits, or amygdules, bound much as nuts in a cake or plums in a pudding within its matrix of sedimentary rock layered deep beneath the glacial sand, silt, and boulder clay characteristic of this still largely neglected midsection of the peninsula. This was "low content rock"—no more than 2 to 4 percent copper, and that widely scattered and finely distributed—and it required new, more sophisticated technology to cost-effectively extract.

In time, the Copper Range—called by locals simply "the Range" or "the District," and which *ranged* along a quasi-serpentine seam thrusting diagonally southwest-to-northeast fully one hundred miles from the village of White Pine in western Ontonagon County through the heart of the Keweenaw on out to Copper Harbor—expanded to include nineteen lodes and more than sixty mines, each boasting a wildly varying number of individual shafts, each sitting athwart and transverse that seam's veins.

Still left unexplored and so untapped, however, was what would prove the peninsula's greatest mother lode—and singular salvation—the geological freak of the precipitously pitched (fifteen to eighty degrees; called "the dip") felsite "Great Conglomerate" main seam a dozen miles north of the Pewabic. A two-mile-long, twenty-foot-thick, sinuous cable of "native" copper—anfractuous as some prose—it wound, looped, torqued, and twisted through its surrounding thin strata of sandstone, shale, and pebblized pudding-stone.

But once the extent and nature of that underground umbilicus had been determined, the fate of the Keweenaw became, for the foreseeable future, fixed—cast, as it were, in copper. The Calumet Conglomerate, a name soon to be invoked only in hushed, even reverential tones, was about to become not only the most valuable lode ever discovered in the Copper Range—as, too, the largest single deposit of native pure copper in the world—but for the ensuing quarter of a century and beyond, the source of the most profitable subterranean copper store on earth.

The Conglomerate, insofar as Franklyn could ascertain, had shaped the fate of the future of the land beneath which it lay wombed as surely as its harbor had determined that of New York City or the Mississippi River that of New Orleans. By 1875, the Conglomerate's sixth year of production, of the eight thousand adult males living on the Keweenaw, well over five thousand of them were employed in the copper industry, half of those by the company newly organized to work the Conglomerate *virtually* exclusively (the bootstrap, upstart Tamarack Company shortly would sink six shafts of its own hard alongside), Boston-based Calumet and Hecla.

By then, the peninsula had grown so "civilized," that of Keweenaw County's 540 square miles, almost four hundred acres qualified as "improved"—"scalped," in the local vernacular—and the peninsula as a whole could count among its burgeoning population of 25,000, 30 doctors, 11 lawyers, and 80 saloon-keepers, the latter a number coincidentally matched by schoolteachers. That year alone, C&H, as Calumet and Hecla universally was known, paid out $1.6 million to its shareholders, its fourteen mines yielding more than twenty million pounds of copper a year— the Pewabic, by comparison, hovered around two million—90 percent of the industry's nationwide total. Hecla, by the way, more properly "Hekla," referred to the 4,890-foot active Icelandic volcano (63.98 N, 19.70 W), rather than to the name of the Norwegian yellow butterfly, *Colias hecla*; in the ancient Norse, *hecla* means "volcanic cloud" or, more colloquially, "gateway to hell."

Having sprung "fully panoplied like Minerva from the head of Jove to a commanding position among the wondrous treasure vaults of man," as Michigan's commissioner of minerals put it, the Calumet Conglomerate seemed overnight to have become a behemoth, one global in its reach, albeit one brought to harness and heel only upon the bent backs and laved brows of those who at mortal risk to body and soul alike—and for roughly two dollars per twelve-hour day, unless you were a twelve-year-old boy, in which case you made perhaps half that—literally laddered down each day in the dark to pry by hand from ever deeper beneath the earth, right rock.

And what was right, always was red, the red gold, precisely that referenced in volume 23, number 2, of the *Mineralogical Record*, viz., *Copper crystals from the Calumet and Hecla Conglomerate are usually of the textrahexahedral form. Silver crystallized as cubes modified by the textrahexahedron* h *in small crystals and as elongated, twinned, textrahexahedrons in large crystals. Associated minerals include calcite, quartz, epidote, pumpellyite, members of the chrorite group and, rarely, powellite and barite.*

A matter of getting to it, getting at it, freeing it up, fetching it forth, hauling it out, sorting it through, crushing it small, stamping it clean (using such arcane devices as Evans bundles, Collom jigs, Wilfley tables, et cetera), smelting it pure into ingots and cakes, chuting it out, shunting it on, shipping it east. That there was real wealth to be generated, stupendous profit to be turned, untold reward to be reaped, individual fortunes to be made, all shortly would come to understand, but none of it, not a red copper's worth withal that this backwash, backwoods, godforsaken wilderness place consented to yield it. And what *this* place yielded, always, ever, was only such of itself as it might be *coerced* into yielding.

Deep within, down below, underground, bound-up tight, locked sight unseen far inside the very nethermost quim of the earth, was a bank. And the mighty vastness of its assets, that red bullion, none—neither C&H's founder Quincy Shaw nor its president Alexander Agassiz—might rightly imagine. The northern outback beneath which that bank reposed, the thornveld of that prodigious bush, was a woman who flowed red only as she was content to burn down or bury any who might presume first to break her wide and more widely open, be it with plunger, pickax, hammer or drill, phalli of dynamite or seed of black powder. Each day, day after day, new virgin, over and over again.

It was not until 1893, nearly a quarter century after the company had been up and running—along the way paying out a cumulative $40 million in dividends, an indisputably handsome sum—that C&H bestirred itself to issue its first policy statement to shareholders. Entitled *Sketch of the Calumet and Hecla Mining Company*, the mottled, dog-eared copy Ivan had included for Franklyn's perusal disclosed that "the operation" included C&H-owned lands totaling 23,939 acres in contiguous Keweenaw, Houghton, and Ontonagon counties; 698 company-owned houses; 941 employee-owned homes on company-leased land—a figure that had doubled by 1913; another 3,500 company houses that were employee rented, typically at five dollars a month or eighty cents a room; one company-owned hotel; six company-financed schools, including the only high school, which catered to "practical," vocational, and manual training; and twenty company-financed churches on company-leased land.

Additional company-owned "surface structures" included sawmills, machine, blacksmith, and carpenter shops, foundries, warehouses, barns and stables, powder-houses, shafthouses, engine-houses, hoist-houses, boiler-houses, and eight rock-houses where extracted bulk rock was crushed to manageable size before being conveyed by company-owned railroad—nine engines, four hundred rock cars, 18.5 miles of track—to the company-owned stamp mill four miles away at Torch Lake. A company-financed library was on the drawing boards, as was a natatorium, bathhouse and sauna, health club, bowling alley, baseball diamonds, ice- and roller-skating rinks, a company-run hospital and company-built armory to be leased to the state. The "Outfit" provided, gratis, for heating, lighting, water, sewer, and trash removal.

As Franklyn pored over the report, a single word kept recurring to him, that French one, *ressentiment*, the rancor *secretly* harbored and *covertly* expressed against one's benefactors. One might, he thought, perforce compose upon the subject a brief, not unpleasant riff.

THE RIFF

Being somewhat familiar with his John Stuart Mill, Franklyn knew that roughly fifty years earlier he had written (in *On Liberty*) that

> the only purpose for which power can be rightfully exercised over
> any member of a civilized community, against his will, is to pre-

vent harm to others. His own good, either physical or moral, is not a sufficient warrant. He cannot rightfully be compelled to do or forbear because it will be better for him to do so, because it will make him happier, because in the opinion of others to do so would be wise or even right. The only part of the conduct of anyone for which he is amenable to society is that which concerns others. In the part which merely concerns himself, his independence is of right, absolute, over himself. Over his own body-mind, the individual is sovereign.

In light of which certain questions suggested themselves. Such as, is it possible to be free and dependent at once? Can freedom of ends flourish where dependence of means thrives? Can one acquiesce in one's own autonomy? Can one do another's bidding by that other's sufferance (even as its object may coincide with one's own) without its breeding a welling resentment? Who ought define whatever is meant by "the social good"—a notion typically construed by nation-states to mean law, order, and security, as it is by economic entities to mean unrestricted enterprise, corporate free play, and "justifiable" avarice—and to what extent ought that "good," insofar as it may be said to exist beyond the mental construct of its constructionists, proscribe individual behavior, whether salutary, indifferent, or reprehensible?

How does one learn to exercise right judgment in the making of choices unless one is permitted, mistakenly or otherwise, to choose? And who defines "mistakenly"? Who is to be trusted with the determination of one's self-interest if not the self *it*self? If one consciously, mindfully, deliberately pursues self-derangement—of each of the senses, say—as one may determine such pursuit is to the benefit of one's welfare, or *not*, is that not one's prerogative? Suicide may not be right—or it may in fact be wholly that and that alone—but is it *a* right?

For anyone or anything *else* to impose choices unilaterally, then, ex cathedra upon another, was, in accord with this logic, an act of coercion, where not a violation, not only of that other's intelligence, but of his individuality, singularity, his humanness, its essence, potential, capacity. To treat a theoretical equal as a practical inferior could be only to indulge in moral superiority at the expense of another's liberty, to reduce that other's person(hood) to the means to another's end by depriving that other of choice, self-determination, and the exercise of his free will to conduct

himself in accordance with or contrary to his conscience, however idio-
syncratic, inconstant, contradictory, or perversely contrary.

Conditional love, thought Franklyn, might still be love, but loving
control still was control—the velvet whip is still a whip and the back it
would lash is the same—and control was paternalism's raison d'être: to, in
effect, bribe one into *voluntarily* submitting to bow one's head, as through
the hoop of a noose, *willingly* to the yoke *by one's own hand*. Because father, like master, knows best.

Smothered by a satin pillow or buried alive beneath a ton of fallen
rock, what dies stays dead, does it not?

"'Should a man come to my house with the conscious design of doing
me good,'" Franklyn recalled Thoreau having written, "'I should run for
my life.'"

And this was quite so, thought Franklyn, for the road to hell was
paved with and more harm done by those who would do good than all the
scoundrels in the world. Not for others to monopolize the "good" or capitalize upon its doing. Not for others to define another's needs and desires
as it might suit them because they and they alone might satisfy them, at
their convenience, by their connivance.

"Woe unto thee who would pretend to help men," Franklyn thought.
"And doubly woe unto thee who would presume to control and carrot
them to his personal gain thereby."

Paternalism was bad alchemy. It patronized, condescended, dwarfed,
made a man feel less of himself. How know what one might be or become
deprived of the license to know it? To do wrong. Or right. Or neither. Or
both.

Why C&H would choose deliberately to manipulate the lapis of its
philosopher's stone in such a fashion, then, so literally to lord over and
overlord every phase of life on the Keweenaw sunup to sundown—going
so far, according to Ivan, to assert ownership over time itself by setting its
company clocks a half-hour ahead of "world time" expressly to capitalize
on "working daylight"—to so willfully cultivate such slavish reliance upon
its largesse, would need be one part of his story. Need be, that is, if he was
going to presume to craft one approaching some approximation of the
truth.

Reading further, Franklyn could not help but notice that the report
enumerated that by 1893, a total of eighteen working shafts—a number
that soon was to more than double—had been sunk at intervals down an

avenue cutting southwest to northeast some nine thousand feet along the surface, fanning out still wider underground, and that a 13.5-mile honeycomb of tunnels had been excavated, a figure that by the time Franklyn arrived was approaching one hundred. The newest shaft, Red Jacket—its main hoist-engine-house, the report boasted, contained "the largest and most powerful hoisting engine ever built," an eight-thousand-horsepower, quadruple-drum beast capable of winching up a ten-ton load at sixty feet per second—recently had "cut the lode" after fours years of "sinking" at roughly 3,300 feet, the fifty-seventh "level," "bottoming" at a total depth of 4,970 feet, virtually a mile underground (though eventually subshafts were to be driven that would take her down to the ninety-sixth level, some 9,700 feet—1.8 miles—"the deepest vertical shaft in the world").

By the middle of 1897, according to the figures Ivan had compiled, C&H in its quarter century of existence had produced exactly 1,176,276,471 pounds of refined copper. Two years later, it paid out $10 million in dividends, a historic high, the average payout being $10 thousand per shareholder, a princely sum. By 1900, while neighboring Quincy stock was peaking at $189 a share, C&H was selling at more than $900. But if one had bought in on day one, then stood pat, one had received dividends over that time totaling more than ninety times the value of one's original investment. And if, in 1900, one chose to sell those original shares, one would be cashing out at a profit 110 times that of what they first had cost.

Not that such shares were easy to come by. More than one third of them were owned by just four of Brahmin Boston's first families, the Shaws, Agassizes, Higginsons, and Cabots, each of whom philanthropically funneled large portions of their profits into such cultural institutions as the Boston Symphony Orchestra and the Harvard University Museum. Their prerogative, of course. They had every right to do so, and in so doing they benefited Bostonians, New Englanders, and other Easterners enormously. But perhaps those whose brute labor kept such institutions afloat could be pardoned for damning, as they typically did, "absentee ownership" and the shanghaiing of such wealth as they might have preferred to see invested in making the Keweenaw less . . . Keweenaw-ish. Not one in twenty shares outstanding were owned by those who actually lived on and worked the peninsula. That said, it was C&H that almost single-handedly kept the range in business. Without it, the district at large would scarcely have broken even.

And then, just as the cash cow appeared *so* cash laden, the golden goose *so* gilded that it was impossible to imagine it ever playing itself out, it did—or began to. Copper mines out west, particularly in Montana, the porphyries so-called, were opened up and quickly began not only outproducing U.P. mines but doing so at lower cost. And, while C&H's share of the American market remained highly profitable, it had dwindled to roughly one quarter by 1905, less than one fifth six years later, and a mere 17 percent two years after that.

Then, too, as shafts were sunk ever deeper—the average mine depth in 1913 was four thousand feet—not only did rock become harder and denser, but its copper content declined, "pinched down," as was said, so that that which had contained well above 50 percent copper in 1900—latterly called "Lake" copper, native, pure, to distinguish it from the West's inferior "electrolytic" or refined type—yielded well below 40 percent seven years later. In 1913, from a ton of rock you could expect to refine but fifteen to twenty pounds of ore.

It rapidly was becoming prohibitively expensive to copper-mine. Indeed, the industry remained a viable one in the U.P. owing to a single factor, one over which it exerted negligible control, yet upon which it was singularly dependent: high market demand. The country was in the midst of electrifying itself coast to coast, and consumption of copper—as, too, the price it was fetching per pound, nineteen cents—was at its peak.

At first, such developments scarce resonated, much less repercussed on the peninsula. In his address at the Red Jacket town hall in the summer of 1904, Gene Debs had, according to the clipping Ivan had included, been quoted in the *Copper Country Evening News* to the effect that "what pleases me most is that everything here operates in harmony with no cause for any decided change in the workings. The improvements which this country has undergone since my last visit here seven years ago, the number of large buildings erected, streets paved, utilities uniformly supplied, are a good sign that the people here are prospering. The Keweenaw Peninsula is much blessed in having such a staple product as copper with which to supply the world." Which, if nothing else, was a singularly shortsighted comment in light of mine ownership itself having publicly commented at the time that "were you in need of a business model for an enterprise in which it is impossible to maintain growth and maximize profits, you could scarcely do better than a mine."

That same year, U.P. Copper Range mines counted roughly 16,500 men on their collective payroll, 90 percent of them on the Keweenaw, 85 percent of them foreign born. Three years later, that number had increased by another five thousand, and for the first time in C&H history a single share of stock sold for one thousand dollars. The boom times, it appeared, were primed to continue booming. In fact, as ownership was only too aware, the boom already was well on toward becoming a bubble, as it knew, too, that a bubble, unlike a boom, too easily bursts: *ka*-boom.

Once again it was the numbers that told. The 5,700 men employed by C&H in 1906—3,500 of them underground—produced roughly 100 million pounds of copper. Six years later, 1,500 fewer men—2,000 underground—produced 30 million fewer pounds. That same year, the range as a whole, all eighteen companies, produced an aggregate 250 million pounds. The point being, that for C&H to remain on a competitive footing, for it to maintain its declining share of the market, it would need to tend with renewed vigor to its economies of scale, belt-tighten, retrench, improve efficiency, modernize, technologize, institute reclamation projects, all in the name of squeezing more blood from less stone. It would need, too, to acquire, consolidate, gobble up, and digest as many of the existing Copper Range mines as it might manage.

And to accomplish all this, it was determined—which is to say, C&H president Alexander Agassiz unilaterally decided—that it would need a transfusion of "fresh, copper-enriched blood" of its own, a new paterfamilias, new padrone, patroon and pontiff. It would need his handpicked, self-anointed wunderkind. It would need James "Big Jim" MacNaughton.

BIG JIM

Ivan having made the "great" man's personal acquaintance prior to his own departure from the *Kivini*, the Keweenaw, for Chicago, half a dozen years earlier, he had had occasion to mention the Canadian-born, Keweenaw-reared MacNaughton to Franklyn a number of times, if only in passing.

Big Jim, then thirty-seven, had come aboard as early as the summer of '01, vowing, according to Ivan, "to teach men, if I must, how to eat potato parings." This was just two years before the twenty-one-year-old Molek had himself arrived in Calumet, a *rojak*, countryman, fresh from Slovenia, *stara kontra*, the old country, by way of the Pennslavnia coalfields and steel mills to work the copper mines, lose an arm, learn English, turn socialist, and, eventually, edit *Glasnik*, the "Herald," before quitting over the priest scandal and moving to Chicago.

Product of a year each at Ohio's progressive Oberlin College and the University of Michigan, where he studied engineering, MacNaughton had been general manager of the state's richest iron mine, the Chapin in Iron Mountain, 120 miles south, when Agassiz—who had known Big Jim's father, Arch, when he had run the Lake Linden terminus of the railroad where the company had its stamp mills and where eleven-year-old Jamie had worked the coal docks for a dollar a day and, later, sixteen-year-old Jim had worked as a switch-tender—lured him to C&H at an annual starting salary of $85,000, that much again in company stock, written assurance that his would be "final say" in "all matters concerning day to day operations at the Lake," and the promise of promotion to both the GM's job and a company vice presidency, "to be compensated accordingly as the time shall come."

"All business, all company, all soldier, all command, hard as iron nails, all flint," had been Ivan's impression. "All Protestant, Republican, fierce Highland Scot. Hates unions. Unionism. Believes they are the devil, un-American. Conspiracy, that is his word. Red agitation, those are his words. He, MacNaughton, only MacNaughton knows best. Everyone knows him there, all the men. They know he is fearless, so they fear him. Not respect, fear. Himself, that is their name for him, the Great Himself. Famous, his temper, red as his hair. The men say so great his anger is, he could bite in two a steel hoist rope.

"Famous his ambition, too. Up there he is *kralj*, king, King *Kivini*. Fingers in everything, fist over all. Politics, power, he owns. The Outfit pays 90 percent local taxes, so MacNaughton picks candidate, MacNaughton controls vote, MacNaughton wears crown—'Chairman County Supervisor.' Eight years now he sits that throne, no rival. *Papez*. Pope. *Vsevedni* and *vsemogochni*. Omniscient and omnipotent. Any challenge to his position, authority, is personal. Challenge to him is coup, coup d'état.

"That is a hard place. MacNaughton is harder. You will see when you go to shake his hand."

He also, had Big Jim, been a six-time-elected state representative to the Republican National Convention and continued to chair the board of directors of both the Mineral Range, and the Duluth, South Shore, and Atlantic railroads.

It was MacNaughton, again according to Ivan's notes, to whom President Agassiz had written a most revealing memo. How Ivan had gotten ahold of a copy, Franklyn could not feature, but there it was, a fully intact carbon lifted from official company letterhead, dated Nov. 10, 1901.

"All trouble at the Lake is our own fault," it read.

> We have let circumstances slip. We have been too soft. We too often have chosen the carrot over the stick. Lack of force will be our undoing. Where there exists dissent or discord among employees, it must be swiftly and decisively <u>crushed</u>. Peace is the object but always on our own terms and without negotiation, compromise, doubt, or hesitation. Lay down the law as we may determine, then enforce it to the hilt. Consistent, constant assertion of resolve and resolution is the only way to remain in charge of our interests.
>
> Yield not so much as <u>one inch</u> of our authority in <u>any</u> affair where such interest is at issue lest we lose our advantage and in so doing loose the Red dogs of rebellion and servile insurrection. We cannot be dictated to by anyone.
>
> The key to continued economic health is keeping wages low. Next year will be the first in our history that we will produce less than 50 percent of Lake copper. Wages will be raised whenever <u>we</u> see fit and at <u>no</u> other time. The man who does not like it can seek employment elsewhere or go straight to hell. Let him find his bread and butter there.
>
> There exist three laws and only three: expand reserves, reduce costs, increase production.

It was MacNaughton who had created the company's first "Efficiency Department" two years earlier, as it was MacNaughton who over the preceding decade had spurned all demands to recognize the unionization of "his" workers by the Wobblies and the WFM—by 1913, some five locals and seven thousand to nine thousand members throughout the range, collected under the umbrella Copper Country Trade Union 16, the leadership of which it had pleased MacNaughton to confer with exactly . . . never.

It likewise was MacNaughton who had doubled the percentage of underground mine "captains"—uniformly Cornishmen—deployed to more vigilantly police output and production, as it was MacNaughton who had hired labor spies called "covert operatives" to infiltrate and monitor "his" workers. As it was MacNaughton who had made it official company policy to hire "no more Red Flag Nigger Findlanders"—C&H boasted of employing the lowest percentage of Finns of any mining company in the U.P. As it was MacNaughton who had created an off-the-books, under-the-table slush fund of ten thousand dollars earmarked for the exclusive purpose of buying favorable coverage in the local, state, and national press, including—how did Ivan know these secret, unsavory things?—four thousand dollars a year to the Detroit *Free Press's* political reporter, H. A. Gilmartin.

So, of course, it also was MacNaughton who more recently had introduced the lightweight, one-man, Leyner percussive, hammer-and-water, hollow-bit sink drill. Coined "the widowmaker" by those miners who bitterly opposed it, the labor-saving device threatened to slash by one half the number of requisite skilled miner positions, since the heavier, more cumbersome Rand air-piston drill—it weighed all of three hundred pounds—the one routinely in use for the past thirty years, had required the skills of a two-man team plus a "drill boy" or "tool nipper" properly to operate.

That the new drill made economic sense was inarguable. Words may lie, but numbers do not, and the numbers favoring its implementation were as irrefutable as they had been thirty years earlier when the Rand drill had replaced the old hand drills and production had leaped 20 percent with a corresponding 20 percent reduction in workforce.

Where with the two-man/one-boy drill it had cost almost $8 to mine a "foot" of copper, with the new drill it cost less than $3.50. Where with the two-man drill a miner could drill less than half a foot per shift, with the new drill he could top over a foot and a half. Where with the two-man drill a miner broke or "stoped" 3,500 tons of copper "stamp rock" a year, with the new drill he stoped over six. Had MacNaughton not insisted upon the introduction of the new technology—already in universal use out West—he would, it seemed plain to Franklyn, have been in criminal dereliction of his professional responsibilities. The John Henry myth might make for good balladeering, but it made for bad business.

Not to say that there weren't problems. The new drill might weigh less than half of its predecessor, but at 140 pounds it was still heavy. Its water-injection system tamped the rock dust down—and so lessened the risk of contracting silicosis—but also rendered what had been merely a dusty job—one performed in eighty-five-degree heat and 90 percent humidity—a muddy, sloppy, slippery one instead. The amount of vibration the new drill produced was measurably higher than the old one and so commensurately more likely to dislodge loose rock. More provocatively still, it flew in the face of the entrenched tradition—one first established in the tin mines of Cornwall whence the Cousin Jacks had imported it intact when they arrived in the Keweenaw some seventy years before—of working in teams.

Copper miners, the Macedonian included, were unaccustomed to working alone. Such lone-wolfing largely was unheard-of. Not only did the heavy Rand drill make solo work impracticable, but, much as police officers often work in pairs or with partners, so the miners' buddy system encourage that same fraternal on-the-job ethic, a culture of camaraderie, one of backup and safety net that fostered the formation of underground families—father working with son, brother alongside brother, cousin helping cousin.

It placed a man psychologically less at mortal risk to know that if something went horribly wrong, if unsound hanging rock (shelf, roof, wall) fell, or bad ground floor collapsed, if dynamite went awry, or dry pine timber treated with zinc-chloride whitewash—whether vertical stull, horizontal cross-tie, square set, roof lagging, cribbing, or sill (some shafts were so elaborately timbered they resembled subterranean forest)—caught fire or gave way, if a drill bit broke and became a flying iron missile, or a high-speed tram cart (also called an ore dump or rock skip) piled with two and a half tons of rock leaped its track at eight miles per hour and went runaway, that there were a pair of hawk eyes, hare ears, and hawser arms beside him to attend to his succor. This was some of the noisiest, dirtiest, most air-befouled, badly lit, rat-infested, dangerous work on or inside earth, and any one of a thousand things might go wrong that could cost a man his life and his family its breadwinner.

Once again, the numbers. Whence Ivan had pried them Franklyn did not know, nor could he find anything in the file indicating their source, although he knew it was precisely this sort of data that it was Haywood's custom to wield to his union's advantage. Not that he did not trust to their accuracy. It was not in either man's character to fabricate or fudge.

In the 1850s, 12 men died underground.

In the 1860s, 54.

In the 1870s, 106.

In the 1880s, 195.

In the 1890s, 284.

In the 1900s, 511.

From 1905 to 1911, underground fatalities numbered 61 a year, more than one per week. The worker who died was an uninsured thirty-four-year-old "timberman," a married father of five, and foreign born, typically Slovene, Italian, Cornish, or Finnish, the four groups that in descending order constituted most of the underground workforce. Interestingly, Ivan had handwritten on the angle across the margin on the page that listed these statistics: "Cornishmen accept. Part of job. Comes with territory. Gives pride. Others complain. Finns loudest."

Simple math might reveal that the rate of death per men employed was no greater than in the past, that the rate of death per amount of copper produced was at an all-time low, that Keweenaw mines were, in terms of fatalities, significantly safer than those out West, and that 1912 had seen a precipitous decline in deaths, to thirty-six. But such statistics were cold comfort to the workers and their families. Perception is reality—old saw and dull, but true—and the perception in the summer of 1913 was that more men were dying violent deaths; that the mines, owing to the new drills, were increasingly hazardous; and that the man responsible for the deteriorating conditions was "the Chief," James MacNaughton.

Besides, as Ivan's notes underscored, examining mortality rates scarce told the whole story. A man who worked an entire year underground might have but a one-in-two-hundred chance of being killed in that time, but his likelihood of being maimed, mutilated, and injured so severely that he either lost his job entirely or was forced to take temporary leave was one in three, the highest rate for any profession in the world. Whether a miner was disposed to make one's peace with the fact, as were the Cornish, or wont to protest and buck against it, as were the Slovenes, Italians, and more radical Finns, the mines were a dark, filthy, perilous business. Each time he descended, six days in seven, a man rolled the dice with his life, the very life he was laying on the proverbial line for sixty dollars a month if he was a trammer, seventy-five dollars a month if he was a miner.

MacNaughton could spin his ciphering as it might please him, or bluster, as according to Ivan he once had done in a public lecture: "If a man gets rattled and runs into danger, or if a man fails to use good judgment and stands in the way of danger, it would seem to me that these are contingencies we cannot provide against as long as we continue to use men in the mine, and as far as I have observed, two thirds of our underground accidents are the result of worker carelessness pure and simple—

call it fear deficiency, if you wish—and, in fact, the longer some of our men work in the mines, the more careless they become; the job always has entailed some degree of risk; the men well know this; if they wish to work, they must assume it," in the end, the mines remained the mines. They could kill, and did, more often than not abruptly, remorselessly, horribly, down deep in the dark and the dirt amid the ravening razor-toothed hunger of rats where thousands of men sweated and bled, pissed, spat, chundered, and shat, out of sight of the sun, nor a breath of fresh air to breathe for one's noisome and sulfurous last.

Another of Ivan's files, one labeled simply "LABOR," proved a relatively arid, needlessly detailed recitation of the history of the Western Federation of Miners, the WFM, the union that latterly had become increasingly active in its efforts to organize Copper Range workers. Franklyn was familiar enough with the WFM from his days at the *Trib* to know that it had been foaled from the often bloody difficulties surrounding the "labor wars" in the hard-metal mines of Idaho, Montana, Colorado, Utah, and South Dakota some twenty years before. Widely acknowledged as the most politically radical, tactically militant of all American labor organizations—it boasted some two hundred locals and thirty thousand members out West, where it had won its first strike, the Haywood-led, 1894 Cripple Creek, Colorado, action, and eight years later had secured for Utah's miners the nation's first eight-hour workday—its initial efforts in the U.P. a decade earlier had met, if not with stiff resistance, then with something less than modest success.

The four ad hoc Keweenaw locals it had succeeded in nascently establishing in 1904 either were dead or moribund a year later, a fact painfully apparent from the contents of a letter Ivan had included from M. E. Condon, head of the fledgling Red Jacket local, to Bill Haywood. Dated May 1905, mere months before Haywood's arrest and subsequent year-and-a-half imprisonment in Idaho on the Steunenberg assassination/murder charge, its concluding sentence spoke volumes: "And so, unionism in this place appears for now to be an utter failure where not an outright scandal in which our officials feel free to decamp with local treasuries."

Paternalism is a high-wire act, and no small part of the genius of Jim MacNaughton's aerial routine was to succeed in convincing those who worked for him not only that they were privileged to be doing so, but that they were the blue-chip best of their professional lot. That to be working

for C&H was to enjoy not only job security replete with the material benefits above and beyond industry norms accruing thereto, but the conferral
of prestige, self-respect, and pride.

Insofar as the chief could keep worker expectations low—and
gratitude-cum-loyalty high—he could regularly exceed them, and the
patrons of paternalism could without fear of interference—what Mac-
Naughton was fond of calling "outside agitation," a phrase Franklyn could
not help noticing had in company correspondence eventually been discarded in favor of "terrorist subversion"—persist in purveying their benevolent bill of goods to its beneficiaries, who, however "pinned fast beneath
the velvet thumb," as Ivan put it, were only too glad to purchase them.

A gun had been jumped. It had not been time, yet, in 1905, to endeavor to resolve the internal contradiction—charity of the giver equals
shame of the receiver—that reposed at the heart of such an algebra. For
the time being, the equation, however specious the calculation upon which
it so precariously balanced, held steadfastly unchallenged. Forty percent of
C&H employees had worked for the Outfit fifteen to forty-five years; another third were the sons of fathers who had. Fifty years of memory can
kink a lot of cable, and webs of codependency a half century in the spinning are not so easily unspun, particularly where that web is perceived as
resembling a womb.

Having affiliated itself with the muscle of the IWW in the meantime,
the WFM reappeared on the Keweenaw in the fall of 1908, where it found
that the soil for its sowing had become marginally more fertile. A local
Socialist Club had been created. A slate of socialist candidates latterly had
contested in the Houghton County elections, albeit uniformly without success. Several socialist newspapers were being published; neighboring Hancock's Finnish-language daily, *Tyomies*, the "Worker" or "Workingman,"
boasted a circulation of ten thousand. The Quincy mines had since suffered a three-week wildcat blamed by management on "Socialist Finns
and Italians," and a Finnish trammer strike at the old Minesota mine in
adjacent Ontonagon County had resulted not only in the shooting deaths
of two strikers, but in the closing of the three-hundred-man mine.

Throughout 1909 and 1910, vetted by half a dozen of its more seasoned
organizers, four new WFM locals were established, the largest and most
active at Hancock, no. 200, and at Red Jacket, no. 203, though their collective membership scarcely topped three hundred. According to Ivan, while
MacNaughton went so far as to employ paid informants to monitor their

activities, he expediently chose to pursue no overtly provocative action against them.

In yet another copy of another remarkable letter from the file, Mac-Naughton had written to Agassiz,

> I do not underestimate the nature of our opposition or potential challenge to our authority, but there is nothing in the entire situation here that causes me worry or a moment's lost sleep or missed meal. I will continue to deal with our workers as I ever have— namely, as they <u>deserve</u> to be dealt with. As for any other issue they choose to inject into our affairs, I shall simply <u>throw it out.</u>
>
> I have no intention of duplicating the lamentable fate of our dear friend Collins, but I know our men as I know, too, the nature of the outside agitators and terrorists, and I know that the lawlessness, rioting, physical assault, destruction of private property, and the murder most foul and bloody that the latter would urge upon the former shall find no good standing or willing ear here.
>
> Michigan is not Colorado, Calumet is not Telluride, C&H is not the Smuggler-Union, I am not Collins. Any dynamite here shall confine itself to its proper use—deep beneath the earth, and singly to our profit. So long as the agitators only meddle and dare not menace, so long as the home office continues to close rank behind my decisions as I may determine they redound to its benefit, we needn't concern ourselves that anything that shall arise here cannot be handled to a right finish.
>
> If a fight is to come, then may it please God let it. Let this Haywood come here and find, as he found with our good compatriot, Wells, what awaits his coming. There can only be one outcome—the one I bring about. I know this to be so. In due time, so shall Haywood and his lot.

Mention of dynamite, Collins, Wells, Telluride, the Smuggler-Union, as Franklyn well knew, were explicit references to the exceptionally bloody WFM-led strike at the Smuggler-Union gold mine in Telluride, Colorado, during the protracted course of which the superintendent's office had been dynamited and Arthur Collins, the mine's general manager, shotgunned to death in his living room—by whom, it never was determined—back-shot through a window as he played poker with cronies while holding two pair, aces and eights, spades and clubs, the so-called dead man's hand.

Begun in the spring of 1901, the strike had drug on through the autumn of 1904 when Collins's replacement, MacNaughton's close friend and long-standing correspondent—he had married a Livermore, one of the Boston Brahmin families heavily invested in C&H—the Harvard-educated, polo-playing Bulkeley "Buck" Wells, having narrowly escaped assassination himself, had succeeded in prevailing upon the Republican governor, James Peabody, to deploy five hundred state militiamen who promptly rounded up and bullpenned the strikers at bayonet point, cattled them beneath both mounted Gatling and Nock Volley guns en masse aboard boxcars, and conveyed them out of town literally on a rail. Having arrested and briefly jailed Haywood, Wells then proceeded to mass-hire permanent replacement scab workers, not a few of them from Michigan.

For the WFM a humiliating defeat, for Big Bill Haywood a personal failure, and for Big Jim MacNaughton an object lesson indelible, one he was never to forget, or forswear.

PASTY

Ana Clemenc built a mean pasty. As the Cornish said, "She 'ad a 'ansum 'and at it," this most traditional Cornish meal of miners. The Cornish quip was ancient: "The devil himself is afraid to come into Cornwall for fear of being baked in a pasty," as was the nursery rhyme:

> *Pasty rolled out like a plate,*
> *Piled with turmut, tates, and mate,*
> *Doubled up and baked like fate:*
> *That's the Cornish Pasty.*

Ethnicity aside, everyone who worked underground carried pasty—pronounced "pass-tee"—or, occasionally, slangily, called "oggy"—in their lunch pail. De rigueur. And don't, for fear of scorn, ridicule, derision, and wrath, call it a meat pie or, lord forbid, turnover or tart. Wives, mothers, sisters, daughters, aunts, if your man worked the mines, you, as the saying went, "baked pasty," this art to be mastered. It had been among the first recipes Ana's mother had taught her, along with *zlikrofi*, the Slovene potato, onion, and bacon ravioli, and the dreaded *zganci*, the buckwheat porridge that reminded her of week-old sweat.

As a rule, Slovenes were natural bakers and pastry chefs. Their *potica*—pronounced "po-teet-sa"—was famous throughout the Keweenaw, the savory strudel roll enriched with walnuts and honey. Nor were they strangers to performing white magic with *biftek* and *svinjina*, beef and pork; their *burek z mesom* was a sort of second cousin to the pasty; they called it meat pastry. Had a way with potatoes as well, their celebrated cubed *francoska* garlique. And Ana, as Josef could attest, uniformly virtuoso at them all.

Upon the pasty there were version and variation, and so endless and spirited debate, debate that had grown only fiercer over time. About purse or pocket shape: oblong, rectangular, squarish, round. About size: six-inch, eight-inch, ten. About thickness, height, density. About crust, *croust* in Cornish: made with strong flour or plain, with suet, lard, or butter. About what proportion fat to flour: one half, one third, one fifth. About the crimp of the dough: on top or along the sides, tight enough to keep the devil out or loose enough to let him back out once in. Thin ridge or thick, steam slit or full seal. About texture and consistency: short crust, flaky, hard, or soft. About ingredients: meat, potatoes, turnips, onions, shallots—yes, all agreed, but rutabagas, called by the Cornish "swede"? Leeks? Carrots? Peas? And what sort of meat? Beef or pork, or both? What cut: fillet, rump, shoulder, shin, blade, skirt, chuck. In chunks? Cubes? Slices? Diced small or large? Chopped? Minced? Ground? Sausaged? Old potatoes or new, in slivers or slices or shavings? And what proportion of vegetable to meat? Fifteen percent of the latter? Twenty percent? More? And what proportion of each vegetable to every other. Add parsley for flavor or forgo? Celery? Kidney? Garlic or no? Salt? Pepper? How much and how so? And in what order layer in the ingredients of the filling? Onion first, or turnip? Potato next, or onion? Meat on top, in between, bottommost? Or spread about? And what of the exterior brush or wash? Egg? Milk? Water? Some combination? Complicated business.

There was a rumor then about that some cooks actually were doing the unthinkable: infusing a sauce or gravy into the mix through the pie's posterior, act of barbarism and apostasy. There even was controversy over whether the self-contained, free-standing meal was properly eaten held in the hand, like a burger, or only with knife and fork. There were jokes, japes, jabs, curses, even the occasional cat- and fistfight.

Ana knew she required exactly ninety minutes to properly prepare, fix, bake, establish the rote of her rhythmic routine: forty-five minutes in the oven at 375 degrees to a fine finish, copper brown, another fifteen minutes to sit "on the off," then into the paper jacket, then the enfolding cloth wrap, then down the three-tiered cylindrical tin of the pail, nesting well packed on the second level above the tea and below the *potica*. Proficiently accomplished, pasty kept right warm for hours on end, this exemplary steaming-hot meal, Josef's portable stew, a mile underground.

And it typically was during these precious solitary early morning/ evening moments, the domestic labor at dexterous hand a matter of sheer automatism—she could, she was not too modest to boast, build a pasty in the dark the way a miner could read rock—that she often found herself alone, adrift among the oniony cooking smells, gazing milelong out the kitchen window dreamy with the image of memory; glazed conjurer.

She was back home then, Pine Street location, early bird on the sofa in the front room, her child's nose squashed to the windowpane, the cool smooth of its surface rattling in its sash with mine growl, its bass vibrato nasaling not unpleasantly through her ethmoid bone, mastoid process, eustachian tubes. She felt the faint *brrurr* in her ears, vague dance of dull pins, the mine sound through her head like distant church-organ chords, close as she ever would come to knowing what was down there, that which was so much "older than Christ and deeper than hell."

She watched through the window's upper half, its lower swirled so tall with snow it blocked the bottom black. "The way winter strode the world," she thought, remembering back, "gnawed its ice to glass." She smelled the paraffin glow of deep winter.

In her mind's eye, her father, grandfather, uncles, and cousins muscled out the door, wading through the thigh-high drifts gaining passage down the middle of the snow-tarped street ahead of the rise of the sun, joined gradually by neighbors one by one or in pairs and clots as they paraded off to the pits like night-marching men—off to war, she used to think as a kid—a convergence of silent figures snug in drab grays and laundered khakis toting their tall cylinders of tin. She listened through the glass-quake to their hard-soled big boots crunch the packed snow underfoot like blunt music, muffled din.

She imagined she was one with them then, one of them, the on-trudging male processional blowing white breath, dry ice on air, dreamed that she, too, wore the light like a solitary eye in her head, bright bob of headlamp, scores up and down the street shaping the snowbanks in the shifting shadow-show of their shine. A hundred hard hats high-hung with halo.

Winters, a man off to work in the Monday-morning dark would not see daylight again until Saturday.

She sometimes thought they looked like wraiths, this gleaming gauntlet of ghosts, some spectral posse bent to its apparitional night raid. God knew, she soon would be taller than most.

And then, as she emerged once more from her half trance, it did not seem to her twenty yesteryears past but . . . now, *this* moment, the experience of reexperiencing it, the immersive moment of reexperience that continues, lingers, altered perhaps, recomposed, but vivid, streaming to its source, the old remade new, submerged *whole* within the flow.

The miracle of memory, the way the dead live, breathing the night-light of dreams.

DELVING

That *Julija*/July evening found Josef on night shift, eleven hours down under. Shifts rotated, day or night, week to week. Those on nights went down at seven.

Ana stood at the door, Libby at her feet, as Josef hastily downed his last mug of *kavo* and *mleko*, coffee and cream, chasing it with the habitual mere finger of *slivovica*, plum brandy. Smacked, then swiped his lips. Handing him his pail by the long loop of its handle, she sagged slight-some at the knee to receive his buss upon her dampened cheek, taking care to miss being grazed by the hard visor of his carbide acetylene-lamp helmet, the one he had devoted much of the weekend to fussing with, polishing its parabolic reflector to a purer sheen.

"*Sreeno,*" she said, as she always did. "*Prosim, pazi. Na svidenje. Moz.*" Good luck. Please, be careful. See you soon. Husband. Eat well.

"*Hvala. Pridem takoj. Zena,*" he replied, as he always did. Thank you. I will be right back. Wife.

Opening the door, he stepped beneath the slant of the sun into another sweltering Keweenaw eve. By the time he arrived poached and swum out at the "dry" to strip off and change into his hobs and other work togs before yarding it over to the Red Jacket, he was drenched.

As was his wont, before entering the hundred-foot-high shaft-house to gather with his shift mates beneath the pulleys of the head-frame, there to await the boarding of the "man-car" that would ferry them down below, he crossed himself and delivered up an inoculating prayer. Here, the presence of fear thickened through the moment, a fear to which few, save the Macedonian, were immune. For it never went away, not completely, though, in time, if you were fortunate, you might arrive at that place where you no longer paid it much heed. Either your fear of it faded, the fear of fear, or you made it your friend, took it in hand, placed it in harness, put it to work. Less because you had conquered it, than because you had gained command and control of its conduct, mastered its anarchy, arranged it in such a way as to render it as much a part of yourself as smoking a cigarette, climbing a stair, whistling or walking, jumping rope, eating a pear.

Being afraid is easy. It is having the time to contemplate your fear that makes a man crazy.

Not that you talked about such things, even to your fellow miners, fellow sinners, even to your wife, or priest. Seldom enough to your god.

Josef prayed to the Virgin then, prayed as he always prayed, his prayer the same prayer his father had taught him back when: "Immaculate Sainted Mother who walks beside me, I pray you take my hand, guide my way, be with this sinner who loves and adores you."

His hand was at his neck, its fingers a fist clasped about the white-gold cross of Saint Piran, patron saint of miners, the one once worn by his father, the one he wore now haltered by its tarnished loop of lightweight, thin chain.

"Breathe away my fear as once you breathed the life of our savior into this, our wicked world. O Holy Mother Mary, queen of the immaculate light of the world, light with your perfect goodness every corner of the dark world below. Call on every fine angel. Let each fly through the earth. Let them cool its deepest depths with the speed of their wings. Let them cleanse its unclean air with the breath of their song. What is mined is not mine, but yours. This blessing in your name. Amen."

Crossing himself, he replaced the tiny cross down the damp nest of his shirtfront, noticed in the flesh of the pocket of his palm a perfect impress of cruciform, immaculate imprint of cross—stigmata of Piran? The sure hands of saints.

Tried then and failed to wedge a sprag on what insisted upon scrolling through his mind like a rolling pin, the late news out of north-neighboring Tamarack no. 2, twenty-eighth level—levels occurred every ten to sixteen fathoms, a fathom being six vertical feet—of a death on Friday late shift of one of the Cousin Jacks—he had yet to catch a name, Jim something or other—who while stoping had gone forfeit to loose-hanging rock down a raise.

He had seen the like too many times before, men buried alive beneath a free fall of overhead ground, crushed by a crag so all through that when you went to dig them out, lift them free, they collapsed in your arms invertebrate as laundry. He remembered the last time, a few months back, right here in the Jacket, lending a hand to lever the slab with the pry of a spare stull, jacking her up, hoisting her over, heave-hoing her off, and the sight of the mangled, melon-burst Finn pinned beneath, every feature of his face flattened as jelly spread smooth on a sandwich.

This latest sounded a clear case of carelessness to him. Still, wouldn't do to cast blame, judge too harshly too soon. Everyone knew you could read rock right as weather and still have it go all wrong, that despite every precaution taken. A raise or a winze could be rife with whimsy, hit you up out of nowhere, spur of the moment, blind side, find yourself upended-side down, no time to react no matter how well you thought you had prepared.

Rockbursts and air-blasts occurred without warning. A catastrophic fall of siliceous mass rock, capricious collapse of weak pillar or precipitous slippage along an old fault, caving of overstressed timber—"If the wood starts squawkin'," went the saying, "git to walkin'; if the rats to scamperin', scatter"—an overcharged breast or one concealing an unforeseen hollow or pocket, the resultant, eruptively propulsive onrush of pressurized air fisting through the drift like a fireless fireball at 200 mph could shake down loose roof like stone thunder, jar free an otherwise interlocked square-set, concuss a man's insides to organ soup.

And yet you *wanted* it, dearly wanted it to be human error, the miscalculation of the man, a case of gross negligence, howling incompetence, individual stupidity, of overreaching, underestimating, of violating some praxis of the vocational protocol. At least then you could call it governable, correctable, avoidable, instead of blind chance or bum luck, arbitrary hazard, divine will, or dumb and disinterested nature's, some *fluke*. A man down under felt powerless enough, thought Josef, without the fact being flung in his face each time some jackleg Red Finn or godforsaken Squarehead made a false move.

"Sometimes the best you can do," he thought, "is the power of prayer.

Supplicate, forbear, stay on God's good side, leave it to him, do your work right as the right may be given yours to do, and trust for the rest to old Piran."

It only made sense that a man have faith, some belief in which to abide, even the Macedonian, though precisely what a man like Temelcoff, whose unaccountable habit it was to whistle odd tunes while he worked, a practice no miner would dream of risking any more than he would cross casually beneath a ladder or fail to leave a crumb of pasty behind for the mine-dwelling "knackers"—the mine gnomes, the incorrigible "wee ugly troll 'uns" as the Cornishmen called them—what such a man as that might profess faith *in* remained much the mystery to Josef. Temelcoff reckoned his own percentages, played by other rules, the calculations and minding of which were best his own business.

Well, each to their own. Faith was a private affair. The point was to have some, in *some*thing, then hew to its path, refuse to waver, swerve, go astray. One needn't be overtly pious or observant, but God, so Josef believed, sought out the faithless sooner or later, flushed them out, lice rid from hair, and insofar as they dared turn to his entreaties a deaf ear, backslid or buckled beneath the testing weight of his plan, he had not only the right but the obligation to render of such lax and slackened souls a righteous example. A man—men—must be held to strict true account. God tallied his ledger, of that Josef Clemenc had not a doubt.

To be an unbeliever, much less proclaim one's unbelief, be possessed of the temerity to spread its poison about the pits, was to not only flout fate, but court disaster, and so place one's fellows in jeopardy. No miner wished to work beside a godless sinner or one so foolhardy, so "plain maze" as the Wesleyan Cornishmen put it, as to conceive of himself as above the reach of right superstition. That sort of taint was contagious, and didn't they all know to a man-jack that it could in an instant turn fatal. A fallen soul in a mine was more than a matter of mere theology or metaphor. God might work some of his ways misted in mystery, and other times plain as the nose on high noon. Faith, thought Josef, was rational as arithmetic.

He wondered whether the dead man had left behind family, how many wee ones, whether he knew him or of him. Not likely, though the Jacks with whom he worked the Jacket well might. Not that it was his place to ask. Every death took its toll. You didn't have to know a man or share his language or religion or customs to feel it. It rang down, a pall over all. The Outfit would do right by the family, if family there was, consent to the cost of its compensation and care. Indeed, its reputation was fair gold on the score. Josef had seen it before. No one went starving or was turned out unsheltered who enjoyed the good fortune of being counted one of its flock. God knew, the company was possessed of its charitable side. Josef might owe his life to God's grace, but for its living he knew enough to thank, and that daily, the old C&H.

Of course, it came down to MacNaughton, as most lifely doings did, and while Josef knew Big Jim for the spine-y and hardheaded sort, stiffy man to work for, as one not to be crossed in a scrape, he knew, too, that the Chief could be counted upon to spare a fair listen when it came to matters of family at stake. He wasn't so callused of heart that he put women and children out of their five-dollar-a-month company houses to fend for themselves on the street. Generally allowed them to stay on rent free for a year, forgave them the cost of their coal fuel and doctoring, even doled out a sum from the company aid fund to tide them over as they might require. Josef knew for a fact that that's how he'd done for the Muszalskis after poor J. J. had gone down 'neath the tram cart.

A lot got prated about James MacNaughton, all of it behind his back, most of it crude and contemptible swill. Josef wasn't one of those prone to let his fear of the man spill over into drunk-ugly words, sottish toasts to his imminent demise, boozy threats wrapped in wishes about what had ought better befall him. The Chief might not merit hailing or hosanna, but he no less than any other had his job to do, and if he failed to do it to the liking of some, he did it in a way that put food on their tables, dry roofs over their heads, a hospital at hand for their healing, churches in which they could worship, and schools that taught their children not only how to read, write, and cipher, but how to God-bless America as it rightly deserved to be blessed.

"Credit where such as that is due," thought Josef. "Chief has his faults same as any man. May seem bigger than most to the men, but 'tis the size of the job does the magnifying. There be plenty far worse than the Chief."

Climbing amid the others to clamber aboard the man-car beneath the scrutinizing eye of the top cager, Josef sat his spot shoulder to shoulder and elbow by rib awaiting the whistle-bell that would signal their plunge more than a mile down the dark of the skipway shaft, sheer drop through wind-rush. Another shift in a lifetime of shifts. He'd been "delvin' the pits" since the age of thirteen, though there were times when it felt a mite awful lot longer.

The car—or cage, or ketch, or skip—was a coffin-shaped staircase affair standing upright on end, perhaps twenty-five feet tip-top to bottom, tiered with a dozen staggered benches called circus seats onto which three men per step shoehorned themselves to perch side by side. Attached to the open-faced, oblong car's undercarriage was a series of wheels that fit plumb to a pair of slant-vertically laid rails constituting the track that ran the steep length of the shaft on the precipitous decline to its terminus more than five thousand feet below.

Raised and lowered by the steam-engine hoist that powered the massive, well-lubricated winding drum around which wrapped and unwrapped an arm-thick steel cable that in turn threaded through a heavy metal eye at the top of the car that in turn yet again was rehitched to the cable higher on by a clutch of clamps, cuffs, and U couplings called crosbys, the hoist-man engineer stationed on the surface read a series of binnacle-housed polished brass-and-glass gauges and dials—a sort of pelorus device—to regulate by hand-control both the vehicle's starts and stops at the mine's various levels and the speed at which it traveled, up to one thousand feet per minute.

Everyone knew how much the company prided itself on, took almost a visceral thrill in, such technology—witness the way it had named each engine as if it were its personal progeny: the Superior, at seven hundred thousand pounds the largest stationary engine in the world; the Rockland, the Mackinac, the Frontenac and Gratiot and Houghton, the Seneca, LaSalle, and Baraga, Perrot and Pewabic, the Hancock and Detroit and Onota. At the Red Jacket, the two hoists were the Minong and Siskowit. Combined, they generated an unprecedented 8,000 horsepower, enough to lift ten tons of rock 3,500 feet per minute from depths exceeding 6,000 feet, numbers that meant little enough save to those who recalled how fewer than fifty years earlier the largest hoist on the peninsula was an unnamed eighty-horsepower workhorse that could raise no more than a ton and a half at 500 feet per minute, that from the shallowest depths.

Morris-built, Leavitt-designed, the gleaming monsters were state of the art, and the company spared no expense in maintaining them. Indeed, it was not uncommon to hear grumbling about how the company cared more for its machinery than its men, how such machines were naught but the expression of MacNaughton's enormity of ego, a cavil Josef thought not only stupid but shortsighted. Because what should it rather do, he thought. Cut corners? Let such assets go to seed? Fall into disrepair and obsolescence? Neglect its investment? Hoist upon the cheap?

As far as he was concerned, let the Outfit spend as it might upon its hardware, only made him feel the safer and more secure knowing he could depend upon the soundness of the prodigious gear responsible for fetching up the raw tonnages of rock and ferrying himself and his thousand fellows daily through the earth. Besides, insofar as such investment improved efficiency and hiked profits, might it not, in time, redound to the benefit of all? He frankly did not understand why so many of the men could not permit the company to make a move without their finding fault. For some, far too many in his estimation, such indiscriminate grousing seemed more natural than breathing.

Something of a miracle, thought Josef, these behemoths, leviathans, titans of haulage and hoist. How *not* be impressed? You stood beside one, tall as a building, twice as big as any pair of big barns, shiny-smooth, new as chrome plate, platinum sheet, sidled up to one whirring, thrumming, come alive with the energy of orbits until the bones of your body and blood in your veins were as one with the power of sound, and you felt— what? Insignificant? Intimidated? Diminished? Small? Overpowered? Overmastered? Overcome? Overawed? Well, sure, partly. But something else. Something at your core . . . soared.

You felt privileged and favored, favored with having been afforded a glimpse of the future's face, one of might and size and capacity, vast and prolific as the country itself. Overcooking it? Probably. But a man needed to feel part of something, thought Josef, connected to something bigger than himself, something out there open and ongoing, expanding, still to be done, all that had yet but was certain to come. And the fact that it existed, that he could see it, hear it, touch it, feel its force gathered clean down in his shoes, bleeding up through his spine, rousing his genitals too, an awakening all through each thought that arose as he wondered—that alone was a lot.

So let the Outfit boast as it might that its five dozen engines generated the same amount of power used by a city of a quarter-million people or outproduced the plant at Niagara Falls. Why not? thought Josef. Was that not something justly to boast of, about which a company ought not be proud or its workers be permitted to crow? And enough of the bad-mouthing, backbiting, bitching, and billingsgate, this late idle talk of a strike. *Stoj*, already! Just stop! *Dosti!* Enough!

Working a mine wasn't whittling whistles from soapstone or rounding up cattle, weighing up a smoked butt or rump roast at Wills's butchery on Fifth or out to the Tamarack Co-op. It was what it was: hard work and dirty, dark work and dangerous. If what you were after was something else—a job cleaner, safer, less demanding, difficult—fine, get out, hie yourself to a city or try your hand behind a plow. You didn't cotton to burrowing through earth or boring through stone, then let the sky above be your limit. Ascend! Impress your wish upon any mica-bright star. Call *that* home.

"It may not be the best life in the world," thought Josef, "but it damn well is the *right* one."

So then, he reckoned, don't strike, deprive the man you worked beside, he whom you had labored hard alongside all of your adult working life—your relative, neighbor, countryman, Catholic—of exercising his god-given right to put in an honest day's work or earn that which he required to clothe, shelter, and feed his most loved ones.

The union would have had you believe that all it was after was an equitable "edge," that the deck was stacked, fix well in, the game a rig run on the down-and-down tilt, and that what it wanted, no more, was to level the playing field and even the odds. Except Josef wasn't buying it. There were rules, *the* rules, rules of long standing; they were written, they applied, and everyone had known what those rules were going in.

He knew what Haywood and his ilk were about, and it wasn't merely a larger say or even shake. They were damn cowboys, Stetson-clad agents provocateurs come riding their winged stallions out of the once-wild West expressly to agitate, stir trouble, sow discord, instigate. They didn't aspire to even the odds, they hankered to even the score. Publicity, that's what they were about, publicity and power, the raw of it and real, one king exchanged for another, and to secure the throne they were willing to spill the blood of innocent hardworking men. Too willing, thought Josef.

They spoke sanctimoniously of justice, preached the brotherhood and fraternity of the labor of men, portrayed ownership as Lucifer's spawn and the workers as slaves to its whims, damned those who dared disagree for the devil, but at what cost? Expendable lives? Whose lives? Whose life would that be, exactly? Put a name to it, thought Josef. Conjure a face and tally a count. Own up, come clean, and stop speaking prettily in fiery platitude and incendiary sop, and, for once, well and truly level about the price to be paid in *individual* loss, the human kind. Manifest the integrity of character to consider the damage done to *real* people, the injury inflicted upon a *living* person.

It was called a STRIKE! for a reason, thought Josef. The icon of the upraised clenched fist on their flags was no accident. Their messianic gasconade about smashing this and overturning that and battling and fighting and self-righteously class-warring unto ultimate victory or valiant defeat was language meticulously drawn and purposefully chosen—jingoistic agitprop of calculated crusade.

Men weren't anonymous fodder to be pitchforked before the cannons of canonical ideals, pawns to be pitied or pitted one against the other, insensible pieces on a chessboard to be cunningly played, deployed, shrewdly manipulated, sacrificed upon the altar of slick and apocalyptic slogan. Nor were they hapless martyrs eager heedlessly to crucify themselves in the expedience of the moment for a cause the darker implications of which most of them were able but vaguely to apprehend in their starker, more salient details. They weren't plankton, krill, chum.

Nor was it principle alone at issue, but the placing of the future of families and communities and the livelihoods of tens of thousands at risk, as, too, the continued existence of the industry to which they had dedicated their youth and from which they drew their scabbed and callused identity as men. More hung in the balance—was that not the phrase?—than most of them might be expected reasonably to rightly conceive of.

And then as the going grew too protracted and protractedly grim—this war of attrition they had sparked and spurred on—watch them leave, the Wobblies. Wave them so long as they turned high tail and skedaddled, saddled up, hit the trail. Stand witness as they washed their hands, cut their losses, and slithered the hell out of Dodge in a cloud of red dust—*poof!* up in smoke, don't let the door bang you on the butt on your way out of town—and so onto the next, the next greener pasture, new frontier, clean breast, and clean break. See the varmints vamoose.

And *their* stake in the outcome? The Wobblies? *Their* investment? The extent and depth of *their* selfless self-sacrifice? *Their* role in succoring the families they had exploited and in cleaning up the bloody mess they had made, the mutual distrust and ill feeling they had planted like the bitterest of seeds to persist—to badly mix a metaphor—like the spread of pitched pebbles upon once-placid ponds? One reaps what one wreaks, or one's children do. The Wobblies, thought Josef, left behind naught but woe, misery, and heartache, the sort that lingers, long as the length of long memory.

Everyone has their own dream. For the union, it was power. For the Outfit, profit. For the men, the sort of parity that might lead to prosperity. And each pursued its possession to their own benefit and at the expense of the other. But then, surely the realization of any dream, thought Josef, any dream worth its dreaming, could come only at high cost. A dream may promise reward in its winning, but only after entailing its fair share of loss, if for no other reason than that *Dream cancels dream in this new realm of fact / From which we wake into the dream of act.*

Would he like to see the company inaugurate an eight-hour day, raise wages, extend benefits, ease up on the speed at which it apparently had determined it must introduce the one-man drill? Of course. Did the men have legitimate grievances that too often were blithely dismissed or ignored? Indeed, they did. Could conditions in the pits *and* on the surface stand salutary, timely improvement? Oh, sure. Would joining a union, shouting demands, peddling propaganda, marching in the street, shutting down the mines, engaging in Western-style acts of roughshod intimidation, sabotage, physical violence, or worse ensure the realization of those aims and objectives? Could you, in essence, bluff MacNaughton, or best him at his own game? Could Big Bill take Big Jim? Take him on and win?

Josef knew he wasn't the only one asking himself such questions.

He thought, did Josef, while waiting to descend: "How do you coerce a person back to their faith once they have got shed of it?" How had she put it? That faith lost was twice as sweet as faith had? Sounded utterly mad to him. And, too, quite sad.

You didn't see certain things coming even as they came, unpleasant things, disappointments, small betrayals, larger treacheries, humiliations, arch-heresies, the way they relentlessly crept, tidal as salt through shore's sand. People are unknowable, wives most of all.

Josef knew who and what he was: simple, godfearing, hardworking, content with his lot. Just as he knew that he was at a loss to follow every voluted veer of her plot. Every marriage mounts and mounts up. Day by day the piling high and heaping on, all the shit two people communally shat. Startling, the amount of accumulated manure human beings spread in the course of cohabiting. But how go from enjoying an exalted place in God's plan, one of the flock, elect and anointed one moment, to running with the wolves of the eternally damned in the next? Had she no fear for the state of her soul?

"How dare she," he thought, "quote that damnable Diderot at me, the wretch, some filthy French atheist out of one of her books: 'Mankind shall not be free until the last king is strangled with the entrails of the last priest.'"

This was not what he had had in mind for his life.

Propinquity? Not on this earth. Not in this lifetime. All, Josef knew, get their just due in the end. So would she, eventually.

And meanwhile? Abide, endure, delve, keep drillin' away. And pretend.

BELOW

At the signal from the top cager, the bell clanged, magnisonant. The car jerked once—brattle, clank, jostle, jounce, or perhaps jolt comes closer—then dropped, *kerplunk*, like a trapdoor. On, into, awaaaay and on d

o
w
n

It wasn't that dark, light, space, time, shape, sound, weather, and sight disappeared down there, but that they were rearranged, reordered, and, so, redefined. You might work it, the mine, in, of, among it, every day of your life, but you never would understand it, no more than you did your own wife.

Naturally, no one thought such things, not a man. Here and there a muscle might tense, jaw clench or clasp shut, but no stomach churned, knee shook, asshole unbuttoned. They were all vets, old hands inured and well seasoned, all this was rote.

The man-car gathered speed, shot like a sling, in their ears a *whizzz* like a whistling, their faces feathered with breeze, the temperature hitching: 42 degrees, seventh level; 102 degrees, ninety-second. At each level a snapshot of light, snippet of flicklight before inking again back to indigo; they strobed their way down. Josef's ears repeatedly popped, *psi*. Humid here, grease thick. You always felt flanneled, wet flanneled, even in winter. Shut his eyes, caught a few zs; the ferocity of his snoring was famous among his fellows.

Forty, forty-five, fifty minutes later—a descent, depending on your working level, could take less than a half hour or up to two—having stutter-stopped and restarted severally along the skipway, Josef debouched, wide awake, stepped out and into the pit of the earth, the pith of its sub-terranean pivot, onto the pitched level landing of his level, the fifty-ninth, mainline, near its plat.

Blinked twice, to untangle his eyes, turned right.

A moment's congestion near the shaft's collar as the crew "lit up the sunshine" high on its hats, the carbide "shiner" lamps that burned acety-lene gas—no one donned earplugs, too dangerous; you needed to hear what was coming and if it was death, try to steer your way clear as quick as you could, but then no one wore Mossiers or safety goggles either—scuffed off down the groot of the drift, peeling away each to their stations hived at intervals throughout the honeycomb maze. No singing, hum-ming, whistling, not a word of g'd luck or g'd day, not a wave. None has-tened. Conspicuous lack of levity. Some hocked, then spat.

Josef saw: down-drift, a cannular chute of tapering corridor, twenty to twenty-five yards wide, its channel straight as a forearm thrust hard miles through earth's belly; low-sagging roof high enough for a tall man com-fortably to stand on tiptoe and upreach his arms, its rough, indetermi-nately colorless rock shored with massive timbers of joining, joist, pillar and column, berm, bolster, buttress and brace, fat beams bulwarked above, aslant and athwart with square-set, stull, lagging and cribbing of hemlock and maple and birch; reddish stearic-acid lamplight filming gritty and dim.

Saw too: the candlepowered light show of thirty-six illuminated hel-mets, its ambient parade of light woovils buttering yellowly across rock wall as they trudged deeper in—down haulage tram rail, past low sollars and mill-ways, along the frieden side-tracks and spurs where the extra tram carts were parked—on out to where the tunnel outfanned in off-shoots and tributaries to cleared cross-cuts and chambers, vault-ceilinged caverns called stopes, some as capacious as 500 feet across, 1,500 feet high, most nearer 100 by 100. An acre of ground stoped was the minimum weekly expectation.

Josef smelled: exposed bowel of earth, expelled bowel of man, bladder too, stale urine, old stool, human expulsion, some damp amalgam of gas, oil, grease, graphite, creosote, nitro, cordite, black powder, burnt charcoal, carbons and naphthas, resins, rosins, ammonia, methane, sulfur, and oxide of hard-metal mineral. There can be a cleanliness to new-turned earth, but this wasn't that. Rather, *eau de mine*, attar of explosion, its singed rusty fumes at his mind like a bucket of slops.

Josef heard: whir of compressor, hum of pump, sputter of pipe, hiss of hose, water dripping *plink-plank plink-plunk*, traveling loud on the loose; heard men backbent to their work way back, high up, low down in the stopes, raises, winzes, going at it with ram of shovel, punch of pick, hammer, and gad, gobbing up bad ground, mucking it back, lagging it on to lay off the slough; heard afar the first of the drill thunder, growl of driven bit, vowel chew at raw stone, baritone bite of burred rowel into rock. To make yourself heard, you had to speak in a shout.

Josef felt: little enough, frankly, save the heat and humidity, sweat alive to his knees, less trickle than splurge, the prickly presence of not enough breeze, and, underfoot, the on-running iron tracks for the rumbling rock trams the Cornishmen preferred to call buggies.

Josef thought: not of Ann, his marriage, Big Jim, Big Bill, neither of union nor strike, not even of his designated purpose in his disgruntled life—no, not even of God—but of all of himself gathered and aligned as an ax to its aiming to the chore near at hand. Thought, that is, only of the unthinking moment and connecting its cuff to the sleeve of the next, of what he was doing and must do when he arrived at his breast. Because down below, there was room for naught but *carved* thought, posture of *attacca*.

The danger—well, there were many dangers, they were countless, but perhaps the greatest lay in taking *anything* for granted. Every moment every nerve on sheer red alert. You could explain the science of demolition to anyone willing to listen, a matter of knowledge and technique, but this, the degree and extent to which you must narrow your mind to naught but exam for hours on end—more than twenty years in the pits and only now was Josef beginning to grasp, manage, direct, and apply it.

The Macedonian had been born with it, the facility full-blown. For Temelcoff it was no more an issue than the color of his eyes, which was why he appeared to go about his shifts possessed of a quality of dance, flight through the jungle, underground swan. He was a miner, the acrobatic best, but he was known first as a "scaler," top level, top shelf, one of the few most adept at drilling high up and way back at the most acute and contorted angles in the least accessible pockets and tucks of the steepest grizzly drifts, dog raises, sheer-faced winzes. Aerialist and choreographer.

But for everyone else it was work, hard work, maximum effort to summon and, over the course of a shift, *sustain* one's best, the very aspect of the job that separated those who did it from those who did it . . . better. A keenness of interrogation and clarity of reconnaissance, eleven hours a day. Psychic muscularity, the mustering that wherewithal. It was *that*, rather than the purely physical feats or the specter of the dread and the danger, that made the job so . . . depleting.

A miner got to know so he knew things, and not all of them were about the way to woo dynamite or blow red rock to shatter and red smithereen. And some of what Josef knew was that while stone may with some difficulty be persuaded to surrender the secrets of its scheme—veins, arteries, faults, fissures, cutways and fractures, seams, this capacity to trust to the wisdom of one's fingers to decipher the legibility of rock as one might any Braille—the *real* trouble lay deeper, embedded in the caverns of the mind.

BLAST

The grim job of keeping alive drained their energy.
The diggings of physical habit made deeper the
deeper grooves from which thought could not rise.

MAXWELL BODENHEIM

The subterranean miner that works in us all,
how can one tell whither leads his shaft
by the ever shifting, muffled sound of his pick?

HERMAN MELVILLE

The expression "to make a clean breast of it" had its origins here. When a "breast"—*brist*, in Cornish—or "face" of rock, as in "facade" or "fascia," had been "end-worked" by a miner in a drift, prepped, so to say, "trimmed up," squared away so as to be "clean" for drilling "the rounds of the set"— the intricately precise, collimated pattern of inset "cuts" or blast-holes, the cylindrical hollows that once bored through or "sculmed" to their proper depth would be loaded (as bullets to their jackets) with "powder," viz., dynamite, in advance of their being "charged up" and "shot" with their tiger-tailed furze—when that "ready" phase of the job was arrived at at last, one had at hand what was known down below as a "clean breast."

Josef stood alone and naked to the waist at his "cut station" before his "clean breast"—five feet across, seven high, its "foot-wall" beneath, "hanging" above—enveloped in his aura of stink, boots swampy-wet with taupe-colored glop because the ground at his feet was goopy with muck; it was dank. Indulging a breather while smathering red sweat from each pore, eyes raccooned with red dust, torso emblazoned, he felt muscle-numb with soreness, physically spent or approaching it after the better part of an arm-jarring, ear-ringing shift on the "Widowmaker," the drill the mine captain preferred to call the Rock Terrier.

The blisters on his hands seemed never to heal. The inlaid calluses there reminded him of hand-hardened hearts.

The round-stock, star-bit, hollow-drill steels Josef employed—the hand-forged bits ran the gamut from piston, leyner, hexagon, and square shank, to cross, six-point, X, double arc, and carr—came in graduated sets. The starter steels used to break open the job typically measured three inches in diameter, a foot in length. As the job progressed and each of the blast-holes was drilled three, five, as many as six feet down through and into rock, the replacement steels staggered gradually both downward in diameter—this to prevent the bit from "fitching," that is, jamming, seizing, or hanging up inside a hole, a common problem with wet drilling—and upward in length, arriving at last at the finisher steel, one and a quarter inches in diameter, fully eight feet long.

Depending upon the character of the rock, a six-foot-deep round could wear out one thousand pieces of steel. Didn't happen day in day out, but Josef had run into hard patches so hard, they chewed up steel as if it were sponge.

It was the stub end of his shift, last ninety minutes before "going back up to grass." All blasting was confined to time windows at the quarter hour before the close of both the half and full shifts, during which time the blast-site was combed for soft ground and unsound rock, timbered ("stulled") where necessary, monitored for unbroken mass rock requiring further blasting with black powder—a process called block-holing—and, finally, its leavings—called, alternately, slag, scrag, scraw, slart, groot, gangue, batch, or tailing—shoveled up and loaded onto tram cars before being shouldered over to the hoist area by the muckers. Sundays, the day off, was called the "all clear" or "clear the air."

Having broken down, dismantled, and abandoned his drill for the day—when up and working, a Leyner Sink Rock Terrier resembled an extraordinarily long-barreled, needle-nose mounted machine gun, one carriage-clamped or "saddled" to a vertically adjustable, horizontal T-bar, which in turn was bolted to a stationary floor-to-ceiling vertical steel column big around as drainpipe—he was poised to assault and bring down this wall, to "fire the holes," "shoot the face," and "pull rock," before leaving it to the day shift to muck with their square-point scoops and round-point spoon shovels, some Finn to load up and tram out the tonnage of "shot rock" and "throwback," rubble of ore intermixed with "leave it" and "poor rock," the noncopper basalt and lava.

So he didn't, frankly, envision the whole continent in front of him, or ponder the Conglomerate's dipping northwest out beneath the floor of the largest lake in North America before cropping back up again forty-five nautical miles out at Isle Royale, or contemplate the fact that he was a mile down, deep as any man had ever gone inside earth's history, or remind himself that it was the summer of 1913 on the Keweenaw and that his life felt to him as if it was or would soon be taking a turn.

His mind, rather, was, as it had best be, on placing danger in harness, risk on leash, peril at his behest and his bading. He knew that there were those who conceived of their jobs as "fighting rock," who insisted that the stone was their opponent, the one they were being paid to destroy, but it was an attitude that made little sense to him. Too brutish, crude, needlessly adversarial.

Standing before the breast, arms akimbo, Josef let his eyes walk the algebra and geometry of the set one last time, scrutineer. He was more scrupulous about his breasts than a copy editor a page. The fastidiousness never hurt. You might see something you had missed. One after the other, left to right, he inventoried the diameter, depth, design, and arrangement, slope and angle of the nineteen blast-holes. Signature of convulsion.

He apprehended the legibility of their meaning as he did his own handwriting, knew it better than the shadow pattern of the whiskers of his face. It was the nature of the task at hand, its thousand variables, idiosyncrasies, quirks, and foibles, its singularity in a word, that governed the hole pattern and firing order you used to drive a drift, sink a shaft, open a stope. Each job had to be tailored to its specific objective. The shift boss or mine captain told you what was required; it fell to you to see that it was done right-well and efficiently.

Josef knew the intricate cuneiform of each of the classic blast patterns and the ways to marry and amalgamate them should the need arise: the Wedge (both horizontal and vertical), the Center (three hole or four hole), the Checkerboard, the Square, the Side, the Bottom, the Spiral, the increasingly popular Diamond Burn, as he knew, too, how to finesse any subtle variation or nuanced departure upon each as the dynamic of the job might dictate.

You didn't deep-punch high-pressure punctures in hard-metal rock willy-nilly, not a mile down you didn't, haphazardly stuff in as much dynamite as a hole could hold, hook up a furze, "spit" or torch its tail, sprint for cover, and wait for the blast to blow, *ka-blewie*. Behind each of these nineteen holes was science and art. The former lay in the physics of detonation, explosion, demolition—the proper load of proper explosive, controlled burn of furze, the sequentially timed detonation of "shooting the holes," and the managed "peel-back" and "pull," fall and launch or "throw" of the face, the amount, piece size, and trajectory of its shotrock. The latter lay in interpreting the innate motif of the ossature of the rock you were interrogating, because until you could see inside stone, see *through*, see deeply enough to recognize and calculate its qualities, hold the sight of its face inside your head as you held the face of your own wife or child in the huddle of your hands, until you could discern the interior meaning of its image, its mien and what it masked by the illuminated caress of the eye of the light in your head, until rock was one with vision, you might call yourself a miner, might do your job with technical competence, even ease, but you had yet to learn what it *meant* to mine.

It never would have occurred to Josef to call himself a sculptor, or even a stonecutter, and, in fact, he was not one. But there was that relationship to stone and its alteration, that comity of working with rock, shaping it to a purpose—whether to persuade it by brute force to yield up its bullion, or to coax it by chip and chisel to free a fettered form. In both cases, the code of the rock worker was in the carve of his signature, whether the secret chevron of chisel, insignia of drill, engraving of sledge, or inscription of sawtooth. Writers of rock, into and on, drill bit as quill point.

Not as far-fetched as it sounds. One could glimpse the impulse *shaped* into the timbering where, like totem poles, men had carved and whittled masks and visages along the face of the wood, as, too, across certain walls where they had spalled and etched, as with acid, glyphs and pictograms—cave art.

Satisfied that the pattern was the one he wanted, that it was arranged, aligned, angled precisely the way that would, if not calm, at least *conduct* the chaos of collapse, upheaval, and propulsion, Josef retreated around a corner and some eighty feet down a cross-drift to his "dry-ass." This was the out-of-the-way niche where he previously had stowed not only his drill and his lunch pail—empty now, save for the few bites of pasty he would be leaving back for the pesty knackers after knocking off—but several twenty-five-pound wooden crates stacked with dynamite, each cartridge nesting in its cushion of sawdust; the puck-shaped tin of blasting caps or "primers" containing one hundred inch-and-a-half open-ended, quarter-inch-diameter mercury-fulminate-charged copper casings; and the 150-linear-foot coil of white double-tape furze line he formerly had cut from the tractor-tire-size iron spool of the stuff located near one of the satellite powder magazines back up and off drift.

Having scared up a spot where he might perch semicomfortably on a reasonably flat ledge of exposed rock, he lifted over one of the ATLAS POWDER WORKS, DOLLAR BAY–stenciled crates, used a wooden chisel to pry off its cleated-down lid, fetched up the furze coil and tin of primers, and sat down, laying the lid flat across his lap; surgeon's table.

Fishing a jackknife, crimpers, and wood-peg punch-holer from his pants pocket, he placed the tools atop the lid alongside the tin and coil before—this gesture redolent of a photographer unspooling a roll of developed film to the light—eye-measuring exactly eight feet of furze, which he severed cleanly from its coil with the knife blade, using the lid as a cutting board. Then, extracting a single number-six primer from the tin and holding it like a bullet between the thumb and first two fingers of his left hand, he worked the end of the furze into the open end of the casing with his right—thread through needle's eye—before applying the crimper, or "capper," like a pliers, pinching the primer's copper skirt snug to the furze. Josef considered the tool a luxury; he knew there still were those, old hands mostly, who insisted on using their teeth.

Lifting out the first of the cartridges from the crate at his feet, eight inches of waxed-paper candlestick one and an eighth inches in circumference packed rigid among kaolin or fuller's earth with twelve ounces of oily gray explosive—dynamite came in varying strengths graded by percentage of nitroglycerin content sliding upward at 5 percent increments from a low of 10 to a high of 70; these were 60, potent stuff—he used the peg-punch to auger a hole in the cylinder's side or "waist" roughly halfway along its length, inserted the primer cap through the opening, burrowing it well down inside, then punched a second eyelet higher up nearer the tube's fore end, through which he laced the tail of the furze so that its length hung free, clear and away.

Thus did Josef Clemenc prime his first round, a procedure he had performed thousands of times in the past and which he now proceeded to duplicate in rapid succession another eighteen times, taking care to crop each furze progressively shorter, in staggered lengths, to coincide with their firing order, in this case the four-hole center-square cut pattern he had spent the shift drilling.

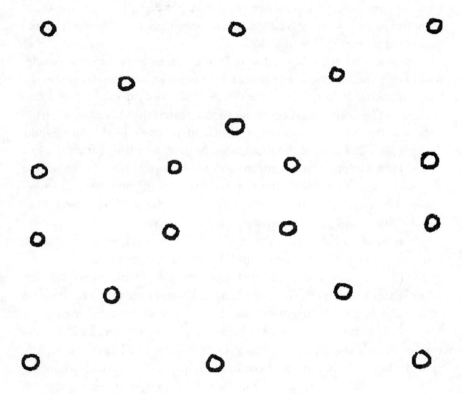

The short-cropped furzes—the shortest being just shy of six feet—were designated for the eight "cut" or "burner" holes located across the center of the breast, each of which Josef had drilled on the oblique toward dead center, and which were designated to blow first to "pocket out," jolt loose, and uniformly weaken the face. The next longest were reserved for the five "reliever" holes at the inside top and bottom, then the three "trimmer" holes across the top edge to maximize "pull," finally the longest—

roughly eight feet—for the three "lift," "lifter," or "kicker" holes across the bottom edge, all of which were designed to create "heave." This particular set did not, as he had determined it, employ "back," "breast," or "skimmer" rounds.

Josef knew the rule of thumb, of course—he had heard it talked around that some engineer had come up with it—two pounds of powder for every cubic yard of conglomerate, but in practice he preferred his own: three-quarters to seven-eighths full load per hole. To put it another way, a six-foot-deep hole took a load of seven or eight eight-inch cartridges, or from five to six pounds of "charge." So, nineteen holes, nearly one hundred pounds of dynamite. Mean kick.

It took Josef three laps, "dry-ass" to breast, to ferry over the powder and primed cartridges. These latter he arranged in firing order across the metal mucking or "turn" sheet, the three-by-six-foot rug of three-eighths-inch steel plate positioned on the ground to catch the shotrock, it having been fetched over and laid out by a pair of muckers in the meanwhile. Having unlidded each of the four crates, he drew a cartridge from the first and slit it open lengthwise stem to stern with his jackknife, doing his best to avoid skin contact with the nitro inside. In sufficient doses, as Josef could well attest, it saddled a man with a headache so excruciating it became a chore both to see straight and think clearly.

Placing the filleted cartridge alongside the primed ones, he repeated the operation eighty more times until the mucking carpet resembled nothing so much as an enormous baking sheet echeloned with cannolis. Then, plucking up a clutch of split cartridges, he walked over to the foraminous breast and began chuting them one after the other, scrolled mail to its pigeonhole, columnarly down the bore-rounds. Once primed and loaded, primer rounds last in, the nineteen furze tails extruded from the wall in strands, laces, clothesline, and cords, their lanyards and whangs hanging down and coiling away across the face. Stone a-sprout with spaghetti, white licorice whips.

Propped off to the side of the breast was what appeared to be a long broom handle, and this Josef took up as a sponge-rammer tamping rod, or "loading stick," wielding it like an eight-foot-long harpoon. Gripping it with both hands, knuckles white, he plunged it repeatedly and without pause down the throats of each of the nineteen holes in swift succession, mashing the incised cartridges one atop the other with enough force and compression to coarctate and backfill every interior gap and air pocket with compaction-packed explosive. True aim was all. You dearly did not want to dislodge a furze from its cap. More often than not that meant a misfire, and misfires too often meant trouble. Tamp too gingerly, on the other hand, and the result was a "blow out"; too much air left in the hole and the dynamite would fail to get hot enough to explode, idly slow-burning instead.

With each thrust he emitted a grunt, until grunt was gasp, gasp groan, and the sweat flew from his body in flows. His shoulders ached, arms burned, the small of his back was damaged sponge. Thirsty now, he would not take water, never did on the job, had trained his body to do without. Mine camel.

Tossing the javelin aside—job almost at an end now—he bent forward, folding at the waist, stood up, bowed his back to an arch, removed his helmet, raked a dirty hand through soppy hair, replaced the helmet, muttered something inaudible, perhaps unprintable, began plugging the scant space remaining in each of the holes between the top of the primer round and the rim, lip, or "collar" of the hole—six, eight, twelve inches—sealing them full up with "stemming" and "leave it"—dry clay and drill cuttings, the gangue previously barrowed over from the stem shed—then picked up the rod and, one by one, resumed tamping down each of the holes yet again.

Josef was aware that there were those whose agenda it apparently served to characterize all this as "backbreaking labor." Indeed, he knew it was the going euphemism: backbreakinglabor. Rolled off their tongues as a single slick block. But he just thought of it as work, steady work, hard work, perhaps, but no harder than it was honorable. A job, nor just any job, but his, what he did. Not that he hadn't known men who had broken their backs doing it, hearts as well, but . . . not him. Josef Clemenc was a miner proud to be one, and now, having drilled his set, loaded his round, and charged his face, he was prepared to spit the furzes, fire the holes, shoot the breast, then call it a day. Head to grass, *domov*, home.

He reached for his rat-tail.

The rat-tail, or "spitter"—also called a "sparkler"—was a twelve-inch furze severally notched through its sheath down to its inner powder core, the number of notches corresponding to the number of holes to be fired, so that each time a flame-up spit from a new notch as the furze burned along its length, that newest spit was applied to the furze next up for its lighting in the firing order.

Josef slipped the rat-tail from his pocket, grasped it by its neck, lifted it to his helmet, touched its terminus to the carbide, caught a whiff of smoke upon contact followed by the sensation of heat at his fingertips as it flared up, then—*fffrit*—spat. Now he would as he must—rapidly, smoothly, calmly, above all with the confidence of a man who knows he has done everything right and can do what remains to be done better still, do it perfectly.

Piece of cake.

"Happy birthday," he thought. "Light the candles."

Addressing the breast face on the square, he applied the flame of the rat-tail to the first of the furzes, cut hole number one, the one in the center, left top. It smoked, sputtered, spritzed spark, caught. So, in order, did the remaining eighteen. Double-tape furze burns at roughly thirty-five to forty-five seconds per linear foot. He had something like three minutes now, more than enough time to make it back to dry-ass.

Shouting, "Fire in the hole! Fire in the hole! Fire in the hole!" he walked without rushing or backward glance to his niche and there stood to silent prayer, contemplating the strangeness of the image: stone on fire. Template of explosion. Attitude of brisance.

It was quiet. *Tiho.*

When the *wha-huuump* of the first report sounded—he could detect the concussion on his fingertips lightly pressed to the rock wall beside him, as, too, up through the soles of his feet, in his teeth—his ears began counting: "One." Pause. *Thump.* "Two." Pause. *Thump.* "Three." Pause. *Thump* . . . Out of his hands now. He could only wait and listen, feel.

Misfires occurred all the time, hang-fires less frequently, part-fires, or "stinkers," less frequently still, but all three were nothing to be regarded with anything but dread. When a hole failed to fire, *some*one had to go back, scout it out, probe around, track it down, fall to its extraction hand-scraping and scooping, sculming the unfired hole with a drill spoon and pick, and to do so according to company policy, "with alacrity and expedition." Sometimes that someone was the shift boss, more often it was a miner, usually the one who followed up the job next shift since, blasting being confined to shift's end, no one could chance doubling back straightaway owing both to the afterhover of nitro fumes—nitrous-oxide-filled "bad air" would choke you down, choke you up tight, choke you right off—and residual loose rock.

Any whichaway, misfires were a bane. If you were lucky, they tipped their own hand, gave their game away as a convex mass of left-behind, still solid, unfractured rock. But you weren't always lucky, and then you were left to hazard a mess not of your making. It had happened to Josef on more occasions than he wished to recount.

"Sixteen." Pause. *Thump.* "Seventeen." Pause. *Thump.* "Eighteen." Pause.

Pause.

Pause.

Pause.

Number nineteen fired off: *thump.*

One short. "Shit!" Missed hole. One of the lifts, middle bottom. He would need to tell Brothers, the shift boss, so he could pass word onto the boss on next shift. "Shit!" He hated this, hated leaving behind misfires. It had happened to him before, of course, but . . . *wha-huuump.*

Ha! Hang-fire then, *not* misfire. "Good," he thought aloud. "Thank God."

Suddenly he was wearied in every muscle, steeped in depletion, crash of a drug clean through. Job done, shift over, sense of completion. Grabbed his tin, reached inside, withdrew the remnants of pasty and placed them in a row upon the ledge.

"There you go," he thought. "Have at, wee ones."

Then, emerging from his niche, he rounded the corner and headed off up-drift toward the shaft, and grass. The light in his head was bright with beam and he imagined he could see miles through red earth; when it shone up the scuttle of a rat down a stull, he could scarce be troubled to muster a smile.

The whistle blew, shift end's signal. But then it blew again, more sharply, or so it seemed to him. Which was wrong, very wrong. And again, meaning trouble. And then more shrilly still, and staccato. And kept on, and kept on, and kept on.

Josef picked up his pace, broke into a slow trot. Men suddenly were everywhere, convoked, converged, on-gathering. The drift was amassed with the momentum of exchanged looks, low words, expressions of alarum and no laughter. Brothers, the shift boss—Josef could just make him out through the ranks of the still orderly herd—stood near the mouth of the shaft, waving them on as if he was a coach at third base and they were runners rounding for home.

The screaming of the whistle arrested, guillotine of silence, all of

God's world above and below holding its breath, poem's caesura. And now Josef could hear it being passed back and along, low murmur, its ripple passing on through, handed off like a gun, man to man: The Word, arrived: STRIKE!

Josef heard curses, heard their opposite, heard the high bounce of emotion, wounded, celebratory, worried, relieved, raw as the mixed news of its moment.

Josef had gone hungry before. If he had to, he would go hungry again. He and Ana could do as they would, scrape on by.

But the children.

And so wondered why, Josef Clemenc, wondered why, every time, anywhere, it was innocence, always innocence, the first to fall victim to everything.

RED JACKET

* * *

When Franklyn awoke, he did so with a start—jolt, actually—owing to the stridulant whistling from the mines. Lying there not a little miffed—as a rule, he was unkindly disposed to being jolted—he fingered his prick before flopping it aside, fluke, fired up a fag, kicked aside the bedsheets, and barefooted it across the arabesque-carpeted floor to wash, brush, floss, and shave, the while coughing free of his phlegm-clogged lungs, clearing his percaled throat, raking the roof of his mouth as if endeavoring to expectorate a sock.

Gazing bleary-eyed at the wayward, none-too-attractive self-image in the mirror before him, he recited aloud a few lines from Bogie Bodenheim's poem "The Miner":

Those on the top say they know you, Earth—they are liars.
You are my father, and the silence I work in is my mother.
Only the son knows his father.
We are alike—sweaty, inarticulate of soul, bending under thick
   knowledge.

Hastily dressing, not bothering to button his vest, he proceeded downstairs and out the front door, notebook containing contact info hip-pocketed, pen slotted at his breast, ignoring everything, cursing his lot, hell-bent haphazardly on caffeine, hacking, headachy, wholly preoccupied with the sensation that his ears were bleeding sounds down the cylindrical sides of his neck, in scrolls.

Out in the street, he crossed over to its sunny side and there lit up again, sucking sharply in as deeply as he could muster the breath. Had he been able to devise a method of doing so without endangering himself, he would, he thought, have smoked in his sleep, all through the night, preferring to believe that he was doing not only his lungs but the rest of his cardiovascular system a favor, treating each to the same flavorful taste of minty, Irish-spring-like, high-alpine refreshment that his tongue and its receptors, despite the hematomas and cankers induced, found so exhilarating.

By the time he entered the café, cindered, sooty, ash-strew down his shirtfront, billowing vapors from his head like a crematory vent, he was onto yet another day of mindless chain-smoking, its reassuring, quotidian rhythm. Franklyn Shivs smoked cigarettes the way some writers use parens: prodigal punctuation. Not enough time in a day nor burley in all the boundlessly mapped world.

THE KID

Slipped, then, into a lumpily cushioned, not uncramped window-side booth—pane filmed with short-order fume—impatiently ordered a pot of java thick enough to prop a plastic spoon, and asked of the waitress, if with but partial success, directions to the offices of both the local telegraph and of *Glasnik*.

"And all this whistling," he added. "What the hell's going on?"

"Strike," she answered.

"That right?" Trying to be casual.

"Yep. Been coming."

"You don't seem real, I dunno, upset or anything."

"Not. Why should I be? 'Bout time. That all, then?" And when he nodded: "Be right back with that pot."

Barely bothering to glance up when the *tra-lee-la* of the bell over the front door signaled the arrival of another patron, he did so enough to register that the customer was a kid, one with a dog off its lead, an underfed foxy-faced pup, its ribs caging through in slats. Ratter breed with a roughened coat cockled with burrs, which, as Franklyn could not help but notice, rendered him much a match with the kid, who, he thought, could only just have emerged from the pages of a Dickensian fiction after having spent the sleepless night previous prowling some garbage scow berthed on the outskirts of town. The kid, who wore a greasy newsboy cap yanked down over one eye and sported a plug of chewing tobacco in his bulging cheek, could not have weighed seventy-five pounds sopping wet. Classic.

"Please, sir," he began, sidling over a mite warily, eyes sidecast, "do you think you might spare anything? For me and my dog? Pal's hungry something fierce. We've not et a scrap since Monday. He'll do tricks for you, won't you, Pal?" He turned to the dog. "Watch."

The dog was into his third, conceivably his fourth, adroitly executed hind-legged, kangaroolike hop across the floor when the proprietor of the place, having emerged girthily aproned from the kitchen in a fit of scowling displeasure, or so Franklyn surmised from the expression scrawling itself upon his sweat-reddened face, lumbered over and, screaming at the kid in a foam-laced spray of invective, roughly grabbed the yelping dog by the nape of the neck before opening the door and, as one might a bucket of slops or swill, flinging him into the street before turning on the kid, who, meantime, had begun pathetically to wail as he trailed after him.

"Pal!"

"Goddamn it! I've told you before, you runty little beggar, keep the goddamn mutt outta my place, or next time, I swear to god, I'll grind him up for sausage and feed him to the cats! Now"—he hooked the kid's ear, corkscrewing him out the door as the kid howled or, rather, brayed in pain—"get the hell outta my place. I see your shitty face in here again, I'll set the coppers on ya wet on rain." And, so saying, proffered him the full sole of a thumping boot square flush in the scrawny backside, sending him sprawling after his pet.

"Aw, shit!" muttered Franklyn beneath his breath, rump-sliding out of the booth as the side of beef strode by on his way back to the kitchen. Catching him just so with a purposefully lowered, perfectly timed, exquisitely aimed shoulder cuff driven hard up under the rib cage, while not enough to plant him on the floor, he nonetheless succeeded in knocking enough of the air from the man's lungs—"Hunnmmphh!!"—that he buckled at the knees, if not nearly enough to suit Franklyn.

"Oh, sorry," said Franklyn, quickly. "Didn't see you there. Entirely my fault. Trust you're not hurt. Really. Sorry, old sport."

And before the man—or, as Franklyn now conceived of him, the motherless pigfucker and might the everlasting curse of a cockhatted god light slantwise upon the brow of the bloody big-arsed gibbosity of a belly-moving agnathan whore's get—could summon the wherewithal to respond, Franklyn headed, still coffeeless, out the door to act upon his impulse, one that he considered less noble—or ennobling—than irksome. He didn't have time for this sort of thing.

The kid was kneeling in the street, hunched over his dog.

"He okay?" asked Franklyn, taking a knee beside them.

The kid's lip was quivering, his face tear-streaked as he sniffled around his words.

Appeared scuffed up some, but otherwise no worse for the wear. "Yeah, think so." He was petting the dog all over, digging behind his ears while the dog licked him appreciatively in the face. Terriers don't terrorize.

"How about yourself? Okay?"

"Sure." For the first time, he looked him in the eye. Still wary, Franklyn noticed.

"Tell you what, why don't we go scout us up another place? You know one where they like dogs?"

The kid's eyes widened up, brightened some, too. "Sure. Pechauer's. Over on Fifth."

"Sounds good. So we'll go there. Catch us some breakfast. On me. You game?"

The kid nodded, said nothing.

"Okay." Franklyn got to his feet. "Come on then, but you lead the way. I'm new around here."

Hooking the dog up under an arm, the kid stood.

"By the way, my name's Frank." Extended a hand.

"George," said the kid, shaking it. Appeared to be mulling something over. "Nobody calls me that, though." Adjusted the dog, gentle jounce. "Well, 'cept my ma."

"So, what's it everyone else calls you?"

"CK," he said.

"All right then," said Franklyn. "CK it is."

"Wanna know why?"

"Only if you wanna tell me." They achieved the sideway, sidled down it, side by side.

"It's 'cuz I'm Cornish."

"Me, too. Partly. How about that? Couple of Cousin Jacks. So what's the K stand for? King?"

"Nah." Big smile, longer pause, unsheepish. "Kid."

"Ah," said Franklyn. "Sure. Shoulda guessed. Cornish Kid."

"Yep." With pride. "And this here's Pal. Say hey, Pal." The dog barked, once.

"Smart dog."

"Yep. Smartest ever."

"So, CK, Pal Cornish, too?"

The kid—the Kid—drew up, serious, solemn even, brow knit. "Dunno. Maybe. How can you tell?"

"Well, does he like pasty?"

"That's his favorite."

"Then I'd say he's Cornish."

The Kid took a moment, pondering, resumed walking. "Yep." Settled matter. "Pal's Cornish, too."

"Thought he might be. So that makes him CP, right?"

"What?"

"Well, you're CK, he's CP. CK's CP. Cornish Pal."

Thought a moment. "'Spose." And, after another, longer. "Nah. Just Pal. Pal's good enough."

"Oh, sure. Pal's great. Just saying."

"Yeah. Pal."

"Hey, CK, any idea where the telegraph office is at?"

Franklyn had downed naught but his customary pot of coffee, content—tickled, actually—to watch the Kid wordlessly and without once coming up for air wolf down a head-high stack of flapjacks—"griddlecakes," they called them up here—drowning sopped-through in a pool of maple syrup an inch deep, even as he fed Pal a couple of rashers of bacon and link sausage, all in record time. Having "et," then, the three of them stood on the sidewalk outside.

"Western Union? Sure. Right there." He pointed either up or down street, depending. "That big building with the clock on top. Opera house. See it? Inside there."

"Thanks. Need to go on over, get in touch with my boss back in Chicago, let him know I made it up in one piece. Hey, I'll probably be around town awhile. Staying at the Arlington, over by the depot. Drop by sometime. Bring Pal."

"Mean it?"

"Something else you should know about me, CK: I *always* mean it—'cept when I'm kidding." Smile. "Of course I mean it. Any time." He extended a hand, pressing the silver dollar into the Kid's cupped own. "Don't go spending that all in one place now, okay? Listen, Kid, gotta run."

"Jeez, Frank, thanks." The Kid turned the coin over severally in his hand, eyed it up close, hefted it some, the realness of its weight. "Look-it, Pal, a whole dollar! We're rich!" Pal woofed, twice.

"See ya, CK, and good luck with the rats out to the dump now." He bent down, belly-rubbed the dog's chest. "See ya, Pal. Go get 'em."

"See ya, Frank," said CK, stuffing the money about as deeply down a pants pocket as money conceivably could go.

Good luck? thought Franklyn, as he headed off down or up street. The only luck was rotten luck. Poor kid, poor soul. From the little he had gleaned over breakfast: father, James, dead in the Tamarack mines three years; oldest brother, Cleo, dead of the diphtheria two; three younger ones—Buck, Herb, Babe—left to him to shepherd and herd; widowed mother, Alice, reduced to taking in other people's laundry, letting out spare rooms, feeding her brood from their postage-stamp-size garden and what her company compensation check might fetch from the Tamarack Co-op plus the little CK brought in from peddling newspapers, picking the local thimble berries, the nickel bounty the county anted up on dead rats, his apprentice steeplejack work. The Kid climbed, apparently—smokestacks, water towers, lighthouses, church steeples, shaft-houses—no height too high or angle too awkward. Problem was, the work wasn't regular, and when it was, didn't pay squat.

Reminded Franklyn of a bird, scavenger kicked from its nest, ousted magpie, jackdaw, jay, the ones that patchwork their lives from the bits and pieces they rummage on the wing. The Kid was eleven years old and already dead set on dropping out of school. Didn't stand a chance.

CK talked way too much and with far too much shine in his eye about "going down," thought Franklyn. Couldn't wait. Itched to see where his father had bought it, and, too, take the measure of himself, reckon how he stacked up, whether he was "man enough," man as his pa. CK idolized those underground workers, stood in childlike awe, thought them "the bravest men in the world." Well, at least he had a dog, a nickname, and, now, a dollar to show for them. Franklyn wondered if he would see him again. He hadn't been feigning. Wouldn't mind it a bit. He liked the Kid.

LAY OF THE LAND

Glasnik's offices were on Seventh Street, number 103, a low-slung, kennel-like wooden structure adjacent to Miha "Mike" Klobuchar's Saloon and Bowling Alley. Red Jacket was chockablock with taverns—back at the hotel Franklyn had counted upward of seventy-five in Polk's *Houghton County Business Directory*, another twenty-five in neighboring Laurium—and most of the Slovene ones were clustered on Seventh: Klobuchar's, Jerman's, Shaltz's, Shertk's, the National—which everyone called Schmalzel's, Drazich's, Grahek's, Kasun's, Muhich's, Sepic's, Shimetz's, Srebenak's.

Franklyn had the names Ivan had provided him in his notebook: John Plautz (Americanized, he would learn later, from the Slovene Plavec), Klobuchar's brother-in-law. And Math Kobe. Both, according to Ivan, employed by *Glasnik*.

Having seen to the telegram, what he needed now was someone, hopefully either this Plautz or Kobe, to point him in the right direction, put him onto Haywood and MacNaughton; he needed interviews. Then get to know the town, quick-read the lay of its land, acquaint himself, first-hand.

Every reporter assigned to a story in an unfamiliar place knows the feeling, being at sea. You spin, flounder, float, tread water before finally hitting your improvised stride, finding your stroke, some wayward groove, connect the dots, their rhythm and pace, succeed in getting on top of things catch-as-catch-can by the seat of your pants, *ambulando*, at least enough to swim discernibly forward instead of drifting aimless in place. The facts were everywhere around him thick as schooling minnows, if, for the moment, but twice as slippery. He had only to lure them to the surface, reel them in, land them like perch, or eels. He needed what every needy reporter needs: stories, ones he could compose and dispatch, right quick.

Opening the door to the newspaper, he walked inside, was immediately greeted by the homey smell of newsprint. Long, narrow space, galleylike; Mergenthaler Linotype; sizable gasoline-driven printing press, a rotary, down at its far end; pair of smaller handpresses nearby; unopened tin tubs of ink aligned along the floor. Along one wall, a team of paper-capped, neoprene-aproned, ink-smudged women were occupied selecting and setting by hand fonts of type from widemouthed metal trays. Nearer the front, next to the sole window, the editor's vacant desk, and beside it,

a smaller one, vacant as well. Low shelves lined thick with ledger books
the size of atlases bowed and sagged; three of the four walls were stacked
straining toward the ceiling with old, yellowing, not-yet-tattered newspapers.

The chief typesetter, as he would prove, ambled over, introduced himself, inquired cordially of his business.

"I'm looking"—had recourse to his notes—"for John Plautz or Math
Kobe," said Franklyn matter-of-factly.

Maks Buh sized him up and down but decidedly did not eye him, as
is said, sidelong or wise. "Kobe doesn't work here anymore. Doesn't live
here anymore, for that matter. Moved away, year back. 'Spect Johnny's at
his tavern. Usually is, this time of day. Block over, on Sixth, 329." Pause.
"Anything else?"

"No. Thank you, sir. Do much appreciate it."

"Mind if I ask why?"

"Nothing to speak of. Friend of mine's a friend of his. Asked me to
look him up. Say hey."

"Ah." Agreeable. "This friend of yours, he's a name?"

"Molek. Ivan Molek."

Buh grinned. "Ha! Wee Van, you, say! You're up from Chicago then,
is it? And your own name, sir? If you don't mind."

"Not at all. Shivs. Frank Shivs." Franklyn remained unexpansive.
Didn't know this Buh from a bag of bolts.

"*You're* Shivs?" His eyes were *O*'s.

"Why? There's a problem?"

"That there's none, none at all. My hand, sir." He reached across the
counter. "Honor. Been expecting you."

Franklyn shook it, bewildered, as Buh unfastened his apron and
tossed it aside, informed his crew he'd be right back, swept around the
counter, motioned for Franklyn to follow him out the door.

"I'll walk you over then. Run interference. Better that way. Johnny
quit the paper a while back, but he continues all for the men, which is
more than I can say for *this* fuckin' rag." Toss of head over back of shoulder. "Used to be something when Wee Van and Kobe and Johnny were the
ones. Now?" Spat in the street, punctus; enough left unsaid. "The editor's
a sot for sale to the highest bidder, and the owner wouldn't know news
from nursery rhymes."

Franklyn couldn't resist. "Some distinction there I'm missing?"

"Ha!" As they walked, Buh remarked, "We read *Proleterac* all the time. Now *that's* a newspaper, real one, have to be or Van'd have naught to do with it. He found a jewel, Mr. Shivs, when he hired you on, if you don't mind my saying. All the boys know your stuff. Won't say we always understand every word of it, but we know a right heart in the ink."

"Don't mind your saying it, Maks," said Franklyn. "What I mind is the Mister. Please, don't. It's Frank, just Frank, okay?"

"All right then, Frank. So here we are. Johnny'll be beside himself pleased."

They slid into the inviting dark of the tavern, which, even at this hour, matutine, was amber-tinged, siftings of maroon. Few were the saloons where, upon entry, day or night, stepping through all light-blind, Franklyn Shivs did not experience this moment of visceral delight. Bars were treasures, oases of spirit, spirits alike, and someday, he promised himself, he was going to write an ode to every one he ever had patronized. Lengthy ode, then, the more florid the better. Because what, he often wondered— well, not often, but now and then—was not to like?

However stale, sour, malty, or hoppy, grapy, grainy, however infragrant with tobacco, aromatic with piss, however greasy and stained, they smelled . . . good. The precise odor of *should*; *eau d'ought*. Their dark-aged wood, the dim, dingy, yet rutilant light so easy on the eyes. Their bar tops—oak, zinc, brass, mahogany—smooth as a baby's bottom or deckled as an acne-vulgarized kid's, the lot put you in touch, earth of your matter, place to repose, heart in head, head in hand. At a bar, as he considered it, you perched, elevated, stooled high as a heaven, surveyor of your patch of the world as it spun, happy-houred, king once again, however uncastled. You had a saloon, no matter how far from home, you had a home, port in a storm, one warm, dry, well stocked: refuge. In even the surliest, unkempt, tumbledown, you were *welcome*, or in time would be, come to be, befriended or left alone as you wished.

Moreover, up here, as he soon was to learn, there was more to it still, for the saloon as *entity* was the place, home away from home, with which the new man in-country touched first base upon arrival, as, too, the one to which he returned to cash his paycheck, pay his fraternal dues, witness on his behalf when applying for citizenship, serve as his interpreter as the need might arise. Barkeep as concierge and benevolent translator, then, decipherer of the code of new custom.

Less than an hour and many a dead soldier later, Franklyn had been offered, and for the slightest fraction of what he was being charged at the hotel, new quarters in the spare room over the saloon—it had its own entrance by way of an exterior shingle-covered staircase around back, boasted an honest-to-god cold-water shower to boot—and was being personally escorted on a shank's-mare tour of the town and environs by John Plautz, the man who had been Ivan's immediate and—as he was quick to make clear—altogether reluctant successor at *Glasnik*. Plautz seemed to know everything about and everyone in Red Jacket, Laurium, and Calumet Township worth knowing. Not surprising. He had been born, reared, and spent all of his forty-five years there, first-born son of the community's first veterinarian.

"Dad must be responsible for half the canine population of Red Jacket," the ruddy, round-faced, rounder-bellied Plautz told Franklin. "Well, the Slovene part anyway."

Affable fellow, Plautz, thought Franklyn, sunny of disposition, quick to laugh, fine wavy head of raspberry hair, flamboyant walrus mustache to match, and one helluva tenor, as Franklyn had occasion to discover when the man, after hoisting a *pivo* or three, a beer, had launched unbidden into a rendition of "Pobratimijo," the Slovene "Song of New Friendships." Comprised one-quarter of a rather notorious traveling quartet, the Four Horsemen—notorious for its nakedly "bawdy" repertoire—along with Leopold Junko, baritone, Jaeger Shvajger, baritone-*deux*, and Josef Clemenc, basso profundo. All in all, so he pegged him, a most valuable man to know.

"Do not want to discourage," he had told him back in the *limuzina*, the saloon, "but you cannot talk to MacNaughton. Easier I should talk to Woodrow Wilson. He will not, not to you. Avoids reporters. All secrets, that one, head low. Hides from the publicity, good, bad, no matter. Believes he has no need of it. He is right.

"Camp to his house, mansion on Calumet Avenue, catch him coming, going, church, Opera House when there is a show. Otherwise"—shook his head—"keeps to company property. Takes his meals at the club."

"The club?"

"Miscowaubik Club, M Club, company club, private playpen for the bosses. Billiards, bowling, squash, bars. Guard dogs there." Shrugged. "Makes sense."

"How so?"

"Talk. Rumors. Threats. Dynamite."

"Really!"

Shrugged again. "These cowboys, they do not play games. Company calls them gunmen. Hired guns. Gunslingers. Wobblies."

"Haywood?"

"Nothing they can pin, make stick. Smart man, Bill. Only just sailed for Europe. Karlsbad. Austria. Labor summit. International Mining Congress. Keeps his hands clean."

"Coming back?"

"So he said, as he can. Did not say when."

"Then who's in charge?"

"Big guns out of the National. Colorado men. Denver."

"Names?"

"Guy Miller. Platform sort, speechifier, smooth with the words. Spellbinder socialist, they call him. Silver tongue. Wants to bring in Mother Jones."

It was out before Franklyn could retrieve it. "Oh, Christ!"

"What? What is wrong?"

"Nothing. Know her some, is all. Way back."

"And? Folk hero to these men."

"Oh, sure. Right, no question. Miners' Angel, all that. And nervy? Hell, yes. But hateful, John. No bend, not an inch. A spiteful, mean-spirited, sanctimonious, coldhearted old lady incapable of listening to any point of view save her wretched own. Personally? I find her impossible to stomach. Miller brings her here, he brings trouble."

"Well, if you say. I do not know. But I think Miller, he already has it settled in his mind. Trouble, that is *just* his game."

"So who else then? I mean, besides this Miller."

"Charlie Mahoney, veep of Denver, executive board. Word is, national wanted to wait, not ready, but now that it has come . . ." Yet another shrug. "So they bring in Mahoney, strike while the iron still is hot. Also, Mor Oppman, John Lowney, Yank Terzich, Howie Tresidder, Stevie Oberto, L. J. Verbos—which he is, all mouth—Billy K. Holawalsky—now there is a mouthful—Manny De Meio—very musical, makes me a-wanna sing: 'Man-eeee, Day, M-eye-ohhhhh'—Joe Cannon. All these, Denver men. I should say Eddie LeGendre, too, and Gus Kerr, Angus Kerr, lawyers here the union signed up. Good men. Also Charlie Hietala, local bull down to

Hancock, one who pushed the calendar, called the vote early. Finn, typical, his way or none." Paused. "Oh." Smiled. "And Ben, Ben Goggia."

"And?"

"What?"

"The grin."

"Just that Ben's the peach, good man, cut above. And such looks—oy! can I say oy?—you never saw. Adonis, that one. Regular here, when you can drag him away from his—how do you say?—constituency, when he can ruggle out, away from under."

"How do you mean, constituency?"

"This you never have seen. In town two seconds and"—finger-snap—"they are onto him, lions on lamb. Young, old, married, not, their eyes are on him like hands. Fun to watch, him fighting them off—and failing. Funnier because only last month he leaped the broom. Does not stop them, though. Here, our weaker sex is not."

"You married, John?"

"Am. Yes."

"Children?"

"Three, one to come. You?"

Franklyn shook his head. "No, no children."

"Wife?"

"No, no wife either."

Plautz waited, *a*waited, the explanation.

"Can't say," said Franklyn, without being asked. "Thought it might happen, once, briefly. When it didn't, stopped looking, stopped without really knowing it, that I'd stopped, or why."

The expression on Plautz's face was quizzical, the very word.

"What I mean is," Franklyn continued, "*I* didn't stop, *it* stopped, on its own, you know? Petered out." Laughed, nonplussed at his ineloquence. "Let's just say I don't miss it. No regrets. Leave it at that."

"But, Frank—god knows I fly no flag for marriage, hard work, every day—but how can you know what you miss? If you never have had it? To miss."

"Ah, terrific point, John. How indeed? What I mean is, I do not think about it—ever."

"Ever?"

"Not if I can help it, and I always can help it."

"And when you cannot? What then?"

"Oh! *Then!* Well, *then* I go to brothels, or read unreadable poetry, or scrutinize inscrutable paintings, or listen to unlistenable music, or get stinking drunk, blotto, do what anyone singularly lacking in imagination and character would do: brood, self-recriminate, wallow, curse the world, and thank my lucky stars." Laughed, uneasily.

"Sorry," said John Plautz, "did not mean to pry. It is just, most men of an age, our age, want children, a son, carry forward the name."

"Noticed the same myself. They do. I don't. They're vain. I'm—well, I'm as vain as the next guy, I suppose. My vanity just leans toward keeping it for myself, to myself, not sharing it, bequeathing it, giving it away, saddling some poor, defenseless, unsuspecting innocent with all the baggage that goes with it, which, in my case, is more and messier than you might wish to know."

"Ach." Dismissive hand wave. "You just have yet to meet. Good that you wait. More should, maybe. Plenty of time."

"Oh, sure, time, lots of time, nothing but, everywhere you look, all the time in the world."

Back at the hotel, packing up to make the move over to the saloon, a scant four-block hop, Franklyn considered what a godsend the obliging John Plautz had been and how the Red Jacket, Laurium, and Calumet Township he so generously had volunteered the better shank of his morning to ushering him around—reconnoitering firsthand, up close, street level, introducing him, solicitously paving his way—was a place unlike any he ever had seen or could have conjured from Ivan's voluminous notes. Well, he thought, words on a page, one or one million, never do do justice, do they? Live up to real life or anything else, save, perhaps, themselves and the white space surrounding their sound.

Who knew, could have known, a city boy like himself, that such a place existed in Midwestern America, circa 1913. For it did not strike him as America at all. Geography and landscape were part of it, of course—the proximity of the great, metallic, ocean-broad lake on the one hand, the raw, scabby, ocher sand-scrub and scraggle, duff and glooming dark loom of untrammeled pine forest on the other. But it was more than the peninsular, elemental isolation of the place, the sense of outback, outpost, palpable presence of endmost extremes, or the singular flora, fauna, and geology. It was, rather, the mines, their ubiquity. And the people, their—how say it?—self-apparent otherness, prevailing foreignness, and how the extent and range of their elbow-by-rib diversity was taken, seemingly by one and all, so matter-of-factly for granted.

What was obvious at once was that much as the culture and character of a town like, oh, say, Iowa City (or Gambier, Ohio) was distinguished, determined, largely dominated by its universities and the academic communities they spawned, so, likewise, Calumet/Red Jacket/Laurium by its mines and the polyglot immigrant population they attracted. You could not venture a step, assay a breath, that the coppery fact did not sidle up, all brass, and spank you—sights, sounds, flavors, fragrances—flush in the face, or insinuate itself beneath the sole of your skin.

As John had butlered him down Calumet Avenue to the idle chat and chewed fat of fellow passersby—amputees abounded, noticed Franklyn, as did the blind, the poulfoot, and kyphotic—a number of them peddling hot pasty from cloth-covered, white wicker punnets, most of whom Plautz had greeted warmly by name and from whom Franklyn had succeeded in catching but the occasional wayward word of thickly accented English—"eighteen languages spoken here, low guess," John remarked at one point, "some say thirty"—his self-appointed guide dog had easeled the lay of the land, scaled, shaped, sketched it for him in a way he found most helpful.

Had urged him, first, to conceive of that boulevard-broad, trap-rock-surfaced street, Calumet—it being the main thoroughfare along which the C&H-owned, round-the-clock streetcar line ran—as "an arrow shaft slashing on the diagonal," southwest to northeast through the heart of the community. On one side of the wide slant, to the immediate west, the bustling, roughly six-square-block commercial district of Red Jacket with its Seventh Street saloons, Fifth Street emporiums, and Sixth Street clock-towered, C&H-owned, 1,200-seat Theater and Opera House, where Modjeska, Caruso, Bernhardt, Fairbanks, Russell, Sousa, Wallace Beery, William S. Hart, and John L. Sullivan himself all had performed at one time or another. Clearly, the district's pride and joy.

When Plautz, eager to show it off, had invited him to tour its lavish interior, Franklyn had found himself not only demurring, but doing so in much of a cold sweat.

"I am sure it is a wonder, John, but I haven't been inside a theater in more than ten years. Bad experience once. Stayed away ever since. Not the superstitious sort, don't spook, but theaters give me nightmares. Appreciate the offer, but, you will forgive me, I shall have to pass."

The other side of the boulevard, to the adjacent east, harbored the more sedate, though not prim, roughly twelve-square-block residential area of Laurium and its own crown jewel, the five-year-old, forty-five-room, 13,000-square-foot mansion of Thomas Hoatson, owner of the Calumet and Mining Company: elephant-hide-covered walls, pure silver-foil ceilings, so forth and so on.

"Some call us Mirage City," said Plautz. "When you are in Calumet, you are in Red Jacket, but when you are in Red Jacket, you are not in Calumet, and when you are in Calumet, you are in Laurium, but when you are in Laurium, you are not in Calumet. And, of course, when you are in Red Jacket *or* Laurium, both of which are in Calumet, you are in neither one nor the other."

Plying along the middle border of the towns was a comparatively narrow, paved-ground, two-mile-long stretch of working corridor, Mine Street by name. Studded at irregular intervals with the many C&H mine entrances, fully a dozen and a half, according to John, the lot was interspersed with the heavily mortised-and-mortared, brick-and-mine-rock C&H "surface structures": machine, blacksmith, drill, forge, and pattern shops; hoist and rock, gear and man-engine houses; boiler and warehouses; the enormous, sublunate railroad roundhouse; the handsome, elaborately masonried administrative buildings; the C&H company hospital; the 40,000-volume C&H public library with its 1,040-square-foot basement pool.

More formidable still were the 120-foot-high, stagger-roofed, ungainly looking, steel-skeletoned chute-and-ladder shaft buildings and the spindlier, yet more massive red-hearthstone, reverberating-furnace smokestacks—150 feet high some of them, nine feet in diameter—thrusting out of the earth like enormous organ pipes—or, alternatively, immense bassoons hurled like javelins down from the very heavens.

Transurban mines, so they struck Franklyn, mines that those who worked them, as those who did not, lived close atop, near amid, hard astride. Nor so much as a hairsbreadth, literally, between town and mine, family and work, life and death, between the praying above and blasting below. Streets, buildings, walkways, yards, and gardens, all owned by the Outfit, all silted with siftings of mineral talcum the russety rust color of blood churned with sand; rubigo. And come sundown, then—oh my and oh yes!—its glow glowing dull orange, poured gravy *l'orange* muted and filmed over all: cast-iron facade, metal cornice, terra-cotta sunburst, column, pilaster, oriel, turret, Richardsonian Romanesque and Renaissance Revival.

The surrounding nearmost company-built, shack-and-shanty, saltbox ethnic residential enclaves as well, all within easy walking distance each of the other: the "Jackets" Blue, Red, and Yellow; the "sections" Annex and Depot; the outwesterly Tamarack and North Tamarack locations around which yet another eight mines were clustered; as well as Swedetown-on-the-Hill (populated not by Swedes, but Poles and Finns), Raymbaultown, Albion, Newtown, Frenchtown, Bumbletown Hill, Caledonia, Corktown, Limerick, Florida, Sing Sing, Shoepack Alley, Waterworks Road; at the more southerly Osceola location, another six mines, one of which, number three, had been the site eighteen years earlier of the deadliest underground blaze in U.P. history; the northmost locations of Centennial and Centennial Heights, and so slanting northeasterly up Calumet Avenue and in quick succession on out of town: South Kearsarge, Wolverine, North Kearsarge, Allouez, Ahmeek, Mohawk, Seneca, the lot accounting for twenty mines more.

All the names, so many they merged. How remember, much less map each correctly in the mind? And each arrayed and mantled as if nothing could be more natural on God's earth than to be far-flung-and-fielded across a vast honeycombed hollow a mile down, twelve more as wide. Stamp a foot too vigorously, Franklyn could not help thinking as he and Plautz strolled, leap and land too hard, pound the ground with a frustrated fist, and how not suspect that one must only tumble through, bottoms-up, buried to one's eyeballs in China itself.

There were certain towns, thought Franklyn, the streets of which were as the walls of a room, a *living* room perhaps, one lung'd and alive, and upon which was written a text that could be read as a relief map is read. An artifice, one of built form, assembled and constructed so that it expressed a dimensionalized human nature. And this is why man deliberately chose, always had chosen, insofar as the choice was afforded him, to build and live in cities. The proportion of a certain perspective, one contoured and textured, structure made manifest. An illusion, of course, such self-delineation, the notion that life hung tidily together—or untidily, for that matter—organized as grids, aligned as any tract, ordered as a quadrant, divided by lines, summed up neatly in boxes, precincts, shires, parishes, wards, districts, realms, dioceses sectored and sectioned into stanzas and chapters.

The pages of towns are written in code. You can live the length of your lifetime in the same one, vast as Chicago, huddled as Red Jacket, and never begin to decrypt the contents of their cubism. Cities contain secrets within their closed covers, behind their battened shutters, curtained windows, locked doors. What you see on city streets, thought Franklyn, is mainly window dressing or public posture, the show owners make of petting their children and parading their pets.

"So what do you think?" John Plautz had asked him as the whirlwind tour had neared its end. The tavern was right around the corner. "What are you thinking? I can tell, something on your face, in your eyes."

"I think," Franklyn had answered as they continued walking, "that this strike, as all strikes, will in time run its course, and in the running, and in the end, prove unlike any I ever have covered, or heard about."

At which Plautz, pulling up in front of his place of business, had nodded in agreement, curiosity piqued but saying nothing, wistful, portentous, sage, until he had said, "But why do you say so? What do you see?" Extracted a pack from a pocket, lit up a *Helmar*.

"What I see," Franklyn had said, "is that everything here is too bound up in everything else, everyone too on top of one another, too wrapped up, too close, tied too tight to the same stake, entwined like strands of rope. Too . . . caged, inside the same cage, and only so much food to go around."

Franklyn had sun-visored his eyes with a hand then. "What I see is that all this could far too easily, far too quickly become little but an intractable death hug. Tinderbox." And had forced a smile. "But hey, I'm nothing but an outlander, what do I know? It'll probably last a week or two and I'll be on my way home, the union boys will have won their concessions, peace, justice, and prosperity will reign throughout the land, and you'll be rolling in the dough on account."

Plautz had been perfectly sober. "What *you* know, Frank, is Haywood."

"Used to, some. And you"—he had paused—"know MacNaughton."

"Not much."

"Enough."

"Enough, yes."

"So looks like I'll be sticking around awhile, that your point?"

"No point. But awhile, yes."

"How long you think?"

He had shrugged, then smiled, then frowned. "Religious, Frank?"

"Not to kneel, no."

"Believe in heaven?"

"Not lately."

"Not hell either?"

"More likely. If I were a betting man, be quicker to wager on the latter than the former. Least *it* makes *some* sense. The place one goes to learn humility, by being humbled, eternally."

Plautz had laughed. "So fetch your things over, settle in upstairs"— jerked his head in the direction—"make yourself to home. At least"—a twinkle had entered his eye—"until hell freezes over, or breaks loose."

"Ah, yes. Plumb forgot. It does do that up here, doesn't it? Freeze over."

"Been known to. Winters. Some few."

"Winter! You think it'll be winter?"

"Not before. Maybe after."

"Lasts a long time up here, right?"

"'Til spring." Had laughed again. "The Long White, Finns call it. Time of colored glasses."

"Colored glasses?"

"Specs, to wear against the white. A man can go blind."

"Well, I'll need to tell Ivan then, see what he wants me to do."

"Tell him hello from me. Wee Van. Miss him. Good man. Better friend."

"I will." Franklyn had paused. "Winter, huh?"

He had nodded. "Spring, maybe. That, or before that . . ."

"What?"

"The torch. What you said. Burning one another down, at the same stake."

What Ivan wanted him to do—no surprise—was to stay on, do his job, cover the strike, file stories, as long as there were stories to file. Take what occurred as it came, day to day, one at a time, or two. His wire in response to the one Franklyn sent down had been somewhat unambiguous upon the point:

STAY. WORK. WRITE. NEWS. TELL PLAUTZ: *ZDRAVO* AND *HVALA*.

Fine, then. Underway, the thing begun. Now he would go in sleuth of the thick of it, report what he saw and might hear. Strangest of strangers in the strangest of strange lands, where, in for a penny, apparently, all in for the lot of his life.

He needed a beer.

Ana, when she heard it, the whistling coming from the mines, already had been up for hours, occupied out back, slaving over her kiln, babushka-ed, didymium-lens goggled, leather aproned and gloved. So at the very moment the whistling erupted—triggering the discordant accompaniment of Libby's plaintive howling—she was withdrawing from the 2,100- to 3,000-degree F. furnace-bright maw of the glory hole her iron blowpipe.

Gobbed molten at its knob end with a sand/soda/salt/lime goo the viscous consistency of Karo syrup, she nimbly spun the pipe's handle, long as a didgeridoo, as she removed the electuaried mass, deftly torquing and rotating it radially, sure hands twirling it on the swivel before swinging it away and lifting it up and airborne. Then, planting her lips firmly to the long tube's open mouth, she blew.

The knobbed gob of gathered goo—the moile, or ambitty—glowed the successive colors of cobalt, sulfur, nickel, then copper, before appearing to shudder and throb, belly, blister, blobble, finally to orb to phosphor transparency—taffy globe of glass.

Bracing the blowpipe capped with its captured form—structure of breath, air of shape; it never would have occurred to her to call it sculpture—in the Y-crotch of her free-standing yoke, she grabbed a second rod, the punty, insinuating it carefully at the base of the rapidly cooling mass even as she fished a three-corner file from her apron pocket. Using it to quick-slash a breakmark near the pipe end before snapping the piece cleanly off, she transplanted it to the lower temperature of the annealing oven to relieve the stress across its surface.

No one was more surprised than Ana, then, when, with a crisp *skree-tle*, it promptly imploded: cullet. First time she had lost a piece this way in years.

"So, Libs," she spoke good-naturedly to the dog, "think it was your howling?" When the dog barked, she laughed. "No, me either."

She knew what those whistles meant, what they signified. It almost was too neat. The inauspicious, nor less ominous neatness, it occurred to her, of stock fiction. Cheap-jack symbolism: The Moment of Boding Foreshadow.

Latching closed the door of the kiln, she used her teeth to tug off her gloves by their fingertips, slid her goggles up to nest atop her head, gathered her tools, tongue-clucked to the dog, and headed back to the house to hand-pump a quick bath in the sink before her husband arrived, her every thought close-quoted in sighs: the way a strike, when it comes, can shatter.

READ ALL ABOUT IT

Ivan played Franklyn's first story, datelined CALUMET, front page above the fold, upper-right, beneath a forty-eight-point headline in boldface Cheltenham type running across three vertical columns:

MICHIGAN MINERS' STRIKE SHUTS DOWN COPPER RANGE ACROSS UPPER PENINSULA

Then two subdecks, the first in thirty-six-point ital:

THREE DOZEN MINES HIT
VIOLENCE WIDESPREAD
NATIONAL GUARD CALLED IN

The second in twenty-four-point Caslon:

**Worker demands rebuffed as company bosses vow
never to recognize Union**

The full text of Franklyn's story ran:

CALUMET—Spurned in its ongoing efforts to arrange a meeting with copper-mine managers to air its demands, the Western Federation of Miners (WFM), representing five union locals claiming some 9,000 members across Michigan's Upper Peninsula, halted work Wednesday afternoon at three dozen mines, effectively shutting down the state's copper-producing industry which last year accounted for a reported $40 million in revenue.

The WFM, which repeatedly had petitioned mine ownership to formally recognize the union as the only legitimate collective bargaining agent on behalf of the roughly 15,000 copper miners employed by 21 companies here, is demanding institution of an 8-hour workday, a uniform $3.50 daily minimum wage for all miners, $3 for all trammers, the abolishment of the so-called one-man mine drill, and a permanent system to address worker grievances.

On behalf of ownership, James MacNaughton, General Manager of Calumet & Hecla (C&H), the largest and most profitable of the state's copper-mining companies, issued a statement declaring, "The Calumet & Hecla and other companies under its management will never recognize the Western Federation of Miners which has sent active gunmen into this district with the avowed intention of committing acts of physical intimidation and violence. Every leader of this strike is from outside this district which until the WFM undertook its campaign was a peaceable and prosperous community."

The statement continued: "It is and remains the policy of the company to listen to the concerns of every man in its employ. However, the demands for a meeting, as the issues to be addressed at that meeting, were presented not by men employed by any company, but by the outside gunmen of the WFM. Consequently, such a meeting could not, and will never, take place.

"The history of the Federation is well known, as are its tactics, which include riots, assaults, destruction of property, and bloodshed. Much of the leadership responsible for such lawlessness and violence presently are on the ground here. Evidence of same is too voluminous to enumerate, but includes the assassination of Superintendant Collins of the Colorado Smuggler's Union mine, the dynamiting of Mr. Bulkeley Wells, also of the Smuggler's Union, and the base and cowardly murder of ex-Governor Steunenberg of Idaho."

Replying to GM MacNaughton's statement, C. E. Mahoney, WFM Vice President, dismissed the general manager's characterization of his union organizers as "absurd," stating, "There are not now, nor have there ever been so-called WFM gunmen in this district. Equally absurd is the charge that the cause of this labor action is agitation on the part of so-called outsiders. The cause of this strike is what it always has been and will continue to be until our demands are met—the desire on the part of the workers that their concerns be granted fair, equitable, and good faith hearing by ownership, beginning with formal recognition of the WFM as exclusive representative on their behalf in the resolution of all such matters."

In the wake of Wednesday's walk-out, numerous running clashes erupted between marauding mobs of strikers and nonstrikers estimated to approach well over 500 on each side. The majority of the attacks occurred on C&H properties in and around the town of Red Jacket where the company operates most of its mines. These involved simple fistfights as well as assaults with weapons such as rocks, bricks, clubs and pipes, ax handles, two-by-fours, sandbags, brickbats, railroad ties and iron bolts, although several gunshots also were heard. As of this writing, no deaths have been reported across the district and no arrests made, but some two dozen strikers and nonstrikers have sustained injuries serious enough to require their hospitalization.

In response to what he termed "the anarchist violence," Houghton County Sheriff James A. Cruse on Thursday telephoned Michigan Governor Woodbridge Ferris to request that he immediately dispatch 3,000 National Guardsman to restore order in the district which comprises over 1,000 square miles in Houghton County alone. The first of these troops, 18 infantry companies under the command of Brigadier General Pearley L. Abbey, presently are billeted in and around the C&H-owned Calumet Light Infantry Armory in Red Jacket. The General reports that another 26 infantry companies have been deployed as far north as Keweenaw County and as far south as Painesdale/Seeberville, some 20 miles away. Artillery, cavalry, mounted signal, engineer, and hospital and ambulance corps are encamped in a sprawling, hastily erected tent village spilling beyond the armory grounds and stretching up and down main thoroughfares here. For the moment, Upper Michigan's Copper County literally is an armed camp subject to martial law.

Additionally, Sheriff Cruse reports that he has placed over 50 men of the Waddell-Mahon Corporation of New York City on the county payroll with plans to "hire on more as circumstances may warrant." These "Waddies," as they are called, described as "professional strikebreakers" by the sheriff, are the same men, all of them licensed to carry firearms, who have been hired to battle the WFM in previous labor actions, most of them in the western mines. Reports indicate that another 60 have been hired by various mine managers in the district, including half a dozen by GM MacNaughton to organize and train his own squadron of company guards.

While no outbursts of mass violence similar to those on Wednesday have occurred since the arrival of the National Guard, the military has been dispatched on numerous occasions to respond to isolated incidents of arson and repeated alarms of the dynamiting of company buildings, particularly the Red Jacket shaft-house and the C&H Miscowaubik Club, the favored after-hours gathering place of company management recently placed under round-the-clock militia protection.

As of this writing, the strikers and their organizers appear content to stage protest parades—one on Sunday was estimated by authorities to number well over 3,000—picket mine entrances, attend union rallies and strategy meetings at their Dunn's Hall headquarters in downtown Red Jacket, and to wage rhetorical war led by stump speakers such as WFM organizer Guy Miller, the "Socialist Spellbinder."

It was Miller who on Sunday exhorted a crowd of several thousand strikers from his platform at the Palestra amphitheater, the same from which presidential candidate Theodore Roosevelt delivered his campaign speech only last fall, that "while the Governor of Michigan cannot be bothered to come north—and were he a man of clean conscience and common decency he would come, be a trammer for a day; hell, for an hour—while the governor lounges comfortably upon his throne in Lansing from which high and mighty perch he sees fit to answer the just demands of workingmen with the cold steel of bayonets, all you need do is stand firm with your arms folded in right resolve for the next 10 days and you will see how the chief, MacNaughton, will be begging you fellows to save the whole Conglomerate Lode from caving in. And you will do it, too, when he treats you square."

Miller, who states that he has been in contact with the octogenarian labor activist Mother Jones, the so-called Miners' Angel, reports that he expects her to arrive "for an extended stay sometime next week from the coalfields of West Virginia, where she has been working tirelessly for the United Mine Workers" on behalf of the miners there.

Meanwhile, railroads in the region report a steady exodus of local residents. According to spokesmen, well over 1,500 have departed the district by train since the beginning of the strike on Wednesday, having purchased tickets for "destinations from Cobalt to California."

At present, then, the mood here is less one of heightened tension than creeping uneasiness as the two sides, with the National Guard the sole buffer between them, endeavor either to break or to outlast the current stalemate. As the strike headed into its second week, the situation may have been summed up best by Red Jacket saloon-keeper John Plautz, who commented, "It will be a while, still, before either side sees the advantage of taking it upon itself to budge. In the end, it is a matter of who blinks first, gives a little to get some back. That, or who is first to call the other out. Make a move. Risk the showdown. No mistake, neither side is bluffing. Both boast they alone know the right of it. And both, I think, are playing for keeps."

Only later did Franklyn learn that it was the Cornish Kid who was responsible for stringing from the clock tower of the Opera House, some seventy feet in the air, the enormous banner that the union had paid him to unfurl there for Sunday's big parade:

GOOD ENOUGH TO WORK FOR THE BOSSES,
BUT NOT GOOD ENOUGH TO TALK TO THEM

Only later, as well, did he learn that as soon as the strike was called, the instant those whistles had blown, Nikolai Temelcoff, leaving his family behind, had hopped the first train west to go in search of "keenlier lodes."

The days of perfection were over.

MOTHER

Along with what doubtless was every other ambulatory soul within a twenty-mile radius, Franklyn was at the depot when Mary Harris "Mother" Jones—only latterly anointed "Our John Brown in Petticoats" by a press that seemed never to flag in its dubious habit of bestowing upon those public figures it deigned to adopt as its own what it considered colorful, if wrongheaded, cognomens (Harriet Tubman, it immediately occurred to Franklyn, would have been by far the more apropos)— Franklyn was there when the buzzard-faced, apiculate-beaked, witch-jawed, wire-bespectacled, spun-sugar-haired crone stepped defiantly unassisted from the train and, with a dismissive wave of her ancient wing, loudly declaimed her disinclination to take advantage of the largesse of her ragtop-down, union-arranged, Chalmers automobile for the three-block ride to WFM headquarters at Dunn's Hall, the union conventicle on Sixth Street.

"Do I look like the pope to you?" she declared crustily, striding her strident way through the largely adoring mob. "I'll march with my boys, if you don't mind!"

Attired, despite the stifling heat, in her trademark head-to-toe black bombazine and velvet, including the antique pancake bonnet, she was flanked by Mahoney, Miller, Ben Goggia, and a woman—middling aged, pterodactyl shouldered, not unsubstantial of bosom and girth—who had debarked the train with her arm in arm, appearing to enjoy an altogether easy familiarity in her presence.

Notebook in hand, Franklyn elbowed his way near as they walked, musing as he did so on how much he genuinely loathed such wolf-packing. Reporters were everywhere, avalanching their shouted questions at the osseous old woman in black. The strike, if not yet full-blown national news, was fast tilting in the direction, just as it already had become, at least for the moment, the biggest story in the Midwest. Western Union latterly had hired on five extra operators to handle the overflow at the Opera House.

Side-winging through the ubiquitous press of the press until he was within earshot of Goggia, Franklyn shouted, "Ben!" The two were friendly. The past ten days had seen to that.

"Frank," yelled Goggia, "over to Dunn's. She'll take questions there." Then, as Franklyn jostled up near, Goggia, apprehending the game, lowered his voice. "I'll make sure you get her to yourself, after." Winked.

"Thanks, Ben. Prince. Owe you one."

"Forget it. Least I can do."

Franklyn smiled. "See you there." Turned to go. Turned back. "So who's the pilot fish?" Nodded toward the younger woman walking arm in arm, barely keeping pace with her older companion.

"Ella? Ella Reeve Bloor, National Socialist Press Association. Talk she's writing up the old lady's biography."

"Ah." And hoofed it straightaway to the hall, where, stationing himself against a wall alcoved in the shadow of a nearby stairwell, he watched and listened to Mother Jones, ensconced in her union-furnished rocking chair, adroitly field the fusillade of questions lobbed her way by reporters from the AP, UPI, the dozen-plus local rags, each of the Detroit, Minneapolis, Milwaukee, and Chicago papers, and one fellow, a "camera correspondent" out of Cleveland, who was "filming" the entire shindig for *Pathé's Weekly* "newsreels," images that shortly were to find their way into theaters not only across the country, but in Europe, Russia, and the Far East.

Ella Bloor, Franklyn noticed, did not for so much as an instant leave her companion's side or alter the worshipful expression altared upon her face, even as the old lady's responses—Mother Jones could only have heard each of these questions a hundred times before, he thought—struck him as little but so many canned polemics and agitprop. It was only when Miller had shut down the session and Goggia shooed the reporters out the door that Franklyn stepped forward, if only to find that the woman's memory, as past reputation attested, was as preternatural as her mind was unnuanced. Unfazed, she did not, as is said, skip a beat.

"Frank Shivs," she said.

"Mother."

"How many years then?"

Resisting the temptation to reply, "Too few," he replied, "1905, 6. What's that?"

Shifted in the rocker. "Ella, Franklyn Shivs. Frank, Ella Reeve Bloor, National Socialist Press."

Franklyn touched his hand to his hat brim, locked eyes. "Ma'am."

Ella Reeve Bloor's eyes were not cold, just flat. Less vacant than blank. Tough read. She nodded, said nothing.

"Frank used to work the labor beat for the Chicago *Trib. Proleterac* now, isn't it, Frank? Ivan Molek."

"It is."

"Good man."

"None better."

Shifted again, began rocking, squawk of rhythm. "Fire away."

"Just a few."

"Good. Long ride. Don't hold together way I used to."

"Look well held to me, Mother, don't mind my saying." Which she did. Eighty-three years old and each one as hard-won as worn well, a woman armatured of fine-gauge cable . . . and hot spit.

"Don't mind a bit." She almost smiled. "Clean living." Franklyn knew she was a professional teetotaler, as that she eschewed tobacco, as that she was bluntly open about not having been with a man for—well, some good long while. "So?"

"You know your presence here ups the ante."

"Whole point."

"Two weeks in and no violence to speak of since day one."

"That so? And how many concessions from ownership? How much justice for the boys? Name me one issue of real substance that has been settled in our favor or so much as acknowledged as such by management."

"Two weeks. Takes time, you know that."

"I do. Time"—she paused—"and other things."

"Needn't."

She sighed. "Look, I hate violence, and *you* know that. Had people telling me for more'n twenty years to pack a pistol. Never have. Broke with the Wobblies on account. Those boys are too damn reckless. Don't misunderstand, Billy Haywood's a fine fellow, be proud to stand beside him anytime, anywhere, but I favor drama, not guns and bombs. Theater, that's the way to go at it. Boston Tea Party, not Harper's Ferry or O.K. Corral."

"And from where the power of such theater?" he asked.

Now she did smile, however crookedly.

"Right," said Franklyn. "Numbers, and the threat of force implicit in them."

She sighed, again. "I've been at this game, fighting this *war*, for twenty long years, which is more'n long enough to know that if you threaten, then fail to back up those threats, don't hold fast to a certain line no matter the setbacks and do it in large enough numbers, amass enough common purpose and solidarity and, yes, *might*, you accomplish nothing."

"No, Mother," said Franklyn, "you accomplish something all right. You provoke reaction. Backlash."

"Which is why we cannot fail and why we shall not fail and why we have won before and will win again. We are right, they are wrong; we have the numbers, they have only themselves, selves that are soulless and small and selfish. Shells."

"Shells they may be, but those shells have the money—and the law."

"Details. Their day is done."

"Confident, aren't you?"

"Why not? I know my boys, I know my history, and I know that our enemies are on the wrong side of it. They already are part of the garbage bundled to its barge. All we need to do is untie it from its dock, let the current catch it, wave so long."

"Untie it," said Franklyn. "Very good. But there's the rub. That knot's wound so tight, so snarled, so . . . grannied, it requires a shears to free it. Amputation."

"Sometimes, yes. Sometimes that's so. You're right. Sorrows me to say it, Frank, but it takes what it takes, and what it takes ain't always so pretty. Hardly ever is—pretty."

"And all the while," he replied, "those aboard that barge, the Mac-Naughton's, doing all in their power, considerable power, to stop you." How was it, he wondered, that he found himself sparring with this woman—pointless. "Mother, you can wield the shears all day, in the end, look around—*they've* got the bullets."

"So they do, and about that I'll say this: militia have no business, none, in an industrial dispute. This is not a revolution." She waved a dismissive hand, ancient hand. "No matter, militia or no, we have the numbers."

"Right. And here is the problem with numbers." Now he was lecturing her. What had gotten into him? "You stir them up, shake the hive—you're good at it, no one would say different—but once stirred and shaken, then what? How control them? How harness the hornets, their anger? It's a high wire you walk, Mother, and no nets to catch those you would honey up there with you."

"Honey? Never used honey in my life. Feed it to 'em like I always have—strong medicine, no sugar. Those boys wouldn't listen otherwise. They know they can count on me to tell 'em straight. Any power I have, that's it." Steely now. "The truth."

She stopped rocking. "We done?"

"One more. Will you meet with MacNaughton?"

"No. Why should I? He wants to talk, he knows where to find me. Speech tomorrow, then do as I always do, visit the neighborhoods, meet with the families, sit with the wives and children, listen and pray. Here's a quote for you, exclusive, Frank, for Ivan, in advance, preview of my speech." Rustled in her skirts, fished out a paper, adjusted her spectacles, cleared her throat:

"'Any woman married to a measly man who would refuse to join the union is degrading herself should she acquiesce in his decision. It is up to the women to raise their voices in their own homes and take the fight to the streets in behalf of their men, no less those men—if they can be called men, for such as they are weak-kneed and no-account toads not fit to have a woman live with them—who refuse to do so themselves. No strike was ever lost that women did their rightful part to win.

"'And to those wives who would plead that the duties of motherhood prevent their doing so, I say, take your children with you! Carry them in arms, push them in carriages, have them march hand in hand beside you! You are blessed with the great opportunity to teach them the *real* facts of life! Never mind if they call you not ladylike. You are *woman*like. God-almighty made the woman. The ownership gang of thieves made the ladies, the ones who live for no reason but to please their husbands and pa-rade their wealth before the poor and hungry, turning the thumbscrews of despair and envy into the very vitals of those who in reality are their sis-ters. It is the gang of thieves who puts rags on the real women and deco-rates their own with all the fancified finery of the nation.'"

Her eyes narrowed, hooded down, enough, thought Franklyn, that at farther remove they might have appeared closed, as in prayer, or death. "'Someday, and soon, there will come another John Brown, and he—or she—will tear this nation end to end if this . . . inequity, does not stop!' There. How's that? Enough?"

"Your call."

"Quits then. Done in. Gotta rest up for tomorrow."

Ella Bloor was at her elbow, helping her from the rocker.

"Write it up good, Frank Shivs," said Mother Jones, leaning on her broad-shouldered companion. "I know we don't exactly see eye to eye. Don't have to, not if you do your job the way your boss wants it done.

"Think I don't know about you?" Tapped her temple. "Too much up here for your own damn good, always was. Put your mind to it, you can set the angels reading."

Pocketing the notebook, he muttered his pro forma thanks for her having been so generous with her time. Mother Jones said nothing, merely flipped an absent hand somewhat vaguely in his direction as her putative biographer ushered her toward the stair, which is when he felt a hand cupped to his shoulder.

"Frank."

"Ben, thanks for that."

"Get what you needed?"

"Oh sure. Aces. Good stuff. More than enough."

"Good. Listen. Tomorrow. Big speech. Palestra. Laurium. One o'clock. Rest of the week we've got her visiting all up and down the range. Welcome to ride along. Lemme know."

"I will. Thanks. See you over to Plautz's later?"

Goggia edged him toward the door. "Can't say. I'm the minder. Sorta have me apron-stringed."

"Or hog-tied." Franklyn laughed. "Not to worry. She turns in early. No night life for Our Mother of the Mines."

He nodded. "Except"—glanced toward the stair as he lowered his voice—"it's not just the old lady. Ella, too."

"You mean she actually leaves her side? Got the impression she was attached by invisible wires or something. Marionette strings."

"Nah. Truth is, Ella's up to her eyeballs same as the rest of us. Mother stirs 'em up, Ella follows through, hands-on. Woman's Auxiliary we've got going down to Hancock? She's wild to do the same right here, only bigger. Should work, too, once the old lady sets 'em on fire."

"Hellfire, sure. Don't see why not."

"Anyway, that's my end. National's got me working distaff side."

"Jeez, Ben." Franklyn grinned. "Wonder why. Something to do with your fashion sense, must be. You know how the ladies like the cashmere." For a union organizer, Ben Goggia was awfully partial to manicured nails, meticulously barbered hair, well-trimmed vibrissae, spit-shined shoes, physique-tailored cashmere suits, and a tan even and deep as amber.

"All right, all right," he replied, good-naturedly. "It's like the old lady said before, you play the hand you're dealt, right?" Shrugged. "Play to your strength. I don't mind. So far so good. We seem to be making some inroads."

"Oh, I'm sure. Inroads. Clearing the brush. Dredging the swamp. Beating the bush. Bush after bush. Very good."

"It's a living."

"And wouldn't we all love to live it. You're a lucky man, Goggia. Lucky stiff."

When he opened the door, Franklyn walked through. "See you when I see you then. Keep the flag flying, Ben."

Swell guy, Ben. Everything John Plautz had said and half again as much. Pushing out onto the street, too hot, sunny, high nineties, Franklyn for the briefest moment found himself light-blind as his thoughts strayed back to Mother Jones. Might have sworn she didn't look a day older than the first time he had seen her, but then he half suspected she had looked ancient even when she had been young, this woman who never had met an admirer whose administration she failed to admire.

Ana Clemenc had set her mind to it, to go hear Mother Jones at the Palestra in Laurium on the two-week anniversary of the strike. Why not? Wednesday was her day off from the hospital. Everyone she knew, including her own parents, George and Mary—hell, everyone she *didn't* know seemed to be going. Besides, it didn't cost a copper. Mother Jones was famous, a famous *woman*. However much Josef might disapprove, what was the possible harm?

"You are not going."

"I am."

"I forbid it."

"Fine, Josef. You forbid it. I am going."

"Why?"

"Why not?"

"Because I forbid it. Because she is who she is."

"Which is what? In your opinion."

"Trouble. Red trouble. Outside trouble. Troublemaking socialist Red who talks black poison against those who put this roof over our heads, these clothes on our backs, that food on our tables."

"No. It is you, Josef. You put those things. The roof. The clothes. The food. You work. You risk your life. You *give* your life. Every day. You are paid. Not enough. Not fairly. But you are paid, and with what you are paid it is you who puts these things. Tell me this is not true."

"It is one *part* of the truth. It is not all. This is what they wish you to forget and would deny. But wishing it, denying it, that does not make it so. I do not own a mine, I work one. That is what I am, what I do, all I do, that is all I wish to do, and be. To be, what I do."

"No, Josef. You are more, much more than what you do. I know you are more, even if you do not. You are a man. One, yes, alone, I know. But you are not alone. You are one among many. Thousands. Tens of thousands. Without you, the many, there is no mine, no Outfit. Without you, all of you, without the ones who work it, a mine is nothing. A dark hole.

Without a meaning. It is you who make it live, give it purpose. It is the miners who make the earth below breathe to life above. Why cannot you see it? Why will you not?"

"Because those are just words, Ann, pretty words. Maybe they even are true ones, some. But words, just words are what they are."

"Which is? In your opinion."

"What I said, words, more words, the sound of air. That is what your Mother Jones is, wind, one that blows ill, blows through here, our home, like she belongs. She does not belong because she does not know. How could she? Was she born here? Does she live here? Will she die here? Has she worked below? Has her family? A single one? Has she ever *been* below?"

"I have not, Josef. I have never been, below. Would you say I do not know?"

"You know. Your grandfather. Father. Uncles. Cousins. You know enough."

"Yes, I do. I know enough to go and listen and hear for myself. What are you afraid of, husband? That if you go, you will hear something for which you have no answer? That if your wife does, she will return a Red as well as a godless one?"

"It is this business, Ann, all that is happening. No good can come of it. It is wrong. Two weeks now. A man should work. What sort of man would rather march than work? Listen to others make speeches than work? Rely on those who have no business here to see to their welfare and that of their families?"

"Once, wife, this was God's country, good, Catholic country. Now? What is it now? Why, Ann? Why trust to strangers, the very ones who throw men out of their work? Who keep them from doing the work they would do? *Should* do. Who see all men as only one thing, one big thing, all the same, no different one from another, what they call a union."

"Because that is the choice, Josef. There is no other. The war has come. It is here. It has found us. You cannot choose to turn away, to hide. You can run, that you can, as some already have. You can leave. But if you stay, then you must fight, or suffer what comes in its coming."

"So you will go."

"I will."

"And nothing I can say—"

"Nothing."

"Then you will go, as you will, as you do, always. But—I will not."
"You will not come with your wife."
"I will not, wife. Ann, I cannot."
"No, Josef. You will not."
"As you wish. As you say. I will not."

Franklyn's second story largely concerned Mother Jones and her Palestra speech, a stemwinder he felt compelled to quote at no little length. Whatever else she was or was not, she was good copy. Even Ivan was interested in selling as many newspapers as he might, and as his recent wire had indicated, coverage of the strike had boosted circulation by, so he estimated, more than half.

EXTRA PRINT RUNS. READERS CANNOT GET ENOUGH.

In any event, the old lady had been in top form:
"I want you to use your brains, not your hands," she had declared. "Your masters want you to use your hands. Don't do it. Don't carry a gun or pistol. If the other fellow goes after you, use your fists, black his eyes so he can't see to shoot. You don't need to fight. Just be firm. But peaceful. Use your brains and wake up to the fact that you have the power, not them. They cannot operate the mines without you. This ground belongs to you, not them.

"The militia has no place here. Militarism is a disease in America. Shame on you girls who talk and laugh with the soldiers who have come to shoot your fathers. I've had experience with militia. Fine fellows, out of uniform. Dress them up, they'll clean hell out of you soon as ask you to move on at the point of their bayonets.

"But don't blame them. Who elected the scab governor who sent them here to camp on company ground and protect company property and ensure the right of scab workers to cross picket lines? It is the same in every strike I have been a part of. The government protects the interests of the money classes. What's the matter with you? Wake up and let it sink into your beery brains that you need elect the right men to public office.

"The capitalists are organized. The doctors are organized. The lawyers are organized. The corporations are organized. And all to skin you. Everyone is organized but you fellows. It is up to you to change the way of it. No one can do it for you. You must hold out until the operators grant every concession demanded of them by the Western Federation of Miners."

Ivan ran with the story as he had the first. He was selling more newspapers now than he ever had in his life. Wee Van's instincts had been right. For all of Franklyn's mandarin existential carping, all his aesthetic effetism, all his insufferable sottishness and bouts of self-indulgent black melancholia, all his unrelentingly tedious, vocal perseverating about his purported loathing of the profession, in the clutch he reverted true to form; he delivered. He might, as Ivan knew he doubtless would, abase himself for it, be left with little but self-recrimination in the morning, but Wee Van's man in Michigan was a reporter born to it and bred. Ivan Molek had little doubt: cut Frank Shivs wide open and what you would find running through his veins was newsprint. Black as ink.

It was just before or after Mother Jones departed the Keweenaw to head out to Colorado (Ella Bloor in custodial tow)—mission triumphantly accomplished: feathers ruffled, hive shaken, bombs metaphorically thrown, call to arms fanfared and bugled, labor action recast now in every high hue and Fauvist color of holy crusade—there to get herself arrested and jailed yet again for her participation in yet another coal miners' strike, that Franklyn noticed—the thing literally was thrust in his face by a newsie upon his emerging from a late breakfast at Pechauer's—the inaugural issue of a new newspaper, a free triweekly called the *Miner's Bulletin*. Edited, as he was shortly to learn, by Guy Miller and Ben Goggia and published in Hancock on the presses contributed to the cause by the Finnish socialist daily *Tyomies*, it scarcely was serious journalism. And yet, in no small part because it was not gun-shy about naming names, it immediately caused an uproar.

> ITEM: "Those, like Henry Warren, who sell themselves cheap to the bosses in hopes of becoming a 10-cent boss themselves, are doing nothing but sucking scabbing. Warren recently quit playing his slide trombone for the Salvation Army in order to have more time to lick through the sole of the jackboot to be able better to taste the toejam."

ITEM: "The idiot-faced Duke Jacaba, who presently is in search of boardinghouses to keep scabs, is little but a two-legged rabid jackass eager to jump into bed with anyone who would slip him the nickel finder's fee to pimp his shameful services."

ITEM: "Having descended from a family of trash pickers and lately been a chambermaid in livery stables and swamper in saloons, the unclean John Walter has chosen to dirty his drawers still further by becoming part of the sorry collection deputized by Bully Cruse. Such dirty work ought suit Walter to a T."

Had there been less at stake, Franklyn would have found such puerile stuff wholly hilarious. As it was, he was but mildly amused. That anyone would take such propaganda seriously was beyond him, and yet, as time proved, they did, both sides, a fact that only underscored, thought Franklyn, how polarized and entrenched their positions had become. Scarce three weeks in, and management and labor remained worlds apart, each speaking its own language, each in a code neither was willing to trouble itself to decrypt.

So it was the next day—had Mother Jones hightailed it by then? seemed to Franklyn she had—that MacNaughton announced, first, that he had directed the emptying of all C&H powder-houses as the first step in the eventual return of all stockpiled dynamite to its manufacturers. And, second, that any C&H employee participating in the strike henceforward would be denied reemployment, and that those seeking to return to work would be required both to withdraw from all and any organized unions, to disavow specifically the WFM, and to sign a statement pledging nonsupport for and nonparticipation in all strike activities. In effect, to take a loyalty oath.

And then MacNaughton did something that even Franklyn considered a deliberately provocative overplaying of his hand. He ordered an enormous, high-wattage searchlight installed atop the octagonal number-two shaft-house, directing that it be left on all through the night, every night, night after night, weekends included, to be manned by an armed operator (one Martin Coppo, as it turned out, father of seven, who would die ten years later in a Red Jacket mine-shaft fire).

The *Miner's Bulletin* immediately tagged the thing "MacNaughton's Eye" and "The Spider's Spy in the Sky" and began running a regular, soon-to-be wildly popular column entitled "Seen by the Searchlight." What was next, it asked, barbed wire and attack dogs?

The mood of the moment, it struck Franklyn, now had arrived at a pass so ominous, he could not help wondering much the same himself.

AND MEANWHILE

Down in Lansing, in Washington, D.C., at C&H corporate headquarters in Boston, 12 Ashburton Place, in the very shadow of Beacon Hill . . .

Unbeknownst to Franklyn—unbeknownst, that is, until Goggia confided the gist of it to him some while later—strenuous back-channel efforts, so-called, by cooler heads, so-called, had been undertaken to settle the strike.

Michigan governor Woodbridge Ferris, desperate to pull the Guard out as soon as possible—it was costing the state some $15,000 a day to keep it there—agreed to Mahoney's request to act as mediator between the two sides. When the proposal was conveyed to MacNaughton, he rejected it out of hand, writing to the governor, "The only assistance we require of the great Commonwealth of Michigan is that it guarantee the immediate safe return to work of those employees who wish to do so without interference of molestation, a right which the laws of the state assure them."

Ferris then dispatched an envoy, Circuit Court Judge Alfred Murphy, to the Keweenaw to meet with both sides on a "fact-finding mission," the end result of which was a report acknowledging that "the workers have real grievances" and that management, MacNaughton in particular, was "unfair, arrogant, and as obtuse as the Bourbons." It continued: "If an employer can force a man to withdraw from a labor union, it likewise can compel him to withdraw from any political, religious, or social body as a condition of employment. This is fundamentally un-American in the first instance, and in the second leaves strikers little choice but to continue to endure desperate hardship rather than acknowledge any such right of their employer."

The report, of course, changed nothing, but did find its way into the hands of U.S. Secretary of Labor William Wilson of the then barely five-month-old Labor Department, who assigned it to John Moffitt of the Bureau of Immigration, who in turn dispatched to the Keweenaw Special Investigator Walter Palmer to do essentially what Murphy already had done, gather facts and meet with both sides "in an effort to find some basis for mediation," an effort effectively torpedoed by MacNaughton upon his informing Palmer that, as far as he was concerned, "there is absolutely nothing to mediate, arbitrate, or confer about."

Moffitt, meanwhile, had taken it upon himself to travel to Boston for a meeting at C&H corporate with company president Quincy Adams Shaw Jr. and company vice president Rodolphe Agassiz, in which he succeeded in securing the former's promise to visit the U.P. "sometime within the next two weeks." It was a visit that never occurred because MacNaughton, whom Shaw trusted implicitly, intervened to stop it as soon as he received wind of it.

Frustrated but not yet resigned, Secretary of Labor Wilson then ordered Moffitt to the Keweenaw to meet face-to-face with MacNaughton, an encounter that proved approximately as productive as all the others when the latter declared that he neither wanted nor needed a "go-between," that he considered "any striking miner a de facto member of the WFM, whether he confesses to such membership or not," and that "what the United States Department of Labor ought rightly do is apply the pressure of its offices to convince the WFM that since its demand that the company grant it recognition is utterly futile, it should immediately withdraw from the district, as it is naught but a scourge on this place."

MacNaughton then concluded the meeting with the declaration, "I am determined to drive the Western Federation of Miners from the copper fields of Michigan if I have to fight all winter to do so." And when Moffitt suggested that "the price to be exacted in your doing so must only be inhuman, particularly as it inflicts suffering upon the women and children in such a cold country, women and children who, after all, are but innocent victims," MacNaughton replied that "the price to be paid makes no difference to me. I will let grass grow in the streets before I will treat with the terrorists."

Undeterred, the redoubtable Wilson then contacted U.S. Congressman Andrew Peters of Massachusetts to arrange another meeting with Shaw and Agassiz in Boston, hoping to end-run MacNaughton. Shaw, however, was having none of it. "I will do nothing over Mr. MacNaughton's head," he declared, "and that includes going north. Jim MacNaughton is my authority on the ground and he has, as he must have, my full and unquestioned trust and confidence. I will not second-guess his judgment in these matters."

And there it stood, even as Governor Ferris precipitously ordered the pull-out of fully one-half of the National Guard, the WFM began doling out the first of its relief payments to strikers only to find itself quickly facing insolvency, and James MacNaughton hired the Burns Detective Agency, the four-year-old national private security firm out of Chicago, to shadow WFM organizers who he was convinced had begun stockpiling an arsenal, importing weapons, and making bombs.

READ ALL ABOUT IT

Ten years earlier, Franklyn had made such little reputation as he yet possessed off his work on the Iroquois fire—which is precisely how he thought of it, *off*. Ever since, he conscientiously had sidestepped those stories likely to place him in too close proximity to physical violence. Not that violence per se troubled him more than it did the next person. He was, having seen his share of it, no more averse to brute brutality, as he considered it, than the average beat cop. What rankled him, rather, was the notion that in writing about it, he inevitably was falsifying it, cheapening, valorizing, elevating, aestheticizing it, this treachery of wielding words to capture *in* words the uncapturable, what never was intended to be captured that way. Because violence, like sex, overwhelmed the word. Pen and paper were not up to it. The quill—at least his—quailed.

TWO MINERS KILLED, TWO WOUNDED IN COPPER COUNTRY CLASH WITH DEPUTY SHERIFFS

WORKERS' HOME RIDDLED WITH BULLETS DURING BLOODY MELEE NEAR SEEBERVILLE

Two deputies arrested and charged with murder, four others still at large

CALUMET—Two copper miners were shot to death here Thursday afternoon, and two others critically wounded when Houghton County sheriff's deputies initiated a running gun battle outside the miners' Seeberville boardinghouse, some 20 miles south of Calumet. According to authorities, the deaths are the first associated with the copper-mining strike poised to enter its fourth week across the Keweenaw Peninsula of northern Michigan.

Killed were Alois Tazan or Tijan, 18, and Steve Putrich, 20, both striking miners in the employ of the Copper Range Consolidated Co. The wounded are strikers John Stimac, 21, and Stanko Stepic, 23. Both were conveyed by ambulance to the Copper Range Hospital in Tri-Mountain, where they remain in critical condition, Stimac with a gunshot wound to the stomach, Stepic with gunshot wounds to the arm and back.

Arrested and charged with second-degree murder in the deaths of the strikers were sheriff's deputies Edwin Polkinghorne and Harry James, both of the Seeberville/Painesdale area. Also charged were Thomas Raleigh, Arthur Davis, William Groff, and Joshua Cooper, all employees of the Waddell-Mahon Corporation of New York City, working as hired deputies for the Houghton County sheriff's office. Polkinghorne and James presently are being held in the Houghton County jail in lieu each of $10,000 bail. Murder warrants have been issued for the arrest of the other four men who as of this writing continue to elude authorities.

Investigations into the incident are ongoing on the part of both the Houghton County district attorney and the Houghton Country sheriff's office. County D.A. Anthony Lucas, on the basis of preliminary findings, has characterized the shootings as "wanton murder, a shameful affair, entirely unjustified." County Sheriff James Cruse has declined comment, save to challenge the jurisdiction of the district attorney's office in the matter.

According to eyewitness Joseph Putrich, proprietor of the boardinghouse and brother of the deceased, he was outside seeking relief from the 102-degree heat with his 21-month-old child and watching his boarders bowl tenpins in the adjoining yard, when he noticed a party of six men walking rapidly toward him just as one of his boarders, John Kalan, emerged through the front door. According to Putrich, "One of the six pointed at Kalan and yelled, 'That's him! That's one of them!' A second man," later identified as Polkinghorne, "then yelled, 'I want you! You are under arrest! Come with me!'" When Kalan refused, backpedaling into the yard, according to Putrich, Polkinghorne followed, grabbing him by the arms and shouting, "Come with us, you son of a bitch!"

When Kalan continued to resist, Polkinghorne and another of the men, later identified as Raleigh, drew billys and began pummeling him about the head until Kalan managed to yell to his fellow boarders playing tenpins, "Come on, boys! They are trying to take me away!"

According to a neighbor, striking miner Evangelista Lencioni, the boarders then rushed to his aid, wrestled Kalan away, and spirited him to the rear of the boardinghouse and into a toolshed, the six deputies in pursuit, revolvers drawn. After a brief scuffle and standoff, according to Lencioni, the six deputies turned to leave, but as they were crossing the yard, one of them, later identified as Cooper, was bashed in the back of the head with a tenpin hurled from the shed. Again according to Lencioni, Cooper staggered from the blow, then whirled and fired his revolver, hitting Steve Putrich, before barging through the door of the boardinghouse itself, discharging two more shots as he did so even as his fellow deputies began firing through the first-floor dining room, bedroom, and kitchen windows on both sides of the building.

Inside the boardinghouse, eight boarders, two women, and three children—one of them a 7-month-old baby, the others 3 and 4 years old—were pinned in a crossfire that Lencioni characterized as "a tumult of shots," and another neighbor, Emilio Guidi, described as "so many shots it sounded like war." One of those shots left Alois Tijan mortally wounded at the foot of an interior staircase. Another grazed the forehead of the infant, Fabian Putrich. Out in the yard, the baby's uncle, Steve Putrich, waited until the barrage had quieted, then staggered, bleeding profusely, into the boardinghouse kitchen, where he instructed his sister-in-law to "send my money to my children," according to Antonia Putrich, before crawling upstairs on his hands and knees and into his deathbed.

Stanko Stepic, meanwhile, shot in the arm and back, attempted to crawl after Putrich, only to make it partway up the stair before tumbling back down, coming to rest on a landing where, pillowed in blood, he lay moaning. John Stimac, shot in the belly, lurched from the dining room and out the front door, fleeing into the nearby woods, where he remained hidden overnight until being taken to the hospital in the morning.

According to authorities, what triggered the incident was Kalan and Stimac's decision to take a shortcut to the boardinghouse through off-limits company property near the Champion Mine that, until the day before, had been patrolled by the National Guard, but that owing to a recent reduction in such forces had since been placed under the the supervision of the sheriff's deputies. Warned by them against trespassing on private property, the pair of striking boarders disregarded the advice, eluding deputies long enough to use the shortcut and arrive safely at the boardinghouse, which is where the deputies spotted Kalan as he emerged through the front door.

In the wake of the killings, a WFM rally at the Palestra amphitheater in Laurium attracted a throng estimated to number well over 5,000. There they listened to union organizers denounce Governor Ferris as "an accessory before the fact," accuse Sheriff Cruse of having "hands dripped with blood," and castigate C&H General Manager James Mac-Naughton as "the chief tool of the Boston Coppers who grow fat by keeping its workers lean."

The strike marks its one-month anniversary next week, and while nonstriking workers—English speakers mainly, Cornish, Irish, Scottish, some few Swedes—continue to trickle back to work in the face of organized harassment and sporadic violence, much of it perpetrated by the mothers, wives, sisters, and daughters of striking miners, most evidence points to the resolve of the strikers remaining unshaken.

As one striker, Paddy Dunnigan, put it, "We are ready to go back to work. To a man, that is what we be wanting. No one likes the way things are now. But the bosses must come halfway before we can meet them in the middle. We want only what is fair. We know the Outfit is no devil, but it must change around its thinking that the union is. The union is just the men, the same men as before, speaking all together at once instead of a lonely one at a time. We are not against the Outfit, we are for it; we just want it to listen better. It pretends to be deaf, and because it plays deaf, it *acts* dumb."

In the aftermath of what already were being commonly referred to as "the murders," Franklyn had trained it on down to Seeberville on his own to speak to witnesses, assess the scene, reconstruct for himself as best he might what in fact had occurred. There, two things had struck him immediately.

One was the sheer number of bullet holes, outside, inside, sprayed all over, walls, floor, ceiling, stairs, every first-floor room of the house, broken glass, splintered wood, pocked plaster everywhere. He counted the holes. "30+" he had jotted in his notebook. "A fury here. Fusillade. Excessive."

The other was the conviction on the part of everyone he had spoken with there, that the incident ran deeper than appearances might indicate, that what had happened could not be accounted for or explained away as a simple case of trespass gone awry, or overzealous law enforcement, or even a labor/management conflict spun regrettably, violently out of control.

"Look at the names," one of the neighbors, Giovacchino Guidi, had told him. "There is your truth. In the names."

So he had. Putrich, Tijan, Stepic, Stimac, Kalan, Grubetich, Mutka, Stiglich, Ozanich, Briski, Pintar—all Croatian. Polkinghorne, Cooper, Davis, Groff, Raleigh, James—all not.

One of the neighbors told Franklyn that he had heard two of the gunmen congratulating themselves on "taming the hunkie tigers." Another said he had overheard one of them boasting about having "taught the Slav boys a lesson." When one of the Italian boarders next door had meandered over after the shooting had ended, he claimed that Raleigh, known around the neighborhood as "the little black fellow" or "the ugly-faced one who rides a horse," ordered him to leave, or "I'll give you one in your stinking Wop back."

One of the qualities that rendered the Keweenaw so remarkable, quite extraordinary, really—Franklyn had noticed it straightaway, anyone would have—not only was how many ethnic nationalities made their homes there—John Plautz had ventured the number 30 before proceeding to tick them off as if reciting the alphabet: Slovenes, Croats, Serbs, Armenians, Austrians, Hungarians, Poles, Germans, Italians, Greeks, Turks, Russians, Bohemians, Rumanians, Lithuanians, Chinese, Swedes, Finns, Norwegians, Danes, the Irish, Scottish, Welsh, Cornish, English and French, French-Canadians, Mexicans, Cubans, Syrians, Jews, the Lebanese—but how many of them lived side by side. And, all things equal, in relative equanimity. Which, he thought, was precisely the point, that they lived side by side, each next to next, strictly, rigidly subdivided.

Right here, for instance, in Seeberville, its single, literally dirt-poor street contained four boardinghouses separated one from the other by little more than an alley's worth of side yard. And yet, in one house, nothing but Croatians. In another, nothing but Italians. In the third, all Finns. In the fourth, Poles. Back in Red Jacket, each of the surrounding "locations" was identified as "belonging" to this or that ethnic group, so much so that one more often heard references to Slavtown or Finntown, Krautville or Mick City, than to Yellow Jacket or Blue Jacket, Bumbletown Hill or Caledonia. Suburbs, yes, but ghettos first or, to be more generous, enclaves—zones and sectors. And, if you knew enough to know, there were microdivisions *within* the locations. In Tamarack, say, where the Cornish Kid lived, you had Bulltoad Hill, Grasshopper Hill, Behind-the-Store, Tamarack-on-the-Hill, North Tamarack. A community, yes, but one wholly fissiparous and fissile.

The chamber-of-commerce types, thought Franklyn, could tout harmony in diversity, invoke the recently coined metaphor of the melting pot to their heart's content. Truth was, some clichés are true: birds of a feather do. For all the commingling across cultural lines, all the inevitable exposure to different languages, religions, customs, cusines, all the on-the-job elbow-by-rib coworker fraternization and close-knittedness foaled by the very shared harshness of the environment itself, the region remained fundamentally segmented and stratified, even insularly tribal, where not downright clannish: English speakers on top, Western Europeans next, Eastern Europeans next, Scandinavians, Hispanics, Middle Easterners last.

And this, as Franklyn was learning, was less a matter of one group endeavoring to promote at the expense of another their own identity—cultural, racial, ethnic, religious, so on—than it was a matter of self-preservation, ensuring a degree of familiarity, or, rather, familiarness, maintaining a certain level of personal ease and psychological comfort and security: kith and kin. So that, yes, regrettably, certain long-standing prejudices, baseless stereotypes, the imaginary tensions accruing thereto, were preserved along with them.

Seeberville had cost two innocent men their lives. It had galvanized—regalvanized, actually—the striking community and had highlighted the element of brute thuggishness that so many suspected always had defined the Waddell-Mahon men, as it also had served as a reminder of the snap violence that so often erupts in the course of such protracted, bitterly contested labor actions. But for Franklyn, it had above all exposed the fissures and rifts, the *volatility* that lurked, much as did the winzes and drifts of the mines themselves, not so *very* far beneath the surface of a place that in less extraordinary times scarcely a soul beyond those who lived there would have bestirred themselves to notice.

Only last week, Franklyn had read a story in the *Evening Copper Journal*, one of the handful of local pro-management rags with lapdog access to the man—the *Mining Gazette* in Houghton and the *Calumet News* the others—in which MacNaughton had commented, "Calumet & Hecla has working for it any number of nationalities. Slovenes, Croats, Austrians, Hungarians, Italians, Poles. They come from all over the world because they wish to work for our company, and many of them are industrious and loyal employees.

"But what you must never forget is that they do not know our language. They do not know our customs, or our laws, or our ideals. They are not Americans, not yet, and they must be taught, with patience and forbearance and a firm hand, as one would a child, what is expected of them and how they might best behave to realize their dreams. They must be made to believe, they must believe deep in their hearts, that what is best for the company is best for the country, and so ultimately best for them and for their families.

"It is those without such belief whom you now see blindly following the lead of the union gunhands and outside agitators, for no man who would believe, and does believe, no man who understands what it means to be a *true* American, ever would join in such lawless action."

The hottest September in recent memory, so they said. Ninety, ninety-five degrees by midmorning, every morning. Freak heat. John Plautz, who kept strict track of such things, traced it thirteen years back, 1900. But that had been but a single, anomalous day. This was relentless, week after week of sheer scorchers, no respite, recourse, no relief.

Humidity didn't help either. Swelter.

"Not good," Plautz had informed Franklyn. "Means a Long White."

The heat only added—difficult to imagine it doing otherwise—to the sense of stalemate perched over the peninsula like unbroken cloud cover.

"So, John, what do you hear? Haywood. Any word?"

Behind the bar, John Plautz shrugged through the sweat. "On his way back, soon I think. Out West first. Denver, then here. Depends."

Franklyn swigged at his beer, conceivably his first of the day. "On what? Do you know?"

"Timing. Word is, National may have him wait."

"Wait. For what? How long? Why?"

"Grand finale. They hope they will not need him."

"Odd logic."

"They think he raises hopes."

"Well, sure."

"Too high maybe. And then . . ." Plautz washed, rinsed, rag-dried glass after glass, slid them to their overhead rack. "Can you imagine? Mac-Naughton?"

"What? If Haywood showed up?"

Plautz nodded. "Heat like this, this late, brings out the rabid dogs."

Franklyn laughed, long-swallowed. "Don't doubt it. Set the chief to frothing."

"Frothing, sure. But there is a man with a bite worse than his bark."

"So I hear. And Haywood, sure to bite back."

Franklyn stared at a middle distance, glazed.

"Troubles?" said Plautz. "I can help?"

"Don't see how, John. Still trying to reckon a way to MacNaughton. Asked for a sit-down three times, all I get is the brush-off. Only talks to certain papers, locals, ones in his pocket, then to work some angle. Tough crab to crack. I don't like reading him secondhand in somebody else's paper. Neither does Ivan. Wants an interview, as he should, as do I." Drained the glass. "Not your problem." Unstooled himself, fished a nickel from his pocket, slid it across the bar top. "I'm off. Gotta go see Ben."

"Give him my regards. Does not come around much anymore."

"Busy man these days." Grinned. "The ladies."

AND MEANWHILE

Down in Lansing . . .

The WFM, having hired fifty-six-year-old Clarence Darrow—the same Darrow whom Franklyn had known briefly in Chicago, Lee Masters's profligate law partner, the one Lee once had described to him as "that barrel of slops," the same Darrow who had won acquittal for Bill Haywood in the Idaho assassination case seven years before and who eleven years hence would keep teenagers Leopold and Loeb from the electric chair before monkeying some with the Scopes trial the year following—that Darrow now decided to take another shot at ending the strike behind the back and over the head of MacNaughton.

Meeting with Governor Ferris in the state capital, he proposed that the governor give arbitration another try, this time omitting the condition that the companies recognize the WFM as long as they acknowledged the workers' right to organize. Darrow was convinced that it was the WFM in particular, not union*ism* in general, that was the stumbling block to beginning negotiations. Ferris was not optimistic. Darrow had yet to deal directly with MacNaughton. Ferris had. Darrow could not conceive that the GM would not recognize the right of workers to organize "before he dies." Ferris could. Quite easily.

Darrow then pressed the governor to call a special session of the state legislature in order to launch an investigation into the conditions in the mines and to establish a state board of arbitration, as well as to pass a law forbidding county sheriffs to hire deputies from other states. Ferris briefly considered the idea before deeming it politically unfeasible.

Darrow pressed ahead. Then, he suggested, issue an ultimatum to the mine managers, forcing them to arbitration. And, countered Ferris, since such an ultimatum was not legally binding, if MacNaughton called his bluff? Then withdraw all Guardsmen from the region and seek to end the strike by fiat, replied Darrow. Easier said than done, said Ferris. He had the power to withdraw the troops, but ending the strike by fiat required the approval of the state legislature, and he hadn't the votes to pull it off.

In the end, aside from the fact that Darrow and Ferris hit it off, developing a warm, what would prove lifelong friendship, the best Ferris could manage was to summon MacNaughton to Lansing where he "went at him from every angle," not a one acute or oblique enough to effect a dent.

The employer is the one with the power, Ferris told MacNaughton, therefore the employer should be the one to offer the olive branch. MacNaughton replied that as he had nothing to hide, he welcomed a legislative investigation. He had "from day one assumed an arbitrary attitude about not a single point, save one: that the WFM must absolutely evacuate the district before I, or any of the managers, will treat with the men."

Following MacNaughton's departure, Ferris met again with Darrow. Together they drafted a proposal providing for the withdrawal of the WFM from the district. A copy was mailed by Ferris to MacNaughton covered by a handwritten note reading: "I write to you as one friend to another where the interests of humanity are at stake. Accept this offer, or one similar to it, and the strike will shortly be settled."

The telegram MacNaughton sent in response read: **CANNOT ACT**

ALONG LINES YOU PROPOSE. CONDITIONS HERE MAKE SAME IMPOSSIBLE.

Ferris exploded. Going public with his exasperation, he declared that he would request a federal investigation into the strike. "If anyone can show me how this can be brought to an end," he said, "please, let me hear from them at once."

Who the governor heard from at once was the WFM, which, having been spurned, in its opinion, one time too many, now issued a statement of its own: "Henceforward, any proposal for ending the strike here must include as its precondition, recognition of the Western Federation of Miners."

RECRUITS

Ben Goggia still was a boy when he immigrated to America from Italy in 1893. Fluent in Italian and English, he could speak enough Slovene and Croat to get by and knew just enough Finnish, as he was wont to jape, "to get myself into deep trouble." Although he was one of those at National who initially had counseled against the strike as "premature," Denver was paying him three dollars a day plus expenses to organize the women of both Houghton and Keweenaw Counties into "Auxiliaries," something he had done before, with ringing success, during the labor actions out West. The strategy, which was as simple as it was sound, had everything to do with sex and using it as a weapon, which, as Franklyn was quick to aver, struck him, at least in affairs of the female sort, as mighty redundant.

"Won't argue," Goggia had laughed, "because who could?"

They were sharing a quick one at a cocklegged table near the back of Plautz's saloon before Goggia's late-afternoon meet with Miller, Dunn's Hall.

"But it works both ways," Ben had continued. "Not just the women using themselves against the men—scabworkers, soldiers, deputies—but the men *permitting* themselves to be used. The women hold the natural advantage in this equation precisely because they are weaker, which is to say, they are perceived to be, by the men, who perceive themselves to be stronger, which the women know they are not, save physically, of course. The trick is to turn that perceived weakness, the women's, into their strength. Work it to their advantage. Turn the tables, so to say. Which, believe me, to a woman, is something they have little trouble understanding how to do. Second nature."

"Nah," said Franklyn. "First."

"Ha! Right. So, we organize them, bring them together, listen to their concerns—which are every bit the equal of their men, talk to them about ours, and then we start planning. Parades, marches, pickets, working the line, so forth."

"So forth?"

"Works two ways. If the woman's husband is experiencing, let us say, a certain difficulty in coming to grips with doing the right thing, joining us, joining up, we encourage her to make it more difficult for him still, at home, mealtime, bedtime, so on—you catch the drift."

"And the other way?"

Goggia looked sheepish. Handsome as all get-out, sheepish nonetheless. Perhaps, thought Franklyn, even handsomer for the sheepishness. "How to put it? We give them permission to, well, act upon their, uh, natural impulses."

"Meaning?"

"Meaning, for example, if a woman, or women, were out taking the air, say, a leisurely stroll about town, perfectly harmless, and—strictly by coincidence, you understand, pure serendipity—she, or they, happened upon a scab on his way to work, and she, or they, found that she, or they, were naturally offended, or understandably angered, or suddenly filled with an uncontrollable passion, unbridled fury, rage even, at the fact that this so-called man was, in effect, taking money out of their very purses, depriving, in effect, their families of the resources required to scrape by day to day, even snatching the very food from their own children's mouths, well, then, it could be considered—what?—excusable? understandable? reasonable? just? moral? brave? necessary? *right?*—were she, or they, to make her, or their, feelings known—in word, and deed."

"Deed?"

Ben didn't look sheepish anymore. "We are what, seven weeks into this thing, eight now? So, save for Seeberville, of course, we've had two months of little but words. Nothing wrong with words, they have their place. I'm not suggesting anyone stop talking, writing, making speeches, holding meetings, but those things are—well, they're didactic, and, at this stage, they're too damn passive. What we need, need now, is"—emphasis—"MOVEment.

"I've seen it before, out West. Every strike assumes a life of its own. As time passes, it develops its own timing, momentum. A strike breathes, each one a little differently, way a fire breathes. You have to know when to blow on its coals, apply the bellows, when to kindle and stoke it, feed it to keep it alive and flaming, otherwise it smolders along for a while, smokes some, but eventually . . ." Shrugged.

"And you think now is that time."

Nodded. "I *know* it's that time. You go through enough of these, you can sense it, feel it in your bones. Hard to explain."

"Well," said Franklyn, "no one wants to see it turn uglier that it is already, but if you say it's time to turn the heat up, who am I to question? Besides, you'll do what you do, I'll write about what you do, and that's what we both get paid to do. So"—he leaned in closer—"what *will* you do?"

He smiled. "Not that I don't trust you, Frank. You're the best reporter up here, New York boys included, and, the job aside, I consider you a friend. But that would be telling, and I can't, and I won't. What I will do is tip you when the time comes."

"That'll do," said Franklyn, smiling. "Thanks, Ben. So any suggestions about how I can get to MacNaughton? Boss is all over me, wants a sit-down, yesterday already."

Goggia thought a moment, harrowing a hand through his slicked-down high hedge of black hair, *en brosse*. Drummed knuckle on tabletop, piano-played with fingertips, squeeze-toyed with fist. "Maybe. How bad you want it?"

"Bad as you can imagine. Worse."

"Okay. See what I can do. Need to run it past some people first, but there may be a way. *May* be. Let you know when I do."

"Miracle, Ben. All aces."

"Nah." Drained his drink, pushed away from the table, rose to his feet, leaned back and down in, voice behind the hand. "If what I've got in mind works, believe me, you'll be doing us a bigger favor than I'm doing you."

Man of some mystery, Goggia, thought Franklyn, watching him disappear through the door, mystery and no little resource. One thing for certain, Ben Goggia ran a whole lot deeper than he had suspected when the two first had met. For three dollars a day, the WFM was getting far more than merely its money's worth.

————

September 13, 1913, Franklyn Shivs awakened early. Not that he ever had fallen off, not completely. Too hot. Decided to cold shower, do something elaborately involved with loofah and pumice; the cold water was warm. Managed to brush, floss, gargle with anise or an anise substitute, shave, clip some nails, run a comb, dress in freshly cleaned clothes, however weather-inappropriate. He was sweating elvers and eels before he had buttoned the second-to-last button on his vest. Then, chancing a last glance in the mirror, tugged at his vest tails, shot his cuffs—left, then right, the pair at once—tipped his hat at himself, bracketing its brim between thumb and forefinger and, swooshing right to left across the prow, muttered that which he had been muttering every day of his life from the moment he first had learned the phrase: *integer vitae scelerisque purus.*

Goggia's note awaited downstairs at the bar. John Plautz handed it wordlessly over. Accepting it in commensurate silence, he flipped it open. Not a note, actually, an address, one printed all in caps on the inside cover of a matchless matchbook, the outer half of which was adorned with a mainly naked Negress, nosebone school.

He read:

ELM AND EIGHTH. ONTO YELLOW JACKET. 8 A.M.

Yellow Jacket, as Franklyn knew, was the residential neighborhood adjacent to C&H's Red Jacket Shaft, deepest mine on the peninsula—on earth, in fact—the one with the largest, most powerful hoist engine, and, so, the most heavily patrolled by Guardsmen. Not a walled or barbed-wired fortress, not yet, not even a citadel or compound, but one of the first—second, in fact, after the immediate vicinity of the M Club—to be publicly declared off-limits and curfewed, a place verboten to all but its residents who for some time had been required to carry on their persons proof thereof. If Goggia was targeting Yellow Jacket, he not only was being deliberately provocative, he was courting conflict, inviting an "incident."

Franklyn fobbed the pocket watch from his vest and glanced at its face. Time enough for an eye-opener, wake-up call, pick-me-up, starter gun, top-o'-the-mornin', hair of the dog that bit ya. He did not typically do this. He did it now. The tavern was empty, chairs upside-down and tabletopped.

"Tequila, John, please. Straight on."

Didn't sit, but bellied up, foot propped to bar rail, elbow to bar top.

"New one on me," said Plautz, pouring.

"Yes, well, stiffy'll do me good this day, I've a hunch."

"That so?" Steadied the glass across. "Regarding?" When Franklyn hesitated, Plautz said, "Didn't read it, you know." Gestured. "Your match-book there."

"Oh, sure! No. I know. That's okay. I dunno. Reporter's day. Some-thing set to break."

"Break? What should break is this heat."

Franklyn nodded. "What *should* break is this fucking strike," he thought, said instead, "And MacNaughton." Sipped.

"Homesick?"

"Never felt so at home in my life." The tone of his voice was the tongue in his cheek. "Wouldn't leave here now if Ivan ordered me back and doubled my pay. Man finds his paradise, oughtta know enough to ap-preciate it. Grass don't get much greener than this, either side of the fence." Took a full mouthful, swished some, swallowed; excellent!

"Ach! Who needs Chicago anyway? What's Chicago got that Red Jacket ain't?"

"Couldn't say," said John Plautz, feigning. "Never been." He paused. "Cooler weather?"

"Ha! Right. Cooler weather—and fewer bugs." Emptied the glass. "Well, smaller ones anyway."

ENGRENAGE

Returning home after having heard the old lady speak, Ana found herself already mulling how best to *do* something, contribute something of posi-tive material substance to what the old lady had convinced her must be couched only in the vocabulary of crusade. Not that Ana conceived of it as a religious experience, but, well, it had all the earmarks. She hadn't yet been—the word they use now—radicalized, she hadn't had her—the words they would use later—consciousness raised, but that day she had traveled some distance in the direction.

Not so surprising, really. For four decades her kith and kin had been— one hesitates to say paying the price or bearing the burden, too clichéd, but certainly invested in, as at the mercy of, the very issues Mother Jones had spoken to. Her grandfather had burned to death in Osceola number two. Her father, George, had been there beside him, watched as his own father, seared to log char, had died in his arms, the son barely escaping himself, then only with bum lungs for the trouble, the black damage the smoke had done. He never ceased to complain, George Klochubar, of smelling to himself like a crematory: "Wake up with the taste in my mouth, go to sleep with it on my tongue. Ashes." More recently she had lost a cousin. An uncle had fractured his spine. Her mother, Mary, had worked her entire adult life as a maid in the Laurium mansions to make the proverbial ends proverbially meet.

So when Ben Goggia and Ella Bloor had beat the bushes—advertised, campaigned, canvassed, actively recruited women to organize themselves into an auxiliary similar to the one in Hancock and Houghton—*take to the streets! man the bartizans! mount the barricades! uproot the cobblestones!*—she had been among the first to volunteer, immediately making enough of an impression that Goggia had on more than one occasion lobbied the MacNaughton-obsessed reporter from *Proleterac* to write up her story.

"Not to harp, but I'm telling you, Frank," Goggia had remarked the last time they had spoken, "this girl, the one I've mentioned to you before, she's the"—had overmodulated the word—"au-then-tic article. Besides being gorgeous—and tall, tallest woman I ever have seen, towers over me, over six feet easy—she has got . . . something."

"Something?" Franklyn had asked, genuinely puzzled.

"Some, I don't know, quality. Of flint, maybe. Heart. Not frivolous, fragile, you know, the way a woman can be fragile."

"Not fragile," Franklyn had replied. "Morphadyke? Or just mule headed?"

"Dyke? Hardly. All woman. No, I mean"—searching—"presence. Fills her space, its moment, and not afraid to do that, put herself out there and take what comes, get knocked down and get back up. Resilient, maybe that's the word." Paused. "Or dauntless. 'On the scrap,' that's what they call it up here. No back-down. Indomitable. There!"

Franklyn, unable to restrain himself, had sighed world-wearily. "Have to tell you, Ben, I've had my share of doings with statuesque women, and frankly?—I'd rather have a root canal absent anesthesia. Gimme a dame that tops out at five-two, any day. But if you say she's something special . . ."

"Oh, nothing but. And for a woman, one in these parts, educated. Would I steer you wrong? Have I ever?"

Franklyn grinned, fished out pen and notebook. "Name?"

Spelled it for him.

"What's that? Clemenc. Croatian?"

"Slovene."

"Age?"

"Dunno. Early, mid-twenties maybe."

"Married?"

Nodded. "No kids. Husband's a miner, the Outfit, though from what I'm getting, less enthusiastic about what we are doing than he might be. About what *she's* doing."

"So where do I find Our Lady of the Treetops?"

"Centennial Heights, thereabouts. Northside. Or Dunn's."

Franklyn dutifully jotted down the information, pocketed the pen, flipped closed the cover, shoved the notebook into the rear hip pocket of his pants, and, forthwith and promptly, forgot all about it.

Throughout August, into September, Ana gradually acquired something of a local reputation. You caught sight of Ana Clemenc prowling, patrolling, policing, picketing, you immediately thought: trouble. Became the bane and bête noire of Red Jacket's streets, though there were those who used other, less evocative names.

Compiled, in not unshort order, quite a résumé—and rap sheet:

Beat—slapped, actually, across the face—a scab near the Red Jacket train depot.

Hurled rocks at mounted deputies near Kearsage.

Verbally cursed out and spat at scabs, relieving them of their lunch buckets on their way to work near Sixth and Oak.

Knocked unconscious a sergeant of the Guard with a thrown rock outside Tamarack number-five shaft.

Pelted elderly scab workers with sticks, stones, and rock-loaded tin cans near Centennial Heights.

Assaulted scabs with rotten eggs and brooms dipped in human excrement, again in the Heights.

Succeeded in hog-tying a scab, then kicked him in the groin and clawed his face near North Tamarack.

Struck the wife of a nonstriking neighbor in the face with a broom, in the Heights.

Wrecked the gardens of nonstriking workers, again in the Heights.

Attempted to yank a scab from a streetcar in Laurium.

Wrestled a scab to the ground in Centennial Heights, dressed him in woman's clothing, applied woman's makeup to his face, then led him through the streets at the end of a rope.

Wrested a lunch pail from a scab and beat him over the head, on Mine Street.

Assaulted three scabs with a coal shovel, Mine Street.

Slingshot stones, bloodying scabs on their way to work at Osceola.

Attacked a contractor carrying a tin lunch pail on Fifth Street, punching him in the face. Arrested along with six other Slovene women and Ben Goggia, the group was briefly jailed before being charged with assault and battery and resisting and interfering with law officers in the performance of their duty. Arraigned and released on their own recognizance, they were ordered to appear in court eight days later.

Perhaps most visibly—the press jumped on it straightaway—each morning, weekends included, she strapped herself into a leather harness, girdling it about her waist and up over her shoulders, to carry a six-by-eight-foot American flag flown from a ten-foot-high staff at the head of a banner-waving procession of strikers and their families, marching two miles south from Centennial Heights to Osceola through the heart of Red Jacket, heat notwithstanding.

A woman with much on her mind, as, too, in her heart and her soul, and that not the half of it, because then she went home, to her husband.

The night before the following morning, that of September 13, the night of the day after the day after Ana's arrest—the neighbors heard loud voices issuing from the Clemenc home on Lincoln Street.

Perhaps they were slightly louder this time than they had been in the past, or perhaps it simply was the uncommon stillness of the night that night—sounds lifted, carried, crisp and keen—but they were the kind of sounds that in their battering tone, particularly if you were a child lying in your bed in your house next door or across the street, *yanked* your attention to them. After which they distressed you enough that, as they continued—rising, falling, rising again, first his, then hers, clashing, colliding, clouting as they caromed—if you were a young boy, you were apt to shudder in your sheets, and if a girl, shed silent tears.

Because you knew that people, adults like your own mother and father—the sounds were not *entirely* unfamiliar, you had awakened once or
twice in the past to some few of them in your own house—were saying
mean, cruel, vicious things to each other, *at* each other. And even if the
words themselves and the meanings of the words were not always the sort
you immediately understood, what you heard and remembered were the
voices, the sound of them, the tone: too loud, too big, clubbing down hard
as steel pipe, the way it socked into you and made you aware of how soft
and how deep was the pit of your stomach.

And then you heard them stop, the voices, likethat. And then silence.
And then a door slam. And then another. And silence. More silence. And
then, only silence.

Winding his way over to the address Ben had provided, Franklyn was
obliged to thread his way through a roiling and weltering throng. Here
were—his ability to calculate such things on such occasions was of necessity becoming increasingly well refined—well over 1,000, perhaps 1,500
people, decidedly more women than men, who had taken to the heat-
addled streets, not a few of them on horseback, one of whom—he could
see him clearly enough a couple of blocks yonder in what appeared to be
the van of the mass—was Ben Goggia.

The horse was black and long maned, slick-glossy with lather, and
when, fractious, it reared, Franklyn immediately discerned two things.
One, that Ben was a seasoned hand with horseflesh. And two, that he
looked exactly like the captain of a cavalry troop, one that at the moment
found itself flat afoot. Not that Franklyn ever had seen the captain of a
cavalry troop, but when it came to cavalry-troop captains, he imagined the
way that Ben looked is how they must look or, if not, ought. He cut, did
his friend, a dashing figure.

As Franklyn neared the head of the march at Eighth and Elm—less a
march or procession, actually, than a collectivized jam of placard-waving,
forward-shuffling humanity—he found it harder to make headway. Here
the street was more crammed, tightly clogged, many of the demonstrators
having locked arms, human chain link. It was only then that he caught
sight of the seven khaki-uniformed, mounted Guardsmen ranked side by
side and stretching from one side of the street to the other, barring the

way. A block beyond lay Yellow Jacket. The gap between the Guard and those it faced was perhaps sixty feet, certainly no more than seventy-five.

The marchers quieted. Less hush, than lull.

"You will not stop us!" This was Ben. His spirited horse stamped some, hoof clops on cobble of stone, pumped its great head up and down, mane flown, spray of lather. "We are for Yellow Jacket and mean to make our way!"

The vanguard, taking his words for their own, erupted in a vast, iterated chant rippling rapidly toward the rear, crescendo: "You will not stop us! You will not stop us! You will not stop us!"

One of the Guardsmen, whose name Franklyn later was given as "Clarence J. Miller of downstate Ypsilanti"—pronounced "Yip-sa-lan-tee"—prodded his horse forward at a deliberate pace into and across the open intersection. When he reined up so near that Ben might have reached across and touched him, Franklyn noticed that the holster flap on his sidearm was unbuttoned.

"Listen, you greasy little Itie," spat Miller, resting his hand upon the burled walnut butt of his government-issue pistol, "you've got exactly ten seconds to back off and take your Wop friends here with you, the stinking lot."

Upon which he began, slowly, to count.

Made it all the way to three before Ben interrupted him. "Clear off, tin-soldier boy," he said evenly. "We are coming through."

Never made it to four, because it was then that one of the marchers at the front—Franklyn never did get a name—pounced forward and, with the staff of his American flag, thrust its fore end, as one might a bayonet, at Miller's midsection, then at his face.

"No!" shouted Ben, as Miller parried the flagstaff with a forearm, knocking it to the ground before—this name he did get—Tony Stefanic scooped it up and went at Miller more savagely still. As the remaining Guardsmen spurred their mounts forward, one of them sabered Stefanic across the back as another impaled the flag upon his blade, jaggedly ripping it as he jerked the staff from Stefanic's grip.

Suddenly, the flag was everything. It was as if, Franklyn wrote later, whichever side assumed and maintained possession of it must win not only the day, but the strike itself. Watching at relative remove from the side way, Franklyn saw one of the striking marchers, marching strikers, whichever, the twenty-four-year-old Frankie King, grapple with one of the Guardsmen for control of the staff. Wresting it away, King swung it Crockett-like wildly at the soldiers, one of whom, saber upraised, screamed, "Let go the flag, you son of a bitch, or I'll run you straight through!" At which King—thank god, thought Franklyn—apparently reckoned it best to comply. He let go.

The flag lay in tatters, its staff in splinters in the street where both the Guardsmen's and Goggia's own horse now trampled them.

And then, out of nowhere—nowhere, at least, that Franklyn later was able to pinpoint—an extraordinarily tall, uncommonly beautiful woman clad in red, white, and blue—red bonnet, white blouse, long blue skirt—leaped not ungracefully in light of the dearth of grace in the circumstances, nor less bravely, into the midst of the frayed and affraying horses. Somehow retrieving the flag from beneath their hooves, she stood straight, full height—in her case, one helluva an altitude; what Franklyn later would describe as a "veritable ascension"—holding the flag horizontally across her body, and, as Franklyn scribbled her words furiously in his notebook, screamed at the Guardsmen, "Kill me! Come ahead! Do your worst! Kill me! Run your swords through! Run them through this flag! I will not move back! What are you waiting for? If this flag will not be my shield, I will die with it! Come! Here I am! Why do you wait?"

Just where, exactly, at what precise moment in her, as Franklyn phrased it in his story, "disquisition of defiance," her right wrist was filleted open to the bone by one of the swordsmen, even Ana herself would not venture to say later. The exceptionally bloody gash, she would remark, "barely registered." But it was owing to the shock of the wound—"crucifixion wound," Franklyn hurriedly jotted—that, knees buckling, she dropped the flag, and, enough of her wits apparently still about her, shrieked as she sagged to the street, "There! Go ahead! There is the flag! Upon the ground at last, where the likes of you would have it! There! Go ahead and stomp upon its colors! Trample your country underfoot!"

By which time a second troop of mounted Guardsmen—Cavalry Troop B, Lieutenant J. Herbert Ferris commanding—had galloped swiftly up accompanied by a double-timing phalanx of bayonet-wielding foot soldiers and a billy-flailing contingent of sheriff's deputies, and the crowd—he noticed Ben side-wing the wounded woman up a-spraddle behind him—was dispersed without further velitation or incident down side streets, along sidewalks, across yards, retreating less headlong than heat-flogged toward Dunn's Hall.

It was, as Franklyn considered it later, just too theatrically perfect. Save that it had not been theater at all. Whatever else she might be—and his job lent him the perfect pretext with which to pursue *that* particular fact—the woman clearly was no actress. Not that he permitted the truth to get in the way of his writing it up that way. Franklyn Shivs might not believe in heroes—or heroines, but he knew good copy when he saw it, as he knew, too, how to midwife a legend, however empurpled in prose.

As he walked back toward Dunn's, where he would spend the next hour listening to strikers regale one another with "flag stories," each one more improbably inflated than the next, he pondered why it was that, when he had seen her go down, he had had to stop himself—as once he had done so long ago in a wintry Chicago alley—from racing to her side.

"You would think," he thought, "that a guy would have learned a thing or two along the way."

Or maybe—nope—you wouldn't.

AND MEANWHILE

Marches, demonstrations, rallies, processions, mass meetings, parades, incidents of sporadic violence aside, as September folded into October and the heat finally, mercifully broke, of the 2,765 Guardsmen the governor originally had deployed to the peninsula, he had ordered all but 213 to stand down. In effect, he washed his—and the state's—hands of the strike, abandoning the fate of the Copper Country to those principals who lived and worked there: let them thrash it out for themselves as they might manage to do so, peacefully or otherwise, or short of that, go to hell.

In rapid succession:

—Spurred by the "near riot" of September 13, and fearing a precipitous spike in lawlessness, if not an outright rash, attorneys for seventeen of the mining companies, led by the firm Rees, Robinson, and Petermann, C&H's regular company lawyers—the firm was then defending the assailants in the Seeberville murders—joined in filing an injunction to halt all striker picketing, mass demonstrations, and harassment of nonstriking workers. The local judge in the case, Patrick O'Brien, granted the companies' request. Nine days later, at the urging of the WFM's LeGendre and Kerr, he reversed himself. When the companies then joined in filing a second injunction, O'Brien rejected it out of hand. At MacNaughton's fuming insistence, Rees, Robinson, and Petermann immediately appealed to the State Supreme Court, which nine days later reinstated the original injunction with a proviso permitting the strikers to parade "off company property" and conduct "peaceful" meetings. When the injunction was violated, not to say flouted, mass arrests were made and the offenders remanded to O'Brien's court, where he pronounced them guilty, then promptly suspended their sentences, explaining, "It is enthusiasm for their cause, not the deliberate breaking of the law that accounts for their behavior. The Court understands their struggle and acknowledges the legitimacy of their right to retain membership in a labor organization. To agitate for improved conditions in the workplace is the right of any citizen. The law is simply the concrete expression of those rules that experience teaches us are to be applied in the best interests of *all* the people, and new experience necessitates its new interpretation." He then advised the sheriff's office to "use better judgment in enforcing the order of the Court in the future."

—Acting to fill what they perceived as the vacuum created by the departure of the Guard, MacNaughton and other managers enlisted the services of the notorious Ascher Detective Agency of New York City—notorious because it boasted of having "broken sixty-nine strikes and counting"—importing well over one hundred "professional armed guards and hotel men," as they described themselves, to augment the county sheriff's force of local deputies and Waddell-Mahon men. More to the point, they were to act privately in the managers' behalf and only at their behest. MacNaughton knew what few others did: what was coming. Already on its way to the U.P. was the first wave of those out-of-state scissor-bill replacement scabs that he had recruited and hired—some 1,600 all told—in contravention, it ought be mentioned, of his late-July avowal never to stoop to such a tactic, and they would be needing the strong-arm protection of what their critics quickly took to calling the "goon squads."

—The sheriff's office released figures revealing that as of October 1, there had been 191 strike-related arrests since commencement of the strike, resulting in six convictions, forty-eight outright dismissals, and one acquittal, with 136 cases still pending.

—The exodus from the region continued and increased, surging toward three thousand workingmen plus families.

—Local merchants, businessmen, and professional men, alarmed by loss of revenue, the damage done to perceptions of the area as one friendly to investment, entrepreneurship, and enterprise, and the proliferation of WFM-backed "Cost Stores"—strike benefits increasingly were paid in coupons redeemable only at these so-called commissaries—banded first into the moderate Copper Country Commercial Club, then into the more shadowy, militant, grassroots Citizens' Alliance (CA). While the CA, which variously claimed between five thousand and ten thousand members, had no acknowledged leaders or spokesmen, it was an open secret that each of the area banks—Calumet State, First National, Merchants and Miners, and State Savings in Red Jacket/Laurium, as well as Houghton National, Citizens National, and Superior National in Houghton/Hancock, all of whose solvency, willingness, and ability to extend credit to local businessmen was determined by the health of the mines—was heavily invested in setting much of its agenda. CA members were encouraged to identify themselves by wearing a red-white-and-blue button beneath their lapels, to attend clandestine mass meetings, to erect roadblocks and barricades to impede parading strikers, to cut off the extension of credit— "end the tick"—to all union members, and to act as the eyes and ears of the local, increasingly striker-hostile press. The latter being how Ana Clemenc found herself portrayed variously as "a ruffian radical agitator," "an outright communist," "that lawless, insane woman," "the well-known atheist anarchist protest leader," "the rough-talking, ringleader jailbird terrorist," and the subject of an editorial opining that "if she does not come to her senses soon and moderate her behavior, at least in public, she is certain to come to a low end at the hands of those who would end the strike by any means." The organization, which in time Franklyn discovered operated out of the back rooms of the high-toned Douglass House Hotel in Houghton, also began printing and publishing a free newspaper of its own—printing and distribution costs borne solely by C&H—titled *Truth*, the first issue of which read in part: "The poisonous propaganda of destructive socialism, violence, intimidation, and disregard of law and order must end and end immediately. It is a menace to the future of the Copper Country. The Western Federation of Miners and their outside agitators, hired gunmen, and professional terrorists must depart the region at once. Henceforward this is our battle cry: THE WFM MUST GO!" It likewise began its serialization of the biography of Albert Horsley, aka Harry Orchard, aka "The Dynamite Killer," the self-admitted WFM-paid assassin and killer of seventeen men, including Idaho governor Frank Steunenberg eight years previously, an act, according to the biography, that was undertaken on orders issued by William F. Haywood.

—Taking stock of their increasingly precarious finances, and with autumn fast approaching, WFM leadership decided to redouble its efforts to win the strike before the onset of winter. National had had on hand since shortly after the advent of the strike some $150,000. Throughout August and September it had disbursed roughly $10,000 a week in worker benefits. Thereafter, that sum was more than doubled. (This amounted to three dollars a week for a single man, up to seven dollars a week for a married man with five or more children, nine dollars a week in "special cases.") Meanwhile, it stepped up its fund-raising through the creation of a statewide strike fund that soon was grossing some $30,000 a month, as well as among its own locals out West and other unions, chiefly the United Mine Workers and United Brewery Workers. Nonetheless, striker disgruntlement, owing to what were perceived to be insufficient benefits and/or their inequitable disbursement, grew steadily toward open dissension. By the second week in October, the eleventh week of the strike, so-called worker solidarity had begun seriously to erode, in places actually to crack, often along both political and ethnic lines. That week, mine managers released figures to the press that created a firestorm. While only a third of the workforce south and north of Red Jacket had returned to work, and while most of the smaller companies remained shut down drumhead-tight, at C&H, 100 percent of surface laborers were back on the job, along with well over half of its underground force, the majority of holdouts being—as always, it was MacNaughton's wont to balkanize every situation at every opportunity—"Slovenes, Hungarians, Finns, and Italians, in that order." (Ninety-eight percent of Cornishmen reportedly had gone back down.) Whether and to what extent such numbers could be trusted, the report accomplished much of its intended purpose, further demoralizing those thousands of strikers still holding fast—it was the received wisdom, after all, that "as C&H goes, so goes the strike"—as, too, wedging deeper the rifts of nationality and political faction among the highly heterogeneous rank and file. One of the first top-level casualties of the internecine bickering over how the strike ought to proceed was Guy Miller, scapegoated by his own bosses for being too strategically moderate and rhetorically radical at once. Before the month was out, so was he, having been summoned back to Denver, a chess move that only underscored how polarized union leadership had become, one faction advocating tactical escalation to include snipers, dynamiting, arson, and physical assault, the other insisting that concessions still could be won through a policy of patience, persistence, and renewal of negotiations.

So that as the leaves blazed toward the cresting of their death colors and Franklyn Shivs ensconced himself, as latterly had become his wont, at one of the several acanthus-leaf-carved, claw-foot mahogany tables in the elegant upstairs reading room of the Red Jacket Library to compose the latest in the series of roughly thirty stories he had filed during the course of the strike, the facts as they stacked up on the ground included: a legally hamstrung, financially problematic union riven by internal dissent and losing more members each day, locked in an ongoing war of attrition with a collusive, collective ownership possessed of apparently unlimited financial resources—though Franklyn would not learn until later just *how* unlimited; C&H alone had on hand $1 million in ready cash, $1.25 million due in bills receivable, 16 million pounds of copper ingot ready for market, and another 8 million set for smelting—that not only had yet to make a single concession to workers while beefing up its private security forces, but had shrewdly succeeded in enlisting the local business, banking, and newspaper communities to its side, even as it enjoyed increasing success in luring its employees back to work.

ANA ELEMENTAL

The first time Franklyn Shivs met Ana Clemenc, she was celled—or the cell was Ana'd, perhaps, she dwarfed it so—standing on the wrong side of a locked bank of floor-to-ceiling blackened bars, her back to him, less broadly wingspanned than long-waistedly contoured.

Ben Goggia, standing beside him, spoke up first. "Ann."

An armed guard stood at the far end of the cellblock. When she wheeled about, it immediately was clear that she had not been crying, had not been for some good long while, a lifetime perhaps.

"Ben!" She smiled broadly, took a step forward. "You are out!" Her blouse was raddled with dried blood, collar to waist.

"They posted my bond this morning," he said. "You'll be out of here before nightfall. Not to worry."

"Oh"—she glanced Franklyn's way inquiringly, rubbing at her wrist—"I am not worried. Getting to be my second home." It was her third or fourth or fifth arrest, this time for inciting a melee between some five hundred strikers and mounted Guardsmen and deputies on South Hecla mine property. Guns had been drawn, sabers brandished, nine strikers arrested, including Goggia, all save herself since released.

When she hesitated, Goggia interjected, "Ana Clemenc, Franklyn Shivs. Frank, may I present Mrs. Ana Clemenc."

Franklyn half stepped forward, touched his hand to his hat brim. "Pleasure."

"And mine, Mr. Shivs."

"Ann, Frank's the reporter I've spoken about before."

"Yes, I remember," she said. "*Proleterac*. Chicago."

Goggia nodded. "Mind if he asks you a few questions? He's thinking of doing a story." Glanced Franklyn's way. "Right, Frank?"

"Only with Mrs. Clemenc's consent, of course." Franklyn deliberately skipped a well-timed beat. "And full cooperation." Emphasized the "full."

"Certainly," she said. "You have them, both. But," she addressed Goggia, "could we wait? Ben? Would that be okay? Not to be difficult, but I would prefer we do this"—she nodded toward the guard—"once I have cleaned up, someplace where we can speak . . ."

"More freely?" Franklyn completed the sentence for her.

"Frankly, yes." She looked at Franklyn, decidedly not batting her eyes or their lashes, which, Franklyn noticed, were as long as they were luxuriantly thick. "Of course, if you have a deadline, we shall just have to—"

Franklyn shook his head. "No, no deadline. Thirty-six hours before I file."

She appeared much relieved. "Good. Then first thing after the parade tomorrow morning?" She looked back to Goggia, solemn. "All set?"

He nodded. "Expecting five hundred, could be a thousand. Mass hooky." Turned to Franklyn. "Children's parade. That's what we're calling it. Mothers keeping their kids back from school to march. Should make one helluva impression."

Franklyn addressed himself to Ana. "Where? Would you like to talk? After the parade, I mean."

"Library. Fourth floor. Know it?"

"I do, but . . ."

"I know a place." She took another step, curled a hand to a bar. "Private room. No whispering."

"Fourth floor it is," he said. "See you there. And"—he paused—"thank you, Mrs. Clemenc."

She sighed. "Well, Mr. Shivs, if we are going to do this, perhaps you could do us both a favor and learn to call me Ann. Or Ana. Either will do." Then reached an arm through, open handed.

Franklyn took it lightly in his own. "Ann." Mustered a smile. "But only if you promise to return the favor."

Outside, in the street, Goggia asked, "So?"

"Tall," said Franklyn, as they sauntered. "Very tall."

"That's it? Tall?"

"Okay. Lovely. Very tall, and very lovely, and . . ."

"And?"

"Very, mmm, dedicated. To her—well, I just had the sense that—she takes herself awfully seriously, doesn't she?"

"Takes her *role* seriously," said Ben. "The cause, yes. What we're trying to accomplish here."

"But her*self*," said Franklyn.

"Wouldn't know. Can't say I know anything about her, not in the way you mean. Know she and her husband are no longer together, that he moved out some weeks back, apparently gone back down for the Outfit. She doesn't volunteer a lot on that score; I don't ask. None of my affair. Why? That's important?"

"Might be, the sort of story I have in mind. I mean, she's good copy, great copy, no question. Look at the way the New York boys picked up on her after the flag thing. Me, too. All of us, guilty. Joan of Arc of the Northwoods, all that. Which is fine, except it's slick and shallow and glib and whatever it is we do to people when we write about them, turn them into some goddamn lie, some fucking *fiction*!" He spat, punctuation, self-disgust splutch in the gutter.

Goggia drew up short. "Frank, whoa! What the hell? Said it before, you're working it better than any reporter up here. And you know how I know? Because there's stuff you write, sometimes, I want to wring your fucking neck. You write for our side, sure, but we're not exactly catching any breaks from *Proleterac*, right?"

Franklyn smiled. "And speaking of that, I'm as close to MacNaughton now as I was the day I got off the train. I keep asking, he keeps dodging." When Goggia frowned, his frown conveyed enough that Franklyn was compelled to ask, "What?"

"Closer than you know, Frank." Here was Plautz's. Goggia was as serious as Franklyn ever had seen him. "Chances are, it's going to get real ugly around here real soon—don't ask how I know, I just know—and when it does, chances are, you're going to get what you want—and then some." He laughed. "But you take your shot with Ann first." Paused. "Now for the best, later for the garbage."

All equal, his "shot with Ann," as Ben had described it, went, Franklyn felt, remarkably well. So well, in fact, that the first story he wrote about her—first, so it would prove, of dozens—was picked up by several of the wire services. Enough of them that, if only after some fair amount of editing to soften what even Franklyn could not dispute was, on balance, its pro-strike slant, it ran in papers all over the world.

Ivan, rather too floridly in Franklyn's opinion, headlined it:

ACROSS THE WARRING SKIES OF THE WILD NORTHWOODS, A BLAZING STAR IS BORN— FIGHTING ANNIE CLEMENC

When Ivan triumphantly wired him about it—it was an unprecedented coup for the paper, about which Franklyn was genuinely happy for his boss—he was surprised, if not entirely pleased, for it inspired in him the suspicion that the story, a rather unsparing portrait in his opinion, must only have failed on some profound level.

That it portrayed a heroine of sorts was true enough. If one was wont to argue that point, if one was bent upon contending that she was more villainess than otherwise, that her criminal public behavior over the past three months was less admirable than deplorable, then, yes, one was going to take exception to the tone and sensibility of the piece. The problem, as he considered it, was that, much as with his treatment of Bill Haywood so many years before, his subject had become something of a lightning rod. Aside from Haywood, after all, she was the most lawless person he ever had encountered.

What the world wanted, so Franklyn presumed, was what the world always wanted: the all-white of her or all-black, the self-martyring backwoods Joan of Arc, or the fire-breathing anarchist dragon lady. Fair enough. Save that Franklyn was not about to write such a story. Ana was

Ana, not Joan, Medusa, Cassandra, or Messalina. What is gray is gray, not black or white, and gray was his favorite color. Lucky thing, too, because for Franklyn Shivs, every last thing, Ann included, had long since dyed itself every shade of it and hue.

So perhaps the wire services had cottoned to the comet imagery of the headline. Or perhaps, because his was the first and only piece out there just then treating upon its subject in quite the way that it did, they felt compelled, while holding their collective editorial nose, to go with it. Or perhaps it was a slow global news day/week/month and they were famished for copy. Or perhaps it was the David-versus-Goliath element, the very one to which too many editors were as addicted as a junkie to his high. Or perhaps, as Franklyn was more prepared to believe, there was something about the woman herself, the very fact that she *was* a woman, one who—go ahead and say it—behaved out of her sex, that connected with and/or tapped into some *geist* or gestalt of the moment.

Whatever the explanation, the story, apparently, had hit a nerve, though not, as Franklyn well knew, because any of those responsible for running it really cared or gave a damn about Ann herself. Journalists care about the subjects of their stories approximately as much as cops care about the victims of their perps or surgeons the objects of their scalpels. Which is to say, a little, for a while, in the abstract, as it serves such of their self-interest as the circumstances of the moment may dictate and determine.

And it was this that Franklyn always found so infernally difficult, the lesson he had taken away from the Iroquois fire and been obliged to live with ever since. It wasn't the profession itself that was the problem—the profession, he reckoned, was honorable enough, though to hear it described as "noble" never failed to trigger in him the impulse to mount a salvaging party to rescue the beleaguered word from ignominy—it was the way that its gatekeepers insisted it be practiced. Because that way was frankly dehumanizing and, finally, dishonest.

He had been doing this now for—what?—thirteen years? Too long then. And if he knew anything at all about the game and its rules, it was that the only way to play it and win, to report and write a story of real worth, was in a procession of improvised, aikido-like steps as the story spontaneously led you—Mr. Tabula Rasa—one forward, two back, another three to the side, but always moving from its margins toward its inner core. True, sometimes you penetrated through only to find no one home and nothing there, or not much. And sometimes you were permitted to penetrate only so far and no farther. And sometimes you were invited to plunge as far as you could and even so never began to touch bottom. But penetrate and plunge you had must. And to do so successfully most often required less detachment and distance, not more. Required a form of intimacy—the giving of oneself *all* to one's subject in the name of receiving in return one's reward: the story, its truth.

That day in the Red Jacket library then, up on the fourth floor, the attic, really, past the stacks and heaps of old books, journals, magazines, newspapers, scrolled maps, outdated atlases, obsolete almanacs, lopsided globes, ornate bronzed bookends wrought into jungle animals and musical instruments—lions, elephants, flügel- and French horns—and the sun slanting dusty through the half-moon window beneath the high-peaked, open-raftered ceiling, that was the day the penetration began—or might have been said to.

"So," she said.

"How do you know this place?" he asked.

"Before everything . . . else, I spent my life here."

"Really."

"Well, not here *exactly*. Downstairs. With everyone else. A bookworm. You're surprised."

"No, not surprised, wouldn't say, but—"

"The literacy rate, here in town, Calumet Township, guess."

He shrugged. "No idea. I imagine—"

"Ninety-eight percent."

"Really!"

"See, you *are* surprised. Do not feel badly, everyone is. You have seen all the newspapers sold around town on every street corner, all the magazines to which the library subscribes, hundreds, in every language. They have even got *Proleterac* down there. People read, and are proud to. Not always in English, no, but in their native language, they can and do.

"So, victim of a curious nature, I explored, found this. The cellar is a good place, too, but busy, and humid. They have a bathhouse down there, swimming pool. I like it up here."

"Me, too."

She smiled, as Franklyn construed it, warmly. "So?"

"What?"

"Ask. Ben says to relax, not to worry, about saying anything. That if I say it wrong, you will fix it, make it right."

He smiled. "Did he?" Something occurred to him. "So, if they have *Proleterac*, then . . ."

She smiled again. "I try not to read about the strike, too upsetting. Ben says you are the best reporter up here." She paused, as is said, pregnantly. "I wish I could write. I mean, *really* write. Used to try a little, when I was young, poems and things, a diary."

"Still have it?"

"What?"

"The diary."

"I do not know. That was long ago. I was a little girl. Why?"

"Never know. Any little thing."

She shook her head. "Girl stuff. Girlie. I would be embarrassed to show it now. Especially now."

"Ah, the other Ann."

"Yes, well, before all this began, I did have a life after all."

"So tell me about it, that life."

"There is not much to tell. Certainly nothing a big-city reporter from Chicago would find interesting."

"Try me. And by the way, I live in Chicago. I am from Wisconsin. Grew up on a dairy farm. Farm boy, that's me."

"Really! So how did you end up in Chicago, then?"

"Newspapers where I lived, around Milwaukee, weren't hiring. Some in Chicago were."

"So you always wanted to write? For newspapers?"

"To write? Always. Also wanted to eat. You're young, no experience, your choices are newspapers or ad agencies, and the former lets you out more, out from behind your desk. The leash is longer. I liked it, in the beginning."

"No more?"

"Not so much, no."

"Why? What happened?"

"Nothing in particular, everything in general. I grew up, I suppose, much as anything. Learned you need a stomach stronger than the one I ever was able to cultivate. Can one cultivate a stomach? Anyway, that, plus, well, my values, such as they are, don't match up so well with the ones that drive the business. Power leaves me cold. No one's fault, that.

"I don't know." He gazed fixedly out the window. "I'm sure I'm wrong. My colleagues, the ones who are good at it, find the variety—how every story is new and fresh and exciting and so on—the very quality about the job that most appeals." Shrugged. "That, and the notion that what they do *matters*. Not to sound gratuitously jaded, but I don't. I find it . . . tedious, and enervating, and *always* fleeting. Unlike myself, my—what? conjurations?—ideas, dreams, words, which I find matter very much—to me."

He looked at her. She was rapt, or so appeared. "Well"—he grinned—"I suppose everyone is convinced that they and they alone are the most profound, charismatic, self-evolved human being walking the face of the earth."

She shook her head. "Not me."

"Well, you should. What harm? Besides, what you're doing here—well, you're *doing* it. Something. And even if you fail, you'll have tried. You'll know you tried."

"Oh, but we cannot fail," she said, soberly. "We must not." Now it was her turn to stare milelong through the windowglass. "Because it *does* matter, because we are right, and they are wrong, because changes need be made, conditions bettered, and because, Frank, I will never give up."

He felt something—where?—when she spoke his name, a vague—what?—sensation of being touched? Sounded different, somehow, coming from her. Felt himself flush. And, so, why did this always happen? Beautiful women—and now this *deeply* beautiful one—forever upending his appleless applecart.

"People," she continued, "most of them, I find, are allergic to sacrifice or even to being inconvenienced, made to feel a little uncomfortable. I know most of them have sacrificed a lot already. They sacrificed when they came to this country, a strange, unknown place, hard place, left the life they knew—relatives, friends, language, customs, the *fit* of where they lived—left all of it behind to start over. That is a lot. I know this and I do not forget, not for a second. My own family . . ." She trailed off.

"Yes?"

"We were poor, poor enough that some of us died for it, poor enough that I knew we were poor, even as a child, and this is something a child should not know. To be poor, that is nothing to be proud of the way some are proud, nor to be ashamed of the way others feel shame, it just *is*. But a child, a *child*, Frank, should not know it. For a child to know it, that is poor beyond poor. That is—I learned the word only later—impecunious. It breaks the parents' hearts, that their children know. And then, when the child is older, they begin to know that their parents know that they know. The hurt is there, always, in everyone's eyes, the sadness. Our story, the story of our people here, it always carries with it that sadness.

"Of course"—she forced a smile—"I was tall. No one could see my own eyes so much."

"So exactly how tall are you? If you don't mind?"

"Over six feet. One inch and one half more. Tall."

"No. Statuesque."

She laughed. "Ha! The writer. All right. Statuesque. I like that better anyway."

"And then, what? You married?"

She leaned her forehead lightly to the windowpane, its cool. "Yes, I married. I was young, very young."

"Ben says he's a miner."

"Yes, the Outfit."

"And he's gone back down?"

"A few weeks back, yes. He—Josef—it is difficult for him, hard on him. He loves what he does, his work, loves the mines. That is who he is. They say a miner is a miner even when he is not mining, and that is Josef. He is a man very set in his ways. He believes as deeply as do I. We believe differently. I did not know how differently, did not realize. Now, I do."

She sighed, turned back around, looked at Franklyn. "He cannot live with himself and live with me, too. He finds it impossible. So he withdraws. And this is not difficult for him, because he has a retiring nature. So he disappears into silence, his long silences, down some well of his own digging, and I am left to wonder at his decency.

"I cannot find it in myself to blame him for this. Not only am I a wife who does not stand by her husband, I am one who refuses to do so in public. That is how he sees it. So do others. But I do blame him for something. I blame him for going back down, and for this I call him stooge and lackey and helot, and for this"—the hands at her sides, both hands, were fists—"no, this I do *not* forgive."

"So—he's left you?"

"We no longer share our lives. I live with my parents now. So, you see, we all must sacrifice. Different sacrifices for different people."

"I had no idea, Ann. I *am* sorry. Surely you will reconcile, once this is over, whichever way it goes."

She shook her head. "I think, now, that if it had not been this, it would, in time, have been something else. Perhaps it is better this way, a blessing. We could love each other, but we could not be happy, make each other happy, and if love is not all for happiness, then"—she swiveled both wrists, upturning her palms—"what?"

"Children?" ventured Franklyn. "Family?"

She bit her lip while he winced at the force with which she did so. "Yes, children. Do you, Frank? Have children?"

"Never married."

"Yes." She took this in her stride. "But do you have children?"

Head-shake. "No, no kids."

"Would you *want* them?" He must have appeared discommoded by her question, because, as he shrugged, she hastened to add, "I mean, did you ever? Have regrets? I only ask because Josef wanted them so *very* much. Those were what mattered to him most, job and family." She scowled. "And his church."

"So what do *you* want, Ann? And don't say to win the strike. I mean for yourself."

"But that *is* for myself, winning. It is what matters to me most. I did not realize how much until it happened, but now that it has, that really is *all* that matters. It is surprising how much.

"Slovenes have a tradition they call Heart Culture. Perhaps you have heard of it." When he allowed as how he had not, she continued. "It is an attitude of kindness, common decency, good humor, extreme generosity toward others, community responsibility, communal experience, coming to the aid of those in need or distress, Good Samaritans. I was reared so."

"Fair enough," he said, "but there are thousands still out, yet you are the only one who does what you do. I mean, in the way that you do it."

She shook her head. "No. There is Ben. There is Mor Oppman. There is—"

"But they're pros, Ann. Ben's a pro. It's what he does for a living, takes his lumps, what he's paid to do. Oppman, too. You seem to have materialized out of homegrown nowhere, thin air. First time Ben mentioned you to me, that's how he talked about you, something heaven-sent."

She smiled. "Ben is a peach. He has been very good to me, good friend. Helped elect me president."

"President?"

"The Woman's Auxiliary."

"I didn't know! Congratulations! When did this happen?"

"Only just now."

"They're paying you, I hope."

Smiled again. "Not enough, and too much. Enough to quit my hospital work. I would do it for free."

"I am certain you would." His leg had fallen asleep; massaged it. "Almost finished, I think."

"So soon?"

It was out before he knew it, pure reflex. "*Too* soon." When she looked at him, wondering, he cleared his throat. "I mean, you've been terrific, to put up with me. No fun, all these questions from a perfect stranger."

"I hardly think we are strangers, Frank. Not anymore. At least, I would like to think we are not. Are we, Frank? Strangers? Still?"

"No, not strangers."

"Good then. That pleases me, very much."

Reddening—why? "One last question."

"As many as may please you."

"All right." He grinned his blush away. "Two then. You mentioned you don't read the papers, too aggravating."

"I refuse."

"But surely you have heard it around, some of the names you are being called."

"One or two."

"Socialist, anarchist, communist, atheist, terrorist."

"Lot of 'ists,' no? They use a broad brush."

"Are any of them the least bit accurate?"

"All of them," she answered matter-of-factly. "All of them and any number of others. More than one soldier and thug deputy has suggested that I would be better off in a whorehouse. They can call me anything they want, call me streel since it so seems to please them. I just want to win."

"The problem with labels, though," he said, "is that if you repeat them often enough, some of them tend to stick, and in their sticking distract, detract, get in the way, make it easy for others to be dismissive or contemptuous or—well, not to think about what you might prefer they think about."

"People like to reduce," she replied. "Nothing new in that. They believe reduction equals clarity, that the narrow mind is the coherent one, the rigid mind the consistent one, that the one that aligns life into slots and assigns it its pigeonholes is the ordered one. That is human nature, too, and it is why you see the union say and do some of the things it says and does. It must appeal to a broad number.

"It is a question of moral clarity, moral certainty. That is what Ben says, that people like moral certainty. To tell you the truth, so do I."

"Well, yes," he replied. "Ambiguity annoys most people. The problem is, without it there is no understanding, but then, perhaps understanding is overrated. Still, you run the danger, don't you, of shifting the focus off the issues and onto yourself? At least, you end up making yourself one of the issues, you and your tactics."

"Ben and I have talked about this. You are not all wrong, but so far as I represent the union, I *am* the issue, the, in Ben's words, 'living embodiment of the issue,' a symbol. It sounds like a lot, but that is only because MacNaughton continues to choose to make recognition—and not even recognition anymore, but the mere presence of the union—the issue.

"I live here. I always have. My parents lived here before he came around. I am not going anywhere, and he has no right to suggest that because people who have lived here all their lives and sacrificed much choose this moment to unite and unionize, they must leave. Despite what he may think when he looks in the mirror, James MacNaughton is not God."

"But, Ann, he does not need to be. He need be only who he is, MacNaughton, the Chief, C&H GM. You will pardon the comparison, but you begin to sound like Mother Jones herself."

At this, her eyes widened, then softened as she construed what Franklyn had intended as gentle criticism for high praise. "She is a great woman. I could only hope to follow her example in some slight way. But I thank you for saying it." She paused. "You said you had another question."

"About your parents. You mentioned that you were living with them."

"For now."

"So that would be the place to find you then, I mean, when you are at home, not . . . striking."

"I suppose. I really am not there much. Why?"

"Well, it is just, if I need to ask any follow-up questions, or if it makes sense to speak with you in connection with other stories, it probably would be helpful, in the event I can't track you down or find Ben, to have an address."

"And if I need to speak to you?"

"Oh, I'm at Plautz's, spare room above the tavern, staircase around back. Feel free."

"I know," she said. "Just testing." Extended her hand. "Here." Nodded at his pen and notebook. "I will write it down for you."

As she received the tools of his trade, first one, then the other, she grazed his hand with her fingertips, whisk of flesh, not even—skin whisper. His hand felt as if it had been branded by a feather feathered with fire.

Returned them to him, not touching.

When he glanced in the notebook later, he noticed that she had included not only her address—the house off Sixth around back of the firehouse—but the location of her bedroom, "1st floor, n.w. corner, window."

So Franklyn wrote his story, and, thereafter, as much at her invitation as with her permission—he soon discovered that she rather unabashedly adored, as certain people will, seeing her name in print—he became, at Ivan's behest, her chronicler and documentarian. Attached himself to her, barnacle. Not exclusively, of course. Other papers ran their share of "Tall Annie" or "Big Annie" stories, but none of them covered her in the same way, to the same saturating extent, ubiquitously, day after day, enjoying unfettered access day and night, telling the story of the strike essentially through her, which is to say, using her to tell it, her sensibility wedded to his.

Just why that wedding worked as well as it did, Franklyn never thought to question. Not every match is made in heaven, of course, but the one between Ana Clemenc and Franklyn Shivs, for a while anyway, was nigh celestial.

There were more children's parades, hundreds, thousands of kids decked out in their Sunday best carrying their PAPA IS STRIKING FOR US signs through the center of town. Impressive, affecting, and, at last, precisely as effective as every other parade staged by the union. Franklyn noticed the Cornish Kid bringing up the rear at one of them, straggler, Pal alongside. The Kid's own Sunday best appeared decidedly less better by half than the rest. When Franklyn waved, he and the dog came scampering over.

"Frank!"

"Hey, CK! On the march, eh?"

"Yep." He was beaming.

"The new army."

"Yep. Hey, Frank, where you been?"

"Around."

"'Cuz I went over to where you said you were staying, and they said you'd left."

"Nah. Moved, that's all. Plautz's tavern. Know it?"

"Sure. Over on Seventh."

"Right. I'm up above, upstairs. So come over sometime. Bring Pal. We'll catch a bite."

"Mean it?"

"What do *you* think?" When the Kid glanced anxiously down-street at the receding procession, Franklyn said, "Go on. Don't wanna get left behind. You're the rearguard. Most important place of all."

"Okay. See ya, Frank."

"See ya, CK. Bye, Pal."

The dog barked, and the Kid took off, bob- and/or shavetailing it headlong, side-flinging a final look back over his shoulder. As Franklyn waved, he could see, even at that distance—the Kid was all smiles.

AND MEANWHILE

As Ben Goggia so presciently had forecast, as October raced to catch up with November the lawlessness and violence became steadily more frequent and widespread.

Ahmeek Mine supply clerk Bill Guy Wilkins was shot in the left leg as he walked to work. Near Houghton, an exchange of gunshots claimed the lives of a deputy, Jim Pollack, and a striker, Joe Minerich. Outside Dunn's Hall, a striker, Phil Mihelcich, was critically wounded by a pistol shot fired by a deputy, Lloyd Lyman. Near Hancock, outside the Quincy Mine, one deputy and three strikers were wounded by gunshots when a gathering of rock-chucking picketers resisted mass arrest; some seventy shots were fired in the ensuing clash. A deputy, Ed Beaudoin, was stabbed in the neck by an unidentified assailant in Red Jacket. A striker, John Vuhich, was arrested and jailed for 120 days for attacking a deputy, Walter Rost, with a shoemaker's awl. The first incident of dynamiting occurred on October 18 when a section of train track was blown up near Copper City, eight miles north of Red Jacket, missing by a matter of minutes the mail train carrying a contingent of fifty new Ascher men. Five days later, a Northwestern train headed for Red Jacket with thirty-five imported scab workers was mobbed south of Hancock, and every window of their two coach cars smashed. The following day, a Mineral Range train carrying deputies and Guardsmen destined for Calumet was twice riddled with bullets, once at Swedetown Hill, north of the Quincy Mine, a second time near Osceola, just south of Red Jacket. No one was injured, but evidence indicated that more than one hundred shots had been fired. Not long after, telegraph wires serving Michigan State Telephone, Western Union, and the Copper Range Railroad were cut. A dynamite bomb exploded outside Mrs. Alina Salminen's Centennial Heights boardinghouse the day after ten Ascher men moved in. A pair of barns used to billet Guardsmen were firebombed and burned to the ground. When Hungarian miners broke ranks with the union and went back down, their homes near Allouez Mine, hard by Copper City, were emblazoned in red paint reading, BLACKGUARDS! BEWARE! DYNAMITE! The homes of mine captains, most of them Cornish, became prime targets for arson and vandalism. At the Ahmeek Mine, just north of Allouez, one of the massive smokestacks serving shafts one and two was dynamited. The stack remained intact, but the explosion, which was heard ten miles away, damaged half a dozen surface structures, including the main engine-house.

The Houghton County sheriff's office released figures revealing that arrests, recently running roughly 150 a week, were sharply on the rise and expected to escalate in the weeks ahead. Among the latest arrests, Ana Clemenc and Ben Goggia for their "hooligan leadership" of a predawn, torchlight, "haranguing march" down Calumet Avenue, resulting in the mass arrest by mounted Guardsmen of some hundred strikers "upon whose persons were found brass knuckles, improvised billies, slingshots, razors, and blackjacks." Convicted on two counts of assault and battery in circuit court on November 10, their sentencing was put off until after the new year, and they were released on their own recognizance.

And then, just as matters seem to have turned from bad to worse, they turned again—worse still.

TRIPLE MURDER IN MICHIGAN COPPER COUNTRY

UNKNOWN ASSAILANTS KILL THREE IN THEIR BEDS

Painesdale residents were vocal opponents of strike

50,000 MARCH TO PROTEST ESCALATING VIOLENCE

CALUMET—Three outspoken opponents of the northern Michigan copper mine strike, now heading into its fifth month, were killed here shortly after midnight Saturday, when unidentified gunmen wielding high-powered rifles opened fire on their Painesdale boardinghouse near the Champion Mine, some 20 miles south of Red Jacket. Authorities' search of the nearby woods, identified by eyewitnesses as the locale from which more than 40 shots were fired, turned up no evidence of the perpetrators.

Killed while they slept were Thomas Dally, 43, Harry Jane, 25, and Arthur Jane, 22. Dally was owner of the Baltic Street boardinghouse, home to the Jane brothers and more than a dozen Cornish miners. The Janes recently had returned from Toronto, Canada, having departed Painesdale at the commencement of the strike. Wounded in the unprovoked attack was 13-year-old Ellie Nicholson, a next door neighbor. According to her doctors, the girl's wounds, while serious, are not thought to be fatal.

Although Houghton County sheriff's deputies in the heavily patrolled neighborhood saw numerous muzzle flashes issue from the woods, and at least one deputy discharged his weapon in their direction, the gunmen made good their escape and presently remain at large. The Houghton Country sheriff's office reports that there currently are no official suspects in the case, but acknowledges that "in all likelihood" the murders are "strike-related."

Reaction to this latest outbreak of violence on the strike-torn Keweenaw Peninsula has been immediate, intense, and widespread. Supporters of the strike were quick to point the finger at what they called "rogue elements" among law enforcement here, "amateur deputies, thug Waddies, and goon squad Ascher detectives," as they characterized them, "bent upon turning public opinion against the strike by any and all means at their disposal, up to and including capital crime." Opponents of the strike are equally convinced that those responsible are "union mercenaries, paid gun-throwers, foreign agitators, hireling conspirators, and agent provocateur WFM whoremongers and terrorists who will stop at nothing to plant the red flag of socialism and the black flag of anarchism over local industry and enterprise."

Following the funeral for the three victims on Wednesday, an estimated 50,000 people poured into the streets of both Houghton/Hancock and Red Jacket/Laurium, an expression of mass frustration with the violence that continues to plague and paralyze their communities. Spearheaded by the Citizens' Alliance, a grassroots group of community activists and business, professional, and religious leaders claiming a membership of 8,000, the protesters staged a flurry of parades and mass meetings featuring speakers such as the Reverend J. R. Rankin of Houghton's Grace Methodist Episcopal Church.

"The WFM," declared Rev. Rankin before an enthusiastic audience of 8,000 inside Red Jacket's newly opened Colosseum, "is a hotbed of socialism which is the enemy of the home, the family, the community, of law and order, good citizenship and good morals, and the arch-enemy of the church and the gospel of Our Lord, Jesus Christ. Therefore, let us in the name of God, act. Let us drive the alien architects and agitators of this trouble forever from our midst. Let us forcibly remove and deport the devils. Let us send them back to the slime of the oblivion whence they came." His speech received a standing ovation.

According to Special Prosecutor George E. Nichols, recently assigned by Michigan Governor Ferris to the Houghton County attorney's office, "The Copper Range now seems to me to be on the verge of civil war, if not anarchy. Both sides are openly arming themselves. Threats of violence against both pro- and antistrike leaders have become routine. We are sitting on a powder keg."

So, the postludial turning, nor, thought Franklyn, need one be a reporter to sense it. Some endgame had commenced, and it was to be played out and to its nadir, increasingly in the dark.

Emboldened by the magnitude of the turnout, antistrike forces began to mobilize in a way and to an extent unprecedented. The remaining Guardsmen, Sheriff Cruse and his deputies, Wadell-Mahon and Ascher men, the county district attorney, and CA members began openly to act in coordination and concert. The contusive pandour.

There was widespread talk, some of it loose, some of it not, of lynching strike leaders. Individual acts of vigilantism, whether actively encouraged or tacitly tolerated by law enforcement, increased precipitously. Strikers were ambushed, mauled, ridden down on horseback, shot at and shot, their homes vandalized and illegally entered and searched at gunpoint, their occupants manhandled and pistol-whipped. The printing and distribution of *Tyomies*, the Finnish socialist daily, was disrupted repeatedly. Franklyn did his best to chase down and document each of the incidents, but they were too many by half, and by the time he was able to ascertain with certainty the facts, such matters inevitably reduced themselves to he said/he said.

Less ambiguous was the peninsula-wide campaign undertaken to disarm workers. Kicked off by the CA announcement that gun shops and hardware stores no longer would sell guns to strikers, numerous raids to confiscate weapons were conducted—from Allouez and Ahmeek in the north, to South Range in the south—always on horseback, always at night, always in force, always wielding the same baseball-size riot sticks massproduced in the C&H carpentry shops.

The South Range union hall was raided by an armed posse of four hundred at three in the morning. Twenty high-powered rifles and ten Colt automatic pistols were removed, forty Finnish strikers arrested and charged with unlawful assembly, the union hall padlocked and boarded up, to reopen some weeks later as a branch of the Houghton County sheriff's office. In Red Jacket, the WFM commissary on Pine Street was rousted in the predawn hours and fifteen rifles, shotguns, and revolvers, and three hundred rounds of ammunition confiscated. At Franklin Location, near Quincy, twenty rifles, four revolvers, six swords, a shotgun, two sticks of dynamite, and furzes were removed from over a dozen homes. At Ahmeek, the entire village was cordoned off by mounted Guardsmen and one hundred feet of furze, rifles, shotguns, and revolvers removed. In nearby Copper City, more high-powered rifles and shotguns were taken, on the heels of which a second Houghton County sheriff's office branch was established. Union organizer Mor Oppman was arrested when his rented room was raided, and two half sticks of dynamite were found in the pockets of his closeted coat.

For the moment, then, the world teetered on its transport, tethered to that which it could not transcend, trying its best to retrieve that which somehow had gone forfeit, even as the question in Franklyn's mind, the question that had been there from the first, loomed ever larger: to what extent, and in precisely what fashion, could the energy, money, organization, and management behind such activity be traced to James Mac-Naughton?

What there could be little question about was the exquisitely timed joint announcement that issued now from carteled mine management: "As of this day, and hereafter, in all Copper Range mines, an eight-hour workday and new worker grievance procedures are hereby in effect. Likewise the policy that all employees who do not return to work as of January 1, 1914, will be immediately replaced by workers imported into this district for that express purpose."

One could almost hear, thought Franklyn, the soughing of the wind as it abandoned certain sails.

AND MEANWHILE

—WFM leaders Vice President Mahoney, Yanko Terzich, and John Lowney returned to national headquarters in Denver, leaving Ben Goggia and Mor Oppman to carry on as best they might while they met with Haywood to discuss whether the time had come for him to make his appearance on the Copper Range.

—Judge O'Brien, officially petitioned by Goggia and Oppman for the WFM, issued an injunction at the application of attorneys LeGendre and Kerr, restraining the Citizens' Alliance and its members from "interfering with or molesting by threats or intimidation" union organizers and members, an injunction that did not prevent Sheriff Cruse from issuing his own order that Sunday parades and mass meetings henceforward would be considered unlawful assemblies, or disclosing that he had increased the number of sworn deputies at his disposal to 2,100.

—U.S. Congressman William MacDonald, Progressive Party representative from the Keweenaw, solicited President Woodrow Wilson to launch a federal investigation into "a strike that hangs over me personally like a nightmare, having turned my district into a perfect hell."

—At the request of the Houghton County Board of Supervisors, Judge O'Brien impaneled a twenty-member special grand jury, empowering the district attorney to compel testimony from WFM leaders and others about their strike activities.

—Clarence Darrow, on behalf of the WFM, contacted Governor Ferris seeking to reopen arbitration, in response to which Ferris dispatched Grant Fellows, Michigan attorney general, to the Keweenaw, where he remained ten days before reporting back to Ferris that he found "the district quiet as a country churchyard."

—U.S. Secretary of Labor William Wilson, speaking before an American Federation of Labor convention, castigated James MacNaughton and Michigan's copper-mining companies, C&H in particular, as profiteers possessed of "a false conception of the title to property, title created by law not primarily for the welfare of the man to whom it is conveyed, but for the welfare of the community, a trustee for the welfare of society. There can be no conciliation between employer and employee that does not presuppose collective bargaining, and there cannot be collective bargaining that does not presuppose trade unionism." To which MacNaughton promptly replied: "Such political bunk is worthy only of a peanut politician; a man in Mr. Wilson's position should be above it. Mr. Wilson offered his services as mediator in the strike in Michigan. His services were declined. The good judgment displayed by the mining companies in doing so now is apparent to everyone."

BEDDING BEN

The banging at his bedroom door awakened him in the dark, reeling him from bed fractionally still asleep, fully erect and comparably naked. The pounding sounded to him like mortar rounds.

"Who's there?"

"Frank! Open up! It is Ann!"

Fumbling for and finding his trousers hung neatly upside-down from the chairback beside the bed, he lifted them up and away, yanked them clumsily on, buttoned them hastily up, unlatched and opened the door as she barged through while he closed and locked it behind her. Somewhere behind him she stood breathing heavily as he reached for and lit the lamp beside the bedstead, shadowing up the walls.

"Frank, they have Ben! Jumped him. Dragged him off. I tried to follow, but could not. There were too many, so many . . ."

Barefooting over, he placed his hands upon her shoulders; she tensed. "Who, Ann? Who took him? Who has him? Where did his happen? When? How long ago?"

She wasn't crying hysterically, crying at all, really, but she clearly was badly shaken. Something akin to whimpering kittened and crocheted her words. "I do not know. I did not recognize them. I tried. Voices. They wore masks, hoods. Black hoods. It was late, dark, very dark. We just were leaving, locking up. Dunn's. We were out in the street, talking, and suddenly, I do not know, out of nowhere, we are surrounded, and . . ." She looked at him, imploring, just sane enough to be distraught. "I did not know where else to go. We must find him!"

"We will. *I* will. I'll roust MacNaughton from his bed if I have to."

This was not bravado, false or otherways. He had to find Goggia. Not doing so did not occur to him. The world and everything in it might be gray as gothica and twice as grotesque, but that didn't mean that on occasion you didn't find yourself faced with a black-and-white moment, one that you had best know what to do with, because if you didn't, then you *were* lost. Then you were beyond absurd. Then you were pointless.

And now she *was* crying, sobbing silently in shudders all through. Taking her by both hands—quavering, impossibly icy hands—he led her over to the bed, sat her down. "Here," he said as calmly as he could muster its management in the moment. "Sit here. Stay here." Squeezed them, still trembling, where they lay in her lap, quietening them some, then reached for his shirt, socks, shoes. Vest. Coat. Overcoat. Hat.

Somewhere along in here, between shoes and vest, perhaps, vest and coat, she said, "I am coming with you."

"No, Ann," he replied. "you are not. You are staying here. I don't know what's out there, and neither do you. What we both know is, whatever it is, I have a better shot at getting him back on my own. Agreed?"

When she nodded her assent, he asked, "What time is it, do you know?"

She shook her head. "Late. Must have been close to one when we were closing up."

"Okay. Oppman?"

"Mor? I do not know. He was not with us."

"Okay, good. That's good." He walked to the door, unlocked it, slewed about. "I'll get him back, all right?"

She nodded. "How?"

He smiled, feigning sangfroid. "It's a story, Annie. My job, information. Pound the pavement, knock on doors, the right doors, ask around, a hundred questions if I have to, raise holy hell if it comes to it, buck the damn tiger." He paused. "Cold, Ann, cold as a cod when I need be." Smiled again. "Hey, did I ever tell you I can see in the dark?"

When she shook her head, he tried to be lighthearted. "Yep, cross my heart." Crisscrossed it. "'S true. What the Eskimos call *qaumaneq*, inner searchlight, that's me. Do my best work after dark, vampire. Takes more heart than you might think, being implacably hateful. Takes tons."

She forced a smile, weak one. "Frank?"

"Ann?"

"Those men."

"Yeah?"

"They had guns."

It was a couple of long hours before first light—following a good three quarters of one spent sizing up the scene, furiously working his sources in the saloons, checking with the police, the hospital, the trains (twenty-three in and out of town in the course of a day)—when Franklyn literally tripped over what they had dumped there. Out of town just south, out past MacNaughton's house, the moonlit-defined clump on the side of road, where, come sunup, someone would have been sure straightaway to have spotted him. Meant to be found, then. Special delivery. Unmisconstruable message. Because in the misshapen shape he was in, he wasn't going any damn where anytime soon.

For a moment, Franklyn took the heaped-up heap for an animal, dead one. Doe perhaps, small bear, gray wolf. But then the clump moaned a little, twitched some, and he knelt to it, bent to, blindly feeling, endeavoring to Braille a human figure from the naked form that lay fetaled there.

This, this here, was a human haunch, definitely a man's. This, right here, was a hip. Up here, an elbow. Around over here, a shoulder. So then surely this was a neck. And this, this was . . . what? What *was* this?

His hand came away, wet. Gooed. With glop. "Crassamentum?" he thought. Held it up, in front of his face, scared, and then more than scared. His asshole puckered, unbuttoned, rebuttoned. Studied his hand, left hand, its palm, as if it were a mirror, steadying.

They say blood appears black in the moonlight. Okay, yes, some black here, oil-spill smears. Christ! But the rest of it appeared less black than . . . gray? Lighter, anyway. What was this, gray? This gray stuff? Felt it with the fingers of his other hand, right hand, some doughy spatter-all between thumb and forefinger. Slippery. Slurry. Slush. Lump of sponge. Brioche. Or, no—sponge*like*. Without the spring, the spring back. Inert. Smutch. And mixed in amid, something pebbly-pieced, harder, gravied grains and kernels of—what?—silica? sand?—like—what?—tooth chip? bone bit?

Aw, no!

Hunched over him, leaned closer in, just enough light to delineate a face the vaguely unfamiliar features of which were raw meat and mush. A pair of eyes, their lids, a nose, its nostrils, a pair of lips, teeth, tongue, a mouth, two ears—checking, each, in order—Okay, all there, but each of them . . . off, oddly rearranged, slidden taffylike, Picasso-like, just enough out of place that—well, it was as if his face was a wheel of Brie placed in the sun, then forgotten about while it melted some before being returned to the icebox. Each of the coordinates, his facial coordinates, askew. *En deshabille.* Some things dangled, others flapped, still others oozed, the rest were mangled, not a one of which had oughtta a-been.

Franklyn shrugged off his coat and tucked it, capelike, about Goggia's shoulders. "Ben! Ben! Can you hear me?" More moaning, gurgling, miscellaneous animal sounds. Franklyn was at his ear. "Ben, it's Frank, Frank Shivs. We need to get you up. Sorry, Ben, but you need to stand up. Think you can make it to your feet?"

Franklyn swung around to Goggia's backside, insinuating his arms beneath Ben's own, surcingling them about his torso, planting his feet shoulder-wide. "Ben, I'm going to lift, lift you up now. Lean against me. Use me to prop up. Counterweight. I'm a tree. Find your feet against me. Okay? Hoist then—on three. Here we go. Ready? One. Two. Three!"

Franklyn was not a large man, but then, luckily, neither was Ben. It took several tries, game try after try, the final one eliciting—or, rather, extracting, tonsiling, *tearing* a sound from the mutilated man that was to remain with Franklyn always, but at last he was up, if not entirely upright, and though Ben proved less ambulatory than not, and though his splenius had been wrenched free of its footing so that his neck failed to support the deadweight of his head which drooped and lolled grotesquely, they soon enough were alternately snailing and turtling, drag-footedly crow-hopping in the direction of the hospital.

As they hobbled on, Franklyn did his best to calm and comfort his friend with the only first aid he knew: his words, like water, flowed. Step by unsteady step, word after word, he sentenced his friend along, wove bandages of the ones that occurred, applied cold compresses of their texture, sutures of tone, relieved his thirst as best he might with the chromed water tongued of their turning. But what he had none of, did Franklyn Shivs, yet needed now most of all, what he never had had, and yet what his friend required now more than anything else in the world, was precisely that which he could not provide, had *never* been able to provide.

He could proverb and pray, whistle and sing, rhyme, recite, and recount, he could chant, incant, wisecrack, and riddle, but when it came to the morphine of stories—real morphine, real stories, those that might momentarily blunt, ease, soothe, and allay, if not lift him free of his pain, triage and *transport*—when it came to once-upon-a-time and happily-ever-after, Franklyn Shivs, once again, ever as always, was fresh out.

Stories—damn them!—were his bane.

Dark still when Franklyn returned to his room. Cat-pawing the exterior stair, he did his best to unlock the door quietly as a cat burglar, step through, close it behind him silently as a jewel thief.

Soundless as a monk.

Ann was asleep in his bed. Removing his bloody coat, he began unbuttoning his bloody vest. Which is when she awoke. He heard her—sheet rustle.

"Ben. Did you find him?" Half-still-drunk-asleep talk, drifty-dreamy.

"Yes. It's all right. Go back to sleep. We'll talk later."

When she yawned and stretched, rolled over and reached for the lamp, he said, "No, leave it."

"But what happened? Where is he?" She sat groggily up, propping herself by a pillow, drew her knees to her chest beneath the covers.

Perching on the side of the bed, his back to her, he began removing his shoes.

"Hospital. He's safe. Good hands."

"Hospital?" She was lifting fully awake now, enough to be alarmed. "What happened?"

He sighed mentally. "I don't know. I don't know that yet. He was beaten, badly beaten."

"How badly?"

"Badly."

Long silence. She smoothed across the bed, close enough to lay a hand on his shoulder. "Will he live?"

His shoulders sagged. A shoe dangled ridiculously from his hand. It suddenly occurred to him that, more ridiculous still, he was wearing his hat. "I don't know. They don't know. Touch and go. The doctors said they wouldn't know for a while, several days. He was barely conscious when I found him. By the time I left, he wasn't. Broken ribs. Collarbone. Punctured lung. The worst was his head. All stove up, stove in."

"I want"—her voice softly cracked—"I want to go see him."

He turned to her. Even in the dark, he could tell she was crying. He gently found the back of her head, drew her face toward him, pressed its cheek to his shoulder, his free hand outspread, webbed through the thick lacing of her hair. The fragrance of her sleep, troubled sleep, enveloped him there.

He dropped the other shoe.

"Annie, we can't. Not right now. The doctors said no visitors until he's out of the woods. Trust me, you don't *want* to see him, not yet. Let him heal some, mend. Ben's a proud man. He wouldn't want you seeing him this way."

He felt her tears through his shirt. The wet stain of them stung.

She lifted her head from his shoulder. "Bastards!"

"Yes," he said. "We'll find out who. Promise."

"How, Frank? And even if we do, what then? The law is against us now. It has turned. It is what they want, this. They let it happen."

He suddenly felt as tired as he ever had in his life, a weariness in muscle and bone deep and all through. He ached both in body and mind. Needed to sleep, consumed by the need, descent of a lead-weighted drape. She sensed it, drew him into bed beside her, laid his head on the pillow, unhatting him. He closed his eyes as she unbuttoned and removed his shirt, undid his trousers.

"Here," she said, "lift up."

He raised his butt, already half adrift as she tugged off his pants and tossed them aside. Naked now.

"I should go home," she began.

"No," he managed, fading. "Stay. Please."

He was falling, fast. She did as he had bade. Nestled to him. Laid her head on his chest. Rise and fall. Closed her eyes. Cant-hooked an arm about his waist. She needed to hold and be held. Listened to the strong sounds of his heart, the way their rhythms revved down and rhymed. Felt her own as it stirred, fully filling.

When she awoke, it was daying toward antelucan gray, downy feathers through the window the framed color of snow, and her head was still where it was. Sleep of the dead. His muffled snores. She kissed his chest, butterflied her head beneath the blanket, tongued the contours of his belly, her face smoothing lower, skating mouth a migration. Outside, overhead, she heard the high sound of last geese; chevron.

She opened wide the wings of her lips, and flew south.

ANA

✦   ✦   ✦

It had snowed unceasingly during the night, increasingly, as if the sky were a ruck bulging overfull with the stuff and while they were sleeping had unlaced itself, unstuffed its stuffing, shaken itself utterly empty, then rummaged about for more, repeated the process all night long at longer length. They awoke to white, this whitened world above and below socked in hip-high; no sun. Or, rather, just enough of one to be aware of how much one already missed it.

This, by the way, is not picking up where one left off, but a week or two later. Ben was alive, but damaged, damaged enough that at the first opportunity he had been train-lifted back home to Denver. The two of them had been there to see him off, not that he recognized them or, perhaps, even understood that they were there. He still scarcely was recognizable himself. Ann had found it difficult to maintain her composure, and later, had spectacularly failed.

Shagging hard on after that night of pile-driven snow came the unconscionable cold snap, one so wind-*full* that left-out pets died, as did pastured and paddocked farm animals. The cold seemed impossible, possessed of a personality, a singularly unpleasant one, that of a bayonet, say, the kind that stapled horizontal hurt to a body, hammered pitons and nails. Unpleasant enough that in the years to come those who made it through unscathed, as those who did not, would yarn stories about it. Lacinating legend of winter; white myth.

And then, around noon, after a morning of intermittent letup and lull, it commenced to snowing again. Harder. Graupel. Matzo-ball snow. Those in the mines stayed there. It was safer gone to ground, underground, away from weather, where, however befouled, it was warmer and drier. Less white.

As accustomed as those Yoopers were to gales, whiteouts, snow squalls, and blizzards, this one was different. People caught out in it, caught too far out, lost fingers, toes, noses, ears. Some lost entire faces. Some, more. And too far needn't be so far, because you couldn't see your hand in front of your face. Everything you were familiar with, everything you knew like the back of that very hand, had gone forfeit to the staggering white and the white wind that roiled it, snirkling your soul in barbed wire, ensnarling your mind along with it, balling them both to white tumbleweed and blowing them out to white sea. The storm was insane, and insofar as you were in and of it, you became insane yourself.

Once it had passed, once the winds had slacked some and the snow subsided enough that you could discern the flaked, flurry slant of it—for it continued to snow with abandon and periodic stretches of real wrath until the following midmorning when it began to diminish toward merely an old-fashioned earnestness before petering out at last—the numbers were quick in their coming. The weather station at Copper Harbor reported winds in excess of fifty miles per hour, temperatures well past twenty-three below zero, a snowfall of thirty-nine inches with impassable drifts high as rooflines, a snow that "lowered the eaves to icicle-kicking level," as they put it.

People with second and third stories climbed out their windows, clambering onto their neighbors' rooftops. Kids somehow lugged their sleds up there and, like ski jumpers, sledded their slant or, if they didn't own sleds, used cardboards and crates the parts of which they had paraffined. So until the removal crews could commence and complete their jobs—the snow wasn't plowed or shoveled from the roadways, but flattened, "pancaked" or "panked" where it lay using horse-drawn, five-foot-diameter drum rollers—this is how people walked to work or into town, how children made their way to school, striding the high pathways across the very tip-top of the sheep-whitened world. Snow empire. Stranded white kingdom come, and fallen.

WHITE MOMENTS

At the first opportunity, they went strolling, or, rather, *a*-strolling, out in it. Her idea. Frankly, he could have done without, but she was intent, not to be dissuaded. The sun was out, thank-you-Jaysus-glory-be high, all of it in every burnished lumen, up high in a cerulean sky achingly clear enough to walk through and out the other side, and when its light—a most over-zealous light, as he conceived of it—hard alighted, it bounced off everything in sight with an acuity he found literally breath-breaking. Because everything it bounced off was bright white, the brightest, circum-ambient spanking bright white in the history of the whole wintry world. Glints sprayed like splinters, angry as spark salt, before landing full-brunt a-thrash on his eyes. "Sheet glare," they called it up here. One's very eye-lids were scarce protection enough.

The pair of indigo-and-rose-colored-lens glasses she thoughtfully had supplied him from home helped some. As did the snowshoes, tra-versing hill and dale hither and yon such steeped ground. And, too, being bundled up—flannel long-john underwear, woolen stockings, two pairs of pants, thicker sweater over never-thick-enough one, vest, wide woolen scarf, black woolen watch cap (he adamantly refused to wear a balaclava—dumb), hooded tan parka, rabbit-fur-lined gloves, big duck-canvas thick-tread cramponless boots, the whole nine yards, thensome.

"Must look like a couple of damn fool Sherpas," he grumbled to him-self, "Everesting around this way."

She had, she said, a place she wished to show him, special place, secret place. Did he think he was up to it? Just yonder, a mile or two. Well, sure, he said, I'm game, the good sport lying through his ch-ch-chattering teeth, the clacking so loud he could not credit how she did not hear it and so deliver him, frozen soul, from this subarctic evil. But, in the meanwhile, Lead on, O Faerie Princess of the Wintry Northern Wasteland.

So, off they trudged, snowshoeing. Trundle, tramp, floppit-and-scrunch, lake-bent through the yard-deep, untrammeled, fresh-fallen snow that in its furred-fleecing of the surrounding landscape had softened its lines, smoothed out its angles, smothered its contours into camel humps and half moons, scallops, saucers, crescents, scoops, bumps the size of bulls, parameres and kyphoses, hollows big as buffalo wallows, sea turtle knobs, a world curvesome and boss-backed, thick-cushioned in parabola white and reshaped as rondure.

The unstriated countryside looked combed and combed over. It was exactly, he thought, as if the sky had been an enormous cumulus cloud that had descended to earth, divested itself of its cloudiness, this load of cloud, then reascended, having left its white weight behind. Something half cruel and extravagantly ice-hearted, but voluptuous, too.

She knew, he soon learned, about the phenomenon of "sky maps," the navigational tool used by Eskimos to keep them true to course, maintain a right bearing. In an essentially featureless, monotonic snow-and-ice land-scape saturated in glarelight, one apt to half-cock scale and a-skelter depth perception, the natives looked to the sky to discern right location by way of "ice blink," the light and dark color-patterned in the sky. The way snowed-in land appears yellow-white, the field ice white-yellow, the pack ice pure white, the sea/lake ice gray-white. They weren't straying far enough that they would need rely upon the method, but it comforted him some that she had knowledge of such.

Because winter up here was rugged. Hard. Indifferent and disquiet-ing. And could be just grotesque enough to cause distress, madness, and mutilation, entice people to tear at their eyes, shear their clothing to tat-ters, slash their flesh with sharp knives, dine on dog shit and scat, run naked and shrieking into the snow as if pursued by invisible snow bats.

And not just the cold of it, but the lack of light, the light defeated, its palette of grays and Cimmerian gloom day after day, the way it shut down, closed off, swept color away until you felt felled by achromatopsia. The way winter pressed, prodded you back and inside, drove you deep toward retreat, shrunk your mind, its size, down to dirt and debris. Tenebrous time. A season capable of seizing you by the throat, kneeling hard on your heart, making you weary of the world, its full weight, every ounce of your life, waking morn after morn to two thousand scavenger crows frozen corvid, foot-bound fast to a butcher's black boneyard.

They bowed their heads as they plowed ploddingly onward, horse-tailed white smoke from their nostrils and mouths that the wind fetched off in flanges; city steam grates. The air was so cold, so clean, you could actually smell it, he thought, the purity of it, the cold a drain through the air, pulling the life from the very atmosphere. So cold you might have sworn you could hear it, the sound of cold: *skreetle, scritchett, skaaaaak.*

At intervals, she glanced back as they trod. At intervals, as he followed in her snow steps, he would raise a hand in the universal "I'm okay" ges-ture. At longer intervals, she reined up to permit him to catch up. At longer intervals still, he caught up, and they stood side by side, exchanging a few breathless words, those of his conspicuously more breathless than those of hers.

"Okay?"

"Fine."

"Sure?"

"Yep."

"Then why are you bent over at the waist with your jaw wide open and your hands claws at your knees?"

"Are they? Hadn't realized. Just checking."

"For what?"

"To make sure they're still attached to my legs."

And she, with some effort, laughed, and he, with more effort, strenuous effort, laughed, and she said, "Ready?" And he said, "Just a sec." And breathed up from his boot soles, cigarette lungs, and beat his chest like congas, and said, "Okay." And she shoved off. And he shoved after.

Turned out that where they were off to was a densely timbered stretch of fir forest overlooking a sheltered lakeside cove that, in spite of the cold, he could see was fetchingly pretty; *très* pelagic. The tall trees, their boughs bent and deflexed with undisburdened snow weight, looked like white-bearded wise men standing upright on stilts. Arm hooped in arm, they gazed out across the ocean-vast lake, blue metal scoured gray.

Having caught what remained of his breath, he piped up first. "This is your place." As much statement as question, kept his eyes glued straight on.

Sensed her nodding beside him. "I saw a spirit here once." The half-dozen words she never had been able to muster the nerve to say to her husband now spoken through swirling whispers of steam. "In there, through the trees. We spoke."

He willed his eyebrows to remain unrisen, commanded his forehead please not to knit. "In words? To each other?"

She was silent a moment. "I think so. Not certain. Seemed so."

"Just the once?"

"Never came back. Too afraid." Paused. "Not upset, awed. Sense of wonder. This is the first I have been, since that day."

"Do you feel scared now?"

When he turned to look at her, she already was looking at him. Shook her head. "No. Not with you." Too cold to kiss—tongue to faucet, lips stuck to pump handle—they smiled instead, trying not to shatter their features.

"What did it say, the spirit?"

"I do not remember everything. Some of what I do, I do not understand, still. The encounter was brief, but seemed several lifetimes. It was about"—she hesitated—"shedding skins, I think. To find out what is underneath, or is not. About how hard that is and how few do it or can, look honestly at themselves, into themselves, through themselves truly naked, nakedly, and not be dismayed or disgusted by what they see."

"Did you?"

"What?"

"Did you look?"

She nodded: solemnity. "Yes. That was my charge. It told me to."

"And?"

"I changed."

"How? How do you mean?"

"I looked, and what I saw was another, an other, one that was a stranger to me, but also *was* me. The original me." She placed her gloved hand on the breast of his coat. "I am sorry. I am making no sense."

"Oh, no! I wouldn't dare to say about the spirit, but what you are saying, *that* makes sense. Please, go on."

"Well, it was not who I was, the way I was reared, been taught, the way I was then, who I had become, the way others wanted of me, for me, the way I was living. But now I knew. It—she—was there. And now I had to live with her, and soon there no longer was room. She was growing larger, every day, so much larger, until finally there only was room enough for one. For her, or for me."

"What did you do?"

"I let it be, let it happen, let *her* happen. I knew I could not stop her even if I had desired it, and I did not desire it. Her heart was so much bigger, stronger, her heart beat so much louder than mine."

"So, the Annie I am with now, right now," he said, "right here, this Annie I am speaking to, this is a different person than before? One I never knew?"

"Different, yes, but the same. It is not that the old Ann is dead, Frank, or all gone. Left behind, maybe, a little, like a shadow. Or put aside, on a shelf, trunked in an attic, but still *my* attic, *my* trunk, *my* shelf, *my* shadow. Do not worry, Frank"—she chuckled—"I am me, still me, all me, all *of* me, and maybe I am more.

"When you shed a skin—and this the spirit did not tell me, this I was left to discover on my own, for myself—when you shed your skin in order to grow another, one newer, better, tougher, you do not throw the old one away. You do your best to bury it in a shallow grave, a grave that only you know, one only you can visit, to which you can pay your private respects, one you and you only may disinter as you wish."

"And have you? Disinterred?"

"No. Never. I will never. It lies where it rests—in peace."

On their way back they saw a heron, *Ardea herodias*. Or rather, she saw it, first. Herons are solitary hunters, and this one, a great white, must have been foraging when it was caught out. Now it was frozen stiff, upright in place, standing at attention on the single spindle of its leg, neck-tucked and feathered in ice. Sculpture of sentinel. The wind ruffled its wings.

She, of course, wanted to bury it. He, of course, did not.

"It's dead," he said, saying the perfectly obvious.

"That is why," she said.

"It's a bird," he said, more lamely still.

"That, too," she said.

Actually, as birds went, he didn't mind herons. Liked the way the word was spelled, for one thing. He/her/hero/heron. Lot going on there, lot going for it, something peculiarly androgynous. King/Queen. *Rex/Regina*. Which he found oddly appealing. Beautiful and handsome both, especially on the hunt. Striding, stately, solitary. Mad, though. Had to be. To stand alone, death-still for hours at a stretch, never dozing off, so much as blinking, not an altered move, tonically immobile, just to catch a stupid fish or a frog. Mad, yes, and magnificent. So precise and delicate, fine-boned, fragile as glass. Every moment, threatening to snap itself in half. Flying body of fracture. Suicide bird.

So, of course, they buried it. He did, while she watched. Off with the snowshoes, down on his knees, using one of the shoes to quarry the long, shallow grave, then scoop the great bird out and lay it gently down on its side, careful of its beak, prowess of splinter, snow-blanket it over again, where, as he assured her, it only would be dug up later by some marauder beast.

"Thank you," she said.

"De nada," he replied.

"We will remember this," she said.

"You will," he replied, stifling the impulse to plunge his face deep into a snow dune and open his eyes wide as they would go.

"It is winter now," he thought, "and everywhere you look, you're snow-blind."

Everywhere, these dark satanic mills.

UNDER THE CALDERA

With Ben gone and Haywood yet to arrive—though his arrival now was talked around on every side—Ana took it upon herself to follow through on a notion that she and Ben had discussed once or twice in passing. Namely, that should the strike string out, limp along, drag through to Christmas, the families must not be deprived, the children especially, of celebrating the holiday as they normally would, at least insofar as the matter might be arranged. So that with the strike at low ebb—announcement of the eight-hour day coupled with Ben's near-fatal beating and the subsequent nonar-rest of a single of his assailants had bleached much of the starch out of all but the hardiest of hard-core holdouts—Ana dedicated herself to organizing the grandest, most extravagant Christmas party for the children of Calumet that they ever had experienced.

At least, that is what she did when she and Frank Shivs were not sequestered in his room above the saloon, working together to obliterate everything but themselves and the increasingly calisthenic moments they more often, if still discreetly, shared. Discreetly, that is, as far as *they* were concerned, because so oblivious were they to themselves as a couple that gossip, as gossip will, already had begun to spread about Calumet like scum on summer ponds. Impossible to keep her in purdah.

"Frank. Hey. Come here."

In the bar, behind the bar, John Plautz. An unseasonably warmish, late-December day, holidays upcoming.

"John. Hey. What's up?"

"Frank, Josef Clemenc, you know this name?"

"A little. Not to shake hands, no."

"Josef Clemenc, we sing together, in church, out, all our lives, little boys. His voice, it is down from the angels. Good friends, Josef and me."

"Good to have good friends, John. I imagine."

"Yes, good, very good. So my friend, he is married. Works below, and while he works, still, he is married."

"That so?"

"Yes, married. But his wife, she has notions, other notions."

"Notions?"

"She gets involved. The strike."

"Ah. Yes. Well, she's hardly alone there, is she?"

"Oh, sure, right. But she gets involved so much, she forgets herself. And then, she forgets him. Forsakes. Moves out of their home."

"Sorry to hear."

"Sorry, yes. Everyone is sorry. And then"—he motioned Franklyn closer, lowered his voice—"then she forgets herself *so* much, she takes up with another, another man, some," spat the word, "stranger."

"These things happen, John. All the time."

"Sure they do, sure. But," he erupted, grotesquely purpling, "NOT IN MY PLACE!"

And just like that—no by your leave, howdy-do, no so long or godspeed—that was that. If Plautz knew, then how many others? Josef? Her parents? Troubling. For his own reputation he might care little enough. Hers was another matter entirely. Certainly it would do nothing but damage the cause of her . . . cause should word of their—what? assignations? liaison?—become public knowledge.

And so, that very day, Franklyn Shivs, evictee, moved back to the Arlington, his old room. Outlander, non-Yooper, Chicagoan, damn writer to boot, this unmitigated menace to the social order. Well, he thought, good to be put in one's place on occasion, as, too, to be reminded of one's base and truer nature.

To anyone less besotted and smitten, the exchange with Plautz would have served to prompt the soberest of redoubled reflection. What, after all, did he think he was doing, screwing not only the wife of a married man, but the most publicly loathed and admired woman on the peninsula. Instead, it did nothing of the kind. Served only to send him tumbling toward . . .

Why booze was such an occupational hazard, to which even the most talented, especially the most talented, so often fell prey, was not a subject that particularly interested him. Reporters had too much time on their hands, or not enough. They spent too much time in saloons, or not enough in church. They spent too much time on the job, or not enough at home. They were scandalously underpaid. Their bosses routinely were autocratic sots themselves, or not. They witnessed too much of the coarse, black worst of human nature. They were ceaselessly under the gun of daily deadline. If they had a perfectionist bone in their bodies, they could rest assured that in time that bone would be stomped on and crushed. The reasons were endless, and each an excuse.

Franklyn was thirty-three years old, years during which, so it often struck him, he had spent far too much time deliberately sidestepping what it pleased him to call "the Grand Entangle," committing to no one, engaging "real" life the less, cultivating what he was fond of referring to as "the Unaffiliated Mind." Pathetic, of course, and equally depressing, and, had pathos and depression less suited him, he doubtless would have bestirred himself to more effectively resist the temptation to wallow in their midst as does a shoat in its slop. But they did. Suit him. And, so, from most things, was content, too content, still to flee.

"Whom do I love?" he asked himself, "besides myself? What do I commensurately value? What have I contributed, much less created? The contraband of column inches? Which amounts to what, exactly? Or need it amount to anything? Ambition is responsible for more horror in this godless world than even religion, and Plato doubtless was right when he admonished us to hold fast to the thing we already hold fast, up to and including despair."

So found himself wondering, "When, at last, does anyone begin to apprehend that everything is not about oneself? When, please god, does everyone begin to acknowledge that none of it matters as much as anyone may believe? And how, pray tell, do I go about having my cake and eating it too? Because I cannot—can I?—live—not properly, correctly, in the *right*, not anymore—without this woman.

"And yet, should we continue . . ."

Perhaps, together, they could devise a way to ease themselves out of this. Let go. Leave off. Just—behave. Perhaps it was not yet too late. Save that he knew what he had yet to acknowledge, most of all to himself. She had annihilated him, rendered him disarticulated, gone clean to fragment. The capacity for such release was, he knew, not in him.

"You are going to get drunk," he told himself. "You need to do this. You owe it to yourself. You must get drunker than you have ever been in your life, which is *real* drunk, and when you are so drunk that you can sprout chitin down your spine, chew tails off scorpions, see through shining suns and out their other side, then and only then are you going to do something . . . rash."

For drinking of this sort—self-recriminating, solitary, purposeful, *sober*—Red Jacket simply would not serve. His mug was too familiar about town, as the town too familiar to him. He needed, for the moment, to abscond.

Leaving word for Ann at the Italian Hall above the A&P on Seventh where he knew she was spending most of her time preparing the Christmas party, he settled his affairs at the hotel, packed his vitals and necessaries neatly in his valise, then hiked over to the train station, purchased a one-way ticket, and hopped the Kelockity for Hancock.

He knew a flophouse, fleabag hotel down there, the Xanadu. Actually had a bar, the Farolito, so-called, Little Star, Little Lighthouse. He would go there, begin the ritual exorcism there. It was fully his intention to be back in Red Jacket by Christmas. Gave him the better part of a week. As the train jerked out of the station to slug its ten miles south, or chug there, he half hoped that he would make it.

"Mescal," said Franklyn; magic word.

It was early. Save for the barkeep, he was alone in the bar, fixed gaze in the mirror while he listened to the grandfather clock in the corner keep incorrect time to the slow beat of his heart. He was bent upon disgracing himself before day's end.

"If one wishes to live *right*," he thought, "one must"—he believed this with all of his heart (such as it was)—"be at least a *little* broken up, go *some* to pieces, time to time."

The bartender placed the spool-slim cylindrical glass on the zinc bar top before him, poured. Franklyn requested a wedge, and when it came hoisted a Melvillean toast to himself in the mirror: "*Give me, ye gods, an utter wreck, if wreck I do.* Bottoms up!" Then tossed back the drink, sucked the lemon, motioned the barkeep to keep pouring, repeated the ritual a second time, then a third, felt his mind slow just enough to require a more deliberate effort to summon a focus.

Who among us can honestly say he is not being dragged under forever?

The strike increasingly was looking like a bust. Ben Goggia had been beaten to within an inch of his life and shipped home. Franklyn had yet to land his interview with MacNaughton. Bill Haywood was still just a ghost. He had been kicked out of his room, having alienated the most generously decent man he had met in the last five months. And he was (apparently) publicly involved with a beautiful, beautifully sexual woman who made him feel more fully alive than he ever had felt in his life, but who believed in what she believed with an ardor so ardent, it actually frightened him, and who, in any event, by the way, was married.

So perhaps now was the time to ask Ivan if he could come home.

Perched on his bar stool, he took stock of his surroundings. In the mirror, the grime-filmed, nearly opaque windows behind him indicated it was morning. A frame-and-chicken-wire cage behind the bar before him hutched a black-and-white rabbit gnawing a tent peg of raw carrot. The a-kiltered shelves flanking the elaborately carved, once-rich dark wood of the much-nicked and gouged back-bar were canopied by an underlit, badly cocked, sagging lead-glass awning some ten feet across. Rows of bottles and decanters, glass soldiers of all shapes, sizes, colors— "crystal phalli," he thought—every kind of tequila known to man, liqueurs galore, oversized mason jars fruit-rind-filled with aguardiente glozened, scarcely reflecting the whey-weak light from the windows. For an instant, he thought he could see himself—paraprosopia—miraged across their bellies, wombed there aglow and distorted. When he smiled at himself, his many faces frowned back, misshapen to forceps.

Studied the bartender. Uncommonly short, almost dwarfish, thin to asthenia. Uncommonly lacunose. Wassail-bowl head upon which precariously balanced a tarboosh-looking, fezzy thing. Uncommonly young, dark-haired, dark-skinned, swarthy and mestizo-looking, bespectacled google eyes behind thick-lensed horn-rims. He openly was leafing through a one-hand magazine while chomping gape-mouthed on chocolate peanuts, cashews, perhaps. When he read, his browned lips visibly moved. When he walked, he limped. When he breathed, he did so through the sewer of his mouth, his tongue lolling wet-brown with chocolate, fat turd of toad.

Rising unsteadily from his stool, Franklyn shuffled over to a window, swiped a peephole with his shirt cuff. Out in the street, the graying, groaty snow was heaped irregularly high and dirty. Nuggets of coal, kernels of cinder, grains of chunk salt and sand lay grittily strewn up and down the sidewalk. He watched a grizzled, bent-backed young man wearing cloth gloves with cutaway fingertips wheel a barrow of horse manure down the middle of the street, periodically stopping to stoop and retrieve the clumps and cakes that jounced free. A foxfur-hooded old woman scurried down the sidewalk carrying a carton of eggs like a loaf of stale bread—i.e., under her arm.

This, he knew, was Front Street. Running east to west, it was sandwiched between the bottom of the steeply pitched, multitiered hill rising

hard up behind it, and the wide river bulge known as the Portage onto
which it squarely faced. Looking through the window to the opposite
shore, Franklyn could see the buildings of Houghton, the larger and
wealthier of the sister towns. High atop the arched brow of the thickly
wooded upslope behind the bar, hundreds of feet directly overhead, he
knew that the shaft-houses and smokestacks of the Franklin and Quincy
mines thrust skyward like Popocatépetl itself. Symbol of something, or
controlling metaphor, some trope *twee*, *louche*, *infra-dig* at once.

Returning to the bar, he rapped the top with a knuckle, on-waved for
another pour, found his thoughts straying in a certain direction. To do
without her, the honorable thing perhaps—no, not perhaps, the honorable
thing—was impossible. New anatomies, discovering each other's bodies,
secret places, recumbent paths and passageways, every reclining pleasure
still to explore. Mutual spell. Bewitched.

But carry on as ever? Her reputation as an agitator was one thing—
she rather relished it, in fact—but adulteress? In such a place as Red
Jacket? With the likes of him?

He would need remain here until he could reckon the right of it, right
way. Entirely necessary that he stay here until he could fish the solution
from the bottom of this glass, where he was convinced it must lurk, just
beyond reach. Somewhere in the mescal, he knew, bobbed the answer.

Laying his head sidewise, cheek down upon the bar top, he gazed
glazy-eyed into the liquid. "Where are you?" he said aloud. Then, jacking
bolt upright, raised the glass to the reflection in the mirror. "To Mne-
mosyne," he said, "goddess of memory, mother of Muses." Tossed it back,
becoming vaguely aware of his bladder.

"Perhaps I should go outside, pee, migrate down-street to the next
bar," he thought.

Heard the whispers then: *"Dégringolade, dégringolade, dégringolade,"*
spreading up from inside, open-side out to his ears.

A pair of freshly unshaven, rough-looking customers entered laughing loudly, jostling rough-and-tumble through the front door, roughhous-
ing. One of them, he noticed—how not?—had but a single arm.

Franklyn called the mestizo over. The man's face was a felony, one
committed against the idea of a face. Severally cratered, pitted as a pin
cushion, fretted with seams like shoemaker stitches, its darker blotches
alternated irregularly with its ragged, more reddened ones, lending him

the aspect of a half-breed whose warpaint has been applied bereft of look-ing glass or right sobriety. "Whatever they're having," he said, pawing a twenty-five-cent piece onto the bar top as he nodded at the two who had taken up their place at the far end of the bar. "On me." Then, sliding down from his stool, and taking his freshly replenished glass with him, he walked outside.

The fresh air assailed him—swack of two-by-four. "Whoa!" he mut-tered, tearing up. Took a nip; fume burn. Backpedaling off the sidewalk, he stepped into the street, arched his back, craned his neck, wiped his eyes, permitting their scrutiny to climb the talused hillside rung by ladderback rung. Against the sky, its white-and-blue field, he could just delineate the burnt, baked-redbrick chimney-top of one of the great smokestacks, its caldera belching smoke dark as dung.

Apparently he had remained outside longer than he had presumed, long enough that when he reentered the saloon, it appeared to him, his incliningly queered vision, to be littered with patrons, as that the light at the windows had gone from milk-glass white to soot gray. A piano was playing somewhere, or perhaps it was a nickel-slot pianola: "Stamboul Nights":

> *Rose of Stamboul O coral Queen—*
> *teased remnants of the skeletons of cities—*

> . . . .
> *ATLANTIS ROSE drums wreathe the rose,*
> *the star floats burning in a gulf of tears*

He scrounged around, rummaged up a back room with tables, sank heavily into a chair, lit a cigarette. He noticed an old woman playing domi-noes at the next table—the woman of the fox-fur hood and eggs?—save that now she was wearing a black faux-cashmere rebozo and drinking tequila, Añejo, he noticed. So bought her a round, wondering as he did so whether the twenty-eight black-and-white game pieces belonged to her or to the bar. Her fishhook-handled shepherd's-crook cane hung at risk from the table edge, swaying some each time she moved a piece. Reminded him of a scavenger eel, *Electrophorus electricus.*

Began to sense that he was losing touch with himself, his situation, track of his bearings, while at the same time remaining altogether clear about his doing just that; moment of porphyria. He suspected he was or was becoming not only stuporously drunk, but squiffed, as is said, quite stiff. Always dearly loved his arrival at this pass. Suspected it was late in the day, yet knew it still was early morning. "Oh well," he thought, "no day decently begins 'til the moon comes up anyway." Began experiencing difficulty recalling his name, would remember, forget, get it wrong. Difficult to focus on such trifles. Labored to riddle his reality, boustrophedonic.

What kind of heartbreak was he causing? Knew he was, must be, but to whom? His brain resisted arriving there, kicked against being dragged plumb with its own thought. It was back there someplace, left behind—with her, probably. Worked to lug it forward; sooner lift himself wrongside up by his own ankles. Stubbed out his cigarette in a beanbag ashtray, fumbled for another, when it suddenly occurred to him that what he needed more than anything else in the unquenchable world was another drink. Figuratively kicked himself for not thinking of it sooner.

Using the table lip to push up from his chair, he bowed deeply at the waist to the old woman before steadying his way toward the now deserted bar. The mestizo, seeing him coming, had his pour waiting in advance. Winking his thanks, Franklyn retrieved the glass and ambled over to the window. Across the waters, Houghton appeared to glitter like a gathering of lanterns, the surface of the Portage flaring yellowly, lacy with reflection. Reminded him of urine stains.

"Ann," he thought he thought, reboantly, "why aren't you here with me now?"

He wanted her, to take her in his arms, each one, feel the fit of her flesh to his own, smell her through every high light in his head, tell her . . . what? What did he wish to tell her? Something important, eventful, momentous, something essential and abiding and irrevocable and—he couldn't re . . .

. . . The floor of the bar was inlaid with red flagstone the color of wine gravy. Ichor. Why hadn't he noticed it before? And the way it rolled, bucked, pitched, heaved like the foredeck of a ship sailing high seas. Or kayak white-watering. Other images. He could walk on water when he had to, waltz on very air; sequoia on an island of bonsai. Having arrived at that moment of Celtic clairvoyance, the sort you drank to stave off, quell down, beat back, he was, he romanticized, become Rilke's panther *un*caged, at last.

He hadn't touched a bite all day, suddenly had an overpowering, un-appeasable taste for jackrabbit. The way they leaped, joint of hip and hind part. Turning, he eyed the cage behind the bar.

What was this hunger, his thirst, but lust? What else could it be? And what was lust? Could one name it? Define? Must it matter itself down to crux of mere loin? It was Ann, wasn't it? Sure it was. Its name was calamity, and it had come for him at last, come to consume him before he collapsed. "What have I done? What must I do? What, ask?"

Heard the damn whispers again: *"Calamity, calamity, calamity."*

How live lustily the time of one's life, live it up to the hilt, every moment? Within every word its own anarchy, he thought. Must the body dissolve before the mind can take flight?

And now the lights of Houghton blinked out one by one. He saw them go. So, so long. It was all quite dark now, dark and quite quiet. Hush. The Portage was pitch, and with it his mind. Transparent as tar. His thought was black, stabbingly clear, clear as pain cut unstemmed in its branching. Clean, as char.

At peace with himself and, too, as one. Utterly lucid, lucidity itself, lucid as delirium—or derangement, the distinction being everything. What must mean, he thought, cannot be.

A man must, he thought some more—insofar as he was in the moment capable of it—strive to arrive at the required state of helplessness and equilibrium, the receptivity they afforded, must return as he can to the Garden all misty-wet with recent rain, where, cards properly played, he might be open to inspiration, salvation, sanctuary, some special knowledge, prophecy, say, or obsession, some . . . deliverance. From himself.

He needed to sit again. His breathing, he suddenly realized, was not right; aerophagic. His lungs, he sensed, were working too hard to express themselves, give vent to the self-enunciation—enunciation, or annunciation?—of dyspnea.

"Yes, something decidedly new is in the wind," he thought, "and it blows only ill. Who among us might know what air we breathe?"

Slumping to the flagstone, he splayed upon the floor, sprawled there, watching undismayed as his wits rolled waywardly away toward the bar, marbles emptied each from a pocket. "Come back," he thought. "Come back." Reached to retrieve them as does a baby a rattle, but his arm wouldn't lift, numb at the elbow on down to his wrist, wrist to the tips of his fingers; glove anesthesia. So, "Goodbye and good riddance. Godspeed."

Feet padded past him, stepping around. Heard a dog-whistle whistling, unhappy tune. Burying his head in his hands, useless hands, he noticed that they had developed minds of their own, each two.

When he looked up again, his surroundings had begun slowly to dis-
integrate, disagglutinate, dissolving in their disaggregation down around
his ears until they had painted him into their last intact corner. Backboned
to the wall, he prepared to defend it with his life against . . . some modal-
ity of the visible, perhaps.

"Not without a fight," he muttered.

Everything now sfumato. His thought—"Am I a good person?"—
gone to the melt in the milt. "But I am not nice, no. I drink too much, lie
not enough, save to myself. So wear your soul on your sleeve as you will,
you scortatory weasel, your sleeve is soiled and beshat. Every profound
spirit needs a mask, and everything we have words for is dead and dead
and dead on arrival. Dead as the hole in your heart."

Ann would rescue him. She must. Willed himself hang on, hold on,
hold out, conjure her face, right here.

Love finds you only to find you out, unmasks. Love never is blind but
sees straight on, around, on through. And should you flee from the sight
of yourself, the one you see mirrored in her eyes? Sooner outrun your own
shadow.

Where was she now, and why wasn't she here?

What did he know of love? Fucking algebra. Never any good at his
ciphers.

Making love. Now there, that was another matter. Then he could
make his half feel wholed, couple with his own most compatible complement, contemptible twin, all the ways a man wishes to penetrate a woman,
yet without rupturing the soul, the spirit throughout the living bread of
her body, devoured as if unto one's own.

Yeah? So?

So perhaps they could live out their days in full sun, he thought, at
home. Come home each to the other. Perhaps that was possible. A new
place to repose.

Tough one, love. Knew nothing about it, save that when you flee from
it, you set something else free, and whatever else it may be, that which is
freed, is foul. Condemn yourself and, too, the other. Mortify thou, yes, and
thee.

She wasn't coming to his rescue after all, was she? All that was a lie, wasn't it? She wasn't Petrushka's valentine pivoting unpained on its pin. She wasnt even the Marines. She was where she was, back there. And he was here, left to make it out of here on his own—or not at all.

"You self-preening sciolist!" he thought. "Every vapor you breathe is dead upon its draught, as vile and unsound as its breather!"

Could he will his hand function long enough to fetch up a cigarette, much less light it? Wedgwood-blue packaging outspread with tobacco-brown wings. But before he tried, he needed another drink.

Contemplated this, challenge. It would mean getting to his feet. Or hands and knees. Contemplated this as well. It would mean somehow getting up on all fours. Or, he could just banana himself seal-like along on his belly, or flop forward, flipper himself like a beached fish, wriggle his way along like an inchworm, sidewind like a snake or an eel, barrel roll as if snowballing a snowball downhill. The possibilities seemed suddenly endless—and each more impossible than the next.

Someone was going through his pockets. No, two, there were two of them, one to each side. On his left, he recognized the old domino woman in the rebozo. To his right, the dwarf mestizo. Vermin. Spiders. The pair were in it together, of that he was certain, the way they worked in synchronized tandem, seasoned ensemble. When he tried to stop their damn arachnid pawing, the old woman whapped him a swift one in the face with the blunt crook of her cane. Gutta-percha, or possibly Zermatt alpenstock. Through the bonfire of blood he saw stars, yet, mercifully, felt remarkably little.

"Now hold on," he rasped, tasting what he suspected was blood as they continued roughly rifling his clothing, "this is preposterous. I'm the press. Check my wallet, it—"

"Shut!" said the mestizo. "Shut yer fuckin' *boca* or . . ."

He watched as the dwarf waddled quickly over to the bar, snatched the rabbit from the cage by its scruff, gimped back, dangled it before his face, and, brownly grinning, snapped its neck clean as a wishbone before stuffing it tail first, still warm, into his gaping mouth.

Had to hand it to him, did make an effective gag.

And then, at last, he was being carcass-dragged outside, feet first—they had, he noticed, removed his boots—his jackrabbit-stuffed head bouncing off a doorstep, scraping across the sidewalk, banging off a curb—

his teeth involuntarily bit down, *goosh* of innard—suffering yet another blow to the head, and another, another still; dwarf kicks. Left to freeze to death, choking on buttocks of bunny, sack of limp laundry in the midmost of the street.

Through blurred vision he caught sight of a horse tethered cater-corner beneath a streetlight perhaps half a block away. Ann-sent, he was certain. "Pegasus," he thought. "She couldn't come herself, so she sent me," he could scarce believe it, "Pegasus."

He couldn't hear his own groans as he staggered to his stocking feet—too much blood-slosh in his ears—lurched slanting toward the beast. The cold had begun to spur and rowel-dig. Falling and side-wheeling, falling and swaying, falling and lunging, pratfalling and on-pitching, he somehow made it across the street, somehow fumbled the reins free of the lamp-post, somehow hoisted himself aboard crosswise like a corpse, one hand clutched to horn, the other clenching cantle. On for dear life.

The horse just stood there.

"Go, horse," he wanted to say, but was unable to manage it around the rabbit. "Oh yeah," he thought. Unhorned his right hand, yanked the rabbit from his mouth by its head as if his mouth were a hat, and let it flop-per, stuffed toy, to the ground. Spat fur. At which the horse immediately turned of its own accord and, slow saunter, clopped away. Just where, he did not know, nor did he care. Away. Away was good enough.

Not far, quarter mile, half, enough to jounce his stomach into an on-going state of propulsion, catapult, somerset, yaw, his jack-in-the-box head to emulsion and gelatin, he serial-vomited intermittently en route before the horse drew up in front of a three-story, brick-and-clapboard building. The sign over the entryway, the one finning slowly into focus through swollen, fast-closing eyes, read HOTEL SCOTT. Noticed the street sign, corner of Reservation and Quincy. This could be only Hollywood good fortune. The Scott, he knew, was where the National billeted its organizers until such time as it could find for them more permanent digs.

"Good a place as any," he thought, releasing his twin handholds before flumping limply to the ground where he lay haphazardly crumpled among pastern, fetlock, cannon, and hoof. "Damn, I'm thirsty." And passed out.

Someone briefly considered throwing a dead dog down after him, but, noting the erratic fluctuation of the hour, with no little politic effort, if more panache, refrained.

SORE-EYED SIGHT

The Stetson-clad figure standing in the threshold of the doorway filled it. Largely.

"I'll say this for you, Tribune, you got yourself one rock-hard head there. Lucky thing, too. Just hope you thrashed back good as you got thrashed."

Franklyn was on his back, pillow-propped in bed, just swum awake, and speaking of his head, it hurt. *Fucking* hurt.

"What the hell, Bill. What happened?" Hurt more to talk.

"What happened, kid," said Bill Haywood, entering the hotel room and pulling up a chair, "is you got the living shit kicked out of you. Clocked cleaned. Ashes hauled. Real beauts. Haven't seen a pair of shiners like that since Colorado. Gives a whole new meaning to the expression 'beat to a bloody pulp.'" He paused. "Know who?"

Franklyn worked to recall. Wasn't much. "Farolito."

"Yeah. No-account bar down the way. So?"

Right away something was eating at him like a panic. "How long have I been out?"

"Can't say. Only pulled in this morning. One of the boys says they found you out in the street. Thought you was dead as daisies. One of 'em recognized you. The vest. Hauled your sorry ass in here."

He suddenly remembered. "What day is it?" Lifted his head from the pillow. Christ, it *did* hurt. Everything from his neck up, catastrophe. Afraid to touch his face. Something felt broken, or nearly. "Did I miss Christmas Eve? It's not Christmas Eve yet, is it?"

"Christmas Eve?" Haywood laughed. "Why, you expecting something special under the tree? Nah, you didn't miss Christmas Eve. Day after tomorrow."

Franklyn lowered his head gingerly to the pillow, mumbled, "Thank God."

"So," said Haywood, "the Farolito. Bar fight? Somebody objected to something you wrote? Thought your weskit too fancy? What?"

Decided not to shake his head, massaging his temples instead. "No. I dunno. I was in there. Must've got drunk. Mescal. Rolled, I think. Least two. More maybe."

"Yeah, well, that'll happen with the mesc*aline*. Oughtta know. Happened to me often enough. Then you learn."

"What?"

"Stick with what's softer—which is everything else. So"—he leaned closer, forearm on thigh, lightly slapped Franklyn's own—"good to see, Tribune. Long time. How's the world been treating you? I mean"—flipped a hand—"aside from all this." Quickly added, "By the way, scrounged around, got you a spare pair of boots." Tilted his head toward the closet. "Seems somebody took off with your'n."

The best he could muster was "Thanks." No recall of having lost them. "The world's shit, Bill, you know that. You do your best to duck through without having to eat too much of it, that's all. I'm all right. Yourself?"

Shrugged. "They've got me up here for the strike. One fucked-up mess, so I'm told. But you know as much about that as I do, probably more. What's your take on it?" He paused. "By the way, read most of your stuff. Typical Shivs."

"Meaning?"

"You walk the line, son, you walk that line. Always have. One thing I picked up on from the start—heart's in one place, head another. What saves you, barely, is your knowing it. Must make for an interesting life."

Franklyn tried smiling. "Sometimes. Other times it just makes for—"

"Doubt?"

"And confusion," he said. "Or regret. Man's gotta fish or cut bait, right? Crap or get off the crapper. Do this or do that. Easy as—"

"Lighting a furze."

Franklyn stared hard at him. "Sure. Easy as that. What's the plan?"

"No plan. Up to Red Jacket tomorrow. Meet with the men."

"MacNaughton?"

The way he snickered, snuffling, Franklyn wished there had been a spittoon handy. "Scots son of a bitch. I've cracked harder than him. Will, too, before I leave here. That skull's for the dogs."

"Dogs, Bill? Or worms."

"His choice. Either'll do. Been dealing with the like all my life. Only thing the MacNaughtons understand: force. Seen it over and over again. They'll never understand the men, don't care to, 'cause to them the men aren't men. They're part-men, half-men. They may be men, but not men like themselves. They're less. Beneath 'em."

"Don't disagree. Seen it myself."

"So that's the seed of it then, poison seed. And everything after poisoned, too. Starts there. The MacNaughtons aren't afraid of the union. They don't *like* it. Costs them. Profits. What they're really afraid of is the men believing they're as good as themselves, good as they are. Not just saying it—speechifying, rallying, marching, picketing it, all that—but *believing*. That they're equals. Makes 'em froth. Makes 'em wanna beat down the spirit of it. It's the spirit spooks 'em, 'cause in the spirit's the power."

"No use for MacNaughton myself, Bill. Just wish I could sit down across from the man. Ask him some questions. Measure his mind. I can't help thinking, must be something to it. More."

"Why? What for?"

"C'mon, Bill. No one's the devil." Tried to smile. "Well, hardly anyone. What can it hurt to know your enemy, keep 'em close?"

"Know all I need to know," said Haywood. "Know enough. Know the tough guys like him need to stomp the weak to make theirselves feel strong. Know the powerful like him are the ones do the least while making others do more, then pocket the credit to themselves."

"So why not know more? About MacNaughton. I mean, if there *is* more."

"See? Now right there, that's just you all over. People call me reckless, but the way you run around trying to understand every damn last reason behind every last damn thing." Shook his head. "Ask me, you're the one's foolhardy.

"You want more? Fine. Go get it. Get more. Happy hunting. Your job, not mine. Other fish to fry."

"Or fritter."

He laughed. "'Fraid that's your department there, Tribune." Got to his feet. "Listen, I'm the early train tomorrow. You're feeling up to it, I could use the company. You may look like hell, but your mind's working okay, tongue better. Besides, I reckon you could use the ex-clu-*sive*."

Franklyn chuckled. His head was a clock tower; it gonged. "That'd be my privilege. Wow. Big Bill Haywood himself."

Haywood horselaughed, spanked his thigh. "Some night though, wasn't it?"

At first, Franklyn fumbled the reference, then, "Oh. Yeah. It was. Saved my life."

He was at the door. "Saved your *foot*, is all." Wistful. "Only wish we could have saved the Club. Fucking best in all the old U.S. of A. Hands down. I miss it." Paused, good eye measuring before alighting upon a middle distance, reposing there some. "You gotta wonder sometimes."

When he failed to continue, Franklyn interjected, "Yep. Sure do. 'Bout what?"

"Country. Way it's going. Where it's headed. Seems like sometimes . . ." Trailed off. "Ach," brightening, "you just rest up, Tribune. Sleep it off. Morning comes early these days."

"Good to see you, Bill. I mean it."

And he then was out the door, closing it behind him, and Franklyn was left alone to contemplate what he was going to say to Ann when next he saw her. Because as he closed his eyes, praying the right words might materialize across the backs of his lids like aerograms their sky, he still hadn't the crust of a clue.

James MacNaughton wrote to Governor Ferris: "Insofar as is it in my power to prevent it, no wife, no child, no family shall want either for clothing, food, fuel, or a good Christmas dinner this holiday season. Calumet and Hecla, through both the Salvation Army and Associated Charities, shall provide the money to guarantee that there shall be no cheerless firesides. What is more, it now is the official policy of this company to be lenient and forgiving in getting its men back to work. It is difficult, I don't hesitate to say, to keep from becoming terribly blue at moments such as these, and as time progresses, one finds that more frequent and longer vacations are required to keep one's soul pulled together. It has been by my calculation some five months now since I have seen my own family intact and settled at home."

He then wrote a pair of five-hundred-dollar checks to the two charities on his personal account, instructing that they be used to "insure that every striker's child has a Christmas remembrance, and that the identity of its source remain undisclosed, concealed, and strictly anonymous." This, at a time, as everyone knew, when his own family—his wife of twenty-one years, Mary, and their two daughters, nine-year-old Mary and twenty-year-old Martha Lois, just then pregnant with his first grandchild—was far and farther away, having been escorted from the U.P. under armed guard at the outset of the strike, and his home under close and constant watch by his staff of personal bodyguards.

The half hour—twenty-two minutes, actually—he had Bill to himself on the train up from Hancock, would, felt Franklyn, score a nice coup for the paper. Characterizing himself as "the mine owners' self-fulfilled prophecy come at last to pass, their worst fear arrived fully in the flesh," Haywood scarce had been retiring about castigating his own union for having been "too soft and too timid, too tame for too long," vowing that "from here on, the fighting shall be done on our terms, not theirs, and it will be done with all gloves off." Asked to explain what "all gloves off" meant, he had replied—Franklyn, of course, had done him the favor of cleaning up his grammar and syntax—"The task before us is to do a lot with a little, do it selectively and to maximum effect and in a way that makes the cost the bosses must pay too expensive for them to continue to behave as they have in the past. The time for more words is over. No more speeches, no more parades, no more pointless chasing after our own tails in the streets. The time is now to reopen the ball. They will recognize this union, or they will pay a price they are not prepared to pay."

Franklyn debarked the train with the headline already Linotyping itself in his head:

WILLIAM F. HAYWOOD ARRIVES IN COPPER COUNTRY APPEARANCE MARKS SHIFT IN STRIKE STRATEGY VOWS REDOUBLING OF PUSH FOR UNION RECOGNITION

In fact, so preoccupied was he with its mental composition, Franklyn scarcely noticed the cloud of smoke inside which huddled the clutch of men—black slouch hats brims tugged low, three-quarter-length buttoned-down cloth coats, collars turned up ear high—down the platform at its far end, smoking cigars, cigarillos, cheroots, cigarettes, consulting one another, curmurring, so conspicuous in their collective effort to appear inconspicuous. But he did notice. As he noticed, too, that Bill Hayward noticed, before him.

When Haywood noticed Franklyn noticing him noticing, he smiled. Knowingly. And winked.

ITALIAN HALL

For the past week, Ann, who had been entrusted with a union-disbursed budget of some three hundred dollars, had spent most of her time prepping the Italian Hall for the early-afternoon and evening children's parties expected to draw at least 1,500 kids and their parents. Admission, restricted to union-member families and their friends, was to be scrupulously monitored by hawkeyed bouncers and doorkeeps. And it was there that Franklyn found her on Christmas Eve morning, shortly after his arrival back in Red Jacket.

The Italian Hall occupied the northeast corner of Seventh and Elm, a block down from the Red Jacket town hall and fire station on the same side of the street. The Opera House was on the side opposite. Dunn's was a block over.

Built on the same site to replace and upgrade the wooden, ship-lap-sided structure that five years earlier had burned to the ground on New Year's Eve only minutes behind the departure of a thousand partygoers, it was a formidably imposing, broad-shouldered, two-story building of clean brown brick, more tan and sand than sienna and sere, crowned by a roof-embedded flagstaff thrusting fifty feet skyward from which flew the Italian colors.

Owned by the Società Mutua Beneficenza Italiana, the local Italian mutual-benefit society, which leased the subdivided street-level space to Dominick Vairo for his saloon and to the Great Atlantic and Pacific Tea Company, managed by Charlie Meyers, for its dry-goods store, the organization routinely rented the cavernous (3,200-square-foot), high-ceilinged (eighteen-linear-foot), multiwindowed (seven side-by-side arching double-sashed panes, fifteen feet high) second story with its elevated stage (five vertical feet) for dances, meetings, wedding receptions, ice-cream socials, parties.

Entering the hall, Franklyn immediately noticed Ann—her back was to him—supervising the decoration of the triumvirate of white-flocked, silver-tinseled Christmas trees—indigenous red pines festooned with pink-and-blue crepe-paper streamers, tricolored garlands, popcorn strings, candy canes—positioned strategically about the stage. He likewise noted the large cardboard boxes and flammable wooden crates and barrels stacked and aligned near its rear, brimful with stuffed stockings, mittens, and scarves, heaped high with what appeared to be penny candies and confitures.

The main floor had been arrayed with hundreds of spindle-backed wooden folding chairs arranged in plumb rows, and by the time he had navigated the narrow center aisle and approached the front, she just was placing, sans benefit of ladder, a star—or no, as he moved closer he could see it was an angel—or no, not at all, but a golden, spread-winged Pegasus, crowning glory atop one of them.

Should he say something or wait until she turned round? Too late. She saw him before he could utter a sound. The expression "their eyes met" was perfectly inadequate to describe what their eyes did then, sharing the momentary frisson of recognition, its fullness, the soaring shiver of joy, the several lifetimes of call-and-response searching, before falling each down the wells of the other, there to drink deeply of . . . et cetera.

Charging across the stage, she descended the stair to one wing and, hems hiked, raced to him—he noticed that everyone, the black-clad Ella Bloor included ("Ella Bloor?" he thought. "What the hell?!")—had ceased what they were doing in midgesture to quite openly stare—tenderly bracketed his battered face with her hands, kissed him flush upon his split and puffy lips.

"Frank." She was breathless, which is to say, breathing hard, labored *putt-putt* gasps. "My god! What *h-happened*?"

"Looks worse than it feels," he said, which was not altogether untrue; fast healer. "I'm fine." He permitted her to caress his face. "Little dustup down to Hancock is all. You should see the other guy." Paused, glanced about. "Quite the bash. I'm impressed." Drew her a ways down the aisle. "So when did Miss Bloor pull into town?"

"Same day you left. She has been a godsend, Frank."

He let it pass. "Haywood's here. Rode up with him on the train."

She arched a brow. "What? Already? We heard he was on his way, *after* the holidays."

"That's Bill. Everything sub rosa. Anyway, *some*body knew. Watchers all over him at the station. Means business, though. From here on it's everything for keeps. If I know Bill, and I do, gonna get real nasty, real fast."

"I will need to speak with him."

"Of course, and you will, later. Right now, got the kids counting on you. Can't disappoint the charges."

He failed to mention the exchange he and Haywood had had on the train.

"This Clemenc woman," Haywood had said, "the one they call Big Annie, Fighting Annie, they tell me she's the authentic article. Nothing stops her. Willing to walk through fire barefoot. You've had"—he trawled for the right word—"doings."

Franklyn was only half surprised. "That's my fault," he had begun, "I . . ."

Haywood had raised his hand in the universal stop-right-there gesture. "Don't care about fault. Only care about whether what they say is true. Is it?"

"It is. Yes."

"And the boys, they like her? Admire? Respect? What? I got my sources, but in *your* opinion. It's important, Frank, that I know what *you* think."

Yes, apparently it was, important enough for Bill Haywood to have called him by his given name for the first time.

"She gives them hope, Bill, the ones still out. Simple as that. It is not enough, of course, but it is something, all they have. Because she will not quit. Because she believes. Because she is not afraid to say anything, and do anything, the world's dirty work." He had pondered whether to say what he had said next. "A lot like you."

"And the others?"

"They hate her. She shames them, reminds them, all they could be, should be, aren't. Her mere presence is a reproach. She's been spat on, shat on, called names, threatened, humiliated, lost friends." Paused. "And a husband."

"Sounds a serious woman, dangerous even."

"Serious? Oh, yes. Dangerous? Maybe. Less so now than before. The numbers aren't there, Bill, not anymore, you know that. Now she is more a danger to herself than anyone else. She is not stupid; she is losing and she knows it. Human nature. The more desperate, the more rash, dangerous. Temerarious, the very word. Hides it, hides it like a pro, but I see it, have seen it. Part of our doings, as you put it. I won't have her hurt, and I won't let her hurt herself. There's enough hurt to go around without Ann having to eat more of it. At least, alone."

"You're hitched up, then? I mean, you're playing her hand along with her?"

"C'mon, Bill, I'm a reporter, not a player. I write about this stuff, that's all, and I do my best to do my best while I'm doing it, even when my best is for shit. Any more than that"—he had shrugged—"I figure that's everyone else's problem. Except Ann, Ann's mine, so I'll take on what comes with her."

Franklyn had paused then, gazed out the train window, seeing nothing as everything passed by. "No, I'm not playing her hand along with her. She's perfectly capable of playing it for herself any way she sees fit. But if you want to know whether I'm sitting alongside her at the same table, watching her cards, counting her chips, looking out so she's not cheated or four-flushed, then, yes, I am."

"You'll forgive me, Tribune, but sounds an awful lot like love to me. Sounds like something, anyway."

"Does it?" He had turned away from the window then, laughing. "Cupid's arrow?"

"More like a gunshot."

"Ha! Well, you could be right. *Her* bullet, smack between *my* eyes."

Leaving Ann and Ella Bloor—back in town, according to Ann, from Schenectady, New York, fresh off covering a winning strike against the General Electric Company there—at the Italian Hall, Franklyn headed for the Arlington. Needed to clean up, slip into fresh duds, grab a bite. Flanging the collar of his coat up around his ears, he drew up in midstride, fished out his pack, salt-shook free a fag, lit up, inhaled. Pewtered day. Seriously stratus. Wide-wale corduroy clouds. Burr-cold.

He was about to enter the hotel when he heard his name being hallooed from across and down the street. Turned to see the Kid and his dog racing over, skidding to a stop across the thin skin of snow-ice.

"Hey, CK. Hi, Pal. Merry Christmas."

The Kid looked at him wonderingly. "What happened to your face, Frank? Looks like somebody beat you up. Bad."

"What, you don't think it's an improvement? It was nuthin'. My fault. Hey, going to the Christmas party?"

"Where? Over the Italian Hall? Might. Dunno. They take dogs?"

"Good question. They should. Tell you what, hide him under your coat, keep him quiet, muzzled down, no one'll notice."

"You goin'?"

"Yep. Soon as I get cleaned up." Nodded toward the hotel. "You should go. Why not? Presents. Santa Claus."

"Santa Claus!! That's for babies."

"What? You don't believe in Santa? C'mon, CK! You gotta believe in Santa."

"No, I don't. Don't believe in the Easter Bunny neither. Or the Tooth Fairy. None of that stuff."

"Free food, too. I know you believe in free food."

Smiled.

"Like what?"

"Cookies, peppermints, gumdrops, licorice, salt-water taffy, popcorn, punch, apples and oranges, sugarplums, figgy pudding. Hot cocoa and chocolates. Jujubes, CK. Think I saw Jujubes. And fruitcake, your favorite. So what? It's all free."

"Pasty?"

"Uh, no. Not that I saw."

"'Cuz Pal likes pasty."

"I know."

"Likes cookies, too, though. They got gingersnaps? He likes ginger-snaps."

"Gingersnaps? Sure. Think I saw some gingersnaps. And saffron cake and seedy buns, currant cookies, cardamom drops, rhubarb pie, muggety hog's pudding, star-gazy, figgies, fairings."

The Kid thought about this, mulled. "Okay, maybe I'll go. You going?"

"Right over, after I change."

"Promise?"

Raised his hand like a pledge. "Scout's honor."

"Okay. See you over."

And they were off, down the street, though not before the Kid turned around and, on the backpedal, yelled, "Hey, Frank!"

"What?" he shouted.

"Your face."

"What?"

"It's really ugly." And, laughing, disappeared down some side alley.

———

As Franklyn Shivs, late as usual, approached the Italian Hall walking north up Seventh Street, he experienced no premonitory sense of déjà vu. Noticed some generic commotion at the entrance was all, which he took for some generic commotion at the entrance. But when, as he drew closer, the commotion began incliningly to resemble an actual ruckus, something deep buried in his brain, limbic region, tripped and triggered in tandem: alarum.

He smelled nothing, eyed the sky for smoke; nope.

Reporter's sixth sense, call it that. Something right here right now was decidedly *off*, which, in *his* world, meant that here, quite possibly, was a story.

Later, he was to recall that part of what tipped him off was the way the increasingly vocal hysteria of the wide-eyed civilians purposefully milling about outside the double doors, so nakedly jarred with the utter nonchalance, even cavalier indifference of the several blue-suited deputies and khaki-uniformed Guardsmen huddled some ways off down the sidewalk, softly laughing behind the hand. The way that disparity lifted into high relief the contrasting behaviors, each of the other. Couldn't reconcile them. Incongruity. One definition of news.

People, men, were struggling mightily with the doors. Had the outer pair thrown open, but couldn't shoulder the inner pair inward. Something was on the other side, inside, barring them. Couldn't batter-ram them to give so much as an inch—jammed, shut fast. He heard what sounded like the word "watra" exchanged repeatedly among them.

Glancing at the deputies and soldiers, who continued to betray no emotion save a half-furtive amusement, he backed into the street, scanned each of the seven windows overhead for some sign. Nothing, neither face nor fist. The lights were on, he noticed, but the panes of tall glass blinked back at him empty as altars.

The fire escape around back! Trotted down the side alley of the building, then around to its rear. Bottom rung, just there, leaped, grabbed hold, hoisted himself up before torquing his body at the waist, skating his butt onto the metal-grid landing. Fetching to his feet, he took the steps up to the back door two at a time, only to find it locked from inside. Shouted, pounded, kicked, pile-drove a shoulder cuff. Nothing. Heard what sounded like a stampede of roller skaters through the door.

Hastily unlacing and removing a boot, he heaved it heel first against the transom's glass. The boot disappeared through the shatter as the oblong pane exploded in a spray of splinter and shard and he felt the fallen weight of glass, its thorns crowning his hat brim, then the trickling descent of some warmth down his forehead, followed by its wetness at an eye.

"Shit!" he barked aloud, tugging off his gloves before brushing the blood away with his left hand as he rubbed at his forehead with the heel of his right. Held it out before him, its red palm hemachrome-bright. He dreaded the sight of his own blood almost as much as he resented it, and for a moment he felt lightheaded. Clutching at the railing, he leaned his weight into and against it at the hip before righting himself enough to flick yet more blood away before slipping back into his gloves. Then, scouting a relatively glass-free handhold spot on the transom frame, he removed his other boot, clenching it with his teeth by its tongue before springing for the spot with both hands.

Free-hanging from the frame by his stronger right, he removed the boot from his bite with his left, using its heel to knock free the remaining jagged pieces still icicled and iceberged along its border, tossed the boot inside before pulling himself up and over, through and on in, dropping stocking-footed to the floor, where he landed amid a garden of glass. Slivers shived through sock.

Tightroping gingerly on his heels, he gathered up his boots, navigated his way clear of the razor field and, after surmising that he was backstage and leaving bloody footprints in his wake, station-crossed his way—hurt like hell—to a short flight of steps leading up to an elevated floor where, he noticed, first, that the curtain had been lowered; and, second, that Ann was rocking silently, slump-shouldered on the floor just behind it, cradling what appeared to be a small child in her lap. Opposite him on the other end of the stage, among the gaily wrapped presents now haphazardly strewn at the base of one of the Christmas trees, was arrayed row after row of—"Neat, tidy, precise," he thought to himself, and then the cliché, "laid out like cordwood"—corpses. Even from where he was standing, he could tell they were young, oddly unmarked.

"Dolls," he thought. Curiously perfect. No blood, not a blot.

And then he was back at the Iroquois, back in hell, outside himself, high above, outlander still. And then from out of nowhere, a dog, small dog, terrier, ratter breed, came scampering over, rose up on its hind legs, and pawed whimpering at his pants legs before dropping to all fours and licking at his feet.

Without fully apprehending what he was doing, dream, he stooped down and scooped him up, hugging him to his chest, digging his fingers behind an ear as he nuzzled at his neck.

"That's okay, Pal," he whispered absently, as the dog's ears pricked. "You stay with me, okay? Let's go see Annie. Think she may need us."

It was only when the dog licked him, lapping his face, that he tasted his own blood. A moment or two more before he realized, his blood was stained with his tears.

The nationally distributed newsreels recorded by newsreeler Will Peacock for Chicago's Gaumont Picture Company served up the accounts of what rapidly became known as "The Italian Hall Tragedy" in theaters coast-to-coast. Authorities, officials, town fathers, mine owners, survivors, all were interviewed. Ella Reeve Bloor was interviewed. Ana Clemenc was not interviewed because she was not up to being interviewed. She could not talk around the devastation.

The Osceola mine fire of '96 had killed thirty adult workingmen. But this, December 24, 1913, was the worst single day of death in the history of Michigan's Upper Peninsula: sixty children aged two to sixteen, another fifteen adults, eleven of them women, eight of those mothers who died with their children.

Having escorted the wordless Ann to his hotel, each step an agony, in agony himself, he undressed her in silence, put her to bed with Pal, and when the front-desk clerk, Mertz or Murtz, knocked on the door to tell him, "You can't have dogs in here, mister," replied as evenly as he could manage it, "Later. We'll talk about it later." Then handed him a dollar, hush-money.

Washragged his face and feet, applied styptic pencil to his wounds, changed into a fresh pair of socks, stuffed pairs of clean underwear down the bottoms of his boots, laced them double tight and double tied, kissed the semicomatose Ann on the forehead and, instructing Pal to keep vigil, eggshelled his way back to the hall to report the story.

To intuit poetry, terrible poetry, from the roll call of the dead, *"Killed in a jam through a false alarum call of fire by a person or persons unknown."*

Lempi Ala, 12, Herman Ala, 60, Sanna Aaltonen, 39, Sylvia Aaltonen, 3, Wilama Aaltonen, 9, Will Biri, 7, Ivana Bolf, 9, Katarine Bronzo, 21,

Victoria Burcar, 9, Joseph Butala, 7, Nick Cvetkovich, 33, Jenny Giacoletto, 9, Katarina Gregorich, 10, Edwin Heikkinen, 7, Eino Felpus O. Heikkinen, 10, Eli Issac Heikkinen, 9, Ina Isola, 33, Tilma Isola, 5, Barbra Jesic, 25, Rosie Jesic, 5, Uno Jokepil, 13, Anna Kalunki, 9, Brida Kalunki, 42, Efia Kalunki, 8, Johan Kiemaki, 7, Katarina Klarich, 7, Kristina Klarich, 11, Mary Klarich, 9, John Koskela, 10, Anna Kotajarvi, 4, Anna Kotajarvi, 39, Mary Krainatz, 11, Hilja Lanto, 5, Maria Lanto, 40, Sulo Rubet Lauri, 8, Mary Lesar, 13, Rafael Lesar, 2, Arthur Lindstrom, 12, Lydia Luoma, 10, Alfred Lustic, 7, Elina Manley, 26, Wesley Manely, 4, Ella Mantanen, 8, Mathias Mantanen, 10, Y. H. Mantanen, 13, Agnes Mihelchich, 7, Elizabeth Mihelchich, 5, Paul Mihelchich, 9, Walter Murto, 9, Edward Emil Myllykangas, 7, Johan Myllykangas, 10, Abram Niemala, 24, Maria Niemala, 22, Annie Papesh, 6, Mary Papesh, 14, Kate Petteri, 66, Saida Raja, 10, Terresa Renaldi, 12, Elma Ristel, 6, Emilia Rydilahti, 16, Heli Rydilahti, 13, John Saari, 5, Elida Saatio, 11, Mary Smuk, 5, Antonia Staudohar, 7, Elisina Taipalus, 4, Edward Takola, 9, Lydia Talpaka, 10, Kaisa Tuippo, 45, Mamie Tuippo, 10, Johan Westola, 48, Hilja Wualukka, 8.

READ ALL ABOUT IT

Franklyn's story ran this way:

74 DIE IN COPPER COUNTRY CHRISTMAS PANIC

FALSE FIRE ALARM TRIGGERS MASS CALAMITY

Holiday Party Ends in Gruesome Tragedy

FIVE DOZEN CHILDREN AMONG THE DEAD

CALUMET—Seventy-four people, 60 of them children aged 2 to 16, died here during a Christmas Eve party thrown for the families of striking copper miners when a cry of "Fire!" by a person or persons unknown sparked a headlong rush toward the exit of the hall where the celebration was being held. Wednesday's tragedy was the single most lethal event in the history of Michigan's Upper Peninsula, eclipsing by more than half the death toll recorded as a result of a fatal mine fire near here 17 years earlier.

Preliminary investigations by fire officials indicate no evidence of a blaze, leading to widespread speculation among survivors that the motivation behind the bogus warning may have been to cause the very panic that in fact ensued.

According to Houghton County Sheriff James Cruse, whose office is heading the investigation into the tragedy, "It is impossible to pinpoint at this stage the source of the alarm or why it occurred. It may have been an honest mistake or simple misunderstanding. It may have been a deliberate prank or practical joke. It may have been something of a more serious nature. It is quite possible that we may never know."

Spokesmen for the copper miners' union, the Western Federation of Miners (WFM), were quick to call for both state and federal investigations into the tragedy. "We have it from numerous reliable eyewitnesses," said secretary of Calumet WFM Local 203, John Antilla, "that a man wearing a Citizens' Alliance badge is responsible for the false alarm. What we know for a fact is that no striker, or anyone in sympathy with the strike, caused this catastrophe."

Informed of the incident, James MacNaughton, General Manager of Calumet & Hecla, the state's largest copper-mine concern, immediately made available the services of the company hospital, its doctors, ambulances, and company automobiles. "This is a horror," declared MacNaughton, "the worst disaster ever to befall this community. I personally extend the sympathy of our company and, on behalf of all the mine owners of the Upper Peninsula, say to the members of the bereaved families, you are in our prayers."

According to party organizer Ella Reeve Bloor of the WFM Women's Auxiliary, some 500 children and their parents, perhaps 700 people total, were gathered in Red Jacket's Italian Hall where they sang carols, recited poems, and were awaiting the late-afternoon distribution of holiday presents by Santa Claus, when the cry of "Fire!" was heard at the back of the second-story hall, initiating the stampede down a staircase to the hall's front door where a bottleneck soon formed that resulted in a mounting logjam of bodies so entangled it took rescuers over an hour to clear it. Doctors at the scene attributed all of the deaths to either suffocation or internal injury due to "rupture and crushing."

Fund-raising efforts on the heels of the tragedy have been immediate, ongoing, and widespread. Contributions to a Houghton County victim's-aid relief fund presently stand at more than $25,000, according to fund organizers, $5,000 of it from the Boston owners of Calumet & Hecla, Quincy Shaw and Rodolphe Agassiz, who in their public statement of sympathy declared, "In the face of this unbelievable catastrophe, all bitterness and ill-feeling that has existed in your community during the past months must be wiped away that the healing might begin. This tragedy is an affliction that is common to all. Now is the time for the alleviation of suffering, not for idle speculation upon the casting of blame."

Distribution efforts, however, have so far met with both stiff and uniform resistance. The prevailing sentiment among those most affected by the tragedy was perhaps best summed up by union organizer William F. Haywood, who declared, "The Western Federation of Miners will bury its own dead. These are our people, and it is our sacred privilege to do so. No aid will be accepted from those who only yesterday were denouncing as undesirable citizens the very people they now presume to assist.

"You cannot fight a man whose money you are taking at the same time. That would be blood money. These offers are far too little, much too late, the tardy sympathy of blood-sucking vampires. Our advice to anyone who is approached to accept charity from such elements is to take an ax to their black hands. It is sympathy of this very kind that put Christ upon the cross."

Meanwhile, in light of conflicting eyewitness testimony, speculation surrounding the incident continues unabated. Interviews with survivors point to the cause as everything, from a chimney fire or blazing Christmas tree, to the mother of an overheated young girl who, in asking for water, was misunderstood to have said *watra*, the Croatian word for fire. Still other reports blame an intoxicated patron from a nearby saloon, a group of deputies in the street outside, and a mysterious "dark-skinned, heavy-set, bearded man wearing a Citizens' Alliance button and Christy hat." It is this latter version that at present has gained wide currency among survivors, though confusion and lack of consensus about the facts runs so rife that there remains serious question as to whether the alarm issued from outside or inside the hall.

Less in doubt is that emotions here persist as raw as they are heated. According to union organizer Haywood, Sheriff Cruse has advised him that "should I remain in this district, even his protection should not protect me from being lynched," an assertion the sheriff does not dispute.

"For five months," said Haywood, "this community has lived under a reign of terror condoned by the state. It has been bullied by hired thugs and goons, terrorized by vigilantes, and cheered on by a local press that applauds the trampling of both flag and Constitution by the mine-owners cabal. If you wish to know who is responsible for the lives of the little children sacrificed at the Italian Hall on the eve of our Saviour's birth, you need look no farther than James MacNaughton, who is the dark power behind every sinister act undertaken in this place. Their lives are on his head and his alone. He is a mass murderer."

Reached for comment in reaction to Haywood's remarks, Mac-Naughton declared in a written memorandum obtained exclusively by this newspaper, "Any charge by Mr. Haywood that I had any part in the tragedy is categorically false. If he has positive proof to back up his accusation, let him bring it to light. Otherwise I would suggest that he keep quiet, as his presence in this district is that of an outside agitator whose express purpose is to incite riot, encourage mayhem, spread anarchy, and to stop at nothing, murder and assassination included, to ensure that his private ambitions are realized.

"We all know Mr. Haywood's history. He is a named assassin who trades in the worst sort of violence for hire. Such a man has no place in decent, law-abiding company. He has no place in this community. He is a cancer whose place is among the nest of union serpents and scorpions who dwell among the rocks and weeds from under which they periodically crawl to wreak their peculiar brand of un-American havoc. Let him leave here or suffer such of the consequences as may befall him should he choose to stay."

Funerals for the victims are scheduled for Saturday, Sunday, and Monday. They are to be buried in the local Lake View cemetery, where three mass graves presently are being excavated. More than a dozen undertakers have been enlisted to prepare the bodies. According to a union spokesman, an invitation has been extended to the well-known Chicago attorney Clarence Darrow to give the graveside speech.

EXCLUSIVE

In approaching MacNaughton for reaction to Haywood's remarks about him, remarks that Franklyn and *Proleterac* had been slipped for exclusive publication, Franklyn had been startled, first, to find no armed guards on patrol outside the general manager's home. Second, once he knocked, to be granted admittance beyond the front door. Third, to be escorted, after some little while of waiting, into the outer vestibule, during which he heard an exchange of loud voices down a long corridor, into the general manager's presence. Fourth, to secure his consent for an interview— or rather, audience. And, above all, to find that James MacNaughton was perfectly aware of who he, Franklyn Shivs, was.

The Italian Hall calamity had occurred at approximately 4:30, 4:45, so that by the time Franklyn had seen to Ann, returned to the hall, grimly examined each of the corpses—no Kid, no trace—and spoken with everyone he had needed to speak with, it was entirely too late to be entirely at ease about respectably paying a visit on a man as busy as James MacNaughton was bound to be at such a time, so late indeed that he entertained second thoughts about waiting until morning to do so.

But he was playing a hunch. Should he arrive at the mansion on Calumet Avenue to find it dark, he would leave. Should he find a sufficient number of lights still blazing, he would convey to the guards that he needed to speak to the general manager on a matter of—yes, he would go ahead and use the phrase—"the gravest and utmost urgency." Which is why he in advance had transcribed from his notebook onto a separate sheet of paper Haywood's exact words.

Should it come to it, he would use that paper as his calling card, a passe-partout, to run whatever gauntlet of go-betweens he might encounter. James MacNaughton might despise newspaper reporters on general principle, but unless his arrogance far exceeded his wisdom, there was no way he could afford to leave unanswered the charge—"mass murderer"— that Haywood had leveled. At a minimum, he would need, so Franklyn was wagering, to draft a written response in kind, and a written response would do quite nicely.

So when he discovered the windows of the estate lit up like bonfires— no surprise, really, given the juxtaposition of the worst human disaster in U.P. history/the U.P.'s most powerful man—then found himself negotiating unmolested the winding farolito-lined, inlaid copper-ingot-studded flagstone pathway to the house, no one was more surprised than himself when, after employing the prodigious Caledonian lion's head solid-copper knocker affixed to the shiny beaten-copper front door, it swung soundlessly open upon its well-oiled hinges and he found himself greeted by a salt-and-pepper-haired, bespectacled man markedly older than himself.

Inquiring after his business, the greeter, with an air less frosty than officious, showed him into the well-appointed foyer, lifted the folded sheet of paper from his outstretched hand with a swift *pluck*, bade him with an open hand of his own to have a plush seat, and disappeared down a long corridor into the presumed bowels of the lion's den.

Then it was the loud voices pitching with no little resonance down the hallway, followed by the reappearance of the same gentleman who said simply, "You will follow me, please," and Franklyn found himself being led down a runner-carpeted, gleaming hall of middling breadth and astonishing length—the copper lateen walls shone like new pennies—before turning sharply right to climb a narrow, uncommonly steep and low-ceilinged—the lack of clearance obliged him to stoop some—oddly twisting, copper-stepped staircase around a mezzanine gallery, cryptoporticus, and toward a closed copper door.

"Like going to see Skrymir himself," he thought.

When his escort knocked twice, a voice answered, "Come," the door was opened from the inside, and Franklyn limped through and into James MacNaughton's office to find him sitting behind an enormous copper goose-neck-lamp-lighted desk flanked by two men he immediately recognized as the company lawyers, Allen Rees and A. E. Petermann.

"Leave us," said MacNaughton to the pair. Franklyn noticed that the GM was holding the piece of paper, unfolded in his hand; dead letter.

"You are certain," said Rees.

"Allen, please," said MacNaughton.

"Jim," said Petermann, "for the last time, I counsel you to reconsider. Certainly you need to offer a response, but let us craft—"

When MacNaughton demonstratively sighed, then openly glowered at his attorney, Petermann cut himself short, shrugged, and, along with his partner, headed for the door. As he brushed past, he muttered, "We know you, Shivs, and we know your whore. So how's the face? Hurt? Sure looks like it hurts." And before Franklyn could duck away, patted him, hard, on the badly bruised cheek.

"Sit," said MacNaughton. As Franklyn heard the door close behind him, the GM gestured with an open hand to one of the trio of matching massive leather armchairs arrayed in a crescent before the desk.

Franklyn hobbled over, leaning forward to smooth his hand over the glossy desktop before settling in. "Sheet copper," he said; high-polished to within an inch of its life.

Rising from his chair, MacNaughton walked over to a sideboard, lifted a crystal decanter. "Cognac?" he asked. "I know your preference is mescal, but . . ."

When Franklyn, brought up decidedly short by the reference, indicated his approval, he unstoppered the neck and poured, returning with a pair of snifters, one of which he handed over. Lowering himself into his chair, the GM lifted his glass. "To the dead. May they each one rest in peace."

Franklyn said nothing, sipped, fished out his pen and notebook. Important that he get it all, word for word.

"So"—MacNaughton picked up the paper, lowering his rimless spectacles some to study at it—"Haywood wishes the war to continue, does he? On the backs of sixty dead children? Then he shall get his wish." Looking up, he noticed Franklyn's jotting. "Off the record, until I say otherwise. Agreed?"

Closed and placed the notebook in his lap.

"It really is too bad. He injures no one but those he would pretend to help. Our people suffer this unspeakable horror, and he immediately is interested in nothing but assigning blame. All this"—he slapped at the paper with the back of his hand—"is so much lunatic nonsense. I am a father myself."

"So is he," said Franklyn.

"Yes, which makes his madness all the more unpardonable. Were he any sort of *decent* father, he would be with his family now, as would I, circumstances permitting. He has no business in this place, as he has less business still making such despicably slanderous remarks designed to do nothing but inflame and exploit the emotions of those who at this moment are at their most raw, tender, and susceptible. If he really cared about them as he claims, he would put his union's money where his mouth is. He would shut up and fund their grief, not try to profit by it.

"There are people in this community, more than a few, who now face certain starvation owing to him and his ilk. Today's tragedy notwithstanding, it pales in comparison to the real tragedy, which is the way so many have been led astray by total strangers who favor victory at any price. Even were such a victory to come, after all that has occurred, it would be but a pyrrhic one.

"Haywood is little but a cheap opportunist, one sadly lacking in morality and conscience and, despite what he may believe, without power, not the sort that really matters. He is a flea who means to me exactly what any flea means and who will be treated by me as any flea would be treated."

Reaching into his coat pocket, he withdrew his wallet, purposefully waggling it beside his head. "Do you see this? This is mine. This is my pocketbook. And I refuse to *arbitrate*"—the word was larded with sarcasm—"as to whose pocketbook it is. I do not need to *arbitrate*. It would be the height of stupidity to *arbitrate*. No one can compel me to *arbitrate*. Because it is mine, and no one else's. The matter already is settled. It is settled in my mind."

Lifting the snifter to the light, he marveled it some, swirling the amber liquor in its bowl, glints and sheens, coating its convex sides before indulging a smooth and generous swallow. "So that if anyone wants it, this which is mine, there is one way and one way only to have it, and that is to come and get it, to try to take it, by force."

Franklyn needed to ask the question, so did. "At the risk of sounding naïve, why must it always be this way? War? Is there no way short of this mutual extermination, burning one another at the stake, to achieve some sort of just settlement, reach a middle ground? Is there no way to execute this war humanely? Must it *always* be the Rough God?"

MacNaughton shook his head. "But I do not consider this a war of extermination, sir. No one has a gun to anyone's head or knives to their throats. This is America, not some feudal kingdom of lords and princes. Those men who do not wish to work and play according to the rules we have laid down are perfectly at liberty to go elsewhere. Indeed, I would prefer that they do so. Despite what you and others may think, I take no pleasure, none, in engaging in such combat, because I know what the outcome must be."

"Which is?"

He sat back in his chair, holding his snifter up, out, and underhanded, cradling its bulb in his palm, fingers scissored at its stem. "Mr. Shivs, I know power. I have been around it most of my life. I understand it and how rightly to use it, as I am paid to use it."

"Paid well," ventured Franklyn.

"That is none of your affair. I am paid what I am worth as my superiors may deem and determine it, and not a copper more. I am paid fairly. The issue is not what I am paid. The issue is what is possible and not possible. The issue is that Haywood knows nothing about power. He *thinks* he knows, but that is *all* he knows. How could he? Know more? He and his band of blackguards never have possessed any of the real stuff. It would be laughable, were it not also so pathetic."

"If knowledge is power," said Franklyn, "then Bill Haywood has power enough. He knows the men. He knows that they are kept from thinking for themselves owing to the circumstances imposed upon them by others, just as he knows that those doing the imposing are unable to think beyond sustaining their power to do so."

MacNaughton rose from his chair, walked around his desk, lowered himself into the armchair next to Franklyn's. He smelled of spice gum, clove, anise, licorice, witch hazel, something. Reeked of resolve. His resin-slick auburn hair was parted rule-straight down the middle of his scalp. Franklyn noticed that his hairline had radically receded, that he was prematurely gray at the temples. His smartly tailored, finely woven, worsted wool suit fell midway between char and charcoal gray, no pinstripes, nailheads, herringbones, houndsteeth, glen or windowpane plaids. He filled it full with sturdy presence, set-jawed will. The four-in-hand tie knotted neatly at his four-finger, stiffly starched white collar, was a rep. Boiled shirtfront. No galluses apparent.

"And that, Mr. Shivs," he said, crossing his legs, clamping both hands to a knee, and leaning forward, "is the great myth. He may know *some* men—Western men perhaps, he must, or he could not have become what so many take him for—but he does not know these. Neither do you. I do. I know their hearts, and in their hearts the strike is over. Especially now, after today. In fact, it was over the day it began; their hearts just required the necessary time to come to the understanding, arrive at the acceptance."

"Or resignation."

He shrugged. "Understanding, acceptance, resignation, defeat. Perhaps you would care to explain the distinction. I fail to see one. I have labored in this position for more than a decade now, and in that time I have operated by one rule above all. When a miner dares lift his head above his station, hit it, hard. There are no Molly Maguires here, sir, because I will not permit them to exist."

"Mr. MacNaughton, I have been covering this strike since its inception."

"Yes, I am well aware of that."

"And I have been covering it for a socialist newspaper in Chicago."

He smiled, revealing a mouthful of porcelain-white teeth straight as picas of type aligned in their tray. "Aware of that as well."

"Yes, well"—Franklyn was startled; had he read his copy?—"I have tried in doing so to be as straightforward as humanly possible. I have tried to steer clear of the sort of partisanship and bias that is the bread and butter of other newspapers. I do not doubt that on occasion I have failed to do so, but I have made that effort in good faith because I believe it important that I do so."

"Yes, it is, and you have."

"You have read—"

"Yes, I have. Had I not, you would not be sitting here, in spite of your affiliation."

"Yes, well, my affiliation, as you call it, is perhaps something less—or, rather, other—than what you may presume it to be, my contempt for the so-called common man being exceeded only by my disdain for the salariat, but that aside—"

"Your affiliation is with Haywood and the Clemenc woman, and before he met with . . . what he met with, the organizer Goggia. And, if you will pardon my saying so"—he lifted his glass—"this." It was not a question.

"The three persons you mention are friends. I consider them personal friends."

"My point exactly."

Franklyn forged ahead. "As for the other, the booze, that, as you might say, is none of *your* affair. It is a matter between myself and my . . ." Shaking his head, he cut himself short.

MacNaughton, tight-lipped, cold-stared him, then broke into a not unfriendly, even warm, distressingly contagious smile. "Fair enough. But then spare me your haddle about the *straightness* of your coverage. It has been decent, on occasion even honorable, but it has never been straight. You slant, Mr. Shivs, you slant—you just do it differently than the rest. You don't so relentlessly grind its ax, for which, I suppose, you are to be commended." He paused. "That said, my lawyers, the men who were here when you came in, do not trust you." Another pause, longer. "But then, frankly, neither do I."

This did not parse, thought Franklyn. "So why not just give me a prepared statement then? That's what they wanted you to do, wasn't it, your attorneys? Something measured, concise, vetted, careful. Something *composed*."

He nodded. "Curiosity. You intrigue me, Shivs, is the long and short of it. Does that surprise you?"

"Of course it does."

"Yes. Of course. It would, as it should. Still, you've been up here longer than anyone else, any newspaperman I mean, save the hometowns, of course, and I know you've pestered for interviews on any number of occasions. Persistent chap. I like persistence. Persistent myself. Persistence pays. And, as I say, I find your reporting"—searching for the word—"an exception. Especially in light of the nature of the publication in which it appears. And then, tonight, you show up here, my home, far too late, disreputable hour, with this perfectly preposterous paper." Looong pause. "But you aren't, are you."

"What?"

"You do not believe. You are not one of . . . them."

"I'm a newspaper reporter, Mr. MacNaughton."

"Yes. Chicago *Tribune*. Once."

"Right. And next you are going to tell me what brand of skivvies I wear."

He laughed. "Believe it or not, there are some things I do not know, and do not *want* to know. The manufacturer of your underwear may well head the list."

Franklyn could not help it; he laughed in spite of himself. Sipped. "You had me rolled, didn't you? Hancock. Farolito."

"Not at all. Had you followed, shadowed, no hand in what happened. Regrettable, that. Consider a moment; what conceivably would have been the point?"

"Some sort of warning? Message delivered? Ann Clemenc?"

"That, Mr. Shivs, I daresay, is entirely your affair, pardon the expression. Better she should be a pain in your arse than in mine. If I might, however, a word to the wise. Insofar as you have succeeded, and you have—not without the assistance of your ink-stained comrades, granted, still, largely, mainly yourself—insofar as you have turned *Missus* Clemenc into some sort of *folk* heroine, permit me to suggest that to the extent you presently have her, um, ear, so to speak, you consider whispering in it that she would do well not to oblige you to turn her still further into a . . . *martyr.*"

Franklyn felt the chill as intended, even as he riled to the bait. "Now hold on, what do you mean, sir? What are you saying?"

"You heard me."

"Yes, I did. Now, you hear me. Call off your jackals. If you are intent upon going to war with Bill Haywood, well, reckon he can take care of himself. As for Ana Clemenc, back off. You're so god-almighty convinced the strike is over, leave her be."

"She complicates things. Needlessly."

"She is a woman, sir, her job. Besides, she goes her own way."

"Be that as it may, one's patience frays. There are those in my employ who—well, let us just say that as their patience wears thin, so the ice upon which she skates. I am doing you a favor, Shivs. I am doing *her* one. I cannot be held responsible for every last action in this district. I control what I control. That is a lot, but it is not everything. Accidents, regrettably, happen."

Rising from the chair, he circled back to the other side of the desk, clutched its edge with both hands, shoulder-wide, leaned his weight. "I like you, Shivs, I do. Don't trust you to walk my dog, but like you well enough—as your sort goes. So let me tell you something that I suspect, as a reasonable man, you already know. All this . . . silliness is going to be over soon, sooner than you may believe, and then everyone, yourself included, will go back to living their lives, and everything that has happened here, in the last five months I mean, today excepted perhaps, is going to be forgotten, save as some bitter reminiscence about a minor inconvenience and momentary disruption over a shot and a beer.

"The strike will end, the men will go back to work, I will continue to run these mines, Haywood will leave to go stir up trouble elsewhere, you will return to Chicago to write your Red propaganda, the world will keep spinning on its axis, and the sky for even an instant will not so much as totter, much less fall. And through it all, the rich sons in Boston, and their sons after them, shall continue to rule the universe and their company to turn a profit until such time as it becomes apparent, as in time it shall— and that time, Mr. Shivs, believe me, is one we both shall live to see; we have the facts, we are able to forecast, the District's threshold of maturity has been reached and exceeded—that the lode is played out.

"So, if you care for this woman at all, as you so clearly do, god knows why, hark to and heed my advice. Either take her out of this district until the end is over, òr use such influence as you may exert to make her understand"—he unhooked his spectacles an ear at a time and placed them upon the desktop—"that after today, she continues in her agitation, her private little passion play, at her own expense, and at her peril.

"This is not, please believe me, an idle threat. I am, as I say, doing you both a favor. Her fight is lost, her day is done, her dream is in fact a nightmare. Unionism has no home here, no hold. There is no worker revolution. Red socialism, as black anarchy, is a myth. Haywood's coming is merely a last gasp."

"Not socialism," Franklyn heard himself saying, incredulously, "justice."

"No, sir," the GM rejoined, "*not* justice, power. The former is but a word, one whose definition changes day to day and hour to hour, in truth changes moment to moment. Two dollars an hour, three dollars an hour, four dollars an hour. Three-man drill, two-man drill, one-man drill. Details. Fine print. Trivia. No, it is the latter, sir, it is power that is reality, the only reality, the one that defines itself and is the definer, and that, in the end, is all that endures and lasts."

"So might makes right? Law of the jungle?"

"Right has nothing to do with it, Shivs. Neither does wrong. There is only what is possible and what is not. The men striking is possible, the men winning the strike is not. The men joining the union is possible, the union winning recognition here is not. Haywood visiting this district is possible, his remaining here is not. Ana Clemenc dreaming her dream is possible, her dream coming true is not.

"Is this just? Perhaps, perhaps not. That is not for me to say, nor do I stay awake at night pondering the answer to such questions. What it is, is real, it is reality as it presently exists in this place and will continue to exist. It is the reality that power, the use and application of power, has created and nurtures and maintains, and insofar as that reality is harsher, harder, less forgiving for some than for others, insofar as it is inequitable, that is only its nature.

"As for the rest"—he shrugged—"it is all so much role-playing. We— you, I, the men, their families—we all have our jobs to do, and whether we do them well or poorly, whether they are done by us or by others, still, they must be done. You see how it is. It would behoove you to see. It would behoove her."

Franklyn emptied his glass, rose to his feet, walked to the sideboard, and, back brandished to MacNaughton, helped himself to another cognac. Gesture of effrontery, two fingers' worth. Then turned and, openly swigging as he did so, commenced to pace even as the chief resumed his seat behind the desk where he toyed idly with the copper-wrought orrery atop it.

"What I see," said Franklyn, feeling emboldened, "is that you, and those like you, are comfortable, and that others, and others like them, are not, and that in a world of division, distinction, and inequity, this is the one that seems to matter most to most people, the one to which they most passionately aspire, to be comfortable, materially and elsewhere.

"And I see, also, that *because* you are comfortable, because you *possess* comfort, you hide behind the word 'power'—hard word, word of the world's winners—to ensure that you will remain in possession of that. And that there is, in itself, *of* itself, nothing wrong with that, not a thing, nothing at all, to use it, power, as camouflage and insulation and aphrodisiac and, above all, as armor. Nothing wrong, because not only is it in the nature of power to be used in such a fashion, it is *human* nature that it ought be so used. Handed the same power, the powerless would behave in *precisely* the same way. You will argue the point, and that is fine, but there is no difference, you see, no difference that really matters, not a jot, between yourself and those you overlord."

"Oh, piffle!" said MacNaughton. "That all men are alike, all equal, is exactly what the world would like to believe, what socialism would like to believe. Lot of fofurraw and clatterfart. That the distinctions between people are merely a function of social and economic engineering not having yet properly ironed them out is the biggest lie going.

"All men are *not* created equal, or as they are, then some, obviously, more equal than others. If I might be permitted to contradict Balzac—behind every great fortune does *not* lie a great crime."

"Perhaps," said Franklyn, "perhaps so, but that does not absolve you and those like you of your sins, and your sins, which are legion, and which are the sins of all the world, all history, every cycle of season and spiral of time, quickly reduce themselves to but a single one: you hoard. Not as certain rodents do, vermin, as a matter of season and survival, but gratuitously. Not thoughtlessly—everything with those like yourself always is done by design, with single-minded preparation and purpose, according to premeditated plan, no spontaneous moment, God forbid—but gluttonously, greedily, without felt regard.

"You hoard—wealth, knowledge, power—that you might bequeath. Self-serve."

Franklyn raised a hand behind his head, stop sign, knowing in advance what was coming. "Charity? Philanthropy? Patronage? Funding, underwriting, do-gooding? Oh, most certainly, as you and those like you may define and determine it. Very good, all kudos and accolades, garlands and gratitude. The Boston Symphony, Harvard University, the Athe-

naeum, all thank you thrice over." Wheeled about, softly: "And"—pause—
"so"—pause—"what?"

He could see MacNaughton from here, across the room, cone-lit by
the gooseneck, respectacled now and watching him, metaled of eye, wary
as a wolf, lobo. So what was he fiddling with beneath his copper-topped
desk? Call button? Alarm? What does he think, thought Franklyn, that
I'm . . . *armed*?

"So how much is enough? Hmm? Eh, MacNaughton? When is
enough enough? When is enough enough not only to bequeath but re-
invest, voluntarily, in the men, their families, lives, *their* comfort. When?
When do the men come first?

"Of course, you are perfectly correct to say that power defines, con-
verts all questions of truth and beauty into its own question in order to attack and suppress them, eliminate them, abolish them. Consumes all
before it, all in its path, the paint and canvas both, brushes, too. But the
picture, image, its shape and form, line, the genius of the thing itself, that
lies in its application, no? Power's put-use, the way of it. Character, sensibility, proportion, perspective, weight and measure, conceit and posture,
angle, slant. These values at play, their right worth. Apply it wrongly, use
power poorly, and all is shite."

He sensed that his voice was getting louder, but couldn't be certain, so
continued. "Which, seems to me is what we have here, up here. Too much
shite, for far too long, and you unwilling to lift a finger to put it right. You
unwilling to risk your *fuck*ing salary to set it square. You interested in not
much at all, save to parrot, 'Power, power, power,' and for the rest, to *them*,
'Fuck-all.'

"Well, power is *merde*, sir, when a man who has it, possesses it, understands it, is intimate with it, the ways and means and hows of it, a man capable of playing it like violins, who knows power like verse, permits
himself to become the instrument that mangles its meant poetry to little
but plodder's prose. It is the stink of that that is on you, ground in beneath
the skin, and nothing you can do to wash it sweet.

"I won't say I agree with Bill Haywood that their deaths are on your
head. It is too easy, nor strictly true. But let me ask you: of those people who died today, how many do you reckon ever heard a poem rightly
sung in its soaring or, having heard, spread their wings, falcon to the
flight? How many might yet, had they lived, become swans? How many of

those children might have created loving work of real worth had they lived on?"

He suddenly found himself wanting to say much more, yet perfectly unable to say it. Falcons? Swans? What was he going on about? Lot of infernal rubbish. Syllabub. The track of his thought off its rails, rails and rudder both. Mumbled, "Vultures." And again, "Vultures."

"Mr. Shivs, please, have a seat. No need to shout."

Had he been shouting? Oh my. As Franklyn returned to his chair, plopped into it, he noticed that the top drawer of MacNaughton's desk had been drawn open and that the GM's hand was resting there, inside of it. Now he withdrew the hand—at which Franklyn immediately tensed, until he saw that what it contained was but a single sheaf of stationery—said coolly, "If you wish, Mr. Shivs, to compare the people of this place to birds, might I suggest that the more apropos imagery is the penguin. They are flightless, huddle in colonies, are singularly susceptible to disease and death, yet winter remarkably well and are easily led. A most nonaggressive, conflict-averse fowl."

Closed the drawer. "But here. To business." Removed a pen from its inkstand and began writing, nail scratch across fabric. "You ought to feel free to use this as you see fit. My considered response to Haywood's ill-considered remarks." Continued writing, without looking up, asked, "If I might, how is it that a man like yourself finds yourself favored by such a man? More to the point, why do you so favor such a man?"

"Romantic readiness," answered Franklyn.

"Pardon?"

"I never have known a man, an individual, so open to becoming or so willing to become, to keep on coming, striving spontaneously toward an elusive, possible horizon that only he can see."

The GM replaced the pen in its stand, rolled a blotter to the paper, seesaw, teeter-totter. "You make him sound like a visionary."

"Do I? Well, yes, I reckon he is, in his way. Searcher, I should say, searcher-in-action. To understand Bill Haywood you need first get past his past, the violence in it, that being the only thing most people see. Because what informs the center of the man's soul is only the sharpest of contradictions.

"On the one hand, he dreams, radically, bravely, pipe dreams if you will, of the one great union of all workingmen, and the power, as you rightly have said, that arises from that amassing. On the other, he values nothing so much as individualism and independence, the unproscribed freedom to go one's own way, follow one's own private star unmolested. Utterly American that way. It is the loner hero he venerates above all."

"Cowboy."

"Well, Nietzschean cowboy anyway. Wrangler, gun hand, maverick gambler. Bounty hunter."

"Saboteur." He paused, recited, "'To find the Western path / Right thro' the Gates of Wrath.'"

"Blake. Impressive. Your point?"

"That your visionary Mr. Haywood is but a common assassin."

"Acquitted."

"Most deplorable miscarriage of justice this country ever has been compelled to swallow."

"Still, acquitted, and wears the stain proudly."

MacNaughton slid the paper smoothly across the copper as Franklyn leaned forward to receive it, folded it once, lifted it in acknowledgment and thanks, inserted it between the leaves of his notebook.

"I will not gainsay that William Haywood can be remorseless," said Franklyn, "even militantly so. It is the very quality that alienates so many who would sooner be his allies. But, in like measure, so is he capable of a great and quite selfless compassion."

"So *you* say," said MacNaughton. "I say that the most dangerous liar is the one who not only believes his own lies, but is willing to act upon them. You will pardon my skepticism, sir, but that side of the beast I never have seen."

"I have. Indeed, I have been its recipient, and on more than one occasion."

"Ah. That explains it then. The beneficiary."

"Some. Explains some, not all."

"Yes? Please—continue."

"His heart is in the right place, simple as that. You will call it a violent heart, fine. I call it a passionate one, impassioned one. Either way, it is in the right place. It is with those who dwell under the hill, wrong side of the rails, those who have not and not enough—power, wealth, opportunity, education, freedom, comfort. Poetry. Love. The means to fly high, and higher. He hopes on their behalf.

"Is he a zealot? Better to ask whether excess in the name of justice is a vice."

"Excess, sir? Excess!? You flatter him, Shivs. Lawlessness, anarchy, violence. The man hasn't the capacity to behave otherwise. Every zealot is the same. Having satisfied himself that he has identified the one true evil, he proceeds in his self-righteousness to act evilly himself in the name of eliminating that evil, the while brooking no opposition to his actions. Thus is dissent suppressed, doubt disdained, criticism dismissed as disloyalty. And this, surely you have noticed, he never fails to describe as his *sacred duty*.

"No, sir! Rigidity and regimentation of thought, orthodoxy, dogmatism, demagoguery, these are the tactics of the zealot, just as his weapon is brutality."

MacNaughton fobbed the pocket watch from his vest, tripped open its face. "Late," he said, glancing at the time. Rose from his chair as Franklyn aped the gesture. "Edifying," he said, "all this, really. I would add only that, in the days and weeks ahead, come what may, you endeavor to remember that as Haywood *hopes* on their behalf, Calumet and Hecla puts them to work, pays them a living wage, feeds, clothes, and shelters them, affords them a free education and medical care, and provides them paid places in which to worship as it may suit them to do so.

"Do the math, sir, do the math. And then, having done it, you tell me, which amounts to more."

Reaching across the desk, he extended his arm, proffered his hand. Franklyn grasped it in his own, felt the crush. No callus.

"If you would like, I can make arrangements to have that looked at," he said. "I'm no doctor, but it appears something may be broken."

Franklyn shook his head. "I'm fine. Looks worse than it is. Nothing time won't heal right as the mail. Appreciate the offer, though."

MacNaughton shrugged. "Suit yourself. Change your mind, offer stands." Paused. "One thing we can agree on. God willing, no more days like today."

Franklyn nodded. "God or no God, no more."

CK

Returning to the hotel, Franklyn looked in on Ann—sleep of the dead—attended to the dog, changed into fresh foot wraps, slipped out, found a saloon, Curto's, where, ignoring as he might the blood pump through his head and throb at his feet, he worked backboothed into the night on his story, preoccupied with the underlying meaning of his encounter with MacNaughton—Haywood could jactitate as it pleased him, he thought, the MacNaughtons of the world were untouchable—if distracted more so by his failure to have turned up the Kid among the victims.

That something was alarmingly wrong was alarmingly clear. The dog never left his side, ever. All Franklyn knew was that he lived at Tamarack location, the Hill, somewhere, one of the "tree" streets. Elm? He never had bothered to get an address. If it came to it, he could hike over there, ask around, knock on some doors. First, though, he would check in at the hospital. Which, when he did, and having done so, is where he found him at last.

Above the sheets, his face, white as oolite, was pristine, perfectly un-marked, peaceful, if exceedingly drawn and drained. And, thanks to the nurses, clean as Franklyn ever had seen it. His jackstrawed hair even bore something approaching the hint of a part.

"We have made him as comfortable as possible," the doctor, Simon-son, told him. "He is feeling no pain at all. The injuries are all internal. The odds of him making it through the night are not good. We have done all we could. A matter, now, of waiting for the inevitable to happen, the body to run its natural course."

"What are you saying, Doc?" asked Franklyn. "You're telling me he's not going to make it?"

"Barring a miracle . . ."

"But he's a kid, Doc, just a kid. Looks fine. You don't know him. He's a fighter. All scrap."

"Sometimes, some things, no matter how hard we battle . . ." Simon-son shrugged. "His lungs, heart, the crush. There is irreversible damage. It is nothing short of inexplicable that he still is breathing. The others, those who sustained similar injury, died instantaneously."

"His mother?" Franklyn asked, absently.

"We don't even have a name," said Simonson. "Found no identifica-tion on him at all."

"George," said Franklyn automatically. "Name's George Olds. Tama-rack location. One of the tree streets, I think. No one's come around ask-ing for him?"

Simonson shook his head. "Not that I am aware, no. Not yet anyway."

"You can get word to his family?" Franklyn asked mechanically.

Simonson nodded. "Olds is a Cornish name, isn't it?"

"Yes, it is," answered Franklyn mindlessly.

"Wonder what he was doing at the hall then. Must have snuck in somehow."

The full weight of it was falling now, come crashing crashing down. He tried to hold it off, fend, ward, stave, parry, shoulder it back, hurl it away. No place to run, fewer to hide. The world flattened him anyway. His knees sagged. Needed to find a chair, did, sat, sank heavily into it, head in his hands, then locked between his knees, short of breath.

He asked, please, for a glass of water.

"You look unwell," said Simonson. "Perhaps I should have a look at those bruises. May be breakage."

Franklyn waved him weakly away. "I'm fine, Doc, thanks." The words huffed themselves out, expelled in gasps. "Little lightheaded, is all. Haven't eaten all day." Labored, half panicked, to regain the regularity of his breathing. Clammy palms. His heart was wild in his throat.

When a nurse arrived with the water—quaffed it all down, dreg and last dollop—he heard Simonson, miles off, order her to fetch up an orange on the double, quartered.

What was the meter of grief, he wondered, or was there one? Time signature, clef, key. Whatever it was, try as he might, he could not seem to fall in lockstep with its measure. Plumb out of poetry. He figuratively rifled his pockets. No poesy, not a punctus. Verseless at last, and *un*versed.

Look at this, at him, lying there, unbecome. Too young. Still as moonstone, white as spring rain. Nonsense, vile nonsense, imbecile death, stupid waste. Poesy imparts pleasure but can't put things right, back right, unbreak what is broken, bodies, minds, lift a boy light to his feet or rekindle the light in his head, yield back his youth, unsnuff a life, render unto him the vested years of his future, that which by rights he is owed.

Can't reunite a kid with his dog.

This was not his milieu, not at all. Every tether of thought untied, cord uncorded, umbilicus cut, every chalaza wrenched free of its shell. His brain was as stormy as shrapnel; smelled the charnel-charred sound of his sight. Heard himself cursing aloud. Cursing himself. Cursing Mac-Naughton. Cursing Bill Haywood. Cursing himself. Cursing himself. Heard himself saying his name.

Rose unsteadily to his feet, placed his moist hand upon the Kid's pale brow, brushed away a comma of hair, held it there, tenderly. Then turned and reeled, wounded, pursued from that place. Then turned and headed anywhere, anywhere at all, but there, away from there, chevied by Simonson's beckoning voice and the soughing of the dying souls of every child from the Iroquois to the Italian Hall down all the corridors of time out of time, 'neath the same sad refrain:

De mortuis nil nisi bonum.

The Pied Piper of Nothing. The poet of prose-laden pain.

OUTSIDE LOOKING IN

Odd word, perhaps, "picturesque," to describe a funeral. But it was. No getting around it. Picture-postcard.

Sunday after Christmas, early afternoon after church, through the snow, the fall and the float of it, lacy as spindrift, gentle as eiderdown beneath a gauzed-frosty sun. From thirty-two churches, or thirty-three, the steeple bells chonged as they trod. Five thousand, four thousand, six thousand black-frocked and hatted down Fifth onto Pine, old Shoepak Alley. Three thousand maybe. Moms, dads, brothers and sisters, grandmas and grandpas, uncles, aunts, cousins, playmates. Thirty-nine foreshortened white coffins, pall borne shoulder-high, each lain neatly with flower and wreath. Fourteen caparisoned, horse-drawn black carriages. A horse-drawn sleigh, a sled, sledge, a dray, cutters and carioles, cartage of cortege.

Two miles of on-marching mourning.

Ana Clemenc walked the processional's prow harnessed into her flag. No stars this time, stripes, pattern, design or insignia. Just a flag, one immense as a ship's sail, red as merlot. Its staff was draped in black crepe.

It was said that she stared straight ahead, head high, eyes crying icicles, *stilettos of a frozen stillicide.* The brass band at her back blew its dirges. Fifty Cornish miners, shelving for the moment their antipathies, sang hymns: "Rock of Ages"; "Nearer My God to Thee"; "Jesus, Lover of My Soul," as fifty thousand watched, weeping, wailing, brought low and bereaved along the milelong route past the company houses of Yellow Jacket, Red Jacket shaft, past Tamarack-high-on-the-hill. Out to Lake View they trudged, tramping to the five battlefield-long trenches—three for Catholics, two for Protestants—that had been hacked out of the flint-hard earth the day before by a battalion of still-striking miners.

Clarence Darrow having pled illness, William F. Haywood delivered the graveside eulogy in his stead: "We mourn for the dead," he said, "as we keep faith with the living and admonish and call to account those responsible for this suffering. What we want from them is not sympathy, not charity, neither handshake nor handout. What we want, what we demand, what we will have, is the justice both the dead and the living deserve.

"This tragedy will not unite this community but occasion its division still further, still deeper. It will mark the new beginning of the struggle renewed. We will meet all acts of coercion here on with not only noncompliance, but active, positive acts of our own."

Franklyn Shivs was not there. Should have been, but having permitted himself, his heart, to get in the way of the "story," he couldn't. Could not. He was in a bar, Pal in his lap, drinking beers, feeding the dog bar scraps; little guy liked potted soused herrings.

No one knows what guilt is, guilt and regret and remorse. The world hasn't the first crust of a clue. If it did, it would stop all its clocks, dismantle the sun, and grind to a halt in midorbit. But it doesn't. Never does. It just / spins / on.

After Italian Hall, Ana changed. Franklyn couldn't pinpoint it, but something in her nature hardened, soured, grew horns against the horror and the responsibility she felt in having played a part in its perpetuation. Their lovemaking was how it expressed itself first, which is to say, impressed itself upon him in a way he could appreciate. It was as if owing to some piece of her having been fractured or broken, perhaps having died along with those children, she needed to feel more alive than ever, redoubled and renewed. Her way, as he reckoned it, of healing. So, they made love more often, if at her behest more than at his, and when they did, more . . . desperately, exigently, with a sense of animal abandon and ardor. Which, as far as Franklyn was concerned, was easy to do, easiest thing in the world. No rules, limits, proscriptions, boundaries. No reason to be humble, cautious, generous, considerate, but everything unharnessed, drunk.

Outside the bedroom was, as is said, another matter. Not that they didn't . . . mesh. They were all right. They were fine. But it was harder now. More moments of collision and clash, of coarctation. Whereas before she had been driven, now he sensed that she was consumed, obsessed, and that this turn in her soul, if that is what it was, was not one that redounded to her benefit, or theirs. But, as he discovered, little he might do to arrest it.

He began to fear for her life.

Dissenting opinion no longer interested her, rational exchange so much the less. It no longer was enough to "defeat the enemy" or "vanquish the opponent"; now it must be "destroyed," "annihilated," "obliterated," trampled underfoot, gleefully stomped upon, if at all possible, "humiliated."

To her one side, Ella Bloor. To her other, Bill Haywood. She was traveling in heady company, and that company was on a mission. Suicide mission, Franklyn might have argued, as he dared to, once, the time he had quoted de Gourmont at her: "'Nothing exists except by virtue of injustice. All existence is theft paid for by other existences; no life flowers except in a cemetery.'"

To which she had replied, "He is wrong, Frank. You are wrong. You could not be more wrong—or more wonderful."

"But," he said, "for beauty to exist, love to govern—I know this in my bones—politics must disappear. Power must."

"But why should it?" she asked. "It never will, not in a hundred or a million years will it. This, now, here, is all that we have, all we shall ever, and so we must do with it the very best that we can, because the world is not a perfect place, and that is why we must only try to make it better. Better is the best we can do, all we can do, because . . . we are . . . human."

"Yes," he said, "and never enough. People are beasts, the world their shithouse, so why bother, why try, why devote the little time one is handed, no more than the blink of an eye, to such . . . futility? As power cannot be destroyed—you are correct—all one can do is keep it from destroying oneself and, if one is lucky, those one loves. A full-time job, that. Full enough."

"I love my people," she said.

"I don't know what that means, *your* people. Your class? Tribe? Race? Sect? Your collective cultural myth? Your gene pool? What? What does that mean exactly?"

"My countrymen. I love them."

"I don't understand what love has to do with that. I can understand loving a person, a single person, everything that makes that individual that individual and no one else. I even can understand loving a dog. I cannot understand loving a people."

"But you need not understand, Frank. When you love, you love. Understanding need not be part of it. You feel this, or you do not." She pressed a hand, palm flat against her chest. "Here. In the heart."

"Fine. Then I do not."

"Yes, I know. Such feeling is not for everyone. It is for the very few, those whose hearts see out, see outward, see wide."

"And mine?"

"Sees in, sees inside, sees deep, deep down, sees itself, narrow, all through, and . . ."

"Yes?"

"Sees mine."

For her, it reduced itself to this: that a man was abused and ill used, beaten down, used up, and then discarded. A man who otherwise would be fully alive experiencing his measure of joy was dead now, not because of who he was in the deep sum of his parts, not because his name was Sid or Murray, Solly or Cy, but because of what he did for a so-called living. That to remain alive, subsist, survive, he must die. And she could not leave the fundamental unfairness of that, the contradiction of it, alone, but was *called* to act toward its correction.

So she was on a mission, one that called to her with a fervor that rivaled, he felt, their sessions in bed, and yet he had no proof of what that mission was, save that it was secret, kept a secret from him, from all, save those few who knew about it.

It being his job, he tried to find out, finger the one thread that would unravel the sweater. But Ella Bloor flatly refused to talk to him, Haywood was better at keeping his own counsel and keeping it close to his vest than any man he ever had known, his cronies were not to be cultivated, and Ana herself was intent—as, he assumed, she had been instructed—upon keeping him purposely in the dark.

Dozen of exchanges, each the same:

"What's up?"

"What do you mean?"

"What's Bill got up his sleeve? What plans?"

"You do not want to know."

"Of course I want to know. I'm in the knowing business."

"Curiosity killed the cat."

"Don't intend to get killed. Intend to eat the canary."

"Leave it be. Best that way."

"But something *is* up, right? I mean, I'd have to be blind not to see it."

"Perhaps. Something."

"How much do you know?"

"What I need to know. What I am told."

"Not everything?"

"I do not know. I am not told whether what I know is everything, or something, or anything at all."

"I thought you trusted me."

"I do. This is not about trust. It is not about us. Our talking about this now, this way, *that* is trust. It also is love."

"Love?"

"Yes, love. Your ignorance is our love. Its gesture. It keeps you . . . clear. Above and away."

"Bill doesn't trust me, does he?"

"Bill adores you."

"Adores, but doesn't trust."

"He trusts you to tell the truth as you see it."

"So, what then? If I get too close, he thinks my vision will blur, cloud, fuzz, what?"

"He thinks your vision is not his. He thinks your way of seeing is your own way, that it is most clear at a distance. Is he wrong?"

"Maybe. Partly. Depends on how far, how far away he thinks I need be kept to see clearly."

"Far enough is fair enough. His words."

"Right, and he gets to say how enough is enough."

"Yes, he does."

"Because he is Haywood."

"Yes, because he is Haywood."

As it was a new year, they decided, in commemoration, to go swimming. Which is to say, she did, decided. Moment of whim. On occasion, she had them, and when she did, he must indulge this side of her, the one he treasured most.

Now, in Calumet, Michigan, in the dead of deep winter, unless you were Finnish, in which case any freezing body of water would do, there was but one place to do that, the bathhouse pool in the library basement, and that wasn't going to work, because she not only wanted to go swimming, she wanted to go swimming starkers, which, okay, greatly appealed to him, but . . . how?

Well, she knew a way in, she said. She had been going there since a child, and knew an illicit way in. After closing, after dark, Sunday night, they would meet around back. The library was neither patrolled nor watchguarded, had no security whatever save the old locks on its windows and doors. Easy as the effractive flip of a jackknife. Apparently, no one had considered that such a paltry thing as a book possibly could be of interest to a self-respecting thief, and, in fact, in its fifteen years of operation the building never had been burglarized or a single one of its 35,000 volumes shanghaied. They would slip in sight unseen by a cellar window and none the wiser.

Oh, and don't forget, she told him, not to bring your trunks.

AND MEANWHILE

An inquest into the Italian Hall, what now was being called "Holocaust," was convened. Seventy witnesses over three days filed through the Red Jacket town hall to give testimony to town fathers, the outcome of which was but more muddle and increased ill will.

Newspaper reporters, state and federal officials, labor representatives, politicians, lawyers swarmed the district. A U.S. senator, James E. Martine of New Jersey, charging that continued Keweenaw labor unrest "threatens the peace and order of the entire nation," had read into the *Congressional Record* a New York *World* newspaper editorial declaring that "Houghton County is not a community of self-governing American citizens, but one of aliens brought thither to serve the monopoly, and ruled from Boston in defiance of law and in despite of democratic institutions."

James MacNaughton, in the company of a coterie of private armed guards, traveled by train to Boston, where he met with Shaw and Agassiz to report, "As far as I am concerned, the strike is over. We now have more men actively employed than before the strike began. We are producing twenty-thousand fewer tons of rock each month, but we shortly shall be back up to and even exceed previous levels." Upon his return, as if to punctuate the point, he ordered the searchlight dismantled and removed.

Clarence Darrow arrived in Lansing for a series of meetings with

Governor Ferris, accomplishing nothing. Upton Sinclair, arguing for federal intervention, wrote President Woodrow Wilson that "the outrages in Michigan's Upper Peninsula afford an unexampled opportunity to prove to American labor whether the new freedom has any meaning for them," accomplishing nothing. American Federation of Labor (AFL) president Samuel Gompers dispatched union representatives to the Keweenaw to "conduct an investigation of affairs there," accomplishing nothing. The Michigan Federation of Labor, urged by the WFM National in Denver to declare a statewide sympathy strike, flatly refused, prompting Guy Miller to denounce both the AFL and MFL as "cowardly, do-nothing organizations directly responsible for the loss, should it come, of the Michigan copper-mine strike," accomplishing nothing.

Shortly after the new year, Governor Ferris visited the district for the first time since the strike's commencement to announce that he was ordering the withdrawal of all sixty-six of the remaining Guardsmen, and to comment that "Red socialism in the Upper Peninsula has been working ruin for five or six years, and, in my humble judgment, the right kind of peace will never reign until there is an entirely different spirit cultivated. The fundamental principles of Christianity must be worked up in all of our labor relations."

He then dismissed the strike as "something that ought never have happened, had only the union stayed away and permitted the miners to treat with the owners as miners instead of unionists," logic so perfect in its tautologizing and specious in its circularity that it left little room for effective rebuttal.

On the other hand, what it accomplished, was nothing.

AT SWIM-TWO-(LOVE)BIRDS

The moonlight through the windows played through the bank of panes glancing dancey across the water's surface, flirting with Ana Clemenc's wet and naked figure. Hadn't Franklyn had something like this once before, another place, planet, another time, different woman, one almost as tall, no less voluptuous? But surely this was neither the time nor the place. Could two women conceivably be more unalike, after all, than Ana Clemenc and Margaret Anderson? Could two women be more the same? Their souls? Could any man as imperfect and incomplete as himself be less qualified to say?

Dare he swim over? Endeavor to reach out, embrace, touch, and caress, shape himself to her? Possess? He suddenly was convinced that should he do so, should he try, she must only vanish before his eyes, up and evanesce, or sink from sight. How was it, after all, that he was deserving of this? Of her? Here, now. He felt to himself a fraud, one blessed, to be sure, anointed, one smiled upon and star-caped; imposter nonetheless.

"Relax and enjoy," he silently admonished himself. "This will not come 'round again. Why must you always hold on to your thought, clutch to it so, cling like a claw, hide behind and outside? Stop and let go, Latty. Just let go and go to her. In from the cold, this moment."

Dark in here, save for the moon. Couldn't risk lighting the wall lamps. The pool was long. He took a large, lung-y breath, silently submersed himself, swam eyes open, frog-kicking underwater toward where she was standing waist-deep and immaculate as magnet. Halfway across the pool, he shut his eyes. He would find her without them. Sense the spot sight-less, vibration and force field, become pure sonar. Aquatic bat.

Surfacing soundlessly a couple of feet behind her, insuperably pleased with himself, he heard her say, "Frank? Frank? Where are you? Come on. Cut it out," before he bent at the knees and submerged again. Finding bottom, he rolled onto his back, then kicked gently once, forward, just enough to slide his head between her outspread legs before allowing him-self, face upturned, to float upward.

Wrapping his hands around the back of her thighs, still underwater, he thrust the length of his tongue, dart-deep inside her, pressed his face to the saddle of her pelvis, tugging her hips toward and onto it. Moment of resistance, then release and response.

She ground herself, epicentered to the pocket of his open mouth, sag-ging slightly at the knees and splaying them open, ballerina, as he withdrew his tongue, then slid the flat of its breadth up and against her there, back down, up again, 'round and 'round, doing more than licking. Minnow ballet.

Running out of breath, he jackknifed his body through her legs, sub-tending eel, and stood up, smiling, swiping the wet hair from his eyes be-fore kneeling before her, altar, to continue what he had begun, as she clutched the back of his head with both hands and brought his face to and up into her, sintered there.

Face still buried at her crotch, he lifted her at the waist, easing her back down, then settling her gently onto her back, helping her float, one arm girdled 'round her waist, the other cradling her buttocks. Her fullish breasts Tetoned the water's skin. She moaned as he felt her buck, then shudder, then again, and again, and then she was palm-slapping the water, pounding it with both fists, rolling her head side to side as she rhythmically shouted in affirmation of the deity neither of them believed in.

Later, after a cigarette shared mainly in silence, he perched, back upright on pool's ledge, while she, standing in the water, great heron, redolent of the fragrance of chypre, of oak moss and amber, iris and musk, bent over him, a-grasp at greatest length, returning the favor.

"She is Eve," was all he could think. "She can only be. Ana is Eve."

OUT OF TOWN ON A RAIL

The hard line Haywood had drawn in the sand in the wake of Italian Hall was, Franklyn knew, from Bill's point of view, the only one worth drawing, but in light of the resentment it foaled, among not only his opponents but those suffering genuine hardship, those in dire need of more relief than the union could hope to provide, it inevitably could prove only self-defeating. If looking $25,000 worth of gift horse in the mouth was perceived by its givers as a grossly insulting act of ingratitude, it likewise was viewed by many if not most of its potential receivers as tantamount to cutting off one's nose to spite one's face.

Franklyn had seen it before, the way Bill Haywood's starchy dogmatism alienated so many of those who agreed with him in principle, yet found his uncompromising tactics in practice pig-iron-headed, unbending, and extreme, the while providing the perfect pretext for those who disagreed with him in the first instance to dismiss him as little but a lunatic, radical Red.

Not that James MacNaughton was less dogmatic, but the GM was possessed of the resources—and clout—to back up his rhetoric, his *diktats* and decrees, in a way that Bill Haywood was not, could not. Indeed, what had become apparent as the strike entered its sixth month—apparent, that is, to Franklyn and all but an estimated 2,500 hard-core holdouts—was that with C&H back up and operating at full capacity, and with the Quincy mine at fully three quarters, barring some force majeure or dramatic eleventh-hour infusion of union money, or short of direct federal intervention, the strike had begun to breathe its last. If the Outfit could survive the damage already inflicted—its average dividend payout since the strike's commencement had plunged from $3,480 to $755, and its stock value from $711 to $350—then it had the resources and wherewithal to survive anything.

The story, as Franklyn was able to piece it together later that evening, was that Haywood had left his room at Hancock's Hotel Scott to go to dinner with Charles Tanner, the union's traveling auditor, sometime around 6:30 p.m. Upon returning from their meal around eight, they had discovered postprandially awaiting them in the hotel lobby both Sheriff Cruse and J. W. Black, a CA member and manager of the M. Van Orden Company in Houghton, the latter in fact Governor Ferris's eyes and ears on the ground. The four of them then adjourned to Haywood's room, where Cruse informed Haywood that their visit was an introductory one on behalf of what he called "The Committee of Six."

Opening the door to the hotel room, Cruse motioned for those waiting in the hallway outside, the aforesaid six, to enter. These proved to be Frank Schumaker, town president of Red Jacket; Joseph Wills, town president of Laurium; Dr. M. A. Thometz, a Calumet dentist, CA member, and treasurer of the community's fund-raising relief committee; Laurium banker and CA member James T. Fisher; Houghton banker and CA member John Rice; and C&H attorney A. E. Petermann. Only MacNaughton himself appeared to be missing.

Thometz asked Haywood why he insisted upon refusing the $25,000 in aid in light of the alleviation of suffering it might provide, to which Haywood responded that he had refused and would continue to refuse, that he considered the money tainted and wished no part of it. Petermann then demanded that Haywood retract his statement charging MacNaughton with responsibility for Italian Hall, to which Haywood replied that he would retract not a word as retractions of the sort were a function of falsehood and that no word he had spoken fit that description. Petermann then declared that should he, Haywood, persist in clinging to such a radical and unwarranted line, he, Haywood, would need accept responsibility for anything that might happen to him in consequence. Without waiting for a reply, the eight men then filed from the room, closing the door behind them.

Haywood immediately got on the room telephone to call Ella Bloor in Red Jacket, only to have a clutch of men burst through the door as he waited to be connected, demanding that he come with them. According to Tanner, the hallway was packed with men, more than a dozen, several of them armed with drawn automatic pistols. When Haywood lunged for the bureau drawer where he kept his own weapon, the men fell upon him "like a pack of rabid wolves."

Embrangled by a pair of men on either side, Haywood's arms were pinned back. When another approached from the front, Haywood head-butted him to his knees, only to be buffaloed by a pistol butt to his right temple. When the gun discharged, accidentally or otherways, the .32-caliber bullet entered Haywood's back, lodging near the spine.

Both Haywood and Tanner then were manhandled out the door, roughhoused down the stair, and bulldogged into the street where, according to Mrs. A. J. Scott, the hotel owner's wife, roughly fifty button-clad men, most of them armed, awaited. She heard a cry of "Throw him off the bridge," another of "Lynch him," another still of "String him up," before the pair were hauled on the run across the Portage swing bridge toward Houghton. According to eyewitnesses, the two were ceaselessly kicked and pummeled en route, Haywood's face beneath his glass eye being gashed open to the bone with brass knucks.

The brutal treatment continued the mile and a quarter to the Copper Range train depot where the armed mob merged with an even larger mob amassed on the platform, led, according to Tanner, by a "tall, smooth-shaven, well-dressed man who emerged from a long, black automobile," walked up to Haywood, grasped him by the throat, spat in his face, and "cursed him for a godless Red cur assassin," before telling him, "We are going to let you go this time. If you show your face here again, you will be hanged."

He then rifled Haywood's coat, coming away with his wallet, before turning the pair over to Deputy Sheriff W. B. Hensley, who later claimed that, if not for his intervention, Haywood "would either have been hung from the Portage Lake bridge, or thrown off it." Ushering both men into the train station to await the arrival of the 9:35 southbound for Chicago out of Calumet, Hensley, weapon drawn, stood guard at the door while the mob outside gradually thinned.

———

Answering an infernal banging on his hotel-room door, Franklyn was startled to discover Ella Bloor standing in the hallway. Inside her heavy frock, she appeared decidedly out of sorts.

"Mother Bloor," he said, all lemons.

"Annie," she replied, matter-of-fact and no-nonsense. "Is she here?"

"Why, yes," he said, "she is." And before he could invite her in, she was edging past him into the room.

"Ann! Come! Come now! They are onto Bill!"

Ana was lounging on the bed, playing tug-o'-sock with Pal. Bolted off and onto her feet. "Who? Who is onto Bill?"

"Lynch mob."

"Where?"

"Houghton. We need go. Now."

Franklyn fetched Ann's coat from the wardrobe while she tugged on and laced up her boots, helped her into it while she grabbed her hat and scarf. Then, sliding his own from its hanger and double-checking its pockets for his notebook and pen, he assured the dog he would be right back, dimmed the lights, and, locking the door behind him, hastened to join the murmuring women already halfway down the staircase.

By the time they arrived at the Copper Range depot, Haywood already was on the train, having been hustled there along with Tanner under Hensley's protection and by his largesse. The deputy, as he made it a point of repeatedly mentioning, had paid cash out of his own pocket for two one-way tickets.

Franklyn, Ana, and Ella Bloor finally were able to locate him, if only after much frantic sleuthing, in his Pullman car, private compartment, lower berth, propped on his side by an elbow, naked above the waist, blood-sopped towel pressed to his cheek. A porter informed them they had only minutes. The train was set to pull out.

Hensley stood by the compartment door, warily guarding.

"It's all right, sheriff," said Haywood. "Could you give us a moment? Say our goodbyes?"

Hensley, begrudgingly, stepped outside.

"The door," Haywood called after him.

"Be brief," said Hensley, and reluctantly snapped shut the door.

"What now?" said Ella Bloor.

"Carry on," said Haywood, in wincing discomfort. "See it through as we have discussed. This changes nothing. You might wire Denver for me, alert them to what's happened here."

"Will you be back?"

"Soon as I can manage it. Been shot before. Don't expect there's much to this one. Scratch, I can feel it. Doc'll dig it out, patch me up, good as new. You two"—he looked from Ella to Ana and back again—"know what to do."

"Do we await your return?"

"You do not. Time counts, now more than ever, every second. The one big blow." He looked at Franklyn. "Not a word, Tribune, savvy? Write up the rest for all that it's worth, but not a word about this."

"But I don't even know what *this* is, Bill. The one big blow. What blow? How big?"

Haywood shook his head, tried to. "None of your concern. Better off not knowing."

There was a rap on the door, porter. "Pulling out. Next stop's Winona. Get off now or get off there, but it'll cost."

"Coming," said Franklyn, placing his hand on Haywood's shoulder, gently squeezing. "Look after yourself, Bill. See you when we see you."

"Thanks, Tribune. You look after these two, hear? Special ladies."

Ella and Ana said their so longs and godspeeds, and then the three of them were out of there and off, and then the train was gone.

At each major stop along the way—Iron Mountain, Green Bay, Milwaukee, finally Chicago—Haywood spoke to the press, informing it in every embellished detail about what had happened, expressing his confidence that the strike still would be won. Arriving in Chicago, he was wheelchaired from the train, head battened in bandages, clothes tattered and streaked with what it pleased him to characterize as "the blood of martyrs."

After calling for a doctor, he spoke with reporters for more than a half hour inside Union Station in advance of being conveyed to St. Luke's Hospital, though not before disclosing that he not only had survived an assassination attempt and narrowly escaped the clutches of a noose-wielding lynch mob, but had been personally assaulted and threatened with his life by James MacNaughton himself, a charge he knew to be patently false. Bill, as Franklyn knew and forgave him, had long ago become less person than personage, one possessed—whether by dint of inescapable circumstance or deliberate and calculated choice—of and by his persona. And this, the brazen dissembling—what Bill himself called "my taradiddling"—whether in the name of himself or of the ideals he over time had come to personify, was something he apparently expected ought be accommodated, if not pardoned, as part and some parcel of the public performance that had in sad fact—sad to Franklyn, at any rate—become inseparable from the private man.

In fact, MacNaughton had spent the evening at the Miscowaubik Club and could produce the witnesses to prove it.

"When MacNaughton had that shot fired into my back," he told them, "it was not Bill Haywood alone who took the bullet. It was every miner in Michigan, every miner on the continent. It was a shot in the back of the working class, of the union, and into the back of all of organized labor."

When he caught wind of the charge, MacNaughton could scarcely be bothered to reply. "Mr. Haywood's accusation is typically false. In fact, it is rank nonsense. I spent the evening in Calumet. I was nowhere near the Portage on the night in question. I will dignify his fictions with no further response."

C&H attorney Rees was slightly more expansive. "If what befell Mr. Haywood is illegal," he remarked, "then we are willing to stand it. None of our men were involved, and those men who were, exercised the greatest restraint possible under the circumstances. The only regret we have is that such positive action was not taken sooner. We won't have him or his kind in this district, and no power on earth can force them down our throats."

On January 24, 1914, seventeen men named in a bill of indictment, for "assault and other wrongs committed with the intent to do the said William F. Haywood great bodily harm less than the crime of murder to the great injury of him," were acquitted by a Houghton County grand jury presided over by Judge Patrick O'Brien.

One of the jurors was James MacNaughton's personal chauffeur.

AURORA ABIDING

Two people had been murdered at Seeberville, another three at Painesdale. Ben Goggia had barely survived being stomped to death. Seventy-four people had died inside the Italian Hall. The Cornish Kid had had the young life crushed from his young body. Bill Haywood had been back-shot, beaten, nearly lynched, run out of town literally on a rail. And now, Ana Clemenc fell so deeply, mysteriously ill—blinding headaches, lingering high fevers, sustained algors, dehydration, creeping numbness in each of her limbs, pneumonia in both lungs, tormina, bouts of delirium, tenesmus, pemphigus—that, unable to extrapolate a coherent diagnosis from her symptoms—"apoplectic neuritis" was their professional conjecture, "presenting with incipient paraphora"—her doctors feared not only for the baby they discovered she was carrying, but for her very life. At home, in bed, alternating between hallucination and convulsion and force-fed liquids laced with artemisia absinthium, she was nursed, in shifts, by her mother and Ella Bloor.

All Franklyn knew, at first, was that she was taken poorly—during her first bedridden week he had looked in on her at irregular intervals to find her mostly sleeping, brought her sweets, flowers, various bijoux and bibelots, a honey-lacquered music box that played "Garryowen" in three-four time, a cameo ivory-and-alabaster locket of Joan of Arc—but had no real sense of how serious her illness was or the extent of its complications. Until, that is, Ella Bloor showed up, unannounced as always, at his hotel room.

"She could die."

"What!? What are you saying, Ella?"

"The doctors say they can do nothing for her. They can keep her sedated, force fluids, make her as comfortable as possible. Beyond that . . ."

"This is preposterous. I'll put her on a train, take her to Chicago, let the doctors there examine her, someone who knows what they're doing."

"We've discussed this. The doctors say she can't be moved."

"She's strong. If the doctors can't say what's wrong, if they don't know how to diagnose, then how can they prescribe and prognosticate? They don't know. Bunch of nosebone-wearing gourd rattlers." Dog in arms, he paced, stopped, stared out the window. "She's strong."

"She is with child."

For a moment, Ella Bloor thought that he had not heard. Offering no gesture of recognition, he stood before the window, staring through it, digging his fingers at the dog's ears.

"Frank, she is pregnant. She is carrying your child."

Still he did not move. "We were careful," he said softly.

"Not careful enough, apparently."

"How far along?"

"The doctors say first trimester. Two and a half, three months."

Shuffling to the bed, he placed the dog on one of the pillows, sat down, shook his head, sighed. The sound was not nearly large enough to fill the enormity of the moment. He felt suddenly small. Again.

"I don't . . ." he began, left off. "What do the doctors say? Will the baby, I mean, her being sick, what does it mean for the baby?"

"Another thing they don't know. If she pulls through," shrugged, "who knows?"

"So she could lose it? Puerperal fever?"

"That always can happen."

"She never said anything, never mentioned it, never hinted at it, not a word."

"She did to me. Wasn't sure. Knew it was possible, that's all. Was going to tell you only once she knew for certain."

"Right. All right. What else?"

"What?"

"What else did she say? About, um, having a baby, this baby, the idea of it."

"She should tell you that herself. Not my place."

"Come on, Ella, out with it. She's in no condition to be telling me much of anything just now. From what you say, may not be for some time." He paused. "I'm the father." Strange, insuperably *strange* words.

She looked through him, sagged some. "She said if she was, if it was true, she would be thrilled, that she felt no shame and could be made to feel none."

"Of course, she wouldn't."

"Her concern was all for you, for what your feelings would be, your reaction." She waited.

"She thought I'd run?"

"Not run. Be upset, angry, displeased, take it badly. Not want it."

"It's a shock, that's all. I wasn't . . . I mean, I hadn't considered, we hadn't talked about . . . I'm just a little, uh, unprepared I guess. I thought she couldn't . . . I mean, I know she and her husband had tried and it never had happened and so . . ."

"It was him, apparently."

"Well, sure. Right. So, now . . ."

"So now we need to get her back right again, on her feet, need to get her healthy. It helps her, you know, when you're there. Hold her hand, talk to her. I can tell. There's a calm."

"You think?"

"I know." A silence. "Frank, there's something else." Something in her tone, a momentousness, unmistakable, something coming, sense of uh-oh. "Do you recall when we saw Bill off on the train?"

"Of course."

"Do you recall when he talked about what he called the one big blow?"

"Of course I recall. Been trying to reckon what the hell he meant by it ever since. Annie won't say, you don't say, can't dig up a single source who's willing to say a damn thing, on the record or off. Drinking water's suddenly laced with *omertà*."

"Yes, well, there's a reason for that, the . . . circumspection."

"Is that what you call it, Ella? Circumspection? Try secrecy. Try *sub rosa, sub silentio, en cachette*. Try fucking silence."

"As I say, all with good reason."

"Which is?"

"What I am about to say remains in this room, agreed? Not outside these four walls." When Franklyn nodded his assent, she continued. "It had been Bill's intention, before he was shot, to hit back hard at the mine owners. We know the strike is not going well. The union is down to its last few thousand dollars. At most, we've a couple thousand diehards still with us.

"C&H always was the linchpin, the prize. If we could shut it down and keep it shut, keep it shut long enough, we could win. The others, Quincy and so on, Tamarack, South Range, Champion, Tri-Mountain, the rest are small potatoes."

"Right," he said. "I know all this. Old news. Except C&H is back and up and running at full strength, so . . ."

"So we need to strike the one big blow that will turn things back around, take it to the next level."

"What level? What are you talking about?"

"We—the union, I mean, Bill—has been stockpiling certain resources in a number of out-of-the-way locations to be brought to bear at the appropriate moment. We—Bill—have determined that that moment is now. It would be better, of course, were he here to put the plan in motion himself, but, regrettably, the thing must go forward without him. And it will, go forward." She paused. "Without Bill." Paused again. "And now, without Ann."

Franklyn's head was at sea, or out to. What did Annie have to do with any of this? What resources? What out-of-the-way locations? What plan? And why, it suddenly occurred to him, was she telling him all this? He looked at her, saying nothing, thunderstruck—or dumbfounded.

"Yes, Frank. Ann. She had her part to play, as I have mine. As, now, do you."

And now his head was perfectly clear. "No, I don't," he said evenly. "Not unless the part you want me to play is to tag along to report and write about whatever it is that is going to happen. Apart from that—no, I don't."

She smiled. "More than tagging along, I'm afraid. Though, of course, once the thing is done, you ought feel free to write about it to your heart's content. Indeed, we should very much hope that you would."

"I am not involved in your business, Ella, whatever it may be. You know that. All your gambade and gambol with scalpel and bistoury. I just—"

She cut him off. "One promise. One favor."

"What? What are you talking about?"

"Promise me you will talk to Ann first, before you make your decision."

"What decision? What do you mean, talk to Ann? How? You tell me she's sedated, she sleeps, or when she's awake, she's delirious with fever."

"She has her lucid moments. She's weak. She can't carry a conversation, true, but she can tell you enough, what you need to know. Talk to her. She knows I'm here, that I'm telling you these things. You're the father of her child, Frank."

"Yes, I am."

"So, will you talk to her?"

"Of course."

"When?"

"I don't know. You tell me."

"In the morning. The fever dips some in the mornings. Tomorrow morning."

"Fine. Tomorrow morning. When? What time?"

"Eight, make it eight. Let her get down some broth first. It helps."

"Eight. Good. Eight it is. I'm there."

Waiting until Ella Bloor was sufficiently gone, he slipped into his hat and coat, lit a cheroot, snugged the dog well up under and buttoned well in, tucked safely warm to a breast, then made for Mark Curto's saloon. It was, he noticed as they strolled, a night extraordinarily crisp and cloudless, its powder-horn moon drawn down near enough to imagine fastening it about one's shoulders like an alchemist's cape. The sky appeared *live*-wired, galvanic with waver of pulse light, lucent with surcharge so palpable, you could envision depositing it deep in your pocket, to call upon in a pinch, perhaps, or fritter away like the time of your life.

"Oh my, Pal!" he exclaimed aloud. "What stars! Billions!"

He wished upon nary a one.

Having emerged from Curto's drunk again, tediously so, he and Pal somehow made it out to her lakeside spot to see, better see, more clearly to see what he had beheld overhead upon exiting the bar. He never had seen them before, not even as a kid, yet, somehow, knew straightaway what they were.

The sky was hallucinating.

The Finns, the ones he knew, called it *revontulet*. Seneca, he knew, had called them *chasmata*. The sky was an easel; some fugue-possessed Cubist was up there creating its canvas. Way up there, some Duchamp-drunk mad painter on high.

He fossicked around and found a sawn tree stump stubby-flat enough to sit save some few fossae and fossettes. Kicked it ice free, brushed off some snow, turned the collar up on his coat—why, he did not know, for he felt immune to the cold, that numb—and, tucking its tails up beneath him, sat beheld and beholden, filled with benison and blessing.

And thought, then, of his father. How had *he* felt when he had found out, been given the news? Had he hoisted a few? More than? And why wasn't he around now to be asked? And would he have been able to answer, had recourse to the words, given himself permission to use them? Probably not. Still, he would have liked to have asked him, just as he doubtless would have liked to have been asked in return. By his son. This was the loss, great loss, he understood now. That he never would speak with his father as one adult to another, father to father, about sons.

"A father, Pal," he said aloud. "Me, a dad. *Me*. How about that?" And thought how anyone can be one, how it was the being *of* one that mattered, not the siring, the fathering, but the being there and doing. Presence.

The northern lights don't always blaze. Common misapprehension. In fact, they seldom do. Some film is photosensitive enough, some cameras so sophisticated that their exposures can make them appear to, but they don't typically emblazon the heavens in spangles, berobe them boldly in brilliance, rainbow ribbons of fulgour and fiery flambeaux. The northern lights are not unfailingly nova and napalm, not to the naked eye. Ghosty-diaphanous often as not, *pale* fire: white-green, salmon pink, apricot saffron.

But sometimes, however seldseen, they can be, pure splendor. The aurora borealis is a sight to be seen first with the eye, of course, but there are times when you can feel it deep in your lungs and all the way down to your shoes. The Eskimos say that if you gently whistle, the lights will inch nearer until they have entered inside you.

So does it do—can it ever?—to describe what he saw as he sat there? Word it like he once had worded so much else? But—why? A man could go mad and, too, on and on.

"Perhaps sentences *should* quail before it," he thought. "The high life in those lights. Cower and run for the woods."

Beauty, like terror, is beyond the right reach of words.

"Look, Pal. See 'em? Helluva thing, heavenly thing. Wish Annie was here."

Inside his coat, the dog barked.

"Yeah, me too." Keeper.

Next morning, less bright than early, he came to her vaguely hungover, if no longer than for both to say what needed to be said. If he had wondered before whether there was anything he would not do for her, now he knew.

"You must," she had told him. "For me and for us, you must. And, too, for my people, *our* people. Refuse, and you shall never again laugh or love, sleep soundly or partake of true joy. Fruit will cease to taste, seasons to sweetly smell, colors will divest themselves of their hues, and the very air you breathe will remind you of the death from which you cannot run, its pursuit your living hell."

Which, as he considered it later, was hitting rather below the belt, if—okay—just as well.

Must love be earned?
  Must love prove itself first to be true?
  Must love be put to the test beyond the means of the flesh?
  Must love survive fire, weather storm, to flower to its fullest feeling?
  What must love profit us?
  What is it required of love that it *do*?

No gainsaying it, it had shaken him to see her that way, one so irrepress-
ibly full of life laid so inexplicably low. She scarcely had been able to lift
her head from where, face chalk-gray of pallor, it lay pinned to its pillow,
working weakly to muster a smile. He never had seen her that way, could
not have imagined. He would, she said, need to "pick up the slack" for the
both of them now, need to do as she asked.
  It had shaken him to see her.
  If not sufficiently shaken that, upon leaving her side, he could shake
free of the words that kept reeling through his mind like a tape: *Satiety of
love is a form of death, too.*

Test run, dry run, nothing more. That was the proposition. Preliminary
sally and probe. Bill wished to send a message, wished to discomfit and
spook, but also, just as critically, to observe and record the response and
response time. So, a reconnoiter of sorts. And he—as Bill knew, Ella had
concurred, and Ann had implored and beseeched him—could pull it off
precisely because he had been there before, MacNaughton's mansion.
That, at least, was their logic, that he would, toted satchel in tow, look less
suspect than any of them. That they would reckon the only weapon it possibly could contain, was words.
  And bring the dog with, they said, to make it look the more innocent
still.
  The dummy bomb was a wooden box, eight inches square, four high,
packed with ten pounds of facsimile dynamite and a hundred fulminating
blasting caps, over which was laid a layer of cotton saturated with cyanide
of potassium and sugar. And, slanting over that, a cork-sealed bottle of

sulfuric acid. In the cork was a pin, and attached to the pin was a rigged fish-line trip wire. When the satchel was opened—*kaboom.*

In theory.

Crude.

Place the phantom package gently upon the stoop, turn around, walk calmly away. Plenty of time. Witless. Idiot's work.

Bill. Ella. Ann. Each, in their way, had fingered the perfect candidate. They had succeeded in recruiting their man.

"LET NOT THE PILGRIM SEE HIMSELF AGAIN"

When he regained consciousness—how many weeks later?—Ana was there, leaning over him, speaking directly into his ear, the rind of it left, careful of his wounds. Later, he wondered how long she had been standing there, trying to buoy him back, yank him 'round, reel him free with the winch of her words. Through the gauze that hived his head he could not feel their warmth as she spoke, the breath of them there. As, of course, he could not see her, see anything, delineate linen-light from dark, or dove-gray.

What had happened? Where was he? Why? How long had he been lying here? What was going on? Why was he thinking these thoughts? He tried to blink inside the bandages. Tried again. Something felt exceedingly wrong.

He did not immediately identify the voice as hers, her words as quite words. Heard only indistinct sounds, inklings of garble, distant vocables endeavoring to forge their way from afar, fizzing and faint through a foreground of fuzzing—clicking, clacking, crickling, crackling, an intermittent dull-tinny, echoic ring—acoustic urtication. Vaguely human, it struck him, but—well, like someone shouting under motorized water, gurgling and gargling at submersive remove. Gradually—veil by veil?—his mind unlayered enough to outline the shapes of the words at his ear. Contour of audition.

Something had gone terribly, horribly wrong, she said. Wrong satchel. Live bomb. The explosive must prematurely have detonated. Something must have tripped it. He had caught the brunt of the bomb's blast with his body, the worst of it above the shoulders. The doctors had likened it to a combat wound, she said, concussive blunt trauma, flash burns. It was a miracle he still was alive, that his head hadn't been blown clean off its anchorage. All that had saved him, she said the doctors had speculated, was the obliqueness of the angle at which it had absorbed the impact, the *slant*, the truth at which the concussion had told.

He was "out of the woods" now, she said, out of imminent danger. The swelling on his brain had significantly subsided. There had been, miraculously, no major internal injuries. Notwithstanding, there was damage. His pelvis was fractured in three places. He had lost three of the fingers and the thumb on his left hand. Lost teeth. His nose was shattered. Jaw wired shut. His vocal chords were lacerated, eardrums badly punctured, *biauriculae* mangled.

None of this was the bad news.

"They tried their best to save your eyes, Frank, but the shrapnel—I'm so sorry, my love . . ."

He let it sink in, fought not to fight it. Encoached in his body cast beneath a single white sheet, flat on his back in the hospital bed, unpillowed head that of a mummy's, neck diapered thickly with batting and bandages, coffered as a coffin, he tried to remember that which he could not, never would, see with the eye of his mind—the only one left him—that which his unsighted eyes failed to recall.

It suddenly occurred to him to wonder whether they were open or closed. They felt open, but when he closed them inside the dressings, he could not feel the difference; this feeling of not feeling. Shuddered at the strangeness of absent sensation, shuddered more as it dawned on him what that meant, must portend. The taste of his tongue was fat as a toad; morphine coat. Tasting blood in his nose, he clutched at the sheet with his good hand, the one not obliterated to stub, crumpling a flag of it with his fingers, held on. Crash-landed alien. He wondered at the *utter* absence of light. Wondered, "What of the dog?"

Frank, the police are involved, she said. Technically, he wasn't under arrest, not yet. She wasn't even supposed to be here. A friendly nurse, old friend, had snuck her in. But once he was well enough to respond to their questions, they would be coming around. The rumors were rampant and none sounded hopeful. There were whispers, louder each day, that the police already had made up their minds that he was a saboteur in the pay of the Wobblies, that his job was just a cover.

She had wired Ivan, who had wired up the money she had used to secure the services of LeGendre.

He wondered who had found him, to whom he owed his life, the little of it left him, then damned that person to eternal perdition. His thoughts still drifted in that direction, impelled toward the past, one to which he clung as a shipwrecked sailor to a scrap of bobbing hull.

Look how white everything is, how quiet, how snowed-in.
I am learning peacefulness, lying by myself quietly
As the light on these white walls, this bed, these hands.
I am nobody; I have nothing to do with explosions.

He couldn't think about this any more. Closed his eyes—or did not, hard to tell—climbed aboard his magic carpet, rose swiftly into the air, hovered a moment, and, saluting farewell to his friends gathered on the raft of ground below—the *one*—floated morphined back to sleep.

Gaze upon white long enough, as he shortly would be learning, and it gradually grays to gray.

Charged with attempted murder, he was steered into the courtroom on a cot. His hearing had improved, but he could not stand or sit upright for long stretches. LeGendre battled honorably, but the outcome was fait accompli. The proceedings lasted less than a week. Found guilty, he was sentenced by Judge O'Brien to ten years without possibility of parole, to be served in the state penitentiary at Marquette. "Only the prisoner's physical condition," declared O'Brien, "prevents the court from imposing the maximum penalty allowable under the law. In light of the nature of that condition, however, any threat he potentially may pose to the welfare of society is, in the court's considered opinion, significantly mitigated.

"May these proceedings serve as warning to all those who would presume for any reason, whatever their motives, to take the law of our land into their own hands. To choose to play with fire is to risk being not only burned, but blinded."

Poetic, he thought. But where the justice?

Ivan had wanted to be there. Couldn't, of course. Had a paper to put out and no one he might count upon properly to put it. Wired up some dear words instead.

SORRY I AM NOT THERE. TO SEE. WOULD BE. GOOD LUCK. KEEP
BRAVE THE HEART. NO CRIME TO ME. NOT GUILTY. YOU DO RIGHT,
FRANK, RIGHT BY THE RIGHT. YOUR PLACE I HOLD OPEN. WHEN
YOU COME BACK. I CALL YOU HERO. IVAN.

These words that Ana, since miraculously recovered—miraculous being the doctors' word; her several symptoms had severally subsided as precipitously as they had presented—had had to read to him.

Franklyn served his time while Annie bided hers, remaining in Calumet
with her family where, while formalizing her divorce from Josef and enduring the strike's official end—Easter Day 1914—she gave birth to the
baby she immediately refused to have baptized.

The train trip to Marquette was 120 miles, yet in all those years she
visited him but once, some two months after the birth of their daughter,
when they were married by the prison chaplain. He did not want them,
new mother, new bride, new daughter, making such a journey. Wanted
her to remain at home, rear Darwina, lavish her with love—and truth—
the daughter he made her swear she never would bring anywhere near that
benighted place.

"I will not have it, Ann," he told her hoarsely in his new voice, gravel
through grate; sounded to himself like a burro, all bray. "I should go mad
were she to see me here this way, yourself as well. You must respect my
wishes, Ann. You must stay away. I know how much it is to ask, too much,
but—try to understand, it is not everything."

He promised he would write, find a way, enlist an amanuensis, that he
would write her every day, epithalamiums.

"I will do as you ask, Frank," she said, nonplussed. "I will try. What
you are asking is not fair. It is indefensible, the worst hardship, we both
know this. It may even be wrong. But I will do as you ask. I will do my best
to obey because you are my husband, because I am your wife, because you
are the father of my daughter, and we love you with our lives."

VISITATION

The trial made some little news back in Chicago. Not the front-page variety, no splash or sensation, tabloidish uproar, but it merited its below-

the-fold, inside-page play. Which accounted for the day, months and months later—or perhaps it was years, difficult to say—when Franklyn was fetched from his cell on the arm of a guard to the visitors' hold, where, having been seated at a table, he was greeted, nor awkwardly, by the only man it ever had occurred to him to call true friend.

"Frank, forgive me. I had to come."

He recognized the voice straightaway, and it made him want to weep. Couldn't, of course. When you lose your eyes, you lose your tears.

"Glad you're here, Floyd." When Franklyn extended his right hand in the voice's direction, Floyd took it too quickly in his own, gripping too tightly. "Welcome to the ashram." Paused. "So, appears I fucked up, eh?" Mustered what he imagined was a smile. "Fine mess, all this."

"Appears so," said Floyd Dell, too startled to relinquish his hold. His friend looked to have aged ten years since last he had seen him, sounded another ten years older than that. The dark glasses he wore but partially hid the rubble. Scars broad as handprints radiated from beneath the lenses, wrapped in jagged blazes back past each temple like wings of wayward lightning—Mercury's helmet, petasus. His neck, Floyd noticed, appeared stitched together, sewn in place, moonscape of welt and keloid weal.

"Ruined," thought Floyd. "My friend is a ruin."

"It's all right, Floyd, you can let go. Sort of selfish about it these days. Only one I have left, you know. Grown partial to keeping it close to the vest."

"Ach, sure, sorry." Unclasped. "Read about it in the papers. Swatty sends his regards, Marjy, too. They treating you decently here? If not, I'll see if I—"

"Oh, sure, decent enough. Three squares, all that. Guards go easy on the blinds. No threat. Got me slaving in their broom works, trustee. You need a bristle bound, I'm your man. Art of the clean sweep." He forced a laugh. "Made the rags, eh?"

"Well, stands to reason Molek was all over it."

Franklyn nodded. "Sent up the clips. Had a guard read them off. Damn white of him to say what he said—martyr to the cause, brother in arms, fallen knight of the pen. Ivan's a peach."

"Nothing you didn't deserve. *Trib* couldn't resist, of course."

"And?"

"Nothing. Played it square. Buried it though, page six."

"That sounds about right." He shook his head. "Pricks. And Floyd?"

"Frank?"

"You can dial it back some. I'm blind, not deaf. My hearing loss is only partial, but the part left is keen as a bat."

"Oh, was I doing that? Sorry. Didn't realize."

"Not a problem. You'd be surprised. Happens all the time."

A silence, neither uncomfortable nor awkward, but one between friends still friends.

"What the hell, Frank? What happened? Why? Guys like us don't die for our causes. We write for them. Christ!"

So he told him, all about it, the last soul he was ever to tell, the last he would consent to speak of it, reporter's version. ". . . And the next I remember, I'm coming to in the hospital and Ann's at my ear giving me the news that I'm blind, part deaf, can't talk, can't walk, telling me the cops are swarming all over it and I'm as good as gone, roast goose."

"Shit!"

"Yes. Precisely. That says it. Shit. Gooseshit. And shit cubed."

"Sorry, Frank." A halt, and then: "I need ask you something, as a friend. I feel I need to, ought to, but—"

"Out with it, Floyd. No word too ugly, not between us."

"Fine then. Frank, what the *hell* were you thinking?"

Franklyn smiled, scarecrowed, then removed his specs while Floyd involuntarily clenched his hand to a fist before lifting it like a punch to the open O of his mouth, biting down hard on the back of his knuckles. Where his friend's eyes should have been, once had, were a pair of lidless hollows, scoops of mangle, horribly chewed cud. His face looked uneyed by acid, zigzag of scar and of gum. Aprosopia and opacity; un-windowed soul.

"Truth? Wasn't Floyd, wasn't thinking at all. Thought a lot about it, as you can imagine. Comes down to this, I suppose: 'twas a loving gesture."

"Ah, yes. No doubt. Could only have been."

"Yes, a loving gesture. And so, entirely thoughtless. Of course, I know better, knew better then. No man acts, much less out of love, and walks away the same as before, unscathed. The piper only pipes for a fee."

"No good deed goes unpunished, eh?" When his friend shrugged, Floyd continued. "And would you again? Knowing what you know? I mean, now. Regrets?"

"Oh, sure, nothing but." Paused again. "Do it again? Dunno. I had come to a place, Floyd, arrived at its moment, you know? One of *those*.

Sort most of us live to skirt, hedge, duck, avoid. It found me, that's all, or I caught up with it."

"Ever the poet-philosopher, even now. Ever the mordant sage."

"Morbid? Nah. Macabre, maybe, not morbid."

"Mordant, Frank." Voice raised a notch. "I said 'mordant.'"

"Ha! Well, then, how not? One goes on living, no? Isn't that so? For laughs and love, if nothing else. For laughs and love in a time and place where laughter and loving are more precious than poems.

"Funny. All I ever wanted was to haunt my own life. Not the world's, not my wife's, and here it's come back 'round to haunt *me*. You don't find that funny, you've not the sense of humor I recall."

"Well," said Floyd, "imagine it helps. Don the brave face. One does as one must, whatever it takes. Personally? I couldn't. Haven't the temperament—or character—or strength of spine."

"No, Floyd. You could. No cakewalk, god knows, but you could. Anyone can. One suffers what one must withstand."

And now they both listened. Neither spoke, no more words. That was the peculiar sound they both heard. Strange, that neither had noticed it before.

"One of the lessons one learns in prison, Floyd—and the lessons, believe me, are countless—is that life is in the moment, and that its living takes its time. The trick is simply to waste along with it, fall in line, and to treat disappointment and defeat with the deference due them. And know what? Goddamnedest thing. What they are due, is everything."

Franklyn leaned across the table, lips behind his hand. "The secret, *cheri*, is to not do anything, but that most perfectly. And this is as good a place as any to do that. To leave undone that which can be left, but beautifully. Pain is just a latitude, son. Comes possessed of its own climate. And in weathering its ways, we all are the same, as one. I've been raped in the bung. It stung. But, Christ, it didn't *kill* me."

"You mean to say—Jesus, Frank!—you were . . . you've been . . . buggered? Christ!"

"Relax, Floyd. Figure of speech. My point is that what goes on in here is not *so* very different from what goes on outside. No sex, champagne, no caviar, no. Ain't summer camp, that's for sure. But when you think about it, as I do, all day, every day, every hour of the day, what happens is *mostly* the same—nothing to speak of, less to write home about.

"The moments pass. Some come, some go, some few linger longer. No one sees them, each so much one like the other, every other, one another. No one notes their music. No one much cares. None is alive enough to feel them as they flow, or hear them on the air. Love in, death out. Old news.

"We all find ourselves boxed inside the same locked and lidded cube. Only difference is, here mine's a little smaller, blacker, a lot less easily shed. Only difference is, mine is a zoo."

Paused again, for a much-needed breath—his lungs still weren't right, on occasion let him down unaccountably—pyramided his arms, braided his few fingers, propped his chin on their ledge. "Floyd, you are the only man I ever loved and damn well ever will." Extending his good arm, the one still attached with a whole hand, he slid it across the table. Floyd did the same. They touched.

"So listen to me now. Time will only bend so much, and the best any of us can do is deflect it some. Tick here, tock there. Tilt it toward—what? A better present? Less bitter end? I don't know. No one does. I'm out of answers, Floyd, if not out of words." He leaned back, taking his hand with him. "Perhaps I always was." He shrugged. "Or wanted to be."

Franklyn was not surprised when Floyd asked then—it *had* to come— "So what is it like? Being blind. To live with that, every day? What was taken away."

"Frightening, at first. Confusing, of course. Demoralizing. The sense of loss. Diminution of everything—one's manhood, humanity, all that. But then, in time, one learns to render unto shadows the darkness duly due them."

"Meaning?"

"Meaning that while something clearly is over, something else is more clearly begun. The streaming through. *That* doesn't stop, just because you can't see. The question remains: is it coming for me? So, I no longer can see it as it comes. So what? Perhaps, now, I no longer wish to. Let what's coming come. Let it come as it comes.

"Because here's what matters more, Floyd, and I don't mean Ann, I don't mean my daughter, though, of course, without them, the meaning of them, this all would be harder. No. What I mean is, every word is a melody waiting to be played, set in motion, and so they are, they depart, move, we see them go, wave farewell, one by one they leave the stage, each one a note fifed upon a flute, the music a thread through the pages of our lives, never finished, abandoned only, but each one meant to be beautiful, very beautiful.

"Being blind doesn't change that. Neither does being in prison. Would I rather my sight, my liberty? Sure. I am not mad, after all. But all this, the way it is, doesn't change a thing. That what I did, I did for Ann, and for my love of her, and her beauty, and not some dogma, doctrine, cause, or crusade, some fucking idea or ideal or the so-called morality twisted therein.

"Besides, incarceration always is more appalling in the abstract, the idea of it, its trope, than it is as lived experience. Endurable, less endurable, unendurable as the moment may determine, that which we are capable of imagining always is worse than real life. We fabricate, invent, artifice, then shudder at the fears our fictions foal."

"But all you've given up."

"But, Floyd, I've given up nothing, or not so very much. I've had some few things taken from me, true. Here and there a rug pulled out from under. But consider, none of us gets out of here alive, and in the meantime we endure. That's our job, and it's seldom Sweet Lorraine. Besides, taken all in all, I'd say I've lost less than I've gained."

"You mean the wife and child."

"Yes. I mean someone to love, besides myself, or ideas, or pictures, or words."

"Brave, Frank. Do you mind if I use that word? You're brave, not to be bitter."

"Oh, I've my moments, but that's what they are, *all* they are. Moments. Just moments. And what I've learned about moments, Floyd, is that there always are more where they came from, endless supply. Wherever you look, they're there, inside. Some will be worse, others worse still, and, on occasion, some will be less so. Like today, with you.

"As a kid—don't know if I ever told you this—but as a kid, I spent most of my time in the muck, ankle-deep. My folks owned a swamp, my second home. And do you know how you survive in a swamp? By not letting it bog you down, that's how.

"Do you know what a water strider is? *Gerris remigis*? Yes? The pond skater? Jesus bug? I used to study its moves by the hour. The way it walked on water, tiptoe and scull-sprint, one hundred body lengths per second, perfect equipoise of surface tension and drag. That's the same as a six-foot-tall man swimming four hundred miles per hour. Fast as miracle.

"I'm still that kid at heart, Floyd. And for the rest? Hey, fuck 'em. And bugger their children besides. They'll find no bullets in *my* back."

"No," said Floyd, "I imagine they won't. Still, damn shame."

Franklyn sensed it. "You need to be going, no? Long trip back. Glad you came. Means a lot, more than you know."

"Soon enough. I should. So, after they turn you loose, what plans?"

"Who knows? Move back to Chicago, maybe. Brush up on my Braille. Mobility training. Get a dog. Won't use a cane—drives them nuts here. Meet my daughter. Love my wife. Make love to her. A book maybe." He shrugged, slipped his glasses back on.

"Book?"

"What else am I gonna do? Blind men write, don't they?"

"Well, sure. Didn't mean to imply . . . Sure, why not? Thought about what?"

Shrugged again. "Nothing in particular. It'll come as it comes, or it won't. I've never planned a word I've ever written. How does anyone know what they know until they write it down, word for word after word."

"Well," said Floyd Dell, "you'll let me know how it goes. Let's not lose track. Keep in touch. Any help I can be—publishers, reviewers, critics—count on me. Least I can do."

"Thanks, Floyd. We'll see"—he laughed—"whether I have in me anything worth getting out—and down. I suspect I may, but who am I to say? And even if I do, need I share it? Should I? Is that the right thing to do? Use the little time left me that way? Perhaps I'd be better served just churning out brooms. Well"—he waved it off—"not your problem. Not at all."

Floyd needed to go. Franklyn stood up, outstretched his hand. They shook. Then, without letting go, Floyd slid around the rim of the table and embraced him. Mutual bear hug. "I'll write," said Floyd Dell.

"You'd better. My regards to Marjy. And tell Swatty I'm still waiting on that masterpiece."

"Aren't we all."

"Indeed, we are. The whole world, just holding its breath."

The guard was at his elbow.

"Keep well, Frank."

"See ya 'round the campus, Floyd." He laughed, at himself. "In a manner of speaking. You keep holding their feet to the fire, hold down the fort. Someone's gotta see to the dirty work. Might as well be a man with a mind, and a soul twice as big as his heart."

And then the guard led him away, back to his cellblock, back to his cell, the intolerable, ubiquitous stink of it, where Franklyn Shivs lay on his bed, curled to a question mark—or ampersand—alone in the dark, trying to fend off the tortured shrieks and torturing screams of a thousand grown men on every side while he inventoried in every fine detail each of the fictions he had just told his friend. You tried not to resent your life, and you failed, failed wretchedly, over and over again.

"Canceled history," he muttered to himself. Reduced to corpse's candle.

He was lost. It was chaos. How does one set about perfecting the art of reordering the soul that refuses rightly to be ordered or suture a new history beneath one's flesh?

So, the great falling now, downward and inward, the easing into the solitude of silence, its Long White, year-round.

"Kill them," he told himself. Every word an assassin, every sentence its own executioner. "Kill them. Kill them all."

So while her husband sat out the great war, blind, mute, in self-imposed silence and *durance vile*—and envying, too, Bill Haywood, if less his freedom and liberty than his remaining good eye—and the world convulsed on its axis, and the Continent insanely exploded, blasting itself into the sort of collective disfigurement that, by comparison, rendered of Franklyn's own little but that of a kid whose fireworks have gone off in his face, Ana reared their daughter with her parents' steadfast help in the very home where she once had been reared herself, regularly writing him of their child's precocious progress.

And when the Two Mothers, Mary Harris Jones and Ella Reeve Bloor, invited her—"Big Annie" now, coast to coast—to join them on the lucrative national lecture circuit, she wrote Franklyn that, desperately in need of the money, she had decided, "I feel we can ill afford to look this gift horse in the mouth, not at this time.

"It is an opportunity, Franklyn, to make some real money for once, and as much as I feel sorely the sacrifice of absenting myself from our daughter at such an inopportune moment, I feel I would be doing her future, and ours, a disservice were I to decline what so fortuitously has fallen our way. Besides, perhaps my words can do some good. So much remains to be done, after all. The struggle goes on. The wicked continue their war upon the righteous.

"Rest easy, husband, in the knowledge that our daughter is to be left in loving hands. She is with family. I must do this. Try to understand, it is much my duty to go. I owe it to Darwina. I owe it to myself and to you. I owe it to all the suffering, voiceless workers to raise my own in their behalf, all those who continue to labor deprived of their due by the very sufferance of those clay gods who comprise their deprivers."

There was more, but that was enough. Franklyn had the letter read and reread to him, multiple readings in rapid succession, with each recital endeavoring with declining success to stifle his increasingly mixed feelings, one of which was a creeping uneasiness, yet another grave and mounting misgivings. Certainly he was possessed of no wish to begrudge Annie the doing of anything she felt bounden to do. She would, he knew, do as she would in any event. She was upon the subject of her precious "workers" not to be right-reasoned with. What profit served in kicking against his stall? None. None at all.

Still, he didn't like it. Troubling enough, he thought, that at the first opportunity she chooses to put money ahead of motherhood, her vaunted "sacred duty" ahead of her child. More distressing still that she has fallen so beneath the spell of the Mother Joneses and Bloors of the world that she is willing to travel to the ends of the earth—the first leg of the tour, she had written, was to take her to Milwaukee, Chicago, Indiana, Ohio, Pennsylvania, West Virginia, onto Washington, D.C.—to do their rhetorical bidding.

He despised her being used this way, permitting her notice and notoriety, her currency, such as it was, to be manipulated and capitalized upon. "Minor fame," he thought, "can only be worse than none at all."

Not that she didn't have a point. They indeed could use the lucre, however filthy.

Still, one might have thought that all the death and disfigurement—and the birth of her child—would have tempered her enthusiasm, leavened her resolve, moved her to a measure of self-reflection, moderation, lowered the pilot a notch on her flame. Instead, it seemed only to have fueled it, where not indiscriminately fanned. That hers was a prodigal spirit, he knew. It was part of why he loved her so. That this in a real sense was largely his doing, he also knew. Who was more responsible for the creation of the creature the newsreels knew as "Big Annie," after all, than himself? But he couldn't help reading into what she had written a note of something far too susceptible to being wooed away by the worries and weights of the world.

For pity sakes, who needed the world? She was all the world he needed, wanted, ever again. He wished nothing but to put himself down, come to rest outside history, home at last, blind and blessed beside her, to inhabit her every margin. But he needed be honest with himself. How long had they been together prior to his being sent away? Five months? Six? By time's measure, it might be argued, not nearly long enough. And then all the hazard shared, violence witnessed, the way the high drama and emotional peripeteia had exaggerated everything, heightened and intensified the mutual passion, fractured all perspective, reason, right judgment, inevitably rendered the relationship wholly—what?—theatricalized? Farly-fetched? Overwrought? In any event, one to be pursued more blindly than not on little but faith and, so, perhaps, as he considered it now, not entirely to be trusted.

And so what did *this* bode? He did not know, could not have said. Perhaps he was borrowing trouble. Perhaps he was jumping the gun. Perhaps he was being consummately silly, or petty, or jealous, or arrantly dumb. Or perhaps he simply loathed the Mothers *deux* just that much. But now, having considered it in that light, it was none of those, but only this: he was right, and she? Wasn't.

You looked around, and what you saw, the little you saw, were capable of seeing, sickened you, until, having arrived at your immaculate moment at last, the realization that it is impossible to choose not to choose, declare, take sides, pledge an allegiance, align, forswear . . . He had looked life square in the eye, his own in like measure, and what he had seen there was trickery, mirage, illusion, and loss. This sleight, of sight.

"To be human," he thought, "is to be a killer. This is what we do. And where we do not, that is doing too. We cause as much pain as we feel, wreak the ruin we receive, harm and hurt even as we rationalize our doing so in the name of whatever aesthetic or system of belief seems best to comport with the circumstances of our moment, living moment.

"There are no noncombatants. In heaven perhaps, but not here. Life leaves no one alone, those who would stand aside and demur least of all. Everything, everyone, try as one might to flee from the truth, is the product of everything and everyone else."

Like it or not—and like it Franklyn Shivs *did* not—all is linkage, connection, consequence bereft of control. Life is impossible when we permit our reason to rule our appetites or rule *out* our basest affections.

HISTORICAL MARKERS

By the time Franklyn was released from prison—1924—the world had become to him a stranger, as he in like measure to it. Faster now, smaller, darker, more dangerous, the world, or, rather, the moment, when it might have veered this way or that, what the history books speak of as the "watershed" or "tipping point," had arrived and long gone. Revolution and war, mainly, had seen to that. Had he been capable of consulting a map, he would have recognized but a fraction of the names and shapes arrayed thereupon.

Lenin had died earlier that year, as had Woodrow Wilson. Stalin had inaugurated his purges, and Hitler just had been sentenced to five years in prison for his participation in the Beer Hall Putsch—he would serve but nine months, during which he would write *Mein Kampf.* J. Edgar Hoover had been named head of a new government agency called the Federal Bureau of Investigation, and the case of Leopold and Loeb, Darrow for the defense, dominated the news.

Franz Kafka had only just passed, as had Joseph Conrad and Anatole France, and some upstart Frenchman named André Breton was touting a new aesthetic he called Surrealism, which he unhelpfully defined as "pure psychic automatism." Serious readers were plowing their way through Thomas Mann's just-published *Magic Mountain*, Forster's *Passage to India*, Ford's *Some Do Not . . .* , and an old, recently rescued Herman Melville work entitled *Billy Budd, Foretopman.*

A musical called *No, No, Nanette* was playing in Chicago, and on the radio one could dial between the Paul Whiteman Orchestra's new renditions of Gershwin's "Rhapsody in Blue" and Berlin's "What'll I Do," or such popular tunes as Gus Khan's "It Had to Be You," Berlin's "Tea for Two," or Ma Rainey's more outré "See See Rider," though Bessie Smith's version of "Down Hearted Blues" still was going strong. Rudolph Valentino, while still the rage, was old news. D. W. Griffith's *Birth of a Nation* older news still. As were birth-control clinics, and something else clearly less beneficial, even shamelessly inimical, the inauguration of the Pulitzer so-called Prizes. Prohibition, and the Judas Eye speakeasies it had spawned, was half a dozen years along, women had had the vote long enough to elect their first governor, and Eugene O'Neill almost had penned enough plays to single-handedly drag the American theater toward some semblance of seriousness.

Ten years, an entire decade, a lost generation, nor to a soul more than himself. A World War. Revolution in Russia. A May Fourth Movement in China. Genocide in Armenia. An Easter rebellion in Ireland. Fascism in Italy. Killer influenza everywhere; the Spanish flu had killed twenty-one million worldwide. Dada, come and gone. The Bauhaus, going strong. Henry James, Jack London, Apollinaire, Proust, Buffalo Bill—*requiescat in pace.* A "Harmonium" and a "Wasteland," a "Mauberley." The calligrammes of Apollinaire and elegies of Rilke. *Dubliners, Portrait, Ulysses*— all done; the *Wake,* begun. Valéry's *La Jeune Parque,* his *Charmes,* the first volume of his *Varieté.* Lu Xun's "Diary of a Madman." WCW's *Kora in Hell.* Freud's "Memory and Melancholia."

And someone—he never was able to track down just who, though he was possessed of his certain suspicions—had, at interesting, if dubious, intervals, been sending him Firbank: *Vainglory, Inclinations, Caprice, Valmouth, The Flower Beneath the Foot.*

Airplanes and automobiles. Tanks, automatic rifles, poison gas. Dial telephones and commercial radio. The world's first news broadcast. Vitamins, insulin, frozen food. The atom had been split with alpha rays, yielding hydrogen, and the going theory was that once upon a time, in a galaxy not so *very* far away, the continents, too, had split, before, tectonically plated, drifting off one from the other. So, we all had had our origin in . . . *fragments!* Free-floating fragments, this most correct of all possible metaphors.

Ten years, a lifetime ago. He was forty-four, but in age alone. The rest of him felt ancient as weather.

Three years earlier, a broken Bill Haywood had moved to Moscow, where Emma Goldman had moved before him. The Wobblies were dead issue, anarchism deader still, the WFM deadest of all (the CA, disbanded at strike's end, had been replaced by the Anti-Socialist League, which immediately had coerced the relocation of the newspaper *Tyomies,* after fifteen years in Hancock, to Superior, Wisconsin).

Floyd Dell, officially divorced from Marjy at last, was nine years in Greenwich Village editing *The Masses* magazine, deflowering Edna St. Vincent Millay, mentoring John Reed, and resurrecting Stony Island Avenue on Washington Square.

Sherwood Anderson, having finally gotten around to writing his masterpiece—*Winesburg* had been published in 1919 to altogether merited accolade and acclaim (Franklyn had had the reviews and portions of the book read to him in jail)—was living unhappily in New Orleans with wife number three (of what, all told, would prove an insufficient five).

And Ivan Molek had risen to the editorship of *Prosveta*, "The Enlightenment," Chicago's socialist daily.

As for Franklyn Shivs, ex-con, he was at the moment of his release heels over head in love with a woman—or the idea of one—who had proved herself consummately capable of abiding by her promise to permit him to flagellate himself in solitude and peace.

Such abiding! Such heroism, really. He could conceive of nothing so miraculous as that, or more foreign to his own nature. He marveled at her certainty. Loathed and despised it. Needed it. Loathed and despised his need. Furious with himself.

There is but one reason to place another human being, one's inamorata most of all, upon a pedestal, and that is to shove her off, watch her fall, and for no reason save that one can. To lay her as low as oneself. Teach her abjection. Make her feel what it means abjectly to crawl.

HOME UPON A HELL

The last thing Franklyn wanted was to remain in Calumet.

The strike, as Ana had kept him abreast of its progress during his incarceration, officially had ended—petered out, perhaps, is closer to the truth—on Easter Sunday 1914, after eight months and twenty-one days, when, over Haywood's halfhearted objections, the union had significantly trimmed worker benefits and the strikers had voted five-to-one to end the work stoppage, a gesture that, by then, was little but a formality.

Now, ten years later, the region was in the midst of an economic freefall following the collapse of the copper market some five years earlier and the contemporaneous rise of the auto industry downstate. People were fleeing the Keweenaw in swarms, twenty-five thousand in the past three years alone, as C&H began for the first time to operate in the red.

On the other hand, neither was he eager to return to Chicago. The thought of reconnection was one he found not only dispiriting, but wrong. "The form of a city changes faster, alas!, than the heart of a mortal," Baudelaire once had observed, and, for now, change was the last quality toward which he felt charitably disposed. Except, he didn't know where else to go.

So he went, they did, the three of them, home, to Chi-town. Home, to begin making a home—or living an opéra bouffe. To count the hours, tally the cost, decipher the odds, and, in time, to launch the narrative that, it would not have occurred to any of them then, would prove noteworthy mainly for the magnitude of the mistreatment each of its members must perpetrate, one upon one, or the other.

When you are blind, he had discovered, the wind makes you happy because it makes you aware that there is something there—trees, say, or leaves. Its sound fills the emptiness, trumps the nothing with something, the audio and acoustics of air. To hear is to see. Like thunder. Thunder's good, too, because it furnishes you a roof, a canopy, a sense of height and up-thereness, celestial capacity. The thunder's your sky. Rain, as well, which, by and through its location, velocity, volume, intensity, its pitch and temperature and weight, renders the insubstantial solid; fragments coalesce—they smelt!—lending to the world some depth and dimension, contour and heft. And birdsong, he had discovered, was beautiful now, as were bell tones and carillon chimes. When you heard their tolling, the very encompassing atmosphere literally assumed the tone shape of their vibration and resonant essence. You lived, then, in those moments, *for* those moments, inhabiting their interior form, reverberation, percussion, breathing the air in, in *peals*.

Being blind in prison, he quickly discovered, was one thing, out in the wild-raw, woolly random world quite another. Existence inside had been same-y, routine, and routine to the newly blind can mean survival, as, too, a measure of dignity. Inside, he had been stewarded, parented in a sense, closely guarded and controlled, yes, but serviced too, shored up and supported, sheltered and provided a degree of managed care, if not caring. Certain expectations were unfailingly met. Prison life was clockwork, itinerary, agenda, schedule. Carceral culture is possessed of form and foundation, mapped according to lines and paths, those you are expected to walk, slots into which you are slid—or coerced, boxes into which you might fit. Regularity, predictability, a scrim of order, however imposed.

It had been infantilizing, no question, narrowing, and it could, as it so often had proved, be by turns dispiriting and infuriating, where not gratuitously humiliating. But it wasn't intimidating, nasty, threatening, or hostile, not as a rule, not once you reckoned its ways. However inflexible, inside was customary. You could rely on certain things. Not all of them were pleasant, of course, but they were familiar, or came to be. Prison was a net. When you fell, it caught you, tossed you roughly back up on your feet. A compass. When you lost your way, it pointed you, however imprecisely, in the right direction.

Inside, sounds strange, there were times when you scarcely missed your own eyes.

Franklyn once had considered routine little but living death, stasis. He remembered those days, the immaturity, arrogance, utter want of humility, the callow, cavalier, cocksure way he had valorized futility. Recalled what he once had told Floyd: "You cannot rely on what you can touch to remain that way. Nothing of the sort ever lasts. Only a dream, a vision, a poem, a thought never changes, never leaves, never absents itself. Only metaphor abides and sustains."

Well, attitudes alter. One grows into one's britches or is brought down a peg—or eight. Something to do less with age, perhaps, than with circumstances, the direness of their straits. Habit, convention, custom, ritual—these were the only anchors remaining to him now. Prison had been harbor, port in a storm, so that now, finding himself once again . . . anchorless, it was like being so far out to sea, so bereft of instrumentation, that he could not rightly tell windward from lee. And so sought dockage, as, too, to shrink the size of his ship, until he had arrived at something more navigable—a cramped South Side flat easy walking distance from Prairie Avenue: a room, a desk, a chair, a *den*, whatever he felt he could comfortably commodore and captain.

Where had he read the remark? "In his state of complete powerlessness, the individual perceives the time he has left to live as a brief reprieve." He had heard it said that in the dark, things don't get in the way, and it was true, some things did not. Ugliness, for one—though it bears mention that some objects that visually are ugly are tactilely quite beautiful—the things that you knew were there anyway. Those the Irish called the *peaca suil*, for another, the sins of the eyes. But other things did. Imagination, mainly. It was everything that was not there, but might be, that was so intolerable. It was beauty.

Ann tried to help, so did Darwina. His pair of polestars. Without them—who knew? How live when you cannot see advancing across your field of vision, even as you hear the rev of its gathering roar, the surge of the approaching tsunami? The light at the end of *his* tunnel? Couldn't see it, save in his dreams, where it looked awfully like the beam of an oncoming train—or full moon about to engulf him.

Ana was no longer "Big Annie," "Tall Annie," "Fighting Annie." All that had played out its string, long past. Currency seldom lasts; flavor of the month. Figure of romance? Object of nostalgia? Curio of curiosity? Historical footnote? Archival oddity? Not even that. She worked as a laundress now, like her mother, twelve-hour days cleaning up the mess others had made, Prairie Avenue matrons, the messes they were too busy to bother with. Seamstress work, too. He didn't like it, but they needed the dough. Still, as much as he hated it, she liked it less.

Hard enough to drag oneself through the day without having to remember what was, used to be, what once had been everything, without knowing what you knew, without looking in the mirror and seeing what you saw there, all of your everything behind you, the present your ongoing past. There is nothing quite so pathetic as the fallen and forgotten heroine, nor to a soul less than the fallen one herself.

And then there was her husband, whose husbanding—his of her—was what it wasn't: she, in fact, was husbanding him. He did little but sit bathrobed, unshaven in his chair, where, when not drinking—he had the stuff delivered while she was at work, had reconnected enough to know a local bootlegger—he scribbled illegibly in his notebook, the while complaining of Ménière's syndrome in his remaining good ear.

How was it, she thought, *when* was it, that the world had turned itself so upside down and wrong-side out? How did these things happen? Did one do them to oneself, or were they done to one? Who to blame? The world? God? The hands of merciless time?

So, naturally, she let herself go, much as he already had gone to pot. Not right away. These things take time. But, *in* time, she got fat, while he remained blind, a fact he could feel when he felt her. And unemployed, and increasingly drunk, and uncommunicative, and insular, like his dad, or purposefully saturnine, while she thought, "How chide him?"

Perhaps she reckoned that owing to his being unable to see, it didn't much matter. Why bother, make the effort? Or perhaps it was that, being from a place like Calumet, she found the impersonal glamour of the city less than everything her mind had cracked it up to be or its empty promise of excitement more or less than she could handle. In any event, she grew huge and hugely enormous while Darwina incliningly remained the sole epoxy between them. Because they both loved her, doted, hung on for dear life. And a good lot to hang on to—big girl, like her mom.

Their daughter was the best of them both.

FATHER AND DAUGHTER

"Winnie, do the other kids ever tease you? Are they mean?"

"Why, Daddy? Why would they? No."

"Well, you know. Because you have a father who can't see and wears dark glasses all the time, like a mask, and these ugly scars." Which he had himself never seen, of course, save with the tips of his fingers. "C'mon, Win, I *am* kinda different than other daddies, wouldn't you say?"

"Yeah, okay, but not in a bad way. They don't tease. They just ask questions sometimes, that's all."

"Like?"

"I dunno. Like, what's it like? How come? Does it hurt? Did you come that way? One time Sadie asked if she could see underneath. Graham wanted to touch it. Stuff like that."

"So what do you tell them?"

"Nothing. To ask you."

"Ask me?"

"You know, if they wanna know, to ask you, not me. How I am supposed to know?"

"Right. But they never do."

"What?"

"They never ask."

"Nope."

"Why, do you think?

"'Cause they're scared to. Some of 'em don't even like to look."

"And some do."

"Yeah. I tell 'em to quit it."

"Why?"

"'Cause it's not nice. You can't see back."

"It's okay, you can let 'em look, doesn't bother me. They're just curious. It's natural."

"Yeah, I know, but it's not right."

"Why?"

"'Cause I know what they're thinking."

"What?"

"That they wanna make fun, but they won't, cuz I'm there."

"You're my protector, huh?"

"I *am*."

"Thanks, Win, but you don't have to, you know."

"I know, but I *want* to."

"Did Mommy tell you to?"

"Un-uh. Just me."

"That makes me feel good, Win. But try not to be too hard on your friends, and tell 'em not to be scared. Tell 'em I don't bite—*that* hard."

She laughed.

"Hey, Winnie, know what?"

"What?"

"I love you, apple of my eyes, both of 'em."

"I love you too, Daddy."

"Got a smooch?"

"Sure."

She was free with her kisses, generous. Wet kisses warm, fishes and finches, if finches could kiss, or fish. Infinite supply. With him. Lifted up his glasses. That was her way, the code between them. One on the left, tenderly. One on the right, gently. Gestures of healing. He still had feeling there, barely.

He never had seen his daughter's face, could not now, never would. Projected, of course, created a mental image with his fingertips, one he married to her voice, her face arisen of its texture, the tone of its sound. He found that what was said was true, that when one lost one sense, others, another, in compensation grew more acute, sensitive, refined, attuned. He seemed able to "read" with his ears now, detect and perceive, interpret nuances of modulation and inflection, subtleties of rhythm and diction that he could not recall having heard before, at least not with such kerosene clarity. As well as the facility, if that it was what, to "sense" presences, the actual physical sensation, a pressure—alteration of air current?—of an awareness of objects. Not unfailingly, but often enough to steer his way clear of most imminent calamities. What they meant by sixth sense? The way certain animals "scent"? What the Old Top Bard himself had meant when he spoke, in Sonnet 23, of hearing with the eyes?

"Like a bat," he thought. "Antennae of echolocation."

Seeing is knowing. He had believed that once, seeing through and around. He hadn't been wrong, far as he had gone, just hadn't gone far enough. Because *not* seeing, he had come to understand, is knowing too, in a way, its own way. Sightless knowledge. There was that as well, nor less true.

"Daddy?"

"What is it, Win?"

"I wish you could see me."

"Me too, sweetie. But know what?"

"What?"

"Sometimes I can—almost."

"Really? How?"

"Well, when you sit on my lap and read to me, I can smell the way you smell. And when we hug, I can feel the way you feel. And when I kiss you, I can taste the way you taste. And when you talk, I can hear in your voice if you're happy or sad, angry or bored or excited. I can see your face in your voice."

"You can?"

"Yep, I can. Not all the way, but partly, mostly."

"Wow! What parts?"

"What?"

"What parts of my face can you see?"

"All the good parts. I can see all the best parts."

"My eyes?"

"Well, sure, sure I can."

"So what do they look like?"

"Well, there's two of 'em. Right so far? And they're dark brown. And when you're angry, they flash, and when you're surprised, they open up real wide, and they're beautiful, all the time."

"Right! That's right! You *can* see me!"

Wasn't true, of course. She was blank, vacant frame, null and void. Whether she knew this or not, fully understood that he could not see her and never would, was another matter, but it was that very blankness that he cherished now more than any rich or resplendent image he ever had seen, any sight he could vividly recollect, any dream. The nothingness that was her meant more to him than anything in all the rest of the grayed and grayless world.

DOWNHILL, RACING

And then three things happened. Well, more than three things, of course. But things do happen in threes, and so they did now. Three in particular happened that you could point to, name, put a proverbial finger on later, looking back, when looking back was all that remained, when what seemed to matter most, and only, was casting assignable blame.

#1

He began to experience difficulty. He had sensed it that first time, when they had made love, after he had come out. Something was different about fucking blind. One needed to see sex to have it, that always had been a necessity with him. He didn't like making love in the dark. It felt wrong, shorted of circuit somehow. Visual gynocrat. He had to see: faces and genitalia, penetralia, which, as he considered it, had faces of their own. The experience had to be *graphic*. In a sense, sight *was* sensation, sensation sight, the audium was the sensorium and so the converse, and what else, finally, was life? Without eyes, making love felt too much like masturbation, and masturbation, while fun at times—"Cleaner, more efficient, and you meet a better class of person," as Wilde liked to say—in its own moment, was, finally, a lie.

So gradually his appetite waned, until it had abandoned him altogether. Yet more loss, loss upon loss. But this, he found, more than he might gracefully bear. His sense of himself, already so curtailed, now was limp as old string. Dead-in-the-pants, no creature stirred, no minnow moused. Which, in turn, led to too many inevitable moments.

"What is wrong now?"

"Nothing. Why do you say that?"

"You are not here again. I can feel it. You are someplace else."

"That's not true. What do you mean? I'm here. Here I am, Ann. Right here."

"No. You are not. You may be someplace, but wherever you are, here you are not. You are off to wherever you go."

"How can you say that? How do you know where I am? How can you possibly? You're the queen of fucking prolepsis now? I know where I am. How can you presume to tell me where I am or am not? You can read minds now? You don't know."

"Fine. I do not know. I do not know anything. I give up. Let us just not do this."

"Fine. We won't. We won't do it. Anymore. Agreed? Ever again."

"Is that what you want? If that is what you want, fine, we will not. Is that what you want?"

"No, it's not what I want."

"Then what? From me. From me you want what? What is it? Contrition? Remorse? To lay down and die? Is that what you want, Frank? That I should just die?"

"What I want is to go back to the way we were before. You want to know what I want? That's what I want."

"So, let us try. Let us try, at least."

"I do. I do try."

"So try harder. You try harder, and I will try harder, and we will make it work, together."

"But it's not supposed to be this hard, is it? Isn't it just supposed to happen? We shouldn't have to try, to work, so hard. This shouldn't be work, it should be play, fun. For Chrissake, it used to be fun."

"Well, it is not fun for me, either. Do you believe this is fun for me? This has not been fun for me since the day you got out. What happened, Frank? What happened in there? What happened to you?"

"What happened? Whatever you imagined happened, happened. Ten years happened. The discovery that truth leads to nothing but violence, more violence, and that life—and love—are as impossible as one makes them.

"Shall I go on? Because I can, Ann, go on. A bomb, *your* bomb, went off in what used to be my face, and it keeps on going off every moment of every day. I can't fucking"—this next emerged as rather more of a distended, elongated howl than he had intended—"*see* you."

And now she purpled, was purpling. "*My* bomb? Fuck you, Frank. I mean it. Go fuck yourself."

The tongue, he thought, smiling, was a barge, or scow, and it can bear only so much weight before it must divest itself. So, good, very good, truer words never were, or wise. No glossaries of forgiveness begged here or borrowed, no recantations whispered in the ear.

And then there was the muffled sound of a child's soft crying, and a knock on the bedroom door.

#2

For Christmas, Darwina had been given a new sled. Veneered, rich blond wood decking with outspread painted-on wings, red whetted blades, waxed-up runners, adjustable steering prow, stiff white tow rope. A beauty she had named Rosebud. Flexible Flyer.

Most of her girlfriends preferred figure skating, executing their eights

and twirls, leaps, spins, but Darwina was a daredevil sledder, or tobog-
ganer when afforded the chance. Didn't sit upright using the rope as a rein,
but laid full-out, flat on her stomach and chest, headfirst bullet.

The hill wasn't far, a few blocks over, in the park. The older kids liked
it because its four lighted slopes—"The Pipeline," "Lightning," "Runaway,"
and "Bloody Nose"—caught the full face of the sun by day, which melted
the top stratas of snow, which froze to ice at night, and because the hill was
staggered in a succession of steep tiers; you flew their rock-hard scrims
like a ski jumper, scrims so slick you didn't even need a real sled to sleigh
them. A lot of the older kids just used cardboard boxes or wooden crates.
But with a sled, you sped, and Darwina liked speed. Flier of flowstone.
Besides, it got her out of the house at night, which is when things always
were worst, when Mom came home, and the two of them went at it.

Walking mufflered and mittened over to the park, crunch of rubber
boot, toting the sled behind her over hardpack snow—teary-cold, but
windless, a clear-through sky starry as teardrops—she thought about how
much she couldn't stand it, and how it made her sad. More sad than angry,
okay, but angry sometimes, too. She had lost track of the number of times
she had had to play peacemaker. Too many. She didn't like being put in
that position, in between. Wasn't fair.

She could see the bright lights of the hill through the trees. Then,
angling off the walkway, down the curb, crossing the road, she was onto
the pathways of the park. She could hear the kids whooping and laughing,
see some of them throwing themselves like seals down the slant of the
slope, bouncing wildly tier to tier. She saw Graham climbing back up from
below, waved as he waved back.

Arriving at hill's crest, she surveyed it for traffic, chose her chute of
clear, its fall line, then lifted her sled, took her running start, flung herself
headlong and downward smoothing across the glaze of ice, rush of wind
in her face, *whapping* in her ears. All smile. Coast.

She neither saw nor heard the second sled, the longer, larger, much
faster one, the one piloted by the seventeen-year-old boy, football star,
boring down on her, careening crazily from the left and behind, cowcatcher out of control. Nor did she feel it, particularly, when he plowed
into her, shearing over her, embrangling her arm, yanking her from her perch,
driving her head hard to the ice, sending her tumbling sprawled on her back,
arms still hooked into the slots of his sled, sliding limply down the hill.

Nor, having blacked out on impact, could she have been aware of the rooster tail of blood that, as she continued flying tier to tier, head bouncing hard against and off the ice, trailed in her wake beneath the glare of the lights. Or the cockeyed, unnatural angle at which her left arm was hasped like a second elbow beneath the elbow, its exposed and shattered bones—ulna and radius both—poking jaggedly up through her mangled flesh.

The doctors couldn't set the breaks, too much shatter and damage, dead nerve, minced muscle. There are—what?—two, three dozen muscles in the human arm, and most of them, each of the extensors and flexors and so forth, either were severed or a hopelessly mangled mess. Her humerus, they said, still could be salvaged, but her radius and ulnar bones . . . There were no appliances then—rods, bolts, screws, clamps, no slotted plates or Eggers splint, auto- or allografts. To leave it alone, said the doctors, would risk gangrene.

So everything became blame then. When they were of the mind, her parents could impale each other like picadors. Terrible, to have to listen to it, the sound of the knife in their nails.

Somehow, kids see it through, see through it, and Darwina, despite the loss of her limb, remained all spirit and spunk, sheer champ. In time, she even climbed back aboard her sled: Darwina of the Sleighs.

It was her parents. What had been bad before, worsened, until the dread dromedary, that humped, silent intruder, slipped through the cracks, or under the door, clambered in through the windows, down from the attic, up through the floor, lay down upon the hearth, and simply . . . waited. The straw would come, its single strand. Fall silent as shadows. Ruined as worlds.

And when Darwina awoke now, or slipped off to troubled sleep, it was with a camel kneeling knurled upon her chest as if to burst in two beneath its heft the height of her only heart.

#3

He had spent ten years tunneling toward the truth of what remained still beyond reach: to survive the prison of life, one must learn to become a lockpick or safecrack, cat-burgling thief. Takes one to catch one, wasn't that how it went or would eventually go? One learns to serve one's sentence by taking it *a word at a time.*

Still, when he thought about it now, which was not often, not so often at all, really, not nearly often enough, he was the first to admit that he probably ought not have hit her, or, at least, hit her in just that way. So damn hard. The one person in the world he ought better have loved. If only he had thought to use his open hand instead of his fist, or ceased in midkick, or permitted his sobbing daughter in her shrieking to restrain him, instead, in his rage, of flinging her aside like a feather. He still couldn't say why he had done what he'd done. To his *wife*. So blindly struck out. Drawn so much innocent blood.

"Well," he thought, "spend a celibate decade sometime in a ten-by-ten-foot unpadded cell and see how well you handle it upon being set free to wreak as you will."

Remorse, contrition, contrition, remorse, words are just words, they die from misuse or abstention, or are silenced in vitro, censored stillborn. But violence and abuse ever last and live on across tundras of lifetimes, concuss what their sempiternal echo bequeaths.

A blind man, maimed, drunk, hellbent upon making up for time lost—*snaps*—lashes out without aim, flails . . . blindly. In the wild moment, knocks his beautiful wife flat to the floor landing a foot flush to her face. Where, crying and spitting a tooth, she lay bleeding, all six-feet-two of her, two hundred pounds, from both lips and an impacted knee.

So what had set him off *this* time? Did it matter? Really? Something she'd said? Or perhaps just her tone, the way it assailed, never left him alone, tried to paint him with the sound of its colors inside her frame, pin him like pigment enclosed in the box of its borders, cubed and contained.

And then they are gone, packed up and fled, headed north, so she said, back to the Keweenaw—home. And you know that this time it's for good, as, too, for the best. Wife, child, family, love. Life. All these I had lost—*I* had—as if they were no more than spare keys.

The art of losing is not difficult to master, for loss is seldom what we think it is—it *always* is less.

Rising from my chair, I shuffled unslippered in my robes damp with piss to the phonograph, switched it on, unclicked the worn arm from the clasp of its cradle, snicked—fumbling—the needle to the 78's familiar first groove, a pirated recording of Ives's *The Unanswered Question* performed by . . . well, who knew?—shambled my way back and—unshaven, unclean, largely unkeeled—sank into the yellow heaven of my ammonia-soaked chair, its obliterating whiff of orange squash and gin, urine and beer, where it occurred to me that I had gotten it all terribly wrong. What-ever *it* might be, *pretend* to be.

What's ahead, down the road, we wish to see, itch to know, and all we are assayed are questions, more questions.

Placing in succession to one side, then the other, with the exaggerated care of the incrementally inebriated, my inscribed Braille copies of *Prancing Nigger* and *Concerning the Eccentricities of Cardinal Pirelli*, I slipped slipshod and sodden, sloshing sloppily to the floor where, blackly beetled, roach on its back, I commenced to laugh uproariously in salivaed paroxysms and spittled arpeggios, unseemly sprays, Valkyrian peals, foam-enriched brays.

We now **hear** *undeniable rays of light*, Mallarmé said.

But I'm not so certain I ever did.

"Well," I thought, "at least no one can turn the lights off on me, not anymore. My body cannot feel what my eyes should see best, and I can see everything, and everything's black, black beyond *noir*, reversion to void, pure zero, to zed, black with despair and with all I've misspent, black with the wan hope of a moment's tear shed.

"*What cannot be said*, wrote Sappho—didn't she?—*will get wept*.

"God! All the voluptuous millions I've so mindlessly squandered. All the umpteens unseen, left *un*wept."

And why not? As it began begat in darkness, so let it end, beshat.

Memory's wink is a wick, and the wick is wet.

Fishing out a matchbook, I flipped back its cover and, without closing it first, struck a fresh match. Held the flame to my face, let it inch down its length. Felt its heat vector, valence there, weevil some, caress crisscross my scars. Felt the singe surge the tips of my fingers and—stared. Imagined my-self staring. Imagined myself one with the fire. Wet a thumb, pinched it out, second try, smelled the sulfur, inhaled the smoke, burning flesh.

Only the willow tearlessly weeps.

I felt to myself made of wood. Deadfall, tinder, sawdust, scrub. Lit an-other match. Let it burn to its stub.

Let it burn.

When I thought of Darwina—as infrequently as possible, frankly—when I thought of my daughter in those moments when I permitted myself to do so, or, more often, as they intruded unbidden, hit me up unawares, I missed her, desperately, and that with the best of my heart. Regrettably, it being but half there, my heart, and half dead besides, it might reasonably have been argued that that was scarcely enough to suffice, or abide. Not that I did not wish that it might have been otherwise. Of course I did. But that is precisely what my wishing remained: wishing. Besides, better off with her mother. Better off without me.

Not that I didn't write on occasion, if not as often as I might, perhaps should have, but . . .

Not that she ever wrote back.

Not that I ever dared blame her.

Dear, dear love—

The one phrase you can take to the bank without fear of rebuttal: the odds are all—every flop, flip, toss-roll, and spin, every round wheel whirled without reason or unwired rim—every damn one with the host of the house. It's not that there are no winners, dear Win. There are winners aplenty, always have been and will be. It's that the winners are all the same one, the one that's not we.

There is a cost, daughter, you see, to forgiving oneself nothing; it is this: impossibly dear. To recognize that life is monotony, time a cheap trick, and that the loss of them both is the price we must bear. We wait as we wallow, to be shown to our seat, retreat to our den, there to shuffle our papers and piss out our pens, to watch what must end, eyeless in exit, existence a cheat.

Just because you kill something, Win, doesn't mean it is dead. I never stopped loving you, for instance, not for an instant. And yet, it is only when you cease feeling, stop seeing what you feel, that you can get shed of yourself, peel free enough to chance an ascent.

Someday a writer will write, "Hell is other people." Someday a poet will write, "I myself am Hell."

As soon as there is <u>only</u> yourself, there is nobody. And nobody is everyone, everywhere. Mezentius had the right idea.

What quality more abhorrent than zeal?

The cosmos, Win, exists only on paper, a matter of writing. The infinite is only a word, and words are little but puppets. We mouth syllables in the dark. The so-called just and humane are great fools or, where not, greater bores still, where not stupid and

confused. Humanity, justice, compassion—these are words, nothing more, words written in water and smoke. They mean nothing.

What is required of us is to see through them, past them,
around them, to what *is*. What is required is to avoid making
mistakes, even beautiful ones. What is required is to develop self-
sufficiency of singular mind, and its mastery. No beginnings, endings, presence only, and the problem with which we all, in like
measure, are saddled—to be here, now, this moment, as fully here
and now as is humanly possible, present in the presence of the
Present, alive in every neuron to the truth that no life resonates
beyond the walls of its own well; no wake, ripple, no repercussion.
The only echo worth hearing, daughter, is silence, the way it per-
sists, the way its persistence insists that we seek, among our many
myths, the clarity of vision to apprehend the way we must <u>consist</u>.
Everything else is as contemptible and wretched as it is perfectly
pointless.

So then, can I extract from you a promise? No reason you
should keep it, and yet . . . promise me, Win, that you will refuse
to believe what they say, that he who dies in despair has lived his
whole life in vain. I am your father. Listen to me. The truth is,
whether you die alone in despair, or bundled bound warm and at
peace in the grace of your faith succored by family and friends, we
all, no exception, live our lives in vain. There is a reason for this,
the best one in the world: it is because it is the very best any of us
can do. All endings are bitter, daughter. My own shall be no less.
Nothing comes true save the worst of our fears. Our very existence stands as our reproach: guilty! Of being alive. We live less
ramified with life than rammed <u>into</u>.

So a last quote, then, after which I shall cease and desist, never
to trouble you further. From Job 7:11, "Therefore I will not refrain
my mouth; I will speak in the anguish of my spirit; I will complain in the bitterness of my soul," of this world forgone but not
yet endeth, for spite of which "I spit my last breath. At thee."

What comes next, Win, is always the same: you roll the dice—
which are loaded, hazard by chance—close your eyes, if you are
fortunate enough to have them to close, and pray that they never
cease rolling, that the play never ends, that the game might continue, that the music of the moment only swells and outspreads,

surges, swarms, expands, and extends. Because there always is another story, on top, underneath, alongside, the one that goes unheard because unsung, unread because unwritten, unacknowledged because too brute to bravely withstand or forbear. It lies mute in the margins, out of mind, beyond sight—the eye, after all, however musically, can see only what it never can mouth—and we close our ears to the hymns of its silence only at our peril. Which is not our prerogative. Oh, sure, we may as we might, pretend it's not there, and most of us do, but in truth? No, we haven't the right.

Words fail none but the blind.

The good news, it has been said, is that the future exists, the bad that we doubtless shall have little choice but to live in it. What can our being here be about, then, but the need to fall silent at the very moment of exchange and disclosure, of human connection? What else must it mean but that moment? Its wayward vision so valveless, unvaunted, so castaway that it can avail of little but that fate which is one and the same with the plunge of our plight. Its approaching silence, incrassated absence, final as the blindness of peace.

'Tis naught but our devastation, Win, that each of us races to reach. Not love, which probably is not possible, or where it is, is never enough, but the loss that awaits us at the moment we breach, the perishability of all that once mattered, all we misconstrued for our best, and all we believed it must mean. Difficult to argue that man is an <u>entirely</u> useless passion, but there is not a one of us that, time to time, does not have his moments, the very ones to which we are as strapped as is the blast to its bomb.

Life may be fleeting. It seldom is gossamer, diaphanous, sheer. You can't see into or through it, grind it to glass, chisel it lucent, inscribe it in tears. Too opaque, slant, shortshrifted, unclear. You pays down your monies, hazards your choice: <u>maudit or manque</u>. No other, just that, it's the end that appalls. Rapture's the bunk. What descends is what stays, and what stays, stays the same. None, Win, not one, none are that brave.

But buck up, daughter. Not all is loss. Not as long as lack of belief cleanses the mind, and absence of faith the soul. Nowhere is it written, after all, that the blind cannot lead the blind and still emerge smelling like a rose, or whatever is ineluctably worse.

You still are young. You still have all the time in the world to teach your own children the truth of it. About prodigality, yes. And lassitude, too. But

Mid-sentence, enamored of the gesture above all others, I . . . shrugged.

In his den, at his desk, emptied bottle of mescal at his feet on the floor, slumped naked in his chair before the typewriter, head pitched forward come to repose upon the platen, they found what was left of him weeks later. Splooze. Slosh. The stench of him stank.

Difficult, then, through the damage done to the paper by the fester of flesh and its fluids, to make out *exactly* what his last line had been, however blank. The police tried, but the best they could come up with—not that it made to them a soupçon of sense, pure speculation—was something along the lines of: "Indifference, Win—never forget—indifference comes first, before all."

Whatever it actually said, however it ought rightly have read, the most they could say, were willing to say, is that it appeared to have been written, each letter of each word, in CAPS.

We wither, whitening, into the truth; no resolution, less catharsis; truth rhymes with brute.

Or do we?

Perhaps, rather, while marking time, waiting for nothing to happen, the nothing that is everything, we dissolve toward it, blind, besotted, bestank, bounden to see its beauty with none but the withholding eye.

Perhaps, as Franklyn Shivs was convinced, life requires a measure of ruin to render its right-reading worth the writing of its draft, as that those few fragments we would feebly shore, riprap against its wreck, serve neither to save nor to salvage us, but simply, in the moment, for the moment, so long as the moment may last, to arrest—pilfered, impoverished, unparsed—the sundering of our sight; SCRAP.

FAMILY PLOT

◆ ◆ ◆

I wanted to . . . resurrect history that had belonged to me before *memory.*

WILLIAM KENNEDY

No fact was ever less
a fact
than one tortured
into poetry.

WILLIAM LOGAN

We are much more (and sometimes much less) than what we have done.

VALÉRY

See: this much was accomplished. A life, perhaps, was made too little of.

RILKE

Three years before the Great Keweenaw Copper Range Strike, my great-grandfather, James Olds, was killed in the mines at Red Jacket, crushed, then smothered to death beneath tons of fallen rock. What we mean, in fact, when we say "buried alive." One moment living, the next, not.

The weight of that moment fell, at once and as redoubled, upon the heads of his sons, his eldest, eleven-year-old James Cleo, and when Cleo died a year later, his younger brother, nine-year-old George, my grand-father.

His father's death, the arbitrary fact of his sudden absence in his life, his being left so abruptly, achingly fatherless, that loss was, as I recollect him confiding to me on numerous occasions, the defining moment of George's life, as, just as surely, it shaped the manner in which he reared his own children, one of whom was my father, his eldest, another Cleo, as it in turn dictated the rearing of Cleo's own and only son.

The past is concussive; it outdistances us all. A detonation, its reso-nances travel with us far beyond the graves of those with whom we share our name, all those we never knew save as stray image or orphaned strand of story. Every generation processes, each in its own fashion, the failures, frailties, doubts, and debilities of the one preceding it. This warp to the weave of every history's woof.

Upon George's death, in 1982, we discovered that he had left behind a document, one he apparently had been working on during the several years of his retirement. Its last words, those bracketed in parens at the bot-tom of the final page, read (to be cont'd.). It never was. We have what we have, the little we have.

I would have much preferred that he had bestowed upon me his per-mission and blessing in advance of my transcribing it here. Knowing my grandfather, I am confident that that would not have posed a problem, and it is only owing to that knowledge that I am able to muster the temerity to make what surely is so very private, so public.

A distracted, underachieving student, my grandfather left school in the eighth grade. He was not proud of his having done so, and repeatedly called it both the biggest mistake and deepest regret of his life. He was an intellectually curious, highly opinionated man hungry to share his opin-ions, but there were few subjects about which he was more vocal than the value of what he typically called "a quality education." Certainly he did his best to make up for lost time, for he seemed always to be at the beginning, in the middle, or approaching the end of some doorstop-length book, and he enjoyed sharing and discussing their contents, as he did the frank and vociferous jousting among opposed ideas.

Indeed, the undisguised pugnacity with which he invigorated his exchanges, the combative passion of the way he went at it, the contagious way he made it seem so *much* to matter, the declarative, cigar-punctuated manner of his self-expression struck me, the child of a quieter, more sedate, less notionally inclined suburban America, as a sort of manly sport. If my own regard for and sensitivity to both the spoken and written word is keener than not—as, too, my fascination with history and heritage—it is owing, I might argue, in no small part to him. Less raconteur than polemicist, he could, on occasion—especially when telling a story cherry-plucked from his past—be a spellbinder.

During those moments, he made me feel a part of something beyond myself, no small accomplishment. I didn't idolize him—I had other idols in those days: Eddie Mathews, Rocky Colavito, Ray Bluth, Robbie Robinson—but I found my grandfather endlessly captivating, and, too, dear. I enjoyed his company. Adored it, actually. To many—colleagues, friends, family—he was a most difficult, contentious, even irascible man, and yet, I have known few people in my life whose company I have enjoyed quite so much, or for whose presence my appetite was so unconditionally boundless.

I have chosen to reproduce his words raw and unedited, if not entirely unmediated—I have corrected punctuation and spelling errors—not only because I am disinclined to tamper or meddle with his voice, but because, quite simply, it does not need it. Little more than a casual letter writer himself, he valued and enjoyed the act of self-expression, though it would be only shortly before his death that, as he thought to tell me in a handwritten letter, I understood just how much. The pride he took in my professional "choice" was more than a little apparent.

So, best, I believe, that his words be permitted to speak for themselves, though whether what they speak are volumes, surely I am the last to say.

> *it's the work of getting it right*
> *in a moment*
> *no cornball monument*
> *just a statement of who where*
> *when it was what*

DAVID MELTZER

Earlier that year my parents had lost a son, aged one. Then, on June 18, 1910, the most horrible thing happened. My father was in a copper-mine accident that killed him instantly. There was an "air blast" that caused a cave-in, tons of falling rock, and he was crushed under a huge slab that broke every bone in his body. He was thirty-seven years old. He had worked in the mines since the age of ten.

It was early Saturday morning before breakfast. I was eight years old. I threw on some clothes and ran out to Tamarack Mine No. 2 Shaft. I didn't know it then, but No. 2 was what the men called the "jinx shaft," because even though it was the company's best producer, more men had died in it than any other. Almost fifty men died in No. 2 in the thirty years it was worked, twice as many as any other.

I was late. The helmet crew had brought Dad up from underground a couple hours before. I looked for him everywhere. Everywhere I could think to look. When I couldn't find him or anyone to tell me where he was or where they had taken him, his body, I sat there until the day-shift miners came up that evening. One of them took me home for supper.

I don't remember what I was thinking. I don't know if I knew even then. I don't remember feeling anything. I don't remember eating, or if I did, what I ate. I don't remember crying. Maybe I did. I sure did later.

Mother got $1,000 in insurance from Tamarack and was lucky to get that because it was the first year the company had begun carrying insurance on their workers. So Mother was left a widow with five boys. The oldest was my brother James Cleo, eleven years old. A year later, on my ninth birthday, he died of the "black diphtheria." I became the oldest.

To keep the family going, Mother converted our three-bedroom home on Elm Street into a roominghouse for miners. She took one of the rooms for herself, had the four of us sleep together in another, and set the third aside for boarders, six of them in three bunkbeds, sometimes a seventh and eighth on the floor. Tamarack owned our house and set the rent. Mother paid $8 a month.

On the day Dad was killed, I believe I became bitter towards life and everything in it. I missed him all the time. I miss him to this day. Mother was the best, but she wasn't Father. I feel I never had him in my life long enough.

I went right out and got two newspaper routes. I passed out the Minneapolis *Tribune* for 75 cents a week and the *Blade* and *Ledger* magazines for $1.25 a week. In season I picked and cleaned strawberries, raspberries, and thimble berries three days a week and sold them to the rich people. In December of each year I cut down and sold Christmas trees to those who could afford them. I also trapped rats out at the dump and in people's homes. The rats in those days were breeding out of control. The county paid a bounty of 5 cents per tail for rats and 2 cents a head for sparrows. There also were too many sparrows.

In 1913, the summer I turned eleven, the miners went out on strike. All the shafts closed down and our lodgers left to take work in Detroit in the automobile plants. They were paying $5 a day down there, almost double what the mines paid. The strike lasted about a year. It was a bad time. Life was at its lowest.

During that time we had no real income. The only money coming in was what I made on my paper routes and from picking berries and killing rats and sparrows. Mother also collected $7.50 in "welfare" that we picked up each Monday from the County Office above the YMCA. Sometimes, when we went for food, the sausage makers at the Tamarack Co-op Meat Market would throw in a ring of bologna and a ring of liver sausage and a couple good soup bones for free. This is the way we lived, always hungry. No telephone, radio, automobile, no indoor plumbing or electricity, only outhouses and chamber pots, hand pumps and kerosene lamps. We wore hand-me-down clothes and had holes in our shoes.

The Co-op helped keep us going. It had six thousand members and did over a million dollars a year in business. It was huge. Three stories high plus a separate butcher shop with its own sausage makers that made every kind of sausage you could name: sautissa, Swedish potato, Italian dry, sylte, cudighi, cotechino, supressa, Finnish maakana, Polish kiska, lots more. It had its own warehouse out back with its own railroad and a stable for more than two dozen horses it used to make wagon deliveries.

It had everything—clothes, shoes, furniture, hardware, drugs, medicines, groceries, meats. Over one hundred people worked there. They called it the biggest retail store north of Milwaukee, and it sold everything cheaper than the stores in town. If you were a member, you could buy on credit, on the "tick," they called it.

I always thought that if Dad had been alive, he would have quit the mines and moved us to a better place, to Detroit, or the Iron Ore country. Maybe not. The copper mines were all he knew, all our family knew. The Oldses always had been miners, back to the eighteenth century in Cornwall, the Cornubian Orefield, Wheal Uny mine. They worked the tin mines around Redruth, a town of ten thousand people in Illogen Parish. Spalliards, they called them.

The old folks crossed over in 1873. The price of copper and tin on the world market went south after 1866 and there was a depression with the mines laying off workers. They had to leave to live. The saying was that the ones who kept their jobs left for underground without their breakfast and only a half pasty for lunch. The average miner over there didn't make it to forty, and the kids were put down to work at eight.

Either way, with Dad, it was family first. That was his favorite expression, "family first." The union was just beginning to organize the Range when he was killed and he never was a member. He wouldn't have been anyway. He was Cornish. The strike wouldn't have set well with him.

In Calumet, my brothers and the other kids called me by my real name, but a lot of the adults, though not my mother, called me CK, short for "Cornish Kid." I don't know why or how that got started. I was Cornish, but so were a lot of kids. The funny thing was, I wasn't even 100 percent Cornish. Mother was Welsh. It was all right by me. We were proud of being "Cousin Jacks."

Looking back, I spent not enough time at home helping out, and too much time on the streets scuffing around, raising hell. None of us ever landed in jail or got in real trouble with the law, but I came close a time or two. Well, I sure didn't make life any easier for Mother. I took advantage, played hookie from school, pitched pennies, chewed tobacco, broke curfew, shot pool, played cards, hung around the saloons.

Sometime in the autumn, during the strike, when the violence was getting out of hand, our relation down in Ishpeming convinced Mother to move there until things settled down. We stayed through Christmas and New Year's and then went back.

Even before the strike ended and especially after the Italian Hall disaster, the company faced a manpower shortage. They had to import miners from outside. Before the strike the men worked twelve-hour shifts, six days a week, for $2.50 a day. After the strike they worked eight-hour shifts, five days a week, for $3 a day.

Mother took in new lodgers. Most of them were Cornishmen, the "Cousin Jacks." Some were Scandinavians and Hungarians and Slovenes. Room and board included Mother washing and ironing all of their bedding and dirty clothes, including their filthy miners' outfits.

When I left school I became eligible for a job in the mines. I wanted one very badly. The way I looked at it, my childhood was over. I was a man looking to do a man's job in a man's world. After listening to the stories of the miners, the ones who had worked with Dad, the way they described the conditions and hazards they worked under, I had to go down and see for myself. I had to know firsthand. No one could stop me.

Mother had some old-timers try to talk me out of it. She begged me not to go. I wouldn't listen. It was more than being curious. I had to prove something. I had something to prove. That I was man enough to do the job, as much of a man as my Dad. I didn't want his death to be for nothing. I thought I could take his place. I thought I could pick up where he left off and carry on for the family. When I promised Mother that I would quit after three months and get a job on the surface, she went ahead and signed the papers promising that if anything happened to me, she gave up her legal right to sue Tamarack for compensation.

I went out to North Tamarack No. 3 Shaft. It was one over from where Dad had died. They made me a drill boy and miner's helper for $2.34 a day six days a week on the four-to-midnight shift. Everything I made except an allowance of $2.50 a week went to Mother. Because I was so small, Dad's miner's outfit didn't fit me, so I bought my own. Canvas shiner hat with carbide lamp, skullcap, safety boots with hobnails on the soles and heels.

The way I thought about it then, it was a new beginning, the start of the second phase of my life. The way I think about it now, at seventy-eight, is different. I grew up too fast. Life became too serious too soon. The truth is, I was afraid, and I was afraid of admitting I was afraid, even to myself. I spent all my time trying to hide how afraid I was. I was so afraid of my fear being found out, of being called yellow or chicken or gutless by the men I worked with, that I broke my promise to Mother and stayed underground for a whole year.

I hated it. Every second. I hated hurting Mother, hated being scared all the time, scared stiff, having to pretend I was brave, that I was a man. I wasn't a man. I was a kid. A scared little kid.

I hated going down in the ore skip. I still remember the feeling. I can't describe it. Like being swallowed in the dark, by the dark. Like being dropped down a cold hole, a hole of coldness.

I hated the air blasts like the one that killed Dad. The sound of the explosion, the shaking ground and walls, the gush of wind, the dust and falling rock. I was involved in three of them. One buried my partner. I helped dig him out and put him on a drill truck and pushed him back to the shaft and put him on a skip to the surface. He died that day at noon. I knew that could have been me just as easily.

I hated it so much that in order to get out I got myself fired by the shift boss. He liked to pick on me, and one day I snapped and threw my dinner pail at him and cracked him one in the head. That was that. But by then I had got all I wanted from the mines. I had experienced for myself the way Father had lived all those years.

I don't know how he did it. A mile underground, in the dark, the blackness, no control over your own life, no way out. Nowhere to run or hide or put your fear or keep from thinking thoughts of death all the time. Wondering who would be next, when your number would come up. Because it never went away. It never got any better. Not for me. Day after day, the same thing, the same feeling.

And the filth of it. Dust over everything, inside your clothes, at your eyes, inside your mouth, up your nose, in the air you breathed. Gas, smoke, dust. Taking the copper into your lungs. Not enough air. Dirty air. Always too hot or too cold, a furnace or a freezer. Rats big as cats. Relieving yourself where you worked. Eating where you just had relieved yourself.

You felt like you were wrapped inside a big, dark fist, trapped. A fist made of red rock and metal, copper. But there was a smaller one, a tighter one inside your guts squeezing. Who knows what hell is, but that was as close to it as I've ever come or want to. I never prayed for death, but I know some who did, and I understood.

I couldn't do it. It wasn't the work. It was hard work, but I could do it. I wasn't afraid of working hard. It was everything else. Maybe that's what saved me, being so afraid. The men called anyone who had a job up top a girl. Maybe what saved me was my own cowardice. I can say that now. I'm man enough to say that now. There are worse things in life than being called a woman.

When I think of the way it must have been for Dad when he first went down, I can't believe it. He was ten years old. They worked by candlelight. They climbed on hand ladders down through solid rock into the earth. He was braver than me. He must have been. I'll never know for sure because it killed him before I had a chance to talk to him about it.

I would have liked to, though. I wonder how he did it. How he kept from being afraid. When you are ten years old and supposed to be having fun, playing with your friends or doing nothing, goofing around, wasting time, how do you get up every day in the dark, go down into the earth in the dark, work all day in the dark, and come back up in the dark? You couldn't talk about that with any of the other men. You couldn't talk about it with your Mother. You couldn't talk about it with anyone, except maybe your Dad.

So I got fired and started looking for a job on the surface. I didn't care anymore if they called me a girl. Let them. At least I didn't have to go back down. No man who had a choice would have chosen to work in those pits.

That was it for me. I became the last one in our family to work the mines, and the thing I'm proudest of in life is that no child or grandchild of mine ever had to go through what I went through or even think about having to go through it. In my own eyes, that makes me a success, makes my life worth something, it's an accomplishment, I accomplished something. Not as much as some people, maybe, but enough, enough for me. I was the one who got out. I was the one in our family who broke through, the one who left the dark and dirt and death behind. I was the one who said no, no more, and put a stop to it for all time, for all the ones who came after me.

After my grandfather's death, upon discovering the document in his desk drawer, we also discovered, paper-clipped to its back page, a single yellowed sheet of brittle, twice-folded paper. It read:

The following is an extract from the Houghton County Mine Inspector Report 1892-1962, Accident No. 39, June 18, a Monday, 1910, James Olds, No. 2 Shaft, Tamarack Mine:

James Olds came to his death on this date from injuries caused by a **FALL OF GROUND** between the 28th and 29th levels, No. 2 Tamarack. An inquest was held before Justice Rule. The following testimony was obtained:

THOMAS BROTHERS: "I was talking with Mr. Olds when we were surrounded by falling rock. After the rock stopped rolling down the winze, I saw a light going up the winze and I hollered, 'Hello, Jim!' And I heard someone answer, 'Hello!' Then more rock fell and I got out of the track and saw no more light. After I got down I saw Thos. Freeman at the 29th level and I took his lamp and went up again to find my lamp, shiner, and skull cap, which I had lost in the fall. I found the shiner and skull cap, but could not find the lamp. When I went down again, I saw Mr. Billings at the 29th and I asked how he got there. He said he came through the down-right winze. I asked for Jim (deceased) and he said he had not seen him and did not know where he was. As I say, I thought I had heard his voice and I had left the 28th before Jim got there. I then went to the 30th level, and when I learned that Jim was not at the 28th, I went to look for him and found him **BURIED IN ROCK.**"

MINE INSPECTOR DANE: "Did you take down the loose ground before you commenced work?"

BROTHERS: "Yes. We thought everything was perfectly safe."

DANE: "Did you hear the report before the ground fell?"

BROTHERS: "The ground fell as the report sounded. It was the same moment."

DANE: "Did the rock come from overhead?"

BROTHERS: "From the side and a little from the back. It fell downward on a SLANT."

Verdict: We, the jury, find that James Olds came to his death on the 18th day of June, 1910, about four o'clock a.m. between the 28th and 29th levels, No. 2 Shaft, Tamarack Mine, by **AN UNFORESEEABLE, ACCIDENTAL FALL OF ROCK IN THE WINZE, AN INCIDENTAL FALL OF SLANT GROUND.**

Perhaps the past had to settle awhile before music could be made of it.

PETER BALAKIAN

APPENDIX, NOTES, CITATIONS

✦ ✦ ✦

My personal experience with respect to fictions such as *The Moments Lost*, which is to say fictions engaged with, but written *out of*, history, is that readers—some, not all, often, not always—hanker to know how much of the work is "true," and how much is "made up." Indeed, I have had the very question pitched my way on countless occasions in a variety of settings, and while my impulse typically has been to foul it off or take it for a ball high and away, more often of late it strikes me that it may well be a perfectly legitimate one to pose or, at least, somewhat understandable.

Regrettably, it is a question I find myself largely at a loss to answer, not only because it is not my wont to document or keep strict tally of such things, but because work such as *The Moments Lost* is less apt to abide by the conventions of that genre popularly known as "the historical novel," where such a concern might be said more properly to obtain, than it is to purposefully contravene, confound, and cut against their grain.

The painter Willem de Kooning once commented, "The past does not influence me, I influence it." An arrogant remark, to be sure, and yet one to which, if not absent a certain reluctance, I find myself enormously drawn. To replenish the past in the nomenclature of the present, this can only be some part of what work such as *The Moments Lost* aspires to.

That said, it may be worthwhile to include a sampling of some odd few of those instances—over and above the obvious, deliberately anachronistic ones—where, for aesthetic reasons, *The Moments Lost* takes license with what historians are fond of calling "the record."

So, the Chicago *Tribune* was not particularly antilabor in its editorial stance, nor did Chicago's Iroquois Theatre possess an overhead oculus, stained glass or otherwise.

Al Capone, then twenty, did not arrive in Chicago to work for Johnny Torrio until 1919. Prior to that, he was attached as a bouncer and "slammer" to gangster Frankie Yale, a Torrio associate, at his Harvard Inn on Coney Island, Brooklyn, New York.

The Everleigh Club ceased operation in October 1911.

Margaret Anderson, the lineaments of whose character I lifted in part from her three-volume memoir *My Thirty Years' War*, *The Fiery Fountain*, and *The Strange Necessity*, as well as her novel, *Forbidden Fires*, did not pitch her tents on the shore of Lake Michigan until the summer of 1915; in the summer of 1912, she still was living at the YWCA.

Wisconsin's Cave of the Mounds was not discovered until August 1939.

The dial telephone was not invented until 1914, Caesar's Salad until 1924, Rice Krispies until 1928, Bananas Foster until 1951.

The Red Jacket telegraph office was located at 116 Fifth Street, not in the Calumet Theatre and Opera House on Sixth, although telegrams of a public nature often were posted at the latter location for the edification of local residents.

The Red Jacket swimming pool was not located in the library basement—although original plans called for its location in that spot—but in the C&H bathhouse, a separate redbrick structure nearby.

It was not William D. Haywood, but WFM president Charles H. Moyer who was back-shot, beaten, and run out of the Keweenaw in December of 1913. While Haywood had visited the Upper Peninsula at least once previously, three years earlier, after which he had forecast the likelihood of a strike in his article for the vol. XI, no. 2, August 1910 issue of the *International Socialist Review*, by the time the strike occurred, the relentlessly militant Haywood and his IWW had broken with WFM leadership. Indeed, in the eyes of the more moderate, five-foot-six, forty-seven-year-old, asthmatic Moyer, whom Haywood, despite their having shared a jail cell in the past, thought a "labor pimp," Big Bill was persona non grata, owing both to his bitter refusal to publicly condemn violence as a legitimate strike tactic, and to his ongoing flirtation with the American Communist Party. Consequently, as far as we know, he played no role in the Keweenaw labor action whatever.

Finally, about Franklyn Shivs, "the record" remains "dark," save that:

1. he was a Slovenian who worked briefly for George Ivan Molek at *Proleterac*

2. he covered the copper strike for that Chicago newspaper

3. he fathered out of wedlock a daughter named Darwina with Ana Clemenc during the strike, after which the couple married and moved to Chicago's South Side, where Darwina lost a limb in an automobile accident and Ana worked in a millinery factory

4. he apparently was beset by a chronic drinking problem and proclivity for "domestic abuse"

5. he is described by Molek in his memoir as one who "did not have editorial aptitude, and attacked his job with enthusiasm and a certain pathological exaggeration, sitting behind his desk barefooted and dressed in overalls, by this wanting to demonstrate that he really was a worker's proletarian journalist; a blue blood in blue jeans"

6. he was *not* in fact named Franklyn Shivs, but Frank Shavs

The decision to fudge his name was made because he remains throughout *The Moments Lost* more fiction than fact, and so, perhaps, more true. Besides, it *sounds* better—Shivs than Shavs—or, at least, more apropos.

As for Ana Klobuchar Clemenc Shavs, she died of uterine cancer in Chicago in 1956, age sixty-eight. All we know about Frank Shavs is that at his death—we haven't a date, which, in light of William Logan's gorgeous phrase, "to solve in poetry the histories death leaves unanswered," is, perhaps, just as well—he was working as a factory watchman.

Surely there exist other examples of *The Moments Lost* "breaching" the record, but either I have unwittingly forgotten, inadvertently overlooked, or deliberately omitted them, in which case I would expect to be alerted to the "fact" by those whom it may please—and ought feel free—to do so.

> *For most of us, there is only the unattended*
> *Moment, the moment in or out of time*
> . . . .
> *. . . or music heard so deeply*
> *That it is not heard at all, but you are the music*
> *While the music lasts.*
>
> T. S. ELIOT, "The Dry Salvages"

In both homage and gratitude, and in the inclusive, playful, improvisational spirit of *bricolage*, the following are, by the author, cheerfully cited:

1) the line in boldface italics on p. 17, William Carlos Williams
2) the line in boldface italics on p. 21, Willliam Carlos Williams
3) the line in italics on p. 112, Wallace Stevens
4) the line in italics on p. 116, James Joyce
5) the line in boldface italics on p. 149, Gustav Flaubert
6) the line in boldface italics on p. 170, William Carlos Williams
7) the line in italics on p. 244, Hart Crane
8) the passage heading on p. 419, Hart Crane
9) the line beginning "In his state of complete powerlessness . . ." on p. 436, Theodor Adorno
10) the line "I spit my last breath. At thee." on p. 448, Herman Melville

ACKNOWLEDGMENTS

◆　◆　◆

Expressions of deepest gratitude are owed, as they unconditionally are extended, to Eric Chinski, an editor whose brilliance is surpassed only by his integrity. Likewise to Gentleman John Glusman, whose early vetting of the rough manuscript was invaluable. And to Sarah Chalfant and Jin Auh, agent-heroines.

Thanks, also, to Gary Olds and Rodger and Nancylu Arola, keepers of the family flame, and to the working staffs of those institutions whose gracious assistance rendered that which unavoidably was arduous, distinctly less so.

These include: the Harold Washington Public Library (Chicago); the Newberry Library (Chicago); the Chicago Historical Society; the Chicago Institute of Art, Ryerson and Burnham Libraries; the Metropolitan Museum of Art, Thomas J. Watson Library (New York City); the University of Minnesota, Andersen Library and Immigration and History Research Center (Minneapolis); Northern Michigan University, Olson Library and Center for Upper Peninsula Studies (Marquette); Michigan Tech University, Archives and Copper Country Historical Collection (Houghton); Finlandia University, Maki Library and North Wind Books (Hancock); the Keweenaw County Historical Society and Museum (Eagle Harbor); the Houghton County Historical Society and Museum (Lake Linden); the Quincy Mine Hoist Association (Hancock); the Coppertown USA Mining Museum and Archive (Calumet); the Copper Range Historical Museum (South Range); the Bisbee, Arizona, Mining and Historical Museum and the staff of the Bisbee Copper Queen Mine; the Morris County Public Library (Morristown, New Jersey).

Also, to all those connected with the creation, organization, and production of the opera *Children of the Keweenaw* and its attendant activities and seminars, especially Kathleen Masterson and Paul Seitz, as well as to independent researcher Jane Nordberg, and to Nancy Dast, Mark Dworkin, and Max Roberts, thank you.

The primary and secondary sources consulted during the writing of *The Moments Lost* are, regrettably, too numerous to list. I would be remiss, however, if I failed to mention the work of Arthur W. Thurner, Larry Lankton, Clarence J. Monette, Tauno Kilpela, David Mac Frimodig, Paul T. Steele, and Dave Engel and Gerry Mantel. Considered collectively, the research and writing of these authors were of incalculable assistance to this one in deepening his understanding of the place and the people of the Keweenaw, and of a time he often had heard about as a child, but until recently, felt but the most mythic of personal connection.

Finally, I owe a belated doff of the hat to Thom Jones and Earl Shorris, who, virtually alone, know why, and to Richard A. Hulseberg, who was there in advance of the rest. Who knew, eh, Doc?